THE PEN

FOUNDER EDITOR

D0526194

HONORÉ DE BALZAC was born at Tours in 1799, the son of a civil servant. He spent nearly six years as a boarder in a Vendôme school, then went to live in Paris, working as a lawyer's clerk then as a hack-writer. Between 1820 and 1824 he wrote a number of novels under various pseudonyms, many of them in collaboration, after which he unsuccessfully tried his luck at publishing, printing and type-founding. At the age of thirty, heavily in debt, he returned to literature with a dedicated fury and wrote the first novel to appear under his own name, *The Chouans*. During the next twenty years he wrote about ninety novels and shorter stories, among them many masterpieces, to which he gave the comprehensive title *The Human Comedy*. He died in 1850, a few months after his marriage to Evelina Hanska, the Polish countess with whom he had maintained amorous relations for eighteen years.

RAYNER HEPPENSTALL was born in Yorkshire and educated locally and in Calais and Strasbourg. He is the author of seven novels, some verse, much criticism, three volumes of reminiscences and four of French criminal history. Earlier work in translation has included Chateaubriand's *Atala and René* and, in collaboration with Lindy Foord, *Impressions of Africa* by Raymond Roussel. He resigned from the B.B.C. in 1967, where he had worked for more than twenty years as a producer in the Features and Drama Department. He is married, with two children and five grandchildren.

Honoré de Balzac

A HARLOT
HIGH AND LOW
(Splendeurs et misères des courtisanes)

TRANSLATED AND
WITH AN INTRODUCTION BY
RAYNER HEPPENSTALL

PENGUIN BOOKS

Penguin Books Ltd, Harmondsworth, Middlesex, England
Penguin Books, 625 Madison Avenue, New York, New York 10022, U.S.A.
Penguin Books Australia Ltd, Ringwood, Victoria, Australia
Penguin Books Canada Ltd, 2801 John Street, Markham, Ontario, Canada L3R 1B4
Penguin Books (N.Z.) Ltd, 182–190 Wairau Road, Auckland 10, New Zealand

—

Splendeurs et misères des courtisanes first published 1839–47
Published in Penguin Books 1970
Reprinted 1971, 1975, 1977, 1979, 1982

—

Translation and Introduction copyright © Rayner Heppenstall, 1970
All rights reserved

—

Made and printed in Great Britain
by Richard Clay (The Chaucer Press) Ltd,
Bungay, Suffolk
Set in Monotype Garamond

It is, I fancy, generally known that characters from one Balzac novel are likely to reappear in others. The editor of the Classiques Garnier edition lists forty-four characters in the present volume who may also be found elsewhere. Many of them are quite unimportant to the action, while the juvenile lead, Lucien Chardon, *dit* de Rubempré, has been met with only once before and will never be seen again for the best of reasons. The other novel of which he is the hero is *Illusions perdues*, and to that novel this one may, to that extent, be considered a sequel, though within the large framework of Balzac's *Comédie humaine* the earlier novel is classed as one of the 'Scenes of Provincial Life' and the present volume as one of the 'Scenes of Parisian Life', a somewhat arbitrary distinction, since much of the action of *Illusions perdues* takes place in Paris.

In it, we find Lucien Chardon, a young man of modest origins but with some claim to nobility (and to the name 'de Rubempré') on his mother's side, a poet and vain of his looks and determined to put them to use, in the southern town of Angoulême. Taken up by a local *grande dame*, he goes to Paris, sets foot in the literary world but sinks to the lowest depths of journalism, leaves his protectress and becomes the lover of a woman of the town, Coralie, who dies, and returns to the provinces, not merely dejected but shamed by a piece of financial trickery which has got his amiable brother-in-law into trouble. Towards the end of the book, he sets off one morning to drown himself in the Charente, but meets a Spanish priest on a diplomatic mission, who at once takes a fancy to the young man and promises him a great future. Lucien gets into the priest's carriage, and they drive on towards Paris, Lucien's sister presently receiving a letter from him which encloses money and says that she mustn't worry. Lucien is all right, though he feels somewhat enslaved.

The date at the end of *Illusions perdues* is the late summer or early autumn of 1823. The present novel begins early the next year. If the reader wished, he might now simply read on. In the first chapter, he would be duly mystified by the powerfully built man in the domino, but so he would if he already knew *Illusions perdues*. If, on the other hand, he had previously read *Illusions perdues*, he would know that group of horrible journalists. Even an acquaintance with what is probably Balzac's best-known novel, *Le Père Goriot*, might bring back memories of a young man called Rastignac at Ma Vauquer's. Rastignac's brief exchange with the man in the domino might, indeed, tell the reader most of what is presently to be revealed about the Spanish priest. Rastignac, it may be noted, recurs in more of Balzac's novels than any other single character. He is said to have been based on the leading politician, Louis-Adolphe Thiers. However, that is a matter we don't need to bother our heads with here.

In any important sense, it is only in connection with Lucien de Rubempré that we should think of *Splendeurs et misères des courtisanes* as a sequel to *Illusions perdues*. About the supposed Spanish priest, who in the end turns out to be the true protagonist of the novel, we might learn more from *Le Père Goriot* but do not in fact need to know more than the present volume tells us, though, if we cared to study him in depth, there is at the end of *Illusions perdues* a brief passage about him which has become very famous. Of this, more in a moment. I turn now to Esther.

No reader of Balzac has ever met her before or will ever meet her again, though he may have met her mother in *César Birotteau* and her mother's uncle there and elsewhere, most notably in *Gobseck*, a story published in 1830, four years before *Le Père Goriot*, seven before *César Birotteau*, thirteen before *Illusions perdues*, seventeen before the completion of *Splendeurs et misères des courtisanes*. His niece, Sara, a prostitute known as '*la belle Hollandaise*', Esther's mother, was murdered in 1818, but Gobseck, a Jewish moneylender from Antwerp, was not to die until 1830. As the reader will see, had he died earlier, none of the sad events in this book need have taken place. When he wrote *Gobseck*, Honoré de Balzac was a young man of thirty-one. When he finished *Splendeurs et misères*, he was forty-eight and had three more years to live, for he died at the same age as Proust, having achieved at least quantitatively more.

His intention had been to write a novel about prostitution. His title for this was to be *La Torpille*, the professional nickname of the heroine, Esther Gobseck, Sara's daughter. *La Torpille* as projected was in fact written, and much of it was published in periodicals, some under that title, some under the title *Esther, ou les amours d'un banquier*. Projected in 1837, partly written in 1838 and completed in 1843, *La Torpille* now forms Parts One and Two of the present book. After the death of Esther, the book is not much concerned with prostitution, and so the overall title is something of a misnomer, though fully applicable to Parts One and Two. Of the sense of the nickname and first title, I shall need to say something in the course of justifying what I have done with it.

About the forty-three characters in this book, other than Lucien, who occur elsewhere, the reader who wants to follow them up could do much worse than consult Félicien Marceau's book, *Balzac and his World*, readily available in English. The hypothetical reader who knows only *Le Père Goriot* may care to be reminded that one of the Goriot daughters, with whom Rastignac is having an affair, is married to Baron Nucingen, of whom we hear much in the present volume and in three others. In *Le Père Goriot*, Dr Bianchon is a medical student who plays a wholly admirable part. Corentin and Peyrade appear elsewhere, as does the unfortunate Contenson under another name. Mme de Sérisy figured in *La Femme de trente ans*. Clotilde de Grandlieu remains faithful to Lucien's memory in *Béatrix*. But knowledge of all these ramifications can add only marginally to any reader's enjoyment of the present volume. Of the supposed Spanish priest Don Carlos Herrera, whose real name turns out to be Jacques Collin, a little may perhaps usefully be said here.

In *Le Père Goriot*, he appears as the respectable, if disconcerting, Monsieur Vautrin, life and soul of the party at the *table d'hôte* in Madame Vauquer's boarding-house, who was really ... what he turned out to be. The events in *Le Père Goriot* belong to the years 1819–20 (the book was written in 1834). In 1840, a play called *Vautrin* was performed once at the Porte Saint Martin theatre. It is not a good play, but the shortness of its run was due to the fact that the star, the great actor of his day, Frederick Lemaître, made himself up in one scene to look like the reigning monarch, Louis-Philippe. The basis for Lemaître's unfortunate joke (perhaps, indeed, not so intended) was this. It was widely understood, by 1840, that the figure of Vautrin in M. Balzac's famous novel had been based on a real-life police chief, formerly an escaped convict, finally retired some eight years before, who had indeed borne some resemblance to Louis-Philippe, a fact which, after 1830, the date of Louis-Philippe's accession, had frequently been made the subject of comment, doubtless to the detriment of Vidocq. For the real-life figure was that great name in criminological history, François-Eugène Vidocq, the ex-convict who became the founder of the French Sûreté and thus the ancestor of criminal investigation departments throughout the world.

Of course, to say that Vidocq was 'the original' of Balzac's Vautrin is greatly to over-simplify the matter. He has also been said to be 'the original' of Jean Valjean in Victor Hugo's *Les Misérables*. Both these characters in great works of fiction had, indeed, something in common with the real-life Vidocq, but the differences are as significant as the resemblances. This is a matter I study closely in a recent volume. Here, I must content myself with repeating what has been so often said and with qualifying it. The Jacques Collin of the present volume, for instance, owes something to at least four other real-life figures, those of the impostors Coignard and a supposed Count of Montealbano, to a master of disguise, Anthime Collet, and even to the murderer Lacenaire. About Vidocq, there was never the least suggestion of homosexuality. His recorded last words were that he had too much loved women, and he more obviously resembled the noisily jovial Monsieur Vautrin of *Le Père Goriot* than the scarred and ravaged colossus of *Splendeurs et misères*. He hadn't the education to pass himself off in Paris as a priest. Among the incidents in his life which are paralleled in the supposed life of Vautrin (but not at all that of Jean Valjean) is that he was first convicted of forgery (Jean Valjean, a simple peasant, archetypally stole a loaf of bread). And then, at the end, we return to the basic parallel. Jacques Collin, like the real-life François-Eugène, is appointed head of a crime squad, though even here the dates are very different indeed.

By 1830, Vidocq had retired (he was to stage a brief come-back, a benevolent industrial enterprise, paralleled by that of Jean Valjean, having failed). He had first entered police service in 1812, under Napoleon, and was given his own section in 1817, under Louis XVIII. In this novel, Vautrin succeeds Bibi-Lupin, himself an ex-convict, who himself bears some resemblance to the real-life Vidocq, at least in his physical appearance, while a man with a comical name of the same type, Coco-Lacour (himself appointed on the principle of setting a thief to catch a thief, *à fripon fripon et demi*), was in real life Vidocq's first, short-lived successor. The point hardly needs labouring. About the figure of Vautrin, the reader who doesn't know Balzac in a large way may care to be told, however, that, at a supposedly later date, he re-appears in his 'last incarnation' in *La Cousine Bette*, a novel written and published earlier than *Splendeurs et misères des courtisanes*. There the reader would receive the impression that his real name was Vautrin, not Jacques Collin.

How the homosexual thing came in, I don't know. To us, it is certainly there. How much it was there to Balzac is a differ-ent matter. He knew about the existence of male prostitutes, that is certain. He knew that prison life tended to foster homosexual practices. I am nevertheless far from certain that he conceived the relations between Lucien and his Mephis-topheles to be anything like those we now regard as normal between men whom we describe as consenting adults. Not to put too fine a point upon it, if he did, the sum total of sexual services then required of Lucien would be such that we need hardly feel surprised that, on his free evenings, all he wanted to do was recline on a divan and smoke a hookah. The idea of Jacques Collin as homosexual Mephistopheles to a succession of young Fausts was, I suppose, first suggested by Proust. The famous passage I spoke of earlier, towards the end of *Illusions perdues*, shows the Spanish priest halting his carriage and gazing at the early home of young Rastignac.

This passage was described by Proust's Baron de Charlus as 'the *Tristesse d'Olympio* of pederasty' (*Tristesse d'Olympio* being a poem by Victor Hugo meditating amid scenes of lost happiness). It will now retain that flavour for ever. I remain unconvinced that it is what Balzac had in mind. There is, for instance, no suggestion in *Le Père Goriot* or, retrospectively, in the novel before us that the ambitious Rastignac had ever given M. Vautrin or anyone else that kind of pleasure. What Rastignac mainly represented to Balzac was persistent ambition, and at that moment Mephistopheles was plotting a great future for another Faust.

The Translation

POOR workmen blame their tools, and the difficulties of its translator do not ordinarily concern the reader of a novel from a foreign language. The thing should simply read well in its new language and the translator's fidelity to his original be taken for granted. In the present case, there were, however, one or two problems which I hope were insoluble, since I am conscious of not having solved them. Nor can they be effectively concealed. They appear as snags on the surface. The reader is bound to notice them.

Of such unsolved problems the least deeply significant but most recurrently tedious was the dialogue given to Baron Nucingen, the banker, commonly understood to be Alsatian but on occasion referred to, in respect of his way of speech, as a Polish Jew. In the original, Balzac prints all his lines in italics, and he distorts them to the point of near-unintelligibility in a perfectly systematic fashion, always changing certain vowels and, in the case of consonants, *everywhere* substituting a voiced for an unvoiced, an unvoiced for a voiced, consonant, *i.e.*, a *p* for a *b* but also a *b* for a *p*, a *t* for a *d* but also a *d* for a *t*, a *k* for a hard *g* and *vice versa*, *ch* for *j*, *j* for *ch* and so on. I have been less systematic. In the result, I fancy that what Nucingen says is in general a bit less immediately unintelligible, though not much. Whenever I saw dialogue in italics coming up, I groaned and was tempted to give up. I did not feel justified in too much pre-alleviating the reader's inevitable groans. To be largely unintelligible is an essential part of the baron's character. No doubt to the reader, as it was to the translator, it will be a great relief when he finally disappears on page 290, having been replaced briefly by a supposed Englishman.

An obviously difficult but more interesting problem was the underworld slang largely concentrated in Part Four. There was an English equivalent at the time, some of it already to be found among the Elizabethans, some of it oddly surviving in the form of schoolgirl or Mayfair affectation, some wrongly thought to be of recent American importation. Again, I have been somewhat less systematic than Balzac, who, it may be noted, was himself no great authority on the subject, which could be quickly read up from glossaries published in his day, notably that appended to one of the volumes of Vidocq apocrypha, *Les Voleurs*. Not all Balzac's forms can be traced to their sources, however, and some of them suggest that he misunderstood. The most fascinating of all these words was, to me, '*dab*'. I suppose it was of gipsy origin. Certainly it was international, developing in English rather towards the side of practised skill (as in 'dab hand' or 'to be a dab at'), in French towards the side of leadership. At any rate, the reader may be assured that, wherever he reads 'dab' in this translation, he would be reading just that also in French. Odd uses of words, as opposed to the use of odd words, I have sometimes translated literally, as in the case of '*sanglier*' for a priest or '*la Cigogne*' for what is only very loosely equivalent to the office of our Director of Public Prosecutions. This practice will, I hope, not be found to have introduced any new element of confusion.

Felt by criminals to be the seat of the authority they dread at the Law Courts, what they describe (for no obvious reason) as the Stork is perhaps no less oddly described by lawyers to this day as '*le Parquet*'. This term is, I am told, commonly understood in the legal world to derive from the fact that magistrates from the procuracy *take the floor*. They belong, that is to say, to the standing magistracy, the *magistrature debout*, as opposed to the seated magistracy or Bench, the *magistrature assise*. For prosecuting counsel in French courts of assize are magistrates and wear red gowns. They never speak for the defence in criminal cases, any more than black-gowned advocates ever directly prosecute. To the French, it seems odd that a barrister may, with us, even if he is a Q.C., sometimes present, and sometimes oppose, a case brought by the Crown. As Procureur Général in Paris (there are *procureurs-généraux* in the departments, just as there are attorneys general in the American states) M. de Granville was, in effect, both Director of Public Prosecutions and Attorney General, with the important difference that, unlike our Attorney General, he was not a member of the government of the day. The Keeper of the Seals, on the other hand, was. 'Keeper of the Seals' is, in France, simply another title of the Minister of Justice. Like our Attorney General, M. de Granville might himself speak for the prosecution in court, though some lesser *representative of the public ministry* might equally, when not on his feet, occupy that little horse-box where prosecuting counsel sits most of the time and for which also '*le parquet*' is an appropriate name.

Not that we ever, in this novel, find ourselves in court, though in Parts Three and Four lawyers, and especially Parquet *personnel*, abound. The reader will manage, I hope, without knowing much about the French legal system and its ways of proceeding. If he wants to know more, I might perhaps, without immodesty, direct his attention to the relevant chapters in two books of my own, *A Little Pattern of French Crime* and *French Crime in the Romantic Age*. There also he will find something about the Conciergerie and other prisons and the changing organization of the French police, though Balzac, I fancy, is clear enough about all that. I had trouble with the word '*police*' itself, more often meaning police work or police methods than a simple collectivity of policemen, but that needn't bother the reader.

Nor, I hope, need that classification of the types of harlotry, that pornotypology, which so occupied writers in Balzac's time. It was the simplest and most general word of all, '*fille*', which gave me most trouble. We have no word which may equally mean a common prostitute, a serving woman, in certain contexts a nun, and at the same time a daughter of even the most respectable or noble family, and it is with the large general category of '*les filles*' that Balzac's sociology and psychology are concerned. His generalizations are all about what '*les filles*' think, feel and do, not with the possibly more specific thoughts, emotions and actions of '*courtisanes*', '*lorettes*', '*rats*' and '*filles soumises*', let alone with those of little seamstresses or *grisettes*. The cruellest deed ever performed by Vautrin was, I feel sure, suggested to Balzac's mind by the simple linguistic fact that a '*fille*' was also a daughter and that nothing renders a man so vulnerable as a cherished daughter, who may be turned overnight into a *fille publique*. The same thing might occur in an English novel, but the language itself would not bring this about.

The totally inescapable snag was more specific, and there was nothing my conscience would let me do to conceal it. While I was known to be translating this book, a question I was asked by both French and knowledgeable English admirers of Balzac was what I proposed to do about Esther's nickname. The reader would not have been long in finding out, and I fancy he might have been jolted. The English translator of Félicien Marceau's still-quite-recent book on the world of Balzac has, I see, let the name stand in French as '*la Torpille*'. I have been bolder. I have allowed Esther to be referred to as 'the Torpedo', fully aware that this lends her associations we might nowadays think more characteristic of some blonde bombshell, Esther being neither a bombshell nor (except on an early page, through Balzac's forgetfulness) blonde. The word '*torpille*' is French for a numb-fish, cramp-fish or electric ray (not to be confused with the sting ray). 'Torpedo' was the Latin word for this fish. When moored or floating mines were devised as an instrument of naval warfare, we and the French both named them after it. You touched them and got a shock. The French and ourselves now both reserve the designation '*torpille*' or 'torpedo' to the self-propelled weapon originally called a '*torpille locomotrice*' or 'locomotive torpedo'. Neither we nor they now think of a moored or floating mine as a torpedo. The word '*torpille*', it is true, may still be used in French for a numb-fish, cramp-fish or electric ray, but the fact seems to be unknown to most Frenchmen, except perhaps on the Mediterranean. I have certainly found it to be unknown to a university-educated young Breton. The fish itself is, I dare say, less common in our waters.

RAYNER HEPPENSTALL

Contents

PART ONE

ESTHER'S HAPPIEST DAYS

A view of the Opera ball

IN 1824, at the last Opera ball, a number of maskers were
taken with the good looks of a young man walking about the
corridors and the crush-room, with the air of somebody
waiting for a woman kept at home by unforeseen circumstances. The meaning of this way of moving about, by turns
indolent and hurried, is clear only to old ladies and confirmed
loungers. In that enormous meeting-place, the crowd pays
little attention to the crowd, people are only concerned with
their own affairs, even idleness is somehow preoccupied. The
young dandy was so engrossed by his own uneasy quest that
he did not notice the success he was having: the jocularly
admiring exclamations of some maskers, the solemn questioning of others, the biting witticisms and jeers, the sweet words,
went all unheard, all unseen, by him. Though by appearance
one of those exceptional people who go to the Opera ball
with the idea of starting an adventure, which they expect as
one might have expected a lucky number at roulette in Fras-
cati's time, he seemed complacently sure of what the evening
held in store for him; was no doubt the hero in one of those
mysterious little plays for three characters which are the whole
life of an Opera fancy-dress ball, but which only those with
parts in them know of; so that to young women who come
only to be able to say they've seen it, to country cousins,
inexperienced young men and foreigners, the Opera at such
times must appear to be simply the court of boredom and
fatigue. To them, this black, creeping, hurried crowd, coming,
going, twisting and turning, returning, climbing, descending,
like ants on a woodpile, is no more comprehensible than the
stock exchange to a peasant from Brittany who never heard of
the Great Book of the Public Debt. With rare exceptions, in
Paris, the men are not masked: a man in a domino looks
ridiculous. This shows the national genius. People who wish
to hide their happiness may set out for the Opera ball but
fail to arrive, while the maskers absolutely forced to go in
soon leave. A particularly amusing spectacle, from the moment

the ball starts, is that of the flood of those escaping and those wishing to go in jammed at the door. The men in masks are thus either jealous husbands who have come to spy on their wives, or husbands with a good reason not to be spied on, both situations equally laughable. Now, the young man, without knowing it, was being followed by a masker who might have been thought to have murder in his heart, a short, heavily built man who rolled like a barrel. To anyone who regularly attended the Opera, this domino could only conceal some land agent, stockbroker, banker, a well-to-do citizen of some kind suspicious of his unfaithful lady, wife or other. In the best society, nobody looks for unflattering evidence. More than one masker had already laughingly pointed out to another this monstrous individual, others had apostrophized him, several young people had openly mocked him. He stoutly and squarely showed disdain for these shafts which did not carry; he followed where the young man led him, like a hunted boar who cares nothing either for the shot whistling about his ears or for the dogs barking round him. Although at first glance pleasure and uneasiness put on the same livery, the well-known Venetian black robe, and though all at an Opera ball is confusion, the various circles of which Parisian society is composed meet, recognize and observe each other. For some of the initiated, the seemingly unintelligible black book of conflicting interests is so precisely notated that they read it as though it were a novel, here and there amusing. To them, this man was therefore out of luck, otherwise he would have borne some agreed mark, red, white or green, the sign of happiness impending. Was it a question of revenge? Watching the mask so closely following a lucky man, a number of idlers looked again at the handsome face upon which pleasure's aureole was set. The young man aroused interest: the further he proceeded, the more curiosity he awakened. Everything about him clearly indicated habituation to an elegant life. In accordance with a fatal law of our age, there existed little difference, whether physical or moral, between the most distinguished, the best-bred son of a duke and peer, and this pleasant young fellow whom poverty's iron hand once held gripped in Paris. Youth and good looks were able to hide deep abysses in his nature and life, as in so many young men bent on cutting a figure in Paris without capital to support their pretensions, and who daily cast their all upon the all in a sacrifice to the most courted god of this royal city, Chance. Nevertheless, his bearing, his manners, were irreproachable, he trod the classic enclosure like one to whom the Opera crush-room was familiar ground. Who can fail to observe that there, as in every other zone of Paris, there is a mode of being which reveals what you are, what you do, where you come from, and what you are after?

'What a fine young man! There's room here to turn and look at him,' said a masker in whom regular visitors perceived a highly respectable woman.

'Don't you remember him?' replied her cavalier. 'Mme du Châtelet introduced him to you . . .'

'What! it's the little apothecary she was enamoured of, who became a journalist, Mlle Coralie's lover?'

'I thought he'd fallen too low ever to rise again, and I don't understand how he can reappear in Paris society,' said Count Sixte du Châtelet.

'He looks like a prince,' said the masker, 'and it wasn't the actress he lived with who taught him that; my cousin, who knew all about it, couldn't get him out of the scrape; I wish I knew the mistress of this Sargine, love's pupil, tell me something about her that I can rouse his curiosity with.'

This couple who also followed the young man, whispering, were now closely watched by the square-shouldered masker.

'Dear Monsieur Chardon,' said the prefect of Charente taking the dandy by the arm, 'allow me to introduce you to someone who wishes to renew acquaintance with you . . .'

'Dear Count Châtelet,' replied the young man, 'it was she who taught me to find the name you give me absurd. An ordinance of the King has restored to me that of my ancestors on my mother's side, the Rubemprés. It was in the papers, but, as the fact concerns a person of so little consequence, I do not blush at recalling it to my friends, my enemies or the indifferent: you will put yourself in which category you please, but I am sure you cannot disapprove of a step recommended to me by your wife when she was still only

Madame de Bargeton.' (This pretty stroke of wit, which made the marquise smile, caused the prefect of Charente a nervous start.) 'Tell her,' added Lucien, 'that I now bear *Gules, within a tressure vert a bull rampant argent.*'

'Pawing the air for money?' Châtelet ventured.

'The marchioness will explain to you, if you don't know, why this ancient scutcheon ranks somewhat above the Empire chamberlain's key and bees *or* found in yours, to the despair of Madame Châtelet, *née* Nègrepelisse d'Espard. . .' said Lucien with feeling.

'Since you've recognized me, I can no longer rouse your curiosity, and the extent to which you rouse mine could be expressed only with difficulty,' the Marquise d'Espard said to him in an undertone, taken aback by the cool impertinence of the man she had formerly despised.

'Allow me, then, dear lady, by remaining in a mysterious half-light, to preserve my only means of occupying your thoughts,' said he with the smile of a man who does not wish to compromise the luck of which he is certain.

The marquise could not repress a little shrug at feeling herself to have been, in an English expression, so unmistakably 'cut' by Lucien.

'My compliments on the change in your position,' said Count Châtelet.

'I receive them as you intend,' Lucien answered, bowing to the marquise with infinite grace.

'Impudent fop!' the count muttered to Madame d'Espard. 'He has ended by acquiring ancestors.'

'In young people, that sort of conceit, when we're faced with it, almost invariably proclaims luck at the highest level; among people like you, it never bodes any good. Anyway, I should like to know which of the ladies of our acquaintance has taken this fine bird under her protection; I might then begin to enjoy myself this evening. That anonymous letter was probably a bit of mischief contrived by some rival, for the young man was mentioned in it; his impudence had been dictated to him: keep an eye on him. I'm going to take the arm of the Duc de Navarreins, you'll know where to find me.'

At the moment at which Madame d'Espard was on the point of approaching her kinsman, the mysterious masker interposed between her and the duke to whisper to her: 'Lucien's devoted to you, he wrote the letter; your prefect is his greatest enemy, his presence ruled out any explanation.'

The unknown man walked away, leaving Madame d'Espard a prey to astonishment on two counts. The marquise did not know anybody whose face could lie under that mask, she feared a trap, went and sat down to hide. Count Sixte du Châtelet, from whose name Lucien had cut out the high-flown *du* with an ostentatiousness in which one detected a revenge long dreamed of, followed that remarkable dandy at a distance, and presently met a young man to whom he felt he could open his heart.

'Well, Rastignac, have you seen Lucien? He's cast his slough.'

'If I were as good-looking a fellow, I should be even richer than he is,' replied the young swell in a casual but shrewd tone which contained a good deal of Attic salt.

'No,' murmured in his ear the heavily built masker, accentuating the monosyllable in a way that multiplied the raillery by a thousand.

Rastignac, who was not one to swallow insults, stood as though struck by lightning, and allowed himself to be led to a window corner by a hand of steel, which he could not shake off.

'Young cock out of Ma Vauquer's chicken-run, you whose heart failed him in laying hold of Papa Taillefer's millions when the worst of the work had been done, know, for your own safety's sake, that if you don't behave towards Lucien as to a brother whom you might love, you are in our hands without us being in yours. Silence and friendship, or I join in your game and bowl the skittles over. Lucien de Rubempré is protected by the greatest power of today, the Church. Choose between life and death. Your reply?'

Rastignac experienced the vertigo of a man who, having fallen asleep in a forest, should awake beside a famished lioness. He was afraid, but without witnesses: the bravest men then give way to their fear.

'Only *he* could know ... and would dare ...' he said, as though to himself.

The masker gripped his hand to stop him completing the phrase, and said: 'Act as though it *were he*.'

Further masks

RASTIGNAC thereupon did what a millionaire does when confronted with a highwayman: he surrendered.

'My dear count,' he said to Châtelet, to whom he returned, 'if you care for your position, treat Lucien de Rubempré as a man whom one day you will find placed much higher than you are.'

The masked man permitted himself a barely perceptible movement of satisfaction, and returned to tracking Lucien.

'My dear fellow, you've very quickly changed your opinion of him,' replied the justly astonished prefect.

'As quickly,' said Rastignac to this prefect-deputy who for some days past had not voted with the Ministry, 'as those who belong to the Centre but vote with the Right.'

'Are there opinions nowadays? Surely, there are only conflicting interests,' put in des Lupeaulx, who was listening. 'Whom or what are we talking about?'

'The Sieur de Rubempré, whom Rastignac is trying to present to me as a figure of importance,' the deputy replied to the Secretary General.

'My dear count,' said des Lupeaulx with a solemn air, 'Monsieur de Rubempré is a young man of the greatest merit, and so well backed that I should be exceptionally glad to renew acquaintance with him.'

'There's a hornets' nest to bring about your ears, the profligates of the age,' Rastignac preferred.

The three of them turned towards a corner in which stood a group of known wits, men of more or less repute and some of fashion. These gentlemen were pooling observations, epigrams and items of gossip, amusing each other or waiting for amusement. Among this oddly composed troop were some with whom Lucien had once had relations superficially amiable but not without a background of harm done, sly tricks played.

'Well, Lucien, my child, my darling, here we are, patched up, re-upholstered! Where have we come from? We've climbed back on the old horse, have we, with the help of little gifts from Florine's dressing-room? Well done, old boy,' said Blondet, letting go Finot's arm to take Lucien by the waist and press him with unabashed familiarity to his bosom.

Andoche Finot was the proprietor of a review for which Lucien had worked almost without payment, and which benefited from Blondet's contributions, the sagacity of his counsels and the profundity of his views. Finot and Blondet might have been the Bertrand and Raton of La Fontaine's fable, except that the cat finally saw through the deception, while Blondet, though he knew he was being tricked, went on serving Finot. This brilliant *condottiere* of the pen would, indeed, long remain in a condition of slavery. Beneath his dull exterior, behind the bulwarks of stupidity and malice, brushed with wit as a labourer's crust is brushed with garlic, Finot concealed a ruthless will. Gleaning in the fields where men of letters and political schemers scatter ideas and small change, he stocked his barns. His powers put in the pay of his idleness and his vices, Blondet guaranteed his own misfortune. Always surprised by need, he belonged to the wretched clan of outstanding people who so lavishly serve anybody's purpose but their own, Aladdins who lend out their lamps. Their advice is invaluable, so long as their own interest is not at stake. With them, the head acts, the arm hangs limp. Whence their disordered lives, whence the poor regard in which they are held by inferior minds. Blondet shared his purse with the comrade he had injured yesterday; he dined, drank, slept with the one whose throat he would cut tomorrow. His amusing paradoxes justified all. Taking the whole world as a joke, he refused to be taken seriously himself. Young, much-loved, almost famous, of happy disposition, he was quite unconcerned to lay up, like Finot, what he might need in old age. The most difficult form of courage is perhaps that which Lucien needed at the moment, the ability to 'cut' Blondet as he had just cut Madame d'Espard and Châtelet. With him, unfortunately, the pleasures of vanity hindered the operations of pride, greatness's mainspring. His vanity had triumphed in the recent encounter: two people who had disdained him when he was poor and miserable had been confronted with his disdain, his wealth and happiness; but could a poet, like an elderly diplomat, quarrel openly with two supposed friends who had welcomed him when he was poor, who had given him a bed when he was penniless? Finot, Blondet and he had debased themselves in each other's company, had wallowed in orgies where not alone their creditors' money vanished. Like a soldier who cannot see where his courage is best bestowed, Lucien did what countless people do in Paris, he once more compromised his character by accepting a shake of the hand from Finot, by not drawing back from Blondet's endearment. Anybody who was once caught up in journalism, or is caught up in it still, is under the cruel necessity of greeting men he despises, smiling at his worst enemy, condoning actions of the most unspeakable vileness, soiling his hands to pay his aggressors out in their own coin. You grow used to seeing evil done, to letting it go; you begin by not minding, you end by doing it yourself. In the end, your soul, spotted daily by shameful transactions always going on, shrinks, the spring of noble thoughts rusts, the hinges of small talk wear loose and swing unaided. The Alcestes become Philintes, character loses its temper, talent degenerates, the belief in works of beauty evaporates. A man who wanted to take pride in his pages spends himself in wretched articles which sooner or later his conscience will tell him were base actions. You came on the scene, like Lousteau, like Vernou, intending to be a great writer, you find you have become an impotent hack. And so no honour is too high to be paid to those, like d'Arthez, whose character is equal to their talent, who steer an even keel between the reefs of the literary life. Lucien was incapable of a reply to Blondet's patter, the man's mind still exerted upon him an irresistible charm, retained the ascendancy of a corruptor over his pupil, he was, moreover, well placed in the world by reason of his connection with Countess Montcornet.

'Has an uncle left you something?' asked Finot banteringly.

'Like you,' said Lucien in the same tone, 'I take my cut off fools from time to time.'

'Has the gentleman acquired a review or a newspaper?' continued Andoche Finot with the offensive self-complacency of an operator towards one whom he exploits.

'I've done better than that,' replied Lucien, to whom vanity, wounded by the superiority the editor affected, had restored the sense of his new position.

'What have you got, then, dear boy? . . .'

'I have my Party.'

'There's a Lucien party?' said Vernou with a smile.

'Finot, you've been outstripped by the boy, as I predicted', said Blondet. 'Lucien has talent, and you didn't foster it, you wore him down. Old bull-of-the-bog, I hope you rue it.'

Blondet's sensitive nose had caught a whiff of important secrets in Lucien's accent, his bearing, his gestures; easing the rein, he yet, with his words, took a firm hold on the bit. He wanted to know the reasons for Lucien's return to Paris, what he planned, what he lived on.

'On your knees before your betters, Finot!' he went on. 'Lucien is one of us, but he must also be admitted now to that band of strong men to whom the future belongs! Handsome and witty, is he not bound to advance by your *quibuscum viis*? There he stands in his fine Milan armour, the powerful stiletto half out of its scabbard, pennon raised! 'Sdeath, Lucien, where did you pick up that pretty waistcoat? Stuff like that is only discovered by men in love. Where do we live? At this moment, I need to know my friends' addresses, I've got nowhere to sleep. Finot has pitched me out for the night, under the vulgar pretext of a lady having said yes.'

'My dear fellow,' replied Lucien, 'I have adopted a maxim with which I trust to lead a quiet life: *Fuge, late, tace!* I leave you.'

'But I don't leave you till we've squared a sacred debt, eh, that little supper?' said Blondet, who was excessively fond of good cheer and, when he was short of money, liked to be treated.

'What supper?' Lucien rejoined, with a touch of impatience.

'Don't you remember? That's how you can tell when a friend is prosperous: he loses his memory.'

'He knows what he owes us, I'll go warrant for his heart,' commented Finot, taking up the joke.

'Rastignac,' said Blondet, taking the young man of fashion by the arm as he came to the top end of the crush-room by the pillar where the self-styled friends were grouped, 'we're talking of a supper: you must join us . . . Unless the gentleman,' he went on solemnly, indicating Lucien, 'persists in denying a debt of honour; he may, of course.'

'Monsieur de Rubempré, I'll undertake, is quite incapable of it,' said Rastignac, whose mind was not on practical jokes.

'There's Bixiou!' cried Blondet, 'he must come, too: nothing's complete without him. Without him, champagne coats the tongue, and everything becomes insipid, even the spice of an epigram.'

'My friends,' said Bixiou, 'I see you gathered about the wonder of the day. Our dear Lucien has started his own version of Ovid's metamorphoses. Just as the gods turned themselves into local bigwigs and others to seduce women, he has turned Chardon into a gentleman to seduce – eh? – Charles X! Lucien, dear boy,' taking him by a button, 'a journalist promoted lord deserves a great reception. In their place,' said the pitiless clown, indicating Finot and Vernou, 'I'd open the pages of my little journal to you; ten columns of fine words should bring them in at least a hundred francs.'

'Bixiou,' said Blondet, 'an amphitryon should always be sacred to us twenty-four hours before and twelve after the feast: our illustrious friend has invited us all to supper.'

'What, what?' Bixiou persisted. 'What more deserving cause could there be than that of preserving a great name from oblivion, than endowing our indigent aristocracy with a man of talent? Lucien, you enjoy the esteem of the Press, whose fairest ornament you were, and we shall uphold you. Finot, a paragraph in all the Paris leaders! Blondet, a sly rigmarole on your page four! Let us announce the appearance of the greatest book of our time, *Charles IX's Archer*! Let us beg Dauriat not to delay giving us *Pearls*, those divine sonnets by the French

Petrarch! Let us raise up our friend on the royal shield of stamped paper which makes and unmakes reputations!'

'If you want to eat,' said Lucien to Blondet to be free of this growing mob, 'you had no need to use hyperbole and parabole with an old friend, as though I were green. Tomorrow evening, then, at Lointier's,' he concluded smartly, seeing approach a woman towards whom he hurried.

'Oh! oh! oh!' said Bixiou mockingly on three descending notes, evidently recognizing the masker Lucien had advanced to meet, 'this merits confirmation.'

The Torpedo

AND he followed the handsome couple, overtook it, examined it with a shrewd eye, and returned to satisfy the envious, interested to learn the origin of Lucien's change of fortune.

'My friends,' they heard Bixiou say, 'the Sire de Rubempré's fortune is a person long known to you, it is des Lupeaulx's quondam rat.'

A perversity now forgotten, but common enough in the early years of the century, was the luxury known as a rat. The word, already outmoded, was applied to a child of ten or eleven, a supernumerary at some theatre, generally the Opera, formed by some rake for infamy and vice. A rat was a kind of infernal page, a female urchin to whom everything was forgiven. A rat could take whatever it pleased; it was best distrusted as a dangerous animal, it introduced an element of gaiety into life, like the Scapins, Sganarelles and Frontins of the old comedy. A rat was a costly indulgence: it brought neither honour, nor profit, nor pleasure; the fashion for rats faded so completely that few people today knew this intimate detail of the life of elegance before the Restoration until it was taken up as a new subject by one or two writers.

'What, after having Coralie shot under him, is Lucien now to steal the Torpedo from us?' said Blondet.

Hearing this name, the powerfully built masker made a

brief movement which, though he controlled it, Rastignac observed.

'It isn't possible!' rejoined Finot. 'The Torpedo hasn't a farthing to give away, she's borrowed, Nathan told me, a thousand francs from Florine.'

'Gentlemen, please! . . .' said Rastignac, wishing to defend Lucien against such odious imputations.

'Why,' cried Vernou, once kept by Coralie, 'is he then such a prude? . . .'

'That thousand francs itself,' said Bixiou, 'is evidence of the fact that Lucien is living with the Torpedo.'

'What an irreparable loss,' said Blondet, 'to the world of literature, science, art and politics! The Torpedo is the one common whore with the makings of a true hetaira; she hadn't been spoilt by education, she can neither read nor write: she'd have understood us. We should have bestowed on our time one of those magnificent Aspasian figures without which no age can be great. Think how well Dubarry became the eighteenth century, Ninon de Lenclos the seventeenth, Marion de Lorme the sixteenth, Imperia the fifteenth, Flora the Roman republic, which she made her heir, and which in consequence was able to pay the public debt! What would Horace be without Lydia, Tibullus without Delia, Catullus without Lesbia, Propertius without Cynthia, Demetrius without the Lamia upon whom to this day his reputation rests?'

'Blondet, talking about Demetrius in the crush-room at the Opera,' Bixiou whispered to his neighbour, 'strikes me as a little too *Journal des débats*.'

'And without all those queens,' Blondet went on, 'what would the empire of the Caesars have been? Laïs, Rhodope *are* Greece and Egypt. The poetry of the centuries in which they all lived is theirs. This poetry, which Napoleon lacked, for his Grande Armée's widow is a barrack-room joke, was not lacking at the Revolution, which had Madame Tallien! In France now, where thrones are in fashion, one, certainly, is vacant! For my part, I'd have given the Torpedo an aunt, for her mother died all too authentically on the field of dishonour; du Tillet would have bought her a town house, Lousteau a coach, Rastignac lackeys, des Lupeaulx a cook, Finot providing hats (Finot could not repress his reaction as this epigram went home), Vernou would have advertised her, Bixiou would have supplied her witticisms! The aristocracy would come to Ninon's for its amusement, and artists would have been summoned under pain of mortiferous articles. Ninon II's rudeness would have been magnificent, her luxuriousness overwhelming. She would have had opinions. One would have read at her house some banned theatrical masterpiece which might at need have been written for the occasion. She would not have been a liberal, a courtesan is always a monarchist. Ah, what a loss! she should have embraced a whole century, and is in love with a commonplace young man! Lucien will make a gun-dog of her!'

'None of the feminine powers you name ever picked pockets,' said Finot, 'and this pretty rat paddled in the mud.'

'Like the seed of a lily in leaf-mould,' Vernou replied, 'she took up nourishment there, it brought her into bloom. Whence her superiority. Mustn't one have known all to be able to give laughter and joy to all?'

'He's right,' said Lousteau who till that moment had stood by without speaking, 'the Torpedo knows how to laugh and how to make others laugh. This skill of great authors and great actors belongs to those who have penetrated to the depths of society. At eighteen, this girl had already known the highest wealth, total destitution, men at all levels. She holds a magic wand with which she unlooses the brutish appetites so violently curbed in men not without heart who are occupied in politics or science, literature or art. There is no woman in Paris who can so effectively say to the Animal: "Out! . . ." And the Animal trots from its kennel, and it wallows in excesses; she sits you at table up to the chin, she helps you to drink, to smoke. In fact this woman is the salt celebrated by Rabelais, which, sprinkled on matter, animates it and raises it to the wonderful realms of Art: her dress displays unknown magnificences, her fingers drip jewels, her mouth is lavish with its smiles; she gives a sense of occasion to everything; her chatter sparkles and pricks; she knows the secret of onomatopeias themselves highly coloured and lending colour; she . . .'

'That's a hundred sous worth of copy wasted,' said Bixiou interrupting Lousteau, 'the Torpedo is infinitely better value than that: you've all been more or less her lovers, none of you can say she was his mistress; she can have you any time, but you won't get her. You force your way into her room, there is something you want from her . . .'

'Oh, she's more generous than a brigand chief in a good way of business, and more loyal than the best of school-friends,' said Blondet: 'you can entrust your purse or your secrets to her. But what made me elect her for queen, is her Bourbonian indifference to the fallen favourite.'

'She's like her mother, much too costly,' said des Lupeaulx. 'The fair Hollander would have swallowed up the revenues of the Archbishop of Toledo, she ate two notaries . . .'

'And fed Maxime de Trailles when he was a page,' said Bixiou.

'The Torpedo is too costly, like Raphael, like Carême, like Taglioni, like Lawrence, like Boule, just as all artists of genius have been too costly . . . ' said Blondet.

'Esther never had that look about her of a respectable woman,' Rastignac suddenly observed as he watched the masker to whom Lucien gave his arm. 'I bet it's Madame de Sérisy.'

'There can be no doubt about it,' du Châtelet agreed, 'and Monsieur de Rubempré's fortune is explained.'

'The Church knows how to pick its Levites, what a pretty embassy secretary he'll make!' said des Lupeaulx.

'Especially,' said Rastignac, 'as Lucien's a man of talent. These gentlemen have had more than one proof of that,' he added with a look at Blondet, Finot and Lousteau.

'Yes, the lad's cut out to go far,' said Lousteau eaten up with jealousy, 'especially as he possesses what we call *independence of mind* . . .'

'It was you who formed him,' said Vernou.

'Well, now,' Bixiou went on, looking at des Lupeaulx, 'I submit my case to the memory of the Secretary-General and Master of Petitions; that mask is the Torpedo, I'll wager a supper . . .'

'I'll hold the stakes,' said Châtelet interested in knowing the truth.

'Come on, des Lupeaulx,' said Finot, 'see if you don't recognize the ears of your quondam rat.'

'There's no need for outrageous peeping under masks,' Bixiou continued, 'the Torpedo and Lucien will be forced to pass this way again, I undertake then to prove that it is she.'

'He's put to sea again, friend Lucien, has he?' said Nathan who had joined the group, 'I thought he'd gone back to the Angoulême country for the rest of his days. Has he found some way of getting round the English?'

'He's done what you're in no hurry to do, he's paid his debts,' Rastignac told him.

The big masker nodded his head in assent.

'A man has to give up a lot to live within his income at that age, all the dash has gone out of him, he's finished,' said Nathan.

'Not that one,' Rastignac said, 'he'll always cut a figure, and always entertain a loftiness of idea that puts him above most of those who consider themselves superior.'

At this moment, journalists, dandies, idlers, all examined, like so many copers inspecting a horse for sale, the delightful subject of their wager. These judges grown old in the knowledge of Parisian depravity, all clever in one or another way, equally corrupt, equally corrupting, all pledged to insatiable ambitions, accustomed to guess, to imagine anything, had their eyes ardently fixed on a masked woman, a woman to be deciphered only by them. They alone and one or two who regularly attended the Opera ball were able to distinguish, beneath the long shroud of the black domino, beneath the hood, beneath the collar falling over the bosom in such a way as to put in doubt even the sex of the wearer, the roundedness of form, the particularities of carriage and gait, the turn of the waist, the way the head was held, those things which the common eye would most have failed to perceive but which to them were unmistakable. In spite of the formless envelope, they were thus able to recognize that most moving of spectacles, a woman truly animated by love. Whether it was the Torpedo, the Duchess of Maufrigneuse or Madame de Sérisy, the lowest or highest rung in the social ladder, this creature was of admirable creation, the light of happy dreams.

Those aged young men, as well as the youthful ancients, experienced so lively a sensation that they envied Lucien the high privilege of this metamorphosis of a woman into a goddess. The mask was there as though it had been alone with Lucien, for this woman there were no longer ten thousand persons, in an atmosphere heavy and full of dust; no; she was there beneath the celestial vault of Love, like the madonnas of Raphael under a threadlike oval of gold. She didn't feel the nudges, the ardour of her gaze started through the two holes of the mask and was reunited in Lucien's eyes, the very tremor of her body seemed to originate in the movements of her lover. What is the source of this light which shines about a woman in love and marks her out from the rest? of this sylphine lightness which seems to change the laws of gravity? Is it the freed soul? Are there physical virtues in happiness? The artlessness of a virgin, the graces of childhood were disclosed beneath the domino. Though walking separated, these two beings resembled statuary groups of Flora and Zephyr cunningly intertwined by the sculptor's hand; but it was not only sculpture, the greatest of the arts, which Lucien and his pretty domino recalled, but also those angels which the brush of Gian' Bellini depicted playing with birds and flowers below his images of Virgin Motherhood; Lucien and this woman belonged to the realm of Fantasy, which is higher than Art as cause stands above effect.

When this woman, forgetful of everything, was a pace away from the group, Bixiou called out: 'Esther?' The unfortunate creature turned quickly on hearing the name, saw the malicious individual, and lowered her head like a dying person who has just yielded up her last breath. A strident laugh broke out, and the group melted into the crowd like so many startled field-mice darting into their holes at the roadside. Rastignac alone moved no farther away than he needed to in order not to seem to be avoiding the blaze of Lucien's eyes; he was able to gaze in wonder upon two griefs equally deep though veiled: first the wretched Torpedo stricken as though by lightning, then the incomprehensible masker, the only one standing nearby who had not moved. Esther spoke a word in Lucien's ear just as her knees were giving way, and the two disappeared, Lucien bearing her weight. Rastignac followed the charming couple with his eyes, remaining sunk in his reflections.

'How did she come by this name of Torpedo?' said a gloomy voice which struck home to the depths of his soul, for it was no longer disguised.

'It is really *he* who has escaped again . . . ,' said Rastignac aside.

'Quiet, or I cut your throat,' replied the masker adopting another voice. 'I am pleased with you, you kept your word, and there are one or two on your side. Henceforward be silent as the tomb; but first, answer my question.'

'Why, then, this electric ray, this cramp-fish, is so attractive she'd have benumbed the Emperor Napoleon, and she'd numb a man harder to charm: you!' Rastignac answered moving away.

'One moment,' said the masker. 'I am going to show you that you can never have seen me anywhere.'

The man unmasked, Rastignac was at first taken aback to discover nothing of the hideous personage he had formerly known at the Maison Vauquer.

'The devil has allowed you to change yourself completely, except your eyes which could never be forgotten,' he said at last.

The grip of steel tightened on his arm to enjoin perpetual silence.

At three o' clock in the morning, des Lupeaulx and Finot found the elegant Rastignac in the same place, leaning against the pillar where the terrible masker had left him. Rastignac had been to confession with himself: he had been priest and penitent, judge and accused. He allowed himself to be led away to breakfast, and returned home decidedly tipsy, but taciturn.

A Parisian landscape

THE rue de Langlade, like the adjacent streets, runs between the Palais Royal and the rue de Rivoli. This part of one of the smartest districts of Paris will long preserve the contamination it received from those hillocks that were the middens of old Paris, topped with windmills. These narrow streets, dark and muddy, where trades are carried on which do not care about external appearance, take on at night a mysterious physiognomy and one full of contrasts. Coming from the bright lights of the rue Saint Honoré, the rue Neuve des Petits Champs and the rue de Richelieu, where there are always crowds and where are displayed the masterpieces of Industry, Fashion and the Arts, any man to whom Paris at night is unknown would be seized with gloom and terror as he plunged into the network of little streets which surround that brightness reflected in the sky itself. Thick shadow succeeds upon a torrent of gaslight. At wide intervals, a pale street-lamp casts its smoky and uncertain gleam, not seen at all in some of the blind alleys. Passers-by walk quickly and are uncommon. The shops are shut, those still open are of unsavoury character: a dirty wine-shop without lights, a linen-draper's selling eau de Cologne. An unwholesome chill folds its damp mantle about your shoulders. Few carriages pass. Notable among these sinister spots are the rue de Langlade, the opening of the Passage Saint Guillaume and various street turnings elsewhere. The municipal Council has never yet found means to cleanse this great leper-house, for prostitution long ago established its headquarters there. Perhaps it is fortunate for Parisian society that these alleys should retain their foul aspect. Passing that way in the day-time, nobody could imagine what all those streets become at night; they are scoured by singular creatures who belong to no world; white, half-naked forms line the walls, the darkness is alive. Female garments slink by walking and talking. Half-open doors suddenly shout with laughter. Upon the ear fall those words which Rabelais claimed to have frozen and which now melt. Strumming music comes up between the flagstones. The sound is not vague, it means something: when it is raucous, that is a human voice; but if it contains notes of music, there is no longer anything human about it, only a whistling sound. Blasts on a whistle are indeed frequently heard. Provocative, mocking, the click of heels approaches and recedes. All these things together make the mind reel. Atmospheric conditions are changed in this region: it is hot in winter and cold in summer. But, whatever the weather, nature there offers the same curious spectacle: this is the fantastic world of the Berliner Hoffmann. Sent to inspect it, the meticulous clerk would no longer credit his senses once he had returned by the same turnings to decent streets in which there were passers-by, shops and light to see by. More disdainful or more easily shamed than the kings and queens of earlier times, who were not afraid to concern themselves with the courtesans in their cities, modern administration and politics dare no longer look this plague in the face. True, what is done must change with time and place, and measures which affect individual liberty are always a delicate matter; but a degree of breadth and boldness might be displayed in purely material schemes to do with air, light and building. The moralist, the artist and the wise administrator will regret the old Wooden Galleries of the Palais Royal where the sheep were folded which appear wherever strollers go by; and is it not better for strollers to loiter where they are? What happened? Today the most brilliant stretches of the boulevards cannot be enjoyed in the evening by families for what should have been enchanted outings. The Police have failed to make a proper use of what are nevertheless called Passages, to spare the public way.

The girl crushed by a jest at the Opera ball had been living, for the past month or two, in the rue de Langlade, in a house of ignoble appearance. Ill-plastered against the wall of a much larger house, this construction without either breadth or depth, lighted only from the street, yet rises to a prodigious height, recalling the stick up which a parrot climbs. Each floor consists of a two-roomed apartment. The house is served by a narrow staircase against the outer wall, whose course may be traced from outside by fixed lights which feebly illuminate it within and on each landing of which stands a sink, one of the most horrible peculiarities of Paris. The shop and the living quarters immediately above it then belonged to a tinsmith, the owner lived on the first floor, the four floors above were occupied by well-behaved seamstresses to whom the owner and caretaker were indulgent because of the difficulty of letting a house so oddly constructed and situated. The neighbourhood had become what it was by reason of the fact that it contained so many just such houses, of no use to serious Commerce and thus able to be exploited only by unacknowledged, precarious or undignified trades.

Interior as familiar to some as unknown by others

AT three o'clock in the afternoon, the caretaker, who had seen Mademoiselle Esther brought back half-dead by a young man at two o'clock in the morning, had just been holding counsel with the *grisette* on the top floor, who, before taking a carriage to some party of pleasure, had evidenced disquietude about Esther, from whom she had heard no movement. No doubt Esther was still asleep, but she ought not to have been. Alone in her lodge, the caretaker wished she had been able to go up to the fourth floor, where Mademoiselle Esther lodged. Just as she decided to leave her lodge in charge of the tinsmith's son, the said lodge being a mere recess in the wall off the tinsmith's landing, a cab arrived. A man enveloped from head to foot in a cloak, with the evident intention of concealing his costume and station, got out and asked for Mademoiselle Esther. This wholly reassured the caretaker, to whom it fully explained the silence and tranquillity of the recluse. As the visitor climbed the steps above her lodge, the caretaker noticed silver buckles on his shoes and fancied she had glimpsed the black fringe of the sash about a cassock; she went down and asked the cabman, who replied without speaking, in a manner the caretaker understood. The priest knocked, received no answer, heard a quiet sighing from within, and shouldered the door open with a vigour doubtless to be attributed to the power of Christian charity, though in another man it might have seemed mere habit. He hurried through to the second room, and there saw, before a Virgin in coloured plaster, poor Esther not so much kneeling as collapsed in a heap with hands together. The 'little milliner' was dying. Cinders in the grate told the story of that dreadful morning. The hood and mantle of the domino lay on the floor. The bed had not been slept in. The poor creature, stricken to the heart with a mortal wound, had without doubt arranged all on her return from the Opera. The wick of a candle, set hard in the sconce of a candlestick, showed how completely Esther had been absorbed in her last reflections. A handkerchief soaked with tears proved the sincerity of the despair of this Mary Magdalene, whose classic pose was that of the harlot without religion. This final repentance made the priest smile. Inexpert at dying, Esther had left the inner door open without calculating that the air in the two rooms needed a greater quantity of coal to make it unbreathable; the fumes had merely dazed her; colder air from the staircase now brought her slowly back to an appreciation of her woes. The priest remained standing, lost in gloomy meditation, untouched by the divine beauty of the young prostitute, watching her first movements as though it had been some animal. His eyes travelled from the barely animate body to objects in the room with apparent indifference. He studied the furnishings of this room, whose cold, worn red tiles were barely hidden by a wretched, threadbare carpet. An old-fashioned cot in painted wood, surrounded by curtains of yellow-brown calico with a dull-red rose-pattern; a single armchair and two painted wooden chairs, covered with the same calico, with which also the windows were curtained; a grey wallpaper speckled with flowers, blackened and greasy with age; a mahogany worktable; the fireplace cluttered with kitchen utensils of the cheapest kind, two large bundles of firewood broken apart, a stone mantelpiece on which a few glass ornaments stood, with bits of jewellery and scissors; a card of dirty thread, white, scented gloves, a delicious hat propped on the water jug, a Ternaux shawl stuffing a crack in the window, an elegant dress hanging on a nail, a little, uncomfortable sofa without cushions; broken clogs and pretty shoes, laced half-boots fit for a queen, china plates chipped and cracked, the remains of a meal among cutlery of German nickel, the silverware of the Parisian poor; a basket full of potatoes and dirty linen, a clean gauze bonnet on top; a hideous wardrobe, its glass doors open, empty, on its shelves a selection of pawnshop tickets: such was the array of joyous and dismal, wretched and expensive objects which met the eye. These luxuries among the broken fragments, this household so appropriate to the Bohemian life of the limp, half-dressed wench sunk down like a horse dead in its harness, pinned by a broken shaft, caught in the reins, did this curious spectacle give the priest pause? Did he say to himself that at any rate that lost creature was acting disinterestedly to love a rich young man and at the same time live in such poverty? Did he ascribe the disorder in the room to a disordered life? Was his feeling one of pity, or of fear? Was his charity stirred? Whoever had seen him, arms folded, forehead creased with thought, tight-lipped, eye scathing, would have thought him possessed by contradictory impulses and thoughts in which a gloomy distaste and baleful intentions predominated. He was, certainly, insensible to the pretty, round breasts half-flattened against the knees and the delicious forms of a crouching Venus revealed beneath the black material of the skirt, so tensely was the dying woman coiled upon herself; the abandon of this head, which, seen from behind, displayed its white, supple, vulnerable nape, the beautiful shoulders of a nature boldly developed, did not move him; he did not raise Esther up, he did not seem to hear the heartbreaking inhalations by which the return to life was accomplished: it needed a dreadful sob and the terrifying look which the girl cast upon him before he deigned to raise her and carry her to the bed with an ease which betrayed prodigious strength.

'Lucien!' she murmured.

'Love returns, the woman is not far behind,' said the priest with a sort of bitterness.

The victim of Parisian depravity then perceived her rescuer's style of dress, and said, with the smile of a child grasping at something long desired: 'I shan't die, then, without being reconciled to heaven!'

'You will be able to expiate your faults,' said the priest, bathing her forehead with water and holding under her nose a vinegar bottle he found in a corner.

'I feel life not leaving but flowing back into me,' she said after receiving the priest's attentions and expressing her gratitude to him with expressions of unaffected simplicity.

This engaging pantomime, which the Graces themselves, bent on pleasing, could scarcely have bettered, might have been thought at least partly to explain the girl's curious nickname.

'Do you feel better?' asked the ecclesiastic, giving her a glass of sugar and water to drink.

The man seemed to know his way about households of this kind, he knew where everything was. He had made himself at home. This gift of being everywhere at home belongs only to kings, light women and thieves.

A rat's confession

'WHEN you have fully recovered,' the singular priest went on after a pause, 'you will tell me the reasons which led you to commit this latest crime, your attempt at suicide.'

'My story is a simple one, father,' she replied. 'Three months ago, I was living in the disorder to which I was born. I was the lowest and most infamous of creatures, now I am only the unhappiest. Permit me to say nothing about my poor mother, who died murdered . . .'

'By a captain, in a house of ill fame,' said the priest interrupting his penitent . . . 'I know your origins, and know that if one of your sex may ever be excused for leading a life of shame, it is you, who lacked good example.'

'Alas! I was not baptised, and haven't received the teachings of any religion.'

'Then everything can be put right,' the priest went on, 'so long as your faith, your repentance, are sincere and without reservation.'

'Lucien and God fill my heart,' said she with a touching ingenuousness.

'You might have said God and Lucien,' the priest replied smiling. 'You remind me of the object of my visit. Omit nothing concerning this young man.'

'You come on his behalf?' she asked with a loving expression which would have melted the heart of any other priest. 'Oh, he suspected what I might do!'

'No,' he replied, 'it isn't your death but your life which gives rise to concern. Come, explain what the relations are between you.'

'In one word,' said she.

The poor wench trembled at the ecclesiastic's abrupt tone, but as a woman to whom gross incivility has long been without surprise.

'Lucien is Lucien,' she continued, 'the handsomest young man, and the best of living beings; but if you know him, my love must seem to you only natural. I met him by chance, three months ago, at the Porte Saint Martin where I had gone on my day out; for we had a free day a week at Madame Meynardie's where I was. Next day, you will easily understand that I broke away without permission. Love had entered my heart, and had so changed me that, returning from the theatre, I no longer recognized myself: I filled myself with horror. Lucien never knew. Instead of telling him the house I was in, I gave him the address of this lodging where a friend of mine was then living, who was kind enough to give it up to me. I give you my sacred word . . .'

'You must not swear.'

'Is it swearing to give one's sacred word? Well, since that day I have worked in this room, like a madwoman, making shirts at twenty-eight sous on order, so as to live by honest work. For a month I lived on nothing but potatoes, to remain good and worthy of Lucien, who loves me and respects me as the most virtuous of the virtuous. I made my declaration in form to the Police, in order to resume my rights, and I am under supervision for two years. They, who are so prompt to inscribe you on the roll of infamy, show an extreme reluctance to strike your name out. All I asked heaven was to protect my

40

resolution. I shall be nineteen in April: at that age things are easier. To me, it seems that I was only born three months ago ... I prayed to God every morning, and begged Him to grant that Lucien should never learn what my life had been. I bought the Virgin you see there; I prayed to her in my own way, seeing that I don't know any prayers; I can neither read nor write, I have never been into a church, I've never seen God except in processions, out of curiosity.'

'And what do you say to the Virgin?'

'I speak to her as I speak to Lucien, with those sudden impulses of the soul which make him weep.'

'Ah, he weeps?'

'With joy,' she added quickly. 'Poor lamb! we understand each other so well that it is only a single soul we share! He's so kind, so affectionate, so gentle in heart, mind and manners ...! He says he's a poet, I say he's God ... Forgive me! but, you priests, you don't know what love is. And then only those like me can know men well enough to appreciate a Lucien. A Lucien, I tell you, is as rare as a woman without sin; when you meet one, you can't any longer love anybody but him: that's all. But a man like that needs somebody like him. So I wanted to be worthy to be loved by my Lucien. That led to my downfall. Yesterday, at the Opera, I was recognized by some young men who've got no more heart than there is pity in tigers; I could still get on with a tiger! The veil of innocence I was wearing fell; their laughter rent head and heart. Don't think you have saved me, I shall die of grief.'

'Your veil of innocence? ...' said the priest, 'so you treated Lucien with, shall we say, a degree of severity?'

'Oh, father, you who know him, how could you ask me such a question?' she replied with a smile that was radiant, superb. 'A God can't be resisted.'

'Do not blaspheme,' said the ecclesiastic in a gentle voice. 'Nobody can be like God; that kind of exaggeration ill becomes real love, it wasn't a pure, true love you had for your idol. If you had undergone the change you lay claim to, you would have acquired the virtues of youth, you would have known the delights of chastity, the delicacy of shame, those two glories of a young girl. You are not in love.'

Esther made a frightened movement which did not escape the priest, but which in no way affected his imperturbability as confessor.

'Yes, you love him for your own sake and not for his, for the temporal pleasures you are addicted to, not for love itself; gaining a hold on him thus, you did not display that holy trembling which inspires a being upon whom God has set the seal of the most adorable perfections: did you think how you degraded him with your past impurity, that you were corrupting a child with those fearful delights which gave you your nickname, with its infamous glory? You were inconsistent with yourself and your short-lived passion . . .'

'Short-lived!' she repeated raising her eyes.

'How else are we to describe a love which is not eternal, which does not unite us, even to the Christian hereafter, with the one we love?'

'Ah, I want to be a Catholic!' she cried out in a violent, toneless voice that would have obtained Our Saviour's grace.

'Could a girl who received the baptism neither of the Church nor of secular knowledge, who can neither read nor write, nor pray, who can't take a step in the street without the paving stones rising up to accuse her, remarkable only for the fugitive gift of a beauty which illness will perhaps destroy tomorrow; could so debased, degraded a creature, knowing her degradation . . . (unknowing and less loving, you might have been more readily excused . . .), could the eventual prey of suicide and damnation be a fit wife for Lucien de Rubempré?'

Each phrase was a dagger-thrust which went home. At each phrase, the despairing girl's increased sobs and abundant tears attested the force with which light penetrated at once into her intelligence as pure as that of a savage, her soul at last awakened, her nature upon which depravity had deposited a layer of muddy ice, now melting in the sun of faith.

'Why am I not dead!' was the sole idea she expressed amid the torrent of ideas which streamed destructively through her brain.

'My daughter,' said the terrible judge, 'there is a love unconfessed before men, which yet, confided to the angels, is welcomed by them with smiles of happiness.'

'What love?'

'The love which is without hope, when it is the inspiration of a life, when that life is governed by its devotion, when every action is ennobled by the thought of reaching an ideal perfection. Yes, the angels approve such a love; it leads to the knowledge of God. To perfect oneself unceasingly in order to be worthy of the loved one, to make a thousand hidden sacrifices for him, adore him from a distance, give one's blood drop by drop, for him to destroy all self-love, all pride and anger, to spare him even the knowledge of whatever pangs of jealousy he may cause, give him whatever he wishes, even to our own detriment, love what he loves, to keep one's face turned towards him and to follow him without him knowing; religion would have forgiven you such a love, it offended against neither human nor divine law, and led to other courses than that of your filthy pleasures.'

Upon hearing this horrible decree expressed by one word (and what a word? and pronounced in what a tone?) Esther was understandably tormented by suspicion. This word was like a thunderclap presaging a storm to come. She looked at the priest, and was pierced by the sudden chill with which even the bravest are seized in the face of a sudden and imminent danger. No look could have read what was passing through the mind of this man; but the boldest would have seen more to tremble at than to hope for in the expression of those eyes, once pale and yellow like those of a tiger, but over which privation and austerity had cast a veil like that which lies on the horizon in sultry weather: the earth is hot and bright, but the mist renders it indistinct, vaporous, it is almost invisible. A heaviness that was wholly Spanish, deep lines which the countless scars of a dreadful smallpox made hideous, like trampled furrows, scored his olive-skinned, sun-baked face. The harshness of this physiognomy was brought out all the more sharply by the hair which framed it, the tattered wig of a priest who no longer cares about his person, threadbare and of a black which showed red in the light. His athletic torso, his old soldier's hands, his square build and massive shoulders belonged to one of those caryatids which the architects of the Middle Ages have placed before certain Italian palaces, imperfectly recalled by those at the Porte Saint Martin theatre. Individuals of no great penetration would have thought that the strongest passions or circumstances out of the ordinary must have thrown this man into the bosom of the Church; certainly, only the most extraordinary blows of fate could have changed him, if indeed such a nature had been susceptible of change.

What constitutes a whore

WOMEN who have led the life now so violently repudiated by Esther reach a point of total indifference to man's exterior form. They are like the literary critic of today, who may be compared with them in more than one respect and who attains to a profound unconcern with artistic standards: he has read so many books, forgotten so many, is so accustomed to written pages, has watched so many plots unfold, witnessed so many dramatic climaxes, he has produced so many articles without saying what he really thought, so often betraying art to serve his friendships and his enmities, that in the end he views everything with distaste and continues nevertheless to judge. It would need a miracle for such a writer to produce a single book of his own, just as it needs a miracle for a pure and noble love to blossom in the heart of a courtesan. The manner and tone of this priest, who might have stepped out of a canvas by Zurbaran, appeared so hostile to the poor little tart, unable to see him in any such terms, that she felt herself to be less an object of solicitude than the victim of a plan. Incapable of distinguishing between smooth words and fair promises and the unction of charity, for one needs to be very vigilant to notice the bad money palmed off by a friend, she felt as though she were pinned by the claws of a monstrous and ferocious bird which had swooped on her after long hovering and, in her fear, she uttered these words in a voice of alarm: 'I believed that priests were meant to console us, and it is my death you intend!'

At this cry of innocence, the ecclesiastic made a vague

gesture, and paused; he collected himself before replying. During that moment, the two individuals so strangely brought together eyed each other. The priest understood the girl, without the girl understanding the priest. Evidently he gave up some plan which threatened poor Esther, and returned to his earlier purpose.

'We are the doctors of souls,' he said in a gentle voice, 'and we know what remedies are suited to their sicknesses.'

'Much has to be forgiven to unhappiness,' said Esther.

She believed that she had been mistaken, slid down from the bed, prostrated herself at the feet of this man, kissed his cassock with deep humility, and raised towards him eyes bathed in tears.

'I thought I had done all I could,' she said.

'Listen, my child, your fearful reputation has plunged Lucien's family into grief; they fear, and not without justice, lest you lead him into dissipation, into a world of folly . . .'

'It is true, I took him to the ball to awaken his curiosity.'

'You are sufficiently beautiful for him to want to triumph through you in the eyes of the world, to show you off with pride like a prize horse. If it were only money it cost him! . . . but he will spend his time, his strength; he will lose all taste for the brilliant future that has been prepared for him. Instead of one day being an ambassador, rich, admired, famous, he will have been, like so many of the debauched whose talents have foundered in the mud of Paris, the lover of a harlot. As for you, after rising briefly into the world of fashion, you would have gone back to your old life, for you lack the power which a good education gives to resist vice and plan for the future. You would no more have broken with your former companions than you were able to break with the men who shamed you at the Opera, this morning. Lucien's true friends, alarmed by the love you inspire in him, followed in his footsteps and learned all. Anxious and worried, they sent me to you to sound out your dispositions and decide what was to be done with you; they are powerful enough to clear any stumbling block out of this young man's way, but they are also merciful. Know this, my daughter: a person loved by Lucien has rights in their eyes, as a true Christian may adore mire in

45

which, by some chance, the divine light shines. I am here as the vehicle of their benevolence; but had I found you altogether perverted, armed with guile and effrontery, corrupt to the bone, deaf to the voice of repentance, I should have abandoned you to their wrath. That civic and political release, so difficult to obtain, which the Police rightly delays in the interests of Society itself, and which I heard you crave for with the strength of true remorse, I have it here,' said the priest, drawing from his girdle an official-looking document. 'You were seen yesterday, this form is dated today: you may conceive how powerful are those who take an interest in Lucien.'

At the sight of this paper, Esther in her ingenuousness was so shaken by the trembling which an unhoped-for piece of good fortune may cause, that her lips bore a fixed smile like that of an idiot. The priest hesitated, looking at the child to see whether, robbed of the horrible strength which the corrupt draw from their very corruption, and brought back to a fragile and delicate original nature, she would continue impressionable. A deceitful whore, Esther would have acted as in a play; but, returned to innocence and truth, she could have died, as a blind man on whom a successful operation has been performed may lose his sight again on being struck by too vivid a light. This man thus saw human nature to its depths, but remained in a calm terrible by reason of its fixity: he was cold as an Alp, white and close to the sky, impermeable and supercilious, granite-sloped, beneficent nevertheless. The daughters of pleasure are essentially unstable beings, changing without reason from bewildered suspicion to absolute trust. In this respect, they are lower than the animals. Extreme in everything, in their joys, their despairs, their religion, their irreligion; most of them would go mad if they were not decimated by an unusual rate of mortality, and if accidents of fortune did not raise some of them out of the mire in which they live. Nothing could better have illuminated the depths of this horrible life than to see how far one of its creatures may go in madness and yet emerge from it, marvelling at the Torpedo's violent ecstasy at the knees of this priest. The poor wench gazed at the order of her release with an expression which Dante forgot, surpassing the inventions of his Inferno. But with tears came the reaction. Esther rose to her feet, threw her arms about this man's neck, placed her head on his bosom, wept on it, kissed the rough material which covered the heart of steel, and seemed bent on penetrating it. She laid hold of the man, covered his hands with kisses; in a holy effusion of gratitude, yet wheedled him with caresses, lavished fond names upon him, among the honeyed phrases said to him again and again: '*Give it to me!*' with as many varied intonations; enfolded him in tenderness, covered him in glances so rapid they should have laid him defenceless; in the end, numbed his anger. The priest saw how this woman had come by her nickname; he understood how difficult it was to resist the enchanting creature, he all at once unriddled Lucien's love and the charm which had caused it. Such a passion, among its many attractions, conceals a barbed sharpness which hooks especially the lofty souls of poets and artists. Inexplicable to the crowd, such passions are fully explained by that thirst for ideal beauty which is characteristic of creative natures. To purify such a being, is it not to be a bit like the angels charged with leading the guilty back to nobler feelings, is it not to create? What a temptation to bring moral and physical beauty into consonance! What pride in one's joy if one succeeds! What a fair task which needs no instrument but love! Unions of that kind, illustrated moreover by the examples of Aristotle, Socrates, Plato, Cethegus, Pompey, yet monstrous in the eyes of the vulgar, are based on that feeling which led Louis XIV to build Versailles, which has always thrown men into ruinous undertakings: to convert the miasma of a swamp into heaped-up scents surrounded by living water; to put a lake on a hill-top, as the Prince of Conti did at Nointel, or the views of Switzerland at Cassan, like Farmer General Bergeret. In the last resort, it is the irruption of Art into Morality.

The priest, ashamed of yielding to tenderness, sharply repulsed Esther, who sat down, herself ashamed, for what he said to her was: 'You are still a whore.' And coldly he tucked the letter back in his girdle. Like a child with only one thought in her head, Esther could not take her eyes off that place at his waist where the paper was.

'DAUGHTER,' the priest continued after a pause, 'your mother was a Jewess, and you were not baptised, but neither were you taken to the synagogue: your place is in the religious Limbo to which little children go . . .'

'Little children!' she repeated softly.

'. . . Just as in Police files, you are a mere number, without social identity,' went on the implacable priest. 'If love, appearing to you as a runaway, made you suppose, three months ago, that you were reborn, you must feel that since that day you have been truly in a state of childhood. You must therefore conduct yourself like a child; you must change utterly, and I take it upon myself to put you beyond recognition. In the first place, you will forget Lucien.'

The poor girl was heartbroken at this thought; she raised her eyes towards the priest and shook her head; she could not speak, finding that the supposed rescuer was still to be her executioner.

'You will at least stop seeing him,' said the priest. 'I shall take you to a religious house where the daughters of the best families receive their education; there you will become a Catholic, you will be instructed in Christian practices, you will be taught religion; you could leave that place a girl with accomplishments, chaste, pure, well-bred, if . . .'

He held up a finger and paused.

'If,' he went on, 'you feel that you have the strength to leave the Torpedo here.'

'Ah!' cried the poor child to whom each word had been like a note of music at the sound of which the gates of paradise were slowly opened, 'Ah, if it were possible to pour out all my blood here and to receive new blood! . . .'

'Listen to me.'

She was silent.

'Your future depends on your power to forget. Think of the extent of your obligations: one word, one gesture which betrayed the Torpedo kills Lucien's wife; something you said

48

in a dream, an involuntary thought, an immodest look, a sign of impatience, a memory of past dissolution, an omission, a movement of the head which revealed what you know or what to your misfortune has been known . . .'

'Believe me, Father, believe me,' the girl said with the exaltation of a saint, 'to walk in shoes of red-hot iron and to smile, to live wrapped in a spiked corset and preserve the grace of a dancer, eat bread sprinkled with ashes, drink wormwood, it would all be easy, sweet!'

She fell on her knees again, she kissed the priest's shoes, made them wet with her tears, she clasped his legs and pressed her face against them, murmuring senseless words as she wept for joy. Her admirable fair hair hung to the ground and made a carpet beneath the feet of this messenger from heaven, whom she saw hard-faced, unsmiling, when she stood up and looked at him.

'What offence have I given you?' said she in fear again. 'I have heard tell of a woman like me who poured aromatic ointment upon the feet of Jesus Christ. Alas, virtue has made me so poor that I have only tears to offer!'

'Did you not hear me?' he answered in a voice of cruelty. 'I tell you, you must be able to leave the house where I am taking you so changed in your nature and appearance that neither man nor woman among those who knew you will be able to call out to you: "Esther!" and make you turn your head. Yesterday, love had not given you the strength so deeply to bury the woman of pleasure that she should never reappear, she appears again in this adoration which belongs only to God.'

'Did He not send you to me?' said she.

'If, during the course of your education, you caught sight of Lucien, all would be lost,' he continued. 'Think well of that.'

'Who will console him?' she said.

'For what did you console him?' asked the priest in a voice which, for the first time in this scene, betrayed a nervous tremor.

'I don't know, he was often sad when he came.'

'Sad?' the priest asked again. 'Did he tell you why?'

'Never,' she replied.

'He was sad at being in love with a woman like you,' cried he.

'Alas, he was right to be sad!' she continued with deep humility. 'I am the most despicable creature of my sex, and I could only find favour in his eyes by the strength of my love.'

'That love must give you the courage to obey me blindly. If I led you at once to the house where you will be educated, everybody here would tell Lucien that you had gone away, today Sunday, with a priest; that would put him on your path. In a week from now, the caretaker, not seeing me come back, will have taken me for what I am not. So, one evening, say today week, at seven o' clock, you will go out secretly and enter a cab which will be waiting for you at the end of the rue des Frondeurs. Avoid Lucien all week; find excuses, have him forbidden the door, and, when he comes, go upstairs to a friend's room; I shall know whether you've seen him, and, in that case, everything is over, I shan't even return. You'll need a week to put some respectable clothes together and stop looking like a prostitute,' he said putting a purse on the mantelpiece. 'There is in your manner, your clothes, that something so well known to Parisians which tells them what you are. Have you never met in the street, on the boulevards, a modest, virtuous young person out with her mother?'

'Oh, yes, to my cost! The sight of a mother and her daughter is one of our worst tortures, it awakens a remorse hidden in the recesses of our hearts, eating us away! ... I know only too well what I lack.'

'Well, then, you know what you should look like next Sunday,' said the priest, rising.

'Oh,' she said, 'before you go, teach me a real prayer, so that I can pray to God!'

It was a touching sight, that of this priest making the penitent whore repeat the *Ava Maria* and *Paternoster* in French.

'How beautiful they are!' said Esther when she had once gone without mistake through the two popular and magnificent expressions of Catholic faith.

'What is your name?' she asked the priest as he left.

'Carlos Herrera, I am a Spaniard and banished from my country.'

Esther took his hand and kissed it. She was no longer a harlot, but a fallen angel getting up again.

A portrait Titian would have liked to paint

IN a house famous for the aristocratic and religious education received there, in early March of that year, one Monday morning, the boarders saw their pretty company augmented by a new arrival whose beauty incontestably surpassed not merely that of her companions, but the finest points of each. In France, it is extremely rare, if indeed it is not impossible, to meet the thirty celebrated perfections described in lines of Persian verse and carved, it is said, in the seraglio, which a woman needs in order to be wholly beautiful. In France, if general harmony is uncommon, ravishing details abound. As to that perfect and imposing harmony which statuary seeks to render, and which it has rendered in one or two notable compositions, such as the Diana and the Callipygian Venus, it is the privilege of Greece and Asia Minor. Esther came from this cradle of the human species, the homeland of beauty: her mother was Jewish. The Jews, though so often debased by their contact with other peoples, yet present among their numerous tribes strains in which the sublimest type of Asiatic beauty is preserved. When they are not of repulsive ugliness, they display the magnificent character of Armenian features. Esther would have carried off the prize in a seraglio, she possessed the thirty beauties harmoniously blended. Far from deleteriously affecting the fine edges of her figure, the freshness of her complexion, her odd life had given her an elusively feminine quality: no longer the closely smooth texture of green fruit, nor yet the hot bloom of maturity, the blossom was still there. A little longer spent in dissolution, she would have grown plump. That abundant health, that animal perfection of the creature in whom voluptuousness takes the place of thought must be a salient fact in the eyes of physiologists.

51

By a rare circumstance, if indeed it is ever found in very young girls, her hands, incomparably formed, were soft, transparent and white like those of a woman brought to bed of her second child. She had exactly the foot and the hair, so justly renowned, of the Duchesse de Berri, hair no hairdresser's hand could hold, so abundant was it, and so long, that falling to the ground it coiled there, for Esther was of that medium height which allows a woman to be made a kind of toy, to be taken up, put down, taken up again and carried without fatigue. Her skin as fine as Chinese rice-paper, its amber warmth tinted with pink veins, had a sheen without dryness, softness without moisture. Remarkably vigorous, though delicate in appearance, Esther caught attention suddenly with a characteristic most often remarked in faces which Raphael's pencil disengaged to perfection, for of all painters Raphael most closely studied and best rendered Jewish beauty. This marvellous feature was effected by the depth of the arch beneath which the eye turned as though liberated from its setting, its curve sharply defined as the groining of a vault. When the pure and diaphanous tints of youth and finely marked eyebrows clothe such an arch; when the light which slips into the hollow circle beneath it is all a bright rose, there are treasures of tenderness to content a lover, beauties of which a painter may despair. Those luminous recesses where the shadows take on tones of gold, this tissue fine as a ligament and flexible as the most sensitive membrane, are nature's final achievement. The eye is at rest therein like a miraculous egg in a nest of spun silk. But in later life a frightful melancholy may afflict this marvel, when the passions have charred these thin contours, when grief has contracted this network of fibrils. Esther's origins were betrayed by the oriental formation of her Turkish-lidded eyes, their colour a slate-grey which, in the light, caught the blue tint in the black wings of a raven. Only the extreme tenderness of her gaze dimmed their brilliance. In the eyes of the desert races alone may be seen the power to fascinate everybody, for a woman may always fascinate one or two. No doubt their eyes retain something of the infinitude they have contemplated. Can it be that nature, in her prescience, has provided their retinas with some capacity for reflecting back and thus enduring the mirage of the sands, the torrents of sunlight, the burning cobalt of the ether? or that human beings, like others, derive some quality from the surroundings among which they have been developed, and that its attributes stay with them over centuries! This great solution to the problem of race is perhaps inherent in the question itself. The instincts are living facts whose cause resides in some necessity endured. Animal species result from the exercise of these instincts. To be convinced of this truth so greatly sought, it is enough to extend to the human herd an observation recently made on flocks of Spanish and British sheep which, on lowland pastures where the grass is thick, feed close together, while they scatter on hill pastures where the grass is thin. Remove these two breeds of sheep from their native lands, transport them into Switzerland or France: the mountain sheep continues to feed alone, though in low-lying, close-grassed meadows; the valley sheep will feed close together, though on an Alp. The acquired and transmitted instinct is barely modified after several generations. At a hundred years' distance, the mountain spirit reappears in a refractory lamb, as, after eighteen hundred years of exile, the East shone through the eyes and in the visage of Esther. This look cast no dread fascination, but rather a gentle warmth, it caused heartstrings to slacken without surprise, it weakened the hardest will by its mild heat. Esther had overcome hatred, she had astounded the rakes of Paris, and in the end that look and the sweetness of her smooth skin had bestowed upon her the dreadful nickname which already provided the inscription for her tomb. In her, everything was harmoniously in character with a peri of the burning sands. Her forehead was strong and proudly designed. Her nose, like that of the Arabs, was fine, narrow, oval-nostrilled, well-placed, turned up at the edges. Her red, fresh mouth was a rose without blemish, orgies had left no mark upon it. The chin, modelled as though by a sculptor in love, was of milky whiteness. One thing which she had not had time to remedy betrayed the courtesan fallen too low: her torn nails had not yet recovered their elegance, so much had they been deformed by common household cares. The young boarders began with jealousy of her miracles of beauty, but ended in admiration. Before a week had passed they had taken the simple Esther to their hearts, interested by the secret misfortunes of a girl of eighteen who could neither read nor write, to whom all knowledge, all instruction were new, and who was about to bring to the archbishop the glory of the conversion of a Jewess to Catholicism, to the convent the festival of her baptism. They forgave her her beauty, finding themselves her superiors in the matter of education. Esther had quickly taken on the manner, the gentleness of voice, the bearing and attitudes of these daughters of distinction; finally she recovered her first nature. The change was so complete that, at his first visit, Herrera was astonished, he whom nothing in the world seemed able to surprise, and her superiors complimented him on his pupil. These women had never, in their teaching career, met with a nature more amiable, a more Christian gentleness, truer modesty, nor so great a desire to learn. When a girl has suffered the misfortunes which had overwhelmed the poor boarder and expects such a reward as the Spaniard offered Esther, it is almost certain that she will renew those miracles of the first days of the Church which the Jesuits brought about in Paraguay.

'She is an edification,' said Mother Superior kissing her on the forehead.

This essentially Catholic word told all.

A form of homesickness

DURING recreation, Esther discreetly questioned her companions about the simplest things in the world, which to her were like life's first surprises to a child. When she knew that she would be dressed in white on the day of her baptism and first communion, that she would wear a white satin hair-band, white ribbons, white shoes, white gloves, with a white bow on her head, she burst into tears in the midst of her astonished companions. It was the opposite of the scene of Jephthah's daughter upon the mountain. The harlot feared to be understood, she attributed her dreadful melancholy to the joy the spectacle caused her in anticipation. As there is certainly as great a distance between the customs she was giving up and those she was adopting as there is between the savage state and civilization, she exhibited the grace and simplicity, the depth, which single out the wonderful heroine of *The Prairie*. She also, without knowing it herself, was gnawed at by the love in her heart, a strange love, a desire more violent in her who knew all than it is in a virgin who knows nothing, although both desires had the same cause and the same purpose. During the first months, the novelty of a secluded life, the surprises of her instruction, the tasks she was taught to perform, the practices of religion, the fervour of a devout resolution, the sweetness of the affection she inspired, above all the exercise of the faculties of awakened intelligence, all helped to keep her memories in check, even her efforts in creating a new memory; for she had as much to unlearn as to learn. We have more than one memory; the body, the mind, each have their own; and nostalgia, for example, is a sickness of the physical memory. During the third month, the impetus of this virgin spirit, straining with outstretched wings towards paradise, was thus, not tamed, but impeded by a muffled resistance whose origin was unknown to Esther herself. Like the sheep of Scotland, she wanted to feed apart, she could not conquer the instincts developed by debauchery. Was she reminded of it by the muddy streets of Paris which she had abjured? Did the chains of her dreadful broken habits cleave to her by forgotten seals, and did she feel them as, according to doctors, old soldiers still feel pain in the limbs they have lost? Had vice and its excesses so penetrated to her marrow that holy water could not yet reach the demon hidden there? Was the sight of him for whom such angelic efforts were being made necessary to her whom God must forgive for mingling human with divine love? The one had led her to the other. Was a shift of vital force taking place in her, in such a way as to cause suffering? All is doubt and darkness in a situation which science has not deigned to examine, fearing to compromise itself with an immoral subject, as though doctor and writer, priest and statesman were not above suspicion. A doctor stopped by death showed nevertheless the courage to begin studies left incomplete. Perhaps the black melancholy to which Esther was a prey and which darkened her otherwise happy life derived from all these causes; and incapable of guessing what they were, it may be that she suffered like the sick who know nothing of medicine or surgery. The fact is curious. An abundance of wholesome food did not sustain Esther as well as the detestable, inflaming diet it had replaced. A pure and regular life, shared between periods of recreation and tasks deliberately made light, tired the young boarder. The freshest sleep, the calm nights which had taken the place of crushing fatigue and cruel agitation, produced a fever whose symptoms eluded the nurse's finger and eye. Good fortune and well-being after evil and misfortune, security after restless disquiet, were as deadly to Esther as her past wretchedness would have been to her young companions. Rooted in corruption, she had grown in it. Her infernal homeland still maintained its empire, in spite of the dictates of sovereign will. What she hated was life to her, what she loved was fatal. She had so ardent a faith that her piety rejoiced the soul. She loved to pray. She had opened her soul to the light of true religion, which she received without doubt or difficulty. The priest who directed her conscience was in raptures, but her body contradicted her soul at every turn. To satisfy a whim of Madame de Maintenon, who fed them with scraps from the royal table, carp were taken from a muddy pond and placed in a marble tank of clear, running water. They died. Animals are capable of devotion, but man cannot infect them with the disease of flattery. A courtier remarked on this mute opposition at Versailles. 'They are like me,' said the secret queen, 'they regret their obscure mud.' This saying contains the whole of Esther's story. At times, the poor wench was impelled to run out into the splendid convent gardens, she went busily from tree to tree, she pushed her way into shady corners, seeking what? she did not know it, but she was yielding to the demon, she flirted with the trees, spoke unarticulated words to them. At times, in the late evening, she glided like a snake along the walls, without shawl, her shoulders bare. Often in chapel, she remained with her eyes fixed upon the crucifix, and everybody admired her, overcome with tears; but she was weeping with rage; instead of the holy images she wanted to see, flaming nights in which she conducted the orgy as Habeneck at the Conservatoire conducts a Beethoven symphony, those gay, lascivious nights, with their agitated movements and inextinguishable laughter, rose before her dishevelled, furious, brutal. She was outwardly suave as a virgin earthbound only by her feminine shape, inwardly a raging, imperial Messalina. She alone knew of this combat between the demon and the angel; when Mother Superior chided her for making more show of her hair than the rule intended, she changed her way of doing her hair with adorably prompt obedience, she was ready to cut off her hair if the nun had so ordained. Her nostalgia had a touching grace in this girl who would rather have perished than return to the world of impurity. Mother Superior slackened her instruction, and took the interesting creature aside to question her. Esther was happy, she found her company wholly to her taste; she did not feel attacked in any vital part, but her essential vitality was affected. She regretted nothing, she desired nothing. Mother Superior, puzzled by the answers her boarder made, did not know what to think on seeing her thus a prey to devouring listlessness. The doctor was called when the young boarder's condition began to look serious, but he knew nothing of Esther's former life and had no reason to suspect it; there was life everywhere, there was no pain. The invalid responded in a way that discounted all theories. One way remained to clear up the doubts of the learned physician struck by a dreadful thought: Esther obstinately refused to allow herself to be examined by the doctor. At this perilous juncture, Mother Superior had recourse to Father Herrera. The Spaniard came, perceived Esther's desperate plight, and took the doctor briefly aside. After this confidence, the man of science declared to the man of faith that the only remedy was a trip to Italy. The priest did not wish any such step to be taken before Esther's baptism and first communion.

'How much longer will that take?' asked the doctor.

'A month,' said Mother Superior.

'She will be dead by then,' replied the doctor.

'Yes, but in a state of grace and saved,' said the priest.

In Spain, religious considerations take precedence over all others, political or civil, and over matters of life and death; the doctor therefore said no more to the Spaniard, he turned to Mother Superior; but the terrible priest thereupon took him by the arm and stopped him.

'Not a word, sir!' he said.

The doctor, though a church and monarchy man, cast upon Esther a glance full of tenderness and pity. The wench was as beautiful as a lily drooping upon its stalk.

'Then God's will be done!' he cried as he went out.

The very day of this consultation, Esther was taken by her protector to the Rocher-de-Cancale restaurant in the rue Montorgueil, for the desire of saving her had suggested strange expedients to the priest; he tried out two forms of excess; an excellent dinner which might remind the former harlot of her orgies, the Opera which placed images of the world of fashion before her. It needed his sternest authority to persuade the young saint to such profane courses. Herrera so thoroughly disguised himself as a military man that Esther had difficulty in recognizing him; he took the precaution of making his companion wear a veil, and placed her in a box where she could avoid the public gaze. This palliative, without peril to innocence so determinedly reconquered, was promptly given up. The boarder felt nothing but distaste for her protector's dinners, but spiritual repugnance for the theatre, and retreated into her melancholy. 'She is dying of love for Lucien,' Herrera told himself, anxious to sound the depths of this soul and to discover what it could endure. There came, then, a moment at which the poor creature was sustained only by her moral force, and at which the body was near to giving way. The priest calculated this moment with the frightful practical sagacity formerly brought by executioners to their art of putting the question. He found his ward in the garden, sitting on a bench, beside an arbour caressed by the April sun; she appeared to be cold and to be warming herself; her comrades studied with interest her pallor like that of withered grass, her eyes those of a dying gazelle, her melancholy pose. Esther rose to greet the Spaniard with a movement which showed how little life she had, and, let it be said, how little taste for life.

The poor gipsy, the wounded wild swallow, for the second time aroused Carlos Herrera's pity. This minister of gloom, whom God seemed likely to use only for the execution of His vengeance, responded to the invalid with a smile which expressed as much bitterness as kindness, as much punishment as charity. Instructed in meditation, in self-containment as a consequence of her almost monastic life, Esther, for the second time, experienced a feeling of distrust at the sight of her protector; but, as on the first occasion, she was immediately reassured by his words.

'Well, now, my dear child,' he said, 'why have you never mentioned Lucien to me?'

'I promised you,' she replied trembling convulsively from head to foot, 'I swore to you not to pronounce that name.'

'Nevertheless you have not stopped thinking of him.'

'That, sir, is my only fault. I think of him all the time, and when you appeared, I was saying his name to myself.'

'Absence is killing you?'

Esther's only reply was to bow her head like a sick person who already feels the breath of the tomb upon her.

'To see him again? . . .' he said.

'That would be to live,' she answered.

'Do you think of him only with your soul?'

'Ah, sir, love is not divided.'

'Daughter of the accursed race! I've done everything to save you, I abandon you to your destiny: you shall see him!'

'Why do you insult my happiness? May I not love Lucien and practise virtue, which I love as much as I love him? Am I not ready to die here for that, as I am for him? Am I not at the point of death out of a dual fanaticism, for virtue which made me worthy of him, for him who flung me into the arms of virtue? Yes, ready to die without seeing him again, ready to see him and live. God is my judge.'

Her colour had returned, her pallor had taken on a tinge of gold. Esther was again a graceful being.

'The day after that on which you are washed in the waters of baptism, you will see Lucien again, and if you think you can live in virtue while living for him, you shall no more be separated.'

59

The priest was obliged to raise Esther up, for her knees had given way. The poor creature had fallen as if the earth had given way under her feet, the priest seated her on the bench, and when she had recovered the power of speech, she said to him: 'Why not today?'

'Do you wish to deny Monsignor the triumph of your baptism and conversion? You are too near Lucien not to be far from God.'

'Yes, I wasn't thinking of anything any longer!'

'You will never belong to any religion,' said the priest with a profoundly ironical expression.

'God is good,' she replied, 'he reads in my heart.'

Overcome by the delightful simplicity shining in Esther's voice, her looks, her gestures, her attitude, Herrera kissed her on the forehead for the first time.

'The libertines gave you the right name: you will charm God the Father. A few days more, it must be, and after that you will both be free.'

'Both!' she repeated with ecstatic joy.

This scene, observed at a distance, struck both boarders and their superiors, who thought they were watching some operation of magic, comparing Esther with her own self. She reappeared in her true nature of love, pretty, dainty, provocative, gay; in short, she returned from the dead!

Various reflections

HERRERA lived in the rue Cassette, near Saint Sulpice, the church to which he had attached himself. This church, of a harsh, bare style, suited this Spaniard whose religion was of a Dominican flavour. A forlorn hope of the wily policies of Ferdinand VII, he served the constitutional cause, knowing that his devotion must remain unrewarded until the restoration of the *Reynetto*. And Carlos Herrera had given himself body and soul to the *camarilla* at a time when the Cortes seemed unlikely to be dissolved. In the eyes of the world, such conduct proved him to be a superior man. The Duc d'Angoulême's expedition had taken place, King Ferdinand sat on the throne, and Carlos Herrera did not go to Madrid to claim the reward of his service. Protected against curiosity by diplomatic silence, he gave out as the reason for his stay in Paris his lively affection for Lucien de Rubempré, to which that young man already owed the King's ordinance respecting his change of name. He lived moreover, as priests employed on secret missions traditionally live, very obscurely. He performed his religious duties at Saint Sulpice, went out only on business, always in the evening and by coach. The day-time was taken up for him with the Spanish siesta, which places sleep between the two meals of the day, and thus occupies the whole of the period during which Paris is busy and tumultuous. The Spanish cigar also played its part and consumed as much time as tobacco. Sloth is as much a mask as gravity, which is a form of sloth. Herrera lived in one wing of the house, on the second floor, and Lucien occupied the other wing. The two apartments were at once separate and combined by a large reception suite whose antique splendour was as well adapted to the grave ecclesiastic as to the young poet. The courtyard of the house was gloomy. Tall, thick trees shaded the garden. Silence and discretion meet in the habitations chosen by priests. Herrera's lodging will be described in two words: a cell. Lucien's, all luxury and comfort, brought together everything that a fashionable life may require in a dandy, poet, writer, man of ambition, of vice, at once proud and merely vain, careless but concerned with order, one of those incomplete geniuses who do not lack power to desire, to conceive, which is perhaps the same thing, but in whom the power of execution is lacking. Between them, Lucien and Herrera constituted a politician. That was no doubt the secret of their alliance. Old men in whom the mainspring of action has been deflected to the sphere of personal interests, often feel the need for a piece of fine machinery, for a youthful and passionate actor capable of accomplishing their designs. Richelieu looked too late for a fair, white, mustachioed face to cast to the women it was important he should keep amused. With only stupid and uncomprehending young men about him, he was forced to banish his master's mother and terrorize the queen, after having tried to make both love him, lacking those gifts which appeal to queens. However one goes about it, in a life of ambition one is certain to come up against a woman just when such an encounter is least to be expected. However powerful a politician may be, he needs a woman to set against a woman, just as the Dutch cut diamond with diamond. At its moment of power, Rome bowed to this necessity. See also how differently the French cardinal and his Italian successor, Mazarin, exercised authority in their time. Richelieu meets with opposition from the great lords, and puts the axe to their roots; he dies at the height of his power, worn out by the duel in which his only second was a Capuchin friar. Mazarin is rejected by the Nobility and the Third Estate together, in arms, sometimes victorious, able to drive royalty into flight; but the servant of Anne of Austria deprives nobody of his head, woos and conquers all France and forms Louis XIV, who completed Richelieu's work by garrotting them with gold laces in the great seraglio of Versailles. With the death of Madame de Pompadour, Choiseul was lost. Was Herrera penetrated with these high doctrines? Had he taken his own true measure earlier in life than Richelieu? Had he picked Lucien as a Cinq-Mars, but a Cinq-Mars who would be faithful? Nobody was in a position to answer these questions or to assess either the extent or the aim of the Spaniard's ambition. When such questions were asked by those who had caught a glimpse of the association, till then concealed, the answer they seemed to discover was rather horrifying, and Lucien had only been aware of it for a few days past. Carlos was ambitious enough for two, his conduct proved that to those who knew him, and they all believed that Lucien was the priest's natural son.

Fifteen months after his appearance at the Opera, which cast him too soon upon a society in which the priest did not mean to see him until he was fully armed against it, Lucien had three fine horses in his stable, a brougham for the evening, a cabriolet and a gig for the day-time. He ate out. Herrera's predictions had been justified, and the young man was dissolute enough, but the priest had judged it necessary to divert him from the wild love he bore in his heart for Esther. After spending some forty thousand francs, each of his follies only brought Lucien back more vividly to the Torpedo, he sought her obstinately; and, not finding her, she became for him what his game is to the hunter. Could Herrera know the nature of a poet's love? Once the feeling has gone to the head of one of these little great men, once it has scorched his heart and gained access to his senses, the poet's superiority to the rest of mankind is made as evident to him by love as it was by the abundance of his imagination. Owing to a freak operation of his intelligence, the poet expresses nature in images to which he attaches both feeling and thought, and the wings of the latter are attached to his love: he feels and depicts, he acts and meditates, he intensifies his sensations with thought, he triples present felicity with aspiration towards the future and memory of the past; with all this he mingles those pleasures of the soul which make him the prince among artists. The passion of a poet thus becomes a great poem in which merely human dimensions are lost. Doesn't the poet then place his mistress higher than women like to be lodged? Like the sublime knight of la Mancha, he transforms a peasant girl into a princess. He makes his own uses of the wand with which he touches everything to make it marvellous, and sensual pleasure is augmented by the realm of the adorable ideal. His love thus becomes an archetype of passion: it is excessive in every respect, in its hopes and its despairs, its angers, its melancholies, its joys; it flies, it leaps, it crawls, it is quite unlike what agitates the rest of mankind; to *bourgeois* love it is what the eternal torrent of the Alps is to the stream of the plains. Such fine geniuses are so rarely understood that they expend themselves in false hopes; they consume themselves in a search for the ideal mistress, they almost invariably die like rare insects ostentatiously decked out for love-feasts by an all-too-poetical nature, trodden underfoot still virgin by a passing boot; but, another danger! when they meet the form which corresponds to their thought and which often enough is a baker's wife, they do what Raphael did, what the rare insects do, they die in the arms of *la Fornarina*. That was the point Lucien had reached. His poetic nature, of necessity extreme in everything, in good as in evil, had divined the angel in the prostitute, rather brushed by corruption than corrupt: he saw her always white, winged, pure and mysterious, as she had made herself for him, guessing that that was how he wanted her to be.

A friend

TOWARDS the end of May 1825, all Lucien's vivacity had left him; he stopped going out, dined with Herrera, remained pensive, worked, read treatises on diplomacy, sat cross-legged like a Turk on his divan and smoked three or four hookahs a day. His groom was more occupied in cleaning the tubes of this elegant instrument and scenting them, than in sleeking the coats of the horses and decking their manes with roses for a trot in the Bois. The day on which the Spaniard noticed Lucien's pale brow and detected signs of sickness beneath the wild manifestations of stifled love, he determined to sound the heart of the man on whom his life's purposes rested.

One fine evening when Lucien, sitting in an armchair, was mechanically contemplating the sunset through the trees in the garden and through the veil of scented smoke he puffed out with leisurely regularity, as preoccupied smokers do, he was drawn out of his daydream by a deep sigh. He turned and saw the priest standing there, with his arms folded.

'You were there all the time!' said the poet.

'For long enough,' answered the priest, 'my thoughts have been following yours as far as they went . . .'

Lucien understood what he meant.

'I never pretended to have a nature of bronze like yours. For me life is by turns a heaven and a hell; but when, by chance, it is neither one nor the other, it bores me, I am bored . . .'

'How can one be bored when one has so many splendid hopes before one . . .'

'When one doesn't believe in these hopes, or when they are too heavily veiled . . .'

'Enough of this nonsense! . . .' said the priest. 'It would be more worthy of you and of me to open your heart to me. There lies between us what there should never be: a secret! This secret has lain there for sixteen months. You are in love with a woman.'

'So . . .'

'A vile tart, called the Torpedo . . .'

'Well?'

'My child, I didn't mind you taking a mistress, but a lady at court, young, beautiful, with influence, a countess at least. I chose Madame d'Espard for you, meaning quite without scruple that she should be the instrument of your fortune; for she would never have warped your heart, she would have left you free . . . To fall in love with the lowest kind of prostitute, when you cannot, like a king, raise her to noble rank, is a very great mistake.'

'Am I the first to give up ambition and yield to unbridled love?'

'Good!' said the priest picking up the *bocchettino* of the hookah which Lucien had let fall to the floor and returning it to him. 'I take your meaning. Cannot ambition and love be reconciled? Child, you have in old Herrera a mother absolutely devoted . . .'

'I know, my dear,' said Lucien taking his hand and shaking it.

'You wanted a rich man's baubles, you have them. You want to cut a figure, I open the way to power before you, I kiss the dirtiest hands to help your advancement, and you will advance. A little while yet, and you'll lack nothing of what appeals to men or women. Effeminate in your waywardness, you have a virile mind: I have thought of everything for you, I forgive you anything. You have only to speak to satisfy your passions of a day. I have set upon your life the seal which makes others adore it, that of political authority. You will be just as great when you are small; but you mustn't break the press which coins the money. I allow you anything, except weaknesses that would destroy your future. When I open the doors of the Faubourg Saint Germain to you, I forbid you to wallow in the gutter! Lucien! I shall be a rod of iron in your interest, I shall endure all from you, all for you. To begin with, I turned your clumsiness at the game of life into an experienced gambler's touch . . . (Lucien raised his head with an abrupt and angry movement.)

'I removed the Torpedo!'

'You?' cried Lucien.

In an access of animal fury, the poet stood up, threw the gem-encrusted gold *bocchettino* at the priest's face, and pushed him with a violence great enough to throw him down, powerful as he was.

'I,' said the Spaniard picking himself up, his gravity of manner quite undisturbed.

His black wig had fallen off. A skull smooth as a death's head revealed the man's true physiognomy; it struck terror. Lucien sat down again on his divan, arms hanging, overwhelmed, looking stupidly at the priest, who said again:

'I removed her.'

'What have you done with her? You took her away the day after the masked ball . . .'

'Yes, the day after I saw one who belonged to you insulted by rascals I wouldn't lower myself to kick in . . .'

'You flatter them,' said Lucien interrupting, 'call them monsters, beside whom those they guillotine are angels. Do you know what the poor Torpedo did for three of them? One of them was her lover for two months: she was poor, and she picked up her bread in the gutter; he hadn't a penny, he was like me when you first met me, near jumping in the river; this fellow used to get up in the night, go to the cupboard where the remains of this wench's dinner were, and eat them: in the end she discovered his little game; she understood how ashamed he must be, she took care to leave plenty for him, and she was glad to do it; she'd never mentioned it, but she told me in the cab on our way from the Opera. The second had stolen money, but before he was found out she was able to lend him the amount, and he put it back, but afterwards forgot to repay the poor child. As to the third, she made his fortune by putting on an act worthy of the genius of a Figaro; she passed for his wife and became the mistress of a very powerful man who believed her the most guileless and respectable of women. One owed her his life, one his honour, the

66

last a fortune which he still has! And that was how they rewarded her.'

'Shall they die?' said Herrera who had a tear in his eye.

'Ah, that's you as I know you! . . .'

'No, wait, you must know all, mad poet,' said the priest,
'the Torpedo no longer exists . . .'

Lucien flew at Herrera's throat with so much force that
any other man would have fallen again, but the Spaniard's
arm took hold of the poet.

'Listen,' he said coldly. 'I have turned her into a chaste
woman, pure, well-bred, religious, a woman who can hold her
head up; she is under instruction. She can, she must become,
beneath the empire of your love, a Ninon, a Marion de Lorme,
a Dubarry, as the journalist at the Opera was saying. You can
acknowledge her as your mistress or you can stand in the
wings of your creation, which might be wiser! Either arrangement will afford you both profit and pride, pleasure and
advancement; but if you are as great a politician as you are a
poet, Esther will still be just a whore to you, for later she may
stand us in good stead, she is worth her weight in gold. Drink,
but don't get drunk. If I hadn't picked up the reins of your
passion, where would you be today? You would have been
rolling with the Torpedo in the mire of wretchedness from
which I raised you. Here, read this,' said Herrera with the
simplicity of Talma in *Manlius*, which he had never seen.

A paper dropped on to the knees of the poet, and roused
him from the ecstasy of surprise into which this awe-inspiring
utterance had plunged him. He took up and read the first
letter ever written by Mademoiselle Esther.

TO M. L'ABBÉ CARLOS HERRERA.

My dear guardian, will you not believe that in me gratitude takes
precedence of love, seeing that it is to thank you that, for the first
time, I make use of the faculty of expressing my thoughts, instead
of devoting it to describing a love which Lucien has perhaps
forgotten? But I will say to you, man of God, what I should never
dare to say to him, whose presence on earth is still happiness to me.
Yesterday's ceremony poured out the treasures of grace upon me,
I therefore place my destiny again in your hands. Must I die far
away from my beloved, I shall die purified like Mary Magdalene,

67

and my soul will be his guardian angel's rival. Shall I ever forget yesterday's festival? How could I abdicate from the throne of glory to which I ascended? Yesterday, I washed away all my pollution in the water of baptism, and I received the sacred body of our Saviour; I have become a tabernacle to him. At that moment, I heard the choirs of angels, I was no longer a woman, I was born into a world of light, amid the acclamations of the earth, admired by the world, in an intoxicating cloud of incense and prayers, and adorned like a virgin for a celestial bridegroom. Finding myself, what I had never hoped to be, worthy of Lucien, I renounced all impure love, and desire to walk only in the ways of virtue. If my body is weaker than my soul, let it perish. Be the judge of my destiny, and, if I die, say to Lucien that I died for him on being born to God.

This Sunday evening

Lucien raised to the priest eyes wet with tears.

'You know the apartment of fat Caroline Bellefeuille, in the rue Taitbout,' the Spaniard went on. 'Abandoned by her legal gentleman, the wench was in dreadful need, she was on the point of being taken in; I've bought the house as it stood, and she's left with her old clothes. Esther, that angel who wished to rise up to heaven, has come down there and awaits you.'

At that moment, Lucien heard his horses pawing the ground in the courtyard, he lacked strength to express his appreciation of a devotion he nevertheless truly valued at its full worth; he cast himself into the arms of the man he had so lately insulted, redressing all with a single glance and the mute effusion of his feelings; then he rushed down the stairs, yelled Esther's address at his tiger's ear, and the horses set off as if their legs were brisked up by their master's passion.

In which it is discovered that the Abbé Herrera was no priest

NEXT day, a man whom, from his garments, passers-by might have taken for a constable in disguise, walked up and down in the rue Taitbout, opposite a house from which he seemed to be waiting for someone to emerge; his gait betrayed agitation.

In Paris, you will often meet walkers intent in this way, real policemen looking for a soldier absent from his unit, process-servers hoping to catch their man, creditors bent on extorting something from a debtor who has shut himself in, jealous and suspicious lovers or husbands, friends standing guard on behalf of their friends; but you will rarely meet a visage upon which play the hard, brutal thoughts which animated that of the gloomy athlete pacing beneath the windows of Mademoiselle Esther with the meditative savagery of a caged bear. At noon, a casement opened and let through the hand of a lady's maid which pushed back the padded shutters. A few moments later, Esther in a tea-gown came to the window for a breath of air, she was leaning on Lucien; anyone seeing them would have taken them for the original of a sentimental English engraving. Esther then caught the basilisk stare of the Spanish priest, and the poor creature, as though struck by a passing bullet, uttered a cry of fear.

'There's the terrible priest,' she said pointing him out to Lucien.

'That one!' said he with a smile, 'he's no more a priest than you are . . .'

'What is he, then?' said she, afraid.

'Oh, he's an old Lascar who only believes in the devil,' said Lucien.

Caught by anyone less devoted than Esther, this gleam cast on the secrets of the false priest might have proved Lucien's ultimate downfall. Passing from the window of their bedroom to the dining-room where their breakfast had just been served, the two lovers met Carlos Herrera.

'What are you doing here?' Lucien said abruptly.

'Bringing you my blessing,' replied that audacious character, stopping the couple and forcing them to stay in the apartment's drawing-room. 'Listen to me, my darlings. Amuse yourselves, be happy, I ask nothing better. Happiness at all costs, that's my motto. But you,' he said to Esther, 'you whom I raised up from the mud and gave a good soaping all over, body and soul, you won't presume to stand in Lucien's way? . . . As to you, young fellow,' he went on after a pause looking at Lucien, 'you are no longer mere poet enough to let yourself be carried off by another Coralie. We're writing prose now. What could Esther's lover become? Nothing. Could Esther be Madame de Rubempré. No. Well, then, the world, little one,' said he placing his hand in that of Esther who shuddered as though a snake had coiled about her, 'the world must be ignorant of your existence; society above all must not know that any Mademoiselle Esther loves Lucien, and that Lucien is infatuated with her ... This apartment will be your prison, little one. If you want to go out, and no doubt your health will require it, you will go out late at night, when you won't be seen; for your beauty, your youth and the distinction of manner you picked up at the convent would be too promptly noticed in Paris. The day on which anybody whatever,' he said in a terrible voice accompanied by an even more terrible look, 'should learn that Lucien is your lover or that you are his mistress, that would be your last day but one. I procured for that younger son an ordinance which allowed him to bear the name and the arms of his maternal ancestors. But it doesn't stop there! the title of marquis was not granted us; and, in order to regain it, he must marry the daughter of a good family in whose favour the King will do us this grace. The alliance will bring Lucien into the world of the Court. This child, whom I have succeeded in turning into a man, will first become an embassy secretary; later, he will be minister in some little German court, and, with God's help or mine (which is more to the point), will take his seat one day on the peers' benches ...'

'Or the hulks ...' said Lucien interrupting the man.

'Be silent,' cried Carlos, clapping his big hand over Lucien's mouth. 'A secret like that to a woman! ...' he breathed in Lucien's ear.

'Esther, a woman? ...' cried the author of *Marguerites*.

'More sonnets!' said the Spaniard, 'and without rhyme or reason. All these angels turn into women again, sooner or later; and at moments all women are at once ape and child! two forms of life in which we encourage laughter at our cost, if only in boredom ... Esther, my pet,' he said to the terrified young boarder, 'I have engaged as your personal maid a creature who belongs to me as though she were my daughter.

For cook, you shall have a mulatto, which gives style to the house. With Europe and Asia, you will be able to live here for a thousand-franc note a month, inclusive, like a queen . . . of the stage. Europe was a milliner, seamstress and small-part actress, Asia served an immensely wealthy man who was a big eater. These two creatures will be your good fairies.'

Seeing Lucien stand like a little boy before this man who was guilty at least of sacrilege and forgery, she, consecrated by love, felt dread deep in her heart. Without reply, she drew Lucien into the bedroom where she said to him: 'Is this the devil?'

'Far worse than that . . . for me!' he quickly answered. 'But, if you love me, try to imitate this man's devotion, and obey him on pain of death . . .'

'Of death? . . .' she said in yet greater fear.

'Of death,' Lucien went on. 'Alas, my darling, no death could be compared with the one that would strike me, if . . .'

Esther paled and grew faint at these words.

'Well, then?' called out the impious forger, 'haven't you finished daisy-picking yet?'

Esther and Lucien returned to him, and the poor wench said, without daring to look at the man of mystery: 'You shall be obeyed, sir, as one obeys God!'

'Good!' he answered, 'for a reasonable time, you will be able to go on being happy, and . . . you will need only night attire and indoor clothes, that will be very economical.'

Two capital watchdogs

THE two lovers continued on their way towards the dining-room; but Lucien's protector signed to the fair couple to stop. 'I've just mentioned your retinue, my child,' he said to Esther, 'I must introduce them to you.'

The Spaniard rang twice. The two women, whom he called Europe and Asia, appeared, and it was easy to see how they had come to be called by those names.

Asia, who might have been born in the island of Java,

presented frighteningly to the gaze that copper-coloured visage peculiar to the Malays, flat as a board, where the nose seems to have been pushed in with great force. The curious formation of the maxillary bones gave the lower part of the face a resemblance to those of the higher apes. The forehead, though low, did not lack the intelligence of a practised cunning. Two small, burning eyes remained as tranquil as those of a tiger, but were averted. Asia seemed afraid of causing fear. Her lips, of a pallid blue, exposed irregular teeth of a dazzling whiteness. The general expression of this animal physiognomy was one of treacherous sloth. The hair, oily and shining, like the skin of the visage, edged with its two black bands a scarf of rich silk. The unquestionably pretty ears were ornamented with two big black pearls. Asia recalled those quaint beings which figure on Chinese screens, or perhaps rather those Hindu idols which clearly do not exist in nature, but which travellers always discover sooner or later. At the sight of this monster, dressed in a white apron over a stuff gown, Esther shivered.

'Asia!' said the Spaniard towards whom the woman raised her head with a movement like that of a dog looking at its master, 'there is your mistress . . .'

And he pointed to Esther in her house-coat. Asia contemplated the fairylike young creature with an expression almost of pain; but at the same time a suppressed gleam between her small, narrowed eyelids darted like the spark of a fire upon Lucien who, wearing a magnificent open dressing-gown, a frieze shirt and red trousers, his fair curls escaping from beneath a Turkish cap, looked like a god. The Italian genius may recount the tale of Othello, the English genius put it on the stage; but it is nature's right alone to express jealousy more magnificently and completely than either England or Italy in a single glance. This glance, caught by Esther, caused her to clutch at the Spaniard's arm and print her nails there as might a cat which takes hold in order not to fall over a precipice whose bottom it cannot see. The Spaniard then spoke three or four words of an unknown tongue to the Asiatic monster, who knelt to grovel at Esther's feet, and kissed them.

'She is,' said the Spaniard to Esther, 'no ordinary cook, but a master who would send Carême out of his mind with jealousy. Asia knows all that can be done in a kitchen. She will put you up a simple dish of beans that will make you wonder whether the angels have not come down to add the herbs of heaven. She will go every morning to the Market herself, and will fight like the demon she is to get things at the fairest price; her discretion will baffle the most inquisitive. As you will pass for a person who has come from the Indies, Asia will be a great help to you in keeping up the part, for she is one of those Parisians who were born to belong to whatever country they choose. But if you take my advice, you won't be a foreigner . . . Europe, what do you say about it?'

Europe formed a perfect contrast to Asia, for she was the nicest little lady's maid Monrose could ever have wished to play opposite him on the stage. Slender, apparently scatter-brained, pretty as a weasel, with a gimlet nose, Europe presented to the gaze a face wearied with Parisian corruption, the wan face of a child fed on sour apples, lymphatic and stringy, soft and clinging. Her little foot forward, hands in her apron pockets, she wriggled without moving, so great was her animation. At once part-time street-girl and stage extra, she must, despite her youth, already have fulfilled many vocations. Depraved as a whole prisonful of women, she might have robbed her parents and shuffled on police-court benches. Asia inspired immediate fear; but at a glance one understood her, she was a direct descendant of Locusta; while Europe inspired an uneasiness which could only grow as one continued to employ her services; one felt her to be boundlessly corrupt; she would be able, as people say, to rock the hills.

'Madame might come from Valenciennes,' said Europe in a dry little voice, 'like me. Would Monsieur,' she said to Lucien with the air of a schoolmistress, 'care to teach us the name he wishes Madame to be known by?'

'Madame van Bogseck,' replied the Spaniard promptly turning Esther's name about. 'Madame is a Dutch Jewess, widow of a merchant and ill with a liver complaint brought back from Java ... Not particularly wealthy, so as not to excite curiosity.'

'Enough to live on, six thousand francs a year, and we shall complain of her meanness,' said Europe.

'That's it,' said the Spaniard inclining his head. 'The devil take you and your jokes!' he added in a terrible voice as he caught passing between Asia and Europe looks which displeased him, 'you know what I told you? You serve a queen, you owe her the respect due to a queen, you will be as devoted to her as to me. Neither the porter, nor the neighbours, nor the other tenants, nor in fact anybody must know what goes on here. It is up to you to thwart any curiosity which may be aroused. And Madame,' he continued placing his broad hairy hand on Esther's arm, 'Madame mustn't commit the slightest imprudence, you would prevent her if it became necessary, but . . . always respectfully. Europe, you will see to the upkeep of Madame's wardrobe, and you will take trouble over it, so as to economize. Finally, let nobody, not even the most insignificant persons, set foot in the apartment. You two, between you, must learn to do everything here. My little beauty,' said he to Esther, 'when you wish to drive out in the evening, you will tell Europe, she knows where to find your people, for you'll have a footman, one trained by me, like these two slaves.'

Esther and Lucien could think of nothing to say, they listened to the Spaniard and looked at the two priceless specimens he was giving his orders to. To what secret did they owe the submissiveness, the devotion written on these two faces, the one so spitefully pert, the other so profoundly cruel? He divined what Esther and Lucien were thinking, the two of them looking as bemused as Paul and Virginia would have looked at the sight of two horrible snakes, and he said to them in a reassuring aside: 'You can count on them as you would on myself; don't keep any secrets from them, that will flatter them. Go and serve, my little Asia,' said he to the cook; 'and you, my pretty, lay another place,' he said to Europe, 'the least these children can do is give Daddy his breakfast.'

When the two women had closed the door, and the Spaniard could hear Europe moving about, he said to Lucien and the girl, opening his broad hand: 'I have a hold on them!' An observation and a gesture to shudder at.

'Where did you find them?' cried Lucien.

'Well, of course,' the man answered, 'I didn't look for them in court circles! Europe rose from the mire and is afraid of returning to it ... Threaten them with *the good father* when they don't do what you want, and you'll see them trembling like mice when a cat is mentioned. I am a trainer of wild animals,' he added with a smile.

'You seem like the demon to me!' Esther cried becomingly, pressing herself against Lucien.

'My child, I tried to bring you to Heaven; but the penitent harlot will always be a puzzle to the Church; if It found one, she would turn whore again in Paradise ... The advantage you gained was to be forgotten and to take on the ways of a respectable woman; for what you learned there you'd never have picked up in the foul sphere you were living in ... You owe me nothing,' he said, perceiving a delightful expression of gratitude on Esther's face, 'I did it all for him ...' And he indicated Lucien ... 'You are a whore, you will remain a whore, you will die a whore; for, despite the seductive theories of people who keep wild animals, in this world you can't become what you aren't. The bumps man is right. You have the bump of love.'

The Spaniard was, as may be seen, a fatalist, like Napoleon, Mahomet and many great statesmen. A strange thing, nearly all men of action incline to Fatality, just as most thinkers incline to Providence.

'I don't know what I am,' Esther answered with angelic sweetness; 'but I love Lucien, and I shall adore him till I die.'

'Come and have your breakfast,' said the Spaniard abruptly, 'and pray God that Lucien doesn't get married too promptly, or you wouldn't see him again.'

'His marriage would be the death of me,' she said.

She allowed the sham priest to pass first in order to reach up to Lucien's ear, without being seen.

'Is it your wish,' she said, 'that I remain in the power of this man who has me guarded by those two hyenas?' ·

Lucien inclined his head. The poor wench controlled her

75

sadness and kept a joyous expression; but she felt horribly oppressed. It needed more than a year of constant and devoted care before she became accustomed to the two dreadful creatures, whom Carlos Herrera named *the two watchdogs*.

A boring chapter, since it describes
four years of happiness

LUCIEN'S conduct, since his return to Paris, so clearly bore the mark of high politics that it was bound to excite and did excite the jealousy of all his former friends, upon whom he executed no other revenge than that of letting them rage at his successes, his irreproachable comportment and his way of keeping people at a distance. The poet once so communicative, so expansive, was now cold and reserved. De Marsay, taken as a model by the youth of Paris, brought no more temperance to his actions and utterance than did Lucien. As to wit, the journalist had already shown proof of that. De Marsay, with whom many people idly compared Lucien to the poet's advantage, was small enough to chafe at this. Lucien, much in favour with the men who exercised power, so completely abandoned all thought of literary fame, that he was insensible to the success of his novel, reissued under its real title *A Bowman of Charles IX*, and to the stir made by his collection of sonnets entitled *Marguerites*, sold out by Dauriat in a week. 'It is posthumous success,' he replied with a laugh to Mademoiselle des Touches when she complimented him. The terrible Spaniard kept his creature with an arm of steel on the path at whose end the fanfares and profits of victory await the patient politician. Lucien had taken Beaudenord's bachelor apartment, on the Quai Malaquais, in order to be nearer the rue Taitbout, and his counsellor was lodged in three rooms of the same house, on the fourth floor. Lucien now kept only one saddle-horse which he further harnessed to his gig, a manservant and a stable-boy. When he was not dining out, he dined at Esther's. Carlos Herrera so carefully looked after the Quai Malaquais household, that Lucien spent less in all than ten thousand francs a year. Ten thousand were enough for Esther, thanks to the constant and inexplicable devotion of Europe and Asia. Lucien, moreover, took the greatest precautions when visiting the rue Taitbout. He always went by cab, with the blinds down, and made the carriage turn into the yard. Thus his passion for Esther and the very existence of the rue Taitbout set-up, wholly unknown to the world, harmed none of his undertakings or relations; never an indiscreet word escaped him on this delicate subject. His mistakes in that respect over Coralie, at the time of his first sojourn in Paris, had taught him a lesson. In the first place, his life displayed that regularity of good form under which abundant mysteries may be concealed: he remained in society every evening until one o'clock in the morning; he could be found at home between ten o'clock and one o'clock in the afternoon; then he went to the Bois de Boulogne and paid calls till five o'clock. He was rarely seen on foot, in that way he avoided his former acquaintance. When he was greeted by some journalist or by one of his earlier companions, his response was an inclination of the head polite enough not to give offence, but with a hint of deep disdain which discouraged French familiarity. He was thus rid of those whom he no longer wanted to know. A ripe hatred prevented him from calling on Madame d'Espard, who, more than once, had shown that she wanted him to call; if he met her at the Duchesse de Maufrigneuse's or Mademoiselle des Touches's, at Countess Montcornet's, or elsewhere, he behaved towards her with exquisite politeness. This hatred, which Madame d'Espard shared, obliged Lucien to use prudence, for it will be seen how he had revived it by permitting himself a revenge which, in fact, got him a dressing-down from Carlos Herrera. 'You are not yet powerful enough to avenge yourself on anybody whatever,' the Spaniard had said to him. ' When you're on the road, under a hot sun, you don't stop to pick flowers . . .' Lucien had too evident a future and too much true superiority for the young men, whom his return to Paris and his unexplained fortune shocked or irritated, not to welcome the opportunity to do him a bad turn. Lucien, who knew that he had many enemies, was not ignorant of this ill-disposition among his friends. The abbé therefore wisely put his adopted son on his guard against the treacheries of society, against those imprudences which are so fatal to youth. Lucien was made every evening to recount to the abbé the smallest happenings of his day. Thanks to the advice of his mentor, he frustrated the cleverest inquisitiveness, that of society. Guarded by a positively English gravity of manner, protected within the walls raised by diplomatic circumspection, he gave nobody the right or the opportunity to cast an eye on his affairs. His youthful, handsome face had become, in society, as impassible as that of a princess on some royal occasion. Half way through the year 1829, the question arose of his marriage to the eldest daughter of the Duchesse de Grandlieu, who at that moment had no fewer than four daughters to set up. Nobody doubted that, in connection with such an alliance, the King would accord Lucien the favour of restoring the title of marquis to him. The marriage would decide Lucien's political fortunes, and he would very likely be named ambassador to a German court. For the past three years certainly, Lucien's life had been quite beyond attack; even de Marsay had had this to say about him: 'The fellow must have somebody very powerful behind him!' Lucien had thus become quite a figure. His passion for Esther had in its way greatly helped him to play the part of a sound man. A habit of that kind preserves the ambitious from all kinds of foolishness; caring little for any woman, they are not liable to let physical attractions gain the upper hand. As to the happiness Lucien enjoyed, it realized the dreams of a penniless poet, starving in his garret. Esther, the ideal of the courtesan in love, while reminding Lucien of Coralie, the actress with whom he had lived for a year, totally effaced her. All loving and devoted women desire seclusion, the incognito, the life of a pearl in the depths of the sea; but, with most of them, it remains a delightful whim to be talked about, a proof of love they would like to be able to give but cannot; while Esther, still in her dawn of happiness, living hourly beneath Lucien's first burning glance, did not, in four years, feel curiosity for a moment. Her entire mind was set on remaining within the terms of the programme traced by the fatal hand of the Spaniard. Even more! in the midst of her most intoxicating delights, she did not abuse the power which a lover's returning desire gives to a loved woman to question Lucien about Herrera, who, indeed, still terrified her: she dared not think about him. The cunning benefactions of this inexplicable character, to whom Esther certainly owed at once her boarding-school accomplishments, her ladylike ways and her moral regeneration, seemed to the little tart to be on loan from Hell. 'I shall pay for all that one day,' she told herself in fear. Whenever it was fine, she went out after dark by hired coach. She went, at a speed no doubt laid down by the abbé, to one of those charming woods outside Paris, at Boulogne-sur-Seine, Vincennes, Romainville or Ville d'Avray, often with Lucien, sometimes alone with Europe. There she walked without fear, for, when Lucien wasn't with her, she was accompanied by a tall lackey liveried as a huntsman, armed with a real knife, his features and build those of a powerful athlete. This second guardian was provided, in the English manner, with a long, heavy stick, called a quarterstaff and known to singlestick-players, with which several assailants may be fended off. In conformity with an order given by the abbé, Esther had never spoken a word to this fellow. Europe, when Madame wished to return, called out; the runner whistled to the coachman, who was always conveniently within distance. When Lucien walked beside Esther, Europe and the huntsman stayed a hundred yards away, like two of those infernal pages of whom *The Arabian Nights* speak, given by the enchanter to those whom he protects. Parisians, above all Parisian women, know little of the charms of a woodland walk on a fine night. The silence, the moonlight and the solitude have all the soothing action of a bath. In general, Esther set out at ten o'clock, walked from midnight to one o'clock, and returned home at half past two. It was never light in the apartment before eleven o'clock. She bathed, then embarked on a scrupulously careful process of dressing, unknown to most women in Paris, for it takes too long, and is rarely practised by any but the better class of prostitutes or great ladies who have the day to themselves. She was just about ready when Lucien arrived and always offered herself to his gaze like a flower newly opened. She cared only for her poet's happiness; she belonged to him as a thing that was his, that is to say, she allowed him every freedom. Never did she cast a glance beyond the realm in which she shone so radiantly; the abbé had advised this, for it was part of the deep politician's plans that Lucien should enjoy every kind of good fortune. Happiness is without history, and the story-tellers of all countries know this so well that the phrase: *They lived happily*, with or without an *ever after*, has always been the end of love-stories. A happiness so truly fantastic in the heart of Paris can only be explained by its circumstances. It was happiness in its purest form, a poem, a symphony whose four movements were years! All women will say: 'That's a good deal!' Neither Esther nor Lucien had said: 'It is too much!' Finally, the formula: *They lived happily*, was more explicit in their case than in fairy-stories, for *they had no children*. In consequence, nothing stopped Lucien flirting around in society, yielding to the impulses of the artistic temperament and, let it be admitted, the needs of his position. During the time when he was slowly making his way, he performed a variety of services, never mentioned, for certain politicians who needed assistance. In all such matters, his discretion was absolute. He greatly cultivated the company of Madame de Sérisy, for whom, it was said in drawing-rooms everywhere, he did all that was necessary. Madame de Sérisy had taken Lucien away from the Duchesse de Maufrigneuse, who, it was said, didn't want him any longer, one of those things that women put about by way of revenge for a happiness they would like. Lucien was, to put it that way, in the bosom of the High Chaplaincy, and intimate with a number of women who were friends of the Archbishop of Paris. Modest in his discretion, he waited patiently. Marsay's pronouncement, Marsay himself being by that time married and leading his wife the kind of life Esther led, thus showed some penetration. But the submarine perils of Lucien's position will be sufficiently explained in the course of this story.

How a shark met the rat,
and what ensued

WHILE things went on thus, on a fine night in the month of
August, Baron Nucingen was returning to Paris from the
estate of a foreign banker established in France, at whose
house he'd been dining. The estate is about twenty-five miles
from Paris, in the heart of Brie. Now, as the baron's coachman
had sworn he could take his master out and bring him back
with the horses, this coachman was allowed to drive slowly
once night had fallen. As they entered the Bois de Vincennes,
the situation of the animals, the men and the master was as
follows. Well and truly watered in the butler's pantry at the
house of the well-known autocrat of the Stock Exchange,
the coachman, completely drunk, slept, still holding the reins,
so that passers-by would have suspected nothing. The footman, sitting behind, snored like a humming-top from Germany, land of little figures in carved wood, big *Reinganumen*
and tops. The baron wanted to think; but, ever since they had
crossed the bridge at Gournay, the gentle somnolence of
digestion had closed his eyes. From the slackness of the reins,
the horses understood the state of the coachman, they heard
the *basso continuo* of the footman from his look-out post in the
rear, they saw that they were their own masters, and profited
from this brief period of liberty to wander at their will.
Intelligent slaves, they offered robbers the opportunity of
stripping one of the richest capitalists in France, the most
profoundly clever of those to whom the name of sharks has
been finally attributed. At last, being in charge and drawn by
the curiosity which has often been noticed in domestic animals, they stopped, at a crossing, before other horses to whom
no doubt they were saying in horse-language: 'Whose are you?
What are you doing? Are you happy?' When the carriage was
no longer moving, the drowsy baron awoke. He thought at
first that he had not yet left his colleague's parkland; then he
was surprised by a celestial vision which immediately brought
into play his normal armoury of calculation. The moonlight

was so magnificent that you could have read anything by it, even an evening newspaper. In the silence of the woods and by this pure light, the baron saw a woman alone, who, as she stepped into a hired carriage, gazed at the unusual spectacle of a sleeping barouche. At the sight of this angel, Baron Nucingen was as it were illuminated by an inner light. Seeing herself admired, the young woman lowered her veil with a movement of fright. A runner uttered a raucous cry whose meaning was understood by the coachman, for the carriage shot off like an arrow. The old banker's feelings were terribly disturbed: the blood from his feet transported fire into his head, his head sent flames down to his heart; his throat tightened. The unfortunate man feared indigestion, yet, despite this dreadful apprehension, he got to his feet.

'Put zem into a kallop! fast asleep, you pally numskull!' he called out. 'Hundert francs if you cadge up wit zat goach!'

At the words *hundred francs* the coachman awoke, the footman behind no doubt heard them in his sleep. The baron repeated his order, the coachman put the horses into a gallop, and at the Trône toll-gate succeeded in overtaking a carriage very like the one in which Nucingen had seen the unknown goddess, but where the head clerk of some big shop was sitting in state, with a proper little woman from the rue Vivienne. This mistake upset the baron.

'If I had prought George, instead of you, pig stupid, he vould eassily haf found zat lady,' he said to his servant as the toll-collectors came up.

'Ah, your lordship, the devil, I'd say, was behind in the shape of a *heyduck*, and switched me that carriage for his own.'

'Ze toffle does not exist,' said the baron.

M. le Baron de Nucingen then admitted to the age of sixty, women had become totally indifferent to him, more particularly his own wife, of course. He boasted of never having known the kind of love which drives men to folly. He regarded it as lucky to have finished with women, of whom he said, without making any bones about it, that the most angelic among them was not worth what she cost, even if she gave herself for nothing. He was understood to be so utterly surfeited that he no longer so much as paid out a couple of thousand francs a month for the pleasure of being deceived. From his box at the Opera, his cold eyes undisturbedly took in the *corps de ballet*. No meaningful glance darted to the capitalist from that redoubtable swarm of elderly girls and youthful old women, the fine flower of Parisian pleasures. Natural love, artificial and self-regarding love, vain and decorous love; casual love, decent, conjugal love, love on the fringes, the baron had paid for them all, known them all, except true love. This love had just swooped down upon him like an eagle on its prey, as it had swooped on Gentz, adviser to H. H. Prince Metternich. It is well known what follies that aged diplomatist performed on behalf of Fanny Elssler whose rehearsals occupied him far more than the pattern of European interests. The woman who had just overturned the double-locked strong-box called Nucingen, appeared to him like one unique in her generation. It is not indeed certain that Titian's mistress, or the Mona Lisa of Leonardo da Vinci, or Raphael's Fornarina was as beautiful as the sublime Esther, in whom the practised eye of the most observant Parisian could not have detected the least sign betokening a harlot. What particularly stupefied the baron was the noble air of a great lady which Esther, loved, surrounded by luxury, elegance and love, had in the highest degree. Contented love is womankind's holy *ampulla*, it makes them all as proud as empresses. Every night for a week, the baron went to the Bois de Vincennes, then to the Bois de Boulogne, then to the woods at Ville d'Avray, then to those at Meudon, finally round all the outskirts of Paris, without meeting Esther. That sublime Jewish face which he described as *ein fess off ze Pipple*, was ever before his eyes. At the end of a fortnight, he had lost his appetite. Delphine de Nucingen and her daughter Augusta, whom the baroness had started to bring out, did not at first notice the change in the baron. Mother and daughter saw Monsieur de Nucingen only in the morning at luncheon and in the evening at dinner, when they were all dining at home, which only happened on the days when Delphine had guests. But, at the end of two months, in a fever of impatience and a state not unlike that of nostalgia, the baron, astonished at the powerlessness of his millions, grew thin and appeared so profoundly affected, that Delphine secretly hoped to become a widow. She began hypocritically to pity her husband, and again kept her daughter upstairs. She overwhelmed her husband with questions; he answered as the English answer when suffering from spleen, he barely answered at all. Delphine de Nucingen gave big dinners on Sundays. She'd chosen that as her day, after having noticed that, in high society, nobody then went to the theatre, so that on Sunday there was generally nothing to do. The invasion of the commercial middle class makes Sunday as silly in Paris as it is boring in London. The baroness therefore asked the celebrated Desplein to dinner in order to be able to have a consultation in spite of the invalid, for Nucingen insisted that he'd never felt better. Keller, Rastignac, de Marsay, du Tillet, all the friends of the house had made the baroness understand that a man like Nucingen must not die unexpectedly. These gentlemen were invited to the same dinner, and so were Count Gondreville, François Keller's father-in-law, the Chevalier d'Espard, des Lupeaulx, Doctor Bianchon, Desplein's favourite pupil, Beaudenord and his wife, Count and Countess Montcornet, Blondet, Mademoiselle des Touches and Conti; finally, Lucien de Rubempré for whom, for the past five years, Rastignac had conceived the liveliest friendship; but *by order*, as they say in advertisements.

Moneybags in despair

'WE shan't easily get rid of that one,' said Blondet to Rastignac, when he saw Lucien enter the drawing-room handsomer than ever and ravishingly got up.

'It's better to make a friend of him, he's formidable,' said Rastignac.

'Him?' said de Marsay. 'The only people I regard as formidable are those whose position is clear, and his is not so much unattacked as unattackable! Look! what does he live on? Where does his fortune come from? he has debts of sixty thousand francs, I know.'

'He's found a rich protector in a Spanish priest, who wishes him well,' replied Rastignac.

'He's marrying the eldest Mademoiselle Grandlieu,' said Mademoiselle des Touches.

'Yes, but,' said the Chevalier d'Espard, 'they're asking him to buy an estate which brings in thirty thousand francs to assure the fortune he'll his intended, and that needs a million, which is not to be found under any Spaniard's foot.'

'It's a lot of money, for Clotilde is very ugly,' said the baroness. Madame de Nucingen made a point of referring to Mademoiselle de Grandlieu by her Christian name, as though she, *née* Goriot, were of that society.

'No,' replied du Tillet, 'a duchess's daughter is never ugly for the likes of us, especially when she has in her gift the title of marquis and a diplomatic post; but the greatest obstacle in the way of this marriage is Madame de Sérisy's insensate passion for Lucien, she must pay him a great deal.'

'Then it doesn't surprise me to see Lucien looking so solemn; for Madame de Sérisy certainly won't give him a million to marry Mademoiselle de Grandlieu. He doesn't know how to get out of that position, I dare say,' de Marsay replied.

'Yes, but Mademoiselle de Grandlieu adores him,' said Countess Montcornet, 'and, with that young person's help, the conditions may not be so hard.'

'What will he do with his Angoulême sister and brother-in-law?' inquired the Chevalier d'Espard.

'But,' replied Rastignac, 'his sister is rich, and he now calls her Madame Séchard de Marsac.'

'There may be difficulties, but he's a good-looking boy,' said Bianchon rising to greet Lucien.

'Good evening, my dear chap,' said Rastignac exchanging a hearty handshake with Lucien.

De Marsay acknowledged Lucien's greeting coldly. Before dinner, Desplein and Bianchon, who, while joking with Baron Nucingen, examined him, realized that his illness was purely temperamental; but neither of them could divine its cause, so impossible did it appear that this deep politician of the Bourse could be in love. When Bianchon, deciding that nothing but love could explain the banker's pathological condition, mentioned the possibility to Delphine de Nucingen, she smiled in the way of a woman who has long known what to think about her husband. Nevertheless, after dinner, when everybody went out into the garden, the close friends of the household surrounded the banker and wondered whether this extraordinary case might not be illuminated by Bianchon's notion that Nucingen must be in love.

'Do you know, Baron,' de Marsay said to him, 'that you've grown considerably thinner? and you're suspected of having contravened the laws of a financier's nature.'

'Notatoll!' said the baron.

'But indeed,' de Marsay pursued, 'they are daring to say that you are in love.'

'Iss true,' Nucingen answered piteously. 'I am lonking for somezink unkenon.'

'You're in love, you? . . . You're a coxcomb!' said the Chevalier d'Espard.

'To pee in luf at my aitch, I kenow zat nossing coult pe more follish; but can I help? zat is how!'

'With a woman in society?' asked Lucien.

'But,' said de Marsay, 'the Baron can only grow thin like that from a hopeless love, and he can buy all the women who can and will sell themselves.'

'I ton't kenow hair,' answered the baron. 'And I can tell you zis, since Madame de Nischingen iss in the trawink-room. Ontil now, I haf not kenown what luf iss. Luf? . . . I sink it moss pee to grow zin.'

'Where did you meet her, this young innocent?' Rastignac asked.

'Out trifing, at midnight, in ze Pois de Finzennes.'

'How would you describe her?' said Marsay.

'Eine hat off vite goss, pink tress, vite scarf, vite feil, . . . eine truly Pippligle fess! Eyess of fire, a skin off Orient.'

'You were dreaming!' said Lucien with a smile.

'Is true, I vos sleeping like ein teet-pox, . . . ein pox foll off teets,' he continued, 'for I was on my way pack from tinner in ze country wiz mine friend . . .'

'Was she by herself?' said du Tillet interrupting the shark.

'Yo,' said the baron with an air of grief, 'except an heyduck behint ze coach and a mate . . .'

'Lucien looks as though he knew her,' cried Rastignac, catching a smile on the face of Esther's lover.

'Who doesn't know women capable of going out at midnight to meet Nucingen?' said Lucien gaily.

'At any rate, it isn't a woman who goes into society?' queried the Chevalier d'Espard, 'for the baron would have recognized the heyduck.'

'I haf not seen her any place,' replied the baron, 'and is forty tays since I was making ze police seek wizout finding.'

'It would be better for her to cost you a few hundred thousand francs than cost you your life, and at your age, a passion which goes unfed is dangerous,' said Desplein, 'one may die of it.'

'Yo, yo,' Nucingen replied to Desplein, 'what I eat kifs me no nourishment, air is fatal to me. I am going to ze Pois de Finzennes, to see ze pless where I saw hair! . . . Ant zat iss mein life! I haf not peen aple to occupy myself wit ze lest lon: I hef esked mine colleaks to look efter it, ent zey hef het biddy on me . . . For a million, I vish to know zis woman, I should be more rich, for I go no longer to ze Pourse . . . Ask ti Dilet.'

'Yes,' replied du Tillet, 'he no longer cares for business, he's changed, it's a sign of approaching death.'

'Sign of dess,' Nucingen went on, 'for me iss dess, sem sing!'

The simplicity of the old man, a shark no longer, who, for the first time in his life, thought something holier, more sacred than gold, greatly affected this company of old hands at the game: some exchanged smiles, others looked at Nucingen mutely expressing the thought: 'So strong a man come to this! . . .' Then each returned to the drawing-room talking about the event. It was indeed a work of nature to speculate about. Madame de Nucingen started to laugh when Lucien discovered the banker's secret to her; but at the sound of his wife's mockery, the baron took her by the arm and led her to a window recess.

'Madame,' he said to her in a low voice, 'hef I efer said a wort of mockery about your bassions, zet you should mock at mine? A goot vife would help hair husbant in soch matter, not mock et him es you vos doing . . .'

From the old banker's description, Lucien had recognized his Esther. Already annoyed at having seen his smile noted, he took advantage of the moment of general chatter while coffee was being served to disappear.

'What's become of Monsieur de Rubempré, then?' said Baroness Nucingen.

'He's faithful to his motto: *Quid me continebit?*' replied Rastignac.

'Which means: "Who can detain me?" or: "I can't be trained," whichever you please,' added de Marsay.

'While Monsieur le Baron was speaking of his fair unknown, Lucien smiled in a manner which suggested to me that he knew her,' said Horace Bianchon without perceiving any peril in so natural an observation.

'*Gut!*' the shark said to himself. Like all men who are desperately ill, he accepted anything which held out hope, and he promised himself to have Lucien watched, by other minions than those of Louchard, the cleverest Commercial Guard in Paris, to whom, during the past fortnight, he'd had recourse.

An abyss beneath Esther's happiness

BEFORE going on to Esther's, Lucien had to call at the Grandlieu house to spend the two hours which made Mademoiselle Clotilde-Frédérique de Grandlieu the happiest girl in the Faubourg Saint Germain. That prudence which characterized the conduct of the ambitious young man advised him to let Carlos Herrera know immediately of the effect of the smile which Baron Nucingen's portrait of Esther had brought to his face. The baron's love for Esther, and the idea he'd had of setting the police to look for his fair unknown, were anyway happenings important enough to communicate to the man who had taken under a cassock the asylum which formerly criminals had found in churches. And, from the rue Saint Lazare, where the banker lived at that time, to the rue Saint

Dominique, where the *hôtel* de Grandlieu stands, Lucien's way led past his own dwelling on the Quai Malaquais. He found his terrible friend smoking his breviary, that is to say seasoning his pipe before going to bed. More foreign than any foreigner, this man had finally given up Spanish cigars, which he found too mild.

'This is becoming serious,' the Spaniard answered when Lucien had recounted all. 'The baron, who makes use of Louchard to look for our little lamb, might well think of putting a policeman on your heels, and everything would be known. I shall need my nights and mornings to prepare cards for the game I'm going to play this baron, to whom I must above all demonstrate the powerlessness of the police. When our shark has lost all hope of finding his tender prey, I undertake to sell her to him at what she's worth to him . . .'

'Sell Esther?' cried Lucien, whose first reactions were always admirable.

'Are you forgetting the situation we're in?' cried Carlos Herrera.

Lucien lowered his head.

'No more money,' the Spaniard continued, 'and sixty thousand francs of debts to pay! If you want to marry Clotilde de Grandlieu, you have to buy an estate at a million to assure this plain Jane's jointure. Ah, well, Esther is meat I'm going to make this shark swim for to the tune of a million. That's my concern . . .'

'Esther would never . . .'

'That's my concern.'

'It'll be her death.'

'That concerns the undertakers. Besides, what then? . . .' cried this untamed figure, putting a stop to Lucien's elegies by his very stance. 'How many generals died in their prime of life for the Emperor Napoleon?' he demanded of Lucien after a brief silence. 'There is no shortage of women! In 1821, Coralie had no equal, you nevertheless found Esther. After this wench, there will be – do you know who? – the woman unknown! Of all women, that one is the most beautiful, and you will seek her in the princely capital where the Duc de Grandlieu's son-in-law will be minister representing the King of France . . . And then, tell me, young master, will Esther die of that? In any case, can Mademoiselle de Grandlieu's husband keep Esther? But leave it to me, you don't need to bother yourself with all this: it's my concern. Just do without Esther for a week or two, and you shall still go to the rue Taitbout. For the moment, be off and warble outside the gilded cage, and play your part well, slip Clotilde the incendiary letter you wrote this morning, and bring me back one that sizzles! The girl compensates herself for her privations by writing: that suits me! You will find Esther a little downcast, but tell her she must obey. It's a matter of our cloak of virtue, our livery of decorum, of the screen behind which great ones conceal their infamy . . . It's a question of my fairer *I*, of you who must never be under suspicion. Chance has served us better than I thought, working, as I have been these two months, in the void.'

Throwing off these terrible phrases one by one, like pistol shots, Carlos Herrera dressed and prepared to go out.

'You're enjoying yourself, that's clear,' cried Lucien, 'you never liked poor Esther, and you look forward with pleasure to the moment when you can be rid of her.'

'You've never grown tired of loving her, have you? . . well, I've never ceased to execrate the wench. But haven't I always behaved as though I were sincerely attached to her, I who, through Asia, held her life in my hands! A few bad mushrooms in a stew, and everything would have been said . . Mademoiselle Esther is still alive, all the same! . . . she is happy! . . . do you know why? because you love her! Don't play the child. We've been waiting four years for luck to run for or against us, well! it will take more than talent to clear the vegetable fate throws us today: in this turn of the wheel there is both good and bad, as usual. Do you know what was wondering when you came in?'

'No . . .'

'Whether here, as in Barcelona, I could, with the help of Asia, become the heir of an old church hen . . .'

'By a crime?'

'It was the only means I could think of to make your fortune. The creditors are beginning to stir. Once pursued by bailiffs and driven away from the Grandlieu establishment, what would become of you? The devil's bill would have fallen due.'

Carlos Herrera depicted in dumbshow a man's suicide by jumping in the water, then he fixed on Lucien one of those penetrating gazes by which the will of the strong is made to enter the souls of the weak. This riveting gaze, whose effect was to slacken all resistance, made it clear that there were between Lucien and his counsellor, not only secrets of life and death, but also feelings as superior to the general run of feelings as this man was to the baseness of his situation.

Constrained to live outside the world into which the law forbade him ever to enter again, drained by vice and by furious, by terrible oppositions, but endowed with a force of soul which devoured him, this ignoble and great, obscure and famous personality, consumed with a fever for life, lived again in the elegant person of Lucien whose soul had become his. He was represented in social life by this poet, to whom he gave his constancy and his iron will. For him, Lucien was more than a son, more than a beloved woman, more than a family, more than his life, Lucien was his revenge; thus, as strong souls hold faster to what they feel than to existence, he had attached the latter to himself by indissoluble bonds.

Having bought Lucien's life at the moment when the poet in despair was on the brink of suicide, he had proposed to him one of those infernal pacts which are never shown except in novels, but the dreadful possibility of which has often been brought to light at Courts of Assize by famous legal dramas. Lavishing upon Lucien all the delights of Paris life, proving to him that it was still possible to create a splendid future, he had played his part. Indeed, this strange man counted no sacrifice, once his other self was in question. In the midst of his strength, he was so weak against the caprices of his creature that he had even betrayed his secrets to the latter. Perhaps this purely moral complicity constituted a further bond between them? From the day on which the Torpedo had been carried off, Lucien knew on what horrible foundation his happiness rested.

This Spanish priest's cassock concealed Jacques Collin, one of the celebrities of the convict world, who, ten years before, had been living under the respectable name of Vautrin in the

Maison Vauquer, where Rastignac and Bianchon then lodged. Jacques Collin, the chief of gallows-dodgers, known as *Dodgedeath*, escaping from Rochefort immediately he had been returned there, profited by the example of the celebrated Count of Saint Helena: but with some modification in the defective part of Coignard's bold action. To substitute oneself for an honest man and continue with a convict's life is a proposition of which the terms are too contradictory not to contain the seeds of a fatal conclusion, especially in Paris; for, grafting himself on to a family, a condemned man multiplies the perils of such a substitution tenfold. To shelter from all pursuit, mustn't you anyway place yourself above the sphere of life's common interests? A man of the world is subject to hazards which do not weigh on those out of contact with the world. The cassock is therefore the surest of disguises, especially if it can be completed by an exemplary, solitary, inactive life. 'So I shall be a priest,' said the man dead to civic life who nevertheless wanted to live again in the world and to satisfy passions as strange as himself. The civil war to which the constitution of 1812 gave rise in Spain, whither this man of energy had betaken himself, provided him with the opportunity of ambushing and secretly killing the real Carlos Herrera. A great lord's bastard long abandoned by his father, not knowing the woman who had given him birth, that priest was charged with a political mission in France by King Ferdinand VII, to whom the suggestion had been made by a bishop. The bishop, the only man to interest himself in Carlos Herrera, died during the journey of the Church's lost child from Cadiz to Madrid and from Madrid into France. Fortunate in acquiring a personality so much to be desired, and under such favourable conditions, Jacques Collin cut the flesh of his back deeply enough to efface the fatal letters and changed his face with the help of chemical reagents. Transforming himself thus beside the priest's cadaver before destroying it, he was able to give himself some resemblance to his Sosia. To complete a transmutation almost as marvellous as that in the Arabian tale in which a dervish acquires the power to enter, himself being old, into a youthful body by the use of a magical formula, the convict, who spoke Spanish, learned as much

Latin as an Andalusian priest would be likely to know. Banker to all three of the great convict settlements, Collin was rich with the money confided to his known probity, known and compulsory, for between such associates a slip would be paid for with dagger thrusts. To these funds he added what the bishop had deposited with Carlos Herrera. Before leaving Spain, he was able to gain possession of the wealth a guilt-ridden woman had once acquired by murder, promising to see to its restitution. Turned priest, charged with a secret mission which gave him the most powerful recommendations in Paris, Jacques Collin, resolved on doing nothing to compromise his new character, had abandoned himself to the hazards this might bring, when he met Lucien on the road from Angoulême to Paris. This young fellow appeared to the sham priest to be a marvellous instrument of power; he prevented the attempt at suicide, saying: 'Give yourself to a man of God as one may give oneself to the devil, and your fate will change. You will live as in a dream, and your worst awakening can only be the death you were about to embrace . . .' The alliance of these two beings, which made them as one, rested on the force of such reasoning, and was further cemented by Carlos Herrera with complicity cunningly obtained. Endowed with the very genius of corruption, he destroyed Lucien's honesty by exposing him to cruel necessities and extricating him by gaining his tacit consent to bad or infamous actions which left him still pure, loyal, noble in the eyes of the world. Lucien was the social splendour in the shadow of which the forger wanted to live. 'I am the author, you will be the play; if you don't succeed, I am the one to be hissed,' he said to Lucien the day he confessed the sacrilege of his disguise. Carlos proceeded carefully from confession to confession, regulating their degree of infamy by his own progress and Lucien's need. Thus Dodgedeath did not yield up his ultimate secret until the moment at which the habit of Parisian pleasures, successes, satisfied vanity had enslaved the weak poet to him body and soul. Where Rastignac, tempted by this demon, had resisted, Lucien succumbed, more carefully handled, more expertly compromised, conquered especially by his own conquest of a position of eminence and the pleasure it gave him. Evil, whose poetic representation is called the Devil, in his dealings with this man half woman employed its most potent charms, at first asking little of him and giving him much. Carlos's great argument was that eternal secret promised by Tartuffe to Elmire. The reiterated proofs of absolute devotion, like that of Mahomet's blind henchman in Voltaire's play, completed the horrible work of Lucien's conquest by one like Jacques Collin. At that moment, not only had Esther and Lucien used up all the funds confided to the probity of the banker of the convict settlements, who for their sake was thus exposed to the most terrible rendering of accounts, but the dandy, the forger and the harlot were in debt. Just as Lucien was about to triumph, the least pebble under the foot of one of these three beings might bring down the whole fantastic edifice of a fortune so daringly erected. At the Opera ball, Rastignac had recognized the Vautrin of the Maison Vauquer, but he knew himself for a dead man if he were indiscreet, and so Madame de Nucingen's lover and Lucien exchanged looks in which on both sides the semblance of friendship concealed fear. In the last resort, Rastignac would certainly, with the greatest of pleasure, have provided the carriage which led Dodgedeath to the scaffold. The reader will now perceive with what sombre joy Carlos was seized on learning of Baron Nucingen's love, apprehending in a single thought all the advantage to which he could turn poor Esther.

'Right!' he said to Lucien, 'the devil looks after his chaplain.'

'You're smoking on a powder-magazine.'

'*Incedo per ignes!*' replied Carlos with a smile, 'that's my profession.'

The Grandlieus

THE house of Grandlieu had divided into two branches towards the middle of the previous century: on the one hand the ducal house doomed to extinction, since the then duke had only daughters; on the other hand the viscounts Grandlieu who were to inherit the title and the arms of the senior branch. The ducal branch bears *Gules, in a fess three battle-axes or*, with the famous CAVEO NON TIMEO! for device, which tells the family's whole story.

The escutcheon of the viscounts is quartered Navarreins, which gives *Gules, a fess battled or*, and crested with a knight's helm bearing: GRANDS FAITS, GRAND LIEU! for device. At the time of our story, the viscountess, a widow since 1813, had a son and a daughter. Though almost ruined on her return from exile, she recovered, thanks to the devotion of a solicitor, Derville, a not inconsiderable fortune.

Returning in 1804, the duke and duchess of Grandlieu received friendly overtures from Napoleon; he not only had them at court but restored to them all that had come into the Demesne, about forty thousand francs in rent. Of all the great lords of the Faubourg Saint Germain who allowed themselves to be seduced by the Emperor, the duke and the duchess (an Ajuda of the senior branch, allied with the Braganzas) were alone in not later disowning him and his benefactions. Louis XVIII had regard to this fidelity when the Faubourg Saint Germain treated it as a crime; but perhaps, in this, Louis XVIII merely wished to tease MONSIEUR. It was thought probable that the young Vicomte de Grandlieu would marry Marie-Athénais, the duke's last daughter, then aged nine. Sabine, the second youngest, was to marry the Baron du Guénic, after the July revolution. Josephine, the third, became Madame d'Ajuda-Pinto, when the marquis lost his first wife, Mademoiselle de Rochefide. The eldest had taken the veil in 1822. The second, Mademoiselle Clotilde-Frédérique, at the present moment aged twenty-seven, was deeply in love with Lucien de Rubempré.

It is pointless to ask whether the *hôtel* of the Duc de Grandlieu, one of the finest in the rue Saint Dominique, impressed Lucien's mind with its glamour; every time the enormous door turned on its hinges to admit his gig, he experienced that satisfaction of his vanity of which Mirabeau has spoken. 'Although my father was a mere apothecary in Houmeau, I nevertheless enter there . . .' That was his thought. He would have committed other crimes than associating with a forger to retain the right of walking up those few steps, to hear himself announced as: 'Monsieur de Rubempré!' in the big Louis XIV drawing-room, modelled, in the time of Louis XIV, on those of Versailles, where the *cream* of Paris was to be found, that society of the chosen, then called *le petit Château*.

The Portuguese noblewoman, who cared very little for going out, was much of the time surrounded by her neighbours the Chaulieus, the Navarreins, the Lenoncourts. Frequently the pretty Baroness Macumer (*née* Chaulieu), the Duchesse de Maufrigneuse, Madame d'Espard, Madame de Camps, Mademoiselle des Touches, allied to the Brittany Grandlieus, came to visit her, on their way to a ball or returning from the Opera. The Vicomte de Grandlieu, the Duc de Rhétoré, the Marquis de Chaulieu, who would one day be Duc de Lenoncourt-Chaulieu, his wife Madeleine de Mortsauf, grand-daughter of the Duc de Lenoncourt, the Marquis d'Ajuda-Pinto, Prince Blamont-Chauvry, the Marquis de Beauséant, the Vidame de Pamiers, the Vandenesses, old Prince Cadignan and his son the Duc de Maufrigneuse, came regularly to this grandiose drawing-room in which one breathed the air of the Court, in which manners, breeding, temper harmonized with the noble birth of the owners whose high aristocratic style had ended by causing their Napoleonic bondage to be forgotten.

The aged Duchesse d'Uxelles, mother of the Duchesse de Maufrigneuse, was the oracle of this drawing-room, to which Madame de Sérisy had never succeeded in gaining admission, though born de Ronquerolles.

Introduced by Madame de Maufrigneuse, who had persuaded her mother to act on Lucien's behalf, having been mad on him for two years, the charming poet had maintained his position there thanks to the influence of the High Chaplaincy of France and the help of the Archbishop of Paris. He was only admitted nevertheless after obtaining the ordinance which restored to him the name and the arms of the house of Rubempré. The Duc de Rhétoré, the Chevalier d'Espard and a few others, jealous of Lucien, periodically affected the duke's disposition towards him by telling stories of his antecedents; but the pious duchess, much frequented by dignitaries of the

Church, and Clotilde de Grandlieu defended him. Lucien, moreover, was able to explain this unfriendliness by his youthful dealings with Madame d'Espard's cousin, Madame de Bargeton, now Countess Châtelet. Moreover, feeling the need to be adopted by so powerful a family, and impelled by his intimate counsellor to charm Clotilde, Lucien had all the courage of an upstart: he appeared five days out of the seven, he gracefully swallowed the affronts of envy, he outfaced impertinent stares, he answered banter wittily. His assiduity, the charm of his manners, his obligingness in the end neutralized scruple and diminished obstacles. Always welcome at the house of the Duchesse de Maufrigneuse whose ardent letters, written during the course of her passion, were kept by Carlos Herrera, idol of Madame de Sérisy, highly regarded at Mademoiselle des Touches's, Lucien, happy to be admitted to these three houses, learned from the Spaniard to conduct his relations with the greatest reserve.

'One can't devote oneself to several houses at a time,' his intimate adviser told him. 'A man who goes everywhere is nowhere the subject of lively interest. The great protect only those who vie with their furniture, those whom they see every day, who become necessary to them, like the divan they sit on.'

Accustomed to regard the Grandlieu drawing-room as his battlefield, Lucien reserved his wit, his epigrams, his news and his courtier's graces for the time he spent there in the evening. Insinuating, affectionate in his manner, warned by Clotilde of the reefs to avoid, he flattered Monsieur de Grandlieu's little manias. After having begun with envy of the Duchesse de Maufrigneuse's happiness, Clotilde's love for Lucien soon knew no bounds.

Perceiving all the advantages of such an alliance, Lucien played the lover's part as it might have been played by Armand, the latest juvenile lead at the Comédie Française. He wrote Clotilde letters which were certainly literary masterpieces of the highest order and Clotilde replied to them in a strife of genius, furiously expressing her love on paper, which was the only way of loving she knew. Lucien went to mass at Saint Thomas of Aquino's every Sunday, he gave himself out for a fervent Catholic, he preached monarchy and religion in the most impressive manner. He also wrote in periodicals devoted to the cause of the Congregation the most remarkable articles, for which he would take no payment and which he signed only L. He composed political pamphlets, demanded either by King Charles X, or by the Chaplaincy, without accepting the slightest remuneration. 'The King,' he said, 'has already done so much for me, that I owe him my life's blood.' For some days past, the question had been mooted of attaching Lucien to the Prime Minister's office as personal secretary; but Madame d'Espard set so many people on to campaign against him, that Charles X's Jack-of-all-trades hesitated to make a decision. Not only was Lucien's situation insufficiently clear, and the words: 'What does he live on?' which everybody asked as he rose in the world, still in need of a reply; but also benevolent curiosity, as much as that of the malicious, proceeded from investigation to investigation, and discovered more than one chink in the ambitious young man's armour. Clotilde de Grandlieu spied innocently on her mother and father. A few days previously, she had led Lucien to a window embrasure to tell him of her family's objections. 'Own property worth a million, and you shall have my hand, that was my mother's reply,' Clotilde had said. 'They will ask you later where your money comes from,' Carlos had said to Lucien when Lucien reported this supposed last word to him. 'My brother-in-law must have made a fortune,' Lucien had pointed out, 'he can be responsible in law,' 'So all we need now is the million,' Carlos had cried, 'I'll give the matter thought.'

To be more precise about Lucien's position at the Grandlieu establishment, he had never dined there. Neither Clotilde nor the Duchesse d'Uxelles, nor yet Madame de Maufrigneuse, who remained very much on Lucien's side, could obtain this favour from the old duke, so obstinately in doubt was this gentleman about one whom he called the Sire de Rubempré. This element of discrimination, perceived by everyone in that society, keenly wounded Lucien's self-esteem, he felt himself to be merely tolerated. Society has the right to be exacting, it is so often deceived! To cut a figure in Paris without having a known fortune, an acknowledged livelihood, is a situation which no artifice can long render tenable. Thus the higher

Lucien climbed, the more force he gave to the objection: 'What does he live on?' He had been compelled to say to Madame de Sérisy, to whom he owed the support of the Attorney General Granville and of a privy councillor, Count Octave de Bauvan, president of the sovereign Court of Appeal: 'I am running horribly into debt.'

Entering the courtyard of the *hôtel* which could grant his vanities official recognition, he said to himself with some bitterness, thinking of what Dodgedeath had told him: 'I hear everything crack under my feet!' He loved Esther, and he wanted Mademoiselle de Grandlieu as his wife! A strange position! He must sell one in order to have the other. Only one man could carry on this traffic without Lucien's honour suffering, that man was the false Spaniard: both needed equal discretion, each to each. Few pacts are made to which both parties are in turn dominated and dominator.

Lucien drove off the clouds which darkened his brow, he stepped gaily and beaming into the reception rooms of the Grandlieus.

The daughter of a great house

AT that moment, the windows were open, the scents from the garden perfumed the drawing-room, a flower stand in the centre drew all eyes to its pyramid of blossom. The duchess, sitting in a corner, on a sofa, was talking with the Duchesse de Chaulieu. A group of women was remarkable for the diverse attitudes each took from her manner of playing mock grief. In society, nobody is interested in suffering or misfortune, everything is talk. The men walked up and down the drawing-room, or in the garden. Clotilde and Josephine were occupied about the tea-table. The Vidame de Pamiers, the Duc de Grandlieu, the Marquis d'Ajuda-Pinto, the Duc de Maufrigneuse played whist in a corner. When Lucien was announced, he crossed the drawing-room and went to greet the duchess, from whom he asked the reason for the grief depicted upon her visage.

99

'Madame de Chaulieu has just received frightful news: her son-in-law the Baron de Macumer, former duke of Soria, has just died. The young Duke de Soria and his wife, who had gone to Chantepleurs to look after their brother, wrote to tell her of this sad event. The condition of Louise is heart-rending.'

'A woman is not loved twice in her life as Louise was by her husband,' said Madeleine de Mortsauf.

'She will be a rich widow,' said the aged Duchesse d'Uxelles looking at Lucien whose face remained impassive.

'Poor Louise,' said Madame d'Espard, 'I understand, and I am sorry for her.'

The Marquise d'Espard had the wistful look of a woman all heart and soul. Although Sabine de Grandlieu was only ten, she gave her mother an intelligent look full of sly mockery which her mother's stern glance removed. This is called bringing one's children up well.

'If my daughter recovers from this blow,' said Madame de Chaulieu with a maternal look, 'her future will give rise to uneasiness. Louise is very romantic.'

'I don't know, I'm sure,' said the old Duchesse d'Uxelles, 'where our daughters can have picked it up? . . .'

'It is difficult,' said a cardinal of her generation, 'to reconcile the heart and the proprieties nowadays.'

Lucien, who hadn't a word to say, went towards the tea-table, to pay his compliments to the Grandlieu girls. When the poet was a few yards away from the group of women, the Marquise d'Espard leaned over to speak in the Duchesse de Grandlieu's ear.

'Do you believe that that young fellow really loves your dear Clotilde, then?' she asked.

The perfidy of this question can only be understood after Clotilde has been sketched. This young person, aged twenty-seven, was standing. Her attitude permitted the mocking gaze of the Marquise d'Espard to take in Clotilde's narrow, un-modulated figure which closely resembled a stick of asparagus. The poor girl's bosom was too flat to allow of those colonial resources known to the dressmaker as helpful trimmings. Indeed, conscious of the advantages her name gave her,

Clotilde, instead of being at pains to disguise the defect, heroically drew attention to it. With close-fitting gowns, she obtained the effect of the sharp, rigid style which the sculptors of the Middle Ages sought in the figures which stand out so distinctly against the shadow of the niches in which they have placed them in cathedrals. Clotilde stood five feet four inches. To use a familiar expression which has at least the merit of being readily understood, she was all legs. This fault in proportion gave the upper part of her body an appearance of deformity. Of a dark complexion, her hair black and harsh, her eyebrows thick, her burning eyes set in orbits themselves coal-black, her profile arched like a moon's first quarter and dominated by a protruding forehead, she was a caricature of her mother, one of the most beautiful women of Portugal. Nature amuses itself with games like that. One often sees, in families, a sister of astonishing beauty whose features, in her brother, have taken on remarkable ugliness, although there is a likeness between the two. Upon her mouth, which was sunk in, Clotilde bore a stereotyped expression of disdain. At the same time, her lips revealed more of the secret feelings of her heart than any other feature of her face, for affection lent them a charming expression, while her cheeks too dark for blushes and her black, expressionless eyes told one nothing. Despite so many disadvantages, despite the fact that she carried herself like a plank, her education and her breeding had given her looks some element of grandeur, of pride, what is known as *a certain something*, perhaps due to her uncompromising way of dressing, which betokened the daughter of a great house. The strength, the length and thickness of her hair might be considered beautiful. Her cultivated voice was full of charm. She sang admirably. Clotilde was the kind of young person of whom one says: 'She has fine eyes,' or: 'She has a charming disposition!' To someone who addressed her in the English manner as: 'Your Grace,' she once replied: 'Call me Your Thinness.'

'Why shouldn't one love my poor Clotilde?' the duchess replied to the marquise. 'Do you know what she said to me yesterday? "If I am loved out of ambition, I undertake in the end to be loved for myself!" She is witty and ambitious, two qualities which may appeal to a man. As to the man, my dear, he is as handsome as a dream; and if he can buy the Rubempré estate, the King, out of regard for us, will restore the title of marquis to him ... After all, his mother is the last of the Rubemprés ...'

'Poor boy, where will he pick up a million?' said the marchioness.

'That is not our concern,' the duchess went on; 'but one thing is certain, he wouldn't steal them ... And, besides, we shouldn't give Clotilde to a schemer or to anyone at all dishonest, however handsome, however much a poet and young like Monsieur de Rubempré.'

'You're late,' said Clotilde with an infinitely gracious smile to Lucien.

'Yes, I was dining out.'

'You go out into society a great deal these last few days,' said she, hiding her jealousy and her uneasiness beneath a smile.

'Society? ...' replied Lucien, 'no, by pure chance, I've been dining with bankers all week, today Nucingen, yesterday du Tillet and the day before that the Kellers ...'

It will be seen that Lucien had picked up the great lords' tone of witty impertinence.

'You have many enemies,' Clotilde told him offering him (with how much grace!) a cup of tea. 'Someone came and said to my father that you were blest with sixty thousand francs of debts, that before long you'd be cooling your heels in Sainte Pélagie. And if you knew what all these calumnies cost me ... Everything falls on my head. I'm not speaking of what *I* suffer (my father gives me looks which crucify me), but of what you must suffer, if any of it bore the least resemblance to the truth ...'

'Don't worry yourself about that kind of nonsense, love me as I love you, and trust me for a few months,' replied Lucien putting his empty cup down on the chased silver tray.

'Don't show yourself to my father, he would be rude to you; and as you wouldn't put up with that, we should be lost ... That malicious Marquise d'Espard told him that your mother looked after women in childbirth, and that your sister took in ironing ...'

'We came very near to destitution,' replied Lucien, tears starting to his eyes. 'That wasn't calumny, just plain scandal-mongering. Today my sister is more than a millionaire, and my mother died two years ago ... These revelations were being kept for the moment at which I seemed likely to succeed here ...'

'But what did you do to Madame d'Espard?'

'I was imprudent enough to recount, at Madame de Sérisy's, as an amusing story, before Messieurs de Bauvan and de Granville, the action she brought to obtain an injunction against her husband, the Marquis d'Espard, which Bianchon had told me about. Monsieur de Granville's opinion, supported by Bauvan and Sérisy, caused the Keeper of the Seals to change his. They were both afraid of the *Gazette des Tribunaux*, of a scandal, and the marquise was rapped over the knuckles when grounds were delivered for the judgment which put an end to this horrible affair. If Monsieur de Sérisy committed an indiscretion which made the marquise a mortal enemy of mine, I gained his protection, the Attorney General's and that of Count Octave de Bauvan whom Madame de Sérisy told about the peril they'd put me in by letting the source of their information be guessed. Monsieur le Marquis d'Espard was clumsy enough to call on me, since he regarded me as the cause of him winning this infamous case.'

'I'm going to rid us of Madame d'Espard,' said Clotilde.

'How?' cried Lucien.

'My mother will invite d'Espard's children who are charming and already quite big. The father and his two sons will sing your praises here, we can be sure of never seeing their mother again ...'

'Oh, Clotilde! you're adorable, if I didn't love you for yourself, I should love you for your wit.'

'That isn't wit,' she said putting all her love into her smile. 'Good-bye. Stay away for a few days. When you see me at Saint Thomas Aquinas's with a pink scarf, my father's mood will have changed. There's a reply stuck to the back of the chair you're sitting on, it may console you for not seeing us. Put the letter you've brought me into my handkerchief ...'

This young person was clearly older than twenty-seven.

The house of a dutiful daughter

LUCIEN took a cab to the rue de la Planche, got out on the boulevards, took another at the Madeleine and gave the driver the address in the rue Taitbout.

At eleven o'clock, when he reached Esther's, he found her in tears, but dressed as though he and she had something to celebrate! She waited for Lucien lying on a divan of white satin brocaded with yellow flowers, wearing a delicious wrap of Indian muslin, with cherry-coloured ribbon knots, uncorseted, her hair simply caught up on her head, her feet in pretty velvet slippers lined with cherry satin, all the candles lighted and the hookah ready; but she hadn't smoked hers, which remained unlighted beside her, like a token of her situation. Hearing the doors open, she wiped away her tears, leaped up like a gazelle and enfolded Lucien in her arms like a tissue which, snatched by the wind, should wind itself round a tree.

'Separated,' she said, 'is it true? . . .'

'Oh, for a few days,' replied Lucien.

Esther let go of Lucien and fell back upon the divan like one dead. In situations of this kind, most women chatter like parrots! Ah! they love you! . . . After five years, it is still to them the dawn of happiness, they cannot leave you, their indignation, despair, love, anger, regrets, terror, mortification and presentiments are sublime! In short, it is as pretty as a scene in Shakespeare. But, you must understand! women like that aren't in love. When they are all they say they are, when truly they are in love, they behave as Esther did, as children do, as true love does; Esther didn't say a word, she lay with her face in the cushions, and wept hot tears. For his part, Lucien made an effort to raise her and spoke to her.

'But, child, we aren't to be separated . . . What, after nearly four years of happiness, that's how you take a period of absence. Ah, what have I done to all these wenches? . . .' he said to himself remembering that he had been loved like that by Coralie.

'How handsome you are, sir!' said Europe.

The senses have their ideals. When the so-charming physical ideal is accompanied by the sweetness of character, the poetry which distinguished Lucien, it is not too difficult to imagine the wild passion of these creatures so eminently sensitive to the external gifts of nature, and so ingenuous in their admiration. Esther sobbed gently, and her posture betrayed extreme grief.

'Little stupid,' said Lucien, 'haven't they told you that my life is in question! . . .'

At this calculated utterance of Lucien's, Esther stood up like a wild creature, her unknotted hair framed her sublime face like the leaves of a tree. She stared at Lucien with a fixed gaze.

'Your life! . . .' she cried raising her arms and then letting them fall with a gesture which belongs to imperilled women of that sort. It is a moment of truth with them, and must not be disregarded.

She drew from her girdle a wretched scrap of paper, then noticed Europe, and said to her: 'Leave us, girl.' When the door had closed behind Europe: 'Look, *he* wrote this to me,' she went on handing Lucien a letter which Carlos had just sent and which Lucien read aloud.

You will leave tomorrow morning at five o'clock, you will be taken to a keeper's house in the depths of the forest of Saint Germain, you will occupy a room on the first floor. Do not leave this room until I say so, everything will be provided. The forester and his wife may be trusted. Do not write to Lucien. Do not stand at the window during the day; but you may walk out at night under the care of the forester, if you need exercise. Keep the blinds down on the way out: Lucien's life is at stake.

Lucien will come this evening to take leave of you, burn this in front of him . . .

Lucien at once burned this letter with the flame of a candle.

'Listen, my Lucien,' said Esther after hearing the note read as a criminal may listen to his death sentence, 'I won't tell you that I love you, that would be stupid . . . For almost five years now, loving you has seemed as natural as breathing, as living . . . The very day on which my happiness began under the tutelage of that inexplicable being, who put me here as one puts a curious little animal in a cage, I knew that you'd have to be married. Marriage is a necessary part of your destiny, and God keep me from impeding the development of your fortune. This marriage is my death. But I shan't cause you any annoyance; I shan't act like one of those seamstresses who kill themselves with the aid of a little coal-stove, once was enough; the second time, it disgusts you, as Mariette said. No: I shall go far away, out of France. Asia knows secrets from her own country, she's promised to show me how to die without trouble. You prick yourself, *paf*! it's all over. I ask only one thing, my angel darling, not to be told lies. My life adds up: from the day I saw you in 1824 until today, I've had more happiness than there is in the existences of ten lucky women. So, take me for what I am: a woman both strong and weak. Say to me: "I'm getting married." I ask for no more than a very tender farewell, and you won't hear me spoken of again . . .' There was a moment's silence after this declaration, whose sincerity was evident from the simplicity of the words and the accompanying gestures. 'Is it a question of your marriage?' she said plunging one of her brilliant, fascinating glances, like the blade of a dagger into Lucien's blue eyes.

'We've been working at that marriage for eighteen months, and it still isn't arranged,' replied Lucien, 'I don't know when it will be arranged; but it isn't a question of that, my little one . . . it's a question of the abbé, of me, of you . . . we're in serious danger . . . Nucingen has seen you . . .'

'Yes,' she said, 'at Vincennes, did he recognize me? . . .'

'No,' answered Lucien, 'but he's in love with you enough to ruin himself. After dinner, when he was describing you in speaking of your meeting, I involuntarily, imprudently smiled, for in society I'm like a savage amid the traps of a tribe of enemies. Carlos, who spares me the trouble of thinking, finds the situation fraught with peril, he's undertaking to break Nucingen if Nucingen takes it upon himself to spy on us, and the baron is quite capable of that; he spoke to me about the powerlessness of the police. You've lighted a fire in an old chimney caked with soot . . .'

'What does your Spaniard mean to do?' said Esther gently.

'I don't know, he told me to sleep on both ears,' replied Lucien without daring to look at Esther.

'If that's how it is, I obey with that doglike submission I'm so good at,' said Esther slipping her arm through Lucien's and leading him into her bedroom as she said to him: 'Did my Lulu dine well at the infamous Nucingen's?'

'Asia's cooking makes it impossible to think a dinner good, however celebrated the cook at the house one dines at; but the dinner was prepared by Carême as it is every Sunday.'

Lucien involuntarily compared Esther with Clotilde. His mistress was so beautiful, so constantly charming that she had kept far away that monster which devours the strongest loves: *satiety*! – 'What a pity it is,' he said to himself, 'to light on a wife in two volumes! in one, poetry, pleasure, love, devotion, beauty, gentleness ...' Esther was ferreting about as women do before going to bed, she darted here and there, fluttered and sang. You would have thought she was a humming-bird.

'... In the other, name and nobility, race, honours, rank, knowledge of the world! ... And no means of uniting them in a single person!' cried Lucien inwardly.

Next morning, waking at seven o'clock in that delightful pink and white room, the poet found himself alone. When he rang, it was the fantastic Europe who bustled in.

'What is it you want, sir?'

'Esther!'

'My lady left at a quarter to five. In accordance with the orders of the good father, I received a new face carriage paid.'

'A woman? ...'

'No, sir, she's English ... one of those creatures who go out scrubbing at night, and our orders are to treat her as if it were my lady: what are you going to do, sir, with that big gawk? ... My poor lady, how she wept as she climbed into the carriage ... "However, I must! ..." she cried. "I left that poor lamb sleeping," she said wiping her tears; "Europe, if he had looked at me or if he had spoken my name, I should have stayed, ready to die with him ..." Look, sir, I'm so fond of my lady, I didn't let her see her substitute; plenty of ladies' maids'd never have thought of that and broken their hearts.'

'The Unknown is here, then? . . .'

'She was in the carriage, sir, that took my lady away, and I hid her in my room, according to his instructions . . .'

'What is she like?'

'Oh, as good as you can expect in a bargain lot, but she'll manage her part without trouble, if you put your mind to it, sir,' said Europe and went off to fetch the replacement for Esther.

Monsiur de Nucingen at work

THE previous evening, before going to bed, the all-powerful banker had given orders to his personal manservant who, at seven o'clock already, introduced the famous Louchard, cleverest of the Trade Protection men, into a small reception-room to which the baron came in dressing-gown and slippers . . .

'You hef been making fun with me!' said he in reply to the security guard's salutations.

'It couldn't be otherwise, baron. I do what I'm supposed to do, and I had the honour of telling you that I couldn't be mixed up in an affair outside my functions. What did I promise you? that I'd put you in contact with that one of our agents who seemed to me likely to serve your turn best. But the baron knows about the demarcations which exist between men of different occupations . . . When you're building a house, you don't get a joiner to do a locksmith's job. Well, there are two kinds of police: the Political Police, the Judicial Police. The judicial don't do the work of the politicals, and *vice versa*. If you applied to the head of the Political Police, he'd need authorization from the minister to take on your business, and you wouldn't dare explain it to the Director General of the Police of the Kingdom. A policeman who worked on his own account would be sacked. Now, the Judicial Police is just as careful as the Political Police. So nobody, either at the Ministry of the Interior or at the Prefecture, makes a move except in the interests of the State or in the interests of the Law.

If it's a matter of a plot or a crime, well! my goodness, the top men will do what you want; but you must understand, baron, they've got other fish to fry than occupying themselves with the fifty thousand love affairs of Paris. For them like me, we're only supposed to concern ourselves with arresting debtors; and as soon as anything else arises, we take an enormous risk if we disturb the peace of anybody else. I sent you one of my men, but I wouldn't take responsibility; you told him to find you a woman somewhere in Paris, Contenson relieved you of a thousand francs and did nothing. Might as well look for a needle in a haystack as search Paris for a woman suspected of frequenting the Bois de Vincennes, whose description was like that of all the pretty women in Paris.'

'Your Gontenson,' said the baron, 'goot he nit hef tolt me ze truce, instead of tittle me out of a *tausend* francs?'

'Listen, Monsieur le Baron,' said Louchard, 'will you give me a thousand crowns, I'm going to give you . . . sell you, some advice.'

'Must I pay *tausend* crowns for advice?' asked Nucingen.

'I'm not letting myself be caught, baron,' replied Louchard. 'You're in love, see, you want to find the object of your passion, you're withering like a lettuce without water. Only yesterday, your manservant told me, two doctors who came to the house found your condition dangerous; there's only me can put you into the hands of a man clever enough . . . Ah, well, so! if your life isn't worth a thousand crowns . . .'

'Tell me ze name of zis so clever man, *und* count on my tschenerosidy!'

Louchard picked up his hat, bowed, took his leave.

'*Teufel* man!' cried Nucingen, 'what is? . . . wait.'

'Note carefully,' said Louchard before taking the money, 'that I am selling you information pure and simple. I will give you the name and address of the only man who can help you, but he is a master . . .'

'Ton't pee riticulous!' cried Nucingen, 'only Rothschild's name iss vort *tausend* crowns, and only when it iss signed at ze bottom of a bill . . . I give you *tausend* francs?'

'You'd haggle over a gold mine!' said Louchard departing with a wave of the hand.

'I'll hef ze address for a note of five hundred francs,' cried the baron who told his manservant to send his secretary in.

Lesage's Turcaret no longer exists. The greatest, like the smallest, banker has since learnt to exercise his acumen over details: he haggles over the arts, good works, love, he'd haggle with the Pope over an absolution. Thus Nucingen, listening to Louchard, had rapidly calculated that Contenson, being the Commercial Guard's right-hand man, must know the address of this Master Spy. Contenson would let him have for five hundred francs what Louchard hoped to sell for a thousand crowns. His speed of thought showed that if the man's heart was infused with love, his brain was still that of a shark.

'Yourself go, sir,' said the baron to his secretary, 'to Gontenson, the spy of Luchard, ze Commerzial Cart, but take a cabriolet, go quick, and prink him fast here, I await! . . . Return by ze karten kate. *Hier ist* ze key, for it is koot zing nobody see zat man at my house. Take him to de sommerhouse in ze karten. Try to do what I say *mit* intelligence.'

There were people wanting to talk business with Nucingen; but he was waiting for Contenson, his mind was full of Esther, he was saying to himself that before long he would again see the woman to whom he owed these unhoped-for feelings. And he sent everybody away with vague words and ambiguous promises. Contenson seemed to him the most important man in Paris, he kept looking out for him in the garden. Finally, after giving orders for the doors to be fastened, he had his luncheon served in the pavilion which stood in a corner of the garden. Among his office staff, the conduct, the hesitation, of the craftiest, most far-sighted, most politic of the bankers of Paris, seemed inexplicable.

'What's the matter with the chief?' said a stockbroker to one of the senior clerks.

'We don't know, it seems that his health is giving rise to uneasiness; yesterday the baroness called in both Doctors Desplein and Bianchon . . .'

One day, a foreign delegation called on Newton when he was occupied in treating one of his dogs called *Beauty*, who as is well known, took up a lot of his time, and to whom

(Beauty was a bitch) all he said was: 'Ah, Beauty, you don't know what you've just destroyed!...' The foreigners respected the great man's labours and went away. In all the lives of great men may be found a little bitch like Beauty. When Marshal Richelieu went to see Louis XV after the taking of Mahon, one of the greatest feats of arms of the eighteenth century, the King said to him: 'Have you heard the news?... poor Lansmatt is dead!' Lansmatt was a door-keeper in the know about the King's amorous intrigues. The bankers of Paris never knew what they owed to Contenson. Because of this spy, Nucingen allowed a huge deal to be concluded without him, though his part in it was already arranged. The shark's guns of Speculation were every day trained on fortune, but a promise of Happiness detained the man elsewhere!

Contenson

THE famous banker was taking tea, nibbling slices of bread and butter like a man whose teeth had not been sharpened by appetite for a long time, when he heard a carriage stopping at the little door to his garden. Presently Nucingen's secretary brought in Contenson, whom he had eventually located in a café near Saint Pelagia's, where the agent was lunching on the tip given him by a debtor incarcerated with certain privileges which have to be paid for. Contenson, you must know, was a real poem, a Parisian poem. From his looks, you would have seen at first glance that the Figaro of Beaumarchais, the Mascarillo of Molière, Marivaux's Frontins and Dancourt's Lafleurs, those great exemplars of audacious knavery, of cunning brought to bay, of the setback turned to advantage, were mediocrities by contrast with this colossus of wretchedness and wit. When, in Paris, you meet a type, it is no mere man, it is a spectacle! it is no longer a moment in life, but a whole existence, several existences! Cook a plaster cast three times in a furnace, and you get a sort of bastard appearance of Florentine bronze; in the same way, the crackle of innumerable misfortunes, the grip of intolerable situations had bronzed Contenson's head as though the light of three furnaces had paled upon his visage. The tight lines could no longer be unwrinkled, they were eternal creases, white at the bottom. His yellow face was all lines. His skull, a bit like Voltaire's, was as unfeeling as a death's head, and, but for a little hair at the back, could hardly have been taken for that of a living man. Beneath a motionless brow, expressing nothing, moved the eyes of a Chinaman displayed under glass at the door of a tea-shop, artificial eyes pretending to be alive, their expression unchanging. The nose, flat like death's, defied Fate, and the mouth, tight-lipped as a miser's, was at once open and discreet like the rictus of a letter-box. Calm as a man of the wilderness, his hands deeply weathered, Contenson, a small, thin, dry man, had that attitude of Diogenic indifference which never bows to the forms of respect. And what commentary upon his life and customs was written into his dress, for those who know how to decipher a man's costume! . . . What breeches, particularly! . . . a bailiff's breeches, black and shiny like the stuff called *voile* of which barristers' gowns are made! . . . a waistcoat bought in the Temple, but embroidered and with lapels! . . . a coat of black turning red! . . . And all brushed, clean-looking, set off by a watch on a pinchbeck chain. On a pleated shirt-front of yellow cambric shone an artificial diamond pin! Upon the yoke of the velvet collar obtruded the raw folds of flesh like a Carib's. The silk hat shone like satin, but its lining would have yielded oil for two small lamps if some grocer had bought it and had it boiled. It serves little purpose to enumerate accessories, one should be able to paint the enormous pretentiousness imprinted on them by Contenson. There was something tremendously smart about the coat collar, about the newly polished boots with their gaping soles, which no expression in the language can render. In the end, trying to fit these various pieces together, an intelligent man, studying Contenson, would have seen that, if he had been a thief and not a police-spy, these rags, instead of bringing a smile to the lips, would have aroused horror. About his costume, an observer might have said to himself: 'There goes a squalid person, he drinks, he gambles, he has vices, but he doesn't get drunk, he doesn't cheat, he isn't a thief or a murderer.' And Contenson was indeed indefinable until the word 'spy' came into one's mind. The man had professed as many unknown trades as there are known ones. The faint smile on his pale lips, the blink of his greenish eyes, the twitching of his flat nose, showed that he did not lack intelligence. His tin-plate face must conceal a soul of identical substance. The movements of his physiognomy were grimaces drawn out of him by politeness, not the expression of emotions within. He would have aroused fear, if he had not been risible. Contenson, one of the most curious products of the scum which floats upon the waters of the Parisian sink, where everything is in ferment, prided himself above all on being a philosopher. He said without bitterness: 'I have great talents, but they go for nothing, as though I were an idiot!' And he condemned himself instead of accusing others. Find many spies with as little gall as Contenson. 'Circumstances are against us,' he repeatedly said to his superiors, 'we might be fine crystal, we are so many grains of sand, that is all.' His indifference in the matter of costume had a meaning, he cared as little about his everyday wear as actors do about theirs; he excelled in disguise, in make-up; he could have given lessons to Frederick Lemaître, for he could turn himself out stylishly when there was need. In his youth he had forcibly adopted the bohemianism of the back streets. He displayed a lordly contempt for the Judicial Police, for under the Empire he had worked for Fouché, whom he considered a great man. Since the suppression of the Ministry of Police, he had made the best of commercial investigations; but his known ability, his fine touch, made him a useful instrument, and the unknown heads of the Political Police kept his name on their books. Contenson, together with many of the same calibre, played only extras in the drama whose leading parts were allocated elsewhere, when political work was afoot.

'LEAF us,' said Nucingen dismissing his secretary with a movement of the hand.

'Why does this man live in a mansion while I'm in a furnished room ...?' Contenson said to himself. 'He's ruined his creditors three times, he's stolen money, I've never taken a penny ... I am more highly gifted than he is ...'

'Gontenson, my luf,' said the baron, 'you tittled me a note off *tausend* francs ...'

'My mistress was in debt up to the eyes ...'

'You hef a mistress?' cried Nucingen eyeing Contenson with mingled admiration and envy.

'I'm only sixty-six,' replied Contenson, a man whom Vice had kept young, as a fatal example.

'End what does she?'

'Helps me,' said Contenson. 'If you're a thief and an honest woman loves you, either she becomes a thief, or you go straight. Me, I'm still an investigator, semi-private.'

'Hallways you hef need of money?' asked Nucingen.

'Always,' replied Contenson with a smile, 'it's my natural condition to want money, the way it's yours to make it; we ought to suit each other: you give me the stuff, I spend it. You're the well, me the bucket ...'

'Do you wish earn note of fife *hundert* francs?'

'That's a fine question! but do I look stupid? ... You're not offering it by way of repairing fortune's injustice in my favour.'

'Not at oll, I add it to ze *tausand* franc note you hef olready cheat me off; *also* fifteen *hundert* francs I gif you.'

'Good, you give me the thousand francs I took, and you add five hundred francs ...'

'Yo, yo, is *gut*,' said Nucingen nodding his head.

'It's only five hundred francs,' said Contenson imperturbably.

'To gif? ...' replied the baron.

'To take. Ah, well, what does Monsieur le Baron propose to buy with that?'

'I hef been dolt zet in Baris is a man gapable of discover ze woman I lof, end zet you know hiss eddress ... Shortly, he iss master spy?'

'That's right ...'

'Well, gif me z' eddress, end I gif you five *hundert* franc.'

'No kidding?' replied Contenson briskly.

'Here are,' the baron continued, taking a note from his pocket.

'Well, then, give,' said Contenson, holding out his hand.

'Gif I am, let us go see zis man, *und* you hef ze money, for you could sell me many eddress at zat price.'

Contenson began to laugh.

'As a matter of fact, you've got every right to think that of me,' said he with an air of greed. 'The more dastardly our condition, the more need we have of probity. But, look, Monsieur le Baron, make it six hundred francs, and I'll give you a piece of advice.'

'Gif it, end trust to my chenerosity ...'

'I'll chance it,' said Contenson; 'but it's a big risk I'm taking. In police work, you know, you've got to keep your feet on the ground. You say: Come on, let's be off! ... You're rich, you think everything gives way before money. Money counts, that's certain. But with money, in the opinion of one or two leading thinkers in our lot, you've only got men. There are things maybe you never think of, and they can't be bought! ... You can't nobble good luck. So, in police work, you don't do things that way. Do you want to be seen with me in a carriage? we'd be met. Luck can be on your side, or it can be against you.'

'*So?*' said the baron.

'Lord! yes, sir. It was a horseshoe picked up in the street which led the Prefect of Police to the discovery of the infernal machine. Well! if we was to go at night in a four-wheeler to see M. de Saint-Germain, he'd no more care to see you walk in than you would to be seen going there.'

'Is true,' said the baron.

'Ah! he's the man all right, the famous Corentin's right hand, Fouché's strong arm, some say his natural son, he must have had one being a priest; but that's all rubbish: Fouché knew how to be a priest, same as he knew how to be Minister. Well, now, look, you won't get him on the job, see, for less than ten thousand franc notes . . . think about it . . . But the job will be done, and done well. And nobody the wiser, as they say. I shall have to warn Monsieur de Saint-Germain, and he'll arrange a meeting with you in some place where nobody'll either hear nor see, for it's risky for him to do police work for private individuals. But, there, what d'you expect? . . . he's a fine fellow, the king of men, and one who's had to put up with persecution on a big scale, all for being the saviour of France, what's more! . . . like me, like all the saviours of their country!'

'Well, *so*, you will write me when is ze ospicious hour,' said the baron smiling at his own witticism.

'Isn't Monsieur le Baron going to grease my palm? . . .' said Contenson with an air of threatening humility.

'Jean,' the baron called out to his gardener, 'go esk Georges twenty francs ent pring zem here . . .'

'If M. le Baron has no more information than what he has given me, I doubt all the same if the maestro will be able to help him.'

'I hef more!' replied the baron with a secretive air.

'I have the honour to salute Monsieur le Baron,' said Contenson taking the twenty-franc piece, 'I shall have the honour of coming and telling Georges where Monsieur should betake himself this evening, for on police work you should never put things in writing.'

'Is *komisch* how witty zese lads are,' said the baron to himself, 'in police is altogether much as in business.'

Father des Canquoëlles

ON leaving the baron, Contenson walked calmly from the rue Saint Lazare to the rue Saint Honoré, till he came to the Café David; there he looked through the window and perceived an old man by the name of Father Canquoëlle.

The Café David, situated in the rue de la Monnaie at the

corner of the rue Saint Honoré, enjoyed during the first thirty years of the nineteenth century fame of a sort, though limited to the neighbourhood known as that of the Bourdonnais. It was a meeting-place for old, retired merchants or wholesale dealers still in the game: Camusots, Lebas, Pilleraults, Popinots, a few landowners like Little Father Molineux. Every now and then you might see Old Father Guillaume who came there from the rue du Colombier. They talked politics among themselves, but prudently, for the Café David itself was Liberal. They retailed the neighbourhood gossip there, for men so feel the need to jeer at each other! ... This café, like cafés elsewhere, had its eccentric character in Father Canquoëlle, who had been going there since the year 1811, and who appeared so perfectly in key with the respectable beings there gathered, that nobody felt embarrassed in talking politics in his presence. Sometimes the old boy, whose simplicity provided the regulars with many anecdotes, had disappeared for a month or two at a time; but his absences, always supposed due to illness and old age, for he had seemed over sixty already in 1811, occasioned no surprise.

'What's become of Father Canquoëlle?' people merely asked the lady at the cash desk.

'I dare say,' she'd reply, 'that one of these days we shall read of his death in the "Local Notices" column.'

Father Canquoëlle's very pronunciation certified his origins. He said 'une estatue', 'espécialle', 'le peuble' and pronounced the word for a Turk 'ture'. His name was that of a small property called Les Canquoëlles, a word which signifies cockchafer up and down the provinces, and situated in the county of Vaucluse, from which he came. People had ended by calling him Canquoëlle instead of des Canquoëlles, without annoying the old boy, whose view was that the nobility had come to an end in 1793; in any case the fief of Les Canquoëlles didn't belong to him, he was the younger son of a junior branch. Today Father Canquoëlle's garb would seem strange; but between 1811 and 1820 it surprised nobody. The old man wore shoes with buckles of steel cut in facets, silk stockings of alternating white and blue horizontal stripes, breeches in grained taffeta with oval buckles similar to those on his shoes in the way they were cut. A white embroidered waistcoat, an old, maroon-green coat with metal buttons and a ruffled shirt with frills ironed into flat pleats completed his costume. Upon the shirt-frills gleamed a gold locket in which the hair under glass had been arranged in the form of a little church, one of those adorable sentimentalities which reassure men, just as a scarecrow frightens sparrows. Most men, like animals, are frightened or reassured by trifles. Father Canquoëlle's breeches were kept up by a buckle which, in the eighteenth-century manner, held him just above the abdomen. From the belt hung two parallel steel chains made up of smaller chains, ending in a bunch of charms and trinkets. His white stock fastened at the back with a little gold clasp. Finally, his snowy, powdered head was still surmounted in 1816 by the kind of three-cornered municipal hat worn also by Monsieur Try, the magistrate. Father Canquoëlle was fond of the hat, but had recently replaced it (the old fellow believed in keeping up with the times at whatever cost) with the kind of miserable round hat which nobody dares take exception to. A short pigtail, tied with a ribbon, traced on the back of his coat a circular trail of which the grease disappeared beneath a fine fall of powder. Contemplating the distinctive cast of these features, the nose covered with gibbosities, red and worthy of its place in a dish of truffles, you would have attributed an easygoing, foolish, meek character to this worthy and essentially simple old man, and you would have been wrong, like everyone at the Café David, where nobody had ever considered the thoughtful and observant forehead, the sardonic mouth and the cold eyes of this old man cradled in vice, calm as a Vitellius from whose imperial womb he had, as it were, reappeared palingenetically. In 1816, a young commercial traveller, called Gaudissart, a regular client at the Café David, got drunk between eleven o'clock and midnight with an officer on half pay. He was imprudent enough to speak of a plot hatched against the Bourbons, of a serious nature and on the point of exploding. The only people to be seen in the café were Father Canquoëlle who seemed to be asleep, two somnolent waiters and the lady at the cash desk. Within twenty-four hours Gaudissart was arrested: the conspiracy had been discovered. Two men perished on the scaffold. Neither Gaudissart nor anybody else ever suspected good old Father Canquoëlle of having let the cat out of the bag. The waiters were dismissed, the clients watched each other for a year, and they lived in fear of the Police, in concert with Father Canquoëlle who spoke of giving up the Café David, so much did policemen upset him.

Contenson went into the café, ordered a small glass of spirits, didn't look at Father Canquoëlle busy reading the papers; only when he had gulped down his glass of spirits did he take out the baron's piece of gold, and call the waiter, sharply thumping the table three times. The lady at the cash-desk and the waiter both examined the coin with a carefulness insulting to Contenson; but their distrust was justified by the surprise which Contenson's appearance occasioned among the customers. 'Is this gold the result of a theft or a murder? . . .' Such was the thought which crossed the minds of more than one thoughtful and farseeing client, as they looked at Contenson over their spectacles while affecting to read their newspapers. Contenson, who noticed everything and was astonished by nothing, disdainfully wiped his lips with a silk handkerchief only thrice mended, picked up his change, tipped all the coins into a waistcoat pocket whose lining, once white, was as black as the cloth of his breeches, and didn't leave a penny for the waiter.

'Gallows meat!' said Father Canquoëlle to M. Pillerault his neighbour.

'Bah!' M. Camusot, who alone had not shown the least sign of astonishment, announced to the café at large, 'it's Contenson, right-hand man of Louchard, the Trade Protection fellow. Those clowns must be wanting to pick up somebody in the neighbourhood . . .'

Quarter of an hour later, old Canquoëlle rose, took his umbrella and calmly departed.

Must we explain what sort of deep, terrible man lurked beneath Father Canquoëlle's old-fashioned coat, just as Father Carlos concealed Vautrin? This man from the Midi, born at Les Canquoëlles, his nevertheless respectable family's sole domain, bore the name of Peyrade. He indeed belonged to the junior branch of the house of La Peyrade, an old but impoverished family of the Comtat, which still owns the small property of Peyrade. A seventh child, he had come to Paris, with two six-livre crowns in his pocket, in 1772, at the age of seventeen, driven by the vices of a fiery nature, by the brutal desire to succeed which draws many meriodionals to the capital, once they have perceived that the paternal establishment will never supply them with the means to their passionate ends. All Peyrade's youth may be understood if one gathers that in 1782 he was the trusted man, the hero of the Lieutenant-Generalship of police, where he was greatly esteemed by Messieurs Lenoir and d'Albert, the two last lieutenants-general. The Revolution had no police, it needed none. Spying, then very widespread, was called good citizenship. The Directory, a somewhat more regular government than that of the Committee of Public Safety, was obliged to reconstitute a police force, and the First Consul embodied it in a Prefecture of Police and a Ministry of General Police. Peyrade, the man with tradition behind him, found the staff, in concert with a man called Corentin, a more powerful individual than Peyrade, though younger, whose genius was fully recognized only behind the scenes in the police world. In 1808, the immense services rendered by Peyrade were rewarded by his nomination to the leading post of General Superintendent of Police at Antwerp. In Napoleon's mind, police prefectures of this kind were equivalent to such ministries of police as that set up to supervise Holland. After the campaign of 1809, Peyrade was removed from Antwerp by order of the Emperor's cabinet, taken by coach to Paris between two constables, and thrown into La Force. Two months later, he left prison under a guarantee from his friend Corentin, after nevertheless having undergone, at the Police Prefecture, three questionings each lasting six hours. Was Contenson's disgrace due to the great speed with which he had seconded Fouché in the defence of the French coast, attacked in what was known at one time as the Walcheren expedition, a moment at which the Duke of Otranto displayed a strength which worried the Emperor? It seemed probable enough in Fouché's time; but now that everybody knows what happened during the Council of Ministers called by Cambacérès, there is more certainty about the matter. Taken aback by the news of the British attempt, a retaliation for Napoleon's Boulogne expedition, and caught in their master's absence, he having withdrawn to the island of Lobau, where Europe thought he was lost, the ministers did not know what course to pursue. The general view was that a dispatch should be sent to the Emperor; but Fouché alone dared trace out a plan of campaign which, moreover, he subsequently put into effect. 'Do as you please,' Cambacérès said to him; 'but *me, I want to keep my head on my shoulders*, I'm sending a report to the Emperor.' It is well known on what absurd pretext the Emperor, on his return, openly in the Council of State, dismissed his minister and punished him for having saved France in his absence. From that day on, the Emperor was faced with the double enmity of Talleyrand and the Duke of Otranto, the only two great politicians to emerge from the Revolution, and the only two who might have saved him in 1813. The excuse for getting rid of Peyrade was misappropriation of public funds, a vulgar excuse: he had encouraged smuggling by sharing the small profits with high finance. It was rough treatment for a man whose General Superintendency in the Police had been awarded him for services rendered on the grand scale. Grown old in the public service, he knew the secrets of every government from the year 1775 onward, that being the date at which he had entered the General Lieutenancy of Police. The Emperor, believing himself to be strong enough to create the men he needed, paid no attention to the representations later made to him on behalf of a man considered one of the soundest, cleverest and most discreet of those unknown geniuses, called to guard the security of States. He thought he could replace Peyrade with Contenson; but just then Contenson's time was profitably taken up with Corentin. Peyrade was all the more cruelly affected, in that, a libertine and a glutton, his relations with women were like those of a pastrycook fond of delicacies. His vicious habits had become second nature to him: he could no longer do without dining well, gaming, and generally leading the life of a great lord without ostentation such as all men of powerful gifts pursue, once they have acquired an imperative taste for exorbitant pleasures. Moreover, till then he had lived and banqueted on the grand scale without ever being called to account for his expenditure, any more than Corentin, his friend. Cynically witty, he liked things that way, he was a philosopher. And then, a spy, no matter what stage he has reached in the police machine, can no more return to the sort of profession known as honourable or liberal than a convict can. Once marked, once matriculated, spies and condemned men acquire, like deacons, an indelible character. On some men their Social Condition imprints the fatal signs of their destiny. It was Peyrade's misfortune to be infatuated with a pretty little girl, a child whom he knew for certain to be his by a celebrated actress, to whom he had rendered service and who was grateful for three months. Peyrade, who brought his child back with him from Antwerp, thus found himself without resources in Paris, living on an annual pension of twelve hundred francs granted by the Prefecture of Police to Lenoir's old pupil. He installed himself in the rue des Moineaux, on the fourth floor, in a little apartment with five rooms, at two hundred and fifty francs.

The inner workings of the Police

IF ever a man feels the sweetness, the utility of friendship, must it not be that moral leper called by the crowd a spy, by the common people a nark, by the administration an agent? Peyrade and Corentin were thus friends like Orestes and Pylades. Peyrade had formed Corentin, as Vien formed David; but the pupil promptly surpassed his teacher. They had carried out more than one foray together. Peyrade, happy to have divined the merit of Corentin, had launched him on his career by preparing a triumph for him. He compelled his pupil to make use of a mistress who despised him as bait to catch a man. And Corentin was then barely twenty-five! . . . Corentin, remaining one of the generals whose marshal is the Minister of Police, had retained, under the Duke of Rovigo, the eminent position he occupied under the Duke of Otranto. Now, in those days it was the same with the General as with the Judicial Police. In any large-scale operation, the worst crimes were classified and, so to say, farmed out as for three, four or five capable men. The minister, informed about some plot, warned of some corporate machination, no matter how, said to one of the colonels of police: 'What do you need to arrive at such-and-such a result?' Corentin or Contenson would reply after ripe reflection: 'Twenty, thirty, forty thousand francs.' Then, once the order to proceed had been given, the choice of men and methods was left to the judgment of Corentin or the agent designated. The Judicial Police acted similarly in criminal matters under the famous Vidocq.

The Political Police, like the Judicial Police, selected its men mainly from among known agents, regular, matriculated men, the soldiers of that secret force so necessary to governments, despite the denunciations of philanthropists or small-time moralists. But the excessive confidence placed in the two or three generals of the temper of Peyrade and Corentin enabled them to employ unknown persons, for whom they must nevertheless account to the Ministry in serious cases. Now, Peyrade's experience and discretion were too precious to Corentin, who, once the little matter of 1810 had blown over, continued to employ his old friend, consulted him regularly, and subsidized his needs. Corentin found means to pay Peyrade about a thousand francs a month. For his part, Peyrade rendered Corentin sterling service. In 1816, in connection with the discovery of the conspiracy in which the Bonapartist Gaudissart was deeply involved, Corentin tried to have Peyrade brought back into the General Police of the Kingdom; but an unknown influence worked against Peyrade. This is why. In their desire to render themselves indispensable, Peyrade, Corentin and Contenson, at the Duke of Otranto's instigation, had organized, on behalf of Louis XVIII, a Counter-Police in which Contenson and other agents of the highest calibre were employed. Louis XVIII died, in possession of secrets which will remain secret from the best-informed historians. The struggle between the General Police of the

Kingdom and the Counter-Police of the King gave rise to dreadful affairs whose secret was hushed on more than one scaffold. This is neither the time nor the place to enter into detail on the subject, for our Scenes from Parisian Life are not scenes from Political Life; it is only necessary to make plain what were the means of existence of the man known as Old Canquoëlle at the Café David, by what threads he was attached to the terrible and mysterious power of the Police. From 1817 to 1822, the mission of Corentin, Contenson, Peyrade and their agents was often to spy on the Minister himself. This may explain why the Minister refused to employ Peyrade and Contenson upon whom, unknown to them, Corentin caused ministerial suspicion to fall, so that he could make use of his friend, once the possibility of his official rehabilitation had been ruled out. The ministers then had confidence in Corentin, they instructed him to keep an eye on Peyrade, which made Louis XVIII smile. Corentin and Peyrade thus remained wholly in command of the field. Contenson, for long attached to Peyrade, continued to serve him. He had got himself into Trade Protection by order of Corentin and Peyrade. In love with their profession and exercising it to the point of madness, these two generals liked, indeed, to place their cleverest soldiers in all those places where information may abound. Besides, Contenson's vices, his depraved habits which caused him to fall further than his two friends, required so much money, that he needed plenty of work. Contenson, without committing any indiscretion thereby, had told Louchard that he knew the one man capable of satisfying Baron Nucingen. Peyrade was, indeed, the only true agent who could with impunity carry out police work on behalf of an individual. On the death of Louis XVIII, Peyrade lost not only his general importance, but the perquisites of his position as Spy-in-Ordinary to His Majesty. Believing himself indispensable, he had continued in his way of life. Women, good cheer and the Foreign Visitors' Club had made economy impossible to a man who, like all those cut out for the pursuit of vice, had a constitution of iron. But, from 1826 to 1829, in his seventy-fifth year, he began to call a halt, as he put it. From year to year, Peyrade had seen his well-being diminish. He was present at the obsequies of the Police, with mortification he saw the government of Charles X give up the best traditions. From one session to another, the House whittled away the allocations necessary to the existence of the Police, out of hatred for this instrument of rule and bent on moralizing the institution. 'It's like trying to cook in white gloves,' said Peyrade to Corentin. Corentin and Peyrade foresaw 1830 already in 1822. They knew the deep hatred with which Louis XVIII viewed his successor, which explains his indulgence towards the younger branch, and without which the politics of his reign would be a wordless enigma.

As he grew old, Peyrade's affection for his natural daughter increased. For her, he had adopted a respectable way of life, for he wanted to marry his Lydia to some worthy man. Thus, more especially during the past three years, he had sought means to settle down, either at the Prefecture of Police or at the headquarters of the General Police of the Kingdom, in some openly avowable position. He had ended by inventing a post whose necessity, he said to Corentin, would sooner or later make itself felt. It was a matter of setting-up, at the Prefecture, an *information* bureau, to serve as intermediary between the Paris Police properly so-called, the Judicial Police and the Police of the Kingdom so that the central direction could profit by all its disseminated forces. Peyrade alone could, at his age, after fifty-five years of professional discretion, provide the necessary link between the three police organizations, be himself the archivist to whom both politics and the law should address themselves for enlightenment in particular cases. Peyrade hoped in this way, with Corentin's help, to catch both a dowry and a husband for his little Lydia. Corentin had already discussed the matter with the Director General of the Police of the Kingdom, without mentioning Peyrade, and the Director General, who came from the south, took the view that the suggestion ought to come from the Prefecture.

At the moment when Contenson had struck the café table three times with his piece of gold, a signal which meant: 'I have something to talk to you about,' the dean of policemen was meditating the problem: 'Through what person, by

what interest to make the present police prefect take action?'
And he looked like an idiot studying his *Courrier Français*.

'Our poor Fouché,' he said to himself as he walked along
the rue Saint Honoré, 'that great man is dead! our inter-
mediaries with Louis XVIII are in disgrace! Besides, as
Corentin was saying only yesterday, people won't believe now
in the agility or the intelligence of a septuagenarian ... Ah,
why did I ever form the habit of dining at Véry's, of drinking
the finest wines, ... of singing "Mother Godichon", ... of
gaming when I have money! To establish a position, a good
mind is not enough, as Corentin says, it has to be a well-
behaved mind! Dear M. Lenoir told me my fortune when, in
connection with the affair of the Necklace, he cried: "You will
never be anybody!" on learning that I hadn't stayed under
the maid Oliva's bed.'

A spy's household

IF the venerable Father Canquoëlle (he was called Father
Canquoëlle at home) had stayed in the rue des Moineaux, on
the fourth floor, be sure that he had found, in this setting,
peculiarities which favoured the execution of his fell designs.
Situated at the corner of the rue Saint Roch, his house was
without neighbour on one side. As the staircase divided it into
two, there were, on each floor, two completely isolated rooms.
These two rooms overlooked the rue Saint Roch. Extending
over the fourth floor were attic rooms of which one served as
a kitchen, while the other was the bedroom of Father
Canquoëlle's only maidservant, a Fleming by the name of
Katt, who had been Lydia's nurse. Father Canquoëlle's own
bedroom was the first of the two that were isolated, and the
other was his study. A thick party wall shut off the far side of
this study. A casement, from which the rue des Moineaux
could be seen, faced a windowless corner wall. Thus, as the
whole breadth of Peyrade's bedroom separated them from the
staircase, the two friends feared neither eye nor ear when they
talked business in this study expressly designed for their

dreadful trade. By way of precaution, Peyrade had placed a straw bed, a coarse haircloth and a very thick carpet in the Fleming's room, on the pretext of increasing the comfort of his child's nurse. Moreover, he had blocked up the fireplace, using a stove whose pipe passed through the outer wall in the rue Saint Roch. Finally, he had spread several thicknesses of carpet over the tiled floor, to prevent the tenants on the floor below catching any sound. Experienced in the ways of espionage, he sounded the party wall, the ceiling and the floor once a week, and examined them like a man in search of troublesome insects. The certitude of being free there of either witnesses or hearers had made Corentin choose this study as a place for any discussion which he did not hold at home. Corentin's lodging was known only to the Director General of the Police of the Kingdom and to Peyrade, he received there any personages whom the Ministry or the Castle used as go-betweens in grave circumstances; but no agent, no subordinate ever went there, and professional schemes were all worked out at Peyrade's. In this unpretentious room plans were concocted, decisions taken which would provide strange annals and curious dramas if walls could speak. There, between 1816 and 1826, huge interests were analysed and weighed against each other. There were perceived in germ events which all France would feel. There, Peyrade and Corentin, as far-seeing, but better informed than Bellart, the Director of Public Prosecutions, were already saying in 1819: 'If Louis XVIII is holding his hand, if he won't get rid of such-and-such a prince, he hates his brother, then? he wants to leave him with a revolution on his hands?'

Peyrade's door was decorated with a slate upon which apparently meaningless signs and figures might sometimes be found written in chalk. This kind of devilish algebra conveyed very precise meanings to the initiated. Facing Peyrade's shabby apartment was Lydia's, composed of an ante-room, a small drawing-room, a bedroom and a dressing-room ... Lydia's door, like that of Peyrade's bedroom, was made of four thicknesses of sheet iron placed between stout oak boards, with a system of locks and hinges which would have made both as difficult to force as prison doors. Thus, although it was an open house, with a shop on the ground floor and no porter, Lydia lived there with nothing to fear. The dining-room, the drawing-room, the bedroom, all of whose casements had window-boxes, were Flemish in their spotlessness and luxuriously furnished. The Flemish nurse had never left Lydia, whom she called her daughter. The two went to church together with a regularity which gave old Canquoëlle an enviable reputation with the royalist grocer established in the house, at the corner of the rue des Moineaux and the rue Neuve Saint Roch, whose family, kitchen, errand-boys occupied the mezzanine and first floor. On the second floor lived the owner, and the third had been rented, for twenty years past, by a stone-cutter. Each of the tenants had a key to the house door. The grocer's wife took in letters and parcels addressed to the three peaceful households, with all the more willingness in that the grocery was provided with a letter box. Without these details, neither outsiders nor those who know Paris would understand the secrecy and quietness, the unguardedness and security which made the house an exception in the city. After midnight, Father Canquoëlle could weave intrigues and hatch plots, receive visits from informers and ministers, women and girls, without anyone in the world noticing. Peyrade, of whom the Flemishwoman had said to the grocer's cook: 'He wouldn't hurt a fly!' passed for the best of men. He spared nothing where his daughter was concerned. Having had Schmucke as a music master, Lydia was musician enough to compose. She could *wash* a *sepia*, paint in water-colour or poster paints. Peyrade dined every Sunday with his daughter. That day, the old fellow was a father to the exclusion of all else. Religious without being sanctimonious, Lydia performed her Easter duties and went to confession every month. This did not stop her taking some interest in the passing scene. She walked in the Tuileries when it was fine. Those were her only pleasures, however, for she led a mainly sedentary existence. Lydia adored her father and knew nothing of his sinister capacities and shady occupations. No desire had troubled the blameless life of this pure child. Slender, beautiful like her mother, gifted with a delightful voice, her pretty features delicate and mobile in their frame of fair hair, she was like one of those angels, more mystical than real, which primitive painters sometimes placed in the background of their Holy Families. The glance of her blue eyes seemed to bestow light from the sky upon anyone whom she favoured with a look. Her chaste attire, totally devoid of affectation, exhaled a delightful odour of family worth. Imagine an old Satan, father of an angel, refreshed by contact with the divine being, and you will have some idea of Peyrade and his daughter. If anyone had sullied this diamond, the father, to swallow him up, would have devised one of those fearsome traps into which, under the Restoration, fell those unfortunates who subsequently took their heads to the scaffold. A thousand crowns sufficed Lydia and Katt, whom she called her maid.

Turning into the rue des Moineaux, Peyrade saw Contenson; he walked past him, went up first, heard his agent's steps in the staircase, and let him in before the Fleming had shown her nose at the kitchen door. A bell set off by a gate, placed on the third floor where the stone-cutter lived, warned the third and fourth floor tenants when there was a visitor for them. Needless to say, at midnight Peyrade muffled the tongue of this bell.

'What are you in such a hurry about, then, Philosopher?'

Philosopher was the nickname Peyrade gave Contenson, and which that Epictetus of informers deserved. The name Contenson itself, alas! concealed one of the oldest names of the Norman feudality.

'Well, there's ten thousand or so to be picked up.'

'What is it? politics?'

'No, a bit of nonsense! Baron Nucingen, you know, the old licensed thief, is whinnying after a woman he saw in the Bois de Vincennes, and she's got to be found for him, or he'll die of love ... Yesterday doctors were called in for consultation, so his valet tells me ... I've already extracted a thousand francs from him, on the pretext of looking for the child.'

And Contenson recounted the meeting of Nucingen with Esther, adding that the baron had received a little further information.

'Oh, well,' said Peyrade, 'we'll find this Dulcinea; tell the baron to come by carriage this evening to the Champs Élysées, corner of the Avenue Gabriel and the Allée de Marigny.'

Peyrade showed Contenson out, and knocked at his daughter's door to be admitted. He went in joyfully, chance had just put in his way a means to the position he desired. He sank into a fine chair of the Voltaire style after kissing Lydia on the forehead, and said to her: 'Play me something . . .'

Lydia played him a fragment written for the piano by Beethoven.

'That was nicely played, my little doe,' said he holding his daughter between his knees, 'had you realized that we're twenty-one? Time to get married, our father, you know, is over seventy . . .'

'I'm happy here,' she replied.

'I'm the only one you love, so ugly, so old?' asked Peyrade.

'Whom do you expect me to love?'

'I'm dining with you, my little doe, tell Katt. I'm thinking of setting us up, of taking a place and looking for a husband worthy of you, . . . some good young man, full of talent, of whom you'll be able to be proud one day . . .'

'So far I've only seen one I'd care to marry . . .'

'You've seen one? . . .'

'Yes, in the Tuileries,' Lydia went on, 'he was passing, Countess Sérisy was on his arm.'

'And he's called? . . .'

'Lucien de Rubempré! . . . I was sitting under a lime-tree with Katt, not thinking of anything. Beside me were sitting two ladies who said to each other: "There's Madame de Sérisy with the handsome Lucien de Rubempré." I looked at the couple the two ladies were looking at. "Ah! my dear," said the other, "some women have all the luck! . . . That one's permitted anything, because she was born a Ronquerolles, and her husband can afford it." "Still, my dear," replied the other lady, "Lucien costs her a lot . . ." What does that mean, papa?'

'Just rubbish, like most of what these society people say,'

Peyrade told his daughter with a good-natured air. 'Perhaps they were alluding to some political matter.'

'Anyway, you questioned me, and I've answered. If you're wanting to marry me off, find me a husband like that young man . . .'

'Child!' said her father, 'looks in a man are not always signs of goodness. Young fellows endowed with an agreeable exterior meet with no difficulty in early life, they don't need to exert any gifts, they are corrupted by the advances society makes to them, and later they have to pay interest on what they've borrowed! . . . I'd rather find you somebody whom established citizens, rich men and fools leave unprotected to their own resources . . .'

'Such as who, father dear?'

'A young man of unsuspected talent . . . But there we are, my dear child, I know how to rummage in all the garrets of Paris and carry out your programme by presenting for your loving approbation a man as handsome as the bad lot you spoke of, but with a future before him, a man marked out for fame and fortune . . . Oh! I never thought of it! I must have a horde of nephews, and there must be one among them worthy of you! . . . I'll write or get somebody else to write to Provence!'

A remarkable coincidence! at that very moment a young man, dying of hunger and fatigue, travelling on foot from the department of Vaucluse, a nephew of Father Canquoëlle's, came in by the Barrière d'Italie, in search of his uncle. In the dreams of a family which knew nothing of that uncle's destiny, Peyrade represented a word of hope: he was thought to have returned a millionaire from the Indies! Stimulated by fireside-corner novels, this great-nephew, called Theodosius, had undertaken a voyage of circumnavigation in quest of his legendary uncle.

Three men at grips

AFTER savouring the pleasures of fatherhood for several hours, Peyrade, his hair washed and died (the powder was a disguise), dressed in a solid frock-coat of blue cloth buttoned up to the chin, a black mantle on top, shod in heavy boots with thick soles and provided with a map specially made, walked slowly along the Avenue Gabriel, where Contenson, disguised as an old costerwoman, met him outside the Élysée-Bourbon gardens.

'Monsieur de Saint Germain,' Contenson said to him, addressing his former chief by the name he used on the job, 'I've earned five facers through you; but the reason why I planted myself there is, the ruddy baron, before he gave them to me, went looking for information at the House,' by which he meant the Prefecture.

'I dare say I shall need you,' replied Peyrade. 'Dig out numbers 7, 10 and 21, we can make use of them without anybody noticing, either at the House or at Police HQ.'

Contenson went and took up his station again by the carriage in which M. de Nucingen awaited Peyrade.

'I am M. de Saint-Germain,' said the southerner to the baron, raising himself up to the carriage door.

'*Gut*, come in wiz me,' replied the baron, giving the order to move on towards the Arc de Triomphe de l'Étoile.

'You went to the Prefecture, baron? that wasn't right . . . May one know what you said to the Prefect, and what answer he made you?' asked Peyrade.

'Before I will gif five *hundert* vrancs to *ein mensch wie* Contenson, I will know if he hess hearnt zem . . . I hef to ze Prefect of Police said simply set I wished *ein* agent by name Peyrade to employ abroad on a delicate mission, and if I could hef in him boundless confidence . . . *Der* Prefect hes replied you were of cleverest and honestest men. Thet is all.'

'Now that he's learnt my real name, M. le Baron might like to tell me what all this is about? . . .'

When the baron had explained wordily and at great length

in his dreadful Polish Jew's jargon, both his meeting with Esther and the cry of the runner behind the coach, and his vain search, he ended by recounting what had passed at his house the evening before, Lucien de Rubempré's involuntary smile, the belief expressed by Bianchon and more than one dandy present, relative to an acquaintance between the unknown woman and that young man.

'Listen, baron, to begin with you're going to give me ten thousand francs on account towards my expenses, because, for you, this is a matter of life and death; and, as your life is strung together of things like that, we must leave no stone unturned to find you this woman. Oh, you're caught, well and truly!'

'Yo, yo, caught is it ...'

'If I need more, I'll tell you, baron; trust me,' said Peyrade. 'I'm not, as you may think, a spy ... I was, in 1807, general police superintendent in Antwerp, and now that Louis XVIII is dead, I may confide to you that, for seven years, I was the head of his counter-police ... So I can't be haggled with. You'll understand, baron, that you can't precisely estimate the price of consciences to be bought, until you've gone into the matter. Don't be uneasy, I shall succeed. And don't think I shall be satisfied just with a sum of money, there's something else I want by way of payment ...'

'Zo long ass it iss less dan a kingdom ...,' said the baron.

'It'll be a mere nothing to you.'

'Zen I vill pay!'

'Do you know the Kellers?'

'Very well.'

'François Keller is the Comte de Gondreville's son-in-law, and Count Gondreville yesterday dined with his son-in-law at your house.'

'How in devil you know?' cried the baron. 'Iss doubtless Georges who always talk too much.'

Peyrade laughed briefly. The banker thereupon conceived remarkable suspicions of his domestic, watching the man smile.

'Count Gondreville is very much in a position to get me into a place I want at the Prefecture of Police, and within forty-eight hours the Prefect will be giving his mind to it,' Peyrade continued. 'Canvass the place for me, see that the Comte de Gondreville is willing to concern himself with the matter, zealously at that, and that will be sufficient recognition of the service I am going to do you. All I need is your word, for, if you didn't keep it, you would sooner or later curse the day you were born, . . . and it's I, Peyrade, who say that and mean it . . .'

'I am give you my wort off honour I do all vhich iss possiple . . .'

'If I did only what's possible for you, that wouldn't be enough.'

'Ay, ay, ay, it will be frankly, I will persist.'

'That's it. . . . That's all I want,' said Peyrade, 'and a little frankness between us is the best present we can make each other to start with.'

'I am frank,' repeated the baron. 'Where do you want me to put you down?'

'At the end of the Pont Louis XVI.'

'To ze Bond de la Jambre,' said the baron to his footman who came to the carriage door.

'So I shell hef the unknown woman . . .,' the baron said to himself as he drove away.

'A remarkable coincidence,' was Peyrade's reflection as he proceeded on foot to the Palais Royal where he meant if he could to triple the ten thousand francs for Lydia's dowry. 'Here I am, having to investigate the little ways of the young man whose glance bewitched my daughter. I dare say he's one of those men who've got *ladies' eyes*,' he said to himself employing an expression in the special lingo he'd made for his own use, in which his own observations or, rather, those of Corentin were summed up in words in which language was often outraged, but which that fact itself may have rendered more energetic and vivid.

On his return home, Baron Nucingen seemed no longer himself; his dependents and his wife were astounded, the face he showed them was full of colour and animation, he was gay.

'Watch out for the shareholders,' said du Tillet to Rastignac.

They were at the moment taking tea in the little drawing-room of Delphine de Nucingen, just back from the Opera.

'Yo, shoah,' replied the baron with a smile, catching his colleague's little joke, 'I feel much wish to do business . . .'

'You've seen your Unknown, then?' asked Madame de Nucingen.

'No,' he answered, 'I hef only hope of finding her.'

'Does anyone ever love his wife like that? . . .' cried Madame de Nucingen feeling a stab of jealousy or feigning to.

'When she's yours,' said du Tillet to the baron, 'we shall come to supper with her, for I'm curious to examine the creature who's been able to make you look as young as you are.'

'She is a masterpiz off creation,' replied the old banker.

'He'll get himself caught like a beginner,' said Rastignac in Delphine's ear.

'Oh, he makes enough money to . . .'

'To give a little of it back, you mean! . . .' said du Tillet interrupting the baroness.

Nucingen walked about the room as if his legs were giving him trouble.

'Now's the moment to get him to pay your latest debts,' said Rastignac in the baroness's ear.

At that very moment, Carlos, who had been to the rue Taitbout to give his last instructions to Europe who was to play the leading part in the comedy devised to trick Baron Nucingen, was leaving full of hope. He was accompanied as far as the boulevard by Lucien, uneasy at seeing this demi-fiend so perfectly disguised that even he had only recognized him by his voice.

'Where the devil did you find a woman more beautiful than Esther?' he asked his corruptor.

'Little one, you wouldn't find that in Paris. That colouring wasn't made in France.'

'I still feel a bit stunned . . . The Callipygian Venus is less well-made! One might damn oneself for her . . . But where did you pick her up?'

'She was the best-looking tart in London. Drunk on *gin*, she killed her lover in a fit of jealousy . . . The lover was a waster the London police were glad to be rid of, and they've sent this creature to Paris for a while, to let the affair blow over ... The jade was very well brought up. She's a clergyman's daughter, she speaks French as if it were her mother tongue; she doesn't know and never will how she came to be where she is. She's been told that if you liked her, she'd be able to get millions out of you; but that you're as jealous as a tiger, and she's been given the same time-table as Esther. She doesn't know your name.'

'But suppose Nucingen preferred her to Esther ...'

'Ah, you've reached that point already ...,' cried Carlos. 'Now you're afraid that what so frightened you yesterday won't come off! Don't worry. This white-skinned, fair-haired wench has blue eyes; it's the reverse with the lovely Jewess, and there are no eyes but Esther's so to disturb a man as depraved as Nucingen. You couldn't be hiding a plain Jane, after all! When this doll has played her part, I shall send her, in safe company, to Rome or Madrid, where they'll run mad over her.'

'Since she's only with us for a while,' said Lucien, 'I'd better go back to her ...'

'Off you go, my child, enjoy yourself ... You'll have a day extra tomorrow. Me, I'm waiting for somebody I've commissioned to find out what is going on at Baron Nucingen's.'

'Who?'

'His manservant's girl-friend, for you've got to know from moment to moment what the enemy's up to.'

At midnight, Paccard, who ran Esther's errands, found Carlos on the Pont des Arts, the best spot in Paris for a brief discussion which mustn't be overheard. As they talked, the messenger kept his eyes turned in one direction and his master in the other.

'This morning the baron went to the Prefecture of Police, very early, and this evening he prides himself on having found the woman he saw in the Bois de Vincennes, he's been promised her ...'

'We shall be watched!' said Carlos, 'but by whom? ...'

'They've already tried Louchard, at Trade Protection.'

'That was a waste of time,' replied Carlos. 'The only people we have to fear are the Security Brigade, the Judicial Police; and the moment *they* won't move, *we can!* . . .'

'There's something else!'

'What?'

'The chums . . . Yesterday I saw La Pouraille, . . . he's chilled a loving couple and he'd got five thousand nicker . . . in gold!'

'He'll be arrested,' said Jacques Collin, 'it's the rue Boucher murders.'

'What's my orders?' said Paccard with the air of respect a marshal might wear on presenting himself for orders to Louis XVIII.

'You will go out every evening at ten o'clock,' replied Carlos, 'you'll get out fast to the Bois de Vincennes, by way of the woods round Meudon and Ville d'Avray. If anybody's watching or following you, take it easy, make friends, talk, let them think they can bribe you. Talk about Rubempré's jealousy, say he's crazy about *Madame*, say he doesn't want anybody to know he's got a mistress like that . . .'

'Right! Do I go armed? . . .'

'Never!' said Carlos emphatically. 'A weapon! . . . what use is that? except to cause trouble. Whatever you do, don't use that hunting knife. When you can break the strongest man's legs with the throw I showed you! . . . when you can take on three armed coppers in the certainty of flooring two of them before they're out with their small arms, what is there to fear? You've got your stick, haven't you? . . .'

'Too true!' said the runner.

Paccard, who'd been called Old Guard, Big Rabbit, Bang On, a man with a leg like iron, an arm of steel, an Italian's whiskers, artist's hair, sapper's beard, his face as pale and impassive as Contenson's, kept his fiery nature under and held himself like a drum-major which put suspicion off the scent. A man escaped from Poissy or Melun doesn't exhibit this pompous fatuity and this consciousness of merit. Ja'far to the Harun al-Rashid of the hulks, he felt for the latter the comradely admiration which Peyrade himself had for Corentin. This colossus, excessively long-legged, without much chest or much flesh on his bones, moved about on his two pins with solemn gait. His right foot took no step without his right eye taking in the external circumstances with that unruffled speed peculiar to the thief and the spy. The left eye imitated the right. A step, a look! Curt, agile, ready for anything at any minute, but for that intimate foe known as fire-water, Paccard would have been perfect, Carlos used to say, so deeply was he imbued with the gifts indispensable to a man at war with society; but the master had succeeded in persuading the slave to *clear the ground in order to stop the blaze spreading* and so not drink in the day-time. Back at home in the evening, Paccard absorbed in thimblefuls the golden liquid poured out of a big-bellied stoneware bottle from Danzig.

'I'll keep my blinkers peeled,' said Paccard putting his magnificent plumed hat back on his head after saluting the man he called *his confessor*.

And that is how three men each as strong in his own sphere as Jacques Collin, Peyrade and Corentin came to find themselves at grips on the same ground, and to put their genius into a struggle in which each fought for his own passion or his own interest. It was one of those unknown but terrible battles in which all the strength and talent needed to establish a fortune expend themselves in hatred, petty irritations, marching and countermarching, ruses.

Nucingen in the expectation of happiness addresses himself to his toilet

MEN and means, all was secret on Peyrade's side, his friend Corentin being behind him in this exploit, a stupid trifle to them. And so history is silent on the subject, as it is on the real causes of many revolutions. However, the result was as follows.

Five days after Monsieur Nucingen's interview with Peyrade in the Champs Élysées, one morning, a man of about fifty, with that flake-white complexion which society life gives diplomatists, dressed in blue cloth, quite elegantly turned out, conceivably a minister of State, descended from a handsome gig tossing the reins to his servant. He asked the footman who was sitting on a bench in the columned entrance hall, and who respectfully opened the magnificent glass doors to him, if Baron Nucingen was visible.

'What name shall I say? . . .' asked the domestic.

'Tell the baron that I come from the Avenue Gabriel,' replied Corentin. 'If there are people around, take care not to announce the name at the top of your voice, or you'll be thrown out.'

A minute later, the footman came back and conducted Corentin to the baron's study, through the inner apartments.

Corentin exchanged glances of equal impenetrability with the banker, and they greeted each other politely.

'Monsieur le Baron,' he said, 'I came on behalf of Peyrade . . .'

'*Gut*,' said the baron slipping bolts on the two doors.

'Monsieur de Rubempré's mistress lives in the rue Taitbout, in what used to be the apartment of Mademoiselle de Bellefeuille, former mistress of Monsieur de Granville, the public prosecutor.'

'*Ach*, chust round ze corner,' cried the baron, '*wie komisch*!'

'I have no difficulty in imagining that you are wild about this magnificent creature, it was a pleasure to me to see her,' replied Corentin. 'Lucien is so jealous of this girl that he forbids her to show herself; and he must be loved by her, for during the four years since she followed Bellefeuille, both into her living quarters and into her condition, neither the neighbours, nor the porter, nor the owners of the house have ever seen her. This *infanta* goes out only at night. When she drives out, the blinds of the carriage are pulled down, and the lady is veiled. It isn't only for reasons of jealousy that Lucien conceals her: he expects to marry Clotilde de Grandlieu, and he's also the current favourite of Madame de Sérisy. Naturally, he wants to keep both the mistress he has on show and his *fiancée*. And so you are in a commanding position, for Lucien will sacrifice his pleasure to his interests and his vanity. You are rich, this is probably your last chance of happiness, be generous. You will attain your ends through the girl's maid. Give her ten thousand francs or so, and she'll hide you in her mistress's bedroom; it'll be worth that!'

No figure of rhetoric could adequately describe Corentin's sharp, clear, absolute salesmanship; the baron himself greeted it with an expression of astonishment, which his impassible visage had long denied itself.

'I have come to ask you for five thousand francs for my friend, who lost five of your bank notes, a trifling misfortune!' Corentin went on with the smoothest air of command. 'Peyrade knows his Paris too well to put himself to the expense of advertising, and he counted on you. But that isn't the most important thing,' said Corentin changing his tone in such a way as to remove all gravity from his demand for money. 'If you want to avoid grief in your old age, secure for Peyrade the place he asked you for, and you can obtain it without trouble. The Director General of the police forces of the Kingdom should have received a note yesterday on the subject. All that's necessary now is to get Gondreville to speak to the Prefect of Police about it. All you need do, you see, is tell Malin Comte de Gondreville, that it's a question of obliging one of those who got rid of the Simeuse gentlemen for him, then he'll act . . .'

'Here you are, sir,' said the baron taking out five thousand-franc notes and handing them to Corentin.

'The maid's gentleman friend is a tall messenger by the name of Paccard, who lives in the rue de Provence, at a coachmaker's, and hires himself out to run errands for those who can adopt a sufficiently princely manner. You will make contact with Madame van Bogseck's maid through Paccard, a big rascal of a Piedmontese who is rather fond of vermouth.'

This last confidence, elegantly thrown in by way of postscript, was evidently what had cost five thousand francs. The baron tried to guess to what race of men Corentin belonged, his intelligence evidently placing him not so much among spies as among those who organized espionage; but Corentin remained for him much what an inscription is to an archeologist when at least three quarters of the letters are missing.

'Whad iss the jambermait's name?' he asked.

'Eugénie,' replied Corentin who then bowed to the baron and left.

Baron Nucingen, transported with joy, abandoned his business and the premises on which he conducted it and went up to his private quarters in the happy state of mind of a young man of twenty anticipating his first meeting with a first mistress. The baron took out all the thousand-franc notes then in his private strong-box, a sum with which he could have made a whole village happy, fifty-five thousand francs! and put them in his pocket. But the prodigality of millionaires can only be compared with their greed for gain. As soon as some whim or passion is involved, money becomes nothing to these Croesuses: it is indeed more difficult for them to *have* whims than gold. Enjoyment is the greatest rarity in that surfeited life, full of the emotions which arise from great draughts of Speculation, upon which these dry hearts feed. For example. One of the richest capitalists in Paris, widely known for his eccentricities, meets one day, on the boulevards, an excessively pretty little working girl. Accompanied by her mother, this *grisette* walked arm in arm with a young man questionably attired, who swayed his hips in an affected manner. At first sight, the millionaire falls in love with this Parisian girl; he follows her home, he goes in; he listens to the story of a life made up of dances at Mabile's, of days without bread, of work and amusement; he becomes interested, and leaves five thousand-franc notes under a five-franc piece: a misplaced piece of generosity. Next day, a celebrated upholsterer, Braschon, comes to take the wench's orders, furnishes an apartment of her choice, spends some twenty thousand francs on it. The working girl abandons herself to wild dreams: she buys her mother good clothes, she imagines she can get her ex-boy-friend into the offices of an Insurance Company. She waits . . . one, two, three days; then a week . . . and then two. She considers herself obliged to remain faithful, she runs up debts. The capitalist, called to Holland, had forgotten the little seamstress; he never once visited the Paradise in which he had installed her, and from which she fell as low as one may fall in Paris. Nucingen didn't gamble, Nucingen did not patronize the arts, Nucingen had no hobbies; he must then fling himself into his passion for Esther with a blindness upon which Carlos Herrera counted.

After luncheon, the baron sent for Georges, his personal servant, and told him to go to the rue Taitbout, to beg Mademoiselle Eugénie, Madame van Bogseck's maid, to call at his office on important business.

'Look her out,' he added, 'and take her up to my room, delling her zet her vortune iss mate.'

Georges had endless trouble in persuading Europe-Eugénie to come. Madame, she told him, never allowed her out; she might lose her job, etc., etc. Georges, therefore, lauded her merits to the baron, who gave him ten francs.

'If Madame goes out this evening without her,' said Georges to his master whose eyes sparkled like carbuncles, 'she'll come sharp on ten.'

'*Gut!* you will come ant tress me at *neun* hours, . . . mek my hair; for I will look nice es bossible . . . I belief zet I shell be tek to zee my mizdress, where money will be of no count . . .'

Between noon and one o'clock, the baron dyed his hair and whiskers. At nine o'clock, the baron, who took a bath before dinner, dressed like a bridegroom, scented himself, made himself beautiful. Madame de Nucingen, told of this metamorphosis, gave herself the pleasure of contemplating her husband.

'Good God!' she said, 'you do look a fool! . . . Why don't you put a black satin bow on, instead of that white thing which makes your whiskers stand out so? besides, it's *Empire*, it makes you a cosy old man, you look like a former counsellor of the *Parlement*. And for goodness' sake remove those diamond studs, every one of them is worth a hundred thousand francs; that monkey'll ask you for them, and you won't be able to refuse; if you're going to give them to a tart, I might as well put them in my ears.'

The poor financier, struck by the justice of his wife's remarks, submitted with a bad grace.

'Look a fool! look a fool! . . . I hef never told you zet you look a fool when you was mek yourself look your best for your liddle Monsieur te Rasdignag.'

'I should hope you've never thought I looked a fool. Am

I a woman to make that kind of spelling mistake in her dress? Look, turn round! ... Button your coat right up, like the Duc de Maufrigneuse, leaving the top two buttonholes free. In fact, try to make yourself look young.'

'Monsieur,' said Georges, 'here's Mademoiselle Eugénie.'

'Goot-bye, my tear ...,' cried the banker. He led his wife back to the farthest end of their respective apartments, so as to be quite certain that she would not overhear the discussion.

Disappointments

RETURNING, he took Europe by the hand, and conducted her into his room, with a kind of ironical respect.

'Well, my liddle one, you are very lucky, for you are in ze zerfiz off ze breddiest woman in de uniferse ... Your vortune iss mate, if you will spik for me, if you will ect in my inderests.'

'Which I will not do for ten thousand francs, sir,' cried Europe. 'You must understand, Monsieur le Baron, that to begin with I am an honest girl ...'

'Oh, yes. I know I shall hef to bay for your honesty. It iss what in pusiness we gall a gommotidy in shord zupply.'

'And that is not all,' said Europe. 'If Madame doesn't like the gentleman, and it's quite possible! she turns nasty, I'm sacked, and my job is worth a thousand francs a year.'

'De gabidal neeted for *tausend* francs iss twenty *tausend*, end if I gif you zet, you will not pe out of bocket.'

'My, if that's how you're going to talk, big daddy,' said Europe, 'it'll make quite a nice difference. Where are they? ...'

'Here,' replied the baron showing her the bank-notes one by one.

He observed the separate flash which each note caused to dart from Europe's eyes, and which displayed the concupiscence he was expecting.

'That pays for my job, but what about my honesty, my conscience? ...' said Europe lifting up her crafty face and giving the baron a *seria-buffa* look.

'The gonscience is not worth as much as the chob; but, let

143

us say, five *tausend* vranc for zet,' he replied adding five more thousand-franc notes.

'No, twenty thousand francs for the conscience, and five thousand for the job, if I lose it . . .'

'Es you wish . . .,' he said, putting all the notes together. 'But to earn them, you must hite me in your misdress' jember during the night, when she iss alone . . .'

'If you'll promise me never to tell who let you in, I consent. But I must warn you of one thing: Madame is as strong as a Turk, she is madly in love with Monsieur de Rubempré, and you could give her a million francs in bank-notes, without persuading her to be unfaithful . . . It's silly, but that's how she is when she's in love, she's worse than an honest woman, eh? When she goes out in the woods with Monsieur, Monsieur doesn't often stay at the house; she's gone out this evening, so I can hide you in my room. If Madame comes back alone, I'll let you know; you can stay in the drawing-room, I won't shut the bedroom door, and the rest, . . . well! the rest, that's up to you . . . Be prepared!'

'I give you the twenty-five *tausend* vrancs in the trawing-room, gash town.'

'Ah!' said Europe, 'are you as trusting as that? . . . Forgive me for so little . . .'

'You will hef blendy off obbordunidies for tittle me . . . We shell ged to know each other . . .'

'Well, then, be at the rue Taitbout at midnight; but then you'd better bring thirty thousand francs with you. Like cabs, a lady's maid's honesty costs more after midnight.'

'From brudence, I will gif you a gash-orter on de Pank . . .'

'No, no,' said Europe, 'notes, or it's all off . . .'

At one o'clock in the morning, Baron Nucingen, hidden in the attic in which Europe slept, was prey to all the anxieties which may beset a man in luck. He was alive, his blood tingled in his toes, his head was on the point of bursting like an over-heated steam engine.

'From a moral boint of fiew,' he said to du Tillet when he told him of this adventure, 'I hef enjoyed more than five thousand crowns worth.' He listened to the least sounds from the street, at two o'clock in the morning he heard his mistress's carriage from the boulevard. His heart beat enough to take the silk off his waistcoat, when the gate swung on its hinges: he was about see once again the divine, the ardent face of Esther! ... His heart received the sounds of the carriage steps and the slam of its door. Waiting for the supreme moment agitated him more than if it had been a matter of losing his fortune.

'Ha!' he cried, 'that was truly to live! To live efen too much, I shell be ingabaple of anyzing at oll!'

'Madame is alone, come on down,' said Europe appearing suddenly. 'Above all, don't make a noise, big elephant!'

'Pig elevant!' he repeated laughing and walking as though on a red-hot iron grating.

Europe preceded him, taper in hand.

'Zere, gount zem,' said the baron handing Europe the banknotes when they were in the drawing-room.

Europe took the thirty notes with a solemn air, and went out shutting the banker in. Nucingen went straight into the bedroom, where he found the fair English who said to him: 'Is that you, Lucien? ...'

'No, pudivul jild,' cried Nucingen, but stopped short.

He was stupefied to see a woman totally the opposite of Esther: fair indeed where she had been dark, weakness where he had admired strength! a soft night in Brittany where the sun of Arabia had blazed.

'Well, well! where have you come from? ... who are you? ... what do you want?' said the Englishwoman ringing without the bell making any sound.

'I muffled ze bells, but ton't pe afrait, ... I go away,' he said. 'Zet's tirty *tausend* vrancs trown away. Are you inteet ze mistress of Monsieur Lucien de Rubempré?'

'More or less, nephew,' said the Englishwoman who spoke French very well. 'But you, who are you?' she said imitating Nucingen's way of speaking.

'A man who hes peen tittled! ...' he replied piteously.

'Iss a man tittled when he finds a pretty woman?' she asked him jokingly.

'Permit me tomorrow to zent you a necklace, to remint you of de Paron de Nuchingen.'

'Don't know him!...' she said laughing like a madwoman; 'but the jewellery will be very welcome, you great big house-breaker.'

'You will know. Goot-pye, Madame. You are a king's morsel; but I em only a boor panker bast sixty years, and you hef mate me unterstend how much power hes the woman I luf, since your own suberhuman beauty hes not peen aple to make me forget it...'

'Well, zet's fery nice what you say me there,' replied the Englishwoman.

'It is less nice than the laty who inspires de zentiment...'

'You spoke of thirty thousand francs... Who did you give those to?'

'To your scountrel off a mait...'

The Englishwoman rang, Europe was not far away.

'Oh!' she cried, 'a man in Madame's bedroom, and it isn't Monsieur!... How dreadful!'

'Did he give you thirty thousand francs to be let in?'

'No, Madame; the two of us together aren't worth that much...'

And Europe began to cry thief so loud and implacably that the terrified banker made for the door, from which Europe hustled him down the stairs...

'Great scoundrel,' she yelled at him, 'you tell on me to my mistress! Thief!... thief!'

The amorous baron, in despair, was able without affront to reach his carriage which was stationed on the boulevard; but he no longer knew which of the spies to trust.

'Could Madame, by any chance, wish to deprive me of my earnings?...' said Europe turning like a fury upon the Englishwoman.

'I don't know your French ways,' said the Englishwoman.

'I need only say one word to Monsieur, and Madame will be thrown out tomorrow,' Europe insolently replied.

'Zet accorsed maid,' said the baron to Georges who naturally wished to know whether his master was content, 'tittled me off torty *tausend* vrancs, ... put it iss my own vault, it iss my own vault!...'

'So all Monsieur's care for his person was wasted. Oh, dear,

oh, dear! I don't advise Monsieur to take his jujubes for
nothing . . .'

'Georges, I am tying of tespair . . . I feel colt . . . I hef ice
in my heart . . . No more Esther, my friend.'

Georges was always a friend to his master when the circumstances were grave.

First round to the Abbé

Two days after this scene, which young Europe had just
recounted more amusingly than it can be done here for she
added mimicry, Carlos was taking his luncheon alone with
Lucien.

'Neither the Police nor anyone, my dear, must poke his
nose into our affairs,' he said in a low voice lighting a cigar
from Lucien's. 'It's unhealthy. I've thought of a daring but
infallible way of keeping our baron and his agents quiet. You
will go to Madame de Sérisy's, and you'll be very nice to her.
You will tell her, in the course of conversation, that, in order
to oblige Rastignac, who for some time has felt he's had
enough of Madame de Nucingen, you've agreed to serve him
as a cloak to conceal a mistress. Monsieur de Nucingen,
infatuated with the woman Rastignac is hiding (this will make
her laugh) has taken it into his head to employ the Police to
spy on you, who are perfectly innocent of your compatriot's
knavery, and whose interest with the Grandlieus could be
compromised. You will beg the countess to enlist the support
of her husband, who's a minister of State, in going to the Prefecture of Police. Once there, in the Prefect's presence, complain, but do it as a politician who will soon be playing an
influential part in the vast machinery of government. As such,
you understand the Police, you admire them, the Prefect
included. The most highly-skilled mechanics drop oil or spit.
Don't seem really annoyed. You have no grudge against
Monsieur le Préfet; but say that he ought to keep an eye on his
people, and sympathize with him at having to grumble at
them. The pleasanter, the more gentlemanly you are, the

angrier the Prefect will be with his agents. Then we shall be left quiet, and we can recall Esther, who must be troating like a stag in that forest.'

The Prefect at that time was a former magistrate. Former magistrates become prefects of police at too early an age. Imbued with the idea of Justice, concerned all the time with legality, they are too slow to adopt the Arbitrary which critical circumstances quite often call for, when the action of the Prefecture must be like that of a fireman called to put out a fire. In the presence of the Deputy Prime Minister, the Prefect invoked more difficulties than there really are in police work, deplored abuses, then remembered the visit he'd had from Baron Nucingen and the information he'd been asked for about Peyrade. The Prefect undertook to damp down the excesses of his agents, thanked Lucien for coming to him directly, promised him secrecy, and in general seemed to understand the intrigue. Fine phrases about the freedom of the individual and the inviolability of the home were exchanged between the Minister of State and the Prefect, to whom M. de Sérisy pointed out that the major interests of the country sometimes required secret illegalities, crime beginning only when State means were applied to private interests. Next day, as Peyrade was on his way to his beloved Café David where he enjoyed watching the citizens as an artist likes watching flowers grow, a constable in plain clothes accosted him in the street.

'I was just going to your house,' he said in an undertone, 'I have orders to take you to the Prefecture.'

Peyrade hailed a cab and got in, without a word, together with the policeman.

The Prefect of Police treated Peyrade as though he had been the lowest of prison warders, walking up and down the little garden of the Prefecture, which at that time extended along the Quai des Orfèvres.

'It is not without reason, my good fellow, that, ever since 1809, you've been kept out of the administration ... Don't you see what you're exposing us, and exposing yourself, to? ...'

This dressing-down terminated in a crushing blow. The

Prefect harshly announced to poor Peyrade that not only would his annual pension be stopped, but that a special watch would be kept on him personally. The old man received this cold shower with the most perfect calm. Nothing is so immobile and impassible as a man who has just been struck by lightning. Peyrade had lost all his money in the game. Lydia's father had counted on his position, and now he could expect nothing but alms from his friend Corentin.

'I've been Prefect of Police myself, and you're quite right,' the old man said calmly to the functionary then invested with judicial majesty, who started significantly. 'But allow me, without wishing to excuse myself in any way, to point out that you don't know me,' Peyrade continued with a sly glance in the Prefect's direction. 'Your words are either too hard for the former General Commissioner of Police for Holland, or not severe enough for a mere detective. The only thing is, Monsieur le Préfet,' Peyrade added after a pause on seeing that the Prefect was silent, 'remember what I shall now have the honour of saying to you. Without wishing to interfere in any way with *your police* or to justify myself in any way, you will see in due course that, in this matter, someone has been tricked: for the moment, it is your servant; later, you will say: "No, it was me!"'

And he bowed to the Prefect, who remained thoughtful in his astonishment. He returned home, weary through all his frame, seized with cold rage against Baron Nucingen. Only that dull-witted financier could have betrayed a secret otherwise concentrated in the heads of Contenson, Peyrade and Corentin. The old man accused the banker of wanting to avoid payment, once his goal had been attained. A single interview had been enough for him to divine the cunning of the most cunning of bankers. 'He liquidates everybody, including us, but I shall take my revenge,' said the old fellow to himself. 'I've never asked anything from Corentin, I'll ask him to help me avenge myself on this absurd moneybags. Accursed baron! you'll learn what I stoke my fires with, one morning when you find your daughter dishonoured ... But does he love his daughter?'

The evening of the catastrophe which reversed this old

man's hopes, he had aged by ten years. Talking with his friend Corentin, he punctuated his tale of woe with tears, torn from him by the prospect of the sad future he was leaving to his daughter, his idol, his pearl, his offering to God.

'We'll follow the matter up,' Corentin told him. 'First we must know if it is the baron who has given you away. Was it wise of us to keep Gondreville? ... Old Malin owes us too much not to want to sink us; so I'm keeping an eye on his son-in-law Keller, a ninny in politics, who might easily get mixed up with some conspiracy against the older branch in favour of the younger ... Tomorrow I shall know what is going on at Nucingen's, whether he's seen his mistress, who tightened the halter on us like this ... Don't worry. To begin with, the Prefect won't always be there ... The times are ripe for revolution, and revolutions stir the water up nicely.'

A whistled signal sounded from the street.

'That's Contenson,' said Peyrade who put a light in the window, 'and he's got something to tell me.'

A moment later, the faithful Contenson appeared before the two Police gnomes revered by him as geniuses.

'What's the matter?' said Corentin.

'Something new! I was coming out of 113, where I'd lost badly. Who do I see under the galleries? ... Georges! the boy's been sacked by the baron, who suspects him of giving information away.'

'Well, there's the effect of a smile I let somebody see,' said Peyrade.

'Oh, the disasters I've seen caused by a smile! ...' said Corentin.

'Not to mention riding crops,' said Peyrade alluding to the Simeuse affair. 'But, come on, Contenson, what happened?'

'This is what happened,' Contenson went on. 'I got Georges talking by standing him little glasses all the colours of the rainbow, he's still drunk; as for me, I must be like an alembic! Our baron went to the rue Taitbout, stuffed with *seraglio* lozenges. He found the lady you know of. But, here's the joke, that Englishwoman isn't his fair unknown! ... And he'd spent thirty thousand francs getting on the right side of her maid. Talk about stupid. That one thinks he's a great man because he can put big capital to little use; turn the phrase round, and you've got the problem it takes a genius to solve. The baron came back in a pitiable state. Next morning Georges, pretending to be an honest man, said to his master: "Why does Monsieur hire scoundrels like that? If Monsieur had asked me, I'd find his fair unknown for him, the description Monsieur gave me was quite enough. I'll turn Paris upside down." "Right," said the baron, "I'll pay you well!" Georges told me all that, together with a lot of ridiculous detail. But . . . rain falls on the just and the unjust! Next day, the baron received an anonymous letter which said something like "Monsieur de Nucingen is desperately in love with an unknown woman, he has already spent a lot of money for nothing; if he cares to be at the far end of the Neuilly bridge at midnight, and get into the carriage at the back of which he will find the lackey he saw in the Bois de Vincennes, allowing himself to be blindfolded, he will see the one he loves . . . As his fortune may cause him to mistrust the intentions of those who proceed in this way, Monsieur le Baron will be permitted to take his faithful Georges with him. There will be nobody else in the carriage." Without telling Georges anything about it, the baron goes, with Georges. The two of them let themselves be blindfolded and have their heads veiled. The baron recognizes the lackey. Two hours later, the carriage, travelling like one of Louis XVIII's (God rest his soul! there was a king who knew about police work!), stops in the middle of a wood. The baron's eyes are unbandaged, he sees in a stationary carriage his fair unknown, who . . . psst! . . . at once disappears. And the carriage (same caper as Louis XVIII) takes him back to the bridge at Neuilly where his own is still standing. Into Georges's hand had been thrust a scribble thus: "How many thousand-franc notes will Monsieur le Baron drop to be put in touch with the lady?" Georges gives this to his master, and the baron, convinced that Georges is hand-in-glove either with me or with you, Monsieur Peyrade, to exploit him, has put Georges out. That's a right simpkin of a banker! he shouldn't have sacked Georges till he'd slept with the fair unknown.'

'Did Georges see the woman?...' said Corentin.

'Yes,' said Contenson.

'Well,' cried Peyrade, 'what's she like?'

'Oh,' replied Contenson, 'he only had one thing to say: as beautiful as the sun!...'

'We've been fooled by rogues stronger than we are,' cried Peyrade. 'Those dogs are going to sell their woman to the baron at a high price.'

'*Ja, mein Herr!*' answered Contenson. 'So, as I learned you'd received a lot of flowery compliments at the Prefecture, I pumped Georges.'

'I'd like to know who'd tricked me,' said Peyrade, 'we'd soon see!'

'Got to hide behind the wallpaper,' said Contenson.

'He's right,' said Peyrade, 'we've got to get into the cracks, to look and listen...'

'That's a text we must study,' cried Corentin, 'for the moment, there's nothing I can do. And you, behave yourself, Peyrade! Do as Monsieur le Préfet tells you...'

'Monsieur de Nucingen is a good one to bleed,' observed Contenson, 'he's got too many thousand-franc notes in his veins...'

'I thought I had Lydia's dowry there!' Peyrade murmured in Corentin's ear.

'Well, Contenson, we must be off, and let daddy sleep...'

'Ah, sir,' said Contenson to Corentin as soon as they were outside, 'a fine bit of dealing on 'change that would have been for the old boy!... Ho! marry off your daughter for the price of!... Ah, yes, you could write a nice play, an improving one, too, on that subject, entitled: *A Young Girl's Dowry.*'

'You chaps are well-trained, what ears you've got!...' said Corentin to Contenson. 'Yes, yes, Social Nature equips all its Species with the apparatus they will need! Yes, Society is another kind of Nature!'

'That's very deep, very philosophical, what you say,' cried Contenson, 'a professor would make a *system* of it!'

'Keep yourself informed,' Corentin continued with a smile as he and the spy went along the streets together, 'of everything that happens at the Nucingen house, about the fair unknown, ... in a broad way, ... don't get up to any fancy tricks ...'

'I'll watch if the chimneys are smoking!' said Contenson.

'A man like Baron Nucingen can't have a turn of luck without people knowing,' Corentin went on. 'And us, well, to us men are supposed to be open books, and we can't allow ourselves to be taken in by them!'

'Ho, that's as if the condemned man were to amuse himself by slicing the executioner's neck!' cried Contenson.

'You've always got a joke,' replied Corentin whose smile betrayed shallow folds in the plaster mask of his face.

The matter was of extreme importance in itself, quite apart from its consequences. If it wasn't the baron who had betrayed Peyrade, in whose interest was it to see the Prefect of Police? Corentin's problem was to be sure that none of his men was playing a double game. On his way to bed he ruminated the same questions as Peyrade: 'Who is it who's complained to the Prefect? ... To whom does this woman belong?' In this way, all in ignorance of each other, Jacques Collin, Peyrade and Corentin were being drawn together without knowing it; and poor Esther, Nucingen, Lucien were to become involved in the battle already begun, to which the special vanity of policemen would add its own terror.

Mock priest, fake bills, bad debts, feigned love

THANKS to the cleverness of Europe, the most threatening part of the sixty thousand francs of debts which weighed on Esther and Lucien had been met. The confidence of their creditors was unshaken. Lucien and his corruptor could breathe for a while. Like two hunted beasts lapping a little water at the edge of a marsh, they might continue skirting precipices along which the strong man led the weak one either to the gibbet or to fortune.

'Today,' said Carlos to his creature, 'we stake all; luckily the cards have been *nicked* and the *punters* are new to the game!'

For some time, by order of his dreadful Mentor, Lucien had been assiduous in his attendance on Madame de Sérisy. He must not indeed be suspected of having as his mistress a kept woman. He discovered, moreover, in the pleasure of being loved, in the blandishments of society, means to deaden his feelings. It was in obedience to the express wish of Mademoiselle Clotilde de Grandlieu that he saw her only in the Bois or the Champs Élysées.

The day after Esther had been settled in the gamekeeper's cottage, the being who was for her so problematical, so terrible, so much a weight on her heart, came to propose that she should sign three stamped forms, blank but for the tormenting words: *Accepted for sixty thousand francs*, on the first; – *Accepted for a hundred and twenty thousand francs*, on the second; – *Accepted for a hundred and twenty thousand francs*, on the third. In all three hundred thousand francs of acceptances. If you put *good for*, it was simply accommodation paper. The word *accepted* made it what was known as a bill of exchange, and you became liable to imprisonment for debt. For the word *accepted*, anybody who signed imprudently might incur five years' imprisonment, a penalty rarely inflicted in police courts and at Assize only upon hardened criminals. The law concerning imprisonment for debt is a relic of barbarous times which to its stupidity adds the exceptional merit of uselessness, since it never catches rogues.

'It is a question,' said the Spaniard to Esther, 'of getting Lucien out of a scrape. We have sixty thousand francs of debts, and with these three hundred thousand francs we may contrive to become solvent again.'

Having antedated these bills of exchange by six months, Carlos had them drawn on Esther by a man *beyond the reach of the courts*, whose doings, despite the noise they made at the time, were soon forgotten, lost sight of, drowned by the din of the great symphony of July 1830.

This young man, one of our boldest financial rogues, son of a bailiff at Boulogne-Billancourt, was called Georges-Marie Destourny. The father, compelled to sell his office under very unfavourable conditions, left his son, about 1824, without resources, having given him a brilliant education, that mania the lower middle class has about its children. At twenty-three, the young and promising law student had already denied his father by inscribing his card:

GEORGES D'ESTOURNY.

With this card, his personality took on an aristocratic air. Further equipped with a tilbury and groom, he became a man of fashion and frequented clubs. The explanation was simple: he dealt on the Stock Exchange with the money of kept women in whose confidence he was. Accused of playing with marked cards, he came before a court of summary jurisdiction. He had accomplices, young men corrupted by himself, henchmen of necessity, sharers in his elegance and credit. Obliged to take flight, he neglected to pay his debts at the Bourse. The Parisian world, the Paris of the sharks and their clubs, still trembled over this two-fold affair.

In the days of his glory, Georges d'Estourny, a good-looking fellow, good-natured, open-handed as a brigand chief, had patronized the Torpedo for several months. The sham Spaniard based his calculations on Esther's former intimacy with the celebrated swindler, an accident peculiar to women of that class.

Georges d'Estourny, his ambition emboldened by success, had taken under his protection a man who had come from the depths of the provinces to do business in Paris, and whom the liberal party wished to see released from convictions courageously incurred in the battle of the Press against the government of Charles X, whose persecution had somewhat relented under the Martignac ministry. A pardon had been granted to M. Cérizet, that sound manager, nicknamed Brave Cérizet.

This Cérizet, still patronized for show by the leading spirits of the Left, started a firm which was at once a general business agency, a commission agency and a banking house. It was the kind of thing which, in the business world, corresponds to the kinds of domestic servant who announce themselves under Small Advertisements as willing and able to undertake all duties. Cérizet had been very happy to be associated with Georges d'Estourny who moulded him.

Esther, seen as a nineteenth-century equivalent of Ninon,

could pass for the faithful trustee of a part of the fortune of Georges d'Estourny. A blank acceptance signed *Georges d'Estourny* made Carlos Herrera master of his total assets. This forgery was without danger from the moment at which either Mademoiselle Esther, or someone acting on her behalf, was able to pay to order. Having informed himself about the firm of Cérizet, Carlos decided that the man was one of those obscure characters bent on making a fortune, but . . . by legal means.

Cérizet, d'Estourny's real trustee, was the security for large sums then committed to a bull market on 'Change, which allowed him to describe himself as a banker. That sort of thing goes on in Paris; a man may be despised, but not his money.

Carlos called on Cérizet with the intention of working on him in his own way, for by chance he had come into possession of all the secrets of this worthy associate of d'Estourny's.

Brave Cérizet lived on a first floor in the rue du Gros Chenet, and Carlos, having had himself mysteriously announced as calling on behalf of Georges d'Estourny, came upon the so-called banker pale from this announcement. In a modestly furnished office, Carlos saw a little man with thin, fair hair recognizable, from Lucien's description of him, as the betrayer of David Séchard.

'Can we talk here without fear of being overheard?' said the Spaniard rapidly transformed into an Englishman with red hair and blue spectacles, as clean and prim as a Puritan on his way to the meeting-house.

'Why, sir?' said Cérizet. 'And who are you?'

'Mister William Barker, a creditor of Monsieur d'Estourny's; but, since you wish me to do so, I shall demonstrate to you the need for keeping your doors well-closed. We know, sir, what your relations were with the Petit-Clauds, the Cointets and the Séchards of Angoulême . . .'

At these words, Cérizet hurried to the door and shut it, turned to another door leading to a bedroom and locked it; then said to his unknown visitor: 'Softly, sir!' And he examined the sham Englishman and asked him: 'What do you want with me? . . .'

'Dear me!' continued William Barker, 'it's everyone for

himself, in this world. You hold that rascal d'Estourny's funds ... Don't worry, I haven't come to ask you for them; but, at my pressing request, that rogue who deserves hanging, between ourselves, gave me these securities telling me that there might be some chance of realizing them; and, as I don't wish to act in my own name, he told me that you wouldn't refuse me yours.'

Cérizet glanced at the bill of exchange, and said: 'He's not in Frankfurt now ...'

'I know,' replied Barker, 'but he might still have been when he made out these drafts ...'

'I don't wish to be answerable,' said Cérizet ...

'I'm not asking you for anything,' Barker went on; 'you could be forced to accept them, receipt them, and I'll see they're discharged.'

'I'm astonished to see d'Estourny show this distrust of me,' said Cérizet.

'In his position,' replied Barker, 'he can hardly be blamed for putting his eggs into more than one basket.'

'Are you under the impression? ...' asked the petty financier giving the bills of exchange duly acknowledged back to the Englishman.

'... I am under the impression, indeed I know,' said Barker, 'that his cash reserves will remain in your hands, they are already green-carpeted at the Stock Exchange!'

'It is in the interest of my business to ...'

'To show a loss on them,' said Barker.

'Sir! ...' ejaculated Cérizet.

'Look, my dear Monsieur Cérizet,' Barker said coldly interrupting Cérizet, 'you would be doing me a favour by facilitating this encashment. Be so kind as to write me a letter in which you say that you are turning these receipted bills over to me on d'Estourny's account, and that the prosecuting sheriff's officer should regard the bearer as possessor of the three drafts.'

'What is your full name?'

'No names!' replied the English capitalist. 'Put: *The bearer of this letter and of the drafts* ... You will be well paid for obliging me in this way ...'

'How! . . .' said Cérizet.

'By something I shall tell you. You will be staying in France, will you not? . . .'

'Yes, sir.'

'Well, Georges d'Estourny won't be coming back ever.'

'Why?'

'There are at least five people, to my knowledge, who would kill him, and he knows it.'

'I'm not surprised, then, that he should want me to help him make up his little private cargo for the Indies!' cried Cérizet. 'And unfortunately he's obliged me to put everything into government holdings. We already owe money to the firm of du Tillet. I live from day to day.'

'Get well out of it!'

'Ah, if I'd known this sooner!' cried Cérizet. 'I've missed making a fortune . . .'

'One last word? . . .' said Barker. 'Be discreet! . . . you know how; but also, perhaps not so easy, keep your word. We shall meet again, and I'll see you make your fortune.'

Having cast into this soul of mud a hope which would assure his discretion for some time to come, Carlos, still in the part of Barker, went to see a bailiff he could count on, and instructed him to take out an injunction against Esther.

'It will be met,' he told the bailiff, 'it's a debt of honour, we just want to be in order.'

Barker had Mademoiselle Esther represented by an attorney at the commercial court so that judgement could be after trial. The bailiff, enjoined to act with consideration, procured all the necessary deeds and himself went to seize the furniture, in the rue Taitbout, where he was received by Europe. Notice of committal having been given, Esther was ostensibly liable for something over three hundred thousand francs of undisputed debts. Carlos's powers of invention were not much taxed by the arrangement. This game of false debts is played every day in Paris. There are sub-Gobsecks and sub-Gigonnets who, for a small fee, lend themselves to this infamous trick, which they regard as a joke. In France, everything is accompanied by a laugh, even crimes. In this way, **every**body, whether it be recalcitrant parents or the unwilling object of a passion, can be made to comply, under flagrant necessity or a threat of dishonour. Maxime de Trailles had frequently employed the same method, reviving comedies from a forgotten repertory. Carlos Herrera, however, anxious to save both Lucien's honour and that of the cloth, had had recourse to a forgery without danger, but latterly so much practised that the Law had been forced to take cognizance of it. It was said that, in the neighbourhood of the Palais Royal, there was a market in sham securities at which you could buy a signature for three francs.

Before broaching the question of the hundred thousand crowns designed to stand as a sentinel at the bedroom door, Carlos arranged with himself to have another hundred thousand francs paid, provisionally, to Monsieur de Nucingen. This is how.

Acting on his orders, Asia presented herself to the amorous baron as an old woman fully informed about the fair unknown's affairs. To date, those who depict the life of society have brought no end of moneylenders on the scene; but they tend to forget the moneylenderess, the Madame la Ressource of the present day, a very strange figure indeed, commonly to be found under the respectable title of *wardrobe dealer*, and well within the savage Asia's scope, in view of the two establishments she had, one near the Temple, one in the rue Neuve Saint Marc, both run by women in her pay.

'You will call yourself,' he said, 'Madame *de Saint-Estève*.' Herrera wanted to see Asia dressed for the part. The bogus procuress appeared in a robe of flowered damask, made out of the curtains taken down in some distrained lady's dressing-room, with the sort of worn, faded, unsaleable cashmere shawl which often ends its life round such a woman's shoulders. She wore a collarette of once-very-fine but frayed lace, and a frightful hat; but she was shod with Irish brogues, above which her flesh bulged smooth and black.

'Just look at this buckle!' she said showing a piece of very doubtful jewellery on the belt which clutched her kitchen-woman's belly. 'What a beauty, eh? And my neck-ribbon, . . . how delightfully ugly it makes me! Oh, Madame Nourisson has turned me out a treat.'

'Be soft-spoken at first,' Carlos said to her, 'almost timid, mistrustful like a cat; and make the baron blush for having used police spies without appearing to have any reason to be afraid of them. Finally let it be known in a clear and business-like way that you defy all the policemen in the world to discover where the fair one is. Cover your tracks carefully . . . When the baron has given you the right to prod him in the stomach and say: "You dirty old man!" turn insolent and send him away like a lackey.'

Threatened with not seeing the procuress again if he had her watched in any way, Nucingen visited Asia on his way to the Bourse, on foot, furtively, in a wretched shop parlour in the rue Neuve Saint Marc. Those muddy footpaths, how often amorous millionaires have trodden them, and with what pleasure! the streets of Paris know. Madame de Saint Estève, by way of alternating hope and despair, brought the baron to the point of wanting to know everything about the fair unknown, *at any price*! . . .

Meanwhile, the bailiff acted, and acted all the more easily in that, meeting with no resistance at Esther's address, he was able to do it legally without waiting twenty-four hours.

Lucien, taken there by his counsellor, five or six times visited the recluse at Saint Germain. His savage guide considered these visits necessary in order to prevent Esther from pining, for her beauty was their main capital. When the moment came for leaving the forester's house, he led Lucien and the poor harlot to the side of a deserted road, to a spot from which Paris could be seen, and where nobody could hear them. The three of them sat down in the light of the rising sun, beneath the stump of a poplar, before that view, one of the most splendid in the world, which takes in the course of the Seine, Montmartre, Paris, Saint Denis.

'Children,' said Carlos, 'your dream is over. You, my dear, will never see Lucien again; or if you see him, you must just have known him, five years ago, very briefly.'

'So that is my sentence of death!' said she without shedding a tear.

'Ah, well, you've been poorly these five years,' Herrera continued. 'Regard yourself as a consumptive, and die without boring us with your elegies. But you will see that you can still live, and very well! ... Leave us, Lucien, go pick *sonnets*,' he said indicating a field nearby.

Lucien cast upon Esther a begging look, the look of a weak, greedy man, his heart full of tenderness, his character that of a coward. Esther answered with a sign of the head which meant: 'I must listen to the executioner and learn how to place my head beneath the axe, and I shall die bravely.' It was so beautiful, and at the same time so full of horror, that the poet wept; Esther ran to him, folded him in her arms, drank the tear and said to him: 'Don't worry!' a thing said with the eyes and with a gesture, and with the voice of madness.

Carlos explained clearly, without ambiguity, sometimes with words of horrible appropriateness, Lucien's critical situation, his position at the Grandlieus' house, the wonderful life he would have if he succeeded, finally the need for Esther to sacrifice herself to this magnificent future.

'What must I do?' she cried fanatically.

'Obey me blindly,' said Carlos. 'And what could you possibly complain of? It is entirely up to you to create for yourself a happy fate. You are going to become what Tullia, Florine, Mariette and the Val-Noble, old friends of yours, were, the mistress of a rich man whom you don't love. Once our fortunes have been put right, our great lover is rich enough to make you happy ...'

'Happy! ...' she said raising her eyes to heaven.

'You've had four years in Eden,' he continued. 'Can't you live on memories like those? ...'

'I shall obey you,' she replied, wiping a tear from the corner of her eye. 'For the rest, you need feel no anxiety! As you once said, my love is a sickness unto death.'

'That isn't all,' went on Carlos, 'you have to remain beautiful. At twenty-two and a half, you are at your highest peak of beauty, thanks to all this happiness. Become what you were, the Torpedo. Be sly, extravagant, devious, pitiless with the millionaire I'm handing to you. Listen! ... this man is a thief on the World Market, he's been without pity for a great many people, he's grown fat on the fortunes of widows and orphans, you will be their Revenge! ... Asia will come to fetch you in a cab, and you will be in Paris this evening. If you were to let your four years' relations with Lucien be suspected, you might as well shoot him in the head. You'll be asked what you've been doing: you will reply that you have been taken on his travels by an excessively jealous Englishman. You used to have the wit to mislead people in a way that they liked, pick the craft up again.'

Have you ever seen a shining kite, the giant butterfly of childhood, trimmed with gold, planing in the skies? ... The children forget the string for a moment, a passer-by cuts it, the meteor *takes*, in schoolboy language, *a header*, and falls with frightening speed. Thus Esther on hearing Carlos.

PART TWO

WHAT LOVE MAY COST
AN OLD MAN

A hundred thousand francs invested in Asia

FOR a week past, Nucingen had been occupied with negotiating the delivery of the one he loved, most days calling at the shop in the rue Neuve Saint Marc. There, sometimes under the name of Saint-Estève, sometimes under that of her creature Madame Nourisson, Asia reigned among fine costumes at that most horrible stage when gowns are no longer gowns but are not yet rags. The setting harmonized with the face this woman put on, for such shops are one of the most sinister peculiarities of Paris. In them may be found cast-off garments flung there by Death's skinny hand, so that consumptive wheezing may be heard in the folds of a shawl, the agony of destitution in a gown gold-spangled. Fine lace there records the frightful dialogue between Luxury and Hunger. A queen's physiognomy may be almost exactly reconstructed from the way a plumed turban now stands. Prettiness conceals horror! The lash of Juvenal, wielded by the hands of the official valuer, scatters the threadbare muffs, the soiled furs of hard-pressed whores. It is a dunghill of flowers where, here and there, glow roses cut yesterday, sported for an hour, now sniffed by an old creature who is Usury's first cousin, bald, toothless Second Hand, eager to sell what the garment had contained as well as itself, the gown without the woman or the woman without the gown! There was Asia, like a warder in the hulks, like a red-beaked vulture among corpses, in her element; yet more appalling than the hags truly what she pretended to be, seen grimacing behind dirty windows in which the astounded passer-by may sometimes see a treasured souvenir of youth displayed.

After countless irritations and seeing the price go up by ten thousand francs on each occasion, the banker had finally offered sixty thousand francs to Madame de Saint-Estève, only to be met with an ape-like grimace of refusal. After a restless night, after realizing what disorder of mind Esther had brought upon him, after unexpected gains on the stock market, he appeared one morning with the clear intention of paying out the hundred thousand francs which Asia demanded, though determined on extracting a great deal of information from her.

'Made up your mind, have you, then, old flighty?' Asia said to him with a slap on the back.

Humiliating familiarity is the first imposition women of that kind levy on the unbridled passions or desperate needs confided to them; they never meet their client on his own level, but make him sit down beside them on the heap of mud where they squat. Asia, as we may see, obeyed her master admirably.

'Iss no aldernadif,' said Nucingen.

'And a bargain at the price,' replied Asia. 'Women have been sold for more than you'll be paying for that one, relatively. There are women and women! De Marsay gave sixty thousand francs for the late Coralie. The one you want cost a hundred thousand francs new; of course, as far as I'm concerned, you old monster, it's just a matter of arrangement.'

'Pud where iss she?'

'Oh, you'll see her all right. I'm like you: nothing for nothing! . . . Look at the trouble you've stirred up with your *passion*. These young things, you can't expect them to be reasonable. At present the princess is what we call a pretty-by-night . . .'

'Briddy pie . . .'

'Come on, now, don't be a muggins! . . . She's got Louchard on her tracks, I had to lend her fifty thousand francs myself . . .'

'Fooftsy *tausend*! Iss nit bozziple,' cried the banker.

'Lord bless you, twenty-five on account of fifty, goes without saying,' replied Asia. 'That woman, you've got to do her credit, she's as honest as daylight! All she had was herself, she said to me, she said: "Dearest Madame Saint-Estève, they're after me, there's nobody but you that can oblige me, give me twenty thousand francs, and you can take my heart as security . . ." Oh, it's a very nice heart! . . . There's only me knows where she is. If I let on, it might cost me twenty thousand francs . . . Once upon a time, she lived in the rue Taitbout. Before she did a flit . . . (her furnishings was seized! . . . more expense. Bailiff's men are all rogues! As you well know, a big noise on 'Change like you!) Well, she's not stupid, she rented the place for two months to an English woman, a fine-looking woman who had that bit of a thing, Rubempré, for a lover, ... and he was that jealous he made her go out at night ... But, now that the furniture's going to be sold, this English woman has hopped it, specially as she was too expensive for a little shrimp like Lucien ...'

'*Also* you too are panker,' said Nucingen.

'By the light of nature,' said Asia. 'I can always lend a bit to pretty women; it pays, because then you've got two kinds of assets to call in.'

It amused Asia to *ham* the part of these women who are sour enough, but mealier-mouthed, more carneying than the Malay, and who justify their traffic by all kinds of high-sounding arguments. Asia pretended to have lost her illusions, five lovers, children, and claimed she was bilked by everybody in spite of her experience. Every now and then she produced a pawnshop ticket, to show how much bad luck there was in her trade. She gave herself out to be harassed, in debt. She was, moreover, so unmistakably hideous that in the end the baron believed in the part she was playing.

'Well, so, ven I hend ofer ze *hundert tausend* vrancs, where I see her?' he said with the gesture of a man ready to make any sacrifice.

'Oh, you could come this evening, if you liked, by carriage naturally, opposite the Gymnase theatre. It's on the way,' said Asia. 'Stop at the corner of the rue Sainte Barbe. I'll be on sentry-go there, we'll go and find my raven-haired asset together ... Oh, she *has* got lovely hair, my asset! When she takes the comb out, it covers her like a tent. But you know, clever you may be at figures, but you strike me as pretty stupid at everything else; I advise you to keep the child concealed, else they'll stow her away in Sainte Pélagie, and quickly, next day, if they find her, ... and ... they're looking for her.'

'Bozzible berhaps puy pack ze pills?' said the incorrigible Shark.

'The bailiff has them, ... but there's nothing doing. The child flew into a passion and swallowed a deposit they're asking for. But there you are, girls of twenty-two will have their little joke.'

'*Gut, gut,* I arrange zet,' said Nucingen putting on an artful air. 'Is agreet I look efter ziz tings.'

'Well, you great stupid, it's up to you to make her fond of you, and there's no doubt you've got the wherewithal to buy what'll look convincingly like love and perhaps be as good. I place my princess between your hands; she knows she's got to come along with you, I don't care what happens after that . . . But she's used to luxury and consideration. Ah, my handsome! she's the right sort of woman, that one . . . Else would I have given her fifteen thousand francs?'

'Och, *so!* Till zis efening, zen!'

The baron once more set about a nuptial beautification of himself; but, this time, the certainty of success made him take twice the quantity of pills. At nine o'clock, he went to the agreed meeting-place and took the dreadful woman into his carriage.

'Vich vay?' said the baron.

'Which way?' said Asia, 'rue de la Perle, in the Marais, an accommodation address, for your pearl is in the mire, but you'll clean her up!' Once there, the false Madame Saint-Estève told Nucingen with a fearful leer: 'We're going to walk a bit now, I'm not such a fool as to have given the real address.'

'You sink of everysing,' replied Nucingen.

'I need to,' said she.

Asia led Nucingen into the rue Barbette, where, in a lodging house kept by an upholsterer of the neighbourhood, he was taken up to the fourth floor. When, in a meanly furnished room, he saw Esther dressed like a girl of the lower orders working at a piece of embroidery, the millionaire turned pale. Even after a quarter of an hour, during which Asia seemed to be holding a whispered conversation with Esther, the rejuvenated old man could hardly speak.

'*Montemisselle,*' he said at length to the poor girl, 'will you pe so kind es to let me pe your brodector? . . .'

'I cannot do otherwise, sir,' said Esther from whose eyes two big tears overflowed.

'Not cry. I vish I mek you ze heppiest off oll women . . . Let me only lof you, zen you will see.'

'My child, the gentleman will be sensible,' said Asia, 'he knows very well that he is sixty-six past, and will be very indulgent. In short, my little angel, it is a father I have found you . . . Got to *say* that,' whispered Asia to the banker who wasn't looking pleased. 'You don't catch swallows by letting off a pistol at them. Come this way!' said Asia leading Nucingen into the next room. 'You know the form, my angel?'

Nucingen drew a wallet out of his pocket and counted out the hundred thousand francs, which Carlos, hidden yet elsewhere, awaited with lively impatience, and which the cook brought him.

'There's a hundred thousand francs our man's invested in Asia, now we'll make him invest some more in Europe,' said Carlos to his confidante when they were on the landing.

He vanished after giving his instructions to the Malay, who went back into the apartment where Esther wept hot tears. Like a criminal condemned to death, the child had lived on a fairy-tale of hope, and now the fatal hour had struck.

'Little ones,' said Asia, 'where are you going to go? . . . for Baron Nucingen . . .'

Esther looked at the famous banker and made an admirably played, apparently spontaneous gesture of surprise.

'Yo, yo, my child, I am Baron te Nuzingen . . .'

'Baron Nucingen cannot, must not stay in such a kennel. Listen! Your old maid Eugénie . . .'

'Ougénie! of the roue Daidpoud . . .' cried the baron.

'Yes, indeed, the legal trustee of the furniture,' Asia went on, 'who rented the apartment to the fair English . . .'

'Och, I onnerstend!' said the baron.

'As former personal maid to Madame,' Asia continued respectfully indicating Esther, 'she will receive you very comfortably this evening, and the Trade Protection men will never think of coming to look for her in her old apartment, which she left three months ago . . .'

'Zblentit, zblentit!' cried the baron. 'Pesites, I know the Drate Brodection pipple, and I know vot vords to make zem go fast avay . . .'

169

'You'll find Eugénie a sly one,' said Asia, 'I ought to know, I found her for Madame . . .'

'I know her,' cried the millionaire with a laugh. 'Ougénie tittled me dirty *tausend* vrancs . . .' Esther's expression of horror would of itself have led a man of heart to confide his fortune to her. 'Wass mine own fault,' the baron continued, 'I wass jessing you . . .' And he recounted the story of the misunderstanding caused by letting the apartment to an Englishwoman.

'There, you see, Madame?' said Asia. 'Eugénie told you nothing about that, the minx! However, Madame is accustomed to that girl,' she said to the baron, 'keep her all the same.' Asia took Nucingen on one side and said to him: 'With five hundred francs a month to Eugénie, who's feathering her nest very nicely, you shall know everything Madame does, keep her on as lady's maid. Eugénie'll be all the nicer to you for having gypped you once. Nothing so attaches a woman to a man as gypping him. But keep Eugénie on a tight rein: she'll do anything for money, that baggage, she's a horror! . . .'

'*Und* yourself? . . .'

'Me, I'm just reimbursing myself,' said Asia.

Nucingen, a man of such depth, was as though blindfold; he let himself be led like a child. To see the candid and adorable Esther drying her eyes and making her embroidery stitches with the modesty of a young virgin, renewed in the infatuated old man the sensations he had experienced in the Bois de Vincennes; he would have given her the key to his safe! he felt young, his heart was full of adoration, he waited for Asia's departure so that he might fling himself on his knees before this Raphael Madonna. Such a flowering of sudden youth in the heart of a Shark, an old man, is one of those social phenomena which Physiology can best explain. Weighed down by business cares, constricted by ceaseless calculations, by the unending preoccupations of the hunt for millions, adolescence and its sublime illusions reappear, spring up and burgeon, like a prime cause, like a buried seed whose effects, whose magnificent flowering obey the chance of a sun which unexpectedly shines late. A clerk at twelve in the ancient house of Aldrigger in Strasbourg, the baron had never set foot in the world of feeling. Thus he stood before his idol with a thousand phrases whirling in his brain, but finding none on his lips yielded to a brutal desire in which the man of sixty-six was visible.

'Will you come zen to the rue Daidbout? . . .' he said.

'Wherever you wish, sir,' replied Esther rising.

'"Vairefer you vish!"' he repeated with rapture. 'You are *ein Engelein* tescented *vom Himmel*, whom I lof es if I wass a young man zo I hef grey hair . . .'

'Oh, you might as well say white! for it's too fine a black now to be grey underneath,' said Asia.

'Go hereout, file trafficker in human flesh! You hef your money, dribble no more upon zis flower of lof!' cried the banker repaying himself with this vicious apostrophe for all the insolence he had had to endure.

'You old scoundrel! you'll pay for that expression! . . .' said Asia threatening the banker with a Billingsgate gesture which made him raise his shoulders. 'Between the cup and the lip there is room for a viper, and you'll find me there! . . .' she said roused by Nucingen's disdain.

Millionaires, whose money is kept by the Bank of France, whose houses are guarded by numerous footmen, whose person is protected, in the street, by the rampart of a carriage with English horses, fear no misfortune; and so the baron stared coldly at Asia, like a man who had just given her a hundred thousand francs. This air of majesty produced its effect. Asia made her way out muttering in the staircase and, her language excessively revolutionary in tone, spoke of the scaffold!

'Whatever did you say to her? . . .' asked the *virgin at her embroidery*, 'she's a good-hearted woman.'

'She has zolt you, she has ropped you . . .'

'When we are in misfortune,' she answered with a look to rend the heart of a diplomat, 'who will show us consideration or give us money? . . .'

'Poor child!' said Nucingen, 'stay not a minute longer here!'

NUCINGEN gave Esther his arm, he led her away as she was, and installed her in his carriage with perhaps more respect than he would have showed the fair Duchesse de Maufrigneuse.

'You will hef a fine equipage, ze priddiest of Paris,' said Nucingen during their journey. 'Everysing vhich luxury hes of most sharming vill surrount you. *Eine* qveen soll nit be richer zan you. You soll be respect like Cherman prite: I will you are vree . . . Do not veep. Listen to me . . . I lof you druly viz a pure lof. Each tear of you breks my heart . . .'

'Can one truly love a woman one has bought? . . .' asked the poor creature in an enchanting voice.

'Yoseph wass solt by his prothers because he wass goot. Iss in ze Piple. Also in ze East iss legal vife bought.'

When they reached the rue Taitbout, Esther could not without pain behold the scene of her former happiness. She stayed motionless on a divan, checking each tear as it started, without hearing a word of the baron's senseless jabbering, he fell on his knees; she left him there without speaking, allowing him to take her hands as he pleased, barely conscious of what sex the creature was who chafed her feet, which Nucingen found cold. This scene of hot tears now and then falling on the baron's head and of icy feet warmed by him, lasted from midnight until two o'clock in the morning.

'Ougénie,' the baron at last called to Europe, 'zee if your misdress will not go to ped . . .'

'No,' cried Esther springing to her feet like a frightened mare, 'not here, never! . . .'

'No, look, sir, I know Madame, she is gentle and kind as a lamb,' said Europe to the banker; 'only, she mustn't be rushed, you've got to approach indirectly . . . She had so much to put up with here! See? . . . how worn the furniture is! Give her her own way. Set her up, somewhere, nicely, in a pretty house. When she sees everything round her new, she'll feel a bit lost like, and she might think you nicer than you are, and behave like an angel. Oh, Madame has no equal! and you really could boast of acquiring a bargain: kind heart, beautiful manners, bit of a devil when she feels like it, skin like a rose . . . Ah! . . . And wit enough to make man laugh on the scaffold . . . Madame is most affectionate, really . . . And the way she knows how to dress! . . . Ah, well, it may cost a bit, a man's got, as you might say, his money's worth. Here, all her clothes have been seized, her wardrobe is three months out of date. But Madame is so kind, you see, that even I'm fond of her, and her my mistress! So, let's be fair, a woman like that to find herself in a place where the bailiffs have been! . . . And for who? for a scamp who ruined her . . . Poor little woman! no longer herself she isn't.'

'Ezder, . . . Ezder . . .' said the baron, 'go to bet, my enchel? Och! if iss me vrightens you, I zday on ze sofa . . .' cried the baron inflamed by the purest love on seeing Esther still weep.

'Well, then,' replied Esther taking the baron's hand and kissing it with a feeling of gratitude which brought something resembling a tear to the Shark's eye, 'I shall thank you for it.'

And she ran into her bedroom and shut herself in.

'Is in zis somezing strendge,' Nucingen said to himself, feeling the effect of his pills. 'Vot vill zey say at hom'?'

He got up, looked out of the window: 'My garritch iss still zere . . . Soon iss taylight! . . .'

He walked about the room: 'How Matame te Nouzingen vill laugh at me, if efer she knows how I spend zis night! . . .'

He placed his ear against the bedroom door feeling that it was too foolish to be accommodated as he was. 'Ezder! . . .'

No reply.

'*Gottes Himmel!* she still veeps! . . .' he said to himself as he stretched out on the sofa.

Ten minutes or so after sunrise, Baron Nucingen, who had slept as badly as one must in a cramped position on a divan, was awakened with a start by Europe in the middle of one of the sorts of dream one has in such positions and whose disordered sequence is a phenomenon still unexplained by medical physiology.

'Oh, my goodness, Madame!' she was crying. 'Madame! soldiers, police! . . . the Law. They want to arrest you . . .'

Just as Esther appeared at the door of her room, barely covered by a dressing-gown, her bare feet in slippers, her hair loose, beautiful enough to damn the archangel Raphael, the drawing-room door disgorged a wave of human mud, trampling on ten feet towards the celestial creature, posed like an angel in a Flemish religious painting. A man stepped forward. Contenson, the frightful Contenson, placed his hand on Esther's moist shoulder.

'You are Mademoiselle Esther van . . . ?' said he.

Europe, with a back-hander across his face, sent Contenson flying to measure as much carpet as he needed to lie on, all the more readily in that she followed the blow up with a sharp kick in the legs of a kind known to those who practise the art which foreigners call French boxing, but which is more correctly known as *savate*.

'Get back!' she cried, 'nobody lays hands on my mistress!'

'She's broken my leg!' Contenson was complaining loudly as he got up, 'somebody'll pay for that . . .'

Against the background of five minions of justice dressed as such minions are, keeping their frightful hats on their yet more frightful heads, displaying faces of veined mahogany in which eyes squinted, a nose here and there missing and mouths grimacing, stood out the figure of Louchard, attired more decently than his men, but hat on head, face at once sugary and mocking.

'I am arresting you, Mademoiselle,' he said to Esther. 'As to you, my girl,' he said to Europe, 'resistance is useless, and all contumacy will be punished.'

The rattle of rifle-butts on the tiles of the dining-room and the ante-chamber added force to his argument. The Guard had a Guard.

'Why do you want to arrest me?' said Esther innocently.

'What about our little debts? . . .' replied Louchard.

'Ah, that's true!' cried Esther. 'Wait while I dress.'

'Unluckily for you, Mademoiselle, I need to make sure that there is no way of escape from your bedroom,' said Louchard.

All this took place so quickly that the baron had not yet had time to intervene.

'Now am I a filthy seller of human flesh, Baron Nucin-

gen! . . .' called out the terrible Asia as she slipped through the
anks of the minions to the divan where she affected to discover the banker.

'File schtrumpet!' cried Nucingen rising to his feet in
inancial majesty.

And he stepped between Esther and Louchard, who took
uis hat off at Contenson's ejaculation:

'Monsieur le Baron de Nucingen! . . .'

At a sign from Louchard, his men evacuated the apartment
all of them uncovering respectfully. Only Contenson stayed.

'Is Monsieur le Baron paying? . . .' asked the Guard now
aat in hand.

'I am baying,' he answered, 'pud virst I vill know vot
ss.'

'Three hundred and twelve thousand francs and a few
centimes, ready cash, and that doesn't cover the cost of this
arrest.'

'Tree *hundert tausend* vrancs!' cried the baron. 'Is too costly
avakening vor a men who hes spent ze night on a sofa,' he
added in Europe's ear.

'Is this man really Baron Nucingen?' Europe asked Louchard accompanying her expression of doubt with a gesture
which Mademoiselle Dupont, latest *soubrette* at the Comédie
Française, might have envied.

'Yes, miss,' said Louchard.

'Yes,' echoed Contenson.

'I vill enswer for ze lady,' said the baron whose pride was
offended by Europe's doubt, 'let me a vort to her say.'

Esther and her aged suitor went into the bedroom, to whose
keyhole Louchard thought it necessary to apply his ear.

'I lof you more zen my life, Esther; but vhy gif your greditors money vhich vould be invinitely petter in your burse?
You go prison: I arrange puy up zis *hundert tausend* crown
mit hundert tausend vranc, end you shell hef two *hundert tausend*
vranc yourself . . .'

'An arrangement like that,' Louchard called out, 'won't do.
The creditor isn't in love with Mademoiselle, not likely! . . . Is
that clear? he's even keener on getting every penny, since he
gathered you were mad about her.'

'Accursed vool!' cried Nucingen to Louchard opening the door and pulling him into the room, 'you ton't know whad you're saying! I gif you, bersonally, dwendy ber zent, you fixing zis . . .'

'Impossible, Monsieur le Baron.'

'What, sir? you'd have the heart,' said Europe intervening, 'to let my mistress go to prison! . . . Do you want my wages, my savings? take them, Madame, I have forty thousand francs . . .'

'Ah, poor wench, I didn't know you!' cried Esther folding Europe in her arms.

Europe burst into tears.

'I am baying,' said the baron piteously taking out a note-case from which he drew one of those little squares of printed paper which the Bank gives to bankers, on which all they have to do is fill in the amount in figures and written out in full to turn them into orders payable to the bearer.

'It isn't worth the trouble, Monsieur le Baron,' said Louchard, 'my orders are to take payment only in gold or silver money. As it's you, I might be content with bank notes.'

'Toffle tek it!' cried the baron, 'I see your gretentials?'

Contenson handed him three documents folded in blue paper, which the baron took with a look at Contenson, to whom he hissed under his breath: 'You coult have spend ze day better by coming to varn me.'

'How was I to know you were here, Monsieur le Baron?' answered the spy without caring whether or no Louchard heard him. 'You lost, you know, by not continuing to place your confidence in me. You were cheated,' added this profound thinker with a shrug.

'Iss true,' the baron thought. 'Och, my chilt,' he cried on seeing the bills of exchange and addressing Esther, 'you vere ze fictim off a vamous rog, a svintler!'

'Yes, alas,' said poor Esther, 'but he was very fond of me! . . .'

'If I het known, . . . I voult hef noted it for protest end so nullified it for you.'

'You're losing your head, Monsieur le Baron,' said Louchard, 'there is a holder for value without notice.'

'Yo,' he went on, 'is a holter in due course . . . Cérizet! a nullity!'

'Misfortune makes him witty,' said Contenson with a smile, 'that was a pun.'

'Would Monsieur le Baron care to write a note to his cashier?' said Louchard also smiling, 'I can send Contenson with it and dismiss the others. Time's getting on, and everybody will know . . .'

'Horry, Gontenson! . . .' cried Nucingen. 'Ze gashier lifs at ze corner of ze roue tes Madurins and the roue te l'Argate. Here iss a note delling him to go to Keller's or tu Dillet's, in gase we hef not *hundert tausend* crown, for all our money iss at ze Pank . . . Get tressed, my enchel,' he said to Esther, 'you are now vree . . . Olt women,' he cried looking at Asia, 'are more tangerous zen young . . .'

'I'll be off and give the creditor a laugh,' Asia told him, 'and he'll be seeing I'm all right for the day. No ill feelings, Monnessier le Paron . . .' added Madame Saint-Estève with a horrible curtsey.

Louchard took the deeds from the baron's hands, and remained alone with him in the drawing-room, where half an hour later the cashier arrived followed by Contenson. Esther then reappeared exquisitely dressed, though with some air of improvisation. When the money had been counted by Louchard, the baron wanted to examine the deeds; but Esther snatched them as quick as a cat and took them to her desk.

'Are you going to tip the rabble? . . .' said Contenson to Nucingen.

'You showt no gonsideration,' said the baron.

'And what about my leg! . . .' cried Contenson.

'Luchard, you vill gif Gontenson *hundert* vranc of ze change from *tausend* . . .'

'Iss a fery peautiful voman!' said the cashier to Baron Nucingen as he left the rue Taitbout, 'pud she is gosting much to Monnessière le Paron.'

'Keeb zis a zegret,' said the baron who had also enjoined secrecy upon Contenson and Louchard.

Louchard went followed by Contenson; but, in the main

street, Asia who was waiting for him stopped the Trade Security Guard.

'The bailiff and the creditor are there in a cab, they're thirsty!' she told him, 'and you're quids-in!'

While Louchard counted the money, Contenson was able to examine the clients. He perceived the eyes of Carlos, made out the shape of his forehead beneath the wig, and the wig itself looked suspect; he took the number of the cab, while seeming quite indifferent to all that went on; Asia and Europe intrigued him in the extreme. He decided that the baron had been a victim of exceptionally clever people, all the more as Louchard, enlisting his services, had been strangely discreet. The way Europe had brought him down hadn't struck Contenson's tibia alone. 'That was a Saint Lazare kick!' he'd said to himself as he got up.

Carlos sent off the bailiff, paying him well, and said to the driver at the same time: 'Palais Royal, the Steps!'

'Ah! the sly dog!' Contenson thought as he heard this command, 'there's something afoot! . . .'

Carlos reached the Palais Royal at too great a speed to fear being followed. Doubly cautious, he then crossed the galleries, and took another cab outside the Château d'Eau, saying: 'Passage de l'Opéra, the rue Pinon end.' A quarter of an hour later, he was back at the rue Taitbout.

When she saw him, Esther said: 'There are the fatal documents!'

Carlos picked up the deeds and examined them; then he took them to the kitchen fire and burned them.

'Well, that's over!' he cried showing the three hundred and ten thousand francs rolled up inside an envelope which he took from the pocket of his frock coat. 'These and the hundred thousand francs snitched by Asia will enable us to act.'

'Good Lord! good Lord!' cried poor Esther.

'Don't be a fool,' said the ferocious schemer, 'be ostensibly Nucingen's mistress, and you'll be able to see Lucien, he's a friend of Nucingen's, I don't want to stop you having a passion for him!'

Esther saw a gleam of light in the darkness of her life, she took breath.

'Europe, my child,' said Carlos leading the creature to a corner of the boudoir where nobody could overhear a word of their conversation, 'I'm very pleased with you.'

Europe raised her head, looked at this man with an expression which so transformed her withered face that Asia, witnessing the scene through the doorway, wondered whether the interest by which Carlos maintained his hold on Europe might be of greater depth than that by which she herself felt riveted to him.

'But that is not all, my girl. Four hundred thousand francs aren't nearly enough . . . Paccard will give you an invoice for plate amounting to thirty thousand francs, duly receipted; but Biddin, the goldsmith, has been put to some expense. Our furniture, distrained by him, will no doubt be put up for sale tomorrow. Go and see Biddin, he lives in the rue de l'Arbre Sec, he'll give you pawnshop tickets for ten thousand francs. You understand: Esther has had silverware made, hasn't paid for it, but has given it as security, she'll be threatened with a small action for fraud. So, the goldsmith will have to be paid thirty thousand francs and the pawnbroker another ten thousand before the plate can be got at. Total: forty-three thousand francs with expenses. That silver contains a good deal of alloy, the baron will have it replaced, we can bone him on that for a few more thousand-franc notes. You owe . . . what, for two years at the dressmaker's?'

'Call it six thousand francs,' replied Europe.

'So, if Madame Auguste wants to be paid and to stay in business, she must make out a bill for thirty thousand francs over four years. Same arrangements with the milliner. The jeweller, Samuel Frisch, the Jew in the rue Sainte Avoie, will lend you pawn tickets, we've got to "owe" him twenty-five thousand francs, and there'll be supposed to have been six thousand francs worth of "our" jewels in hock. We'll return the jewels to the jeweller, half of them will be paste; however, the baron won't look. In the end, you'll get our gull to cough up a hundred and fifty thousand francs by a week from now.'

'Madame will have to help me a little,' replied Europe, 'speak to her, for she stands there like somebody speechless, and I have to rack my brains harder than three authors writing a play.'

'If Esther starts being prudish, you must let me know,' said Carlos. 'Nucingen owes her an equipage and horses, she'll want to chose and buy them herself. There we shall lay on admirable horses, very expensive, which'll be lame within a month, and then we shall change them.'

'We could manage another six thousand francs on a note from a perfumer,' said Europe.

'Oh,' said he with a shake of the head, 'go gently, from one concession to another. Nucingen's arm is caught in the machine, we want his head. Beyond all that, I need five hundred thousand francs.'

'You'll get them,' Europe answered. 'Madame will soften towards this great imbecile at round about six hundred thousand, and she'll ask four hundred more to love him properly.'

'Listen to this, my girl,' said Carlos. 'The day I lay my hand on the last hundred thousand francs, there'll be twenty thousand for you.'

'What use will that be to me?' said Europe throwing her arms out as one to whom life seems impossible.

'You'd be able to go back to Valenciennes, buy a fine establishment, and become an honest woman, if you wanted; you find people with every kind of taste, that's what Paccard dreams of; there's nothing hanging over him, even his conscience is fairly easy, you could arrange yourselves,' replied Carlos.

'Go back to Valenciennes! ... What are you thinking of, sir?' cried Europe with a frightened air.

Born at Valenciennes the daughter of poor weavers, Europe was sent at the age of seven into a spinning-mill where modern Industry had made too great demands upon her physical strength, and Vice had depraved her too early. Corrupted at twelve, a mother at thirteen, she found herself in the company of the most deeply degraded creatures. In connection with a murder, she had appeared, as a witness, at the Assizes. Being then sixteen, she had retained a shred of truthfulness, and moreover was afraid of the Law, and it was her evidence which sentenced the accused to twenty years' hard labour. The criminal, one of those old offenders in whose constitution the instinct of vengeance is strong, had said in open court to the child: 'In ten years, as if it were now, Prudence' (Europe was called Prudence Servien), 'I shall come back and *bury* you, if I'm *sliced* for it.' The chairman of the Court did his best to reassure Prudence Servien by promising her the support, the interest of the Law; but the poor child was struck down with so profound a terror that she fell ill and remained almost a year in hospital. The Law is a rational entity represented by a collection of individuals endlessly replaced, whose good intentions and whose memories are, like themselves, itinerant. The magistracy in its diverse functions can do nothing to prevent crime, but is constituted only to deal with cases as they arise. A police force entirely devoted to prevention would be a great boon to a country; but the very word 'police' makes legislators nervous, so that they fail to distinguish between the terms 'govern', 'administer', 'make laws'. The legislator tends to absorb everything into the State, as though it were capable of action. The convict is thinking all the time of his victim and his revenge, while the Law no longer gives either a thought. Prudence, who knew her danger instinctively, if darkly, left Valenciennes, and at seventeen came to Paris to hide. She plied four trades there, the best of them playing walking-on parts at a little theatre. She met Paccard, and told him her troubles. Paccard, Jacques Collin's devoted follower and henchman, spoke of Prudence to his master; and when the master needed a slave, he said to Prudence: 'If you're willing to serve me as one might serve the devil, I'll rid you of Durut.' Durut was the convict, the sword of Damocles hanging over Prudence Servien's head. Without these details, Europe's attachment might strike some people as fantastic. Nobody can have known what theatrical stroke Carlos was to prepare.

'Yes, my child, you can go back to Valenciennes . . . Look, read this.' And he handed her the previous day's newspaper pointing with his finger at the following item: TOULON.

The execution of Jean-François Durut took place yesterday ...
From early morning, the garrison, etc.

Prudence dropped the paper; her knees gave way beneath the weight of her body; her life was renewed, for she hadn't, she said, known the taste of bread since Durut's threat.

'You see, I kept my word. It took four years to make Durut's head roll by drawing him into a trap ... Well, finish the job for me here, you'll find yourself running your own little business near where you were born, with twenty thousand francs and married to Paccard, to whom I grant virtue as a pension.'

Europe picked the newspaper up, and with eager eyes read all the details which for twenty years newspapers have never tired of giving about the execution of convicts: the imposing spectacle, the chaplain who always converted the condemned man, the habitual criminal who exhorts his former colleagues, the artillery ready to fire, the kneeling convicts; then the trite comments which change nothing in the running of the penitentiary, where eighteen thousand crimes swarm.

'We must get Asia back into the household,' said Carlos.

Asia came forward, understanding nothing of Europe's pantomime.

'To install her as cook here again, you'll begin by serving the baron a dinner such as he's never eaten before,' he went on; 'then you'll tell him that Asia has lost her money gambling and is back in service. We shan't need a porter: Paccard will be coachman; coachmen stay on their boxes where they can hardly be seen; agents won't spot him there. Madame will set him up with a powdered wig, a three-cornered hat in thick felt with gold braid; that'll change him, besides I'll make up his face.'

'Are we going to have servants with us?' said Asia squinting.

'We shall have honest folk,' replied Carlos.

'All feeble-minded!' was the mulatto's comment.

'If the baron takes a house, Paccard has a friend who can be caretaker,' Carlos continued. 'All we shall need then will be a footman and a kitchen maid, you can manage two people we don't know ...'

Just as Carlos was leaving, Paccard appeared.

'Wait, there are people in the street,' he said.

This simple statement was disturbing. Carlos went up to Europe's room, and stayed there until Paccard came for him with a hired carriage which was brought into the yard. Carlos lowered the blinds and was driven out at a speed to discourage any pursuit. Reaching the Faubourg Saint Antoine, he alighted some little distance from a cab rank which he approached on foot, and thus returned to the Quai Malaquais without meeting inquisitive glances.

'Look, child,' he said to Lucien showing him four hundred thousand-franc notes, 'this, I hope, will do on account towards the price of the Rubempré estate. We'll chance a hundred thousand elsewhere. They've launched these Omnibuses, it's a novelty the Parisians will take to, in three months we shall treble our capital. I know how to handle it: they'll pay a handsome dividend, to make the shares seem attractive at the outset, and build things up fast. It's an idea Nucingen's started up again. Taking over the Rubempré estate, we shan't pay cash down immediately. You'd better go and see des Lupeaulx, and ask him to recommend you personally to a solicitor called Desroches, a sharp rogue whom you'll go to see in his office; tell him to go to Rubempré, and value the land, and you can promise him twenty thousand francs over and above his fee if he can buy eight hundred thousand francs worth round the castle ruins, and guarantee you thirty thousand annual income.'

'You go too fast! . . . Too fast! too fast! . . .'

'At least I move. Let's not joke about this. Go and put a hundred thousand crowns into Treasury bonds, so as to begin drawing interest; you can leave them with Desroches, he's sly but honest . . . Then go to Angoulême, persuade your sister and your brother-in-law to tell a little white lie. Your relations can say they gave you six hundred thousand francs to facilitate your marriage with Clotilde de Grandlieu, no disgrace in that.'

'We're saved!' cried Lucien dazzled.

'You, yes!' Carlos went on; 'but only when you walk out of Saint Thomas Aquinas with Clotilde on your arm . . .'

'What are you afraid of?' said Lucien apparently full of concern for his mentor.

'I'm being watched . . . I must seem like a real priest, and that is very tedious! The devil won't look after me any longer, when he sees me with a breviary under my arm.'

At that moment, Baron Nucingen, helped along by his cashier, reached home.

Profit and loss

'I AM afrait,' said he as they went in, 'zet I héf mate a pad pargain . . . Och, ve shell recover oll . . .'

'Vot iss unvortunade iss zet Mennesier le Paron teglared himzelv,' replied the worthy German concerned only with decorum.

'Yo, my ecknowledged misdress shoult pe in a bosition vorthy off me,' replied the Louis XIV of the counting house.

Sure of having Esther sooner or later, the baron once more became the great financier he was. He again took up the direction of his affairs with so much zest that his cashier, finding him next day, at six o'clock, in his study, checking various securities, rubbed his hands.

'Tecitetly, Mennesier le Paron mate egonomies turing ze night,' he said with a German smile, half cunning, half stupid.

If those who are rich as Baron Nucingen was rich have more opportunities than other people of losing money, they also have more opportunities of gaining it, even while they abandon themselves to their follies. The financial policy of the famous House of Nucingen must be studied elsewhere, but we may point out here that fortunes of that size are not acquired, are not built up, augmented, maintained, amid the commercial, political and industrial revolutions of their time, without enormous losses of capital, or, if you like, levies taken on the fortunes of individuals. Not many new securities are created in the common treasury of the globe. Every corner made represents a new inequality in the general distribution of wealth. What the State demands, it gives back; but what a House of Nucingen takes, it keeps. When it stabs somebody in the back, there are no legal consequences, for the same reason as Frederick II would have been a Jacques Collin, a Mandrin, if, instead of operating on whole provinces by means of battles, he had worked at smuggling or in liquid assets. Forcing the states of Europe to borrow at twenty or ten per cent, making up this ten or twenty per cent from public funds, holding whole industries to ransom by monopolizing raw materials, throwing a line to some large speculator to pull him out of the water while one recovers his drowned enterprise, such pecuniary warfare constitutes the high politics of money. True, for the banker, as for the conqueror, there are risks to be faced; but there are so few people in a position to take part in such contests that the sheep are unaware of what is happening. These great things take place among the shepherds. When people are *hammered*, to use the jargon of the Stock Exchange, it is because they were guilty of wanting to make too much too quickly, and few of us care much what situations a Nucingen or two may bring about. A speculator blowing his brains out, a stockbroker fleeing the country, a notary making off with the savings of a hundred families, which is far worse than homicide; a banker going into liquidation; such catastrophes are forgotten within a few months in Paris and overlaid by the tidal movements of the great city. The huge fortunes of those like Jacques Coeur, the Medici, the Angots of Dieppe, the Auffredi of La Rochelle, the Fuggers, the Tiepolos, the Corners, were at one time acquired without question through privileges due to mass ignorance of the source of all those precious commodities; but, nowadays, geographical knowledge is so widespread, and competition has so narrowed margins of profit, that any quickly made fortune must be either the effect of chance or lucky discovery, or the result of a legal theft. Corrupted by scandalous examples, petty commerce has, in recent years, copied all that is worst in the trading practice of its betters, and vilely contaminated raw materials. Wherever chemistry is practised, what we drink is no longer wine; so viticulture declines. Artificial salt is sold to avoid taxation. The courts are appalled by this general lack of probity. French trade practice is suspect in the eyes of the world, and England has become equally demoralized. The Charter has proclaimed the reign of money, success justifies all in an atheistical age. Thus corruption at the highest levels, despite financially dazzling results and specious self-justification, has become more ignoble than the merely personal corruptness which flourishes elsewhere and provides elements of comic relief, not it is true of the pleasantest, on this great Stage. The Government, afraid of all new thought, has banished from the theatre proper all comedy which reflects the life of today. The Middle Class, less liberal in its views than Louis XIV, trembles at the thought of seeing its own *Marriage of Figaro*, bans any political Tartuffe from the boards, and, certainly, would no longer license *Turcaret*, for Turcaret now is our lord and sovereign. Henceforward, the comic genius must become a story-teller, and the Book is the poet's less rapid but surer weapon.

All that morning, amid the comings and goings, the interviews, the issuing of orders, the five-minute conferences, which make Nucingen's office a great financial Waiting Room, one of his brokers told him of the disappearance of a member of the Company, one of its cleverest and richest members, Jacques Falleix, brother of Martin Falleix, and successor to Jules Desmarets. Jacques Falleix was the accredited Broker of the Maison Nucingen. In concert with du Tillet and the Kellers, the baron had as coldly brought about this man's ruin as though it had been a matter of killing a sheep for Easter.

'Hiss nerf gafe vay,' the baron calmly replied.

Jacques Falleix had rendered great service in the stock-jobbing field. In a crisis, a few months earlier, he had *saved the situation* by bold dealing. But to expect gratitude from Sharks is like hoping to soften the hearts of the wolves of Ukraine in winter.

'Poor man!' said the dealer, 'he so little expected this outcome that he'd furnished, in the rue Saint Georges, a little house for his mistress; he'd spent a hundred and fifty thousand francs on decorations and furniture. He was so much in love with Madame du Val-Noble! ... Now the woman simply has to get out ... Nothing's paid for.'

'*Gut, gut!*' thought Nucingen, 'zis is how I make up lest night's losses ... It iss oll unbait vor?' he asked the stock-dealer.

'Why, yes!' the broker replied, 'what uninformed furnisher would not have given Jacques Falleix credit? The cellar, it seems, is first-rate. And, by the way, the house is for sale, he was going to buy it. The lease is in his name. How stupid! Silver, furniture, wine, carriage, horses, it all becomes a job lot, and what will the creditors get out of that?'

'Tomorrow you come,' said Nucingen, 'I shell hef been to see oll zet, end if zere iss no proceedings in pankruptcy, if oll iss to pe arrenged in friendly menner, you shell offer a reasson-aple brice for ze furnishings, *und* tek on ze lease . . .'

'There won't be any trouble about that,' said the stock-broker. 'Go round this morning, you'll find one of Falleix's friends with the contractors, who want a preferential claim; but the Val-Noble has all their invoices in Falleix's name.'

Baron Nucingen at once sent a clerk round to his notary, Jacques Falleix had told him about the house, which cost at most sixty thousand francs, and he wanted to become its owner at once, so as to enjoy a preferential claim by reason of tenancy.

The cashier (worthy man!) wanted to know if his master would lose anything by Falleix's bankruptcy.

'On ze gontrary, my dear Wolfgang, I shell mek a *hundert tausend* vrancs.'

'No! how so?'

'Well! I shell hef ze little house zis poor toffle Falleix hes been gedding ready for hiss misdress since a year. I shell hef oll by offering fifty *tausend* vrancs to ze greditors, *und* Meister Gartot, my notary, will hef my orders for ze house, for ze owner iss in tiffiguldies . . . I knew oll zet, pud I wassn't sinking. Soon my tivine Esder will be lifing in a liddle balace . . . I owe zet to Falleix: it iss a dreasure, *und* shust rount ze corner from here . . . Oll zet fits me like a clove.'

Falleix's insolvency compelled the baron to go to the Stock Exchange; but he found it impossible to leave the rue Saint Lazare without passing by the rue Taitbout; he already suf-fered from having been several hours away from Esther, he wanted her by his side. The profit to which he counted on putting his stockbroker's spoils made the loss of the four hundred thousand francs already paid out seem excessively easy to bear. Delighted at the thought of announcing to his *enchel* her imminent translation from the rue Taitbout to the rue Saint Georges, where she would be living in a *smoll balace*, where memories would not longer stand in the way of their happiness, he found the paving stones grateful to his feet, he walked like a young man in a young man's dream. At the corner of the rue des Trois Frères, in mid-dream and mid-pavement, the baron saw Europe coming towards him, looking very upset.

'Are going where?' he asked.

'Oh, sir, I was on my way to see you . . . You were right yesterday! I can see now that my poor lady would have done well to let herself be taken to prison for a few days. But do you expect women to know anything about finance? . . . As soon as my lady's creditors knew she was back at home, they came at us like a pack of hounds . . . Yesterday, at seven o'clock in the evening, sir, they pasted up awful bills advertising the sale of her furniture on Saturday . . . But that's nothing . . . My lady's all heart, and once upon a time she tried to oblige that monster of a man, you know!'

'Vhich monsder?'

'Oh, well, the one she loved, you know, d'Estourny, oh, he was charming. He gambled, that's all.'

'He blayed *mit* marked garts . . .'

'Well, what about you? . . .' said Europe, 'what do you do at the Stock Exchange? But let me go on. One day, to stop Georges blowing his brains out as he said he would, she took all her silver and jewels, still not paid for, to the pawnshop. As soon as they learned she'd *advanced* something to one creditor, all the others started making a fuss . . . She was threatened with a court of summary jurisdiction . . . Your angel in that dock! . . . wouldn't it make a wig stand up on your head? . . . She burst into tears, she speaks of going and throwing herself in the river . . . She'll do it, too!'

'If I com' to zee you, I shell never get to 'Chenge!' cried Nucingen. '*Und* I most go zere, for zen I vin somesing for her . . . Go and galm her: I vill bay her tebts, I vill go see her at vour o'clock. But, Eugénie, tell her to luf me a liddle . . .'

'A little, sir, nay, a lot! ... Look, sir, there's nothing like generosity for winning a woman's heart ... Certainly, you might have saved a hundred thousand francs by letting her go to prison, but you'd never have had her heart then ... As she said to me, "Eugénie," she said, "he's been so great, so splendid ... He has a noble mind!"'

'Tit she zay zat, Eugénie?' exclaimed the baron.

'Yes, indeed, sir, she said it to me.'

'Ah, look, here are den louis ...'

'Thanks, I'm sure ... But she's weeping at this moment, since yesterday she's wept as much as Mary Magdalene wept in a month ... The one you love is in despair, over debts that aren't even her own! Oh, men! they sponge on women just as women do on old men ... just think!'

'Zey are oll ze same! ... Gommitting zemselves! ... Ah, one most never gommit oneself ... She most never zign anysing again. I vill pay, but if she ever zign her nem again ... I ...'

'Yes, what will you do?' said Europe firmly.

'*Mein Gott!* I hef no gontrol ofer her ... I most tek charge of her affairs ... Horry, horry, gonsole her, and dell her zat in a mont' she vill pe lifing in a balace.'

'Monsieur le Baron, your investments will bear great interest in a woman's heart! Look ... I can see you are rejuvenated, I'm only a lady's maid, I know, but I've often seen the same thing, ... it is happiness, ... happiness reflects itself ... If you're a bit out-of-pocket, don't worry, ... it'll be made up to you. First, as I was saying to my lady: she'd be the lowest of the low, *a common tart*, if she didn't love you, for you're raising her out of hell ... Once she's got rid of her worries, you'll see. Between ourselves, I can tell you, the night she wept so hard ... What do you expect? ... you've got to earn the respect of a man who's going to keep you, ... she didn't dare tell you all that, ... she meant to run away.'

'Run avay!' cried the baron startled by this idea. 'But I most go on to ze Stock Exchange. Go beck, I vill not com' in ... But I vould like to zee her at ze vindow, ... ze sight off her vill gif me gourage ...'

Esther smiled at Monsieur de Nucingen as he passed before

the house, and he clumped heavily away saying to himself:
'She iss *ein Engel*! 'This is how Europe had set herself about
producing such an unexpected result.

Necessary explanations

AT about half past two, Esther had finished dressing as she
would when she was awaiting Lucien, she looked exquisite;
seeing her thus, Prudence said to her, looking out of the
window: 'There he is!' The poor girl rushed to the window,
expecting to see Lucien, and saw Nucingen.

'Oh, how could you do that to me!' she said.

'It was the only way I could make you look as though you
were paying attention to a poor old man who's going to pay
your debts,' replied Europe, 'for they are all going to be paid.'

'What debts?' cried the creature whose only thought was
to regain her love driven away from her by dreadful hands.

'Those that Monsieur Carlos made on Madame's behalf.'

'But look! there are nearly four hundred and fifty thousand
francs here!' cried Esther.

'And there's still a hundred and fifty thousand; but he took
it all very well, the baron ... He's going to get you out of
here and install you in *ein smoll balace* ... Lord! some people
are lucky! ... In your place, since you've got that man at your
finger-ends, once you've satisfied Carlos, I'd see I had a house
and an income. Madame is certainly the most beautiful woman
I've seen, and the most captivating, but looks don't last! I was
fresh and pretty once, and look at me now. I'm twenty-three,
just about Madame's age, and I look ten years older ... One
illness does it ... Ah, well, if you've got a house in Paris and a
fixed income, you don't have to be afraid of ending up in the
street ...'

Esther was no longer listening to Europe-Eugénie-Prudence
Servien. The will of a man endowed with the genius of corruption had again sunk Esther in the mire with as much force as he
had employed in once raising her from it. Those who know the
infinitude of love understand that its pleasures and its virtues

must be experienced together. Since the scene in her hovel in the rue de Langlade, Esther had totally forgotten her former life. She had continued to live virtuously, cloistered in her passion. Thus, in order to avoid meeting with any obstacle, the wily corruptor had so prepared all that the poor wench, impelled by her devotion, could only assent to knaveries already consummated or about to be so. Revealing as it does the superiority of his guile, the corruptor's way of proceeding in this matter shows also by what means he had subjugated Lucien. The method is to engineer dreadful needs, to dig the mine, fill it with powder, and, at the critical moment, say to your accomplice: 'Just nod, and everything goes up!' Imbued with the morality peculiar to harlots, Esther had once found it natural to exact flattering tribute and judged her rivals purely by what they could get a man to spend. Ruined fortunes are the long-service stripes of these creatures. Counting on Esther's memories, Carlos was not mistaken. Such stratagems of war, such tactics a thousand times employed, not only by women but by spendthrift males, didn't trouble Esther's mind. The poor tart only felt her degradation. She was in love with Lucien, she was becoming the acknowledged mistress of Baron Nucingen: that was the only truth which affected her. That the sham Spaniard should take the money left as a deposit, that Lucien should build the edifice of his fortune with stones from Esther's tomb, that one night of pleasure should cost the old banker so many thousand francs more or less, that Europe should more or less ingeniously take her few hundred francs' pickings out of these, nothing of all that concerned this whore in love; but such was the canker which gnawed at her heart. For five years past she had seen herself white as an angel! She was in love, she was happy, she hadn't committed the least infidelity. That beautiful, pure love was to be defiled. It was not her mind which contrasted the fine, secret life with the vile life to come. It was a matter neither of calculation nor of lyricism, she simply felt undefinedly but with great force that her white was turned to black; pure to impure; noble to ignominious. Ermine to herself by force of will, she could not endure any thought of moral defilement. And so when the baron had threatened her with his love, the idea of throwing herself from the window had come to her mind. Lucien was in fact loved absolutely, and as women very rarely love a man. Women who say that they love, who often believe that they love exceptionally, dance, waltz, flirt with other men, dress for social occasions, at which they look for a harvest of covetous glances; but Esther, without regarding it as a sacrifice, had performed miracles of true love. She had loved Lucien for six years with the love of actresses and courtesans who, having wallowed in mud and impurity, thirst after the nobility, the devotion of real love in all its *exclusiveness* (the word is needed for something so little put into practice). The vanished peoples of Greece, Rome and the nations of the East always shut their women away, the woman who loves ought to sequester herself. It is therefore easily understood that, emerging from the palace of the imagination in which that festival, that poem had been consummated, for the *smoll balace* of a chilly old man, Esther fell prey to a kind of moral sickness. Impelled by a hand of iron, she had found herself up to the waist in infamy without time to reflect; but for two days past she had reflected and felt a mortal chill at heart.

At the words: 'ending up in the street' she rose abruptly and said: 'End up in the street? . . . no, rather end up in the Seine . . .'

'In the Seine? . . . What about Monsieur Lucien? . . .' said Europe.

The name by itself caused Esther to sit down again on a chair, from which she gazed at a rosette in the pattern of the carpet, the tears melting inside her skull. At four o'clock, Nucingen found his angel deep in that ocean of reflections, of resolutions, upon which the female mind floats and from which it emerges speaking words incomprehensible to those not of the convoy.

'Zdop vrowning, . . . my peautiful,' said the baron sitting beside her. 'You shell hef no more tebts . . . I vill arrendge tings *mit* Eugénie, *und* in von mont' you will leaf zis apardment *und* moof into a smoll balace . . . Oh, vot a priddy hant. Let me kizz it.' (Esther allowed him to take her hand as a dog might stretch out its paw.) 'Ah, you gif de hant, but not de heart, . . . and iss ze heart I vish . . .'

This was said with such an accent of truth, that poor Esther turned her eyes upon the old man with an expression of pity which robbed him of his wits. Lovers and saints feel like brothers in martyrdom! Nothing in the world creates so much understanding as shared pain.

'Poor man!' she said, 'he is in love.'

Hearing the word, but not understanding its use, the baron turned pale, the blood danced in his veins, he breathed the air of paradise. At his age millionaires pay as much for sensations of that kind as a woman cares to ask for.

'I lof you as I lof my daughder, . . .' he said, 'and I feel it dere'; he continued placing his hand on his heart, 'zet I con only pear to zee you hoppy.'

'If you were willing only to be my father, I should love you dearly, I should never leave you, and you would see that I am not a wicked or a venal or a calculating woman, as you must think me now . . .'

'You hef done silly tings,' the baron went on, 'like oll priddy womans, det is oll. Let us not tok about zem. Our jop now is to mek moneys for you . . . Be hoppy: I vill be your vather for a tay or dwo, I onnderstent dot you muzd begome used to my poor gargass.'

'Truly! . . .' she exclaimed getting up and throwing herself on Nucingen's knees, putting her arm about his neck and pressing herself to him.

'Druly,' he replied forcing his face into a smile.

She kissed his forehead, she was ready to believe the impossible: that she could remain pure, and see Lucien . . . She wheedled the baron with so much skill that the former Torpedo reappeared in her. She bewitched the old man, who promised to be her father for forty days. Those forty days were needed for the purchase and setting in order of the house in the rue Saint Georges. Once in the street, and on his way home, the baron said to himself: 'I em a vool!' The fact was that, although he may have behaved like a child in Esther's presence, the moment he was away from her he resumed his Shark's skin, just as Regnard's Gambler falls in love with Angélique again as soon as he hasn't a bean.

'Ha'f a million, and not yet efen gaught zight off her legs.

it is too zilly; luggily nopody vill know,' he was saying twenty days later. And he firmly resolved to put up with no more nonsense from a woman for whom he had paid out so much good money; then, when he was with Esther again, he spent all the time he could afford to spend with her in making up for the first moment of brutal approach. 'I gannot,' he was telling himself by the end of a month, 'pe de Edernal Vather.'

Two great loves in conflict

TOWARDS the end of December 1829, on the eve of installing Esther in the house in the rue Saint Georges, the baron begged du Tillet to take Florine there to see that everything was in keeping with the Nucingen fortune, to make sure that the expression a *smoll balace* had been justified by the craftsmen who had been commissioned to make the aviary worthy of its bird. All the devices of luxury as it was known before the revolution of 1830 had made the house a prototype of good taste. The architect Grindot's decorative gifts had achieved a masterpiece. The new marble staircase, the mouldings, the materials, the discreetly applied gilding, the smallest details as well as the large effects surpassed anything of the same order that the century of Louis XV had left in Paris.

'That is my dream: that and virtue!' said Florine with a smile. 'And all this expense is for whom?' she asked Nucingen. 'Some virgin just fallen from the skies?'

'Iss a woman who must go back zere,' replied the baron.

'A way of playing Jupiter,' the actress continued. 'And when are we to see her?'

'Oh, the day of the house-warming!' cried du Tillet.

'Nod until den . . .' said the baron.

'Well, we shall have to get ourselves well and truly brushed up, turned out, positively inlaid,' added Florine. 'Oh, won't the women just be giving their dressmakers and hairdressers headaches that day! . . . When is it? . . .'

'I em not de master.'

'Well, there's a woman for you! . . .' Florine exclaimed. 'How I should like to see her! . . .'

'I also,' replied the baron artlessly.

'What! the house, the woman, the furnishings, all new!'

'Even the baron,' said du Tillet, 'for my old friend is looking very young.'

'We must get him down to twenty,' said Florine, 'if only for a moment.'

During the early days of 1830, everybody in Paris was talking of Nucingen's passion and the unbridled luxury of his house. Talked about everywhere and made constant fun of, the poor baron reacted violently in a manner which may be easily understood and joined the determination of a financier to the passion raging in his heart. At the house-warming he proposed to cast off his part as a kindly father and touch the reward of so much sacrifice. Too easily numbed by the Torpedo, he resolved to deal with this marriage question by correspondence, and so get agreement signed and sealed. Bankers only believe in firm bills of exchange. And so, one fine morning in the New Year, the Shark rose early, went to his office and composed the following letter, written in good French; for if he spoke it badly, there was nothing wrong with his spelling.

Dear Esther, flower of my thoughts and sole happiness of my life, when I told you that I loved you as I love my daughter, I deceived both you and myself. I meant thus simply to express to you the sanctity of my feelings, so different from those which men commonly experience, first because I am old and secondly because I had never loved. I love you so much that, if you cost me my whole fortune, I should not therefore love you less. Be just! Few men would have seen in you, as I did, an angel: I have never cast eyes on your past. I love you at one and the same time as I love my daughter Augusta, who is my only child, and as I should love my wife if my wife had been capable of loving me. If happiness alone can absolve an old man in love, ask yourself whether I am not playing an absurd part. I have made you the joy, the consolation of my declining years. You know very well that, as long as I live, you will live in as much contentment as a woman could hope for, and you must also know well that after my death you will be rich enough for your good fortune to be the envy of other women. Since I first had the pleasure of speaking to you, you have had your share in all the business I did, and you have an account at the House of Nucingen. Within a matter of days, you will occupy a house which, sooner or later, will be yours, if you like it. Will it indeed be as a father that I visit you there, or shall I at last be made happy? . . . Forgive me for writing to you so plainly; but when I am with you, I lack courage, and I am too much aware of you as mistress. It is not my wish to offend you, I simply want to let you know how much I suffer and how cruel it is at my age to wait, when each day deprives me of hope and pleasure. The delicacy of my behaviour is a warrant of the sincerity of my intentions. Have I ever acted as though I were a creditor? You are like a citadel, and I am not a young man. To my complaints you reply that to you it is a matter of life and death, and you make me believe it while I am listening to you; but at home I become a prey to black mortification, to doubts which dishonour both you and me. You seemed to me as kind, as frank as you were beautiful; but now you seem bent on destroying my conviction. Judge for yourself! You tell me that your heart nourishes a passion, a pitiless passion, and yet you refuse to tell me the name of the one you love . . . Is that natural? You have turned a man not without strength into a man of incredible weakness . . . See to what a pass you have brought me! after five months I am compelled to ask you what future there is for my passion? I must know what part I am to play when you are installed in your house. Money means nothing to me where you are concerned; I am not foolish enough to think that such a contempt for money will impress you; but if my love is boundless, there is a limit to my fortune, which I respect only for your sake. Well! if by giving you everything I possess I could, then poor, gain your affection, I would rather be poor and loved by you than rich and despised. You have wrought such a change in me, my dear Esther, that nobody knows me any longer: I paid ten thousand francs for a picture by Joseph Bridau, because you told me that he was a gifted painter and neglected. To all the poor I meet I give five francs in your name. Well! this poor old man, who considers himself your debtor when you do him the honour of accepting anything from him, what is it he asks? . . . All he wants is a single hope, though what a hope it is, dear God! a certainty, rather, of receiving from you only what my passion exacts. The flame in my heart will itself help you to deceive me cruelly. I am ready to submit to all the conditions you impose on my happiness, my infrequent pleasures; but, at least, tell me that the day you take possession of your house, you will accept the heart and the devotion of one who inscribes himself, till the end of his days,

> Your slave,
> FRÉDÉRIC DE NUCINGEN.

'Christ, the old money-bags, what a bore he is!' exclaimed Esther, all harlot again.

She took writing paper and wrote, in letters as big as the paper would hold, the famous Scribe phrase, now proverbial: *You can have my teddy bear.*

A quarter of an hour later, Esther remorsefully wrote the letter which follows:

MONSIEUR LE BARON,

Please pay no attention to the letter you've just received from me, I wrote as though I'd returned to the madness of my early life; so forgive a wretched girl who ought to see herself as a slave. I have never so deeply felt the degradation of my state as since the day I was abandoned to you. You have paid, I am the debt. Nothing is more sacred than debts of dishonour. I have no right to *clear myself* by jumping in the Seine. A debt can always be paid in this dreadful currency valid only on one side: I therefore await your commands. I am willing to pay in one night every penny mortgaged on that fatal moment, and I have no doubt that an hour of me is worth millions, since it will be the last, the only hour. After that, my account will be straight, and I can give up my life. An honest woman may rise again after a fall; but, those like me, we have fallen too low. My decision is so finally taken that I shall beg you to keep this letter as evidence of the cause of death of her who signs herself for one day,

> Your servant,
> ESTHER.

Having sent this letter off, Esther regretted it. Ten minutes later, she wrote a third, as follows:

Pardon, dear baron, it is me again. I did not mean either to make fun of you or to hurt you; I only meant you to ponder this simple piece of reasoning: if we stay as father and daughter to each other, your pleasure will be slight, but it will last; if you insist on the contract being fulfilled, you will have me to grieve for. I won't vex you any further: the day on which you choose pleasure instead of happiness will have no tomorrow for me.

> Your daughter,
> ESTHER.

At the first letter, the baron fell into one of those cold furies which may prove fatal to millionaires, he looked at himself in the glass, he rang. 'A voot path! . . .' he called to his new manservant. While he was taking his foot bath, the second letter arrived, he read it, and fell unconscious. The millionaire was carried to his bed. When the financier recovered consciousness, Madame de Nucingen was sitting at the foot of the bed.

'The wench is right!' she said, 'what makes you think you can buy love? . . . it isn't a commodity. Let's have a look at your letter?'

The baron gave her the various scribbled drafts he'd made, Madame de Nucingen read them smiling. The third letter arrived.

'This is a remarkable tart!' the baroness exclaimed when she'd read the last letter.

'Vot vill I do, Matame?' the baron asked his wife.

'Wait.'

'Vait!' he went on, 'de flesh iss veak . . .'

'Look, my dear,' said the baroness, 'you've been rather nice to me lately, I'll give you a bit of advice.'

'You are kind, I am krateful! . . .' he said. 'Run up tebts if you like, I bay dem . . .'

'The effect these letters had on you will touch a woman more than any amount of expenditure, or any letter, however movingly conceived; see that she learns about it indirectly, you may possess her! and . . . don't worry, it won't kill her,' she said examining her husband.

Madame de Nucingen did not understand the nature of a harlot.

Peace treaty between Asia and the House of Nucingen

'How indellichent Matame de Nucingen iss!' the baron said to himself, when his wife had left him. But the more the banker marvelled at the subtlety of the advice the baroness had just given him, the less was he able to see precisely how he should make use of it; and not only did he think himself stupid, he said so aloud.

The proverbial stupidity of money men is only relative, however. It is the same with our faculties of mind as it is with physical aptitude. The dancer's strength lies in his feet, the blacksmith's in his arms; the market porter exercises himself by carrying great weights, the singer toughens his larynx, and the pianist's wrist becomes strong. A banker is accustomed to weigh and balance different pieces of business and to set interests in motion, just as a writer of vaudevilles is trained in creating a situation and moving his characters about the stage. Conversational wit should no more be demanded of Baron Nucingen than poetic images of the understanding of a mathematician. In any age, how many poets are there who can write prose or who excel on social occasions like Madame de Cornuel? Buffon was dull, Newton never loved, Lord Byron loved hardly anyone but himself, Rousseau was gloomy and near madness, La Fontaine absent-minded. Equally distributed, human energy produces fools, or universal mediocrity; unequally, it gives rise to those incongruities we call *genius*, which, if they were discernible by the eye, would seem deformities. The same law governs the body: perfect beauty is almost invariably coupled with coldness or silliness. That Pascal should be at once a great geometer and a great writer, that Beaumarchais was a first-class businessman, Zamet a remarkable courtier; such rare exceptions only prove the rule of the specialization of intelligence. In the field of calculated speculation, the banker may deploy just as much skill, cleverness, subtlety and high qualities as a brilliant diplomat shows in the sphere of conflicting national interests. If a banker were still remarkable outside his office, he would be a great man. Nucingen multiplied by the Prince de Ligne, Mazarin or Diderot is not a likely human formula, and yet it has borne the names of Pericles, Aristotle, Voltaire and Napoleon. The rays of the imperial sun should not blind us to the qualities of the man, the Emperor also had charm, he was cultivated and witty. Monsieur de Nucingen, purely a banker, with no inventive capacity outside his calculations, like most bankers, believed only in the safe investment. In the matter of art, he had the good sense to seek out, money in hand, the recognized experts, engaging the best architect, the best surgeon, the man acknowledged to know most about pictures or statues, the smartest solicitor, once it was a matter of building a house, looking after his health, buying curiosities or an estate. But, as there are no accredited experts in intrigue or graduate masters of passion, a banker has little guidance when he's in love and cannot be expected to manage women. Nucingen could therefore think of nothing better to do than what he had done before: give money to some Frontin, male or female, to act or think in his place. Madame Saint Estève alone could put the baroness's plan into action. The banker bitterly regretted quarrelling with the odious old-clothes woman. Nevertheless, confident in the magnetic influence of his coffers and the soothing drugs dispensed by the Bank of France on the signed prescription of Garat, he rang for his manservant and told him to inquire, in the rue Neuve Saint Marc, for this horrible widow, asking her to call. In Paris, extremes meet by way of the passions. Vice indissolubly welds the rich to the poor, the great to the small. The Empress there consults Mademoiselle Lenormand. In every age, the great lord has his Cabaret Ramponneau.

The new manservant returned two hours later.

'Monsieur le Baron,' he said, 'Madame Saint-Estève has gone bankrupt.'

'Och, zat iss *gut*!' said the baron beaming, 'she iss in my hand!'

'The good woman is, it seems, given to gambling,' the manservant went on. 'Moreover, she is under the domination of a small-part actor from the outlying theatres, whom, for decency's sake, she passes off as her godson. It seems she's a first-rate cook, and she wants a place.'

'Dese toffles of suportinade cheniuses oll hef ten wayss off earning money, *und zwelf* wayss off zbending it,' the baron thought without realizing that Panurge had once thought something of the kind.

He sent the domestic off in search of Madame Saint-Estève who came next day. Questioned by Asia, the new valet told the female spy of the dreadful results of the letters written by the mistress of Monsieur le Baron.

'He really must be in love with that woman,' said the man-servant in conclusion, 'he nearly died. Me, I advised him not to try again, he'd only be diddled. A woman who's already cost Monsieur le Baron five hundred thousand francs,' he said, 'without counting what he's spent on the house in the rue Saint Georges! . . . But that woman wants money, nothing but money. As I was leaving the baron's, his wife said with a laugh: "If this goes on, that tart will leave me a widow."'

'Damn it!' replied Asia, 'we can't kill the hen that lays the golden eggs!'

'Monsieur le Baron's only hope lies in you,' said the valet.

'It's only natural, I know how to deal with women! . . .'

'Well, here we are, in you go,' said the manservant grovel-ling before her occult power.

'Well,' said the false Madame Saint-Estève entering the invalid's room with an obsequious manner, 'it seems that Monsieur le Baron has had a little disappointment? . . . Ah, well! everyone suffers from the same complaint. Even I've had my troubles. Within two months the wheel of fortune's turned oddly for me! here I am wanting a place . . . Neither of us was very sensible. If Monsieur le Baron cared to place me as cook at Madame Esther's, he'd find me the most devoted of the devoted, and I should be very useful to him in keeping an eye on Eugénie and Madame.'

'Iss not a qvestion of det,' said the baron. 'I em nod yed de masder, end I em dreated like . . .'

'A top,' Asia went on. 'You've made other people spin, Daddy, and now the child's got the whip . . . Well, God is just, you can't deny that!'

'"Chust"?' said the baron. 'I tit not pring you here to hear you moralize . . .'

'Oh, go on, my child, a bit of morality does nobody any harm. It's the salt of life to people like me, just as vice is to the pious. Look now, were you generous? Did you pay her debts? . . .'

'Yo!' said the baron piteously.

'Good. And you cleared her belongings, even better; but

let's face it! . . . that isn't enough: it'll keep her warm, but, you know, the creatures like to have money to *burn* . . .'

'I em brebaring for her a zurbrise, rue Saint Georges . . . She knowss, . . .' said the baron. 'Pud I ton'd vish to be a vool.'

'Well, leave her! . . .'

'I em avrait she let me,' exclaimed the baron.

'And we want something for our money, eh, my boy?' replied Asia. 'Well, listen. It was the public we bilked of these millions, my child! You're suppose to have twenty-five.' (The baron couldn't repress a smile.) 'Well, you'd better resign yourself to the loss of one . . .'

'I vould lose von glatly,' answered the baron, 'but I vill hef no sooner lose it dan a secont iss esk.'

'Yes, I see that,' replied Asia, 'you don't want to say B, for fear you'll have to go as far as Z. Esther is an honest girl, all the same . . .'

'Yo, iss honest!' exclaimed the banker; 'iss villing seddle, ass you bay a tebt.'

'She doesn't want to be your mistress, she feels repugnance. Well, that's likely enough, the child has always had a mind of her own. When you've only known nice young people, you don't think much of an old man . . . You're no beauty, you're fat like Louis XVIII, and a bit of a numskull, like everybody who plays about with money instead of women. Well, if you don't mind another six hundred thousand francs,' said Asia, 'I'll undertake to see she becomes just what you want her to be.'

'Six *hundert tausend* vrancs! . . .' cried the baron with a start. 'Esder is gosting me a million already! . . .'

'Happiness is well worth six*teen* hundred thousand francs, you old fraud. You certainly know men, these days, who've swallowed up more than a million or two with their mistresses. I know women who've even cost men their lives, men who've spilt their heads into a basket . . . You know that doctor who poisoned his friend? . . . he wanted the money to please a woman.'

'Yo, yo, put if I em in luf I em not a vool, not in zis, at least, for vhen I zee her, I vould gif her pordvolio . . .'

'Listen, Monsieur le Baron,' said Asia taking up a Semiramis pose, 'you've been swindled enough like that. As true as I'm called Saint-Estève, at any rate professionally, I'm on your side.'

'*Gut!* . . . I vill revard you.'

'I should hope so, for I made it plain I knew how to take my revenge. Besides, you know, Daddy,' she said casting him a glance to make the blood run cold, 'I have the means to whistle Madame Esther away from you just as I'd snuff out a candle. And I know my woman! When the little trollop has made you happy, she'll be even more necessary to you than she is at this moment. You paid me well, you needed your ears pulling, but in the end you settled! Me, I kept my part of the bargain, didn't I? Well, then, look, I'll make you a new offer.'

'Vot iss?'

'You install me with Madame as cook, you take me on for ten years, I get a thousand francs wages, you pay the last five years in advance (just a gratuity, eh?). Once I'm there on the spot, I shall be able to persuade Madame to make the following concessions. For example, you get her a lovely dress sent round by Madame Auguste, who knows Madame's tastes and little ways, and you give orders for the new equipage to be at the door at four o'clock. You call in on your way home from the Bourse, and you take her for a little run in the Bois de Boulogne. So then this woman has proclaimed herself your mistress, she's committed in the sight and knowledge of all Paris . . . A hundred thousand francs . . . You'll dine with her (I know how to lay out dinners of that kind); you take her to the theatre, to the Variétés, in a box, and all Paris then says: "Look, there's that old swindler Nucingen with his mistress . . ." That flatters both you and her, yes? And all these advantages, as I'm an honest woman, you get for the hundred thousand francs . . . At the end of a week, if you keep it up, you'll have made headway.'

'I shell hef bait out *hundert tausend* vrancs . . .'

'The second week,' continued Asia without appearing to have heard this piteous expression, 'Madame will make up her mind, urged on by these preliminaries, to leave her little apartment and settle into the house you're offering her. Your

Esther has caught a glimpse of society again, she's met her old friends, she'll want to cut a figure, she'll do the honours in her little palace! It stands to reason ... Another hundred thousand francs! And there you are, you're at home. Esther is compromised, ... she belongs to you. That leaves only one trifle, though you think it's the main thing, you old elephant! (Oh, the fat monster, that makes him open his eyes!) I'll see to that ... Four hundred thousand ... But that lot, my love, you don't pay up till next day ... How's that for honesty, eh? ... I trust you more than you trust me. If I can persuade Madame to appear in public as your mistress, to compromise herself, to take everything you offer, this very day may be, then perhaps you'll believe I can lead her to yield up the pass to the Great Saint Bernard. It isn't easy, mind you! ... To get your artillery through, it'll be as hard pulling as it was for the First Consul over the Alps.'

'Vot for so?'

'Her heart is full of love, *razibus*, as you say, you people who know Latin,' Asia went on. 'She thinks she's the Queen of Sheba because she's been washed in the sacrifices she's made for her lover, ... a notion women like that do stuff their heads with! Ah, my little one, let's be fair, it's a beautiful thought! The joker'd die of grief at belonging to you, I shouldn't wonder; only, what I find reassuring, personally, and I tell you this to encourage you, is, there's a good bit of the tart in her still, that one.'

'You hef,' said the baron who had listened to Asia in deep silence and with admiration, 'ze chenius off gorruption, es I hef zet for panking.'

'Just as you say, my angel,' added Asia.

'Oll right for vifty *tausend* vrancs inzdeat of *hundert*! ... End I gif you vife *hundert tausend* de morning efter my driumph.'

'Well, I'll get to work,' replied Asia ... 'Ah, call when you like!' continued Asia with respect. 'MONSIEUR will already find MADAME as soft as a cat's back, and quite disposed to be agreeable to him.'

'*Gut, gut*,' said the banker rubbing his hands. And, having dismissed the frightful mulattress with a smile, he said to himself: 'How zenziple off me to hef a lot off money!'

And he sprang out of bed, went to his office and took up the management of his immense business, with a gay heart.

Abdication

NOTHING could have been more fatal to Esther than the path adopted by Nucingen. The poor harlot was defending her life in defending herself against infidelity. Carlos called this perfectly natural defence *squeamishness*. Not without taking the customary precautions, Asia went to inform Carlos of the discussion she had just had with the baron, and the use she'd put it to. Like himself, the man's anger was terrible; he at once took a carriage, the blinds down, to Esther's, driving into the yard. Still almost white when he went up, the double forger appeared before the poor wench; she looked at him, she was standing up, she fell on to a chair, her legs giving way.

'What's the matter, sir?' she asked him trembling through all her limbs.

'Leave us, Europe,' said he to the lady's maid.

Esther looked at the creature as a child might have looked at its mother, from whom a murderer was taking it away to kill.

'Do you know where you will be sending Lucien?' Carlos went on when he found himself alone with Esther.

'Where? . . .' she asked in a weak voice hazarding a glance at her executioner.

'There where I came from, my jewel.'

There was a red mist before Esther's eyes as she looked at the man.

'To the galleys,' he added in a low voice.

Esther's eyes closed, her legs stretched out, her arms hung down, she went white. The man rang. Prudence came.

'See that she recovers consciousness,' he said coldly. 'I haven't finished.'

He paced about the drawing-room as he waited. Prudence-Europe was obliged to come and ask the gentleman to lift

Esther on to the bed; he picked her up with an ease which indicated his athletic strength. The most violent resources of the Pharmacy had to be drawn on to bring Esther back to awareness of her ills. An hour later, the poor trollop was in a state to listen to the living nightmare, who sat at the foot of her bed, his fixed and glaring eyes two jets of molten lead.

'Little one,' he proceeded, 'Lucien stands between a splendid life, honoured, happy, full of dignity, and the hole full of water, mud and pebbles into which he was going to jump when I met him. The house of Grandlieu requires the dear child to show an estate worth a million before getting him the title of marquess and offering him the hand of that long pole called Clotilde, with whose help he will rise to power. Thanks to us two, Lucien has just acquired his maternal manor, the old house of Rubempré which didn't cost much, thirty thousand francs; but his solicitor, by the luck of the market, has managed to add to it a million's worth of land, on which three hundred thousand francs have been paid. The house, the costs, the considerations paid out to those who provided a front to disguise the nature of the transaction from local people, have used up the rest. True, we have a hundred thousand francs in business which, in a few months' time, will be worth two or three hundred thousand francs; but there will still be four hundred thousand francs to pay . . . Three days from now, Lucien comes back from Angoulême where he's just been, for he mustn't be suspected of having come into money through carding your mattresses . . .'

'No, indeed!' she said raising her eyes with a sublime effort.

'I ask you, is this the moment to frighten the baron?' he asked calmly, 'and you almost killed him the day before yesterday! he fainted like a woman on reading your second letter. Your style is magnificent, I must compliment you on it. If the baron had died, what would have happened to us? When Lucien walks out of Saint Thomas Aquinas's, son-in-law of the Duc de Grandlieu, if you then feel like jumping into the Seine, . . . well, my love, we'll join hands and jump in together. It's one way of making an end. But just think! Wouldn't it be better to live and to be able to say to oneself at every minute: "That dazzling fortune, that happy family" –

for he will have children, ... children! ... (have you ever thought of the pleasure of running your fingers through his children's hair?).'

Esther closed her eyes and quivered gently.

'Well, seeing that edifice of happiness, one says to oneself: "That is my work!"'

There was a pause, during which the two creatures looked at each other.

'That's what I've tried to make of a despair which was for throwing itself in the water. Am I the egoist? That's what love is! Only kings receive such devotion; but I anointed my Lucien king! If I were riveted for the rest of my days to my old chains, I could, I think, retain my tranquillity by saying to myself: "*He* is at the ball, *he* is at Court." My soul and my mind would triumph while my carcass was given over to the *screws*! You are only a wretched female, you love like a female! But with a courtesan, as with all such degraded creatures, love should be a means of becoming a mother, in spite of nature which has stricken you with infecundity! If ever, under the skin of the Abbé Carlos Herrera, they were to discover the convict I was at one time, do you know what I would do to avoid compromising Lucien?'

Esther awaited his reply with a certain anxiety.

'Well,' he went on after a slight pause, 'I should die as black men do, by swallowing my tongue. But you, with your affectations, are putting them on my tracks. What did I demand of you? ... to wear the Torpedo's skirts again for six months, for six weeks, and make use of them to lay hold on a million ... Lucien will never forget you! Men don't forget a being recalled to memory by the happiness they enjoy every morning awaking always rich. Lucien is even *kinder* than you, ... he began by loving Coralie, she dies, fine; but he couldn't pay for her funeral, he didn't act as you were just doing, he didn't faint, poet or not; he wrote six naughty songs, he got three hundred francs for them, to pay the undertaker. I have those songs, I know them by heart. Well, you too, make up songs; be gay, be irresistible ... and insatiable! You hear me? don't oblige me to speak again ... There, kiss Daddy. Good-bye ...'

When, half an hour later, Europe went into her mistress's room, she found her kneeling before a crucifix in the pose which the most religious of all painters gave to Moses before the bush in Horeb, to portray his deep and complete adoration of Jehovah. After saying her last prayers, Esther renounced her fine life, honour as she had come to know it, glory, her virtues, love. She rose.

'Oh, Madame, I shall never see you like that again!' cried Prudence Servien struck almost dumb by the sublime beauty of her mistress.

She quickly turned the cheval-glass so that the poor harlot could see herself. Her eyes still showed traces of the soul ascending to heaven. The Jewish complexion glowed. Moist with tears half-dried by the heat of prayer, her lashes were like foliage after summer rain, the sun of pure love made them sparkle for the last time. The expression on her lips was that of her last invocations to the angels, from whom it may be she had borrowed the martyr's palm in return for the spotless life she offered up. In short, she bore about her the majesty which must have shone from Mary Stuart at the moment at which she bade farewell to her crown, to the earth and to love.

'I should have liked Lucien to see me thus,' she said breathing a stifled sigh. 'Now,' she continued in vibrant tones, 'let's have *a bit of fun* . . .'

At this, Europe stood open-mouthed, as though she had heard an angel blaspheme.

'Why, what's the matter with you, looking to see if I've got a mouthful of cloves instead of teeth? From now on, I'm just a vile and filthy creature, a *thief*, a tart, and I'm waiting for my gentleman friend. So heat up a bath and get my glad rags out. It is mid-day, the baron will no doubt be coming on here from 'Change, I'll tell him that I'm only waiting for him, and I understand Asia is to lay on a fancy dinner, I'll turn the man crazy . . . Come along, jump to it, my girl . . . We're going to have fun, that is to say we're going to *work*.'

She sat down at her table, and wrote the following letter:

My dear, if the cook you've sent me had never been in my service, I might have supposed your intention was to let me know how many times you'd fainted the day before yesterday on receiving my three little notes. (What do you expect? I was very on edge that day, I was dwelling on memories of my deplorable existence.) But I know the sincerity of Asia. So I'm not going to go on feeling sorry for having upset you, since it helped to prove how fond of me you are. We're like that, we poor despised creatures: real affection touches us far more than all the money you can spend on us. Me, I've always been afraid of being a coat-rack on which you hung your vanity. It irritated me to think I was nothing but that. Yes, despite all your fine protestations, I thought you took me for a bought woman. Well, now you'll find me a good girl, so long as you'll always do a little what I say. If this letter may take the place of doctor's orders, you can prove it by coming to see me on your way from the Stock Exchange. You will find fully armed, and wearing your favours, her who calls herself now, for life, your pleasure machine,

ESTHER.

At the Bourse, Baron Nucingen was so jovial, so happy, so easy to please, and made so many jokes, that du Tillet and the Kellers, who were there, could not refrain from asking him for an explanation of his jollity.

'She lofs me . . . Ve shell soon hef housevarming,' he said to du Tillet.

'How much is that costing you?' asked François Keller whom Madame Colleville was said to have cost twenty-five thousand francs a year.

'Nefer hes dis woman, who iss an ainchel, esk me for two bress varthinks.'

'They never do that,' du Tillet replied no less abruptly. 'It's so they need never ask for anything themselves that they equip themselves with aunts and mothers.'

Esther reappears on the surface of Paris

FROM the Bourse to the rue Taitbout, the baron said to his coachman seven times: 'Ve aren't moofing, vy don't you vip ze horse! . . .'

He climbed up eagerly, and for the first time found his mistress beautiful in the way of those women whose sole occupation is to wear fine clothes and adorn themselves. Newly bathed, the flower was fresh, fragrant enough to inspire concupiscence in a Robert d'Arbrissel. Esther was dressed to perfection but informally. A light coat of black rep, trimmed with pink silk, opened on a skirt of grey satin, the costume later adopted by the fair Amigo in *I Puritani*. A neckerchief of English needle-point fluttered about her shoulders. The sleeves of her gown were caught up with piping into the separate puffs which, for some time past, fashionable woman had substituted for the leg-of-mutton sleeves which had begun to seem monstrous. Upon her magnificent hair, Esther had pinned a madwoman's bonnet of Mechlin lace, which looked as though it would fall off but never did, giving her the appearance of uncombed disorder, though one distinctly saw the white parting of her little head between the furrows of hair.

'Isn't it terrible to see Madame looking so beautiful in a shabby little drawing-room like this?' said Europe to the baron as she opened the door to him.

'Ha, vell, go ve rue Saint Georges?' said the baron, still as a pointer before a partridge. 'De vedder iss maknivizent, ve vill drife in de Champs-Élysées, and Matame Saint-Estèfe *mit* Eugénie vill dranzbord oll your glothes, your linen *und* our tinner rue Saint Georges.'

'I shall do anything you wish,' said Esther, 'if you will oblige me by calling my cook Asia, and Eugénie Europe. I've given those nicknames to all the women who've served me, since the first two I had. I don't like change . . .'

'Asia, . . . Europe, . . .' repeated the baron laughing heartily. '*Wie komisch*, . . . you hef soch imachinazion . . . I vould hef eaden a lod off tinners pevore I vould hef colled a gook Asia.'

'Girls like me need our little jokes,' said Esther. 'Can't a woman be fed by Asia and dressed by Europe, when you live on everybody? Is it a myth? There are women who would eat up the whole world, I only want half. So there!'

'Vot a voman Matame Saint-Estèfe iss!' the baron said to himself, marvelling at the change wrought in Esther's ways.

'Europe, my child, I need a hat,' said Esther. 'I should have a black satin bonnet lined with pink, with a bit of lace.'

'Madame Thomas hasn't sent it. . . . Come along, baron, quick! paws up! start your life as a slave, that is to say a happy man! . . . Happiness is a great weight! . . . You have your gig, go to Madame Thomas's,' said Europe to the baron. 'Get your man to ask for Madame van Bogseck's bonnet . . . And whatever you do,' she whispered into his ear, 'bring her the finest bouquet in Paris. It's winter, see if you can't get tropical flowers.'

The baron went down and said to his people: 'To Matame Domas's.' The coachman took his master to a famous pastry-cook's. 'She zells glothes, impezile, nod gakes,' said the baron who hurried to the Palais Royal to Madame Prévôt's, where a bouquet at five louis was put up for him, while his man went to the dressmaker's.

On his way about Paris, the superficial observer may wonder who the fools are who buy the fabulous flowers exposed in the celebrated florist's windows and the early fruit and vegetables at Chevet's, the only place, apart from the Rocher de Cancale, to offer a true and delightful Two Worlds Review . . . Every day in Paris are awakened a hundred and one passions like Nucingen's, bent on proving themselves with rarities which queens cannot afford, and which men offer, on their knees, to whores who, as Asia put it, like to *shine*. But for this little fact, virtuous wives would never be able to explain how a fortune may melt away in the hands of these creatures whose social function, in the Fourier system, is perhaps to make good the ravages of Avarice and Cupidity. Such dissipation is no doubt to the Body Social what the prick of a lancet is to a body afflicted with plethora. In two months Nucingen had watered trade to the extent of more than two hundred thousand francs.

When the amorous old man returned, night was falling, the posy was useless. In winter, the time for driving in the Champs Élysées is between two and four. The carriage nevertheless served to take Esther from the rue Taitbout to the rue Saint Georges, where she took possession of her little palace. Never, let it be said, had Esther before been the object of such devotion or equal outlay, she was astonished; but she carefully avoided, like all such regal ingrates, showing the least surprise. When you go into Saint Peter's in Rome, to make you appreciate the breadth and height of the queen of cathedrals, they show you the little finger of a statue which has I know not what length, and which looks to you like an ordinary little finger. Now, people have so criticized those descriptions, nevertheless so necessary to the historian of his own time, that here we had better imitate the Roman guide. Thus, then, as they went into the dining-room, the baron could not help making Esther feel the curtain material, draped over the windows in royal abundance, lined with white watered silk and trimmed with braid worthy of the corsage of a Portuguese princess. The curtaining was a heavy silk bought in Canton upon which Chinese patience had depicted the birds of Asia with a perfection otherwise to be found only in parchment volumes of the Middle Ages or in the missal of Charles V, pride of the imperial library in Vienna.

'It gost dwo *tausend* vrancs an ell from a milord who prought it pack from de Indies . . .'

'Very nice. Charming! What a pleasure it will be to drink champagne here!' said Esther. 'The froth won't splash the windows!'

'Oh, Madame!' said Europe, 'just look at the carpet! . . .'

'Es de garpet hed been dessigned vor de Tuke Tolinia, who vount it too dear, I pought id vor you, who are a qveen!' said Nucingen.

By an effect due to chance, this carpet, the work of one of our most ingenious designers, was in perfect keeping with the caprices of the Chinese drapery. The walls painted by Schinner and Leon de Lora portrayed voluptuous scenes, thrown into relief by carved ebony panelling, acquired at huge cost from du Sommerard, narrow fillets of gilt discreetly catching the light. Now you may judge the rest.

'You did well to bring me here,' said Esther, 'it will take me a good week to become used to my house, and not to seem like an upstart . . .'

'My houze!' the baron joyfully repeated. 'Den you agsept it? . . .'

'Indeed, yes, a thousand times yes, you stupid animal,' she
aid with a smile.

'Hanimal vould pe enough . . .'

'Stupid is to stroke you,' she continued looking at him.

The poor Shark took Esther's hand and placed it on his heart:
e was animal enough to feel but too stupid to find a word.

'Zee how it peats, . . . vor a liddle vort of avvection,' he
vent on. And he led his *gottess* into the bedroom.

'Oh, my, Madame,' said Eugénie, 'I couldn't stay in there, I
houldn't be able to keep out of that bed.'

'Well, my little elephant,' said Esther, 'this must be paid for
t once. . . . Look, after dinner, let's go to the theatre together.
 have a craving for theatres.'

It was exactly five years since Esther had been near a
heatre. At the moment, all Paris was going to the Porte Saint
Martin, to see one of those plays upon which a gifted cast
•estows a powerful sense of reality, *Richard d'Arlington*. Like
ll essentially simple natures, Esther loved to be made to
remble with fear no less than to give way to sentimental
ears. 'We'll go and see Frederick Lemaître,' she said, 'he's
n actor I adore!'

'Iss a treatful trama,' said Nucingen who didn't at the
noment fancy appearing in public.

The baron sent his man out to book one of the two stage-
evel boxes. Another peculiarity of Paris! When Success, with
ts feet of clay, packs a theatre, there is always a stage-level
•ox free ten minutes before the curtain rises; the management
:eep it for themselves unless some passion of the Nucingen
ype appears to take it. Like first fruits from Chevet's, that box
s a tax levied on Olympian folly in Paris.

It is pointless to describe the tableware. Nucingen had
•rought three sets together: the great, the small and the
nedium. The finest dessert service was, plates and dishes, all
•f it carved silver-gilt. In order not to overwhelm the table
vith investments in gold and silver, the baron had attached
lelightfully fragile porcelain to each service, Dresden china
 osting more than silver services. As to the napery, linen
rom England, Saxony, Flanders and France vied in perfection
vith their flowered damask.

At dinner, it was the baron's turn to be surprised on tasting Asia's cooking.

'I onnerstend,' he said, 'why you coll her Essia: zis iss Essiatic foot.'

'Ah, I am beginning to think he loves me,' said Esther, 'he said something I recognized as a word.'

'I know ozzer,' he said.

'Well, he's more of a Turcaret than they told me!' cried the laughing courtesan at this reply worthy of the celebrated ineptitudes of Lesage's unscrupulous financier.

The dishes were spiced in such a way as to give the baron indigestion, so that he might go home early; it was therefore all that he gained in the way of pleasure from his first evening with Esther. At the theatre, he was obliged to drink innumerable glasses of sugar and water, leaving Esther alone at the intervals. Too predictably for mere coincidence, Tullia, Mariette and Madame du Val-Noble were at the theatre that evening. *Richard d'Arlington* was one of those wild and deserved successes to be seen only in Paris. Watching this play, men all felt that it was possible to throw their legitimate wives out of the window, and the women loved seeing themselves unjustly maltreated. The women said to themselves: 'It's too much, they only push us, ... but how often! ...' Now, a creature of Esther's beauty, attired as Esther was, couldn't *shine* with impunity at stage-level in the Porte Saint Martin. And so, by the second act, the two dancers' box was the scene of a positive upheaval caused by the recognition that the fair unknown was none other than the Torpedo.

'Well, I never, where's she come from?' said Mariette to Madame du Val-Noble, 'I thought she was drowned ...'

'Is it really her? she looks to me thirty-seven times younger and better-looking than six years ago.'

'Perhaps she's preserved herself like Madame d'Espard and Madame Zayonscheck, in ice,' said Count Brambourg, who had brought the three women to the theatre, in a stalls box. 'Isn't it the *rat* you were going to send me to work on my uncle?' he said to Tullia.

'None other,' replied Tullia to her companion. 'Du Bruel, run down to the orchestra, and see if it really is she.'

'Does she give herself airs!' exclaimed Madame du Val-Noble.

'Oh, she has a right to them,' Count Brambourg commented, 'since she's with my friend Baron Nucingen. I'm going along.'

'Can she be the supposed Joan of Arc who conquered Nucingen, the one they've bored us with for three months? ...' said Mariette.

'Good evening, my dear Baron,' said Philippe Bridau entering Nucingen's box. 'So there you are married to Mademoiselle Esther? ... Mademoiselle, I'm just a poor soldier you got out of trouble, at Issoudun, ... Philippe Bridau ...'

'Never heard of him,' said Esther, fixing her opera glasses on the house.

'Matamiselle,' answered the baron, 'iss no longer blain Esther; her name iss now Matame de Champy, efter a smoll esdate I pought her ...'

'If you really want to know the form,' said the count, 'the ladies are saying that Madame de Champy *gives herself airs* ... If you don't want to know me, you might condescend to remember Mariette, Tullia, Madame du Val-Noble,' went on the upstart whom the Duc de Maufrigneuse had ingratiated with the Dauphin.

'If the ladies are nice to me, I am disposed to be agreeable to them,' Madame de Champy said coldly.

'Nice!' said Philippe, 'they're better than that, they call you Joan of Arc.'

'So, if ziz leddies vish to choin you,' said Nucingen, 'I vill leaf you alone, I hef eaden doo much. Your garriage vill bick you up *mit* your pipple ... Zot toffle, Essia! ...'

'The first time out, and you'd leave me alone!' said Esther. 'Really! I shall be stranded. I need my man with me when I leave. If anybody insulted me, I should have nobody to appeal to ...'

The old millionaire's egoism had to yield to the lover's obligations. The baron suffered and stayed. Esther had her reasons for keeping *her man*. If she received her old friends, she wouldn't be as closely questioned in company as she

would been alone. Philippe Bridau hurried back to the dancers'
box and told them how matters stood.

'Ah, she's the one who's taking over *my* house in the rue
Saint Georges!' said Madame du Val-Noble with some bitterness, for she now found herself *on foot*, as they say.

'Probably,' answered the colonel. 'Du Tillet told me the
baron had laid out three times as much there as your poor
Falleix.'

'Are we going to see her, then?' said Tullia.

'Not me!' replied Mariette, 'she's too well got up, I'll call
and see her at home.'

'I don't look too bad, I'll chance it,' said Tullia.

The bold First Subject therefore went along at the interval
and renewed acquaintance with Esther who confined herself
to generalities.

'Where have you just got back from, child?' asked the
dancer who could not restrain her curiosity.

'Oh! I stayed five years in a castle in the Alps with an
Englishman as jealous as a tiger, a nabob; my *nabot* I called
him, my dwarf, for he was smaller than the Bailiff of Ferrette.
And now I've reverted to a banker, *from a Caribbee to a syllabub*,
Florine would have said. And so here I am, back in Paris, so
much in need of amusement, life with me will be just a
Carnival. I shall keep open house. Ah! after five years of
solitude, I need a tonic, and I'm starting on it at once. Five
years of English, that's too long; according to the advertisements, you're supposed to be able to pick it up in six weeks.'

'Did the baron give you this lace?'

'No, that's a bit left over from the nabob ... Am I unlucky, my dear! he was as green as the smile of a successful
man's friend, I thought he'd be dead in ten months. But, my
dear, he was strong as an Alp. Never trust a man with liver
trouble ... I never want to hear about livers again. I've been
too much of a believer in proverbs ... That nabob robbed
me, he died without making a will, and the family put me out
as though I had the plague. So I said to the big boy here:
"You pay for two!" You might well call me a Joan of Arc, I
lost England! and I dare say I shall die in the flames.'

'Of love!' said Tullia.

'Burnt alive!' replied Esther suddenly turning thoughtful.

The baron laughed at all these salacious jokes, but it took him time to see them, so that his laughs went off like forgotten squibs after a firework display.

We live in our various circles, and curiosity is confined to no one sphere. At the Opera, the news of Esther's return ran round the corridors in the small hours, so that, by four o'clock in the morning everybody in the Champs-Élysées world had heard about the Torpedo, and finally knew who was the object of Baron Nucingen's passion.

'Do you realize,' said Blondet to de Marsay in the Opera lounge, 'that the Torpedo disappeared the day after we recognized her here as little Rubempré's mistress?'

In Paris, as in the provinces, everything gets around. The police in the rue de Jérusalem is not so well organized as that of society, where everyone spies on everybody else without knowing that he is doing it. Carlos had never been in doubt about the danger of Lucien's position during and after the rue Taitbout.

A woman on foot

THERE is no more horrible situation than that in which Madame du Val-Noble found herself, and the expression *on foot* renders it to perfection. The carelessness and prodigality of such women prevents them ever thinking about the future. In that exceptional world, far wittier and more full of comedy than it is commonly given credit for, women who are no longer beautiful with the positive, unchanging beauty so easily recognized, those who are loved capriciously, if at all, are the only ones to think about and save for their old age: the more beautiful they are, the less provident. 'Are you afraid of growing ugly, then, that you've started saving . . .?' was a thing Florine had said to Mariette which perhaps indicates one source of this prodigality. Given a financier who kills himself, or a prodigal whose money has run out, in the result these women fall with appalling rapidity from shameless opulence to sheer destitution. Then they fling themselves into the arms of the wardrobe dealer, they sell exquisite jewellery for almost nothing, they run up debts, anything to keep up the appearance of luxury which might help them to regain what they have lost: coffers into which they can dip. The ups and downs of their life sufficiently explain the cost of affairs almost invariably arranged, in reality, as Asia had *fixed up* that of Nucingen with Esther. Those who know their Paris thus understand the situation perfectly when they see in the Champs Élysées, that busy and tumultuous bazaar, such and such a woman in a hired carriage whom, a year or six months ago, they saw in a scrupulously maintained equipage of stunning elegance. 'When you come down to Sainte Pélagie, you must know how to bounce back into the Bois de Boulogne,' said Florine laughing with Blondet over the little Vicomte de Portenduère. Some women are too clever to risk the contrast. They shut themselves away in dreadful boarding houses, where they expiate their former luxury with privations like those suffered by travellers lost in some Sahara; but this doesn't give them the least taste for economy. They venture out to masked balls, they travel about in the provinces, on fine days they appear in their best clothes on the boulevards. Among each other, too, they find the mutual aid often displayed by the proscribed classes. A little help given to another does not cost a lucky woman much, since she can still say: 'That's what I'll wear on Sunday.' The most effective help, nevertheless, comes from the wardrobe dealer. When this kind of usurer is owed money, she rouses and digs into old men's hearts everywhere in aid of her hat and half-boot repository. Unable to foresee the calamity which befell one of the richest and cleverest stockbrokers, Madame du Val-Noble had been caught in utter disarray. She had used Falleix's money to satisfy her whims, and counted on him directly to see to her real needs and her future. 'How,' she said to Mariette, 'was one to expect that from a man who seemed so *good-natured*?' At almost all social levels, *good nature* belongs to the open-handed man, who lends a few crowns here and there without expecting repayment, who behaves at all times according to a code of some delicacy, beyond common, everyday, constrained morality. Some who are thought virtuous and upright, like Nucingen, have ruined their benefactors, and some who have passed through the hands of the police behave admirably with a woman. All-round virtue, the dream of Molière, in the person of Alceste, is extremely rare; it occurs nevertheless everywhere, even in Paris. *Good nature* is the product of a certain graciousness of character which proves nothing. A man is like that as a cat is smooth-furred, as a slipper is ready for the foot. And so, as the expression is understood among kept women, good nature required Falleix to warn his mistress of what was coming and leave her something to live on. D'Estourny, the gallant swindler, had been good-natured; he cheated at cards, but he had put thirty thousand francs on one side for his mistress. Thus, wherever an evening celebration was afoot, women always replied to his accusers: 'THAT'S NOTHING! ... whatever you say, Georges was a good-natured fellow, he had nice manners, he deserved better luck!' Whores don't care for the law, they adore a certain delicacy of feeling; they may sell themselves, like Esther, for some obscure ideal, which is their religion. After barely saving one or two pieces of jewellery from the shipwreck, Madame du Val-Noble was subjected to the terrible weight of the accusation: 'She ruined Falleix!' She was near thirty, and although in the full development of her beauty, she could all the more easily pass for older in that, in such a crisis, all a woman's rivals turn against her. Mariette, Florine and Tullia still invited their friend to dinner, helped her out with money now and then; but, not knowing what her debts amounted to, dared not sound the depths of that gulf. An interval of six years had caused the Torpedo and Madame du Val-Noble to drift too far apart on the shifting tide of Paris for the *woman on foot* now to address herself to the one in her carriage; but the Val-Noble knew well that Esther was too generous not to think sometimes that, as she put it, she had inherited from her old friend, and not to show this if they met apparently by chance. In the hope of bringing this chance about, Madame du Val-Noble attired herself very respectably and walked every day in the Champs Élysées, on the arm of

Théodore Gaillard, whom she was later to marry and who, at the present sad juncture, was behaving very well to his former mistress, inviting her out and sending her theatre tickets. She counted on running into Esther one fine day. Esther now had Paccard as a coachman, for the household had, within five days, been organized by Asia, Europe and him, on the instructions of Carlos, in such a way as to make its rue Saint Georges headquarters an impregnable fortress. On his side, Peyrade, moved by a deep hatred and a desire for revenge, but above all with the aim of setting up his dear Lydia, also took to walking in the Champs Élysées, once Contenson had told him that Monsieur de Nucingen's mistress was to be seen there. Peyrade got himself up so perfectly as an Englishman, and was so effortlessly able to speak French in the twittering English manner; his knowledge of English was faultless, his knowledge of that country's affairs was so complete, as a result of three police missions on which he had been sent there in 1779 and 1786, that he played the part of an Englishman at embassies or in London, without arousing suspicion. Peyrade, who had much in common with Musson, the famous mystifier, so well understood the art of disguise that even Contenson had been known to fail to recognize him. Accompanied by Contenson, disguised as a mulatto, Peyrade studied Esther and her people with an eye which seemed inattentive but which saw all. It was quite natural, therefore, for him to be on the pavement used by those with carriages in fine, dry weather, the day Esther met Madame du Val-Noble there. Peyrade, followed by his mulatto in livery, strolled unaffectedly, like a true nabob thinking only of himself, in the path of the two women, in such a way as to pick up fragments of their conversation as he passed.

'My dear child,' said Esther to Madame du Val-Noble, 'come and see me. Nucingen owes it to himself not to leave his broker's mistress without a farthing . . .'

'All the more as they say he ruined him,' said Théodore Gaillard, 'so that a hint of *blackmail* . . .'

'He's dining with me tomorrow, come then, my dear,' said Esther. Then she whispered in her friend's ear: 'I do what I like with him, he hasn't *had it* yet!' She put the nail of one gloved finger under her prettiest tooth, in the well-known gesture which vividly signifies: nothing at all!

'You've got him where you want him . . .'

'Darling, so far he's only paid my debts . . .'

'What a little pickpocket she is!' cried Suzanne du Val-Noble.

'And when I say debts,' Esther continued, 'I mean the sort that would rock a minister of finance. Now I want an income of thirty thousand francs before the first stroke of midnight! . . . Oh, he's a pet, I'm not complaining . . . He's in a good mood. In a week's time, we shall have the house-warming, you'll be asked . . . Next day, I get the deeds of the house in the rue Saint Georges. You can't decently live in a house like that without thirty thousand francs annual income of your own, that you can lay your hands on when you want it. I've known what it is to be hard up, and I don't want any more of it. There are some acquaintances you've soon had enough of.'

'You who used to say: "Fortune, that's me!" how you've changed!' exclaimed Suzanne.

'It's the air of Switzerland, you grow thrifty there . . . Why don't you try it, child! find yourself a Swiss, and perhaps you've got a husband! for they haven't learnt about women like us yet . . . In any case, you'll come back in love with what can be written in ledgers, a refined and lasting love! Good-bye.'

Esther climbed back into her fine carriage harnessed to the most magnificent dappled greys then to be seen in Paris.

'The woman getting into her carriage,' Peyrade thereupon said to Contenson, 'is attractive, but I prefer the one who is walking, follow her and find out who she is.'

'This is what that Englishman was saying in English,' said Théodore Gaillard repeating Peyrade's words to Madame du Val-Noble.

Before venturing to speak English, Peyrade had tried out a word or two in the language which caused a movement of Théodore Gaillard's face telling him that the journalist knew English. From this point, Madame du Val-Noble proceeded very slowly to where she lived, in the rue Louis-le-Grand, in respectable furnished rooms, glancing round to see whether the mulatto was following. The house belonged to a Madame Gérard to whom Madame du Val-Noble had been obliging in her days of splendour and who now showed her gratitude by accommodating her handsomely. This kindly soul, a respectable woman full of virtues, regarded the harlot as a superior being; she saw her still surrounded with luxury, a banished queen; she confided her daughters to her; and, more naturally than may be thought, the courtesan was as careful about taking them to the theatre as if she had been their mother; the two Gérard girls doted on her. This excellent, worthy landlady was like those sublime priests who see in outcast women a creature to be saved, to be loved. Madame du Val-Noble respected this honest worth, often she envied it as she talked in the evening, lamenting her misfortunes. 'You are beautiful, you can still settle down comfortably,' said Madame Gérard. In any case, Madame du Val-Noble had gone downhill only relatively. The wardrobe of this spendthrift, elegant woman was still sufficiently well furnished to allow her, on occasion, as on the *Richard d'Arlington* evening at the Porte Saint Martin, to appear dazzling. Madame Gérard still graciously paid for the carriages this woman on foot needed for dining out or going to the theatre and returning.

'Well, my dear Madame Gérard,' she said to the honest mother of a family, 'my luck is changing, I fancy . . .'

'Why, Madame, so much the better; but be careful, think of the future . . . Don't run up any more debts. I spend so much time getting rid of people who want to see you! . . .'

'Don't waste sympathy on *dogs* like those, who've all had enormous sums out of me. Look, here are tickets for the Variétés for your daughters, a nice box halfway back. If anybody asks for me this evening and I'm not back, let them go up all the same. They'll find my old maid, Adèle, there; I'll send her to you.'

As she had neither aunt nor mother, Madame du Val-Noble had to have recourse to her maid (also on foot!) to play the part of a Saint-Estève with the unknown whose conquest was to allow her to reassume her rank. She went out to dinner with Théodore Gaillard, who, that evening, had a *party*, that is to say a dinner arranged by Nathan, who was paying off a lost wager, one of those evenings of debauchery whose guests are told: '*There'll be women.*'

Peyrade as a nabob

PEYRADE had not decided without powerful reasons to venture his person upon the field of this intrigue. Like Corentin's, however, his curiosity had been so vividly aroused that, even without reason, he might willingly have been drawn into the drama. At that moment, the policy of Charles X had performed its final evolution. After confiding the helm to ministers of his own choice, the King was preparing the conquest of Algiers, intending that the glory of this achievement should serve as justification for what has been called his last throw. Internally, conspiracies were no longer afoot, Charles X believed himself without adversary. In politics as at sea, there are deceptive lulls. Corentin felt himself utterly becalmed. In such a situation, your real hunter, just to keep his hand in, *for lack of thrushes, kills blackbirds*. Domitian, for lack of Christians, killed flies. Witnessing Esther's arrest, Contenson, with a spy's trained sense, justly appraised the matter. As we have seen, the rogue had not taken the trouble to conceal his opinion from Baron Nucingen. 'For whose benefit is the banker being made to pay for his passion?' was the first question the two friends put to each other. Recognizing in Asia a character from the play, Contenson had hoped, through her, to discover the author; but she slipped through his hands like an eel and hid herself for some time in the Parisian ooze, and, when he found her again installed as Esther's cook, the mulattress's part struck him as inexplicable. For the first time, the two artists in espionage were faced with an undecipherable text, though the story it concealed was certainly shady. In the course of three successive bold attacks on the house in the rue Taitbout, Contenson met with nothing but stubborn silence. While Esther was still there, the porter seemed a prey to terror. Perhaps Asia had threatened the whole family with poison balls in case of indiscretion. The day after Esther left her apartment, Contenson found the porter a little more reasonable, he was sorry to see the last of the little lady who, he said, had kept him going with the remains of her table. Disguised as a commercial broker, he discussed the price of the apartment, and he listened to the porter's complaints with an air of mockery, casting doubt on everything he said with a: 'Really? You don't say?' 'Yes, sir, that little lady lived five years here without ever going out, just as her lover, who was jealous, though he had no need to be, took all sorts of precautions about getting here, going in, leaving. A very good-looking young man, as a matter of fact.' Lucien was still at Marsac, staying with his sister, Madame Séchard; but, as soon as he got back, Contenson sent the porter to the Quai Malaquais, to inquire of Monsieur de Rubempré whether he would agree to sell the furniture in the apartment left by Madame van Bogseck. The porter then identified Lucien with the mysterious lover of the young widow, and that was all Contenson wanted to know. As may be imagined, Lucien and Carlos were taken by surprise, though they did not show it; they gave the impression of thinking the porter mad, and did what they could to persuade him that it was so.

Within twenty-four hours, a watch was being kept on Contenson in his turn, and his activities were reported to Carlos. They left no room for doubt. Disguised as a delivery man from the Central Market, Contenson had already twice brought provisions bought that morning by Asia, and so twice he had set foot inside the house in the rue Saint Georges. Corentin, for his part, was not inactive; but the real existence of a Carlos Herrera pulled him up short, for it at once became clear that such a priest, secret envoy of Ferdinand VII, had come to Paris in late 1823. Corentin must therefore know what reasons led this Spaniard to take Lucien de Rubempré under his wing. That Esther had been Lucien's mistress for five years soon became evident. So the Englishwoman's substitution for Esther must have been performed in the interests of this dandy. Lucien had no visible means of existence, he was prevented from taking Mademoiselle de Grandlieu to wife, yet he had just paid a million for the Rubempré estate. Corentin got the Director General of the Police of the Kingdom to make judicious inquiries of the Prefect and thus learned that, in the case of Peyrade, the complaints had been made by no others than Count Sérisy and Lucien de Rubempré.

'Now we have it!' Peyrade and Corentin exclaimed.

It took the two friends no more than a moment to sketch out their plan.

'The wench must still have women friends,' said Corentin. 'Among them, there must be somebody down on her luck; one of us must play the part of a rich foreigner who'll set her up; we'll see they confide in each other. These women always need somebody to rattle on about their lovers to, that will lead us to the heart of the matter.' Peyrade quite naturally thought at once of adopting his Englishman's part. The life of debauchery he would have to lead, during the time needed to unearth the plot whose victim he had been, appealed to him, whereas Corentin, aged by his work and rather sickly, did not much care for such things. As a mulatto, Contenson easily shook off the watch put on him by Carlos. Three days before Peyrade's encounter with Madame du Val-Noble in the Champs Élysées, the last of Messieurs de Sartine and Lenoir's agents, provided with a passport in perfect order, had disembarked in the rue de la Paix, at the Hotel Mirabeau, arriving from the colonies by way of Le Havre in a small barouche as mud-spattered as if it had indeed come from Le Havre, although it had only come to Paris from St Denis.

Carlos Herrera, for his part, went to the Spanish embassy for a visa, and at the Quai Malaquais made all preparations for a trip to Madrid. This is why. Within a matter of days Esther would be the owner of a private house in the rue Saint Georges, and she would also have scrip for thirty thousand francs' annual income; Europe and Asia were sufficiently cunning to get her to sell this and secretly convey the proceeds to Lucien. Lucien, supposed to be rich through his sister's liberality, would thus be able to make up the price of the Rubempré estate. Nobody could object to this procedure, unless Esther were indiscreet; but she would die sooner than be seen raising an eyebrow. Clotilde had tied a little pink kerchief about her stork's neck, so the argument had been won at the Grandlieu house. The Omnibus transactions already paid threefold. If he disappeared for a few days, Carlos would shake off suspicion. Everything humanly possible had been taken into account, there would be no mistakes. The false Spaniard meant to leave the day after Peyrade had encountered Madame du Val-Noble in the Champs Élysées. However, that very night, at two o'clock in the morning, Asia appeared at the Quai Malaquais in a cab, and discovered the author of the plan thus briefly summarized going over it in detail in his mind as other authors may critically examine the pages they have written searching for faults to correct. Such a man was not to be caught twice forgetting a point like that of the porter at the rue Taitbout.

'This afternoon,' whispered Asia to her master, 'at half past two, Paccard recognized, in the Champs Élysées, Contenson disguised as a mulatto acting as the servant of an Englishman who, for three days, has been walking in the Champs Élysées on the look-out for Esther. Paccard recognized our watchdog, as I did when he was a Market porter, by his eyes. Paccard brought the child back in such a way as to keep his eyes on the rascal. He is at the Hotel Mirabeau; but he and the Englishman exchanged such signs of intelligence, that the Englishman, as Paccard sees it, cannot possibly be an Englishman.'

'There's a horse-fly buzzing around,' said Carlos. 'I shan't go until the day after tomorrow. It was Contenson who sent the porter round here from the rue Taitbout; we must find out whether the sham Englishman is a friend of ours.'

At noon, Mr Samuel Johnson's mulatto servant was solemnly serving his master, who always lunched too well, deliberately. Peyrade meant to pass for an Englishman of the heavy-drinking type; he always went out tipsy. He wore black cloth gaiters up to his knees, padded to make his legs fatter; his breeches were lined with thick fustian; his waistcoat buttoned up to the chin; his blue stock encircled his neck almost up to his cheeks; he wore a small red wig which covered half his forehead; he'd made himself about three inches taller; the oldest customer at the Café David wouldn't have recognized him. From his square-bottomed, black, full-cut, clean English coat, a passer-by would have taken him for an English millionaire. Contenson displayed the cool insolence of a nabob's confidential manservant, silent, haughty, scornful, uncommunicative, now and then permitting himself awkward gestures and ferocious growls. Peyrade was finishing his second bottle when one of the hotel servants unceremoniously introduced into the apartment a man whom both Peyrade and Contenson recognized as a member of the armed constabulary in plain clothes.

'Monsieur Peyrade,' said the constable addressing himself to the nabob and speaking into his ear, 'my orders are to take you to the Prefecture.' Peyrade got up without saying anything and looked for his hat. 'You will find a cab at the door,' the constable said to him on the stairs. 'The Prefect wanted to have you arrested, but he has made do with sending a police officer to demand an explanation of your conduct. You will find him in the carriage.'

'Do you want me to stay with you?' the *gendarme* asked the justice of the peace when Peyrade had got in.

'No,' replied the officer. 'Just tell the cabby quietly to drive to the Prefecture.'

Peyrade and Carlos found themselves together in the same cab. Carlos had a dagger handy. The driver was in his trust, quite prepared to let Carlos out without seeming to notice and without showing surprise if, on reaching his destination, he found a body in the vehicle. No fuss is made about spies. The law almost invariably allows such murders to go unpunished, so difficult is it to see to the bottom of them.

Duel in a cab

PEYRADE cast a spy's glance at the magistrate whom the Prefect of Police had sent him. Carlos's appearance seemed much as it should be: a sparsely covered cranium, deeply wrinkled at the back; powdered hair; then, over soft, red-rimmed eyes which needed attention, a pair of very light gold spectacles, very much those of an office-worker, with double green-tinted lenses. Those eyes bore testimony to a lifetime of ignoble diseases. A cotton cambric shirt with frills ironed flat, a waistcoat of worn black satin, lawyer's breeches, stockings of black floss-silk and shoes tied with ribbons, a long black frock-coat, black gloves at forty *sous*, ten days unwashed, gold watch-chain. He was, to perfection, that type of inferior magistrate paradoxically called a justice or *officer* of the peace.

'My dear Monsieur Peyrade, I am sorry that a man like you should be under supervision, and that you should make a point of deserving it. Your disguise is not at all to the Prefect's taste. If you think that is the way to escape from vigilance, you are mistaken. No doubt you began your journey from England at Beaumont-sur-Oise? . . .'

'At Beaumont-sur-Oise,' replied Peyrade.

'Or at Saint Denis?' the sham magistrate persisted.

Peyrade was troubled. This further question called for a reply. Whatever answer he made could be dangerous. If he replied in the affirmative, that would seem like sarcasm; if the man knew the truth, a denial would be worse. 'He is crafty,' thought Peyrade. He forced himself to smile at the justice, offering his smile by way of a reply. The smile was accepted without comment.

'For what purpose have you disguised yourself, taken rooms at the Hôtel Mirabeau, and got Contenson up as a mulatto?' asked the *officier de paix*.

'The Prefect will do what he pleases with me, I account for my actions only to my superiors,' said Peyrade with dignity.

'If you want to give me to understand that you're acting on behalf of the General Police of the Kingdom,' the false agent said abruptly, 'we'll change direction and go to the rue de Grenelle instead of the rue de Jérusalem. My orders with regard to yourself are perfectly clear. But take care. The matter is not so far considered as one of exceptional gravity, and you could easily make matters worse for yourself. For myself, I wish you no harm . . . But come along, now! . . . Tell me the truth . . .'

'The truth? well, you shall have it,' said Peyrade with a sharp glance at his Cerberus's red eyes.

The pretended magistrate's face remained expressionless, impassive, he was doing his job, all truth was the same to him, he might have thought it all a mere whim on the part of the Prefect. Prefects do have their vagaries.

'I have fallen madly in love with a woman, the mistress of that stockbroker who is travelling for his own pleasure and the displeasure of his creditors, Falleix.'

'Madame du Val-Noble,' said the justice.

'Yes,' Peyrade went on. 'To set her up for a month, which won't cost me much more than a thousand crowns, I've turned myself out as a nabob and taken Contenson as a manservant. That, sir, is so straightforwardly the case that, if you cared to leave me in this cab, where I'll wait for you, on the word of a former Chief Superintendent of police, and to go into the hotel, you can question Contenson. Not only will Contenson confirm what I've just had the honour of telling you, but you will be present when Madame du Val-Noble's maid calls, as she undertook to do this morning, with her mistress's consent to my proposal, or new conditions of her own. An old monkey knows what faces to pull: I've offered a thousand francs a month, a carriage; that makes fifteen hundred; five hundred francs' worth of presents, as much again on parties, dinners, theatres; you see I'm not a penny out when I say a thousand crowns. A man of my age can afford to spend a thousand crowns on his last fling.'

'Ah! Papa Peyrade, you still love women enough to . . .? But I'm not so simple; me, I'm sixty, and I get along very well without . . . However, if things are as you say, I do see that, in order to enjoy your little fling, you must pass yourself off as a foreigner.'

'You can understand that neither Peyrade nor Father Canquoëlle of the rue des Moineaux . . .'

'Indeed, neither one nor the other would have suited Madame du Val-Noble,' Carlos continued, delighted to have Father Canquoëlle's address confirmed. 'Before the Revolution I had a mistress,' he said, 'who'd been kept by the high executioner or Tormenter as he was then called. One day, at the theatre, she pricked herself on a pin, and, as people did then, she exclaimed: "Oh, the torment!" "Is that what it reminds you of?" said her neighbour. Well, my dear Peyrade, for that witticism she left her man. I can see that you don't want to expose yourself to a snub of that kind ... Madame du Val-Noble is a woman for the best kind of man, I saw her one day at the Opera, I thought her very beautiful ... Tell the driver to turn back to the rue de la Paix, my dear Peyrade, I'll go up with you to your rooms and see for myself. No doubt the Prefect will be satisfied with a verbal report.'

Carlos took out of his pocket a snuff-box of black card lined with silver-gilt, he opened it, and offered it to Peyrade with the most engaging air of friendliness. Peyrade said to himself: 'That's the sort of agents they have now! ... good Lord! if Monsieur Lenoir or Monsieur de Sartine were to come back, what would they say?'

'That, I dare say, is part of the truth, but it isn't the whole, my dear friend,' said the false justice of the peace as he finished sniffing up his pinch. 'You've been interesting yourself in the affairs of the heart of Baron Nucingen, and no doubt you're hoping to catch him with a slip-knot; you missed your aim with a pistol, and now you're going to try the big guns on him. Madame du Val-Noble is a friend of Madame de Champy ...'

'The devil! I must watch out!' said Peyrade to himself. 'He's cleverer than I thought. He's playing with me: he speaks of letting me go, but he's still making me talk.'

'Well?' said Carlos with an air of authority.

'Sir, it is true that I made the mistake of trying to find Monsieur de Nucingen a woman over whom he'd lost his head. That's how I come to be in my present disfavour; for it appears that, without knowing it, I brushed against important interests.' (The petty magistrate remained impassive.) 'But I know enough about police work after fifty-two years of practice,' Peyrade continued, 'to leave that matter alone after the dressing-down I got from the Prefect, who was certainly right ...'

'So you would give up your little fling if the Prefect asked you to? That, I'm sure, would be the best way of proving the sincerity of what you say.'

'He's pressing hard! he's pressing me hard now!' said

Peyrade to himself. 'Confound it! agents today are as good as Monsieur Lenoir's.'

'Give it up?' said Peyrade . . . 'I shall await the Prefect's orders . . . But if you wish to come up, here we are at the hotel.'

'Where do you find the money?' Carlos asked him with a close and penetrating look.

'Sir, I have a friend, . . .' said Peyrade.

'Try telling that to an examining magistrate,' Carlos added.

This boldly conceived scene had resulted from Carlos's putting two and two together with the simplicity characteristic of a man of his temper. He had sent Lucien, very early in the day, to Countess Sérisy's. Lucien begged the count's private secretary to go, on the count's behalf, to ask the Prefect for information about the agent employed by Baron Nucingen. The secretary had come back with a note on Peyrade, copied from the summary in his file:

In the police since 1778, arrived in Paris from Avignon, two years previously.

Without fortune and without morality, repository of State secrets.

Domiciled rue des Moineaux, under the name of Canquoëlle, that of a small estate on which his family lives, in the department of Vaucluse, family of good repute.

Recently sought by one of his great-nephews, named Théodose de la Peyrade. (*See agent's report, document No. 37.*)

'He must be the Englishman Contenson is serving as a mulatto,' Carlos exclaimed when Lucien reported what he had been given to understand verbally, outside the note.

Within three hours, this man, whose range of action was that of a general in command, had found through Paccard an innocent accomplice capable of playing the part of a constable in plain clothes, and had disguised himself as a justice of the peace. He had hesitated three times about killing Peyrade in the cab; but as he had forbidden himself ever to commit a murder in person, he resolved to get rid of Peyrade in due course by pointing him out as a millionaire to one or two former convicts.

Peyrade and his Mentor heard the voice of Contenson talking with Madame du Val-Noble's maid. Peyrade then made a sign to Carlos to remain in the first room, with the evident air of adding: 'Now you shall judge of my sincerity.'

'Madame agrees to everything,' said Adèle. 'Madame is at the moment with one of her friends, Madame de Champy, who still has a year's lease of an apartment fully furnished in the rue Taitbout, and will no doubt let her have it. It will be better for Madame to receive Mr Johnson there, for the furniture is still in very good condition, and Monsieur can buy it for Madame by arrangement with Madame de Champy.'

'Excellent, my child. If that isn't a carrot, it's the leaves of one!' said the mulatto to the stupefied girl; 'but we'll share it . . .'

'Well, that's a way for a coloured man to speak!' exclaimed Mademoiselle Adèle. 'If your nabob really is a nabob, he can afford to provide Madame with furniture. The lease runs out in April 1830, your nabob can renew it, if it suits him.'

'Aoh, yes, that will suit me down to the ground!' replied Peyrade with a tap on the maid's shoulder as he entered.

And he motioned significantly to Carlos, who answered with a nod to show that he understood that the nabob must remain in character. But the scene changed suddenly with the entrance of a player over whom neither Carlos nor the Prefect of police exercised control. Corentin appeared unexpectedly. He was passing and, having found the door open, had looked in to see how his old friend Peyrade was getting along in the part of a nabob.

Corentin wins the second round

'THE Prefect is after me again!' said Peyrade in a whisper to Corentin, 'he's discovered me as a nabob.'

'We must get a new Prefect,' Corentin answered his friend in an undertone.

Then, after bowing to him coldly, he examined the magistrate with deliberation.

'Stay here till I come back; I am going to the Prefecture,' said Carlos. 'If you don't see me, you can carry on with your little game.'

Having whispered these words to Peyrade so as not to demolish his character before the maid, Carlos went out, not wishing to remain under the gaze of the newcomer, in whom he recognized one of those blond, blue-eyed natures of a frightening coldness.

'He's the justice the Prefect sent along to me,' said Peyrade to Corentin.

'Him!' replied Corentin, 'you've let yourself be taken in. That man has three packs of cards in his shoes, you can tell from the position of the foot in the shoe; besides a justice of the peace has no need to disguise himself!'

Corentin went down rapidly to confirm his suspicions; Carlos was getting into the cab.

'Hi, *Monsieur l'Abbé*? . . .' Corentin called out.

Carlos turned his head, saw Corentin and stepped into his cab. Corentin nevertheless had time to say through the closing door: 'That's all I wanted to know.' Then: 'Quai Malaquais!' he called to the driver with devilish mockery in both look and accent.

'Well, well,' thought Jacques Collin, 'the game's up, they're on to me now, I shall have to move fast, above all I must know what they want with us.'

Corentin had seen Father Carlos Herrera five or six times, and the man's eyes were not easily forgotten. The first thing Corentin had noted was the squareness of the shoulders, then the blistered face, and the trick of putting on three inches with a false heel.

'So he pulled you up short, eh?' said Corentin seeing that only Peyrade and Contenson were now in the bedroom.

'Who?' cried Peyrade with a metallic vibration in his voice, 'I'll spend my last days putting him on a grill and turning him on it.'

'It's Father Carlós Herrera, probably the Spanish Corentin. Everything is explained. The Spaniard is a high-class procurer who's set himself to making that little man's fortune by minting money with a pretty whore as bait . . . It's up to you to decide whether you'll risk a turn with a diplomatist who strikes me as hellish clever.'

'Good Lord!' exclaimed Contenson, 'he's the one who took the three hundred thousand francs the day of Esther's arrest, it was him in the cab! I remember those eyes, that forehead, those pock marks.'

'Ah! what a dowry my poor Lydia'd have had!' cried Peyrade.

'Keep up the nabob part,' said Corentin. 'To have an eye at Esther's, we must see that she remains friends with the Val-Noble, she was Lucien de Rubempré's real mistress.'

'Nucingen's already been bilked of more than five hundred thousand francs,' said Contenson.

'They need as much again,' Corentin went on, 'the Rubempré estate costs a million. Papa,' said he with a tap on Peyrade's shoulder, 'you shall have a good hundred thousand francs to settle on Lydia.'

'Don't say that to me, Corentin. If your plan misfired, I don't know what I might be capable of . . .'

'You may even get them tomorrow! The abbé, my dear friend, is very cunning, we must give him his due, he's a superior devil; but I've got him, he knows when he's beaten, he'll give in. Just be stupid enough for a nabob, and fear nothing.'

In the evening of this day on which the real adversaries had met face to face in the open, Lucien went to a reception at the Grandlieu house. The company was large. Before all her guests, the duchess kept Lucien by her for some time, and behaved charmingly to him.

'You've been away for a while?' she asked him.

'Yes, Madame la Duchesse. My sister, in the hope of facilitating my marriage, has made great sacrifices, and I've been able to buy up the Rubempré estate and bring it all together again. But my solicitor in Paris is a clever man, he's been able to spare me the claims those in possession of the property would have put in if they'd known the name of the purchaser.'

'Is there a manor-house?' said Clotilde smiling too broadly.

'There's something of the kind, but the best thing will be to use it as building material towards a modern house.'

Clotilde's eyes added flames of happiness to her smiles of contentment.

'This evening you'll make up a *rubber* with my father,' she said in an undertone. 'Within a fortnight, I hope you'll be invited to dinner.'

'Well, my dear sir,' said the Duc de Grandlieu, 'they tell me you've bought up the Rubempré estate; I congratulate you. It answers those who said you had debts. Like France or England, people of our sort can afford to have a Public Debt; but, of course, those without fortune, beginners, mustn't adopt that style . . .'

'The fact is, Monsieur le Duc, that I still owe five hundred thousand francs on my estate.'

'Well, you'll have to marry some girl who can provide them; but I'm afraid you won't find it easy to make a match on that scale in this neighbourhood, daughters round here don't get much in the way of dowries.'

'They have their name, and that does instead,' replied Lucien.

'There are only three of us for whist, Maufrigneuse, d'Espard and myself,' said the duke; 'will you make up the four?' he added to Lucien indicating the card table.

Clotilde came to the table to watch her father play.

'She wants to bring me luck,' said the duke patting his daughter's hands and glancing sideways at Lucien who remained serious.

Lucien, Monsieur d'Espard's partner, lost twenty louis.

'Mother dear,' Clotilde went over and said to the duchess, 'he's been clever enough to lose.'

At eleven o'clock, after exchanging some words of love with Mademoiselle de Grandlieu, Lucien returned home and went to bed thinking of the complete triumph he was bound to enjoy in a month, for he felt certain of being accepted as Clotilde's suitor, and married before Lent 1830.

Next day, at the time when Lucien was smoking several cigarettes in company with Carlos who was sunk in thought, Monsieur de Saint Estève (he gave that name!) was announced.

He wanted to speak either to the Abbé Carlos Herrera or to Monsieur Lucien de Rubempré.

'Haven't they told him below that I've gone away?' cried the reverend father.

'Yes, sir,' replied the groom.

'Well, then, you see this man,' he said to Lucien; 'but don't utter a single compromising word, and don't show any surprise, this is the enemy.'

'You'll hear me,' said Lucien.

Carlos concealed himself in an adjacent room, and through the crack of the door he saw Corentin enter, recognizing him only by his voice, so expert was this unknown great man at transforming himself! At that moment, Corentin looked like an elderly departmental head from the Ministry of Finance.

'I have not the honour of being known to you, sir,' said Corentin; 'but . . .'

'Forgive me for interrupting you, sir,' said Lucien; 'but . . .'

'But it is a matter of your marriage with Mademoiselle Clotilde de Grandlieu, which will not be taking place,' Corentin then added briskly.

Lucien sat down and made no reply.

'You are in the hands of a man with the power, the will, the ability to prove to the Duc de Grandlieu that the Rubempré estate will be paid for with the price a fool gave you for your mistress, Mademoiselle Esther,' Corentin continued. 'It won't be difficult to turn up the record of the court decision under which Mademoiselle Esther was proceeded against, and there are means of getting d'Estourny to talk. The extremely clever manoeuvres used against Baron Nucingen will be brought to light . . . All this can be done very quickly. Give me a sum of a hundred thousand francs and you will be left in peace . . . This does not concern me personally. I am acting on behalf of those who have planned this *blackmail*, that is all.'

Corentin might have talked for an hour. Lucien puffed at his cigarette with an air of perfect indifference.

'Sir,' he answered, 'I don't want to know who you are, for those who undertake missions of that kind are persons without name, as far as I am concerned. I have allowed you to go on talking without interruption: I am in my own home. You don't seem to me to be entirely senseless, let me explain my own dilemma to you.'

A pause ensued, during which Lucien icily encountered the cat's gaze turned upon him by Corentin.

'Either you are basing what you say on facts which are wholly false, in which case I need pay no attention,' Lucien went on; 'or you are right, and if that is so, by giving you a hundred thousand francs, I should leave you the right to demand as many similar amounts as your mandatory can find Saint Estèves to send me . . . In short, to bring your esteemed communication to an end, know that I, Lucien de Rubempré, am afraid of nobody. I have nothing to do with the kind of jobbery you mention. If the house of Grandlieu wishes to be awkward, there are other aristocratic young persons to be married off. Indeed it would be no reproach to me to stay a bachelor, especially if, as you suggest, I conduct my white-slave traffic with so much profit.'

'If Monsieur l'Abbé Carlos Herrera . . .'

'Sir,' said Lucien interrupting Corentin, 'Father Herrera is at the moment on his way to Spain; he has nothing to do with my marriage, nor indeed with any of my concerns. This man of State was kind enough to give me the benefit of his counsel for a long time, but he has accounts to render to His Majesty the King of Spain; if you want to talk to him, you had better take the road to Madrid.'

'Sir,' said Corentin sharply, 'you will never be the husband of Mademoiselle Clotilde de Grandlieu.'

'So much the worse for her,' replied Lucien impatiently pushing Corentin to the door.

'Have you reflected?' Corentin asked coldly.

'Sir, I don't admit your right either to interfere with my affairs or to make me waste a cigarette,' said Lucien throwing his extinguished cigarette away.

'Good-bye, sir,' said Corentin. 'We shan't meet again, . . . but there will certainly come a moment in your life when you would give half your fortune to have thought of calling me back on the stairs.'

In reply to this threat, Carlos made the gesture of chopping a head off.

'AND now to work!' he cried looking at Lucien who had
turned pale at the close of this dreadful conference.

If, among the somewhat restricted number of readers who
care about the moral and philosophical part of·a book, a
single one could be found who believed in the satisfaction of
Baron Nucingen, that single one would prove how difficult it
is to subject the heart of a harlot to any set of physiological
rules. Esther had decided to make the poor millionaire pay
dear for what he called his *tay of driumph*. Thus, at the beginning of February 1830, no house-warming had yet taken place
at the *liddle balace*.

'But,' said Esther in confidence to her friends who repeated
it to the baron, 'at the Carnival, I shall open my house, and I
mean to make my little man *as happy as a fighting cock*.'

This saying became proverbial in the whores' world. The
baron thereupon began to grumble loudly. Like so many
husbands, he became quite absurd, he complained to his
friends, and his discontentment was known everywhere.
Meanwhile Esther conscientiously kept up her part as
Pompadour to the prince of Speculation. She had already
given one or two little parties in order to introduce Lucien to
the new house. Lousteau, Rastignac, du Tillet, Bixiou,
Nathan, Count Brambourg, all the pick of the profligate
crew, were constantly around. As feminine cast in the play she
was putting on, Esther took on Tullia, Florentine, Fanny
Beaupré, Florine, two actresses and two dancers, and Madame
du Val-Noble. Nothing is gloomier than a harlot's house
without the salt of rivalry, the display of clothes, the changing
faces. In the space of six weeks, Esther became the wittiest
and the most amusing of women, the prettiest and the most
elegant of those female Pariahs who make up the class of kept
women. Set upon a pedestal of her own, she savoured all
those pleasures of vanity which charm the common run of
women, but in her case with a secret knowledge which placed

her above others of her kind. In her heart she kept an image of
herself which at once made her blush and glorified her, the
hour of her abdication was always present to her consciousness; thus she lived as two persons, one pitying the other. Her
sarcasms proceeded from that inward division, the contempt
borne by the angel of love, within the harlot, for the infamous
and hateful part played by the body in presence of the soul.
At once spectator and actor, judge and defendant, she
personified the myth so often found in Arabian tales, where a
sublime being lies hidden beneath a degraded exterior,
typified also, under the name of Nebuchadnezzar, in the book
of books, the Bible. Having granted herself life until the day
after her infidelity, the victim might as well amuse herself a
little with the executioner. Besides, the glimpses Esther'd
had into the secretly shameful methods to which the baron
owed his colossal fortune removed all scruple, she liked to
think of herself as the goddess Ate, Vengeance, as Carlos put
it. And so, turn and turn about, she behaved charmingly and
detestably towards this millionaire who lived only through
her. When the baron reached the point of misery at which he
determined to leave Esther, she brought him back to her with
a tender scene.

Herrera, having made a great to-do about his departure for
Spain, had gone as far as Tours. He had then sent his carriage
on to Bordeaux, leaving in it a servant instructed to play the
part of his master, who was to wait for him at a hotel in
Bordeaux. Returning by diligence in the guise of a commercial
traveller, he had secretly installed himself at Esther's, from
where, through Asia, Europe and Paccard, he carefully
directed his machinations, keeping an eye on everything,
especially Peyrade.

About a fortnight before the day chosen for her reception,
the day after the first Opera ball, the courtesan, whose
witticisms had begun to make her formidable, was to be seen
at the Italiens, at the back of the box which the baron, made to
give her a box, had acquired at stage level, in order to conceal
his mistress and not appear in public with her, a few yards
away from Madame de Nucingen. Esther had picked her box
so as to be able to look into that of Madame de Sérisy, in

whose company Lucien was commonly to be observed. The poor harlot's happiness now depended on seeing Lucien on Tuesdays, Thursdays and Saturdays, sitting by Madame de Sérisy. That evening, at about half past nine, Esther saw Lucien enter the countess's box careworn, pale and haggard. These signs of inward distress were apparent only to Esther. Knowledge of a man's face is, with a woman who loves him, like that of the open sea to a sailor. 'Heavens! what can be the matter with him? ... what has happened! Could he be needing to talk to that dark angel, who is a guardian angel to him, and who lives concealed in an attic room between those of Europe and Asia?' Preoccupied with such cruel thoughts, Esther barely heard the music. It will therefore be readily imagined that she didn't listen at all to the baron, who held one of his *engel*'s hands between his own, talking to her in his Polish Jew's dialect, whose singular inflexions must give no less trouble to those who read them than to those who hear.

'Esder,' said he letting go of her hand, and pushing it away with evident signs of bad temper, 'you are not lizzening to me!'

'Look, baron, you mispronounce love as you mispronounce French.'

'*Gottverdommy!*'

'I am not in my dressing-room here, I am at the Italiens. If you were not one of those strong-boxes manufactured by Huret or by Fichet, metamorphosed into a man by some feat of Nature, you wouldn't make so much noise in the box of a woman who likes music. You're quite right to say I'm not listening to you! There you are, fidgetting about in my frock like a cockchafer in a paper bag, and you make me laugh with pity. You keep on saying: "You are zo briddy, I vill like to ead you ..." You old fathead! if I said to you: "You don't annoy me as much this evening as you did yesterday, let's go home." Well, from the way I see you sighing (for if I don't listen to you, I feel you), I can tell that you've dined too well, you're digesting it all. Believe me (I cost you enough to give you a bit of advice now and then for your money!), believe me, my dear, when a man's digestion is as difficult as yours, he

240

can't go on saying to his mistress, whenever it pleases him: "You are zo briddy ..." An old soldier died of behaving like that *in the arms of Religion*, as Blondet put it ... It is ten o'clock, you finished dinner at nine at du Tillet's with a pigeon you mean to pluck, Count Bramburg, you have all that money and truffles to digest, try again at ten o'clock tomorrow.'

'How you are gruel! ...' cried the baron who recognized the justice of this medical opinion.

'Cruel? ...' said Esther with her eyes still on Lucien. 'Didn't you consult Bianchon, Desplein, old Haudry? ... Since you glimpsed the first dawn of your happiness, do you know what you remind me of? ...'

'Off vot?'

'Of a little old man wrapped up in flannel, who every now and then makes a journey from his armchair to the window to see if the thermometer is still at *silkworms*, the temperature his doctor ordered ...'

'*Ach*, how ongradevul you are!' cried the baron in despair at hearing music of a kind which old men in love nevertheless do quite often hear at the Italiens.

'Ungrateful!' said Esther. 'And what have you given me so far? ... a great deal of annoyance. Look, daddy! can I really be proud of you? You're proud of me, I wear your braid and your livery very well. You've paid my debts! ... all right. But you've *snitched* millions enough ... (Ah, ah! don't pout, you know what we agreed ...) to think nothing of that. And that's all you can boast of ... Whore and thief, they go well together. You've constructed a splendid cage for a parrot that pleases you ... Go and ask a macaw from Brazil if it feels grateful to the man who put it in a gilded cage ... Don't look at me like that, you old bonze ... You show your red and white macaw to everybody in Paris. You say: "Is there anyone in Paris who owns a parrot like that? ... and how it talks! how carefully it chooses its words ..." Du Tillet enters, and it says to him: "Hello, you little rogue ..." But you're as happy as a Dutchman with a tulip like nobody else's, you're like a retired nabob, pensioned in Asia by the British government, to whom a traveller has sold the first Swiss snuff-box to play three overtures. You want my heart! Well, now, look, I'm going to teach you how to win it.'

'Dell me, dell me! . . . I vill do oll vor you . . . I like to hear you mek chokes at me!'

'Be young, be handsome, be like Lucien de Rubempré, who is over there with your wife, and you shall have *gratis* what you will never be able to buy with all your millions! . . .'

'I em leafing you, druly you are egsegraple zis efening! . . .' said the Shark, whose face had dropped.

'Good night, then!' replied Esther. 'Tell Georges to raise the head of your bed up, and keep your feet well down, you've got an apoplectic look this evening . . . Darling, don't say I don't take an interest in your health.'

The baron stood up and took hold of the door-handle.

'Here, Nucingen! . . .' said Esther calling him back with a haughty gesture.

The baron at once took up an attitude of doglike devotion.

'Do you want me to be very nice to you and take you back home this evening and give you glasses of sweetened water and cosset you, you big brute? . . .'

'You are pregging my hurt . . .'

'Better than tanning your hide! . . .' she rejoined. 'Look now, fetch Lucien for me, so that I can invite him to our Belshazzar's feast, and make sure he comes. If you make a success of this piece of business, I'll tell you I love you so convincingly, my big Fred, that you'll believe it . . .'

'You are *ein* enjandress,' said the baron kissing Esther's glove. 'I vod villinkly lizzen to inzults by ze hour, if only voss a gind vort at ze ent . . .'

'Mind you, if you don't do what I say, I . . .' she said wagging her finger at the baron as one does at a child.

The baron shook his head like a bird caught in a trap looking pathetically at the birdcatcher.

'Heavens! what can be the matter with Lucien?' said she to herself when she was alone, no longer restraining her tears, 'he has never been so sad!'

This is what had happened to Lucien that very evening.

Trouble on a threshold

At nine o'clock, as usual, Lucien had set out in his brougham for the Grandlieu house. Keeping his gig and saddle horses for mornings, as most young men do, he'd hired a brougham for the winter evenings, and at the best coach-hirers he'd picked one of the finest, with splendid horses. Everything had gone well for him over the past month; the sale of his Omnibus interests at three hundred thousand francs had enabled him to pay off another third of the cost of his estate; Clotilde de Grandlieu, who dressed marvellously, had ten pots of make-up on her face when he entered the drawing-room, and openly avowed her passion for him. A number of highly placed persons spoke of the marriage between Lucien and Mademoiselle de Grandlieu as of something imminent. The Duc de Chaulieu, former ambassador in Spain and for a while Foreign Minister, had promised the Duchesse de Grandlieu to ask the King to grant Lucien a marquisate. After dining at Madame de Sérisy's, Lucien had therefore gone, that evening, from the rue de la Chaussée d'Antin to the Faubourg Saint Germain to pay his daily visit. He arrives, his coachman finds the entrance, it opens, he pulls up before the steps. Lucien, stepping down from his own, sees four other carriages in the courtyard. Perceiving Monsieur de Rubempré, one of the footmen, who was opening and closing the door to the pillared hallway, advances, plants himself at the top of the steps and stands before the door like a soldier returning to sentry-duty. 'His Grace is not at home!' said the man. 'Madame la Duchesse can receive me,' Lucien pointed out to the footman. 'Madame la Duchesse is out,' the man gravely replies. 'Mademoiselle Clotilde. . . .' 'I do not think Mademoiselle Clotilde could see Monsieur in the absence of Madame la Duchesse . . .' 'But there are people here,' replied Lucien conscious of the blow. 'I don't know,' says the footman trying at one and the same time to appear both stupid and respectful. Nothing is more dreadful than Etiquette for those who regard it as the rule of society. Lucien had not failed to divine the

243

meaning of this painful scene, the duke and duchess didn't mean to admit him; he felt the spinal fluid freeze in his vertebrae, and drops of cold sweat appeared on his forehead. This colloquy had taken place before his own personal man-servant, whose hand was still on the carriage-door and who hesitated whether to shut it; Lucien signalled to him that he was about to leave; but, as he climbed in, he heard the sound of people descending a staircase, and the footman called out in succession: 'Monsieur le Duc de Chaulieu's attendants!' 'Those with Madame la Vicomtesse de Grandlieu!' All Lucien said to his man was: 'Quickly, to the Italiens! . . .' In spite of thus making all speed, the unfortunate dandy could not avoid the Duc de Chaulieu and his son the Duc de Rhétoré, with whom he was forced to exchange mere signs of greeting, for they did not speak a word to him. A great calamity at court, the fall of a powerful favourite, is often consummated on the threshold of some closet by the words of an usher with expressionless face. 'How can I let my counsellor know at once of this disaster?' said Lucien to himself on his way to the Italiens. 'What is happening? . . .' He was lost in conjecture. This is what had taken place. That very morning, at eleven o'clock, the Duc de Grandlieu, as he joined his family in the breakfast room, had said to Clotilde after kissing her: 'My child, until further orders, give no more thought to the Rubempré gentleman.' Then he had taken the duchess by the hand and led her to a window corner, to say something to her in a low voice which caused poor Clotilde to change colour. Mademoiselle de Grandlieu saw an expression of surprise appear on her mother's face as she listened to the duke. Then, 'John,' the duke had said to one of the servants, 'here, take this note to Monsieur le Duc de Chaulieu, ask him to give you yes or no for an answer . . . I'm asking him if he can dine with us today,' he said to his wife. The family luncheon had been gloomy. The duchess seemed lost in thought, the duke appeared to be angry with himself, and it was difficult for Clotilde to keep back her tears. 'My child, your father is right, do as he tells you,' the mother had said in a voice of affection to her daughter. 'I can't, as he does, say: "Don't think of Lucien!" No, I understand your grief.' (Clotilde kissed her mother's hand.) 'What I will say, my angel, is: "Wait and don't do anything whatever, suffer in silence, since you love him, and have confidence in your parents' concern on your behalf!" Great ladies, my child, are great because they know how to do their duty on all occasions, and with nobility.' 'What is the matter? . . .' Clotilde had asked pale as a lily. 'Things too serious for us to speak of them to you, dear heart,' the duchess had answered; 'for if they are false, your thoughts would have been uselessly sullied by them; and if they are true, you must remain in ignorance of them.'

At six o'clock, the Duc de Chaulieu had come to see the Duc de Grandlieu who was waiting for him in his study. 'Tell me, Henri . . .' (The two dukes always addressed each other by their Christian names in this way. It was one of their ways of indicating degrees of intimacy, keeping at bay that familiarity which was invading French life, humbling other people's self-esteem.) 'Tell me, Henri, I'm in such an awkward difficulty, that I can only ask for advice from an old friend who's as broken in to the ways of the world as you are. My daughter Clotilde, as you know, is in love with this young Rubempré they've more or less made me promise to let her marry. I've always been against this marriage; but, in the end, Madame de Grandlieu found she couldn't oppose Clotilde's love. When the boy had bought his estate, when he'd three parts paid for it, I raised no further objection. Yesterday evening I received an anonymous letter (you know what weight one should attach to such things) in which it is stated that the boy's fortune comes from a tainted source, and that he lied to us when he said his sister had provided the necessary funds. I am exhorted, in the name of my daughter's happiness and the consideration due to my family, to seek information, the means of finding it being indicated. But there, to begin with, read it.' 'I share your opinion of anonymous letters, my dear Ferdinand,' the Duc de Chaulieu had answered having read the letter; 'but, while you may view them with contempt, you can sometimes find them useful. It is absolutely the same with letters of that kind, as it is with spies. Bar your door to this boy, and let's see what we can find out . . . Look, I know just what to do. Your solicitor is Derville, a man in whom we all have every confidence; he knows the secrets of a great many families, and that may be one of them. He is an honest man, a man of weight, a man of honour; he is clever, he is not without guile; but it's only monetary matters and such that he's clever about, you must use him only to collect evidence you can really trust. At the Ministry of Foreign Affairs we have a man from the Royal Police, who is without equal at discovering State secrets, we often post him on missions. Inform Derville that, in this affair, there'll be somebody under him. Our spy is *a gentleman* who will appear decorated with the Légion d'Honneur, he will look like a diplomatist. This rogue will be the huntsman, and Derville will simply look on at the hunt. Your solicitor will tell you whether the mountain gives birth to a mouse, or whether you must break with young Rubempré. Within a week, you'll know what course to follow.' 'The fellow isn't yet marquess enough to seek a formal explanation if he finds me not at home for a week,' the Duc de Grandlieu had then said. 'Especially if you're giving him your daughter,' the former minister had replied. 'If that anonymous letter is right, it won't matter! You can send Clotilde on her travels with my daughter-in-law Madeleine, who very much wants to go to Italy . . .' 'You take a load off my mind! and I don't know how I shall be able to thank you . . .' 'Let's see what the outcome is.' 'Ah!' cried the Duc de Grandlieu, 'what is this gentleman's name? I must let Derville know . . . Send him along tomorrow, at four o'clock, I'll have Derville here, I'll bring them together myself.' 'The real name,' said the former minister, 'is, I believe, Corentin . . . (a name you won't have heard), but this gentleman will come here under his ministerial colours. He calls himself Monsieur de Saint Something-or-Other . . . Oh, Saint Yves, Saint Valère, one or the other . . . You can trust him, Louis XVIII trusted him absolutely.'

After this discussion, the steward received orders to bar the door to Monsieur de Rubempré, which had just been done.

LUCIEN walked through the crush-room of the Italiens like a drunk man. He saw himself the talk of all Paris. In the Duc de Rhétoré he had one of those pitiless enemies at whom one must smile without hope of revenge, for their blows are inflicted in conformity with the rules of society. The Duc de Rhétoré knew what had passed on the steps of the Grandlieu house. Lucien felt a need to communicate the news of this sudden disaster to his personal and actual privy counsellor, and he feared to compromise himself by visiting Esther's box, where there might be people who knew him. He even forgot Esther was there, so confused were his thoughts; and amidst his perplexities he found himself having to make conversation with Rastignac, who, knowing nothing of what had just happened, congratulated him on his coming marriage. At that moment, Nucingen bore down smiling on Lucien, and said to him: 'Vill you gif me ze bleasure of goming do zee Madame de Champy who vishes to infite you herzelf do our houzevarmink . . .'

'Gladly, Baron,' replied Lucien to whom the financier's appearance seemed providential.

'Leave us,' said Esther to Monsieur de Nucingen when she saw him enter with Lucien, 'go and talk to Madame du Val-Noble whom I see in a box on the third tier with her Nabob . . . Nabobs grow thick in the Indies,' she added with an understanding look at Lucien.

'And that one,' said Lucien with a smile, 'is terribly like yours.'

'And,' said Esther answering Lucien with another sign of intelligence while continuing to speak to the baron, 'bring her and her Nabob here, he is very anxious to meet you, he is said to be extraordinarily rich. The poor woman has already sung me so many sad songs about him, she can't manage with the Nabob; and if you lightened him of ballast, he might be a bit more nimble.'

'You dake uz vor tieves,' said the baron.

'What's the matter with my Lucien? . . .' she whispered to her darling brushing his ear with her lips as soon as the door of the box was shut.

'I'm lost! I've just been refused entry to the Grandlieu house, on the pretext that nobody was at home, both the duke and duchess were in, and five equipages were snorting in the yard . . .'

'You mean the marriage is off!' said Esther in a voice stifled with feeling, for this was a glimpse of paradise to her.

'I don't know yet what they're plotting against me . . .'

'Lucien dear,' she replied in an adorably wheedling voice, 'why upset yourself? you'll make a finer marriage presently . . . I'll earn you two estates . . .'

'Give a supper party, this evening, so that I can speak to Carlos secretly, and make sure you invite the sham Englishman and Val-Noble. That Nabob is the cause of my ruin, he's our enemy, we shall have got him, and we . . .' But Lucien stopped short with a despairing gesture.

'Why, what is it?' asked the poor whore who felt as though she were on fire.

'Damnation, Madame de Sérisy has seen me!' cried Lucien, 'and to make it worse, the Duc de Rhétoré, who witnessed my discomfiture, is with her.'

Indeed, at that very moment, the Duc de Rhétoré was playing upon Countess Sérisy's grief.

'You allow Lucien to show himself in the box of Mademoiselle Esther,' said the young duke indicating both the box and Lucien. 'You who take an interest in him, you should tell him that that isn't done. One may sup at her house, one may even . . . but, truly, I don't wonder now that the Grandlieus have turned against this boy, I've just seen him turned away at the door, on the steps . . .'

'Those creatures are very dangerous,' said Madame de Sérisy who turned her opera glasses on Esther's box.

'Yes, indeed,' said the duke, 'as much for what they can do as for what they want . . .'

'They'll ruin him!' said Madame de Sérisy, 'for according to what I'm told, they're as expensive when you don't pay them as when you do.'

'Not for him! . . .' replied the young duke with an air of surprise. 'Far from costing him money, they give it to him whenever he needs it, they all run after him.'

There was a nervous movement about the countess's mouth which could hardly be regarded as one of her smiles.

'Well, then,' said Esther, 'come to supper at midnight. Bring Blondet and Rastignac. Let's have at least two amusing people, and let's not be more than nine.'

'We must find some way of getting the baron to look for Europe, on the pretext that Asia must be warned, and you can tell her what happened to me, so that Carlos will know about it before he has the Nabob in his power.'

'It shall be done,' said Esther.

Thus Peyrade, without knowing it, must find himself beneath the same roof as his adversary. The tiger was going into the lion's den and the lion would be prepared for him.

When Lucien went back to Madame de Sérisy's box, she, instead of turning her head towards him, smiling and arranging her gown to make room for him beside her, affected to pay no attention to the person who had entered, she continued her inspection of the audience; but Lucien perceived by the trembling of the binoculars that the countess was a prey to one of those powerful agitations by which we expiate inadmissible moments of happiness. He nevertheless came forward to the front of the box, beside her, and planted himself in the opposite corner, leaving a narrow space empty between the countess and himself; he leaned against the front of the box, placed his right elbow on the ledge, and his chin in his gloved hand; there he sat posed in three-quarters profile, waiting for her to speak. Half way through the act, the countess had still said nothing to him, and hadn't even looked at him.

'I don't know,' she said at last, 'why you're here; your place is in Mademoiselle Esther's box . . .'

'That's where I'm going,' said Lucien and went out without looking at the countess.

'Ah, my dear,' said Madame du Val-Noble entering Esther's box with Peyrade whom Baron Nucingen didn't recognize, 'I am happy to introduce to you Mr Samuel Johnson; he is a great admirer of Monsieur de Nucingen's abilities.'

'Really, sir,' said Esther smiling at Peyrade.

'Aoh, yes, very much,' said Peyrade.

'Well, baron, there's a French rather like your own, much as Breton is like Burgundian. It will amuse me very much to hear you discussing finance . . . Do you know what I demand of you, Monsieur Nabob, in return for introducing you to my baron?' she said with a smile.

'Aoh, thenks, I shell be delighted, I'm sure, to make the baronet's acquaintance.'

'Well, then,' she went on, 'you'll have to give me the pleasure of supping with us . . . There's nothing like champagne for binding men together, it's a wax that caulks every seam, especially when you're sinking. Come this evening, we shall have good company! As to you, Fritz darling,' she whispered to the baron, 'your carriage is here, run to the rue Saint-Georges and bring Europe here, I've a word or two to say to her about the supper . . . I've asked Lucien, he'll bring two amusing people with him . . . We'll bring your Englishman to the point,' she whispered into Madame du Val-Noble's ear.

Peyrade and the baron left the two women alone.

Pleasure has its inconvenient side

'Oh, my dear, if you can ever bring that big scoundrel to the point, you'll be very clever,' said Madame du Val-Noble.

'If there was no other way, you could always lend him to me for a week,' replied Esther with a laugh.

'No, you wouldn't keep him for half a day,' rejoined Madame du Val-Noble, 'my daily bread is too hard, I break my teeth on it. Never, so long as I live, will I try to make any Englishman happy . . . They are all cold egoists, pigs dressed up . . .'

'What, no consideration?' said Esther smilingly.

'On the contrary, my dear, the monster isn't *familiar* enough.'

'Not in any situation?' said Esther.

'The wretch calls me Madame all the time, and retains the most abominable calm just when all other men are rather nice. Making love is for him, really, my dear, just like trimming his beard. He wipes his razor, puts it back in its case, looks at himself in the glass, and seems to be saying: "Well, I didn't cut myself." Then he treats me with the kind of respect to drive any woman out of her mind. It amuses this frightful Lord Stockpot to hide poor Theodore and leave him standing about in my dressing room half the day. In fact he deliberately thwarts me in every way. And he's mean, as mean as Gobseck and Gigonnet put together. He takes me out to dinner, he doesn't pay for the cab I come in, if by chance I've forgotten to order the carriage.'

'And in return for all this, what do you get?'

'Nothing, my dear, absolutely nothing. Five hundred francs a month, not a penny more, and he pays for the hire of the carriage. As to that, what sort of thing do you think it is? ... one like those they hire out to grocers on their wedding day to go to the Town Hall, the Church and the Blue Dial ... He maddens me with his respect. If I'm at all nervy and ill-disposed, he doesn't get annoyed, he says: "I aonly wish my lady too doo as she chooooses, for I'm sure nothing is more detestable, no gentleman would thinka vitfra moment, than to say to a nice filly she was just a bale of cotton to be paid for! ... Haw, haw, the buyer is a member of the Society for Temperance and No Slavery!" And the scoundrel remains pale, dry, cold, giving me to understand that he respects me as he would a negro, and that this doesn't come from the heart, but because of his abolitionist opinions.'

'I can't imagine anything more frightful,' said Esther, 'but I'd ruin him, a Chinaman like that!'

'Ruin him?' said Madame du Val-Noble, 'he'd have to love me first! ... But even you wouldn't dare ask him for two farthings. He would listen to you solemnly, and then he would say, in that British manner which makes you feel you'd rather have your face slapped, that he pays you quite enough for the *trifling thing love is in his poor life*.'

'To think that, in our condition, we can meet men like that!' cried Esther.

'Ah, my dear, you're lucky! ... watch that Nucingen of yours.'

'He knows what he's doing, your Nabob?'

'Adèle thinks so,' replied Madame du Val-Noble.

'You know, that man, my dear, might have taken it into his head to make a woman hate him, and so make sure of being sent packing after a certain time,' said Esther.

'Or else he has business he wants to do with Nucingen, and took me on because he knew there was a connection, that's what Adèle thinks,' replied Madame du Val-Noble. 'That's why I'm introducing him to you this evening. Oh! if I really knew what his plans were, what a pretty understanding I could come to with you and Nucingen!'

'Don't you lose your temper,' said Esther, 'and tell him a few home truths from time to time?'

'You'd try, I know, and you're clever, ... but, well, however nice you were to him, he'd kill you with his frozen smiles. He'd say to you: "You knaow, I em anti-slavery, and you are free ..." You'd tell him the most amusing things, he'd look at you and say: "Very good!" and you'd see that, in his eyes, you were nothing but a punch-and-judy show.'

'And when you're angry?'

'Just the same! It's a spectacle to him. You can operate on his left side, under the breast, and it won't produce the slightest effect; his insides must be made of tin. I told him. He replied: "It suits me very well to have a constitution such as you describe ..." And always polite. His very soul wears gloves, my dear ... I shall continue to endure this martyrdom for a few days more just to satisfy my curiosity. Otherwise, I should have got milord called out by Philippe, who is without equal as a swordsman, it'll come to that yet ...'

'I was going to suggest that!' cried Esther; 'but you'd best find out first if he can box, for these old Englishmen, my dear, they can always turn nasty.'

'There can't be others like him! ... No, if you saw him coming to me for orders, at quite unimaginable hours, clearly in the hope of surprising me, and if you saw his curious ways of expressing respect, in the manner, you understand, of a *gentleman*, you would say: "There is a woman truly loved," and any other woman would say the same . . .'

'And yet they envy us, darling,' said Esther.

'Yes, indeed! . . .' cried Madame du Val-Noble. 'Look, we've all more or less, at some time or other, discovered how little they really care about us; but, my dear, I've never been so cruelly, so profoundly, so utterly humiliated by anyone's brutality, as I am by the respect of this big wineskin full of port. When he's drunk, he goes away, so as not to upset the little lady, he says to Adèle, and not to be under two *influences* at the same time: wine and woman. He makes more use of my carriage than I do . . . Oh! if we could only get him under the table this evening, . . . but he drinks ten bottles, and he's only just tipsy: his eyes are blurred, but he sees everything.'

'It's like those people whose windows are dirty outside,' said Esther, 'and who from inside can see everything that happens in the street . . . I know men like that: du Tillet is a fine example of them.'

'Try to have du Tillet, and Nucingen with the two of them, if they could only catch him up in one of their schemes, I should at least have my revenge! . . . they'd reduce him to beggary! Ah! my dear, to fall into the hands of a hypocrite and a Protestant, after my poor Falleix, who was so amusing and good-natured, such a *wag*! . . . How we used to laugh! . . . They say all stockbrokers are stupid . . . Well, his wit failed him only once . . .'

'When he left you without a penny, it let you know pleasure has its inconvenient side.'

Europe, brought by Monsieur de Nucingen, pushed her viper's head in at the door; after listening to the few words her mistress whispered into her ear, she vanished.

The snakes entwine

A T half past eleven that evening, five carriages stopped in the rue Saint Georges, before the door of the famous courtesan: they belonged to Lucien who came with Rastignac, Blondet

and Bixiou, to du Tillet, to Baron Nucingen, to the Nabob and
to Florine recruited by du Tillet. The fact that the windows
were still boarded up was disguised by the folds of the
magnificent curtains of China silk. Supper was to be served at
one o'clock, tapers burned, the small drawing-room and the
dining-room displayed all their sumptuousness. One of those
nights of debauch seemed promised to which only three women
and those men would offer resistance. First there was gambling,
for two hours had to be passed.

'Do you play, my lord? . . .' said du Tillet to Peyrade.

'I have played with O'Connell, Pitt, Fox, Canning, Lord
Brougham, Lord . . .'

'Why not just say countless lords?' Bixiou asked him.

'. . . Lord FitzWilliam, Lord Ellenborough, Lord Hertford,
Lord . . .'

Bixiou studied Peyrade's pumps and bent down.

'What are you looking for?' Blondet asked him.

'Why, the button you have to press to stop the machine,'
said Florine.

'What stakes?' said Lucien, 'twenty francs a trick?'

'I shall play for whatever you wish to lose . . .'

'Isn't he good? . . .' said Esther to Lucien, 'they all take him
for an Englishman! . . .'

Du Tillet, Nucingen, Peyrade and Rastignac got out a card
table and settled down to their whist. Florine, Madame du
Val-Noble, Esther, Blondet and Bixiou stayed talking near
the fire. Lucien passed the time turning the pages of a magnificent book with engravings.

'Madame is served,' said Paccard in a splendid livery.

Peyrade was placed on Florine's left and flanked by Bixiou
whom Esther had engaged to make the Nabob drink beyond
measure by challenging him. Bixiou had the gift of being able
to drink indefinitely. Never, in all his life, had Peyrade seen so
much splendour, nor tasted such cooking, nor seen such
pretty women.

'This evening alone pays back the thousand crowns the
Val-Noble has already cost me,' he thought, 'and besides I've
just won a thousand francs from them.'

'Here's an example for you,' called out Madame du Val-

Noble who was sitting next to Lucien and who with a gesture called attention to all the splendour of the dining-room.

Esther had put Lucien next to herself and held his foot between hers under the table.

'Do you hear?' said Val-Noble looking at Peyrade who pretended not to see, 'this is how you should arrange a house for me! When you return from the Indies with millions and want to do business with the Nucingens, you have to put yourself on their level.'

'I belong to the temp'rance s'iety.'

'Then you'd better drink nicely,' said Bixiou, 'for it's hot in India, isn't it, uncle? . . .'

All through supper, Bixiou amusingly kept up the pretence that Peyrade was an uncle of his returned from India.

'Matame di Fal-Noble tells me you hef a number off iteas . . .' asked Nucingen examining Peyrade.

'This is what I wanted to hear,' said du Tillet to Rastignac, 'the two kinds of gibberish together.'

'You'll see they'll end up by understanding each other,' said Bixiou who guessed what du Tillet had just said to Rastignac.

'Aoh, yes, I'd thought of just the ticket, a comfortable little speculation likely to appeal to a baronet of your kind, . . . very profitable, rich pickings . . .'

'You'll see,' said Blondet to du Tillet, 'that in half a minute he'll be bringing in Parliament and the British government.'

'In China, as a metter of fect, . . . opium, y'know . . .'

'I know,' Nucingen at once said as a man who owned his commercial Globe, 'put ze Enklish Kofernment hess its plens for obening up China *mit* opium, *und* vould nod allow uz . . .'

'Nucingen got in first about the government,' said du Tillet to Blondet.

'Ah, you've trafficked in opium, have you?' cried Madame du Val-Noble, 'I can see now why you stupefy me so, you've got it on the heart . . .'

'Ah, you zee!' ejaculated the baron to the supposed opium dealer pointing out Madame du Val-Noble, 'you are like minezelf: nefer can millionaires mek zemselves luft py vomen.'

'Meself, I'm rather a one for love, my lady,' Peyrade replied.

'Always for the sake of temperance,' said Bixiou who'd just

got Peyrade through his third bottle of claret, and was now broaching the port with him.

'Aoh,' cried Peyrade, 'this is real English port!'

Blondet, du Tillet and Bixiou exchanged smiles. Peyrade had it in him to parody everything, even wit. There are few Englishmen who will not maintain that gold and silver are better in England than anywhere else. Chickens and eggs sent from Normandy and put on the market in London authorize the English to insist that the eggs and chickens of London are superior to those of Paris which come from the same rural area. Esther and Lucien were in a state of amazement in the face of such perfection in the matter of dress, speech and mental character. The drinking and eating, the talk and laughter, went on till four o' clock in the morning. Bixiou considered himself to have brought off one of those victories so amusingly recounted by Brillat-Savarin. But, just as he was saying at the same time as he filled his uncle's glass: 'I've conquered England! . . .' Peyrade answered the ferocious joker with a: 'Fill up, my boy, fill up!' which only Bixiou heard.

'Hi, you others, he's as English as I am! . . . My uncle's a Gascon! he'd have to be, of course!'

Bixiou and Peyrade were sitting away from the others, and nobody heard. Peyrade fell off his chair and lay on the floor. At once Paccard picked him up and carried him to an attic where Peyrade fell into a deep sleep. It was six o' clock in the evening before the Nabob awoke to find that his face was being wiped with a wet cloth and that he lay on a shaky trestle bed, face to face, beside Asia masked and wearing a black domino.

'Hello, Papa Peyrade, are there two of us, then?' said she.

'Where am I? . . .' he said looking about him.

'Listen to me, this'll sober you up,' replied Asia. 'If you don't love Madame du Val-Noble, you love your daughter, don't you?'

'My daughter?' howled Peyrade.

'Yes, Miss Lydia . . .'

'Well? . . .'

'Well, she isn't in the rue des Moineaux any longer, they've taken her away.'

Peyrade uttered a gasping sigh like that of a soldier dying of an open wound on the battlefield.

'While you played at being an Englishman, somebody else played at being Peyrade. Your little Lydia thought she was going with her father, she's in a safe place . . . Oh, you'll never find her! not unless you make good the harm you've caused.'

'What harm?'

'Yesterday, at the Duc de Grandlieu's, entry was refused to Monsieur Lucien de Rubempré. This result was due to your intrigues and to the man you took away from us. Not a word. Listen!' said Asia seeing Peyrade open his mouth. 'You won't get your daughter back, pure and without stain,' Asia went on driving each point home by the stress she placed on each word, 'till the day after Monsieur Lucien de Rubempré comes out of Saint Thomas Aquinas's, married to Mademoiselle Clotilde. If, ten days from now, Lucien de Rubempré isn't received back at the Grandlieu house, you to begin with will die a violent death, without any possibility of warding off the blow which threatens you . . . And then, just as you feel death coming, you'll be given time in your last moments to think this thought: "My daughter will be a prostitute to the end of her days! . . ." Although you've been stupid enough to let us get our claws into the prey, you've got wit enough left to ponder this communication from our government. Don't bark, don't say a word, just go and change your clothes at Contenson's, go home, and Katt will tell you that, on receiving a message from you, little Lydia went out and hasn't returned. If you make any complaint, or go and see anyone, we shall begin where I told you we should finish with your daughter, she's been *promised* to de Marsay. With Papa Canquoëlle, we don't mince our words, or wear mittens, do we? . . . Off you go now and remember not to meddle with our affairs again.'

Asia left Peyrade in a pitiable state, each word fell like a bludgeon stroke. The spy had two tears in his eyes and two tears at the bottom of his cheeks joined by two trails of moisture.

'Mr Johnson is awaited for dinner,' said Europe poking her head in a moment later.

Peyrade didn't answer, he went down the stairs, walked

along the streets till he came to a cab stand, he hurried to Contenson's to undress, without saying a word to Contenson he got himself up as Papa Canquoëlle again, and was home by eight o'clock. He climbed the stairs with beating heart. When the Flemish servant heard her master, she thoughtlessly asked him: 'Well, where is Mademoiselle?' so that the old spy was forced to lean against the wall. The blow was too great for his strength. He went into his daughter's room, in the end fainted with grief on finding the apartment empty and hearing Katt's account of a kidnapping as cleverly contrived as though he had invented it himself. 'Come,' he said to himself, 'we shall have to give way, I'll avenge myself later, I must see Corentin . . . For the first time, we've met our match. Corentin shall leave this pretty lad free to marry empresses if he chooses! . . . Ah! I understand now how my daughter came to love him at first sight . . . Oh! the Spanish priest knows what he's doing . . . Courage, Papa Peyrade, disgorge your prey!' The poor father did not foresee the dreadful blow which awaited him.

When he reached Corentin's the confidential, servant, who knew Peyrade, told him: 'Monsieur has gone away . . .'

'For long?'

'For ten days! . . .'

'Where?'

'I don't know! . . .'

'Oh, my God! I'm becoming stupid! I ask him where? . . . as if we ever told them,' he thought.

At the Belle Étoile

SEVERAL hours before Peyrade was to be awakened in his attic at the rue Saint Georges, Corentin, driving in from Passy, appeared at the Duc de Grandlieu's residence, dressed as a private servant in some good family. In the buttonhole of his black coat might be seen the ribbon of the Legion of Honour. He had given himself a little old man's face, with powdered hair, full of wrinkles, pallid. His eyes were veiled by shell-rimmed spectacles. He looked like some old senior clerk. When he'd given his name (Monsieur de Saint Denis) he was conducted to the Duc de Grandlieu's study, where he found Derville, reading the letter he had himself dictated to one of his agents, the handwriting expert. The duke took Corentin on one side to explain to him all that Corentin knew. Monsieur de Saint Denis listened coldly, respectfully, amused to be studying this great lord, penetrating to the bedrock under the velvet, seeing in the cold light of day a life given over, then and forever, to whist and the position of the house of Grandlieu. Great lords are so simple-minded with their inferiors, that Corentin didn't need to put many questions humbly to Monsieur de Grandlieu before he received the kind of impertinence he expected.

'Believe me, sir,' said Corentin to Derville after being duly introduced to the solicitor, 'it will be best for us to leave this very evening for Angoulême by the Bordeaux diligence, which travels just as fast as the mail-coach, we shall only need to stay there six hours to pick up the information Monsieur le Duc wants. It is sufficient, if I have understood Your Lordship, to discover whether the sister and brother-in-law of Monsieur de Rubempré could have given him twelve hundred thousand francs? . . .' said he with a look at the duke.

'Exactly,' replied the peer of France.

'We should be back in four days,' Corentin went on looking at Derville, 'and neither of us will have left his business alone long enough for it to have suffered.'

'That was the only objection I had to make to His Lordship,' said Derville. 'It is four o'clock, I'm going back to say a word or two to my head clerk, pack my things; and when I've dined, say by eight o'clock . . . But will there be seats?' he said to Monsieur de Saint Denis interrupting himself.

'I'll see to that,' said Corentin, 'be in the yard at the Messageries du Grand Bureau at eight o'clock. If there weren't any places, I shall see to it that they are made, that is the kind of service Monseigneur le Duc de Grandlieu has a right to expect.'

'Gentlemen,' said the duke with great affability, 'I shall not express my gratitude just yet . . .'

Corentin and the solicitor, taking this as a sign of dismissal took their leave and departed. At the moment at which Peyrade was questioning Corentin's servant, Monsieur de Saint Denis and Derville, seated in the half-compartment of the Bordeaux diligence, studied each other in silence as this vehicle left Paris. The following morning, from Orléans to Tours, Derville, who was bored, became talkative, and Corentin deigned to amuse him, while keeping his distance; allowing him to believe that he belonged to the diplomatic corps, and expected to become a consul general through the protection of the Duc de Grandlieu. Two days after their departure from Paris, Corentin and Derville stopped at Mansle, to the great astonishment of Derville who had expected to go on to Angoulême.

'In this little town,' said Corentin to Derville, 'we shall pick up definite particulars about Madame Séchard.'

'You know her then?' asked Derville surprised to find Corentin so well informed.

'I got the driver to talk when I discovered he came from Angoulême, he told me that Madame Séchard lives at Marsac, and Marsac is only a league away from Mansle. I thought we should be better placed here than in Angoulême to unmask the truth.'

'In any case,' thought Derville, 'I'm only here, as Monsieur le Duc said, as a witness to this confidential agent's inquiries . . .'

The landlord of the inn at Mansle, called the Belle Étoile, was one of those big, fat men whom one barely expects to see at a second visit, but who are still there, ten years later, standing at the door, with the same quantity of flesh, the same cotton bonnet, the same apron, the same big kitchen knife, the same greasy hair, the same three chins, and whose stereotype we find in all the novelists, from the immortal Cervantes to the immortal Sir Walter Scott. Are they not all full of culinary pretensions, haven't they all got everything you could desire and don't they all end by serving you a skinny chicken and vegetables warmed up in rancid butter? They all boast of their fine wines, and compel you to drink the local stuff. But from his earliest years Corentin had learnt to draw out of innkeepers things more essential than dubious dishes and apocryphal wines. So he gave himself out for a man easily pleased and perfectly happy to leave all to the discretion of the best cook in Mansle, as he said to the fat man.

'It isn't difficult for me to be the best, I'm the only one,' replied mine host.

'Serve us in the side room,' said Corentin winking at Derville, 'and above all don't be afraid to light a fire, we're numb with cold.'

'It wasn't very warm in the back of the coach,' said Derville.

'Is it far from here to Marsac?' Corentin asked the innkeeper's wife who descended from the upper regions on learning that the diligence had brought her travellers who would be staying the night.

'Are you going to Marsac, Monsieur?' the landlady asked.

'I don't know,' he replied with a certain abruptness. 'What sort of distance is it from here to Marsac?' he asked again after giving the mistress of the house time to see his red ribbon.

'By carriage, it's a matter of a short half hour,' said the innkeeper's wife.

'Do you suppose that Monsieur and Madame Séchard are there in winter? . . .'

'Oh, certainly, they stay there all the year round . . .'

'It's five o'clock, should we find them still up at nine?'

'Oh, till ten, they have company every evening, the *curé*, Monsieur Marron, the doctor.'

'They must be excellent people!' said Derville.

'Oh, sir, the very best,' replied the innkeeper's wife, 'honest, straightforward folk . . . and not ambitious, what's more! Monsieur Séchard, although his circumstances are comfortable, could have had millions, by what people say, if he hadn't let himself be robbed of an invention he'd made in paper-making, so that all the profit goes to the Cointet brothers . . .'

'Ah, yes! the Cointet brothers!' said Corentin.

'Hold your tongue now,' said the innkeeper. 'What does it matter to these gentlemen whether Monsieur Séchard does or does not possess the right to letters patent in paper-making? these gentlemen aren't paper-dealers . . . If you mean to spend the night here at the Belle Étoile, under the stars, as you might say,' went on the innkeeper addressing the two travellers, 'here is the book, and I shall ask you to sign yourselves in. We have a local policeman who has nothing to do and who spends his time plaguing us . . .'

'Confound it, confound it, I thought the Séchards were very rich,' said Corentin while Derville wrote out his name and his qualifications as a solicitor attached to the Court of First Instance of the Seine department.

'There are some folk,' replied the innkeeper, 'who say they're millionaires; but to try to stop tongues clacking is like undertaking to stop the river flowing. Old Mr Séchard left property worth two hundred thousand francs in broad daylight, as they say, and that in itself isn't bad for one who started as a workman. Well, he may have had as much again in savings, . . . for towards the end he was drawing a thousand or twelve hundred francs a year on his property. So, then, suppose he was stupid enough to do nothing with his money for ten years, that would be the lot! But reckon three hundred thousand francs, if it was put out at interest, as people think, then you can see for yourself. Five hundred thousand francs, that's a long way short of a million. If I had the difference, I shouldn't be here at the Belle Étoile.'

'You mean,' said Corentin, 'that Monsieur David Séchard and his wife haven't got a fortune of two or three millions . . .'

'That,' cried the innkeeper's wife, 'is what they reckon Messrs Cointet have, who robbed him of his invention, and all he got from them was twenty thousand francs . . . So where do you expect these honest folk to have got millions from? they were hard put to it in their father's lifetime. Without Kolb, their manager, and Madame Kolb, who's as devoted to them as her husband, they'd have found it difficult to live. What had they then, apart from the house, the Verberie? . . . a thousand crowns a year! . . .'

Corentin took Derville aside and said to him: 'In vino veritas! you find the truth under a bush. For my purposes, I regard an inn as the civic centre of a countryside, the notary knows far less than the innkeeper about what goes on in a small place . . . Look! we're now understood to know the Cointets, the Kolbs and so on . . . An innkeeper is the living register of every incident, he polices the neighbourhood without knowing it. A government needs two hundred spies at most; for, in a country like France, there are ten million honest informers. But still we mustn't trust everything we hear, though in this little town you can be sure something is known about the twelve hundred thousand francs laid out on the Rubempré estate . . . We shan't stay here long . . .'

'I hope not,' said Derville.

'That is why,' Corentin continued, 'I've hit on the most natural way of extracting the truth from the Séchards themselves. I count on you, with your authority as a solicitor, to back up the little ruse I shall employ to make you hear a clear and exact account of their fortune. After dinner, we shall be setting off for Monsieur Séchard's,' said Corentin to the inn-keeper's wife, 'you can see to making up our beds, we want separate rooms. There must be plenty of space *à la Belle Étoile*.'

'Oh, sir,' said the woman, 'we didn't give it that name, the sign was here.'

'The play on words exists in every part of the country,' said Corentin, 'making your guests sleep "out under the stars" isn't a monopoly of yours.'

'Your dinner is now served, gentlemen,' said the innkeeper.

'So where the devil did that young man find the money? . . . Is the anonymous letter writer telling the truth? could it be the savings of some fair lady?' said Derville to Corentin as they seated themselves at table.

'That will be the subject of further inquiries,' said Corentin. 'According to what the Duc de Chaulieu tells me, Lucien de Rubempré lived with a converted Jewess, who gave herself out for a Dutchwoman, and used the name Esther van Bogseck.'

'What a singular coincidence!' said the lawyer, 'I'm looking for the heiress of a Dutchman called Gobseck, it's the same name if you change the consonants round . . .'

'Well,' said Corentin, 'when we get back to Paris, I'll dig up what you need about the consanguinity question there.'

An hour later, the two representatives of the house of Grandlieu left for the Verberie, Monsieur and Madame Séchard's house.

NEVER had Lucien experienced feelings so profound as those with which he was seized at the Verberie when he compared his own destiny with that of his brother-in-law. The two men from Paris would be confronted with the same spectacle as, a few days before, had met Lucien's eyes. There everything spoke of calm and plenitude. At the time at which the two strangers were due to arrive, the Verberie drawing-room contained a group of five people: the parish priest of Marsac, a young man of twenty-five who, at Madame Séchard's request, had constituted himself her son Lucien's tutor; the country doctor, a Monsieur Marron; the mayor of the commune, and an old colonel retired from the service who grew roses on a small piece of land, facing the Verberie, on the other side of the road. Every evening in winter, these four came to play an innocent game of Boston at a centime a trick, pick up newspapers or retail what was in the ones they'd read. When Monsieur and Madame Séchard bought the Verberie, a fine house built of limestone with slated roofs, its outside amenities consisted of a little garden of about two acres. With time, devoting her savings to it, the beautiful Madame Séchard had extended her garden as far as a little watercourse, sacrificing the bits of vineyard she bought and converting them into lawns and rockeries. At that moment, the Verberie, surrounded by a little park of about twenty acres, shut in by walls, was regarded as the most important property in the district. The late Séchard's house and its outbuildings now served only for the exploitation of twenty odd acres of vineyard left by him, plus five small farms producing about six thousand francs, and ten acres of meadowland, situated on the far side of the watercourse, just opposite the park of the Verberie; thus Madame Séchard hoped to be able to take them in the following year. Already, in the countryside, the Verberie was described as a *château*, and Madame Séchard was called the lady of Marsac. In gratifying his vanity Lucien did no more than imitate the peasants and wine-growers. Courtois, the owner of a mill situated picturesquely almost within gunshot from the Verberie meadowland, was said to be negotiating with Madame Séchard over the purchase of this mill. Its probable acquisition would finally give the Verberie all the amenity of one of the finest estates in the department. Madame Séchard herself, who performed her good works with as much discernment as generosity, was both esteemed and loved. Her beauty, with its new touch of magnificence, was coming to its finest point of development. Though some twenty-six years old, she had retained the freshness of youth, enjoying the repose and abundance of a country life. Still in love with her husband, what she respected in him was the man of talent modest enough to dispense with the chatter of fame; to complete the portrait, it is thus perhaps enough to add that, in all her life, her heart beat only for her children and her husband. The tax this family paid to misfortune was, as may be guessed, the grief caused by Lucien's way of life, in which Ève Séchard suspected elements of mystery which she feared the more in that, on his last visit, Lucien had abruptly checked all his sister's questions by saying that men of ambition owed an account of their means to themselves alone. In six years, Lucien had seen his sister three times, and he had written to her six times in all. His first visit to the Verberie took place at the time of his mother's death, and the object of the last had been to beg the favour of a lie necessary to his private purposes. Between Monsieur and Madame Séchard and their brother, this had given rise to a painful scene which left grave doubts in the heart of their sweet and noble existence.

The interior of the house, as markedly transformed as the outside, was comfortable rather than luxurious. It may be judged by a rapid glance at the drawing-room where the company was seated at that moment. A pretty Aubusson carpet, hangings of grey cotton twill decorated with green silk braid, paintwork grained to look like Spa pine timbering, carved mahogany furniture upholstered in grey kerseymere also green-braided, flower stands loaded with flowers, in spite of the season, offered to the eye a well-composed whole. The window curtains of green silk, the ornaments over the fireplace, the frames of the mirrors were exempt from that false taste which spoils everything in the provinces. Elegant and clean, the smallest details rested the soul and the eyes in that poetic element with which a loving and intelligent woman may and should suffuse all in her household.

Madame Séchard, still in mourning for her father, was working in the fire-corner at a piece of tapestry, helped by Madame Kolb, the housekeeper, who took most of the burden of daily chores off her shoulders. Just as the hired carriage reached the first dwellings in Marsac, the regular company at the Verberie was augmented by the arrival of Courtois, the miller, a widower, who wanted to retire and who was hoping to get *a good price* for his property of which Madame Ève appeared very desirous, and Courtois knew why.

'There's a cab just pulling up here!' said Courtois hearing the sound of a carriage at the door; 'and, to judge by the way it rattles it must be a local one . . .'

'No doubt it will be Postel and his wife who want to see me,' said the doctor.

'No,' said Courtois, 'that cab was coming from the direction of Mansle.'

'Matame,' said Kolb (a great, fat Alsatian), 'here iss a zolizitor vrom Baris who vishes to zbeak to Monzieur.'

'A solicitor! . . .' cried Séchard, 'that word gives me the colic.'

'Thank you,' said the mayor of Marsac, a man by the name of Cachan, twenty years a solicitor in Angoulême, who at one time had been instructed to proceed against Séchard.

'My poor David will never change, he's so absent-minded!' said Ève with a smile.

'A lawyer from Paris,' said Courtois, 'have you some business in Paris?'

'No,' said Ève.

'You have a brother there,' said Courtois also smiling.

'Watch out it hasn't to do with old Séchard's succession,' said Cachan. 'The old boy got up to some pretty fishy business! . . .'

On entering, Corentin and Derville, having bowed to the

company and stated their names, asked if they could speak privately with Madame Séchard and her husband.

'Certainly,' said Séchard. 'Is it a matter of business?'

'Purely to do with your late father's succession,' replied Corentin.

'Then please allow our mayor, who was formerly a solicitor in Angoulême, to be present at the discussion.'

'Are you Monsieur Derville?...' said Cachan looking at Corentin.

'No, sir, that's this gentleman,' replied Corentin indicating the solicitor who bowed.

'But, indeed,' said Séchard, 'we're all close friends here, we have nothing to hide from our neighbours, there's no need to go to my study where there isn't a fire... Everything is open and above board...'

'There were things in your father's life,' said Corentin, 'which you might not feel altogether happy to have everyone hear about.'

'Is it something, then, we need to be ashamed of?...' said Ève with a sudden fear.

'No, no, just something that happened in his youth, as such things will,' said Corentin calmly setting one of his numerous mouse-traps. 'Your father gave you an elder brother...'

'Well, the old grump!' cried Courtois, 'he never cared for you, Monsieur Séchard, and he kept that up his sleeve, the crafty old boor... Ah, now I understand what he meant, when he said to me: "You'll see some fun when I'm in my grave!"'

'Don't be alarmed, sir,' said Corentin to Séchard studying Ève with a glance to the side.

'A brother!' exclaimed the doctor, 'but that means the inheritance will be divided!...'

Derville affected to examine the fine first pulls of engravings displayed on the panelling of the room.

'Don't be alarmed, Madame,' said Corentin seeing the astonishment on Madame Séchard's beautiful face, 'it is only a matter of an illegitimate child. The rights of a natural son are not the same as those of one born in wedlock. This child is living in the direst poverty, he is entitled to a sum based on the size of the total succession . . . The millions left by your late father . . .'

At the word 'millions', there arose a cry of perfect unanimity in the drawing-room. At that moment, Derville no longer examined the engravings.

'Old Séchard, millions? . . .' said the burly Courtois. 'Who told you that? some peasant.'

'Sir,' said Cachan, 'you don't belong to the inland revenue, so you can be told just how things are . . .'

'Don't worry,' said Corentin, 'I give you my word of honour, I'm not concerned with Crown property.'

Cachan, who'd just made a sign to everybody to be quiet, now evinced satisfaction.

'Sir,' Corentin went on, 'were there only one million, the natural child's share would still be considerable. We haven't come to institute any proceedings, we simply want to propose to you a gift of a hundred thousand francs, after which we shall leave you quite . . .'

'A hundred thousand francs! . . .' exclaimed Cachan interrupting Corentin. 'What old Séchard left, sir, was twenty acres of vineyard, five little farms, ten acres of meadowland in Marsac and not a penny with it . . .'

'Not for anything in the world,' interposed David Séchard, 'would I tell a lie, Monsieur Cachan: least of all in a matter of this kind . . . Gentlemen,' he said to Corentin and Derville, 'besides land my father left us . . .' Courtois and Cachan vainly signalled to him, he added: 'Three hundred thousand francs, which brings the total value of his estate to some five hundred thousand francs.'

'Monsieur Cachan, what share does the law allot to illegitimate children?' asked Ève Séchard.

'Madame,' said Corentin, 'we aren't Turks, we only ask you to swear before these gentlemen that you collected no more than a hundred thousand crowns in money from your father-in-law's estate, and we shall proceed no further . . .'

'First,' said the former solicitor in Angoulême, 'give us your word of honour that you are legally qualified.'

'Here is my passport,' said Derville to Cachan handing him a paper folded in four, 'and this gentleman is not, as you might fancy, an inspector of Crown lands, you can be assured,' added Derville. 'Our interest is solely to know the truth about the Séchard inheritance, and now we know it . . .' Derville took Ève by the hand, and very politely led her to the far end of the room. 'Madame,' he said to her in a low voice, 'if the honour and the future of the house of Grandlieu were not involved in the question, I should not have lent myself to the stratagem devised by the gentleman with the decoration; but you will excuse him, it was a matter of exposing the lie by means of which your brother gained access to the sanctuary of this noble family. Take care now not to let it be supposed that you gave twelve hundred thousand francs to your brother to buy the Rubempré estate . . .'

'Twelve hundred thousand francs!' exclaimed Madame Séchard turning pale. 'Where can he have found all that, poor fellow? . . .'

'Ah! there,' said Derville, 'I fear that the source of his fortune will turn out to be tainted.'

Ève had tears in her eyes which her neighbours perceived.

'We may have done you a great service,' Derville said to her, 'by stopping you becoming involved in a lie whose consequences may be dangerous.'

Derville left Madame Séchard sitting down, pale, tears on her cheeks, and bowed to the company.

'To Mansle!' said Corentin to the little boy who was driving the hackney carriage.

The diligence from Bordeaux to Paris, which passed that way at night, had one place free; Derville begged Corentin to allow him to take it, claiming business; but, at bottom, he mistrusted his travelling companion, whose cold-blooded diplomatic adroitness seemed to him a matter of habit. Corentin stayed three days in Mansle without finding means to get away; he was obliged to write to Bordeaux and book a seat for Paris, to which he did not return until nine days after his departure.

During that time, Peyrade called every morning, either at Passy or in Paris, at Corentin's, to see whether he had returned. On the eighth day, he left at one address or the other a letter written in their private code, to explain to his friend the manner of death which threatened him, the kidnapping of Lydia and the dreadful fate to which his enemies destined her.

Mene, Tekel, Upharsin

ATTACKED as till then he had attacked other people, Peyrade, deprived of Corentin but with Contenson still beside him, remained nevertheless disguised as a Nabob. Discovered as he had been by his invisible enemies, he thought reasonably enough that he might learn something by remaining on the battlefield. Contenson had set everyone he knew on the trail of Lydia, he hoped to find out in what house she was hidden; but, from day to day, the ever more evident impossibility of discovering anything hourly added to Peyrade's despair. The old spy surrounded himself with a guard of twelve or fifteen of the cleverest agents. Close observation was kept on the neighbourhood of the rue des Moineaux and the rue Taitbout where he was living as a Nabob at Madame du Val-Noble's. During the last three days of the fatal period allowed him by Asia to restore Lucien to his former position at the Grandlieu house, Contenson never left the veteran of the old Lieutenancy General of police. Thus, that poetry of terror which the stratagems of enemy tribes at war create in the heart of the forests of America, and of which Cooper has made such good use, was attached to the smallest details of Parisian life. The passers-by, the shops, the hackney carriages, a person standing at a window, to the men who had been numbered off for the defence of Peyrade's life, everything presented the ominous interest which in Cooper's novels may be found in a tree trunk, a beaver's dam, a rock, a buffalo skin, a motionless canoe, a branch drooping over the water.

'If the Spaniard has gone, you have nothing to fear,' said Contenson to Peyrade pointing out to him the deep calm all about them.

'And if he hasn't gone?' replied Peyrade.

'He took one of my men behind his barouche; but, at Blois my man was forced to get down and couldn't catch the carriage up.'

Five days after Derville's return, one morning, Lucien received a visit from Rastignac.

'I'm in despair, my dear, at having to deliver myself of a mission which has been entrusted to me because of our close acquaintance. Your marriage is broken off without the least hope of you ever renewing it. Never set foot again in the Grandlieu house. To marry Clotilde, one would have to wait until her father died, and he is too much of an egoist to die quickly. Old whist-players stick to their tables. Clotilde is leaving for Italy with Madeleine de Lenoncourt-Chaulieu. The poor girl is so in love with you, my dear fellow, that she has to be kept under observation; she wanted to come and see you, she'd already made her little plan of escape . . . That may be some consolation to you.'

Lucien did not reply. He looked at Rastignac.

'Is it really a misfortune! . . .' his compatriot said to him, 'you'll soon find another girl as well-born and better-looking than Clotilde! . . . Madame de Sérisy will marry you off out of revenge, she can't abide the Grandlieus, they've never invited her to their house; she has a niece, little Clémence du Rouvre . . .'

'My friend, since our last supper I'm not on good terms with Madame de Sérisy, she saw me in Esther's box, she made a scene, and I did nothing about it.'

'A woman turned forty doesn't quarrel for long with a young man as handsome as you,' said Rastignac. 'I know something about these sunsets . . . they last ten minutes on the horizon, and ten years in a woman's heart.'

'I've waited all week for a letter from her.'

'Do something!'

'I shall have to, now.'

'At any rate, are you going to Madame du Val-Noble's? her Nabob is returning Nucingen's hospitality with a supper.'

'They've asked me, and I shall go,' said Lucien with a solemn air.

The day after the confirmation of his misfortune, the news

of which was at once given by Asia to Carlos, Lucien went with Rastignac and Nucingen to the sham Nabob's.

At midnight, in Esther's old dining-room were gathered together almost all the characters in this drama of which the interest, hidden far beneath the surface of these torrential lives, was known only to Esther, to Lucien, to Peyrade, to the mulatto Contenson and to Paccard, who came to wait upon his mistress. Unknown to Peyrade and Contenson, Madame du Val-Noble had asked Asia to come in and help the cook. Peyrade, who'd given Madame du Val-Noble five hundred francs extra for the occasion, found folded in his napkin a piece of paper on which he read these words written in pencil: *The ten days expire at the moment at which you sit down at table*. Peyrade passed the note to Contenson, who stood behind him, and said to him in English: 'Was it you who tucked that in with my name?' Contenson read this *Mene, Tekel, Upharsin* by the candlelight, and stuffed the paper in his pocket, but he knew how difficult it is to detect a handwriting in pencil especially when only capital letters are used, that is to say when the spacing is almost mathematical, since capital letters consist wholly of curves and straight lines from which it is impossible to discover the hand's common habit, so evident in the writing known as cursive.

That supper lacked all gaiety. Peyrade was visibly pre-occupied. Of those young sparks who know how to enliven a supper, there were only Lucien and Rastignac. Lucien was thoughtful and depressed. Rastignac, who had lost two thousand francs before supper, ate and drank with little thought but how to make it up afterwards. The three women looked at each other, conscious of a certain chill. Boredom robbed the dishes of all savour. Supper-parties are like plays and books, they may go well or badly. At the end of the meal, ices with tiny preserved fruits were served in small glasses, the ice and the delicate fruit forming a pyramid. These sundaes had been ordered by Madame du Val-Noble from Tortoni's, whose famous establishment was at the corner of the rue Taitbout and the boulevard. The cook sent for the mulatto to pay the ice-cream vendor's note. Contenson, to whom the boy's insistence seemed unusual, went down and got rid of him by saying: 'Aren't you from Tortoni's, then? . . .' and went straight up again. But Paccard had already taken advantage of his absence to distribute the ices to the guests. Hardly had the mulatto reached the door of the apartment when one of the agents appointed to watch the rue des Moineaux called up the staircase: 'Number twenty-seven.'

'What is it?' replied Contenson hurrying down again.

'Tell the old man his daughter is back at home, and in what a state! my God! he must come at once, she's half dead.'

Just as Contenson returned to the dining-room, old Peyrade, who had been drinking heavily, swallowed the cherry from the top of his ice. Somebody proposed Madame du Val-Noble's health, the Nabob filled his glass with Constantia wine, and emptied it. Troubled as Contenson was by the news he was about to transmit to Peyrade, he was, on his return, struck by the close attention with which Paccard was watching the Nabob. The two eyes of Madame de Champy's manservant were like two steadily burning flames. Despite its importance, this observation could not delay the mulatto, and he bent over his master just as Peyrade replaced his empty glass on the table.

'Lydia is at home,' said Contenson, 'and in a poor way.'

Peyrade let out the most French of French oaths with so marked a southern accent that the deepest astonishment appeared on all the guests' faces. Perceiving his mistake, Peyrade cast off all disguise by saying to Contenson in good French: 'Find a cab! . . . I'm off.'

Everybody rose from table.

'Who are you, then?' exclaimed Lucien.

'Yo, yo! . . .' said the baron.

'Bixiou told me you could play the Englishman better than himself, and I wouldn't believe him,' said Rastignac.

'This is some undisclosed bankrupt,' said du Tillet in a loud voice, 'I thought as much! . . .'

'What an odd place Paris is! . . .' said Madame du Val-Noble. 'If he goes broke on his own doorstep, a man can re-appear there dressed up as a Nabob or strut like a dandy in the Champs Élysées with impunity! . . . Oh! what a luckless creature I am, insolvency follows me around.'

'Most ladies have their familiar,' said Esther calmly, 'mine is like Cleopatra's, an aspic.'

'Who am I? . . .' said Peyrade at the door, 'Ah! you shall know, for, if I die, I shall rise from my tomb to plague you every night of your lives! . . .'

With these parting words, he gazed at Esther and Lucien; then he profited by the general astonishment to disappear with remarkable agility, for he meant to run home without waiting for the cab. In the street, Asia, her head enveloped in a black shawl such as women carried in those days for leaving a ball, caught at the spy's arm, as he left by the carriage entrance.

'Send out for the sacraments, Papa Peyrade,' she said in the voice which had foretold his misfortune in the first place.

A carriage was there, Asia stepped in, the carriage disappeared as though borne away by the wind. There were five carriages, Peyrade's men didn't know one from another.

The oath sworn by Corentin

WHEN he arrived at his country house in one of the quietest and pleasantest streets in the little town of Passy, the rue des Vignes, Corentin, who passed for a business man passionately fond of gardening, found his friend Peyrade's coded note. Instead of resting, he climbed back into the cab which had brought him, had himself driven to the rue des Moineaux and found only Katt there. From this Fleming he learned of Lydia's disappearance and marvelled at his own and Peyrade's lack of foresight.

'*They* don't know *me* yet,' he said to himself. 'People like that will stop at nothing, it remains to be seen whether they will kill Peyrade, if they do I shall have to remain unknown . . .'

The more infamous a man's life is, the more he will cling to it; its every minute is then a protestation, a vengeance. Corentin went away, at home disguised himself as a needy little old man, in a short frock coat turning green, a dog's tooth wig, and returned on foot, impelled by his friendship for Peyrade. He wanted to give his orders to the cleverest and most conscientious of his Numbers. Along the rue Saint Honoré on his way from the Place Vendôme to the rue Saint Roch, he found himself walking behind a girl in slippers, dressed in women's night clothes. This girl, who wore a white bed-jacket, a night-cap on her head, from time to time uttered a sob or other sound of involuntary complaint; Corentin passed her, looked back and saw that it was Lydia.

'I am a friend of your father, Monsieur Canquoëlle,' he said in his natural voice.

'Ah! then you are someone I can trust! . . .' she said.

'Pretend not to know me,' Corentin went on, 'for we are pursued by cruel enemies, and forced to wear disguise. But tell me what happened to you . . .'

'Oh, sir,' said the poor girl, 'I can tell you what it was, but I can't describe it . . . I'm dishonoured, lost, without being able to say how! . . .'

'Where have you come from? . . .'

'I don't know, sir! I ran away in such a hurry, I've been along so many streets, by so many turnings, thinking I was followed . . . And when I met someone respectable, I asked the way to the boulevards, so that I could reach the rue de la Paix! At last, after walking for . . . What time is it?'

'Half past eleven!' said Corentin.

'I escaped just at nightfall, so I've been walking for five hours! . . .' exclaimed Lydia.

'Come along, you need a rest, you'll find your kind old Katt . . .'

'Oh, sir, there'll be no more rest for me! The only rest I want is in the grave; and I shall go to wait for it in a convent, if they think I'm fit to enter one . . .'

'Poor child! you did all you could to resist?'

'Yes, sir. Ah! if you knew among what abject creatures they put me . . .'

'I dare say they put you to sleep?'

'Ah, was that it?' said poor Lydia. 'Still a little strength, and I shall reach the house. I think I'm going to faint, and my thoughts aren't very clear . . . Just now I thought I was in a garden . . .'

Corentin took Lydia up in his arms, where she lost consciousness, and he climbed the flights of stairs.

'Katt!' he cried.

Katt appeared and uttered cries of joy.

'Don't be in a hurry to celebrate!' said Corentin gravely, 'this girl is very unwell.'

When Lydia had been placed on her bed, when, by the light of two candles Katt brought, she recognized her room, she became delirious. She sang the refrains of pretty tunes, and every now and then uttered foul expressions she'd heard! Her beautiful face was mottled with purple tints. She mingled memories of her pure earlier life with those of the past ten days of infamy. Katt wept. Corentin paced about the room stopping at moments to examine Lydia.

'She's praying for her father!' he said. 'Could there possibly be a Providence? Oh! how right I am to have no family . . . A child! it is, on my word of honour, as I don't know which philosopher says, a hostage given to fortune! . . .'

'Oh!' said the poor child sitting up in bed and letting her beautiful hair fall down, 'instead of lying here, Katt, I should be lying on the sand at the bottom of the Seine . . .'

'Katt, instead of weeping and gazing at your child, which won't cure her, you should go and look for a doctor, the one from the Town Hall first, then Messieurs Desplein and Bianchon . . . This innocent creature must be saved . . .'

And Corentin wrote down the addresses of the two famous doctors. At that moment, the stairs were climbed by a man whose step was familiar, the door opened. Peyrade, in a sweat, his face purple, his eyes bloodshot, blowing like a porpoise, ran from the door of the apartment to Lydia's room crying: 'Where is my daughter? . . .'

He saw Corentin's woeful gesture, Peyrade's eyes followed the pointing finger. Lydia's condition could only be compared with that of a flower, lovingly tended by a botanist, fallen from its stalk, crushed by the iron-shod clogs of a peasant. Translate this image into the very heart of Fatherhood, you will understand the blow received by Peyrade, whose eyes at once filled with big tears.

'Somebody's crying, it's my father,' said the child.

Lydia was still able to recognize her father; she got up and fell at the old man's knees just as he collapsed into an armchair.

'Forgive me, papa! ...' she said in a voice which pierced Peyrade's heart at the moment at which he experienced what might have been the blow of a club on his skull.

'I'm dying ... ah! the scoundrels!' were his last words.

Corentin rushed to his friend's side, receiving his last breath.

'Died poisoned! ...' said Corentin to himself. 'Good, here's the doctor,' he exclaimed hearing the sound of a carriage.

Contenson appeared, without the mulatto's make-up on his face, and stood like a bronze statue on hearing Lydia say: 'Won't you forgive me, then, father? ... It wasn't my fault!' (She didn't notice that her father was dead.) 'Oh, what a strange look he gives me! ...' said the poor child out of her mind ...

'We must close his eyes,' said Contenson, lifting the late Peyrade on to the bed.

'What we are doing is foolish,' said Corentin, 'we must carry him into his own room; his daughter is half out of her mind, she'd go right out of it if she saw he was dead, she'd think she'd killed him.'

Seeing them take her father away, Lydia stared in bewilderment.

'That was my only friend! ...' said Corentin clearly moved by the sight of Peyrade on the bed in his own room. 'In all his life, the only thought of money was for his daughter! ... Let that be a lesson to you, Contenson. There is a code for every condition. Peyrade was wrong to become involved with the affairs of individuals, we must concern ourselves only with public affairs. But, whatever happens, I hereby swear,' said he with an accent, a look and a gesture which struck Contenson with fear, 'to avenge poor Peyrade, my friend! I shall discover the authors of his death and those of his daughter's shame! ... And, by my own self-respect, by the few years which remain to me, and which I imperil by this revenge, they shall all end their days at four o'clock, in perfect health, shaved, suddenly, on the scaffold in the Strand! ...'

'I'll help you!' said Contenson equally moved.

Nothing is indeed more deeply moving than the spectacle of

passion in a cold, formal, methodical man, in whom, for twenty years, nobody had perceived the least flicker of sensibility. It is the iron bar molten and melting all it meets. Thus Contenson felt his entrails turn.

'Poor father Canquoëlle,' he went on looking at Corentin, 'he often wined and dined me ... What's more – it's only those with vices of their own who think of such things – he'd often give me ten francs to gamble with ...'

After this eulogy of the dead, Peyrade's two avengers went to Lydia's apartment hearing Katt and the Town Hall doctor on the stairs.

'Go to the police station,' said Corentin, 'the district attorney wouldn't find the makings of a legal action in this; but we shall make a report to the Prefecture, that may produce some effect.'

'Sir,' said Corentin to the Town Hall doctor, 'you will find a dead man in that room; I don't believe he died from natural causes, you'll have to perform an autopsy in the presence of the police superintendent, who will be coming presently at my invitation. See if you can discover traces of poison; you will have the assistance of Doctors Desplein and Bianchon in a few moments, I've called them in to examine my best friend's daughter whose state is worse than her father's, although he is dead ...'

'I do not,' said the municipal doctor, 'need these gentlemen's help to carry on my profession ...'

'Well, all right,' thought Corentin. 'Let us not get in each other's way, sir,' Corentin went on. 'In a few words, here is my opinion. Those who have just killed the father also dishonoured the daughter.'

By dawn, Lydia had finally succumbed to her fatigue; she was asleep when the famous surgeon and the young doctor arrived. The doctor whose business it was to state the cause of death had by then opened Peyrade up to that end.

'Until we feel we can waken the invalid,' said Corentin to the two distinguished medical men, 'would you help one of your colleagues in an examination which will certainly be of interest to you, while your opinion might usefully be shown in the police report.'

'Your kinsman died of apoplexy,' said the doctor, 'there are symptoms of a terrifying cerebral congestion . . .'

'Take a look at him, gentlemen,' said Corentin, 'and see whether Toxicology doesn't show poisons which produce the same effect.'

'The stomach,' said the doctor, 'was absolutely full of various matters; but, without submitting them to chemical analysis, I see no trace of poison.'

'If the characteristics of cerebral congestion are evident, that alone, given the patient's age, would be a sufficient cause of death,' said Desplein indicating the enormous quantity of foodstuffs . . .

'Did he eat here?' asked Bianchon.

'No,' said Corentin, 'he came here at speed from the boulevard, and found his daughter had been raped . . .'

'That's the real poison, if he loved his daughter,' said Bianchon.

'What poison could produce those effects?' asked Corentin not relinquishing his idea.

'There's only one,' said Desplein after examining everything carefully. 'It's a poison from the archipelago of Java, taken from shrubs about which we don't yet know very much, but they're related to the *strychnos* group, and they're used to poison those very dangerous weapons, . . . the *krisses* of the *Malays* . . . At least so I'm told . . .'

The police superintendent arrived, Corentin told him what he suspected, and asked him to draw up a report stating at what house and in what company Peyrade had supped; also outlining the known plot against Peyrade's life and the cause of Lydia's present condition. Then Corentin went along to the poor girl's apartment, where Desplein and Bianchon were examining their patient; but he met them at the door.

'Well, gentlemen?' asked Corentin.

'Put that girl in a clinic. If she turns out to be pregnant and doesn't recover her reason in childbirth, she'll end her days in melancholy-madness. There's no other cure for her state but the maternal instinct, if it awakes . . .'

Corentin gave forty francs in gold to each of the doctors,

and turned to the police superintendent, who was pulling at his sleeve.

'The doctor claims that death was natural,' said this functionary, 'and the fact that he was Father Canquoëlle makes it very difficult for me to write a report, he got mixed up with all kinds of things, and we should hardly know who was at the other end ... People like him often die *by order* ...'

'My name is Corentin,' said Corentin in an undertone to the police superintendent.

The superintendent betrayed surprise.

'So make a note,' continued Corentin, 'it will be useful later, and pass it on only as private and confidential. Crime can't be proved, and I know that the judicial inquiry could be brought to a sudden halt ... But one of these days I shall be turning the guilty parties in, I'm going to keep them under close observation and catch them in some act or other.'

The police superintendent bowed to Corentin and left.

'Sir,' said Katt, 'Mademoiselle does nothing but sing and dance, what shall I do? ...'

'Has something new happened? ...'

'She knows now that her father has just died ...'

'Put her into a cab and take her straight off to Charenton; I shall write a note to the Director General of the Police of the Kingdom to see that she's properly looked after. The daughter at Charenton, the father in a common grave,' said Corentin. 'Contenson, go and order the poor man's funeral wagon ... Now, Don Carlos Herrera, it is between us two ...'

'Carlos!' said Contenson, 'he's in Spain.'

'He is in Paris!' said Corentin in his most peremptory tone. 'In this there is the touch of Spanish genius in the time of Philip II, but I have traps for everybody, including kings.'

The mousetrap catches a rat

FIVE days after the Nabob's disappearance, at nine o'clock in the morning, Madame du Val-Noble was sitting at Esther's bedside weeping, for she saw herself on the slopes of destitution.

'If, at least, I had a hundred louis' income! With that, my dear, one may retire to some small town, and there would always be somebody to marry . . .'

'I could get you that amount,' said Esther.

'How?' exclaimed Madame du Val-Noble.

'Oh! quite easily. Listen. You decide you're going to kill yourself, put on that act; send for Asia, and offer her ten thousand francs for two black pearls in fine glass containing a poison which kills in one second; bring those to me, and I'll give you fifty thousand francs . . .'

'Why don't you place the order yourself?' said Madame du Val-Noble.

'Asia wouldn't let me have them.'

'You're not going to use them yourself? . . .' said Madame du Val-Noble.

'Perhaps.'

'You! who live a life of happiness and luxury, in a house of your own! preparing for a celebration which will be talked of for ten years to come! which is costing Nucingen twenty thousand francs. You'll be eating, they tell me, strawberries in February, asparagus, grapes, . . . melons . . . There'll be a thousand crowns worth of flowers up and down the place.'

'More than that! there'll be a thousand crowns worth of roses in the staircase alone.'

'They say you'll be dressed to the tune of ten thousand francs?'

'Yes, my gown is of Brussels lace, and Delphine, his wife, is furious. But I wanted to look like a bride.'

'Where are the ten thousand francs?' said Madame du Val-Noble.

'It's all the change I have,' said Esther smiling. 'Open my dressing-table drawer, it's under my curl-paper.'

'When people talk of dying, they don't kill themselves,' said Madame du Val-Noble. 'If what you meant to do was . . .'

'Commit a crime, really!' said Esther completing the thought over which her friend hesitated. 'You needn't worry,' Esther went on, 'I wasn't thinking of killing anyone. I had a friend, a woman who was happy, she's dead, I shall follow her, . . . that's all.'

'How stupid!'

'What do you expect, we promised each other.'

'Let them protest that bill,' said the friend with a smile.

'Do as I tell you, and be off. I hear a carriage at the door, and it's Nucingen, a man who will soon be out of his mind with happiness! He loves me, that one ... Why don't we love those who love us, for after all they do everything to please ...'

'Ah, there we are!' said Madame du Val-Noble, 'it's the tale of the herring which is the most interesting of fishes.'

'Why? ...'

'The fact is, nobody's ever discovered.'

'Well, be off, my lamb! I have to ask for your fifty thousand francs.'

'Good-bye, then ...'

Over the past three days, Esther's manner with Baron Nucingen had quite changed. The monkey had become a pussy-cat and the cat had become a woman. Esther lavished treasures of affection upon the old man, she was charm itself with him. Her conversation, void of all malice and acridity, full of tender insinuation, had brought conviction to the banker's dull mind, she called him Fritz, he believed himself to be loved.

'My poor Fritz, I've tried you sorely,' she said, 'I tormented you, your patience was sublime, you love me, I see that it is so, and I shall repay you. I'm fond of you now, and I don't know how it came about, but I would prefer you to a young man. It may be the result of experience. In the end one comes to see that pleasure is simply the small change of the soul, and it is no more flattering to be loved for the pleasure one gives than to be loved for one's money ... Besides, young men are all egoists, they think more of themselves than they do of us; while you think only of me. I am your whole life. And so I shall ask nothing more of you, I mean to prove to you how disinterested I am.'

'I hef gif you nossing,' replied the baron, delighted, 'I vill tomorrow pring you dirty *tausend* vrancs ingome ... Dot iss my vedding bresent ...'

Esther kissed Nucingen so nicely that he grew pale, without the aid of pills.

'Oh!' she said, 'don't think it's for your thirty thousand francs' income that I'm like that, it's because now . . . I love you, my big Frédéric . . .'

'Och, goot Lort! vhy dry me so. . . . I vould hef been so heppy zese tree monts . . .'

'Is it in three per cents or in five, my lambkin?' said Esther playing with Nucingen's hair and arranging it fancifully.

'In tree . . . I hed a lot of zem.'

So that morning the baron had brought her registration in the Great Book of the Public Debt; he had come to lunch with his dear little girl, and to receive his orders for tomorrow, the famous Saturday, the great day!

'Dere, my liddle vife, my only vife,' said the banker joyously, his face shining with happiness, 'dot vill bay your householt gosts to ze ent off your tays . . .'

Esther took the paper without the least emotion, she folded it and put it in her dressing-table drawer.

'So now you're happy, you monster of iniquity,' she said patting Nucingen's cheek, 'to see me accept something from you at last. I can no longer tell you home truths, for now I share the proceeds of what you call your work . . . That isn't a present, my child, it's an act of restitution . . . Come, don't put on your Stock Exchange face. You know I love you.'

'My peautivul Esdher, my enchel of lof,' said the banker, 'ton't pliss zbeak to me like dot, . . . look, . . . it iss oll de zame to me if oll de vorlt tink me a tief, so long ess I em an honest man in your eyes . . . I lof you olvays more *und* more.'

'That is what I intend,' said Esther. 'So I won't ever again say anything to upset you, my little elephant ducky, for you've become as innocent as a babe . . . Heavens, you great scoundrel, you never had any innocence before, the bit you were born with needed bringing to the surface; but it was buried so deep it didn't appear till you were past sixty-six . . . and needed the long arm of love to hook it out. The phenomenon may be observed in the very old . . . And that's why I've come to love you, you are young now, really young . . . Nobody else but me will have known that Frédéric . . . I alone! . . . for you were a banker at fifteen . . . At school, you must have lent bills to your friends and got two back . . .' (She jumped on to his knee as she saw him laugh.) 'Well, you shall do as you please! Lord! go hold men to ransom ... I'll come and help you. Men aren't worth the trouble of loving, Napoleon killed them like flies. Let the French nation pay taxes to the Treasury or to you, what difference does it make! ... One doesn't make love with the Budget, and, goodness me – yes, I've thought about it, you're right – shear my sheep, it's in the Gospel according to Béranger ... Kiss your *Esdher* ... Now, tell me, you'll give poor little Val-Noble all the furniture in the apartment in the rue Taitbout! And then, tomorrow, you'll offer her fifty thousand francs, ... that will settle things for you, kitten. You killed Falleix, there's a hue and cry after you ... To be generous like that will seem Babylonian, ... and all the women will talk about you. Oh! ... you'll be the only great one, the only true nobleman in Paris, and the world is such that Falleix will be forgotten. So, after all, it will be money laid out to some purpose! ...'

'You are right, my enchel, you know de vorlt,' he replied, 'you shell be my atficer.'

'You see,' she continued, 'how I think about my man's business, his standing in the world, his honour ... Off with you, go and find me fifty thousand francs ...'

She wanted to get rid of Monsieur Nucingen so that she could send for a broker and sell her registration that very evening at the Stock Exchange.

'Zo zoon, vhy? ...' he asked.

'Why, yes, pet, they must be offered in a little satin box wrapped round a fan. You will say to her: "There, Madame, a fan which, I trust, will be to your liking ..." They think you're only a Turcaret, they'll see you're a Beaujon!'

'Jarming! jarming!' exclaimed the baron, 'I shall pe vitty now! ... Yo, I shall rebead your chokes ...'

Just as poor Esther was sitting down, worn out with the effort she had made to play her part, Europe entered.

'Madame,' she said, 'here is a messenger sent from the Quai Malaquais by Célestin, Monsieur Lucien's manservant ...'

'Show him in! ... but no, I'll see him in the other room.'

'He has a letter for Madame from Célestin.'

Esther hurried into the outer room, she glanced at the

messenger, who seemed to her the purest embodiment of a street porter.

'Tell *him* to come down! . . .' said Esther in a feeble voice, letting herself fall into a chair after reading the letter. 'Lucien means to kill himself, . . .' she added in a whisper to Europe. 'In any case take the letter up to *him*.'

Carlos Herrera, who was still dressed like a commercial traveller, came down at once, and his glance immediately fell on the messenger when he saw a stranger in the outer room. 'You'd told me there was nobody,' he whispered to Europe. And with an excess of caution he went straight into the drawing-room after examining the messenger. Dodgedeath didn't know that for some time past the famous head of the crime squad who'd arrested him at the Maison Vauquer had a rival already designated to succeed him. This rival was the messenger.

'They're right,' said the sham messenger to Contenson who was waiting for him in the street. 'The man you described to me is in the house; but he isn't a Spaniard, and I'd stake anything there's our sort of game under that cassock.'

'He's no more a priest than he is a Spaniard,' said Contenson.

'I'm certain of it,' said the agent of the Brigade de Sûreté.

'Oh! if only we could be sure! . . .' said Contenson.

Lucien had in fact been away for two days, and advantage had been taken of his absence to lay this trap; but he came back that evening, and Esther's fears were calmed.

A farewell

NEXT morning, as the courtesan emerged from her bath and returned to bed, her friend arrived.

'I have your two pearls!' said the Val-Noble.

'Let's see?' said Esther sitting up and plunging her pretty elbow into a lace-trimmed pillow.

Madame du Val-Noble handed to her friend what looked like two large blackcurrants. The baron had given Esther two of those Italian greyhounds of a special breed, made fashionable by a living poet; she was proud of these and had called them Romeo and Juliet, names which occurred in their pedigree. It would be impossible to praise too highly the charm, the whiteness, the grace of these animals, bred for indoors and in their ways exhibiting something of an English discreetness. Esther called Romeo, Romeo approached on his small, flexible paws, which were yet so firm and muscular they might have been thought rods of steel, and gazed up at his mistress. Esther made as if to throw him one of the two pearls, to attract his attention.

'His name destined him to die thus!' said Esther and threw the pearl which Romeo crunched between his teeth.

The dog uttered no cry, he spun round and fell in the rigidity of death. This happened while Esther was still speaking her brief elegy.

'Heavens!' cried Madame du Val-Noble.

'You have a carriage, take the late Romeo away,' said Esther, 'his death would cause trouble here, let's say I gave him to you, you lost him, put out an advertisement. Hurry, and you shall have your fifty thousand francs this evening.'

This was said so calmly, and with so perfect a harlot's air of insensibility, that Madame du Val-Noble exclaimed: 'You are queen of us all!'

'Come early, and look your best . . .'

At five o' clock that evening, Esther dressed herself like a bride. She put on her lace gown over a skirt of white satin, with a waistband also white and white satin slippers, a shawl of English point about her beautiful shoulders. In her hair she put white camellias, so that she appeared garlanded like a young virgin. Upon her bosom was displayed a necklace of pearls worth thirty thousand francs given her by Nucingen. Although she had finished dressing by six o'clock, she shut her door to everyone, even Nucingen. Europe knew that Lucien was to be introduced into the bedroom. Lucien arrived at seven sharp, Europe found a way to show him in to Madame without anybody noticing his arrival.

At the sight of Esther, Lucien wondered: 'Why not go live with her at Rubempré, far from the social whirl, without ever returning to Paris! . . . I paid five years' deposit on this life, and the dear creature is not of a nature to deny it! ... And where shall I ever find such a masterpiece?'

'My dear friend, you of whom I made my God,' said Esther bending one knee on a cushion before Lucien, 'bless me ...'

Lucien made to raise Esther and kiss her saying: 'What pleasantry is this, my beloved?' And he attempted to seize Esther by the waist; but she drew away with a movement which depicted both horror and respect.

'I am no longer worthy of you, Lucien,' she said letting her tears flow, 'I beg you, bless me, and swear to endow two beds at some hospital ... Prayers in church will only cause God to forgive me to myself ... I loved you too much, my dear. Tell me, at least, that I made you happy, and that you will think of me sometimes ... yes?'

Lucien saw that Esther was speaking in solemn good faith, and he remained thoughtful.

'You're going to kill yourself!' he said at length in a voice whose sound betokened deep meditation.

'No, my love, but today, you see, will be the end of the pure, chaste, loving woman you had ... And I'm rather afraid that the shock of her death may kill me.'

'Don't be in a hurry, my poor child!' said Lucien, 'during the past two days I've made a great effort, and I've managed to see Clotilde.'

'Still Clotilde! ...' said Esther in a tone of concentrated fury.

'Yes,' he continued, 'we wrote to each other ... On Tuesday morning, she's leaving for Italy, but I shall have an interview with her on the way, at Fontainebleau ...'

'Oh, that! what sort of wives do you want, you men? ... planks! ...' cried poor Esther. 'Look now, suppose I had seven or eight millions, wouldn't you marry me?'

'Child! What I was going to say is that, if everything's over for me, I don't want any other wife but you ...'

Esther lowered her head so as not to show her sudden pallor and the tears she wiped away.

'You love me? ...' she said gazing at Lucien with the deepest grief. 'Well, that shall be my blessing. Don't compromise yourself, go out by the hidden door, and act as though you'd gone straight from the hall to the drawing-room. Kiss me on the forehead,' she said. She held Lucien, pressed him to her heart furiously and said to him: 'Go!... Go... or I live.'

When the doomed woman appeared in the drawing-room, there was a cry of admiration. Esther's eyes gave off a light of infinity in which the soul lost itself as it saw them. The blue-black of her splendid hair showed off the camellias. In short, every effect the sublime whore aimed at had been achieved. She had no rivals. She was the very embodiment of the un-bridled luxury with which she was surrounded and adorned. Her wit, too, was at its most sparkling. She ruled the orgy with the cold, tranquil power deployed by Habeneck at the Conservatoire in those concerts at which the leading musicians of Europe attain the peak of execution in their interpretations of Mozart and Beethoven. She nevertheless observed fearfully that Nucingen ate little, didn't drink and was acting as master of the house. At midnight, nobody was in his right mind. They broke glasses so that they shouldn't be used again. Two curtains of Pekin print were torn. Bixiou was drunk for the only time in his life. As nobody could stand up, and the women lay more or less asleep on the divans, the guests were unable to carry out the joke they had originally planned of leading Esther and Nucingen to the bedroom, standing in two lines, holding candelabra and singing the *Buona Sera* from *The Barber of Seville*. Nucingen alone gave his hand to Esther; though drunk, Bixiou, who noticed them, still found strength to say, like Rivarol at the last marriage of the Duc de Richelieu: 'The Prefect of Police should be told ... A foul trick is about to be played ...' Intended as light chaff, this would turn out to be prophecy.

Nucingen's lament

MONSIEUR DE NUCINGEN didn't appear at home till near mid-day on Monday; but at one o'clock, his stockbroker told him that Mademoiselle Esther van Gobseck had sold her thirty thousand francs' inscription on Friday already and had just been paid.

'What is more, Monsieur le Baron,' he said, 'just as I was talking about the transfer, Maître Derville's head clerk came to see me; and, when he realized what Mademoiselle Esther's real name was, he told me she'd come into a fortune of seven millions.'

'Pah!'

'Yes, it seems that she's the sole heir of the old discount-broker Gobseck ... Derville is going to check the facts. If the mother of your mistress was "*la belle Hollandaise*", she inherits ...'

'It voss so,' said the banker, 'she dolt me her live-story ... I vill write a vort to Terville! ...'

The baron sat down at his desk, wrote a little note to Derville, and sent it by one of his servants. Then, after going to the Stock Exchange, he returned promptly at three o' clock to Esther's. 'Madame has forbidden anyone to wake her under any pretext whatever, she has gone to bed, she is asleep ...'

'Ah, ze toffle!' exclaimed the baron. 'Eurobe, it von't tis-blease her to learn dot she is now ferry rich ... She inerids zefen millions. Olt Copsegg iss teat and leafes zese zefen millions, and your misdress iss his zole heir, her mudder peing Copsegg's own nieze, pezites he levd a vill. I vould nefer hef zuspected zet a millionaire, like him, vould leafe Esdher benniless ...'

'Why, then, that's the end of your reign, you old mounte-bank!' said Europe looking at the baron with an effrontery worthy of one of Molière's maidservants. 'Ho! you old Alsatian crow! ... She likes you about as much as one likes the plague! ... Good God! millions! ... but she can marry her lover! Oh! won't she be pleased!'

And Prudence Servien left the baron struck dumb while she went off to be the first to announce the stroke of luck to her mistress. The old man, intoxicated with pleasures beyond his belief, and believing in happiness, had had cold water thrown on his love just as he was coming to a point of something like incandescence.

'She tezeifed me ...' he exclaimed with tears in his eyes. 'She tezeifed me! ... O Esdher, ... O my live ... How stubit I hef peen! Do such vlowers efer crow for olt men? ...

I can puy eferyding, except yout'! . . . O heafens! . . . vot shall I do? vot vill begome off me? She iss right, ziss gruel Eurobe. Vhen she iss rich, Esdher esgabes me. Musd I heng myzelf? Vot iss live widout ze tifine vlame off bleasure vhich I hef dastet? *Mein Gott* . . .'

And the Shark tore off the wig with which he had been covering his grey hair for the past three months. A piercing cry uttered by Europe made Nucingen tremble in his innermost parts. The poor banker got up, tottered on drunkard's legs after draining his cup of Disenchantment, for no liquor is so potent as misfortune. From the doorway of her bedroom, he saw Esther rigid upon her bed, her face blue with poison, dead! . . . He went to the bed, and fell on his knees.

'You are right, she dolt you! . . . I gaused her deat' . . .'

Paccard, Asia, all the household came running. It was a spectacle, a wonder, not a desolation. At first nobody quite knew how to behave. The banker became a banker again, he was suspicious, he committed the imprudence of asking where were the seven hundred and fifty thousand francs of annual income. Paccard, Asia and Europe thereupon looked at each other in so singular a manner that Monsieur de Nucingen left at once, believing that theft and murder had taken place. Seeing under her mistress's pillow a folded package whose softness told her that it contained bank notes, Europe set herself to laying the deceased out properly, as she put it.

'Go and tell Monsieur, Asia! . . . Dying before she knew she had seven million! Gobseck was the late Madame's uncle! . . .' she exclaimed.

Paccard noticed what Europe was up to. As soon as Asia had turned her back, Europe unsealed the packet, on which the poor harlot had written: *To be handed to Monsieur Lucien de Rubempré!* Seven hundred and fifty thousand-franc notes shone before the eyes of Prudence Servien, who cried: 'You could be happy and honest on that to the end of your days! . . .'

Paccard said nothing, his thief's nature was stronger than his attachment to Dodgedeath.

'Durut is dead,' he finally replied taking the sum, 'my shoulder is still unmarked, let's go away together and share this so as not to have all our eggs in one basket, and then we'll be married.'

'But where shall we hide?' said Prudence.

'Here in Paris,' answered Paccard.

Prudence and Paccard went down at once with the speed of two honest people who had turned thief.

'My child,' said Dodgedeath to the Malay as soon as she had given him the gist of what had happened, 'find the letter Esther must have left while I write out a will in due form, then you can take the letter and the draft will to Girard; but he'll have to hurry, the will must be slipped under Esther's pillow before they put seals on here.'

And he drafted the following last will and testament:

Never having loved anyone in the world but Monsieur Lucien Chardon de Rubempré, and being resolved to put an end to my days sooner than slip back into vice and into the infamous life from which his charity raised me, I give and bequeath to the said Lucien Chardon de Rubempré all that I possess at the time of my demise, with the condition that he establish a mass to be said in perpetuity at Saint Roch for the repose of her who gave him everything, even her last thought.

ESTHER GOBSECK.

'That is just her style,' said Dodgedeath to himself.

By seven o'clock the will, copied and sealed, was put by Asia under Esther's bolster.

'Jacques,' she said hurrying precipitately upstairs again, 'just as I left the bedroom, the Law arrived . . .'

'You mean, a justice of the peace . . .'

'No, laddie; there was a justice all right, but there are armed constables with him. The district attorney and the examining magistrate are there, the doors are guarded.'

'This death gave rise to gossip very quickly,' said Collin.

'Look, I haven't seen Europe and Paccard again, I'm afraid they may have filched the seven hundred and fifty thousand francs,' said Asia.

'Ah! the blackguards! . . .' said Dodgedeath. 'That bit of larceny is going to be *our* downfall! . . .'

HUMAN justice, in the form in which it flourishes in Paris, that is to say in its cleverest, most mistrustful, wittiest, most educated form, too witty in some ways, for it interprets the law differently on different occasions, had at last put its hand on the originators of this horrible intrigue. Baron Nucingen, recognizing the effects of poison, and failing to find his seven hundred and fifty thousand francs, thought that one of those odious characters who so greatly displeased him, Paccard or Europe, was guilty of the crime. In his first moment of fury, he made haste to the Prefecture of Police. It was a stroke on the bell which alerted all Corentin's numbered men. The Prefecture, the Attorney General's office, the local police superintendent, the justice of the peace, the examining magistrate, everything was set in motion. At nine o' clock in the evening, three doctors who had been summoned were conducting an autopsy on poor Esther, and a thorough search was being made! Dodgedeath, warned by Asia, exclaimed: 'I'm not known here, I can *dissimulate* myself!' He pulled himself up by the frame of the hinged skylight in his attic room, and, with unparallelled agility, stood on the roof, from which point of vantage he studied his surroundings with the calmness of a slater. 'Good,' he said to himself seeing, five houses away, in the rue de Provence, a garden, 'that will do for me! ...'

'Better come quietly, Dodgedeath!' was the reply made by Contenson who stepped out from behind a chimneystack. 'You can explain to Monsieur Camusot what sort of religious service you're conducting on the roof-tops, Monsieur l'Abbé, and especially why you were running away ...'

'I've got enemies in Spain,' said Carlos Herrera.

'Let's go there by way of your attic, to Spain,' said Contenson.

The sham Spaniard appeared to yield, but, bracing himself against the frame of the skylight, he took hold of Contenson and threw him with such violence that the spy landed up in the gutter in the rue Saint Georges. Contenson lay dead on the battlefield. Jacques Collin returned calmly to his attic, and went to bed.

'Give me something to make me really ill, without killing me,' he said to Asia, 'for I must be at death's door so that I can't reply to anything I'm asked by the *inquisitor*. Don't worry, I'm a priest, and a priest I shall remain. I've just got rid, in a way that will seem quite natural, of one of those who could have unmasked me.'

At seven o' clock the previous evening, Lucien had set out in his gig with a passport made out that morning for Fontaine-bleau, had changed horses once and spent the night at the last inn on the Nemours side. At six o' clock next morning, he went alone, on foot, into the forest through which he walked as far as Bouron.

'That,' he said to himself, sitting down on a rock from which the fair landscape of Bouron may be seen, 'is the fatal place at which Napoleon hoped to make a gigantic stand, the last evening but one before his abdication.'

At daybreak, he heard the rumbling of a post-chaise and saw an open carriage go by with the servants of the young Duchesse de Lenoncourt-Chaulieu and Clotilde de Grand-lieu's maid.

'There they are,' Lucien said to himself, 'come on, let's play this little scene nicely, and I'm saved, I shall be the duke's son-in-law in spite of the duke.'

An hour later, he heard the unmistakable sound of an elegant travelling carriage, the berline in which the two women rode. They had arranged for the carriage to brake hard on the hill outside Bouron, and the manservant who was riding behind stopped the berline. At that moment, Lucien came forward.

'Clotilde!' he cried knocking on the glass.

'No,' said the young duchess to her friend, 'he is not to enter the carriage, and we shall not be alone with him. Talk with him for the last time, I don't mind that: but it must be in the roadway where we shall go on foot, followed by Baptiste . . . It is a fine day, we are well-wrapped-up, we're not afraid of the cold. The carriage will follow us . . .'

And the two women got down.

'Baptiste,' said the young duchess, 'the post-boy can go very gently, we're going to walk for a little way, and you can come with us.'

Madeleine de Mortsauf took Clotilde by the arm, and allowed Lucien to speak. They walked together thus as far as the little village of Grez. It was then eight o'clock, and there Clotilde dismissed Lucien.

'Well, my dear,' she said bringing the long interview to a dignified end, 'I shall never marry anyone but you. I'd rather believe in you than in other men, or my father and mother ... Nobody can offer better proof of attachment, can they? ... Now you must try to dissipate the prejudices you're faced with ...'

At that moment several horses were heard at a gallop, and, to the astonishment of the two ladies, a detachment of *gendarmerie* surrounded the little group.

'What do you want? ...' said Lucien with a dandy's arrogance.

'Are you Monsieur Lucien Chardon de Rubempré?' said the procurator of Fontainebleau.

'That's my name, yes.'

'You'll be sleeping tonight at La Force,' replied the attorney, 'I have a warrant of arrest made out for you.'

'Who are these ladies? ...' exclaimed the leader of the detachment.

'Ah, yes, I beg your pardon, ladies, your passports? for, according to my information, Monsieur Lucien is acquainted with women who are capable of ...'

'Do you take the duchess of Lenoncourt-Chaulieu for a tart?' said Madeleine giving the district attorney a duchess look.

'You are handsome enough,' the magistrate said blandly.

'Baptiste, show our passports,' replied the young duchess with a faint smile.

'And of what crime is Monsieur accused?' said Clotilde whom the duchess wished to help back into the carriage.

'Of complicity in theft and murder,' replied the leader of the constabulary.

Baptiste lifted Mademoiselle de Grandlieu into the berline in a dead faint.

At midnight, Lucien was entered at La Force, a prison situated at the junction of the rue Pavée and the rue des Ballets, and placed in solitary confinement; arrested earlier, Father Carlos Herrera was already there.

PART THREE

WHERE EVIL WAYS LEAD

The salad basket

NEXT day, at six o' clock, two carriages with post-boys, of the kind known in the vigorous language of the people as *salad baskets*, emerged from the yard of La Force and proceeded towards the Conciergerie and the adjoining Law Courts.

Few of those who stroll in our streets have failed at one time or another to meet this type of ambulant prison; but though most books are written exclusively for Parisians, other people may be pleased to find here some description of this powerful instrument of our criminal justice. Who knows? the police forces of Russia, Germany or Austria, the magistracies of countries without salad baskets may find such a description profitable; while, in a number of foreign countries, imitation of this mode of transport would certainly prove beneficial to the prisoners themselves.

This ignoble carriage with its yellow body, raised on two wheels and lined with sheet-iron, is divided into two compartments. The front part contains a leather-covered bench, protected by a splashboard. This is the free part of the basket, intended for an usher and a constable. A strong grating of iron trellis, over the full height and breadth of the carriage, separates this cab from the second compartment in which are two wooden benches placed, like those in omnibuses, at either side of the body, and on these the prisoners sit; they are introduced by way of folding steps through an unlighted door at the tail of the vehicle. The nickname 'salad basket' comes from the fact that, originally, the body being of open work all over, the prisoners were shaken about just like salads. For greater security, in case something unexpected happens, the vehicle is followed by an armed constable on horseback, especially when it is taking those condemned to death to their last ordeal. Escape is thus impossible. Lined as the vehicle is with sheet metal, no sort of tool can bite a way out. The prisoners, carefully searched at the time of their arrest or committal, may at best have concealed about their person short lengths of watch-spring useful for sawing through bars, but powerless with plane surfaces. Thus the salad basket, perfected by the genius of the Paris police, ends by serving as a model for the cellular van which transports convicts to the penal settlement, replacing the frightful tumbril, the shame of earlier civilizations, though Manon Lescaut made it famous.

Accused persons are in the first place taken by salad basket from the various prisons in the capital to the Palais de Justice there to be interrogated by the magistrate in charge of the judicial inquiry. In prison slang, this is called *seeing the judge*. The same persons may thereafter be taken to the Palais from the same prisons to receive their sentences, when it is only a matter of summary jurisdiction; then, when in the eyes of the law we are concerned with serious crime, they are decanted from houses of detention into the Conciergerie, which is the headquarters of justice in the Seine department. Finally, those condemned to death are taken in a salad basket from Bicêtre to the Saint James's barrier, which is the place of execution since the July revolution. Thanks to the work of philanthropists, these unfortunates no longer undergo the torture of transportation from the Conciergerie to the Place de Grève or Strand in a cart exactly like those used by wood-sellers. Such a cart is now employed only to transport the scaffold itself. Without this explanation, we shall fail to understand the joke made by a celebrated murderer to his accomplice as they were pushed into the salad basket: 'Now it's all up to the horses!' It would hardly be possible to face the extreme penalty in greater comfort than that in which it is currently faced in Paris.

The two patients

At present, the two salad baskets leaving so early in the morning were being used somewhat irregularly to transfer two accused persons from La Force to the Conciergerie, and the two prisoners each had a salad basket to himself.

Nine tenths of the readers and nine tenths of this last tenth are certainly ignorant of the considerable differences which separate the words: *inculpé, prévenu, accusé, détenu,* or *maison d'arrêt, maison de justice* and *maison de détention*; everyone, indeed, may be surprised to learn that these distinctions are crucial to any understanding of French criminal law, of which a clear and succinct account will presently be offered them as much for their general instruction as in order that the conclusion of this story may also be clear. The reader's curiosity may, however, be sufficiently aroused, to begin with, when he knows that the first salad basket contained Jacques Collin and the second Lucien, who within a few hours had descended from the very summit of social grandeur to the depths of a prison cell. The attitude of the two accomplices was characteristic. Lucien de Rubempré concealed himself to avoid being seen by passers-by who peered through the grating of the sinister and fatal conveyance as it made its way along the rue Saint Antoine to come out by the river down the rue du Martroi, then through the Arcade Saint Jean under which it had to pass to cross the Place de l'Hôtel de Ville. This arcade now forms the entrance to the prefectoral residence within the vast City Hall. The intrepid convict kept his face against the grill which divided the carriage, peering between the heads of the usher and the *gendarme* who, confident in the security of their salad basket, talked happily.

The tempestuous July days of 1830 caused so great an upheaval that what took place shortly before them has been forgotten. People were so concerned with politics during the last six months of the year, that scarcely anyone still recalls, however strange they may have been, what personal, judicial and financial catastrophes, the annual diet of Parisian curiosity, duly occupied them during the first six months. It is therefore necessary to remind the reader to what extent Paris was then agitated by news of the arrest of a Spanish priest found at the house of a courtesan and by that of the elegant Lucien de Rubempré, future husband of Mademoiselle de Grandlieu, captured on the highway to Italy, at the little village of Grez, the two of them charged with a murder of which the proceeds amounted to seven millions; for the scandal provoked by this case overshadowed for some days the nevertheless prodigious interest of the last elections held under Charles X.

For one thing, this criminal trial resulted in part from an action brought by Baron Nucingen. For another, Lucien, on the eve of being made private secretary to the prime minister, was talked of at the highest level in Parisian society. In all the drawing-rooms of Paris, more than one young man remembered his envy of Lucien when the latter had been singled out by the fair Duchesse de Maufrigneuse, and all the women knew to what extent Madame de Sérisy, wife of one of the most influential of current statesmen, interested herself in him. The victim's extreme good looks were famous throughout the various worlds of which Paris is composed: the world of high society, the world of finance, the world of harlotry, the world of young men, the literary world. For two days past, Paris had talked of nothing else but these two arrests. The examining magistrate upon whom the conduct of the judicial inquiry had devolved, Monsieur Camusot, saw in it a way to his own advancement; and, in order to press on with the matter at the greatest possible speed, had ordered the two accused (or inculpated) to be transferred from La Force to the Conciergerie as soon as Lucien de Rubempré had been brought from Fontainebleau. The abbé Carlos and Lucien having spent, the former no more than twelve hours and the latter half a night at La Force, there is no point in describing that prison which has since been greatly modified; while, as to the committal proceedings, to present them in detail would be a mere repetition of what was to take place at the Conciergerie.

Criminal law for the man in the street

BUT before going into the awful drama of a criminal inquiry, it is indispensable, as we have just said, to explain the usual course of a trial of this kind; its various phases will then be better understood both in France and abroad; the previously uninformed will also be in a position to appreciate the simplicity of criminal proceedings at law, as these were conceived by our legislators under Napoleon. It is all the more important in that this great and finely constructed work is, at the moment, threatened with destruction by the so-called penitentiary system.

A crime is committed: if it is flagrant, the *inculpés* or persons detected are taken to the nearest guard post and put in the cell popularly called a *violon*, doubtless because of the music which is heard there: shouting or weeping. Thence, the prisoner is taken before the police superintendent, who conducts a preliminary investigation and who may discharge him at once, if there has been a mistake; otherwise *inculpés* are taken to the central police station, where the police hold them at the disposition of the district attorney and the examining magistrate, who, according to the seriousness of the case, alerted more or less promptly, arrive and question those in custody. According to the nature of his first findings, the examining magistrate issues a warrant of committal and consigns the *inculpé* to a remand centre or *maison d'arrêt*, of which there are three in Paris: Sainte Pélagie, La Force and Les Madelonnettes.

Note the expression: *inculpé*. The French Code has set up three essential distinctions in criminal law: *inculpation, prévention, accusation.* Until a warrant of arrest is signed, the presumed authors of a crime or misdemeanour are *inculpés*; placed under arrest in due form, they become *prévenus*, they remain purely and simply *prévenus* so long as the judicial inquiry proceeds. Thereafter, the tribunal being convinced that the case against them should be brought before the courts, their condition is that of *accusés*, once the Crown has been advised by the Attorney General that they may appear on indictment before a court of assize. Thus, persons suspected of a crime pass from one to another of three different conditions, are sifted three times before their appearance at a public hearing. At the first stage, the innocent may vindicate themselves in the eyes of the public, the town guard, the police. At the second stage, they stand charged before a magistrate, are confronted with witnesses, and the bill of indictment against them is examined by a chamber of the tribunal in Paris, by a whole tribunal in the provinces. At the third stage, they appear before twelve counsellors, and the judgment of a court of assize may, in the event of misdirection or an error of form, be referred by the accused to the Central Court of Criminal Appeal or *Cour de Cassation*. The jury does not know what popular, administrative and judicial authorities it affronts when it acquits *accusés*. Thus, it appears to us that, in Paris (whatever may be the case under other jurisdictions), an innocent man is unlikely to find himself in the dock at the Court of Assize.

A *détenu* is a man who has been sentenced. Our criminal law has set up *maisons d'arrêt*, *maisons de justice* and *maisons de détention*, juridical differences which correspond with those between the *prévenu*, the *accusé* and the *condamné*. Mere imprisonment carries with it only light punishment, it is the penalty for minor offences; but detention is afflictive and may, in certain cases, involve banishment or other loss of civil rights. Those who nowadays advocate a uniform penitentiary system would thus destroy an admirable penal code according to which penalties were carefully graduated, and the result would be to punish trifling misdemeanours almost as severely as serious crimes. The code instituted by Napoleon, it may be noted, differs greatly from that of revolutionary times which it superseded.

In important cases, like the one before us, the *inculpés* almost invariably become *prévenus* at the outset. The warrant for committal or arrest is issued immediately. In fact, more often than not, the *inculpés* have either taken flight, or they are surprised in the act. Thus, as we have seen, the Police, which is only the means of executing the law, and Justice had appeared with the speed of lightning at Esther's domicile. Even had no motives of revenge been whispered into the ear of the *Police Judiciaire* (as the *Brigade de Sûreté* or crime squad is more properly called), information of a theft of seven hundred and fifty thousand francs had been laid by Baron Nucingen.

The Machiavelli of the hulks

As the first carriage which contained Jacques Collin reached the Arcade Saint Jean, a dark and narrow passage, an obstruction caused the post-boy to stop under the archway. The eyes of the *prévenu* shone through the grating like two carbuncles, despite the mask of a dying man which the evening before had made the governor of La Force think it necessary to call in a doctor. At that moment free, for neither the constable nor the usher turned round to look at *their customer*, those burning eyes spoke so clear a language that a clever examining magistrate, like Monsieur Popinot for example, would have recognized the convict beneath that sacrilegious attire. Ever since the salad basket had emerged from the gate of La Force, Jacques Collin had indeed been examining everything on the way. Despite the speed of their journey, his avid and all-seeing gaze took in the houses from top storey to ground floor. God's grasp of his creation in its means and in its end was not more complete than this man's perception of small variations in the mass of things and passers-by. Armed with hope, as the last of the Horatii was with his sword, he waited for help. To anyone else but this Machiavelli of the hulks, such a hope would have appeared so impossible of realization that he would have lapsed into a mechanical indifference, as the guilty invariably do. None of them thinks of resisting the situation in which Justice and the Police of Paris have plunged those who are duly charged, more especially when they are being kept in solitary confinement, as both Lucien and Jacques Collin were. The sudden isolation of such a man is difficult to conceive: the constables who have arrested him, the police superintendent who first questions him, those who take him to prison, the warders who conduct him to what in literature is called a dungeon, those who take him by the arms to force him to climb into a salad basket, all those who surround him from the moment of his arrest, are silent or make notes of what he says in order to repeat it to the police or the magistrate. This absolute separation, so easy to establish

305

between the *prévenu* and the rest of the world, produces a total overthrow of his faculties, an utter prostration of the mind, above all when he is a man unaccustomed by his antecedents to the operations of the Law. The duel between criminal and judge is all the more dreadful in that among the allies of the Law are the silence of walls and the incorruptible indifference of its minions.

Nevertheless, Jacques Collin or Carlos Herrera (it is necessary to give him one or the other of these names according to the exigencies of the situation) had long been familiar with the ways of the police, the prisons and the legal authorities. This colossus of trickery and corruption had therefore employed all the strength of his wit and the resources of mimicry to act the astonishment, the foolishness of an innocent man, while playing out the comedy of his grave illness. As we have seen, Asia, that cunning Locust, had made him take a poison so tempered as to produce the semblance of a mortal sickness. The intentions of Monsieur Camusot, the police superintendent and the district attorney had thus been defeated by the action of what appeared to be an apoplectic stroke.

'He has poisoned himself,' had exclaimed Monsieur Camusot alarmed by the sufferings of the supposed priest when he had been brought down from the attic a prey to horrible convulsions.

Four policemen had had a great deal of trouble in conveying Father Carlos down the stairs to Esther's bedroom where the magistrates and the constabulary were gathered.

'It was the best thing he could do if he's guilty,' the district attorney had replied.

'Do you think he's ill, then? . . .' had asked the police superintendent.

Policemen question everything. The three magistrates had then discussed the matter, as we might expect, in whispers, but Jacques Collin had divined from their facial expressions the tenor of their speculations, and he had taken advantage of what he perceived to render impossible or nugatory the summary interrogation which is conducted at the time of arrest; he had stammered phrases in which Spanish and French mingled in such a manner as to make nonsense.

At La Force, this play-acting had proved all the more successful in that the head of the detective force, Bibi-Lupin, who had formerly arrested Jacques Collin at Madame Vauquer's boarding-house, was on a mission in the provinces, his place being taken by an agent designated as Bibi-Lupin's successor, a man to whom the convict was unknown.

Bibi-Lupin, a former convict, Jacques Collin's companion at the penal station, was his personal enemy. The source of this enmity lay in quarrels in which Jacques Collin had always come out on top, and in the prestige Dodgedeath had enjoyed among his comrades. Furthermore, for ten years, Jacques Collin had been the good angel of discharged convicts, their chief, their counsel in Paris, their trustee, and in consequence the antagonist of Bibi-Lupin.

A breach of enforced isolation

THUS, although he remained in solitary confinement, he counted on the intelligent and absolute devotion of Asia, his right hand, and perhaps on Paccard, his left, whom he flattered himself he would find once more at his orders when that careful lieutenant had put his seven hundred and fifty thousand stolen francs away. That was the reason for the concentrated attention he gave to everything on the way. A strange thing! his hope was to be fully satisfied.

The two massive walls of the Arcade Saint Jean were clothed up to a height of six feet with a permanent mantle of mud produced by splashes from the gutter; for in those days the only thing which protected passers-by from the incessant passing of carriages and what were called cart-kicks was a succession of posts long ago smashed by the hubs and pipe-boxes of wheels. More than once some quarryman's cart had crushed inattentive people at that point. For long, many parts of Paris were like that. This detail may help to convey the narrowness of the Arcade Saint Jean and the ease with which it could be blocked. If a cab happened to enter from the Strand, while a costermonger was pushing his barrow loaded with apples from the rue du Martroi, the arrival of a third carriage would create an obstruction. Frightened pedestrians hurried by looking for a post to protect them against a blow from those old-fashioned wheel-blocks, which projected so absurdly far that legislation had to be passed to curtail them. When the salad basket arrived, the arcade was blocked by one of those female costermongers whose survival in Paris is all the more remarkable in view of the increasing number of fruiterers. She was so perfectly representative of her kind that a town sergeant, if such had existed at that time, would have let her circulate without making her show her permit, despite her sinister physiognomy which sweated criminality. Her head, tied up in a ragged scarf of cotton check, bristled with rebellious tufts of hair like hog's bristles. Her red, wrinkled neck was horrible to see, and her shawl did little to conceal a skin tanned by sun, dust and mud. Her dress was like dilapidated tapestry. Her shoes grinned in a way to suggest that they were making fun of her face, as pitted and pocked as her dress. And what a stomacher! . . . old sticking-plaster would have been less filthy. From ten paces away, the nostrils of the delicate were affected by this ambulant, foetid scarecrow. Those hands had grubbed everywhere! Either the woman had just attended a witches' sabbath, or she had been discharged from a beggars' hostel. But what looks! . . . what audacious intelligence, what secret life when the magnetic rays of her eyes and those of Jacques Collin met to exchange a thought.

'Get out of the way, you old home for vermin, will you! . . .' cried the post-boy in a hoarse voice.

'Don't you start running into me, gallows lackey,' she replied, 'your wares are worse than mine.'

And in the attempt to squeeze herself between two posts to make way, the barrow-woman obstructed the road long enough for the accomplishment of her plan.

'O Asia!' said Jacques Collin to himself, at once recognizing his accomplice, 'now all will be well.'

The postillion was still exchanging courtesies with Asia and carriages accumulated in the rue du Martroi.

'*Ahé! . . . pecaire fermati. Souni lá. Vedrem! . . .*' old Asia called out with those war-whooping intonations peculiar to street vendors which so effectively distort their words that these become forms of onomatopeia intelligible to Parisians alone.

In the hubbub of the street and amid the cries of all the coachmen who were now held up, nobody paid attention to this wild cry which was taken for that of a street trader. But in Jacques Collin's ear, the clamour of that agreed lingo made up of corrupt Italian and Provençal distinctly conveyed its dreadful meaning:

'*Your poor boy has been arrested; but I shall be there to look after you both. You will see me again . . .*'

In the midst of the infinite joy which his triumph over the Law brought him, for now he could expect to maintain contact with the world outside, Jacques Collin was stricken by a reaction which might have killed anyone but him.

'Lucien under arrest! . . .' he said to himself. And he came near fainting. This piece of news was more appalling to him than the rejection of his appeal would have been had he lain under sentence of death.

Historical, archeological, biographical, anecdotal and physiological history of the Palais de Justice

Now that the two salad baskets are rolling along the quays, the interest of this story requires a few words about the Conciergerie during the time they will take to get there. The Conciergerie, a historical name, a terrible word, a thing yet more terrible, is a part of revolutionary France. It has seen most of the great criminals. If of all the monuments of Paris it is the most interesting, it is also the least known . . . to people who belong to the upper classes of society; but despite the immense interest of this historical digression, it will be as rapid as the course of the salad baskets.

What Parisian, foreigner or provincial is there, though he may have spent a mere two days in Paris, who has not noticed the black walls flanked by three big pepper-pot towers, two of them almost joined together, sombre and mysterious adornments of that stretch of riverside known as the Quai des Lunettes? This embankment begins at the Pont au Change and ends at the Pont Neuf. A square tower, called the Tour de l'Horloge, from which the signal for Saint Bartholomew was given, almost as high as the tower of Saint Jacques-la-Boucherie, indicates the Law Courts and forms the corner of this quayside. The four towers and the walls are clothed with that shroud of black which all north-ward-facing fronts acquire in Paris. Half way along the embankment, by a blank archway, begin those private establishments which went with the building of the Pont Neuf in the reign of Henry IV. The Place Royale was a replica of the Place Dauphine. It had the same style of architecture, in brick framed with freestone piers. The archway and the rue de Harlay mark the west side of the Law Courts. Formerly, the police Prefecture, residence of the speakers of the high judicial court, was attached to the palace. The Audit Office and the Board of Excise there complemented supreme law, that of the sovereign. It may thus be seen that before the Revolution the palace enjoyed that isolation which attempts are being made to create about it once more.

This block of buildings, this island of houses and monuments, where the Sainte Chapelle stands, the most magnificent jewel in the casket of Saint Louis, this area is the sanctuary of Paris; this is the holy place, the sacred ark. To begin with, indeed, this was the whole of the original city, for the site of the Place Dauphine was a meadow within the royal domain and on it was built a mill for the striking of coin. Thence comes the name of the rue de la Monnaie, which leads to the Pont Neuf. Thence also the name of one of the three round towers, the second, which is called the Tour d'Argent, evident proof that it was once used for minting. The famous mill, which may be seen on the original plans of Paris, must have been set up after a time during which money was coined in the palace itself, and was no doubt due to some improvement in the process of minting. The first tower, almost contiguous with the Tour d'Argent, is called the Montgommery Tower. The third and smallest, but best preserved, for it retains its battlements is the Bonbec Tower. The Sainte Chapelle and these four towers (counting the Tour de l'Horloge) precisely demarcate the extent, the perimeter, as a surveyor would say, of the palace, from the time of the Merovingians to the first of the Valois; but to us, in consequence of its many transformations, it represents more particularly the age of Saint Louis.

It was Charles V who, in the first place, gave up the palace to the high judicial court, a newly created institution, and went, under the protection of the Bastille, to live in the Saint Pol house to which the Tournelles palace was presently attached. Then, under the last of the Valois, royalty returned from the Bastille to its earlier *bastille* or small fortress, the Louvre. The first abode of the kings of France, Saint Louis's palace, which is remembered as simply the Palace, the greatest palace of all, is totally buried under the Law Courts, whose cellars it forms, for, like the cathedral, it was built down into the Seine, with such care that the highest water in the river barely covers its lowest steps. The Quai de l'Horloge lies some twenty feet above this structure ten centuries old. Carriages bowl along at the height of the capitals of the supporting pillars of those three towers, whose elevation must formerly have harmonized with the elegance of the palace and created a picturesque effect over the water, since even now those towers stand as high as the tallest monuments in Paris. When one looks out over the vast capital city from the lantern of the Pantheon, the Law Courts, with Sainte Chapelle, still appear as the most monumental among so many monuments. That palace of our kings, over which you walk when you pace about the immense waiting hall, was an architectural wonder; it is still so to the perceptive eyes of the poet who gazes at it in the course of his visit to the Conciergerie. Alas! the Conciergerie has invaded the palace of the kings. The heart bleeds to see how gaolers' lodges, wretched living quarters, corridors, public rooms without light or air, have been carved out of this magnificent composition in which the Byzantine, the Norman, the Gothic, those three faces of art in the old days, were brought together in the architecture of the twelfth century. This palace is to the monumental history of France's earliest times what the Château de Blois is to the times which followed. Just as at Blois, from the same courtyard you can admire the castle of the counts of Blois and those of Louis XII, Francis I, Gaston; so at the Conciergerie you find, on the one site, traces of the earliest people and, in Sainte Chapelle, the architecture of Saint Louis. Municipal council, if you are putting up millions, appoint a few poets with the architects, if you wish to preserve the cradle of Paris, the cradle of kings, in your task of endowing Paris and the sovereign court with a palace worthy of France! The question is one worth pondering for several years before a beginning is made. Build one or two other prisons, like that of La Roquette, and the palace of Saint Louis will be saved.

Continuation of the same subject

AT present this gigantic monument, buried beneath the Law Courts and the embankment, displays many wounds, like one of those antediluvian animals of which plaster casts may be seen at Montmartre; the worst of them is, to have become the Conciergerie! The word itself needs explaining. In the earliest days of the monarchy, important criminals, whether burgesses or villeins (for we must retain this spelling which gives the word its sense of peasant), belonging to urban or manorial jurisdictions, the possessors of *great and small fiefs*, were taken to the King and kept in the Conciergerie. As not many important criminals were seized, the Conciergerie sufficed for the King's justice. It is difficult to determine precisely on what ground the primitive Conciergerie stood. Nevertheless, as the kitchens of Saint Louis still exist, and today form what is known as the Mousetrap, it may be presumed that the original Conciergerie occupied what was, until 1825, the position of the Conciergerie of the high judicial court, beneath the archway to the right of the great external staircase which leads to the Cour Royale. Thence, until 1825, the condemned proceeded to their place of punishment. Thence emerged all the great criminals, all those sentenced for political reasons, the Maréchale d'Ancre like the Queen of France, Semblançay like Malesherbes, Damien no less than Danton, Desrues and Castaing equally. Fouquier-Tinville's office, occupied to this day by the King's attorney, was so situated that the public procurator could see the carts taking away those newly condemned by the revolutionary tribunal. This man of blood could thus cast a last glance over his batches of victims.

After 1825, under the ministry of Monsieur de Peyronnet, a great change took place at the *Palais*. The old wicket of the Conciergerie, scene of all the ceremonies of committal and the neck-trimming of men for execution, was shut down and transferred to its present position, between the Tour de l'Horloge and the Montgommery tower, in an inner yard flanked by an arcade. To the left is the Mousetrap, to the right the wicket. The salad baskets drive into this irregularly shaped yard, where they may stand, turn easily and, in the case of a riot, take protection behind the strong grating of the archway; while formerly their movements were severely restricted by the narrow space which separates the great external staircase from the right wing of the court buildings. Nowadays the Conciergerie, which is hardly big enough for those on trial (there would have to be room for three hundred people, men and women), accommodates neither those first charged nor those already sentenced, except in exceptional circumstances, such as those which brought Jacques Collin and Lucien there. All those held prisoner there must appear before the court of assize. Exceptionally, the magistracy allows there convicted persons from high society who, already sufficiently dishonoured by a verdict in the court of assize, would be too heavily punished, if they served their sentence at Melun or Poissy. Ouvrard preferred his stay in the Conciergerie to that at Sainte Pélagie. At the present moment, Lehon the notary and the prince of Bergues are serving their terms of imprisonment there, by a quite arbitrary but humane dispensation.

The uses to which these premises are put

In general, remanded persons, whether they are going, in the
jargon of the palace, to school, or to appear before a court of
summary jurisdiction, are deposited by their salad baskets
straight into the Mousetrap. The Mousetrap, which lies
opposite the wicket, is composed of a certain number of cells
effected in the kitchens of Saint Louis, where *prévenus* brought
from the various prisons wait either for the court to sit or for
their examining magistrate to be ready for them. The Mousetrap is bounded on the north by the embankment, on the east
by the guard post of the municipal guard, on the west by the
Conciergerie yard and on the south by a huge vaulted room
(doubtless the old banqueting hall), not at present in use. Over
the Mousetrap extends a large interior guardroom, with a
window looking out over the Conciergerie yard, it is occupied
by the departmental constabulary and the staircase ends there.
When it is time for the courts to sit, ushers appear to call out
the names of those who are to appear, constables go down in
number equal to that of the prisoners, each constable takes an
accused person by the arm; and, thus paired, they climb the
staircase, pass through the guardroom and along corridors
which bring them to a room adjacent to the famous Court Six
(of summary jurisdiction). This is also the route taken by
persons on indictment on their way from the Conciergerie to
the Court of Assize, or on return.

In the big waiting room, between the door to Court One
(also of summary jurisdiction) and the staircase which leads
up to Court Six, you immediately notice, on a first visit, an
entrance without door, without any architectural decoration,
an insignificant square hole. Through it come judges and
lawyers on their way along the corridors, to the guardroom,
down to the Mousetrap and the wicket of the Conciergerie.
All the offices of examining magistrates are situated on different floors in that part of the building. These offices are reached
by dreadful flights of stairs, a maze in which people who don't
know the Law Courts always lose themselves. Some of the

office windows give on to the embankment, others on to the Conciergerie yard. In 1830, some examining magistrates' offices also looked out over the rue de la Barillerie.

Thus when a salad basket turns left into the Conciergerie yard, it will be bringing remanded persons to the Mousetrap; when it turns right, it is bringing those committed for trial to the Conciergerie. It was to the right that the salad basket containing Jacques Collin turned to deposit him at the wicket. Nothing could be more forbidding. Criminals or visitors perceive two wrought-iron gratings, separated by a space of about six feet, which are always opened one after the other, and through which everything is so scrupulously examined that people accorded a visiting permit have effectively crossed this space before the key grates in the lock. Examining magistrates, even the Attorney General's personal staff, do not enter without having been recognized. And so, is there any talk of the possibility of communicating or escaping? . . . the governor of the Conciergerie will have on his lips a smile to discourage the most temerarious novelist in his schemes against verisimilitude. The only escape known, in the annals of the Conciergerie, is that of Lavalette; but the certainty of august connivance, now proved, diminished, if not the devotion of the spouse, at least the risk of failure. If they estimate the nature of all the obstacles on the spot, the most fervent lovers of the marvellous must acknowledge that at all times those obstacles were what they are now, invincible. No words can describe the strength of these walls and vaults, they have to be seen. Although the paving of the yard is at a level below that of the embankment, once you are through the wicket, you must go down several steps to reach an enormous vaulted hall whose massive walls are ornamented with magnificent pillars and flanked by the Montgommery Tower, today part of the governor of the Conciergerie's private quarters, and by the Tour d'Argent which contains the sleeping quarters of the warders, turnkeys or screws, whatever you choose to call them. These employees are less numerous than might be imagined (there are twenty of them); their accommodation does not differ from that of what is known as the *pistole*. This name doubtless comes from the fact that formerly prisoners paid a pistole a week for such accommodation, which recalls by its bareness those cold attics in which great men without resources start by living in Paris. To the left in this great entrance hall stands the registry of the Conciergerie, an office set round by glass partitions, occupied by the governor and his clerk and containing all committal records. There, those in various stages of inculpation are entered, described and searched. There it is decided where they shall be lodged, a question whose solution depends on the size of the patient's purse. Facing the counter here, may be seen a glass door, that of the parlour where relations and lawyers communicate with prisoners through a double trellis of wood. Light reaches this parlour from the prison yard, the place of exercise in which prisoners take the air at fixed times.

Illuminated only by such daylight as reaches it by way of two gratings, for the only window giving on to the courtyard in which we arrived lies entirely within the record-office, the atmosphere and the lighting of this hall are perfectly in keeping with what the imagination might have conceived. It is all the more frightening in that parallel with the Argent and Montgommery Towers, you glimpse mysterious, vaulted, forbidding, unlighted crypts, winding beyond the parlour and leading to the dungeons of the queen, of Madame Elizabeth, and the cells for solitary confinement. This maze of freestone has become the basement of the Law Courts, having once seen royal festivals. From 1825 to 1832, it was in this great hall, between a big stove which heats it and the first of the two gratings, that the ceremonial toilet was performed on condemned men before execution. Walking across these flagstones, one cannot but shudder to think what confidences, what last looks and last footsteps they have received.

The formalities of committal

To get out of his frightful conveyance the man at death's door needed the assistance of two constables who took him each under one arm, held him up and carried him to the registry as if in a faint. Dragged thus, the dying man raised his eyes in a manner reminiscent of the Saviour's descent from the cross. Certainly in no painting does Jesus display a more cadaverous, more collapsed face than was that of the sham Spaniard, he seemed at his last gasp. When he was seated in the record-office, he repeated in a feeble voice the words he had addressed to everyone since his arrest: 'I wish to see His Excellency the Spanish ambassador . . .'

'You can say that,' replied the governor, 'to the examining magistrate.'

'Ah! Jesus!' Jacques Collin continued with a sigh. 'Can I not have a breviary? . . . Am I to be forever denied a doctor? . . . I have not two hours to live.'

As Carlos Herrera was to be consigned to solitary confinement, it was useless to ask him whether he claimed the advantages of the *pistole*, that is to say the right to occupy one of those rooms in which one enjoys the only comforts allowed by the Law. These rooms are situated to one end of the prison yard with which we shall be concerned later. The usher and the clerk between them phlegmatically carried out the formalities of committal.

'Mr Governor,' said Jacques Collin in his foreign-sounding French, 'I am dying, as you see. Tell, if you can, at the very earliest moment, tell this examining magistrate that I solicit as a favour what a criminal would most fear, that I may appear before him as soon as he arrives; for my sufferings are truly unbearable, and as soon as I see him, this mistake will be put right . . .'

It is a general rule, criminals always speak of a mistake. Go to the penal settlements, question those under sentence, they are almost invariably the victims of a miscarriage of justice. This expression therefore brings a smile to the lips of all who have to do with prisoners at any stage in the course of legal proceedings.

'I shall tell the examining magistrate of your request,' replied the governor.

'I shall bless you then, sir! . . .' the Spaniard said raising his eyes heavenward.

Once committed in due form, Carlos Herrera, taken under

the arms by two municipal guards accompanied by a warder, told by the governor to which cell the prisoner should be taken, was conducted through the underground labyrinth of the Conciergerie to a room which was perfectly clean, whatever certain philanthropists and reformers may say, but without any possibility of communication.

When he was out of sight, the warders, the prison governor, his clerk, the usher himself, the constables looked at each other like people who seek each other's opinions, and doubt was depicted on all their faces; but at the sight of the other prisoner, all the spectators returned to their habitual uncertainty, concealed by an air of indifference. Except in very unusual circumstances, those employed at the Conciergerie do not show much curiosity, criminals being to them what his clients are to a barber. Thus all the formalities which so disturb the imagination are conducted with greater simplicity than money matters at a bank, and often with more politeness. Lucien's mask was that of a guilty man who has given up hope, for he simply did what was expected of him, he behaved mechanically. Ever since Fontainebleau, the poet had been contemplating his ruin, saying to himself that the hour of expiation had struck. Pale, limp, knowing nothing of what had taken place at Esther's during his absence, he knew himself to be the intimate companion of an escaped convict; a situation in which he could only anticipate catastrophes worse than death. The sole intention his mind was now and then able to conceive was that of suicide. He wanted at any price to escape the ignominies he foresaw like the fantasies of a disordered dream.

Jacques Collin, as the more dangerous prisoner of the two, had been put in a dark cell of solid freestone, into which light only entered from one of those small inner yards, such as are found here and there in the precincts of the Law Courts, situated in the wing in which the Attorney General had his office. This little enclosed space serves as an exercise yard for the women's quarters. Lucien was led in the same general direction to a cell next to the *pistoles*, the examining magistrate having instructed the governor to show him some little consideration.

In general, those who are unlikely ever to find themselves up against the Law entertain the darkest notions about solitary confinement. The thought of criminal justice is inextricably bound up with ideas of torture, of the insalubrity of prisons, of cold stone walls sweating tears, of the coarseness of the gaolers and the food, obligatory stage-properties of drama; but it may be useful to point out here that such exaggerations belong entirely to the theatre, and are laughed at by magistrates, lawyers and those who, out of curiosity, visit prisons or come to observe them. For long, things were indeed terrible. It is not to be disputed that under the former high judicial court in the ages of Louis XIII and Louis XIV, those awaiting trial were flung pell-mell into a single large room above the old reception hall. Its use of the prisons was itself one of the crimes of the revolution of 1789, and to see the dungeons of the queen and of Madame Elizabeth is enough to give one the deepest horror of old judicial forms. Today, however, incalculable harm though philanthropy may have wrought in society generally, it has done some good to individuals. We owe to Napoleon our Code of criminal law, which, more obviously than that of civil law, which in certain respects urgently calls for reform, will remain one of the greatest monuments of that short reign. The new penality did away with a host of abuses and the needless suffering they caused. Though members of the superior classes of society must always feel dreadfully afflicted when they fall into the hands of the Law, we may truthfully assert that its power is exercised with a mildness and simplicity all the greater for being unexpected. Those first charged or subsequently remanded are not indeed made as comfortable as they would be at home; but the requisites of life are found in the prisons of Paris. The pressure of unaccustomed feelings, in any case, frees the accessories of life of their habitual meaning. It is not the body which suffers. The state of mind is so violent that any kind of discomfort, or even brutality, encountered in those surroundings, would be easily borne. In Paris at least, anyone who is innocent will be promptly set at liberty, that is certain.

Lucien, on entering his cell, thus saw a faithful replica of the first room he had occupied in Paris, at the Hôtel Cluny. A bed like those in the poorest furnished rooms in the Latin quarter, straw-bottomed chairs, a table and a few utensils constitute the furniture of one of these rooms, in which two prisoners are often put together when their manners are mild and their crimes of a sufficiently reassuring nature, forgery and bankruptcy for instance. This similarity between his point of departure, full of innocence, and the point to which he had come, the last degree of shame and degradation, was so evident to what remained of his poetic fibre, that the unfortunate young man burst into tears. He wept for four hours on end, in appearance as unfeeling as a figure of stone, but tormented by all his disappointed hopes, stricken to the heart of all his crushed social vanity, his broken pride, all those *selves* which belong to the ambitious man, the man in love, the fortunate man, the dandy, the Parisian, the poet, the voluptuary and the child of privilege. Every faculty in him had been shattered by this Icarian fall.

Carlos Herrera, for his part, once left alone in his cell, paced about it like the polar bear in its cage at the zoological gardens. He minutely inspected the door and established that, the spy-hole apart, no hole had been made in it. He sounded all round the walls, he looked up at the hood through whose aperture feeble light reached him and said to himself: 'This is out of harm's way all right!' He went and sat down in a corner where the eye of a warder applied to the spy-hole would not have been able to see him. Then he removed his wig and promptly unstuck a piece of paper from the inside. The side of this paper in contact with his head was so filthy it seemed part of the tegument of the wig. If Bibi-Lupin had had the idea of removing this wig to establish the Spaniard's identity with Jacques Collin, he would not have been suspicious of this paper, so much did it seem to belong to the wigmaker's art. The other side of the paper was still white and clean enough to be written on. The difficult and minute business of unsticking had been begun at La Force, two hours would have been too little time, half the previous day had been spent on the operation. The prisoner began by trimming this precious paper in such a way as to give him a strip four or five lines broad, which he divided into several pieces; then he replaced his store of paper in its singular repository, having moistened the layer of gum arabic with which it was kept in place. He felt among the hair for one of those pencils, slender as a pin, which Susse had recently begun to make, and which also was gummed into place; he broke off a piece long enough to write with and short enough to keep in his ear. These preparations completed with the speed and dexterity common to old lags who are as clever as monkeys, Jacques Collin sat on the edge of his bed and considered his instructions to Asia, certain of finding her in his path, such was his trust in this woman's ingenuity.

'Questioned summarily,' he said to himself, 'I behaved like a Spaniard who speaks French badly, demanding his ambassador, claiming diplomatic privilege and not understanding what was put to him, all that punctuated with moments of weakness, deep groans, sighs, in short all the humbug appropriate to a man at death's door. I must go on like that. My papers are in order. Asia and I together, we shall make a meal of Monsieur Camusot, he isn't very bright. Now let's think about Lucien, his spirits need raising, at all costs I must communicate with the child, outline his plan of conduct, otherwise he'll give himself away, give me away and ruin everything! ... It must be drummed into him before his interrogation. Then I must have witnesses to the fact of my priestly state!'

Such was the mental and physical condition of the two prisoners whose fate at that moment depended on Monsieur Camusot, examining magistrate of the Court of First Instance of the Seine, sovereign judge, during the time allowed him by the code of criminal procedure, of the smallest details of their existence; for he alone could allow the chaplain, the Conciergerie doctor or anyone else to communicate with them.

The functions of an examining magistrate

No human power, neither the King nor the Keeper of the Seals, nor yet the Prime Minister, can encroach on the authority of an examining magistrate, nothing can stand in his way, he cannot be given orders. He is subject only to his conscience and the law. At a time when philosophers, philanthropists and publicists are all the while engaged in cutting down the forms of social authority, the rights which the law confers on examining magistrates are being made the subject of attacks which are all the more formidable in that they are partly justified, those rights being excessive. Nevertheless, any man in his right mind will see that the authority must remain unimpaired; in a number of ways, its exercise may be made less harsh by broad discretionary means; but society, already shaken by the stupidity and weakness of juries (whose high and august magisterial function should be confided only to selected persons of note), would be threatened with ruin if this column which upholds the whole of our criminal law were broken. The power of arrest is fearsome but necessary, its social danger counterbalanced by its very importance. Distrust of the magistracy would be the start of social disintegration. Destroy the institution, rebuild it on other foundations; require, as was done before the Revolution, that all magistrates be rich men; but believe in it; don't make it an image of society in order to insult it. Magistrates now, paid as public servants, for the most part poor men, have swopped their former dignity for a pride which seems intolerable to many set up as their equals; for haughtiness is a dignity which rests on a slender base. That is the weakness of the institution as we find it today. If France were divided into ten jurisdictions, the magistracy's position could be raised by requiring all magistrates to be men of great fortune, which becomes impossible with twenty-six judicial areas. The only real improvement which may be demanded in the exercise of those powers confided to the examining magistrate, is the rehabilitation of those prisons we call *maisons d'arrêt*. There should be no marked change in the life of those who are merely *prévenus* or remanded in custody. Those prisons ought, in Paris, to be so built, furnished and disposed as to modify profoundly the public's idea of what committal involves. The law itself is good, it is necessary, the way it is carried out is bad and laws are judged morally by the manner of their carrying out. Public opinion in France condemns the man taken into custody but, by a strange contradiction, views him with sympathy once he comes up for trial. Perhaps this is due to the Frenchman's essentially critical attitude towards authority. A lack of consequentiality in the Parisian public was to contribute towards the catastrophe of our present drama; it was indeed, as we shall see, a major factor. To understand the terrible scenes played out in an examining magistrate's office; to appreciate the respective situations of the two belligerent parties, the prisoners and the Law, when what is at stake is the secret kept by the former against the determined curiosity of the latter, we must never forget that those kept in solitary confinement know nothing of what is being said about them in the seven or eight publics which constitute the Public, nothing of what the police and the courts know, nothing even of what newspapers have published about the circumstances of a crime. Thus for such a man to have learnt what Asia had contrived to tell Jacques Collin about Lucien's arrest, is for a line to be thrown to a drowning man. We shall see that, without this, the plan concocted against the convict would have succeeded. This being stated in large general terms, readers not easily moved may well experience the fear to which these three circumstances give rise: sequestration, silence and remorse.

The examining magistrate is worried

MONSIEUR CAMUSOT, son-in-law of an usher to the King's office, already too well known to need any explanation of his alliances and his position, was at that moment in a state of perplexity equal to Carlos Herrera's own, with regard to the judicial inquiry entrusted to him. Formerly chairman of a court in the provinces, he had been extracted from this position and appointed to the magistracy in Paris, a coveted post which he owed to the protection of the famous Duchesse de Maufrigneuse whose husband, a companion of the Dauphin and colonel of a cavalry regiment of the Royal Guard, was as much in favour with the King as she was with *Madame*. For a small but important service rendered to the duchess at the time of a charge of forgery brought against the young Count Esgrignon by a banker in Alençon, he had been promoted from the minor ranks of the provincial magistracy to chairmanship of his own court and subsequently to an examining magistracy in Paris. For the past eighteen months, sitting as a member of the most important court of the realm, he had taken the opportunity to espouse the views of no less powerful a great lady, the Marquise d'Espard, to whom the Duchesse de Maufrigneuse had recommended him; but he had failed. Lucien, as we mentioned at the beginning of the present work, to avenge himself on Madame d'Espard who sought to deprive her husband of control over his estate, had succeeded in bringing the truth of the matter to the eyes of the Attorney General and Count Sérisy. These two great figures once aligned with the friends of the Marquis d'Espard, it was only through her husband's clemency that his wife had escaped the reprimand of the court. The previous day, on hearing of Lucien's arrest, the Marquise d'Espard had sent her brother-in-law, the Chevalier d'Espard, with a message to Madame Camusot. Madame Camusot had at once hurried round to see the marchioness. At dinner-time, back home, she had taken her husband aside into her bedroom.

'If you can send that little fool Lucien de Rubempré before the court of assize, and he is duly sentenced,' she said to him in an undertone, 'you will be made a counsellor at the Royal Court . . .'

'Why is that?'

'Madame d'Espard would like to see that poor young man's head fall. A shiver ran down my spine hearing such hatred speak on a pretty woman's lips.'

'Don't get mixed up with matters at the Law Courts,' replied Camusot to his wife.

'Me, get mixed up?' she went on. 'A third party could have heard all we said, he wouldn't have understood what it was about. The marchioness and I were both as amusingly hypocritical as you are being with me at this moment. She wanted to thank me for your good offices at the time of her action, telling me that, although it did not succeed, she was grateful. She spoke to me of the terrible mission with which you are entrusted by the law. "It is dreadful to have to send a young man to the scaffold, but with that one! justice must be done! ... etc." She was sorry that such a handsome young man, brought to Paris by her cousin, Madame du Châtelet, should have turned out so badly. "That," she said, "is what bad women, such as Coralie, or Esther, bring young men to if they are so corrupt as to live on their immoral earnings!" All this with magnificent speeches about charity, about religion! Madame du Châtelet had told her that Lucien deserved a thousand deaths for almost killing his sister and his mother ... She spoke of a vacancy at the Royal Court, she knew the Keeper of the Seals. "Your husband, Madame, has a splendid opportunity to distinguish himself!" she concluded. And there we are.

'We distinguish ourselves every day, by doing our duty,' said Camusot.

'You'll go a long way, if you act the magistrate everywhere, even with your wife,' exclaimed Madame Camusot. 'Well, I thought you were stupid, but now I'm full of admiration ...'

The magistrate smiled in a manner exclusive to magistrates, just as a dancer's smile is like nobody else's.

'May I come in, Madame?' asked her maid.

'What do you want?' said her mistress.

'Madame, the first maid of Madame la Duchesse de Maufrigneuse came here while Madame was out, and begs Madame, on behalf of her mistress, to go round to the Hôtel de Cadignan, whatever she may be doing.'

'Dinner will have to wait,' said the magistrate's wife thinking that the cabman who had brought her home was still waiting to be paid.

She put her hat on again, got back into the cab, and in twenty minutes was at the Hôtel de Cadignan. Shown in by a side entrance, Madame Camusot waited ten minutes by herself in a boudoir leading to the bedroom of the duchess who appeared looking resplendent, for she was off to Saint Cloud where she had an invitation to the Court.

'My child, between ourselves, a couple of words will do.'

'Yes, Madame la Duchesse.'

'Lucien de Rubempré has been arrested, your husband is conducting the inquiry, I guarantee that poor boy's innocence, I want to see him at liberty within twenty-four hours. That isn't all. Somebody wants to see Lucien alone tomorrow in prison, your husband could be present, if he wishes, so long as he isn't seen . . . I am faithful to those who do things for me, as you know. The King is hoping for much from the courage of his magistrates in the grave circumstances in which he will presently find himself; I'll put your husband forward, I'll recommend him as a man devoted to the King, even to the point of staking his life. Our Camusot will first be a counsellor, then he shall have his own court wherever he likes . . . Good-bye . . . they're waiting for me, you'll excuse me, won't you? You'll be obliging not only the Attorney General, who can't speak out in this matter; you'll be saving the life of a woman who'd certainly die of it otherwise, Madame de Sérisy. So you won't be without support . . . Well, you see how I trust you, I don't need to tell you what has to be done . . . you know!'

She put a finger on her lips and went.

'And me not able to tell her that the Marquise d'Espard hopes to see Lucien on the scaffold! . . .' thought the magistrate's wife as she returned to her cab.

She reached home in such a state of anxiety that at sight of her the magistrate said:

'Amelia, what's the matter? . . .'

'We're caught between two fires . . .'

She recounted her interview with the duchess, whispering it to her husband, so afraid was she of her maid listening at the door.

'Which of the two is the more powerful?' she ended by

saying. 'The marchioness nearly compromised you in the silly affair of getting her husband deprived of control, while we owe everything to the duchess. One of them made me vague promises; while the other said: "You'll first be a counsellor, then you shall have your own court wherever you like!" ... God preserve me from offering you advice, I won't get myself mixed up in Law Court matters; but I must faithfully pass on what is being said at the other Court and what is afoot there ...'

'What you don't know, Amelia, is what the Prefect of Police sent me this morning, and by whom? by one of the most important men in the general Police of the Kingdom, the Bibi-Lupin of the political squad, who told me that the State had undisclosed interests in the case. Let's eat and then go to the Variétés ... We'll talk about it all tonight, when we're on our own; for I shall need your point of view, a magistrate's judgement may not be enough ...'

How bedrooms are often council chambers

NINE tenths of magistrates will deny the influence of wife on husband in such a matter; but, however exceptional such influence may be, there is no doubt that it occurs. The magistrate is like the priest, especially in Paris where the cream of the magistracy is found, he rarely discusses the affairs of the Courts, unless they have already been heard and judged. Magistrates' wives not only pretend to know nothing, but they have enough sense of what is fitting to see that they would damage their husbands if, when they have been taken into some secret, they let the fact be known. Nevertheless, on those great occasions when advancement seems to depend on taking a certain line, many women have, like Amelia, been a party to their husbands' deliberations. In the last resort, such exceptional cases, the more easily denied in that nobody can really know about them, depend entirely on the manner in which the battle between two characters is fought out within a particular household. Now, Madame Camusot wholly dominated her husband. When all was quiet in the house, the magistrate and his wife sat together at the desk on which he had already set out the documents in the affair.

'Here,' said Camusot, 'are the notes the Prefect's office have sent me, at my request.'

FATHER CARLOS HERRERA

This individual is certainly the Jacques Collin called Dodgedeath, whose last arrest goes back to the year 1819, and took place at the home of a certain Madame Vauquer, who kept a boarding house in the rue Neuve Sainte Genevieve, where he lived in hiding under the name of Vautrin.

In the margin, in the Prefect's own hand, one read:

An order has been transmitted by telegraph to Bibi-Lupin, head of the C.I.D., to return immediately to help with the confrontation, he being personally acquainted with Jacques Collin whom he arrested in 1819 with the connivance of a certain Mademoiselle Michonneau.

His fellow-boarders at the Vauquer house are still traceable and may be cited to establish identity.

This so-called Carlos Herrera is the intimate friend and counsellor of Monsieur Lucien de Rubempré, to whom, over the past three years, he has furnished considerable sums, evidently proceeds of theft.

This association, if the identity of the supposed Spaniard with Jacques Collin is established, will serve to convict the said Lucien de Rubempré.

The sudden death of the agent Peyrade was due to a poisoning effected by Jacques Collin, by Rubempré or their minions. The reason for this murder was that the agent had been, for some time past, on the trail of these two clever criminals.

In the margin, the magistrate pointed out a phrase in the Prefect's own hand, which read:

This is a matter of personal knowledge to me, and I am quite sure that Sieur Lucien de Rubempré has basely worked on his lordship Count Sérisy and the Attorney General.

'What do you say to that, Amelia?'

'It's terrifying! ...' replied the judge's wife. 'But let's hear the rest!'

The substitution of the Spanish priest for the convict Collin is the result of some crime more cleverly committed than that by which Cogniard made himself the count of Saint Helena.

LUCIEN DE RUBEMPRÉ

Lucien Chardon, son of an apothecary in Angoulême and whose mother is a Demoiselle de Rubempré, has royal authority for bearing the name of Rubempré. This authority was issued at the solicitation of Madame la Duchesse de Maufrigneuse and of Monsieur le Comte de Sérisy.

In 182 . . ., the young man came to Paris without means of subsistence, in the retinue of Madame la Comtesse Sixte du Châtelet, then Madame de Bargeton, a cousin of Madame d'Espard.

Ungrateful towards Madame de Bargeton, he lived as man and wife with a Demoiselle Coralie, deceased, actress at the Gymnase, till then cohabiting with Monsieur Camusot, silk merchant in the rue des Bourdonnais.

Presently, reduced to poverty by the insufficiency of the means with which this actress supplied him, he gravely compromised his honourable brother-in-law, a printer in Angoulême, by issuing false letters of credit for the payment of which David Séchard was arrested during a short stay of the said Lucien in Angoulême.

This affair determined the flight of Rubempré, who suddenly reappeared in Paris with Abbé Carlos Herrera.

Without known means of subsistence, Sieur Lucien spent, on an average, during the first three years of his second stay in Paris, about three hundred thousand francs which he can only have received from the so-called Abbé Carlos Herrera, but under what right?

He recently, moreover, laid out more than a million on the purchase of the Rubempré estate in order to meet a condition set to his marriage with Mademoiselle Clotilde de Grandlieu. The breaking off of this marriage was due to the fact that the Grandlieu family, to whom Sieur Lucien had said that these sums came to him from his brother-in-law and sister, caused information to be procured from the worthy Séchard couple, notably by the solicitor Derville; not only were they ignorant of his recent purchases, but further they understood Lucien to be heavily in debt.

Furthermore, the estate inherited by the Séchards consists of houses and land; the total amount of ready money was, according to their declaration, no more than two hundred thousand francs.

Lucien was living secretly with Esther Gobseck, it is therefore certain that all the money lavished on this person by her protector, Baron Nucingen, was passed on to the said Lucien.

Lucien and his companion the convict maintained themselves longer than Cogniard in the face of society, drawing their resources from the immoral earnings of the said Esther, formerly a registered prostitute.

Police files

DESPITE the repetitions these notes introduce into the narrative, it was necessary to give them textually in order to show the workings of the Police in Paris. The Police have, as we already saw from the note requested on Peyrade, files, generally of some exactitude, on all families and individuals whose way of life is suspect, whose acts are considered reprehensible. No abnormality goes unrecorded. This universal ledger, this balance-sheet of consciences, is as well-kept as the Bank of France's account of private fortunes. Just as the Bank pricks off the least arrears in regard to payment, evaluates all credits, puts a price on capitalists, keeping an eye on their operations; so does the Police with regard to the public repute of its citizens. In this, as at the Law Courts, innocence has nothing to fear, such action is taken only with respect to misdemeanours. However highly placed a family may be, it cannot avoid this social provision. The extent of its power is equalled by its discreetness. The enormous quantity of reports made by police superintendents, of records, notes, files, this ocean of information sleeps motionless, deep and calm as the sea. If some important accident happens, if there is public disorder or an outbreak of crime, the Law makes its appeal to the Police; and at once, a file is produced on the incriminated persons, the judge is apprised of the facts. These files, setting out the background to what has happened, contain information of which the Law cannot make overt use, they become a dead letter within the walls of the Palais de Justice, but the information is noted and may meet one or another practical need. These are the threads which show on the reverse side of the tapestry of crime, the materials, otherwise unseen, out of which the pattern was made. No jury would accept them as evidence, the country as a whole would rise up in indignation if they were put in at the public hearing of a criminal case. They contain the truth condemned to stay underground, as the truth is everywhere and always. No magistrate could fail, after working twelve years in Paris, to know very well that the courts of assize and of summary jurisdiction conceal half these infamies, which are as it were the nest in which crime is slowly hatched; every magistrate knows well that the Law never punishes half of the outrages and criminal acts committed annually. If the public knew how far the discretion of the Police goes among those of its minions whose memories are long, it would revere these worthy people as it does an Archbishop Cheverus. The Police are thought to be crafty, Machiavellian, what they are remarkable for is their benignity; all they do is listen to the paroxysmal words of passion, hear what information is laid, take notes and keep them. Only in one aspect is their behaviour frightening. What they do for Justice, they do also for the government. In political matters, they are as cruel and as partial as the late Inquisition.

'Well, let's leave that,' said the magistrate putting the notes back in the folder, 'it's a secret between the Police and the Law. In my judicial capacity I shall see what it's worth; but Monsieur and Madame Camusot know nothing about it.'

'Do you need to remind me of that?' said Madame Camusot.

'Lucien is guilty,' the magistrate continued, 'but of what?'

'A man loved by the Duchesse de Maufrigneuse, Countess Sérisy, Clotilde de Grandlieu, can't be guilty,' Amelia replied, 'it *must* be the other man who did it all.'

'But Lucien was his accomplice!' exclaimed Camusot.

'Do you want to know what I think? . . .' said Amelia. 'Let the priest go back to diplomacy whose finest ornament he is, declare the young wretch not guilty, and look for the guilty parties elsewhere . . .'

'How you go on! . . .' replied the magistrate with a smile. 'Women drive straight through the laws to get what they want, like birds in the air, stopped by nothing.'

'Diplomatist or convict,' Amelia went on, 'Father Carlos

will put his finger on somebody who can get you out of this.'

'I'm only a cap, you're the head,' said Camusot to his wife.

'Well, the discussion is closed, come and kiss Melia, it is one o'clock . . .'

And Madame Camusot went off to bed leaving her husband to put his papers and his thoughts in order for the interrogation he must put the two suspects through next day.

A product of the Palais

THUS, while the salad baskets were taking Jacques Collin and Lucien to the Conciergerie, the examining magistrate, after a substantial breakfast, was crossing Paris on foot, with the lack of ostentation common to Parisian judges, on the way to his office where all the documents in the case had arrived before him. This had come about as follows.

All examining magistrates have their clerks, a type of sworn judicial secretary, whose species perpetuates itself without bonuses, without encouragement, a first-rate kind of people to whom absolute discretion comes naturally. From the time of the old high judicial courts to the present day, not a single case of an indiscretion committed by a clerk appointed to judicial inquiries has ever been known at the Palais. Gentil sold the acquittance given to Semblançay by Louise of Savoy, a clerk at the war office sold to Czernicheff the plan of the Russian campaign; traitors like those have generally been quite rich. The prospect of a position at the Law Courts, an office of one's own, professional conscience are enough to make an examining magistrate's clerk a successful rival of the grave, for even graves speak since the introduction of forensic chemistry. Such an employee is the magistrate's own pen. Many people will understand how one may be the spindle of a machine but wonder how one can remain content as a screw-nut; but the nut is content, perhaps it is afraid of the machine? Camusot's clerk, a young man of twenty-two, called Coquart, had come early in the morning to pick up all the documents and the magistrate's notes, and everything was laid out in his office, while the judge strolled along the embankment, looking at the curiosities in the shops, and pondering within himself: 'How to set about a fellow as sharp as Jacques Collin, always supposing it is him? The head of the crime squad will know him, I must simply appear to be doing my job, if only in the eyes of the Police! So many possibilities are out of the question, the best thing might be to enlighten the marchioness and the duchess, by showing them the police notes, and so avenge my father from whom Lucien took Coralie ... If I unmask such black scoundrels, everybody will think I am very clever, and Lucien will soon be disowned by all his friends. Well, I shall see where the interrogation takes me.'

He went into a curiosity shop, his eye caught by a Boule clock.

A form of influence

'NOT to be untrue to my conscience and to serve the two great ladies, if I bring that off it'll be a real feat,' he thought. 'Ah, you here, too Mr Attorney General,' said Camusot aloud, 'looking at medals, I see!'

'It's what's on the other side,' replied Count Granville with a laugh, 'that appeals to all us legal dignitaries.'

And, after looking round the shop for a few moments longer, as though completing his examination, he led Camusot along the embankment, without Camusot being able to suppose that it was anything but a chance encounter.

'I gather you're questioning Monsieur de Rubempré this morning,' said the Attorney General. 'Poor young man, I was very fond of him . . .'

'The charges against him are serious,' said Camusot.

'Yes, I've seen the police records; but they're due, in part, to an agent who doesn't belong to the Prefecture, the celebrated Corentin, a man who's got more innocent necks chopped than you'll ever send guilty men to the scaffold, and . . . But the rogue is out of our reach. Without wanting to influence the conscience of a judge like yourself, I can't help pointing out to you that, if you could convince yourself that Lucien knew nothing about that tart's will, it would show that he had no interest in her death, for she left him a prodigious amount of money! . . .'

'He wasn't there at the time this Esther was poisoned, we know that,' said Camusot. 'He was at Fontainebleau watching out for the passage of Mademoiselle de Grandlieu and the Duchesse de Lenoncourt.'

'Oh!' the Attorney General went on, 'he placed such great hopes on his marriage with Mademoiselle de Grand-lieu (I have this from the Duchesse de Grandlieu herself), it simply can't be imagined that a boy of his intelligence would compromise everything by a stupid crime.'

'No,' said Camusot, 'especially if this Esther was giving him everything she earned.'

'Derville and Nucingen say she died without knowing about the inheritance which had come to her some time ago,' added the Attorney General.

'What's your theory, then?' asked Camusot, 'for something happened.'

'I'd say a crime committed by servants,' said the Attorney General.

'Unfortunately,' Camusot pointed out, 'it is quite in the style of Jacques Collin, for the Spanish priest is pretty certainly that escaped convict, to make away with the seven hundred and fifty thousand francs from the sale of the inscription for annual income at three per cent given her by Nucingen.'

'You must weigh everything, my dear Camusot, but be prudent. Father Carlos Herrera claims diplomatic privilege, . . . but an ambassador who committed a crime wouldn't be saved by his status. Is he or is he not the abbé Carlos Herrera, that's the important question . . .'

And Monsieur de Granville went on his way like a man who does not expect a reply.

'So he also wants to save Lucien,' thought Camusot, who took the Quai des Lunettes while the Procurator went into the Law Courts by way of the Cour de Harlay.

334

A convict trap

ARRIVING in the courtyard of the Conciergerie, Camusot went to the prison governor's office and led him out of earshot, on to the paved area.

'My dear sir, do me the favour of going to La Force, and ask your colleague there whether by a lucky chance he possesses at the moment any convicts who, between 1810 and 1815, were at the penitentiary in Toulon; you might find out whether also you have any here. Those at La Force we'll have transferred here for a few days, and you can let me know whether any of them recognize the supposed Spanish priest as Jacques Collin known as Dodgedeath.'

'Very well, Monsieur Camusot; but Bibi-Lupin has arrived . . .'

'Ah! already?' exclaimed the magistrate.

'He was at Melun. He was told that the matter concerned Dodgedeath, he smiled with pleasure and awaits your orders . . .'

'Send him to me.'

The governor of the Conciergerie was then able to put Jacques Collin's request before the examining magistrate, while depicting the former's lamentable state.

'I meant to examine him first,' replied the judge, 'but not on account of his health. I had a note this morning from the governor of La Force. It appears that this fellow, who describes himself as having been at death's door these twenty-four hours, slept so well, that he didn't hear the doctor, who'd been sent out for, when the latter entered his cell at La Force; the doctor didn't even feel his pulse, he let him sleep; which proves that both his conscience and his health are good. I shall merely pretend to believe in this illness in order to study my man's game,' said Monsieur Camusot with a smile.

'There is always something new to learn about prisoners,' observed the governor of the Conciergerie.

The Prefecture of Police communicates with the Conciergerie, and the magistracy, like the prison governor, as a result of knowing those underground passages, can go from one to the other with great promptness. This explains the miraculous facility with which the public ministry and judges presiding at the Court of Assize may, while the court is sitting, find out whatever they may wish to know. Thus when Monsieur Camusot reached the head of the staircase leading to his office, he found Bibi-Lupin there with speed by way of the waiting hall.

'Such zeal!' the magistrate said to him with a smile.

'Ah! if only it's *him*,' replied the head of the Sûreté, 'you'll see some terrible capers in the prison yard, given only there's a few old lags there.'

'How so?'

'Dodgedeath has swallowed the funds, and I know *they*'ve sworn to do him.'

They signified the convicts whose loot entrusted to Dodge-death over the past twenty years had been dispensed for Lucien, as we know.

'Could you find witnesses to his last arrest?'

'*Sub poena* me a couple, and I'll bring them in today.'

'Coquart,' said the judge taking off his gloves, putting his stick and hat in a corner, 'make out two *sub poena* forms to the inspector's specifications.'

He looked at himself in the glass over the fireplace on the mantelpiece of which, instead of a clock, there stood a bowl and a water-jug, to one side of it a decanter of drinking water and a glass, to the other a lamp. The magistrate rang. After a few minutes his usher appeared.

'Are there any visitors for me yet?' he asked the usher whose job it was to receive witnesses, check their summonses and seat them in the order of their arrival.

'Yes, sir.'

'Take the names of those who've come, and bring me the list.'

Examining magistrates, who must be sparing of their time, are sometimes obliged to conduct several judicial inquiries concurrently. That is the reason why witnesses are often kept waiting so long in the room where the ushers stand and where examining magistrates' bells ring.

'Then,' said Camusot to his usher, 'go and look for Father Carlos Herrera.'

'Ah! so he's a Spaniard now? a priest, they tell me. Bah! it's the Colet trick all over again, Monsieur Camusot,' exclaimed the head of the C.I.D.

'There's nothing new under the sun,' answered Camusot. And the magistrate signed two of those imposing summonses which so disturb everyone, even the most innocent witnesses whom the Law thus commands to appear under heavy penalties, if they fail to comply.

Jacques Collin in solitary confinement
bestirs people

AT that moment Jacques Collin had, in the past half hour, concluded his profound deliberation, and was under arms. Nothing could better portray this man of the people in revolt against authority than the few lines he had traced on his filthy pieces of paper.

The sense of the first was as follows, for it was written in the language agreed between Asia and himself, a slang derived from slang, a thought in cipher.

Go and call on the Duchesse de Maufrigneuse or Madame de Sérisy, let one or the other see Lucien before his interrogation, and let her make sure that he reads the enclosed sheet. Then Europe and Paccard must be found, so that those two thieves are at my disposition, and ready to play the part I shall indicate to them.

Also call on Rastignac, tell him on behalf of the man he met at the Opera ball to come and testify that Father Carlos Herrera bears no resemblance to the Jacques Collin arrested at Ma Vauquer's.

Get Bianchon to do the same.

Put both *Lucien's women* to work to bring this about.

On the enclosed sheet, there was this in good French:

Lucien, don't admit anything about me. To you, I am Father Carlos Herrera. Not only is that your justification; but just hold on a bit longer, and you've got seven millions, plus an unspotted reputation.

337

These two papers stuck together on the written side, in such a way as to make them seem only one sheet, were rolled up tightly in a manner known only to those at convict stations who've dreamed of being free. The whole object had the form and consistency of a ball of much the size of the wax heads thrifty women fasten to needles when the eye is broken.

'If I *go to school* first, we're all right; but if it's the youngster, we're lost,' he said to himself while he waited.

The moment was so full of anguish that this formidable man's face came out in a cold sweat. In the sphere of crime, this prodigious man's instinct for the truth was as sure as Molière's in dramatic poetry, like Cuvier's among the relics of a vanished world. In all spheres, genius is intuition. At a lower level, talent will do. That is the difference between men of the first and those of the second order. Crime has its men of genius. Jacques Collin, at bay, was attuned like Madame Camusot by her ambition and Madame de Sérisy by the love sprung to life under the blow of the terrible catastrophe which threatened Lucien. This was the supreme effort of human intelligence against the steel armour of the Law.

Hearing the heavy ironwork of the locks and bolts of his door cry out, Jacques Collin once more assumed the mask of a dying man; in this he was helped by the intoxicating sensation of pleasure which the sound of the warder's shoes in the corridor brought him. He did not know by what means Asia would make her way to him; but he counted on seeing her in his path, especially after the promise he had received from her in the Arcade Saint Jean.

Asia at work

AFTER that fortunate encounter, Asia had gone down to the Strand. Before 1830, the name Strand had a sense now lost. All that part of the embankment, from the Pont d'Arcole to the Pont Louis-Philippe, was then just as nature had made it, apart from the flagged path and the banking which supported it. Thus, at high water, one could go by boat alongside the houses and into the sloping streets which went down to the river. Along that stretch of embankment, most of the houses had their ground floor raised up by the height of a few steps. When the water lapped against the foot of the houses, carriages drove along the frightful rue de la Mortillerie, now wholly demolished to make room for extensions to the City Hall. It was therefore easy for the pretended coster to push her little cart rapidly to the far end of the quay, and to hide it there until the real costerwoman, who at that moment was drinking away the whole proceeds of the transaction at one of the low bars in the rue de la Mortillerie, claimed it at the spot where the borrower had promised to leave it. At the time, the Quai Pelletier was being enlarged, an old soldier guarded the entrance to the site, and the barrow entrusted to his care was in no danger.

Asia at once took a cab in the City Hall square, and said to the driver: 'To the Temple! and fast, there's money in it.'

A woman dressed as Asia was could, without arousing the least curiosity, lose herself in the huge covered market where all the old rags of Paris are piled up, where a thousand pedlars jostle and two hundred shopwomen cry their wares. The two *prévenus* were barely committed, before she was getting herself rigged out in a low, damp little room over one of those dreadful shops which sell all the remnants stolen by dressmakers or tailors, kept by an old spinster called Romette, from her Christian name Jéromette. Romette was to wardrobe dealers what those ladies themselves are to distressed gentlewomen, a moneylender at one hundred per cent.

'Come on, old girl!' said Asia, 'I need dolling up. I must be at least a baroness in the Faubourg Saint Germain. And let's get it sorted out sharp, eh?' she went on, 'I'm standing with my feet in boiling oil! You know what kind of thing suits me. Bring out the rouge pot, find me some bits of posh lace! and let's have some glittering *trinkets* . . . Send your girl out to get me a cab, and let it draw up at the back door.'

'Yes, ma'am,' replied the old spinster with the submissiveness and the nervous haste of a servant in the presence of her mistress.

If there had been any witness to this scene, he would

quickly have understood that the woman concealed beneath the name of Asia was on her own premises here.

'I've been offered some diamonds!...' said Romette as she did Asia's head-dress.

'Are they stolen?...'

'I think so.'

'Well, whatever the price, my child, you must do without them. We could be having dicks around for a while.'

We may now understand how Asia came to be in the waiting hall at the Law Courts, a writ of summons in her hand, being conducted along corridors and up those staircases which lead to the examining magistrates' offices, asking for Monsieur Camusot, a quarter of an hour or so before his arrival.

A view of the big waiting room

ASIA was no longer herself. Having, like an actress, cleaned off her old woman's face, put on red and white, she had covered her head with an admirable fair wig. Got up exactly to resemble a lady from the Faubourg Saint Germain in search of her lost dog, she looked about forty, for she had concealed her face behind a magnificent veil of black lace. A tight corset held in her cook's waist. Carefully gloved, armed with a rather prominent bustle, she smelled of face-powder like a marshal's wife. Toying with a gold-mounted handbag, she divided her attention between the walls of the Law Courts which she was evidently seeing for the first time and a leash to which might have been attached some pretty spaniel. So remarkable a dowager did not escape the notice of the black-robed population of the waiting hall.

Apart from the barristers without brief who sweep the hall floor with their gowns and who address more eminent counsel by their Christian names, as great lords do each other, to make it appear that they belong to the aristocracy of the Order, one often sees patient young men, kept standing about by solicitors against the possibility that some case at the bottom of the list may be fitted into a gap caused by the late arrival of those awaited in connection with a matter of higher priority. It would be interesting to portray all the varieties of black gowns which walk up and down this enormous room three by three, sometimes four by four, the noise of their chatter booming about the hall, so aptly named, since lawyers are worn out as much by waiting as by their prodigalities of speech; but this is not the place for such a study of the Parisian bar. Asia had counted on these accredited idlers, she laughed quietly at one or two of the jokes she heard and finally attracted the attention of Massol, a young probationer more occupied with the *Gazette des Tribunaux* than with any clients of his own, who laughingly placed his services at the disposition of a woman so well scented and so richly dressed.

Asia put on a tiny little voice to explain to this obliging young fellow that she was here in response to a summons issued by a judge, named Camusot . . .

'Ah! the Rubempré case.'

The trial had a name already!

'Oh! it isn't myself, it's my maid, a girl nicknamed Europe who's only been with me twenty-four hours and who ran away as soon as she saw my porter bring me an official document.'

Then, like any old woman whose life is spent in fireside gossip, egged on by Massol, she went off at various tangents, she told him of her troubles with her first husband, one of the three leading provincial bankers. She asked the youthful barrister's advice on whether she ought to bring an action against her son-in-law, Count Gross-Narp, who was making her daughter very unhappy, and whether she was entitled by law to do as she pleased with her own fortune. Despite his best efforts, Massol was unable to discover whether it was to the mistress or her maid that the summons had been addressed. In the first place, he had merely glanced at this small judicial form of which everyone has seen copies; for rapid issue, it is printed, and examining magistrates' clerks only have to fill in blanks left for witnesses' names and addresses, time at which required and so on. Asia asked innumerable questions about the Law Courts, which in fact she knew better than the lawyer himself did; finally, she asked him at what time Monsieur Camusot arrived.

'In general, examining magistrates begin questioning their prisoners at about ten o'clock.'

'It is a quarter to ten,' she said looking at a pretty little watch, a true jeweller's masterpiece which made Massol think: 'What is it going to please her to do with that fortune! ...'

Massol dreams of marriage

In the course of their perambulations, he and Asia had approached that dark room gazing out on the Conciergerie yard where the ushers collect. Looking out of the window and seeing the wicket, she exclaimed: 'What are those big walls there?'

'That's the Conciergerie.'

'Ah! so that's the Conciergerie where our poor queen ... Oh! I would so like to see the dungeon she was in! ...'

'It can't be done, Madame la Baronne,' replied the barrister giving the dowager his arm, 'people have to have permits which are very difficult to obtain.'

'I've been told,' she went on, 'that Louis XVIII himself composed, and in Latin, the inscription which has been carved in Marie-Antoinette's dungeon.'

'That is so, Madame la Baronne.'

'I wish I knew Latin so that I could study the words of that inscription,' she replied. 'Do you think Monsieur Camusot could give me a permit ...?'

'It isn't his job of course, but he could go with you ...'

'But what about his prisoners?' said she.

'Oh, they can wait,' replied Massol.

'That's true, they've got plenty of time,' said Asia ingenuously. 'Of course I know Monsieur de Granville, your chief procurator ...'

This interjection produced a magical effect on the ushers and the barrister.

'Ah! you know the Attorney General,' said Massol who was thinking how best to ask this chance *client* for her name and address.

342

'I often see him at his friend Monsieur de Sérisy's. Madame de Sérisy is a Ronquerolles kinswoman of mine . . .'

'If Madame wishes to go down to the Conciergerie,' said an usher, 'she . . .'

'Yes,' said Massol.

And the ushers made way for barrister and baroness who presently found themselves in the small guardroom at the head of the staircase from the Mousetrap, a place well known to Asia, forming, as we have seen, as it were an observation post through which everyone is obliged to pass between the Mousetrap and Court Six.

'Ask these gentlemen whether Monsieur Camusot has arrived!' she said watching the constables who were playing at cards.

'Yes, Madame, he's just come up from the Mousetrap . . .'

'The Mousetrap!' she said. 'What's that . . .? Oh! how stupid I am not to have gone straight to Count Granville . . . But I haven't the time . . . Take me, sir, to talk to Monsieur Camusot before he gets busy.'

'Oh! Madame, you're in plenty of time for Monsieur Camusot,' said Massol. 'If you send your card in, you'll be spared the disagreeable business of waiting among the witnesses . . . At the Palais, we do show some consideration for women like yourself, . . . who have cards . . .'

Purposes served by Massol and the little spaniel

At that moment Asia and her lawyer stood directly in front of the window of the guardroom from which the constabulary can watch the movements of people at the wicket of the Conciergerie. The armed constables, brought up to respect the defenders of the widow and the orphan, knowing moreover what privileges went with a barrister's gown, for some while tolerated the presence of a baroness accompanied by her lawyer. Asia allowed herself to listen to the dreadful things the young barrister told her about the wicket. She refused to believe that a condemned man's head and neck were trimmed before execution behind the grill that was pointed out to her; but the sergeant in charge confirmed this.

'How I should like to see that! . . .' she said.

She remained there flirting with the sergeant and her lawyer until she saw Jacques Collin, held up by two constables and preceded by Monsieur Camusot's usher, emerging from the Wicket.

'Ah! there's the prison chaplain who has no doubt come to prepare some unfortunate person for his fate . . .'

'No, no, Madame la Baronne,' replied the sergeant. 'It's an accused person due to be examined.'

'Whatever is he accused of?'

'He's involved in that poisoning case . . .'

'Oh! I should so like to see him . . .'

'You can't stay here,' said the constable, 'he's in solitary, and he'll have to go through this guardroom. Here we are, Madame, this door gives on to the staircase.'

'Thank you, officer,' said the baroness turning to the door and emerging on to the staircase where she cried: 'But where am I?'

Her voice reached the ears of Jacques Collin whom she wished thus to alert to her presence. The sergeant ran after the baroness, seized her by the waist, and bore her like a feather into the midst of five constables who had stood up like one man; for nobody is trusted in that guardroom. That kind of arbitrariness is sometimes necessary. The lawyer himself had twice called out: 'Madame! Madame!' in a tone of alarm, so much did he fear to be compromised.

Father Carlos Herrera, in a fainting condition, collapsed on a chair in the guardroom.

'Poor man!' said the baroness. 'Can that be a guilty man?'

These words, though spoken into the ear of the young barrister, were heard by everybody, for the silence in that dreadful guardroom was deathly. Occasionally privileged persons do obtain permission to see famous criminals while they are passing through that guardroom or along the corridors, so that the usher and the constables charged with conveying Abbé Carlos Herrera made no comment. Moreover, thanks to the conscientiousness of the sergeant who had laid hold of the baroness to prevent all possibility of communication between the prisoner and visitors, a reassuring space was set between them.

'Come along, then!' said Jacques Collin making an effort to stand up.

At that moment the little ball fell out of his sleeve, and the place where it came to rest was duly noted by the baroness whose veil allowed her gaze to move freely. Damp and sticky, the little ball did not roll far, such apparently insignificant details having been calculated by Jacques Collin to assure the success of his manoeuvre. When the prisoner was led off to the upper part of the staircase, Asia dropped her bag in the most natural manner and hurriedly picked it up; but in stooping she had also picked up the little ball whose colour, indistinguishable from the dust and grime of the floor, had prevented it being noticed.

'Ah!' said she, 'that gave me a turn, . . . he's at his last gasp . . .'

'You might think so,' said the sergeant.

'Sir,' said Asia to the barrister, 'take me at once to Monsieur Camusot's; this is the case I'm here for, . . . and he might like to see me before interrogating the poor priest . . .'

The lawyer and the baroness left the guardroom with its sooty, oleaginous walls; but when they were at the head of the staircase, Asia suddenly exclaimed: 'My dog! . . . oh, sir, my poor dog!'

And she made off, like a madwoman, back to the waiting hall, asking everyone if they had seen her dog. She reached the Galerie Marchande, and hurried towards a staircase saying: 'There he is! . . .'

This was the staircase which led to the Cour de Harlay, whence, having finished her performance, Asia made haste to pick up one of the cabs which stand in the Quai des Orfèvres, and she disappeared with the summons in fact made out for Europe whose real names were still unknown to either main branch of the Law.

'RUE Neuve Saint Marc,' she cried to the driver.

Asia could count on the inviolable discretion of a wardrobe dealer called Madame Nourrisson, known also under the name of Madame Saint Estève, who lent her not only her identity but her shop, at which Nucingen had bargained for the delivery of Esther. Asia was at home there, for she kept a room in Madame Nourrisson's living quarters. She paid off the cab and went up to her room after greeting Madame Nourrisson in a manner which gave her to understand that there was no time for words.

Once out of the way of all onlookers, Asia set to work unfolding the pieces of paper with all the care which a scholar might give to unrolling a palimpsest. Having read these instructions, she judged it desirable to transcribe the lines destined for Lucien on to writing paper; then she went down to Madame Nourrisson whom she kept talking just long enough for a little girl about the shop to go and get a cab from the Boulevard des Italiens. Asia had wanted the addresses of the Duchesse de Maufrigneuse and Madame de Sérisy which Madame Nourrisson knew from her dealings with their maids.

These various errands, and the occupation with matters of detail, took more than two hours. Madame la Duchesse de Maufrigneuse, who lived towards the far end of the Faubourg Saint Honoré, kept Madame de Saint Estève waiting an hour, although her maid had passed in through the door of her dressing-room, after knocking, Madame de Saint Estève's card on which Asia had written: '*Called on urgent mission respecting Lucien.*'

'Who are you? . . .' asked the duchess without any show of politeness taking stock of Asia who might well be taken for a baroness by Massol in the waiting hall, but who, on the carpets of the little drawing-room in the Hôtel de Cadignan, produced the effect of a grease stain on a white satin gown.

'I'm a wardrobe dealer, Madame la Duchesse; in matters

like this, you go to women whose profession calls for absolute discretion. I've never given anybody away, and God knows how many great ladies have trusted me with their diamonds for a month, wanting false jewellery exactly like their own...'

'Have you another name?' said the duchess smiling at a reminiscence which this answer brought to her mind.

'Yes, Madame la Duchesse, I am Madame Saint Estève on great occasions, but my business name is Madame Nourrisson.'

'Yes, of course...' said the duchess briskly with a change of tone.

'I can be helpful in all kinds of ways,' Asia went, 'women like me know the secrets of husbands as well as wives. I've had a lot to do with Monsieur de Marsay whom Madame la Duchesse...'

'That'll do!...' exclaimed the duchess, 'let's concern ourselves with Lucien.'

'If Madame la Duchesse wants to save him, she'll need the courage not to waste time about getting dressed; in any case Madame la Duchesse couldn't look more beautiful than she does at this moment. You are pretty enough to eat, on an old woman's word of honour! In short, don't have your carriage brought round, Madame, get in my cab with me... Come and see Madame de Sérisy, if you want to avoid troubles worse nor the cherub's death would be...'

'Hurry, then! I'll come with you,' the duchess then said after a moment's hesitation. 'Between us, we'll give Léontine heart...'

A splendid grief

DESPITE the truly infernal activity of this underworld Dorine, it was striking two when with the Duchesse de Maufrigneuse she was admitted to the house of Madame de Sérisy who lived in the rue Chaussée d'Antin. There, however, thanks to the duchess, not a moment was lost. The two were taken straight in to the countess, whom they found extended

347

upon a divan in a summer house in a garden fragrant with the rarest flowers.

'This is all right,' said Asia looking about her, 'nobody'll be able to hear us here.'

'Ah! my dear! this will be the death of me! Listen, Diana, what have you done? . . .' exclaimed the countess springing up like a fawn, seizing the duchess by the shoulders and bursting into tears.

'Come, Léontine, there are times when women like us mustn't weep, but act,' said the duchess forcing the countess to sit down again beside her on the sofa.

Asia studied this countess with the look peculiar to old reprobates like herself, a look which may search the soul of a woman with the speed of a surgeon's lancet probing a sore. Jacques Collin's accomplice thereupon recognized the traces of a feeling which is rare among society women, true grief! . . . that grief which ineffaceably furrows both heart and visage. No finery about her person! The countess was then forty-five, and the crumpled morning wrapper of printed muslin boldly displayed her uncorseted bust! . . . The black rings round her eyes, her blotchy cheeks spoke of bitter tears. No girdle about her wrapper. The embroidery on her shift and petticoat was frayed. The hair gathered up under a lace cap, uncombed for the past twenty-four hours, showed in all their poverty a thin, short plait and loose ringlets. Léontine had forgotten to put on her false braids.

'You're in love for the first time in your life . . .' said Asia sententiously.

Léontine thereupon caught sight of Asia and gave an expression of fright.

'Who's that, my dear Diana?' she said to the Duchesse de Maufrigneuse.

'Whom do you expect me to bring you, except a woman devoted to Lucien and ready to serve us?'

A Parisian type

ASIA had guessed the truth. Madame de Sérisy, who passed for one of society's most frivolous women, had been attached, for ten years, to the Marquis d'Aiglemont. Since the marquess's departure for the colonies, she had doted madly on Lucien and detached him from the Duchesse de Maufrigneuse, ignorant, as indeed was all Paris, of Lucien's love for Esther. In the best society, a known attachment does more to spoil a woman's reputation than ten secret adventures, while two attachments are obviously worse. Nevertheless, as nobody counted with Madame de Sérisy, the historian cannot guarantee her virtue no more than twice-chipped. She was a blonde of medium height, preserved as blondes are when they look after themselves, that is to say looking no more than thirty, slight without being thin, white-skinned, her hair silvery; feet, hands, body of aristocratic fineness; witty in the Ronquerolles fashion, and consequently as malicious towards other women as she was kind towards men. Her great fortune, her husband's elevated position and that of her brother the Marquis de Ronquerolles had no doubt kept her from the disappointments and rebuffs which any other woman would have had to put up with. She had one great merit: in her depravity she was frank, she openly admitted a taste for Regency customs. Then, at forty-two, this woman, to whom men had till then been agreeable toys and who, oddly, had granted them much because she saw love as a matter of making sacrifices in order to dominate the lover, had been seized at the sight of Lucien by a love like that of Baron Nucingen for Esther. She had thenceforward loved, as Asia told her, for the first time in her life. Such transpositions of youth are more frequent than people think among the women of Paris, even among great ladies, and cause the inexplicable downfall of some of the most virtuous just as they reach the haven of their forties. The Duchesse de Maufrigneuse alone was in the secret of this unbounded and terrible passion whose moments of happiness, from the childish sensations of first love to the giant folly of sensual delight, had made Léontine mad and insatiable.

True love, as we know, is pitiless. The discovery of an Esther had led to a break in such anger as may lead a woman to thoughts of murder; this had been followed by that weakness to which a sincere love abandons itself with so much pleasure. Thus, for a month past, the countess would have given ten years of her life to see Lucien again for a week. In the end, she had reached the point of accepting Esther as her rival, just when the paroxysm of tenderness was to be shattered by the trumpet-blast announcing that last judgment, Lucien's arrest. It had indeed almost proved the death of the countess, whom her husband himself had tended in bed fearing what revelations might be heard in her raving; for the past twenty-four hours, she had been living with a dagger in her heart. In her delirium, she had said to her husband: 'Free Lucien, and from then on I shall live for nobody but you!'

Asia as a peasant from the Danube

'IT won't help to make eyes like a dead goat, as the duchess says,' exclaimed the terrible Asia shaking the countess by the arm. 'If you want to save him, there isn't a minute to lose. He is innocent, I swear it on the bones of my mother!'

'Oh! yes, he is, isn't he? . . .' cried the countess looking at the frightful crone with benevolent kindness.

'But,' said Asia continuing, 'if Monsieur Camusot interrogates him *hard*, with two phrases he can make him guilty; and, if you have the power to get inside the Conciergerie and speak to him, set off at once and give him this paper . . . Tomorrow he'll be free, I promise you . . . Get him out of there, for it's you who put him in . . .'

'I! . . .'

'Yes, you! . . . You great ladies, you never have a penny, even when there are millions behind you. When I allowed myself the luxury of having kids, they had their pockets stuffed with gold! it amused me to see them happy. It's nice to be mother and mistress at the same time! Women like you, you let people you love die of hunger without inquiring into their means. Esther, she didn't just talk, she gave, at the cost of perdition to body and soul, the million demanded of Lucien, and that's what got him into the plight he's in now . . .'

'Poor creature! she did that! I love her! . . .' said Léontine.

'Ah! it's a bit late,' said Asia with glacial irony.

'She was very beautiful, but now, my angel, you are far more beautiful than she is, . . . and Lucien's marriage with Clotilde is so badly broken that nothing will put a new handle on it now,' said the duchess in an undertone to Léontine.

The effect of this reflection and this calculation on the countess were such, that she no longer felt ill; she passed her hands over her forehead, she was young.

'Come along, my child, paws up, and let's be going! . . .' said Asia who saw this transfiguration and divined its cause.

'But,' said Madame de Maufrigneuse, 'if the main thing is to prevent Monsieur Camusot questioning Lucien, we can do that by writing him a note, which a footman of yours can take round to the Law Courts, Léontine.'

'Let's go back to the house, then,' said Madame de Sérisy.

While Lucien's protectresses carried out the orders set down by Jacques Collin, this is what was happening at the Law Courts.

Observations

CONSTABLES carried the dying man to a chair placed facing the window in Monsieur Camusot's office, the latter sitting in comfort at his desk. Coquart, pen in hand, sat at a little table a few yards away from the judge.

The position of the examining magistrates' offices is not a matter of indifference, and if it was not selected with intention, it must be conceded that Chance greatly favoured the Law. These magistrates are like painters, they need the pure, even light which comes from the north, for the face of any criminal before them is a picture they must constantly study. For this reason, they almost invariably dispose their furniture as Monsieur Camusot had done, themselves sitting with their backs to the light, to which the faces of those they are questioning are consequently exposed. Not one of them, after six months' practice, fails to wear either spectacles or a distraught, indifferent air during the course of each interrogation. It was by a sudden change of expression, perceived in this way and caused by a question suddenly put at close quarters, that the crime of Castaing was discovered, just as the judge, after lengthy consultation with the Attorney General, was about to restore the criminal to society, for lack of proof. A small detail of that kind may indicate to those who have given the matter little thought how vital, interesting, curious, dramatic and terrifying a battle a judicial inquiry may be, a battle waged without witnesses but recorded as it takes place. God knows what remains on paper of these scenes so glacially ardent, where the eyes, the tone of voice, a quiver of the facial muscles, the slightest change of colour caused by a new feeling, are signs of no less danger than those noted by savages mutually seeking out to kill each other. The written report can be no more than the ashes of such a conflagration.

'What are your real names?' Camusot asked Jacques Collin.

'Don Carlos Herrera, canon of the royal chapter of Toledo, secret envoy of His Majesty Ferdinand VII.'

Here Jacques Collin must be envisaged as speaking French 'like a Spanish cow', as we say, jabbering in such a way as to make his replies almost unintelligible, so that he had to be asked to repeat what he had said. The Germanisms of Monsieur de Nucingen have already been so much used for decorative effect in the course of this narrative that the reader shall be spared anything here so difficult to read, since it would hold up the speed with which these events reach their outcome.

As a man of what mark the convict
proves himself to be

'You have papers which show these to be your qualifications?' asked the judge.

'Yes, sir, a passport, a letter from His Catholic Majesty authorizing my mission ... You could also dispatch at once to the Spanish embassy a few words which I would write now in front of you, they would claim me. Then, if you had need of further proofs, I could write to His Eminence the High Chaplain of France, and he would send his private secretary here.'

'Do you still claim to be on the point of death?' said Camusot. 'If you were truly as ill as you have never ceased to complain that you were since your arrest, you should be dead by now,' the judge added with a touch of irony.

'I see that an innocent man's courage and strength are on trial!' replied the prisoner gently.

'Ring the bell, Coquart! have the doctor come with an attendant from the Conciergerie. We shall be obliged to take your frock coat off and verify the mark on your shoulder ...' Camusot went on.

'I am in your hands, sir.'

The prisoner asked whether his judge would be kind enough to explain to him what mark this was, and why it should be looked for on his shoulder? The judge was expecting this question.

'You are suspected of being Jacques Collin, an escaped convict whose audacity recoils before nothing, not even sacrilege ...' said the magistrate briskly plunging his gaze into the prisoner's eyes.

Jacques Collin neither quivered nor reddened; he remained calm and assumed a mildly quizzical air as he looked at Camusot.

'I, sir, a convict? ... May God and the Order to which I belong forgive you your mistake! tell me what I must do to spare you persisting in so grave an insult to the Law of Nations, to the Church, to the King my master.'

The magistrate, without replying directly, explained to the prisoner that, if he had once been branded as the law then decreed for those once sentenced to hard labour, a slap on his shoulder would cause the letters to reappear at once.

'Ah! my dear sir,' said Jacques Collin, 'it would be hard indeed if my devotion to the royal cause were now to prove detrimental to me.'

'Explain yourself,' said the judge, 'that's what you're here for.'

'Why, sir! I must have many scars on my back, for I was shot from behind, as a traitor to the country, while I was only faithful to my king, by the Constitutionalists who left me for dead.'

'You were shot, and you're still alive! . . .' said Camusot.

'I had an understanding with several of the soldiers to whom pious persons had given a little money; and in consequence I was stood at such a distance that I received only balls that were almost spent, the soldiers aimed at my back. This is a fact to which His Excellency the Ambassador will be able to testify . . .'

'This devil of a man has an answer to everything. So much the better, I suppose,' thought Camusot, who showed so much severity only by way of meeting the exigencies of legal procedure and police regulations.

Jacques Collin's admirable invention

'How did a man of your character come to be at the house of Baron Nucingen's mistress? and what a mistress, once a common prostitute! . . .'

'The reason why I was discovered at a harlot's house, sir, is as follows,' replied Jacques Collin. 'But before I explain that, I must tell you that it was just as I set foot on the first step of the staircase that I was suddenly taken ill, I was therefore not able to speak to the girl in time. I had learnt of Mademoiselle Esther's intention of killing herself, and as it concerned young Lucien de Rubempré, of whom I am particularly fond, for the holiest possible motives, I wished to do my best to turn the poor creature's mind from the path despair had pointed out to her: I wanted to tell her that Lucien's final appeal to Mademoiselle Clotilde could not succeed; and, by informing her that she inherited seven millions, I hoped to give her back the courage to live. I know very well, my dear judge, that I am a victim of the secrets confided to me. From the manner in which I was struck down, it is clear that I must have been poisoned that very morning; but the strength of my constitution saved me. I know that, for a long time, an agent of the political police has followed me about, seeking to involve me in some disreputable matter ... If, as I asked, at the time of my arrest, you had sent a doctor to me, you would have had proof of what I am now telling you about the state of my health. Believe me, sir, that individuals beyond our reach are violently bent on causing me to be confused with some rogue in order to have the right to be rid of me. It is not all gain to serve kings, they have their petty side; the Church alone is perfect.'

It is impossible to describe the play of facial expression with which Jacques Collin spent ten minutes unfolding this speech, phrase by phrase; everything in it was made to appear so probable, especially the illusion to Corentin, that the magistrate was shaken.

'Are you able to confide in me the grounds of your affection for Monsieur Lucien de Rubempré ...?'

'Can't you guess? I am sixty years old, sir ... I beg you, don't write that down ... It is simply that – but, indeed, must I?'

'It is in your own interest and that of Lucien de Rubempré to tell all,' answered the judge.

'Ah, well, then! he is ... O my God! ... he is my son!' came the murmured answer.

And he fainted.

'Don't write that down, Coquart,' said Camusot in an undertone.

Coquart rose from his table and went to get a small vial of Marseilles vinegar.

'If this is Jacques Collin, he is a consummate actor,' thought Camusot.

Coquart held the vinegar under the nose of the old convict whom the judge examined with a perspicacity common to lynx and magistrate.

Diamond cut diamond

'WE must get him to take his wig off,' said Camusot as he waited for Jacques Collin to recover consciousness.

The old convict heard what he said and felt afraid, for he knew how base was then the expression his physiognomy acquired.

'If you don't feel strong enough to take your wig off . . . yes, Coquart, remove it,' said the magistrate to his clerk.

Jacques Collin held his head forward to the clerk with touching resignation, but thereupon head and face, unadorned, became frightful to see, their true character was exposed. The sight plunged Camusot into deep uncertainty. Awaiting the arrival of doctor and male nurse, he set himself to classifying and inspecting all the papers and other objects seized at Lucien's domicile. After performing its duties in the rue Saint Georges, at Mademoiselle Esther's, the Law had descended upon the Quai Malaquais to carry out a search there.

'You have your hand on letters from Madame la Comtesse de Sérisy,' said Carlos Herrera; 'but I don't know why you should want almost all Lucien's papers,' he added with a sudden smile of irony at the judge.

Perceiving this smile, Camusot understood how much the word 'almost' conveyed.

'Lucien de Rubempré, suspected of being your accomplice, has been arrested,' replied the magistrate wishing to see what effect this news would produce on his prisoner.

'You have done great wrong, for he is every bit as innocent as I am,' the false Spaniard added without showing the least sign of emotion.

'We shall see, for the moment we're still concerned with

your identity,' continued Camusot, astonished by his prisoner's calm. 'If you are really Don Carlos Herrera, the fact would have immediate bearing on the situation of Lucien Chardon.'

'Yes, it was indeed Madame Chardon, Mademoiselle de Rubempré!' murmured Carlos. 'Ah! it was one of the greatest faults of my life!'

He raised his eyes heavenward; and, from the way in which his lips moved, it seemed that he was praying fervently.

'But if you are Jacques Collin, if he was knowingly the companion of an escaped convict, guilty of sacrilege, all those crimes suspected by the Law will seem more than probable.'

Carlos Herrera did not betray a tremor as he listened to the magistrate's cleverly phrased statement, and for his only reaction to the words 'knowingly', 'escaped convict', he held up his hands in an expression of noble grief.

'Monsieur l'Abbé,' the magistrate continued with exaggerated politeness, 'if you are Don Carlos Herrera, you will forgive all that we are obliged to do in the interests of justice and truth . . .'

Jacques Collin divined the trap laid for him solely by the sound of the judge's voice as he pronounced the words 'Monsieur l'Abbé,' for the man's countenance did not change, Camusot was waiting for a look of joy which would have been as it were a first sign of his convict nature, the ineffable pleasure taken by a criminal in deceiving his judges; but he found the hero of the penitentiary armed with Machiavellian powers of dissimulation.

'I am a diplomatist and I belong to an Order in which one takes vows of the greatest austerity,' replied Jacques Collin with apostolic sweetness, 'I understand, and am accustomed to suffering. I should already be at liberty if you had found at my dwelling the hiding-place in which I kept my papers, for I see that those you have confiscated are of very little significance . . .'

This was a mortal blow for Camusot; Jacques Collin had already, by the ease and simplicity of his manner, outweighed all the suspicions to which the sight of his head had given rise.

'Where are those papers? . . .'

'I will describe the place to you if you will allow your

357

messenger to be accompanied by a legation secretary from the Spanish embassy, who will take charge of them and to whom you will be responsible, for they concern my diplomatic status, they are secret documents some of which compromise the late king Louis XVIII. Oh, sir! it would be better . . . But there, you are a magistrate! . . . Besides, the ambassador, to whom I appeal in all this, will appreciate . . .'

The mark is abolished

AT that moment the doctor and the infirmary attendant came in, after being announced by the usher.

'Good morning, Monsieur Lebrun,' said Camusot to the doctor, 'I called you to pronounce on the state of the prisoner you see here. He says he has been poisoned, he claims to have been on the point of death since the day before yesterday; see if there is any danger in undressing him so that we can verify what marks there may be on his body . . .'

Doctor Lebrun took Jacques Collin's hand, felt his pulse, told him to put his tongue out, and looked at him very attentively. This examination lasted about ten minutes.

'The prisoner,' replied the doctor, 'has been very unwell, but at this moment he is in full possession of his strength . . .'

'This apparent strength is due, sir, to the nervous excitement which my curious situation causes me,' said Jacques Collin with the dignity of a bishop.

'That could well be,' agreed Monsieur Lebrun.

At a sign from the magistrate, the prisoner was undressed, he was allowed his breeches, but everything else was removed, even his shirt; revealed, then, to the admiration of those present might be seen a hairy torso of Cyclopean power. It might have been the Farnese Hercules of Naples without its exaggerated gigantism.

'To what end are men thus built destined by nature? . . .' said the doctor to Camusot.

The usher returned with that species of ebony bat which, from time immemorial, has been the badge of their office and which is mildly known as a rod; with it he struck several blows on the place where the executioner had applied the fatal letters. The scars of seventeen holes thereupon reappeared, distributed at random; but, despite the care with which the back was examined, no letters could be made out. The usher did indeed point out that the horizontal of a T might be indicated by two holes as wide apart as the two serifs at either end of that stroke, and that another hole would then correspond with the bottom of the vertical.

'That's pretty vague, all the same,' said Camusot seeing doubt depicted on the face of the doctor from the Conciergerie.

Carlos begged them to perform the same operation on his left shoulder and half way down his back. Fifteen other scars became visible which the doctor studied at the Spaniard's request, and he declared that the back had been so deeply furrowed by wounds, that the mark could not possibly show, supposing that the executioner had imprinted it there.

Thrusts

AT that moment a messenger from the Prefecture of Police entered, delivered an envelope to Monsieur Camusot and waited for the reply. Having read the message, the magistrate went over and spoke to Coquart, but so quietly that nobody could hear what he said. The only thing was that, from a look Camusot gave him, Jacques Collin guessed that new information about him had come from the Prefect.

'I've still got Peyrade's friend on my heels,' thought Jacques Collin; 'if I knew who he was, I'd get rid of him as I did of Contenson. Could I manage to see Asia again? ...'

Having signed the paper written out by Coquart, the judge put it in an envelope and handed it to the messenger from the Delegations office.

This office is an indispensable auxiliary of Justice. Presided over by a police superintendent appointed *ad hoc*, it consists of officers who act in conjunction with the superintendents in any particular quarter to carry out search warrants and even warrants of arrest at the abodes of persons suspected of complicity in crimes and misdemeanours. Those so delegated by judicial authority spare magistrates in charge of an investigation a great deal of valuable time.

The prisoner, at a sign from the judge, was then dressed by Monsieur Lebrun and the male nurse who withdrew, as did the usher. Camusot seated himself at his desk and began to play with his pen.

'You have an aunt,' Camusot said abruptly to Jacques Collin.

'An aunt?' replied Don Carlos Herrera with astonishment. 'I have no relations, sir, I am the unacknowledged child of the late Duke of·Ossuna.'

And to himself he said: '*They're getting warm!*' an allusion to the game of hide-and-seek, which is indeed a childish image of the terrible struggle between the Law and the criminal.

'Bah!' said Camusot. 'Look now, you still have your aunt, Mademoiselle Jacqueline Collin, whom you placed under the bizarre name of Asia in the service of Demoiselle Esther.'

Jacques Collin shrugged indifferently in a manner perfectly in keeping with the expression of curiosity with which he greeted the magistrate's words, the latter glancing at him quizzically.

'Watch out,' continued Camusot. 'Listen to me carefully.'

'I am listening, sir.'

Asia's qualifications

'YOUR aunt is a dealer in the Temple, her business is run by a Demoiselle Paccard, sister of a man under sentence, an honest wench as it happens, nicknamed La Romette. The Law is on your aunt's trail, and in a matter of hours we shall have definite proof. This woman is very devoted to you ...'

'Go on, Monsieur le Juge,' said Jacques Collin with perfect composure as Camusot paused, 'I am listening.'

'Your aunt, who is some five years older than you, was the mistress of Marat of odious memory. It was from that bloodstained source that the nucleus of her present fortune came . . . She is, according to the information I have received, a very astute receiver of stolen goods, though at the moment that cannot be finally proved. After the death of Marat, she seems, by the report I have here in my hands, to have belonged to a chemist sentenced to death in the year XII, for coining. She appeared as a witness at the trial. It was during this association that she picked up some knowledge of toxicology. She was a wardrobe dealer from year XII of the Republic to 1810. She served two years in prison in 1812 and 1816 for procuring minors . . . You had already been sentenced for forgery, you left the banking house to which your aunt had sent you as a clerk, thanks to the education you had received and to the patronage your aunt enjoyed with persons whose depravity she provided with victims . . . All this, prisoner, bears little relation to the elevated station of the dukes of Ossuna . . . Do you still persist in your denial? . . .'

Jacques Collin, as he listened to Monsieur Camusot, was thinking of his happy childhood, at the Oratorian school he had left, a meditation which gave his face a look of real astonishment. Despite the skill of his interrogatory manner of speech, Camusot did not succeed in ruffling that placid physiognomy.

'If you faithfully transcribed the explanation I gave you at the outset, you need only read it over,' replied Jacques Collin, 'I can't change it . . . I didn't visit the courtesan, how should I know who her cook was? I have no connection with the individuals of whom you speak.'

'Despite your continued denial, we shall confront you with persons who may shake your composure.'

'A man who has once been shot is ready for anything,' Jacques Collin answered gently.

Camusot turned back to the confiscated documents while he waited for the return of the head of the crime squad whose diligence was exemplary, for it was half past eleven, the interrogation had begun at about half past ten, and the usher entered and in a low voice announced to the magistrate the arrival of Bibi-Lupin.

'Let him come in!' replied Monsieur Camusot.

On entering, Bibi-Lupin, from whom a prompt: 'It's him all right!' was expected, stood puzzled. He no longer recognized the face of his *customer* in that pockmarked visage. This hesitation struck the magistrate.

'It's his build, his bulk,' said the agent. 'Ah! that's you, Jacques Collin,' he went on examining the eyes, the cut of the forehead, the ears . . . There are certain things which cannot be disguised . . . 'It's him all right, Monsieur Camusot . . . Jacques has the scar of a knife-wound on his left arm, get him to remove his coat, and you'll see . . .'

Once more, Jacques Collin was obliged to take off his frock coat, Bibi-Lupin pulled the shirt sleeve up and pointed out the scar.

'It was a bullet,' replied Don Carlos Herrera, 'see, there are other scars.'

'Ah! and that's his voice!' exclaimed Bibi-Lupin.

'Your conviction is only a piece of information, it isn't a proof,' said the judge.

'I know that,' answered Bibi-Lupin with deference; 'but I'll find you witnesses. One lodger who was at the Maison Vauquer is here already . . .' he said with a look at Collin.

The calm expression on Collin's face did not falter.

'Call this person in,' said Monsieur Camusot peremptorily, his irritation evident despite his air of studied indifference.

This flicker was observed by Jacques Collin who wasn't counting on any sympathy from his examining magistrate, so that a marked apathy covered what in fact was a violent inner search to divine its cause. The usher showed in Madame Poiret of whom this unexpected sight occasioned a slight quiver in the convict, but this trepidation escaped the magistrate whose mind seemed made up.

'What is your name?' asked the judge launching straight into the formalities with which all depositions and interrogations begin.

Madame Poiret, a little old woman white and wrinkled like

362

calves' sweetbreads, dressed in a gown of dark-blue silk, described herself as Christine-Michelle Michonneau, wife of Sieur Poiret, aged fifty-one, born in Paris, domiciled in the rue des Poules at the corner of the rue des Postes, keeper of a boarding-house.

'In 1818 and 1819, Madame,' said the magistrate, 'you resided on premises kept by a Dame Vauquer.'

'Yes, sir, that is where I made the acquaintance of Monsieur Poiret, retired clerical worker, subsequently my husband, whom, for a year past, I keep in bed, . . . poor man! he is very unwell. Thus I ought not to be long away from home . . .'

'At that time a lodger in the house was a certain Vautrin . . . ?' inquired the magistrate.

'Oh, sir! what a tale that was, he turned out to be a terrible convict . . .'

'You took part in his arrest.'

'That is not so, sir . . .'

'You stand before the Law, be careful! . . .' Monsieur Camusot said sternly.

Madame Poiret remained silent.

'Recall your memories!' Camusot went on, 'do you remember the man? . . . would you recognize him?'

'I think so.'

'Is it the man you see here? . . .' said the judge.

Madame Poiret put on tinted spectacles and looked at Father Carlos Herrera.

'He was broad like that, about the same height, but . . . no, . . . though if, . . : Monsieur le Juge,' she went on, 'if I could see his bare chest, I should recognize that at once.'

The magistrate and his clerk could not restrain themselves from laughing, despite the gravity of their functions. Jacques Collin joined in their hilarity, though with moderation. The prisoner had not yet put his arms into the sleeves of the frock coat which Bibi-Lupin had just taken off him; and, at a sign from the judge, he obligingly opened his shirt.

'That is his palatine; but you've gone grey, Monsieur Vautrin,' exclaimed Madame Poiret.

'WHAT do say to that?' asked the judge.

'The woman is mad!' said Jacques Collin.

'Oh, my goodness! if I was in doubt, for his face isn't the same, that voice would be sufficient, I heard it threatening me ... Ah! and that was his way of looking.'

'The criminal investigation agent and this woman could not,' the magistrate went on addressing Jacques Collin, 'have agreed to say the same about you, for neither of them had seen you; how do you explain that?'

'The Law has committed worse mistakes than would result from accepting the testimony of a woman who recognizes a man by the hair on his chest and the suspicions of a policeman,' replied Jacques Collin. 'My voice, my way of looking, my build are found to resemble those of an important criminal, that seems a bit vague to begin with. As to the reminiscence which is supposed to prove that between the lady and my double there were relations which do not cause her to blush, ... you laughed at that yourself. If, on behalf of the Law, sir, you are one half as anxious as I am, for my part, to establish the truth, will you ask this Madame ... Foi ...'

'Poiret ...'

'Poret. Forgive me! (I am Spanish), if she remembers the people who were living in this ... what did you call the house? ...'

'A respectable boarding-house,' said Madame Poiret.

'What kind of establishment is that?' asked Jacques Collin.

'A house at which you breakfast and dine by subscription.'

'You're right,' exclaimed Camusot with a nod of the head which appeared to show agreement with Jacques Collin, so evidently was he struck by the apparent good faith with which the latter showed his willingness to be helpful. 'Try to remember the subscribers who were there at the time of Jacques Collin's arrest.'

'There was Monsieur de Rastignac, Doctor Bianchon, old Goriot, ... Mademoiselle Taillefer ...'

'Good,' said the judge who hadn't taken his eyes off Jacques Collin's face which remained impassive. 'Well, now, this old Goriot . . .'

'He's dead,' said Madame Poiret.

'Sir,' said Jacques Collin, 'I've several times met at Lucien's a Monsieur de Rastignac, attached, I believe, to Madame de Nucingen, and, if he's the young man in question, he certainly never mistook me for the convict with whom an attempt is being made to confuse me . . .'

'Monsieur de Rastignac and Doctor Bianchon,' said the judge, 'are persons of such high standing in society that their testimony, if it is in your favour, would be enough to set you at liberty. Coquart, make out their writs of summons.'

Within a matter of minutes, the formalities of Madame Poiret's deposition were concluded. Coquart read over to her his report of the scene which had just taken place, and she signed it; but the prisoner refused to sign basing his refusal on a lack of knowledge of French legal procedure.

An interruption

'WELL, that's quite enough for one day,' Monsieur Camusot went on, 'you must be feeling the need for a little food, I'll have you taken back to the Conciergerie.'

'Alas! I don't feel well enough to eat,' said Jacques Collin.

Camusot wanted to make the moment of Jacques Collin's return coincide with the time of the prisoners' exercise period in the prison yard; but he also wanted a reply from the governor of the Conciergerie to the order he'd given him that morning, and he rang for his usher to be sent for it. The usher came and said that the woman doorkeeper of the house on the Quai Malaquais had brought him a substantial document relating to Monsieur Lucien de Rubempré. This interruption was to prove so important that it made Camusot forget his design.

'Let her come in!' he said.

'Pardon, excuse me, sir,' said the doorwoman curtseying

in turn to the magistrate and Father Carlos. 'We got so flustered, my husband and me, by the Law, the two times it came, that we forgot we had in the drawer a letter addressed to Monsieur Lucien, on which we had ten sous to pay, what's more, although it was posted in Paris, because it's so heavy. Can you pay me the carriage? Goodness only knows when we shall be seeing our tenants again!'

'This letter was given you by the postman?' asked Camusot after studying the envelope carefully.

'Yes, sir.'

'Coquart, you'd better draw up a report of this declaration. Right! my good woman. Give us your name, your occupation . . .'

Camusot swore the woman in, then he dictated the report.

While these formalities proceeded, he checked the postmark which showed the times of collection and delivery, as well as the date. This letter, it thus appeared, delivered to Lucien's the day after Esther's death, had indubitably been written and posted on the day of the calamity.

We may now judge of Monsieur Camusot's stupefaction on reading this letter, written and signed by one believed by the Law to have been the victim of a crime.

Too much

ESTHER TO LUCIEN

Monday, 13 May 1830.

(MY LAST DAY, AT TEN O' CLOCK IN THE MORNING.)

Dear Lucien, I have not an hour to live. By eleven o'clock I shall be dead, and I shall die without pain. I paid fifty thousand francs for a pretty little black fruit containing a poison which kills with lightning speed. Thus, my lamb, you will be able to say: 'My little Esther didn't suffer . . .' No, I shall suffer only in writing you these pages.

That monster who bought me so dearly, knowing that the day on which I regarded myself as his would have no morrow, Nucingen

366

has just gone, drunk as a bear who has been plied with liquor. For the first and last time in my life, I have been able to compare my former profession as a 'daughter of joy' with the life of love, to juxtapose that tenderness which opens like a flower in the infinite and the horror of a duty which could wish so to annihilate itself as not to leave room for a kiss. I needed this disgust to find death adorable . . . I've had a bath; I should have liked the confessor at the convent where I was baptized to come and confess me, in short to wash my soul. But there's been quite enough prostitution without that, it would be to profane a sacrament, and besides I feel bathed in the waters of sincere repentance. God will do with me as He pleases.

Let's have done with this whining, for you I want to remain your Esther until the last moment, not to bore you with my death, with the future, with God, who would not be good if he tormented me in the other world when I have swallowed so many griefs in this one . . .

I have in front of me the lovely miniature Madame de Mirbel did of you. This ivory panel often consoled me for your absence, I look at it with intoxication as I write you my last thoughts, depict my last heartbeats for you. I shall enclose this portrait with my letter, for I don't want it stolen and sold. The thought of what gave me so much pleasure being mixed up in some shop window with the officers and ladies of the Empire, or with Chinese curiosities, is almost a death in itself. That portrait, my darling, hide it or have it cleaned off, don't give it to anyone else . . . unless such a present could win you the heart of that walking lath in clothes, that Clotilde de Grandlieu, who will cover you with bruises in her sleep her bones are so sharp. . . . Yes, I consent to that, I should still be good for something as I was in my lifetime. Ah! to give you pleasure, or if it had just made you laugh, I'd have held myself close to a fire with an apple in my mouth to roast it for you! My death will then still be of use to you . . . I should have troubled your domestic life . . . Oh! that Clotilde, I don't understand her! To be able to be your wife, to bear your name, not to leave you day or night, to be yours, and still to make difficulties! to do that, you need to belong to the Faubourg Saint Germain! and not to have ten pounds of flesh on your bones . . .

Poor Lucien, darling, disappointed man of ambition, I dream of your future! Come now, you'll sometimes miss your poor faithful dog, that kind-hearted tart who stole for you, who'd have let herself be dragged before the Court of Assize to ensure your happiness, whose sole occupation was to think of your pleasures, to invent new ones, who felt love for you in her hair, in her feet, in her ears, in fact your *ballerina* whose every look blessed you; who, for six years past, thought only of you, so much your creature that I was never more than an emanation of your soul as light is of the sun. But there, for lack of money and position, alas! I can't be your wife . . . I've always provided for your future by giving you what I had . . . Come as soon as you get this letter, and take what you'll find under my pillow, for I don't trust those in the house . . .

You'll see, I mean to make a beautiful corpse, I shall lie down, I shall put myself nicely to bed, I shall *arrange* myself, eh! Then I shall press the berry against the soft palate, and I shan't be disfigured either by convulsion, or by lying in a ridiculous posture.

I know that Madame de Sérisy has quarrelled with you, because of me; but, you see, pussy, when she knows I'm dead, she'll forgive you, you'll just have to make a fuss of her, she'll marry you off well, if the Grandlieus persist in their refusal.

My once-was, I don't want a lot of loud lamentation from you when you learn of my death. First, I must tell you that eleven o'clock on Monday 13 May was just the termination of a long illness which began the day when, on the terrace at Saint Germain, you sent me back to my old career . . . The soul can be hurt like the body. Only, the soul won't just let itself suffer stupidly like the body, the body doesn't help the soul as the soul helps the body, and the soul may find a cure in those very thoughts which lead seamstresses to their bags of charcoal. You held out a whole life to me the day before yesterday when you said that if Clotilde still refused you you'd marry me. It would have been a great misfortune for both of us, I should have been all the more dead, to put it that way; for deaths may be more or less bitter. We should never have been accepted by society.

Believe me! these past two months I've thought a great deal. A poor whore is in the mud, as I was before I went to the convent; men find her beautiful, they get her to serve their pleasure without showing much consideration, they receive her on foot after going out to look for her by carriage; if they don't spit in her face, it's because she's preserved from that outrage by her beauty; but morally, they do worse. Well, now! if the tart inherits five or six million, she'll be sought by princes, she'll be greeted with respect when she goes by in her carriage, she can take her pick of the ancient scutcheons of France and Navarre. Society, which would have hurled abuse at us on seeing two fine creatures united and happy, was always polite to Madame de Staël, in spite of her wild adventures, because she had two hundred thousand francs' income.

The world, which bows before Money or Fame, won't bow before happiness, or goodness; for I should have done good . . . Oh! how many tears I should have wiped away! . . . as many I think as I have shed! Yes, I should have wanted to live only for you and for those in need.

Thinking like that has made death adorable to me. So don't weep and wail, my darling. Say to yourself now and then: there were two good-natured harlots, both of them beautiful, who both died for me, without bearing me any grudge, who worshipped me; raise up in your heart a monument to Coralie, to Esther, and go on your way! Do you remember the day when you pointed out to me the mistress of a poet before the Revolution, old, shrivelled, in a cabbage-green bonnet, in a puce quilted wrap with black stains of grease, hardly warmed by the sun, although she was sitting out in it in the Tuileries, fussing over a horrible pug-dog, the mangiest ever? You know, she'd had lackeys, equipages, a town house! I said to you then: 'It is better to die at thirty!' Well, that day, you found me thoughtful, you did all kinds of silly things to distract me; and, between two kisses, I said to you again: 'Every day pretty women leave the theatre before the play is over!' . . . So you can say, I didn't want to see the last act, that's all . . .

You'll be finding me garrulous, but this is my last tittle-tattle. I'm writing to you as though I were talking to you, and I want my conversation to be gay. Complaining seamstresses have always irritated me; you know I tried to die properly once before, when I got back from that awful Opera ball, where they told you I'd been a whore!

Oh! no, my sweet, don't give this portrait away. If you knew under what waves of love I drowned in your eyes as I gazed at them intoxicated just now at a pause in my writing, . . . if you were able to take back the love I've tried to overlay this ivory with, you'd think the soul of your once-cherished was there.

A dead woman who begs alms, isn't that funny? . . . No, I must learn to stay quiet in my grave.

You don't know how heroic my death would seem to fools if they were told that last night Nucingen offered me two millions if I'd love him as I loved you. He'll feel nicely robbed when he knows I've kept my word and died of him. I did all I could to go on breathing the same air as you. I told this fat thief: 'If you want to be loved as you say, I'll even undertake never to see Lucien again . . .' 'What must I do?' he asked. 'Will you give me two million for him?' . . . No! if you'd seen his face? Ah! I should have laughed, if it hadn't meant tragedy for me. 'Don't answer, then!' I said. 'I can see, you'd rather have two millions than me. Well, it's always nice for a woman to know what she's worth,' I added, turning my back on him.

The old scoundrel will know in an hour or two that I wasn't joking.

Who'll be able to part your hair as I did? Bah! I don't want to think about anything to do with life any longer, I've only got five minutes left, I give them to God; don't be jealous of Him, my angel, I only want to talk to Him about you, ask Him to make you happy in return for my death, and my punishment in another world. I wish I weren't going to Hell, I should have liked to see the angels and find out whether they are at all like you . . .

Good-bye, my pretty, good-bye! out of all my unhappiness I bless you. Even in the grave I shall be

Your ESTHER . . .

It is striking eleven. I have said my last prayer, I am going to bed now to die. Once more, good-bye! I wish that the warmth of my hand might keep my soul there as I place a last kiss on it, and I must just once more call you nice pussy, although you have caused the death of your

ESTHER.

In which we see that the Law is and must be heartless

A FEELING of jealousy contracted the magistrate's heart as he finished reading the only suicide's letter he had seen written with such gaiety, although it was a feverish gaiety, and the last effort of a blind tenderness.

'What is there so unusual about him that he should be loved like that! . . .' he thought repeating what is always said by men who lack the gift of appealing to women.

'If you can prove not only that you are not Jacques Collin, escaped convict, but also that you really are Don Carlos Herrera, canon of Toledo, secret envoy of His Majesty Ferdinand VII,' said the magistrate to Jacques Collin, 'you will be set at liberty, for the impartiality which my office requires of me obliges me to tell you that I have just received a letter from the girl Esther Gobseck in which she avows her intention of killing herself, and in which she gives expression to suspicions about her servants which may well designate them as authors of the theft of the seven hundred and fifty thousand francs.'

As he spoke, Monsieur Camusot was comparing the handwriting of the letter with that of the will, and it seemed to him evident that the letter had indeed been written by the same person who had drawn up the will.

'Sir, you were too quick to believe that a crime had been committed, do not be in a hurry to suppose theft.'

'Ah! . . .' said Camusot casting a judge's glance at the prisoner.

'Don't imagine that I am compromising myself if I tell you that this sum may yet be found,' went on Jacques Collin giving the judge to understand that his suspicion had been noted. 'That poor creature was well loved by her servants; and, if I were free, I should undertake to look for money which now belongs to the being I most love in the world, to Lucien! . . . Would you be so kind as to let me read the letter, it won't take long . . . it is the proof of my dear child's innocence . . . you can't suppose I should destroy it . . . or speak about it, since I'm being kept in solitary confinement.'

'Solitary confinement! . . .' exclaimed the magistrate, 'you won't be presently . . . I'm begging you to establish your identity as quickly as you can, have recourse to your ambassador if you want . . .'

And he handed the letter to Jacques Collin. Camusot was happy to be rid of his difficulties, to be able to satisfy the Attorney General, Mesdames de Maufrigneuse and Sérisy. Nevertheless he coldly and curiously watched the man's face while his prisoner read the letter from the harlot; and, despite the sincerity of the feelings there depicted, he said to himself: 'That really is a convict physiognomy, all the same.'

'That's how they love him! . . .' said Jacques Collin giving the letter back . . . And he showed Camusot a face bathed in tears. 'If you knew him!' he went on, 'his soul is so young, so fresh, he is so magnificently handsome, a child, a poet . . . You can't help feeling a need to sacrifice yourself for him, to gratify his least whim. Dear Lucien, he would bewitch you with his winning ways.'

'So, then,' said the magistrate still making an effort to discover the truth, 'you can't possibly be Jacques Collin . . .'

'No sir . . .' replied the convict.

And Jacques Collin made himself more of a Don Carlos Herrera than ever. To put the finishing touches to his creation, he went up to the magistrate, led him into the window embrasure and adopted the manner of a prince of the Church, speaking in a confidential tone.

'I love that child so much, sir, that were it necessary to be the criminal you take me for in order to avoid some inconvenience befalling my heart's idol, I should accuse myself,' he said in a low voice. 'I should imitate the poor wench who killed herself to his gain. Therefore, sir, I implore you to grant me a favour, that is, to set Lucien at liberty forthwith . . .'

'My duty does not properly allow it,' said Camusot good-humouredly; 'but, whenever compromise is possible, the Law knows how to show consideration, and, if you can give me good reasons . . . Say what you have to say, this won't be written down . . .'

'Why, then,' Jacques Collin continued, deceived by the good humour of Camusot, 'I know all that the poor child is suffering at this moment, he might even attempt to take his own life on finding himself in prison . . .'

'Oh! as to that,' said Camusot with a shrug.

'You don't know whom you'll oblige by obliging me,' added Jacques Collin playing on other strings. 'You'll be rendering a service to an Order more powerful than any Comtesse de Sérisy or Duchesse de Maufrigneuse who won't forgive you for having had their letters in your office . . . ,' said he indicating two scented bundles . . . 'My Order does not forget.'

'Sir!' said Camusot, 'that will do. Think of other reasons you can give me. My duty is as much to the prisoner as to the prosecution.'

'Well, then, believe me, I know Lucien, he has the soul of a woman, a poet, a man of the South, inconstant, lacking in will-power,' Jacques Collin continued, who thought he perceived that the judge had been won over to their side. 'You are certain of the young man's innocence, don't torment him, don't ask him questions; give him this letter, tell him that he inherits from Esther, and set him at liberty ... If you act otherwise, you'll find that it leads you nowhere; while if you just let him go without a thought, I'll explain to you (keep me locked up meanwhile), tomorrow, this evening, everything that seems mysterious to you in this affair, including the reasons why there are people in such hot pursuit of me; but I shall be risking my life, they've been after my head these five years ... With Lucien free, rich and married to Clotilde de Grand-lieu, my earthly task will be over, I shan't care about my own skin any more ... My pursuer is a spy of your last king ...'

'Ah! Corentin!'

'Ah! he's called Corentin ... thank you ... Well, then, sir, are you going to promise to do what I ask? ...'

'A judge cannot and must not make promises. Coquart! tell the usher and the constables to take the prisoner back to the Conciergerie ... I shall give orders for you to be moved to more comfortable quarters this evening,' he added gently with a slight inclination of the head to the prisoner.

The magistrate regains the upper hand

STRUCK by Jacques Collin's request and remembering how strongly he had insisted on being questioned first, giving his illness as a reason, Camusot was again filled with distrust. Lending ear to his unformed suspicions, he saw the supposed invalid go out, walking like a Hercules, no longer putting on those little touches so expertly adopted at the time of his entrance.

'Sir? ...'

Jacques Collin turned.

'In spite of your refusal to sign, my clerk will read over to you his report of your interrogation.'

The prisoner was in excellent health, the movement with

which he came and sat down beside the clerk was a revelation to the judge.

'You've recovered very promptly?' said Camusot.

'I've been caught,' thought Jacques Collin. Then he replied in a clear voice: 'Joy alone, sir, is nature's panacea ... this letter, the proof of an innocence I never questioned ... that's the great remedy.'

The magistrate followed his prisoner with an attentive gaze as the usher and constables gathered round him; then he moved like a man waking from sleep, and threw Esther's letter down on his clerk's desk.

'Coquart, copy that letter! ...'

A melancholy peculiar to examining magistrates

IF it is in man's nature to distrust what he is begged to do when this is against his interests or against his duty, even though he may feel personally indifferent about it, such a feeling is obligatory with examining magistrates. The more the prisoner, whose identity was not yet fully established, saw clouds on the horizon if Lucien were interrogated, the more such a questioning seemed necessary to Camusot. According to the Code and its usages, the formality would not have been strictly indispensable, had not the question of Father Carlos's identity arisen. In all walks of life, there exists some form of professional conscience. Without feeling any particular curiosity, Camusot would have questioned Lucien in the course of duty as he had just questioned Jacques Collin, employing all the ruses which a conscientious magistrate may properly employ. The favour to be done, his own advancement, everything for Camusot was subordinate to a desire to learn the truth, however much this had to be done by guesswork and even if it could not then be published. He drummed with his fingers on the panes of the window abandoning himself to a flow of conjecture, for at such moments thought is like a river passing through many countries. Lovers of truth, magistrates are like jealous women, they give way to endless suppositions and probe them with the dagger of suspicion as the sacrificing priests of antiquity eviscerated their victims; then they come to a halt not at the true, but at the probable, and they end by glimpsing the truth. A woman questions a man she loves as the judge interrogates a criminal. In such situations, a flash, a word, an inflexion of the voice, a moment of hesitation suffice to point to the hidden fact, the betrayal or the crime.

'The way he described his devotion to his son (if it is his son), makes me fancy that he was in that tart's house to keep an eye open for squalls; and, not realizing that there was a will under the dead woman's pillow, he took those seven hundred and fifty thousand francs for his son, *on account*! . . . That's why he promised to see that the money was found. Monsieur de Rubempré owes it to himself and to the Law to throw some light on the social position of his father . . . And to promise me the protection of his Order (his Order!) if I don't question Lucien! . . .'

He continued to think about this.

As we have just seen, an examining magistrate will conduct an inquiry as he pleases. He is free to be devious or straightforward. An interrogation is everything and nothing. That is where the possibility of showing favour lies. Camusot rang, the usher was there. He gave orders for Monsieur Lucien de Rubempré to be brought, with strict instructions that he should not communicate with anybody on the way. It was then two o'clock in the afternoon.

'There is something mysterious,' said the judge to himself, 'and it must be important. The reasoning of my amphibious customer, who is neither priest nor layman, neither convict nor Spaniard, but who is anxious that his young favourite's lips shall not utter some fatal word, is this: "The poet is weak, he is a woman; he isn't like me, who am a positive Hercules of diplomacy, and you will easily wrest our secret from him!" Well! we are going to learn everything this innocent can tell us! . . .'

And he went on tapping the edge of his table with an ivory paper-knife, while his clerk copied Esther's letter. What oddities we betray in the use of our faculties! Camusot considered all the crimes he could think of, but quite failed to think of the one the prisoner had in fact committed, the forging of a will in Lucien's favour. Let those who attack the magistracy's position out of envy reflect on those lives spent in a state of continual suspicion, on the torture these people inflict on their own minds, for civil cases are no less complicated than criminal inquiries, and they may well come to the conclusion that the priest and the judge are in equally heavy, equally galling harness. But every profession has its hair shirt and its Chinese puzzles.

Dangers courted by innocence at the
Palais de Justice

A T a little after two, Monsieur Camusot saw Lucien de Rubempré enter, pale, unkempt, his eyes red and swollen, in short in a state of collapse which allowed him to compare nature with art, true prostration with play-acting. The way taken from the Conciergerie to the magistrate's office between two constables preceded by an usher had brought despair to its height in Lucien. A poet's mind prefers torture to judgment. Seeing this nature so utterly devoid of the moral courage which made the judge himself hesitate and which had just been so powerfully manifested by the other prisoner, Monsieur Camusot felt both contempt and pity before so cheap a victory, in which his most decisive blows would be registered with the ease of a marksman picking off dolls in a fairground.

'Pull yourself together, Monsieur de Rubempré, you are in the presence of a magistrate anxious to repair the harm which the Law does without wishing to when it places a man in preventive detention without good cause. I believe you to be innocent, and you will be set at liberty immediately. The proof of your innocence is here. It is a letter kept by your caretaker in your absence, which she has just brought. In the disturbance caused by the appearance of the police and the news of your arrest at Fontainebleau, the woman forgot this letter which comes from Mademoiselle Esther Gobseck . . . Read it!'

Lucien took the letter, read it and burst into tears. He sobbed without being able to utter a word. After a quarter of an hour, during which Lucien remained deprived of all strength, the clerk presented him with the copy and asked him to sign for this as being *in conformity with the original and to be presented immediately on demand during the judicial inquiry*, inviting him to collate the copy with the original; but naturally Lucien took Coquart's word as to its accuracy.

'Sir,' said the judge with an air of great good will, 'it is difficult, nevertheless, to set you at liberty without going through certain formalities and asking you a few questions. . . . It is rather as a witness that I require you to answer. To a man like yourself, I hardly need to say that swearing to tell the whole truth is not simply an appeal to your conscience, but for the moment a necessity of your position here, which remains a little ambiguous. The truth cannot hurt you whatever it may be; but a lie could bring you before the Court of Assize, and would compel me to send you back to the Conciergerie; whereas if you answer my questions frankly you will sleep at home tonight, and your reputation will be restored by an item in the newspapers which says: "Monsieur de Rubempré, arrested yesterday at Fontainebleau, was at once discharged after a short interrogation."'

This discourse produced a lively impression on Lucien, and observing his prisoner's change of mood, the judge added: 'I repeat, you were suspected of complicity in the murder by poisoning of Demoiselle Esther, there is now proof of suicide, that is all; but a sum of seven hundred and fifty thousand francs which form part of the inheritance has been removed, and you are the sole heir; there, unfortunately, we have a crime. This crime preceded the discovery of the will. Now, the Law has reason to think that a person who loves you, as much as you loved this Demoiselle Esther, allowed himself to commit this crime to your profit . . . Don't interrupt me,' said Camusot imposing silence on Lucien who made as if to speak, 'I am not questioning you yet. I want to make you understand to what extent your honour is involved in this matter. Give up the false, the wretched point of honour which binds accomplices together, and speak the whole truth.'

The reader must already have noticed how excessively out of proportion are the armaments deployed in these battles between prisoner and examining magistrate. Certainly a denial intelligently persisted in contains no defect of form and may be a prisoner's best defence; but plate armour of that kind may become crushing if the questioner's dagger finds a joint in it. The moment denial fails to account for certain evident facts, the prisoner is entirely at the judge's mercy. Take the case of a half-criminal, like Lucien, who, preserved from the initial shipwreck of his virtue, might amend and become useful to his country; he may yet perish in the pitfalls of a judicial inquiry. The magistrate draws up a bare report, a faithful verbal analysis of the questions and answers; but of his insidiously paternal speeches, of misleading admonishments like the one we have heard, nothing remains. The judges of higher jurisdiction and their juries see or hear the results without knowing the means. Thus, to the minds of some worthy people, the jury itself, as in England, might well conduct inquiries. France enjoyed this system for a period. Under the code of Brumaire, year IV, the institution was known as a *jury d'accusation* by contrast with the later *jury de jugement*. At the public hearing itself, if we returned to 'juries of accusation', the trial would be conducted before a royal court, without the presence of jurymen.

In which all those who may have committed
some misdemeanour will tremble at the thought
of appearing before any court whatever

'Now,' said Camusot after a pause, 'what is your name? Monsieur Coquart, take note! . . .' he said to the clerk.

'Lucien Chardon, de Rubempré.'

'You were born?'

'At Angoulême . . .'

And Lucien gave day, month and year.

'You received no patrimony?'

'None.'

'You nevertheless, during your first stay in Paris, spent a fair amount of money, in view of your relative lack of fortune?'

'Yes, sir; but at that time, I had in Mademoiselle Coralie a friend who was almost too devoted to me and whom I had the misfortune to lose. It was the grief caused by her death which led me to return to my place of birth.'

'Good, sir,' said Camusot. 'I commend your frankness, it will be properly appreciated.'

Lucien was, as we may see, embarked upon a general confession.

'You spent a great deal more on your return from Angoulême to Paris,' continued Camusot, 'you lived like a man who should have, say, an income of sixty thousand francs.'

'Yes, sir . . .'

'Who provided you with this money?'

'My patron, Father Carlos Herrera.'

'Where did you meet him?'

'I met him on the highway, at a moment when I was planning to do away with my life by suicide . . .'

'You'd never heard him spoken of in your family, by your mother? . . .'

'Never.'

'Your mother never spoke to you of meeting a Spaniard?'

'Never . . .'

'Can you remember in what month, what year you became attached to the Demoiselle Esther?'

'Towards the end of 1823, at a little theatre on the outskirts.'

'In the first place, she was a charge on you?'

'Yes.'

'Latterly, in the hope of marrying Mademoiselle de Grandlieu, you bought up what remained of the old Rubempré house, with land to the value of a million, you told the Grandlieu family that your sister and brother-in-law had just come into a fortune and that you owed these sums to their generosity? . . . Is that what you told the Grandlieu family, sir?'

'Yes.'

'Do you know why the marriage was broken off?'

'No, sir.'

'Well, the Grandlieu family sent one of the best-known solicitors in Paris to see your brother-in-law. In Angoulême this solicitor learned, from the avowals of your sister and brother-in-law themselves, that not only had they loaned you very little, but that what they had inherited consisted of land and buildings, of some value but hardly amounting to more than two hundred thousand francs ... It won't surprise you that a family like the Grandlieus draws back in face of a fortune whose origins can't be shown ... That, sir, was the point to which you were led by telling a lie ...'

Lucien was chilled by this revelation, and the little strength of mind which had remained left him.

'The Police and the Courts know all they need to know,' said Camusot, 'remember that. And now,' he went on thinking of the father's part adopted by Jacques Collin, 'do you know who this supposed Carlos Herrera is?'

'Yes, sir, but I learned it too late ...'

'How do you mean, too late? Explain yourself!'

'He isn't a priest, he isn't a Spaniard, he's ...'

'An escaped convict,' said the magistrate briskly.

'Yes,' replied Lucien. 'When the dreadful secret was revealed to me, I was indebted to him, I had thought I was associated with a respectable churchman ...'

'Jacques Collin ...' began the magistrate.

'Yes, Jacques Collin,' Lucien echoed, 'that's his name.'

'Good. Jacques Collin,' Monsieur Camusot went on, 'has just now been identified by a certain person, and if he continues to deny his identity, it is, I believe, in your interest. But my purpose in asking you whether you knew who the man is was to bring out another piece of imposture on Jacques Collin's part.'

When Lucien heard this terrifying observation, it was as though a red-hot iron penetrated his entrails.

'Did you know,' said the judge continuing, 'that he claims to be your father by way of accounting for the extraordinary affection of which you are the object?'

'He! my father! ... oh! sir! ... he said that!'

'Did you suspect where the sums he gave you came from; for, according to the letter you have in your hand, that poor girl, Demoiselle Esther, seems to have rendered you the same services as Demoiselle Coralie did earlier; but, for some years, as you have just said, you lived, very handsomely, without receiving anything from her.'

'I shall ask you, sir,' exclaimed Lucien, 'to tell me where convicts get their money from! . . . A man like Jacques Collin my father! . . . Oh! my poor mother . . .'

And he burst into tears.

'Clerk, read over to the prisoner that part of the interrogation of the pretended Carlos Herrera in which he said that he was the father of Lucien de Rubempré.'

The poet listened to the reading in silence and with a look on his face which it was pitiful to see.

'I am lost!' he exclaimed.

'One does not lose oneself along the way of honour and truth,' said the magistrate.

'But you will send Jacques Collin before the Court of Assize?' asked Lucien.

'Certainly,' replied Camusot who wanted Lucien to go on talking. 'Finish what you were saying.'

Two schools of morality

BUT, in spite of the magistrate's insistence, Lucien made no further reply. Reflection had come too late, as it commonly does to men who are slaves of sensation. That is the difference between the poet and the man of action: one abandons himself to feeling in order to reproduce it in living images, judgment follows; while the other feels and judges in a single operation. Lucien remained gloomy, pale, he saw himself at the bottom of the precipice, pitched there by the examining magistrate, whose friendly manner had beguiled him, the poet. He had just betrayed not his benefactor, but his accomplice who, for his part, had defended their position with the courage of a lion, and with skill of the same order. Where Jacques Collin had saved everything by his boldness, Lucien, the clever one, had lost it all unintelligently through lack of reflection.

The foul lie which had stirred him to indignation screened a much fouler truth. Confused by the judge's subtlety, frightened by the speed with which the admitted faults of his life had been turned into hooks to drag his conscience, Lucien sat there like an animal which has escaped the slaughterhouse chopping-block. Free and innocent at his entry into this office, in a moment he had become a criminal by his own avowal. Finally, as a concluding piece of grim mockery, the magistrate calmly and coldly pointed out to Lucien that his revelations had been the fruit of a misunderstanding. Camusot had been thinking of Jacques Collin's claim to paternity, while Lucien, fearing above all lest his alliance with an escaped convict should be made public, had imitated the legendary inadvertence of the murderers of Ibycus.

It is to the glory of Royer-Collard that he proclaimed the regular victory of natural over dictated feelings, to have maintained the cause of the anteriority of oaths by insisting that the law of hospitality, for instance, was binding on a man to the point of annulling the virtue of a juridical oath. He announced this theory in the face of all, before a French court of law; he courageously praised the conspirators, he showed that human obedience was due rather to friendship than to tyrannical laws brought from society's arsenal to meet such and such a case. In Natural Law there are statutes which have never been promulgated, but which are more efficacious than those forged by society. Lucien had disregarded, to his own detriment, the law of solidarity which obliged him to be silent and to let Jacques Collin defend himself; nay, he had brought the charge! In his own interest, that man should, for him, have been and remained Carlos Herrera.

Monsieur Camusot rejoiced in his triumph, he held two guilty men, beneath the hand of the Law he had crushed one of the darlings of fashion, and discovered the undiscoverable Jacques Collin. He would be proclaimed one of the cleverest of examining magistrates. And so he did not harass his prisoner; but he studied that silence of consternation, he watched the drops of sweat on that crumpled face start, grow and finally fall mingled with two streams of tears.

The bludgeon stroke

'WHY weep, Monsieur de Rubempré? you are, as I told you, the sole heir of Mademoiselle Esther, who is without either collateral or direct heirs, and whose estate amounts to almost eight millions, if we can only find the seven hundred and fifty thousand francs which have gone astray.'

This was the final blow to the guilty man. Ten minutes' firm control, as Jacques Collin said in his note, and Lucien would have attained the goal of all his desires! he would have settled up with Jacques Collin, and the two could have separated, he would have been rich, he would have married Mademoiselle de Grandlieu. Nothing displays more eloquently than this scene the power with which examining magistrates are armed by the isolation or by the separation of prisoners, and the value of such a communication as Asia had made to Jacques Collin.

'Ah! sir,' replied Lucien with the bitterness and the irony of the man who makes a pedestal of his crowning misfortune, 'how right you are in your language to speak of *undergoing interrogation*! ... Between the physical torture of olden days and the present day's moral torture, for my part I shouldn't hesitate, I'd prefer the sufferings formerly inflicted by the headsman. What do you still want of me?' he went on proudly.

'In this place,' said the magistrate meeting the poet's sudden arrogance with a haughtiness of his own to which he added a bantering smile, 'only I have the right to put questions.'

'And I had the right not to reply,' murmured poor Lucien whose intelligence had returned to him in all its clarity.

'Clerk, read this interrogation over to the prisoner ...'

'I am still a prisoner!' Lucien said to himself.

While the clerk read, Lucien formed a resolution which obliged him to woo Monsieur Camusot. When the murmur of Coquart's voice came to an end, the poet started as a sleeper may when a noise to which his organs have become accustomed stops.

'You have to sign the report of your interrogation,' said the judge.

'And then you are setting me at liberty?' asked Lucien becoming ironical in his turn.

'Not yet,' replied Camusot; 'but tomorrow, after your confrontation with Jacques Collin, no doubt I shall be able to let you go. The Law still wants to know whether you were or were not an accessory to such crimes as this individual may have committed since his escape, which dates from 1820. However, you are no longer in solitary confinement. I shall write to the governor to put you in the best room he has in the *pistole*.'

'Will it contain writing materials . . . ?'

'You will be provided with whatever you need, I'll send an order to that effect with the usher who will take you back.'

Lucien mechanically signed the transcription, and he initialled the marginal alterations as Coquart directed with all the docility of a resigned victim. A single detail will indicate the state he was in more clearly than any large description. The announcement of his confrontation with Jacques Collin had dried up the drops of sweat on his face, his eyes also dry shone with an insupportable glitter. Suddenly, with the speed of lightning, he became, like Jacques Collin, a man of bronze.

Among those of a character like Lucien, so well analysed by Jacques, these sudden transitions from a state of complete demoralization to one in which the human forces so tauten it is almost metallic, are a distinct phenomenon of the life of thought. The will returns, as water may to a spring; it infuses itself into the constitution prepared for the play of its unknown constitutive substance; and, then, the corpse becomes a man, and the man springs forth full of strength to do battle at whatever cost.

Lucien put Esther's letter to his heart with the portrait she had sent him. Then he bowed curtly to Monsieur Camusot, and walked with a firm step along the corridor between two constables.

'There's a blackguard for you!' said the magistrate to his clerk to avenge himself for the crushing scorn which the poet had just shown him. 'He thought to save himself by giving his accomplice away.'

'Of the two,' said Coquart timidly, 'the convict is of stouter material . . .'

Torture for the judge

'WELL, I can let you go for today, Coquart,' said the magistrate. 'That will do. Send away those who are waiting, they will have to come back tomorrow. Ah! but you'd better go at once to the Attorney General's office to see if he's still there; if he is, ask if he can see me for a moment. Oh! he'll be there,' he went on after consulting a wretched clock of wood painted green with a gilt filigree. 'It is a quarter past three.'

These interrogations, which are so quickly read, being entirely written down, the questions as well as the replies take up an enormous amount of time. This is one of the causes of the slowness of criminal investigations and the length of time which may be spent in preventive detention. For small people, it means ruin, for the rich, it means disgrace; though for them immediate release may largely repair the misfortune of arrest. That is why the two scenes which have just been faithfully recounted had taken up all the time consumed by Asia in deciphering her master's instructions, rousing a duchess out of her boudoir and giving energy to Madame de Sérisy.

At that moment, Camusot, who was thinking of the benefits likely to accrue from his cleverness, took the two reports, read them over and was meaning to show them to the Procurator and ask his further advice. While he was deliberating on this point, his usher returned to say that Madame la Comtesse de Sérisy's personal manservant insisted on speaking to him. At a sign from Camusot, a servant, dressed like one of his betters, entered, looked from usher to magistrate and from magistrate to usher, and said: 'It is indeed to Monsieur Camusot that I have the honour . . .'

'Yes,' replied usher and judge together.

Camusot took a letter handed to him by the domestic, and read what follows:

For a variety of good reasons which you will understand, my dear Camusot, don't question Monsieur de Rubempré; we are bringing you proofs of his innocence, so that he may be immediately set at liberty.

D. DE MAUFRIGNEUSE, L. DE SÉRISY.

P.S. Burn this letter.

Camusot understood that he had committed a gross blunder in setting traps for Lucien, and he began by doing what the two great ladies said. He lighted a candle and destroyed the letter written by the duchess. The manservant bowed respectfully.

'Madame de Sérisy is coming here?' he asked.

'They were bringing the carriage round,' replied the man.

At that moment, Coquart came to tell Monsieur Camusot that the Attorney General was waiting for him.

Weighed down by the mistake he had made in putting the interests of the Law before his private ambition, the magistrate, in whom seven years' practice had developed the cunning which comes easily to any man who has measured himself against shopgirls as a student of Law, felt the need to arm himself against the resentment of the two great ladies. The candle at which he had burnt the letter was still alight, he made use of it to seal the Duchesse de Maufrigneuse' thirty notes to Lucien and the sufficient correspondence of Madame de Sérisy. Then he went to the Attorney General's office.

Monsieur le Procureur-Général

THE Palais de Justice is a confused mass of buildings superimposed one on another, some very splendid, others decidedly shabby, the general effect being spoilt by a lack of any composition among them. The waiting hall is the largest of all known rooms; but its bareness appals and discourages the eyes. This vast cathedral of pettifoggery obliterates what was once a royal court. The Marchande gallery leads to two places of horror. In the vestibule may be seen a double staircase, somewhat broader than that connected with the courts of summary jurisdiction, while folding doors open off the space beneath it. The staircase leads to the Court of Assize, and the door below to a second Court of Assize. There are years when the crimes committed in the Seine department require two courts to be in session at the same time. In that direction lie the Attorney General's office, the barristers' room, their library, the offices of the prosecuting lawyers, those of the Attorney General's substitutes. All these places, for we can only use a generic term, are connected by turret staircases, or by dark corridors which are a disgrace to architecture, to the city of Paris and to France. In its settings, the chief abode of our sovereign justice surpasses the prisons in its hideousness. The chronicler of this time recoils before the necessity of describing the ignoble corridor some four feet wide where the witnesses sit for the upper court of assize. As to the stove which serves to heat the audience chamber, it would do little credit to a bar in the boulevard Montparnasse.

The Attorney General's office is set in an octagonal pavilion which flanks the main body of the Galerie Marchande, on ground recently taken from the prison yard on the side towards the women's quarters. All that part of the Law Courts is overshadowed by the tall and splendid structure of the Sainte Chapelle. Thus it is gloomy and silent.

Monsieur de Granville, worthy successor to the great magistrates of the old High Judicial Court or *Parlement*, had not intended to leave the Palais without a solution to the case of Lucien. He was waiting for news from Camusot, and the judge's message plunged him into that vague meditation which waiting causes even the firmest minds. He was sitting in the window embrasure of his office, he got up, paced this way and that, for that morning he had found Camusot, in whose way he had placed himself, somewhat deficient in understanding, he was full of disquiet, he felt uneasy. This is the reason why. The dignity of his position prevented him interfering in any way with the inferior magistrate's absolute independence, and this case involved the honour, the reputation of his best friend, one of his most zealous protectors, Count Sérisy, minister of State, member of the Privy Council, deputy prime minister, probable future lord chancellor of France, in the event of the death of the noble old man who at present fulfilled those august functions. Monsieur de Sérisy had the misfortune to adore his wife *in spite of all*, his protection extended to her in all she did. The Attorney General could imagine the frightful rumpus which would be caused in society and at Court by the proven culpability of a man whose name had been so often maliciously linked with that of the countess.

'Ah!' he said to himself folding his arms, 'at one time the royal power allowed for the evocation of special cases ... Our mania for equality will be the death of this age ...'

This worthy magistrate knew to what extremes of misfortune an illicit attachment may lead. Esther and Lucien had taken, as we have seen, the apartment in which the Comte de Granville had lived as man and wife secretly with Mademoiselle de Bellefeuille, and from which one fine day she had run away, abducted by the lowest of wretches.

Just as the Procurator was saying to himself: 'Camusot will have done something stupid!' the examining magistrate knocked twice at the door.

'Well! my dear Camusot, how are things going in the matter we talked about this morning?'

'Badly, Monsieur le Comte, read and judge for yourself.'

He handed the two interrogation reports to Monsieur de Granville who picked up his eyeglasses and took them to read by the window. He read them quickly.

'You've done your duty,' said the Attorney General in a troubled voice. 'Everything is out, Justice will run its course ... You have displayed skill of an order which makes it impossible that one should ever dispense with an examining magistrate like yourself ...'

If Monsieur de Granville had said to Camusot: 'You will be an examining magistrate all your life! ...' he could hardly have been more explicit than he was in this apparent compliment. Camusot felt his blood run cold.

'Madame la Duchesse de Maufrigneuse, to whom I owe so much, had begged me ...'

'Ah! the Duchesse de Maufrigneuse,' said Granville inter-rupting the judge, 'it is true, yes, she is a friend of Madame de Sérisy's. You did not yield to any influence, I can see. You did right; sir, you are a shining light in your profession.'

Is it too late?

AT that moment, Count Octave de Bauvan opened the door without knocking, and said to Count Granville: 'My friend, I've brought you a pretty woman who didn't know where to make for, she'd have lost herself in this labyrinth of ours . . .'

And Count Octave was holding by the hand Countess Sérisy who, for the past quarter of an hour, had been wander-ing about the Palais.

'You here, Madame,' exclaimed the Attorney General bring-ing his own armchair forward, 'and at what a moment! . . . This is Monsieur Camusot, Madame,' he added indicating the judge. 'Bauvan', he went on addressing this celebrated govern-ment spokesman of the Restoration, 'wait for me in the Recorder's office, he's still there, I'll join you presently.'

Count Octave de Bauvan understood not only that he wasn't wanted, but also that the Attorney General would be needing an excuse to leave his office.

Madame de Sérisy had not made the mistake of coming to the Law Courts in her magnificent brougham with its blue armorial mantling, its gold-laced coachman and its two foot-men in short breeches and white silk stockings. At the moment of setting out, Asia had made the two great ladies understand that they should go by the hired carriage in which she had come with the duchess; moreover, she had made Lucien's mistress wear that costume which is, for women, what the sombre cloak once was for men. The countess wore a brown overcoat, an old black shawl and a plush hat from which the flowers had been removed and replaced by a veil of thick black lace.

'You received our letter . . .' she said to Camusot whose stupefaction was taken by her as a sign of admiring respect.

'Too late, alas, Madame la Comtesse,' replied the magistrate whose displays of tact and wit were reserved for prisoners in his office.

'How do you mean, too late? . . .'

She looked at Monsieur de Granville and saw the consternation written on his face.

'It cannot, it must not be too late yet,' she added with the intonation of a despot.

What women do in Paris

WOMEN, pretty women of position, such as Madame de Sérisy, are the spoilt children of French civilization. If the women of other countries knew what a fashionable, rich and titled woman is in Paris, they would all think of coming and taking advantage of this splendid queenliness. Women dedicated only to the ties of their position, to that collection of petty laws which we have elsewhere called the Female Code, care little for the laws of men. They say whatever they please, they do not shrink from any fault, any piece of stupidity; for they all know with admirable certainty that they are not responsible for anything in life, except their feminine honour and their children. They utter the greatest enormities with a laugh. In whatever connection, they are likely to repeat what pretty Madame de Bauvan said in the early days of her marriage to her husband whom she had come to see at the Law Courts: 'Finish judging that case, and come along!'

'Madame,' said the Attorney General, 'Monsieur Lucien de Rubempré is guilty neither of theft, nor of poisoning; but Monsieur Camusot has made him admit a crime greater than either of those! . . .'

'What?' she asked.

'He has confessed,' the Procurator said to her in an undertone, 'to being the friend and pupil of an escaped convict. The abbé Carlos Herrera, the Spaniard with whom he's been living for the past seven years, turns out to be the famous Jacques Collin . . .'

Every word the head of the magistracy spoke was like a blow with an iron bar to Madame de Sérisy; but this notorious name was the last stroke.

'And the moral in all this?...' she said in a voice which was a mere breath.

'Is,' went on Monsieur de Granville finishing the countess's sentence for her and speaking in a low voice, 'that the convict will appear at assizes, and that if Lucien doesn't figure beside him as having profited knowingly from this man's crimes, he will be there as a witness who is gravely compromised...'

'Never, never!...' she cried out with a remarkable steadiness of purpose. 'For myself, I should not hesitate between death and the prospect of seeing a man whom everyone knew as my best friend, proclaimed at law the intimate of a convict ... The King is very fond of my husband.'

'Madame,' the Attorney General said distinctly with a smile, 'the King is without the slightest authority over the least examining magistrate in his kingdom or over the deliberations of a Court of Assize. Therein lies the greatness of our new institutions. For myself, I have just congratulated Monsieur Camusot on the ability he has shown...'

'His clumsiness,' briskly rejoined the countess whom Lucien's intimacy with a brigand disturbed far less than his liaison with Esther.

'If you were to read the interrogations Monsieur Camusot caused the two prisoners to undergo, you would see that all depends on him...'

After that statement, which was as far as the Attorney General could allow himself to go, and with a glance of feminine or, if you like, judicial nicety, he walked towards the door of his office. Turning at the threshold, he added: 'Excuse me, Madame! I have a few words to say to Bauvan...'

In the language of society, what that meant for the countess was: 'I can't be a witness to what transpires between you and Camusot.'

'WHAT are these interrogation reports?' then said Léontine sweetly to Camusot who stood sheepishly before the wife of one of the most important men in the country.

'Madame,' replied Camusot, 'a clerk puts down in writing the examining magistrate's questions and the replies of the prisoners, the report is signed by the clerk, the judge and the prisoner. These reports form the basis of proceedings, they determine the nature of the indictment and the appearance of accused persons before the Court of Assize.'

'Why, then,' she continued, 'if one simply destroyed them? . . .'

'Ah! Madame, that would be a crime which no magistrate would dare commit, a crime against society!'

'It's a far greater crime against me to have written them; and, at the moment, this is the only proof against Lucien. Look, read me his report so that we can see whether means cannot be found to save us all. Good God, it doesn't only concern me, who would deliberately take my own life, but also the happiness of Monsieur de Sérisy.'

'Madame,' said Camusot, 'do not imagine that I forgot the consideration I owed you. If Monsieur Popinot, for example, had been in charge of this inquiry, you would have been more unhappy than you are with me; for he wouldn't have come to consult the Attorney General. Nothing would have been known. But see, Madame, everything was impounded at Monsieur Lucien's domicile, even your letters . . .'

'Really! my letters!'

'Here they are, under seal . . .' said the magistrate.

The countess, though troubled, rang as if she'd been at home, and the Procurator's office messenger entered.

'Light,' she said.

The messenger lighted a candle and placed it on the chimney-piece, while the countess identified her letters, counted them, screwed them up and threw them into the fireplace. She then set fire to the heap of paper twisting the last letter and using it as a torch. Camusot stupidly watched the papers burn holding the two records in his hand. The countess, who appeared to be solely occupied with destroying the proofs of her affection, observed the judge from the corner of her eye. She took her time, calculated her movements, and, with the agility of a cat, seized the two documents and cast them into the fire; but Camusot snatched them out, the countess flung herself upon the judge and recaptured the scorched papers. There followed a struggle during which Camusot cried: 'Madame! Madame! you are attacking the very foundations ... Madame ...'

A man appeared suddenly in the office, and the countess could not hold back a cry on recognizing Count Sérisy, followed by Messieurs de Granville and de Bauvan. Nevertheless, Léontine, who meant to save Lucien at all costs, did not let go the fearful stamped paper which she held as if with pincers, although the flames were already singeing her delicate skin. In the end, Camusot, whose own fingers were equally affected by the fire, seemed to be ashamed of the situation, he abandoned the documents; there remained only those fragments, clutched in the hands of the two fighters, which the fire had not caught. The whole scene was over in less time than it takes to read this account of it.

Present laughter

'WHATEVER is the matter between you and Madame de Sérisy?' the minister of State asked Camusot.

Before the magistrate could reply, the countess took the remaining papers to the candle and threw them on to those fragments of her letters which the fire had not yet entirely consumed.

'I shall have to lodge a complaint against Madame la Comtesse,' said Camusot.

'And what has she done?' asked the Attorney General looking from one to the other.

'I burned his interrogatories,' laughingly replied the woman of fashion so pleased with the results of her sudden action that she did not yet feel her burns. 'If that is a crime, why then! the gentleman can begin his frightful scribbling all over again.'

'That is true,' replied Camusot attempting to regain his dignity.

'And so everything has turned out for the best,' said the Attorney General. 'Only, dear countess, you musn't often take liberties of that kind with the magistracy, it might forget who you are.'

'Monsieur Camusot put up a stout resistance against a woman whom nobody can resist, the honour of the robe is saved!' said Count Bauvan with a laugh.

'Ah! Monsieur Camusot resisted? . . .' said the Procurator laughing also. 'That was brave of him, I should never dare resist the countess!'

At that moment, this serious misdemeanour became a pretty woman's joke, and even Camusot laughed.

The Attorney General then perceived that one of the company did not laugh. Justifiably alarmed by the attitude and physiognomy of Count Sérisy, Monsieur de Granville took him on one side.

'My friend,' he whispered, 'this is so painful for you that for the first and last time in my life I shall compromise with my duty.'

The chief magistrate rang, his office messenger came.

'Tell Monsieur de Chargeboeuf to come and speak to me.'

Monsieur de Chargeboeuf, a young advocate serving his three years' probation, was the Attorney General's secretary.

'My dear fellow,' continued the Procurator drawing Camusot towards the window, 'go back to your office, call a clerk and reconstitute the interrogation of Father Carlos Herrera which, as it wasn't signed, may be drawn up again without inconvenience. Tomorrow you'll be confronting this *Spanish diplomatist* with Messieurs de Rastignac and Bianchon, who won't identify him as our Jacques Collin. Sure of being set at liberty, the man will then sign both reports. As for Lucien de Rubempré, let him go this evening, he won't be the one to speak of an interrogation whose record has been destroyed, especially after I've admonished him. The *Gazette des Tribunaux* will announce in the morning that this young man has been immediately released. Let us think now whether the Law suffers in any way from these measures? If the Spaniard is the convict, we have innumerable ways of bringing him in again, and starting a case against him, for we shall use diplomatic channels to find out what he was up to in Spain; Corentin, the head of counter-espionage, will look after him, we shall keep him in sight at all costs; so treat him well, no more solitary confinement, have him transferred to the *pistole* tonight ... Are we going to kill the count, the countess de Sérisy and Lucien for the theft of seven hundred and fifty thousand francs, still pure hypothesis and committed to Lucien's detriment? wouldn't it be better to let him lose this sum than to destroy his reputation? ... especially since his downfall would also bring down a minister of State, his wife and the Duchesse de Maufrigneuse ... That young man is a bruised orange, don't let him go rotten ... This will only take you half an hour. Be off, we're waiting for you. It is half past three, you will still find judges around, let them know if you can get the matter formally non-suited ..., or Lucien will have to be kept here until morning.'

Camusot bowed and went out; but Madame de Sérisy, who was by now feeling the effects of the fire, did not return his salute. Monsieur de Sérisy, who had left the office suddenly while the Procurator was speaking to the inferior magistrate, came back with a small pot of virgin wax, and dressed his wife's hands saying in her ear: 'Léontine, why come here without letting me know?'

'My poor friend!' she whispered in reply, 'forgive me, I must seem out of my mind; but it concerned you as much as me.'

'Love this young man, if fate decrees, but don't display your passion so clearly to everyone,' replied the poor husband.

'Come, my dear countess,' said Monsieur de Granville after speaking for a while with Count Octave, 'I hope you'll be able to take Monsieur de Rubempré home to dine with you this evening.'

This half-promise so affected Madame de Sérisy that she burst into tears.

'I thought I had no tears left,' she said with a smile.

'Couldn't you,' she went on, 'have Monsieur de Rubempré come and wait here? . . .'

'I'll see if I can find ushers to fetch him, so that he needn't be accompanied by constables,' replied Monsieur de Granville.

'You show God's own kindness!' she said to the Attorney General with an effusiveness which made her voice sound like celestial music.

'Women like that,' Count Octave said to himself, 'are truly delightful, irresistible! . . .'

And his mind filled with melancholy as he thought of his wife.

On his way out, Monsieur de Granville was stopped by young Chargeboeuf, to whom he paused to give instructions as to what he should say to Massol, one of the editors of the *Gazette des Tribunaux*.

In which the dandy and the poet are reunited

WHILE pretty women, ministers, magistrates all conspired to save Lucien, this was his behaviour at the Conciergerie. Passing through the wicket, the poet had said at the record-office that Monsieur Camusot allowed him to write, and he asked for pens, ink and paper, which a warder was at once ordered to take to him on a whispered word from Camusot's usher to the governor. During the short time the warder spent in procuring and conveying to Lucien's quarters what he was waiting for, the poor young man, to whom the idea of a confrontation with Jacques Collin was insupportable, fell into one of those fits of fateful meditation in which the idea of suicide, to which he had once already yielded without being able to accomplish it, reach manic proportions. According to certain medical *alienists*, suicide, in some constitutions, is the culminating point of a mental alienation; since his arrest, it had become a fixed idea with Lucien. Esther's letter, read through several times again, augmented the intensity of his wish to die, reminding him of the tragedy of Romeo uniting himself with Juliet. Here is what he wrote.

At the Conciergerie, this fifteenth of May 1830.

I the undersigned give and bequeath to the children of my sister, Madame Ève Chardon, wife of David Séchard, former printer in Angoulême, and of Monsieur David Séchard, the totality of goods and lands belonging to me on the day of my death, after deduction of the payments and bequests which I beg the executor of this will and testament to make.

I request Monsieur de Sérisy to act as the executor of this will.

Shall be paid, first, to Monsieur l'Abbé Carlos Herrera the sum of three hundred thousand francs and, second, to Monsieur le Baron de Nucingen, that of fourteen hundred thousand francs which shall be reduced by seven hundred and fifty thousand francs, if the amounts removed from Mademoiselle Esther's premises are recovered.

I give and bequeath, as heir to Mademoiselle Esther Gobseck, the sum of seven hundred and fifty thousand francs to the charitable institutions of Paris to found a home specifically devoted to registered prostitutes who wish to give up their career of vice and perdition.

I further bequeath to these institutions the sum necessary for the purchase of annual income to the amount of thirty thousand francs at five per cent. The annual interest to be employed, at the end of each half year, to freeing those imprisoned for debt, whose indebtedness shall amount to two thousand francs at most. The governing bodies of these charities shall select the most deserving of those imprisoned for debt.

I beg Monsieur de Sérisy to devote a sum of forty thousand francs to the erection of a monument to Esther in the Eastern cemetery, and I wish to be buried with her. This tomb shall be constructed like the tombs of earlier days, it shall be square; our two effigies in white marble shall lie on top, the heads resting on cushions, the hands joined and raised to heaven. This tomb shall bear no inscription.

I further beg Monsieur le Comte de Sérisy to convey to Monsieur Eugène de Rastignac the gold toilet service at my abode, to remember me by.

Finally, for the same purpose, I beg the executor of my last will to accept the gift I make him of my library.

LUCIEN CHARDON DE RUBEMPRÉ.

This will was enclosed with a letter addressed to Monsieur le Comte de Granville, Attorney General of the Royal Court of Paris, thus conceived:

MONSIEUR LE COMTE,

I entrust my last will to you. When you open this letter, I shall no longer be numbered among the living. From a desire to regain my liberty, I answered Monsieur Camusot's captious questions in so cowardly a fashion, that, despite my innocence, I should be implicated in a degrading court case. Even if I were acquitted, without censure, life would still be made impossible for me, by the susceptibilities of society.

Convey, I beg you, the letter enclosed herewith to Father Carlos Herrera unopened, and to Monsieur Camusot the formal retractation also enclosed.

I do not suppose that anybody would dare break the seal of a packet addressed to you. Confident that this is so, I say farewell to you, paying you herewith my last respects and begging you to believe that in writing to you I testify to my gratitude for all the kindness you have shown your defunct servant.

LUCIEN DE R.

TO THE ABBÉ CARLOS HERRERA

My dear abbé, I have received nothing but benefits from you, and I have betrayed you. This unintended ingratitude must be my death, and so, when you read these lines, I shall no longer exist; you will not be there to save me this time.

You freely gave me the right to cast you off whenever it suited me, flinging you to the ground like a cigar butt, but I found another and totally senseless way of bringing about your ruin. To free myself from an awkward situation, taken in by the clever question of an examining magistrate, your spiritual son, he whom you adopted, allied himself with those who would murder you at any cost, by establishing an identity, which I know to be impossible, between you and a French criminal. Need I say more?

Between a man of power like yours and myself, of whom you tried to make a greater figure than I had it in me to be, there can be no silliness exchanged at the moment of final separation. You wished to make me powerful and glorious, you have flung me into the pit of suicide, that is all. I have seen this giddiness approaching for a long time.

As you once said, there is the posterity of Cain and that of Abel. Cain, in the great drama of Humanity, is the opposition. You descend from Adam by this line in which the devil still blows on that fire whose first spark was struck in Eve. Among that demonic progeny, there appear from time to time, terribly, one or two of massive constitution, who sum up in themselves all human energy, and who are like those feverish animals of the wilderness whose form of life calls for the vast spaces they find there. People like that are dangerous in society as lions would be in the heart of Normandy: they must feed on something, they devour common men and browse on the money of fools; their play is so perilous that they end by killing the humble dog they have made a companion of, an idol even. When God chooses, such mysterious beings may be Moses, Attila, Charlemagne, Mahomet or Napoleon; but when He allows these giant instruments to rust on the sea-bottom of a generation, they become only Pugatcheff, Robespierre, Louvel and Father Carlos Herrera. Endowed with power over tender souls, these are drawn to them and ground small. In its own way, the spectacle is great and beautiful. It is that of a brightly coloured poison plant which fascinates children in the woods. It is the poetry of evil. Men like you should dwell in caves and never come out. You made me live with your giant's life, and I have paid for it with my very existence. So I take my head out of the Gordian knot of politics and give it to the slip-knot I have tied in my cravat.

To make amends for my fault, I am sending the Attorney General a formal retractation of all that I said at my interrogation; you will know how to turn this document to your advantage.

According to the provisions of a will drawn up in due form, you will receive back, Monsieur l'Abbé, the sums belonging to your Order which you so imprudently laid out on my behalf, in consequence of the paternal tenderness you bore me.

Farewell, then, farewell, mighty monument of evil and corruption, farewell, you who, set in the right road, could have been greater than Jiménez or Richelieu; you kept your promises: I am become again what I was on the banks of the Charente, after owing to you the dream and its enchantment; but, alas, it is not now the river of my own countryside where I was going to drown the petty transgressions of my youth; but the Seine, and the deep pool I chose is a dark cell in the Conciergerie.

Don't feel regret for me; my contempt for you was no less than my admiration.

LUCIEN.

I the undersigned hereby declare that I totally retract what is contained in the report of the interrogation to which Monsieur Camusot subjected me today.

Abbé Carlos Herrera commonly described himself as my spiritual father, and I must have been misled by the examining magistrate taking this word in another sense, doubtless without intention.

I know that, for political ends and in order to annul secret information concerning government inner circles at the Tuileries and in Spain, certain agents of diplomacy are trying to establish an identity between Father Carlos Herrera and a convict by the name of Jacques Collin; but Father Carlos Herrera's confidential disclosures to me on this point have had to do solely with his efforts to obtain proof either of the demise or of the continued existence of Jacques Collin.

From the Conciergerie, this 15th May, 1830.

LUCIEN DE RUBEMPRÉ.

The difficulty of committing suicide in prison

THE fever of suicide communicated to Lucien a great lucidity of mind and that manual activity which authors know when they are a prey to the fever of composition. This state of feeling was so strong in him that these four documents were written in the space of half an hour. He put them together in one packet, closed it with sealing wafers, stamped these forcibly with his arms by means of a signet ring he wore on his finger, and placed it in a prominent position in the middle of the floor, on the tiles. Certainly, it would have been difficult to behave with greater dignity in the false position in which so much infamy had put Lucien: he was preserving his memory from disgrace, and he was repairing the harm done to his accomplice, in so far as the wit of a dandy could cancel the results of a poet's trustfulness.

If Lucien had been in one of the solitary-confinement cells, he would have come up against the impossibility of there executing his design, for the only furniture in those freestone boxes is a sort of camp or guardroom bed and a bucket for imperative natural needs. There is no chair or stool, nor even a nail in the wall. The bed is so firmly fixed to the floor that it cannot be moved without a labour which would be bound to be observed by a warder, for the iron-framed spy-hole is always open. Moreover, when a prisoner's behaviour is considered uncertain, he is kept under observation by a member of the armed constabulary or other policeman. In the rooms in the *pistole* and specifically in that to which Lucien had been transferred on account of the consideration the examining magistrate felt impelled to show a young man belonging to Parisian high society, the moveable bed, the table and chair, may help the occupant to commit suicide, though not without some difficulty. Lucien wore a long blue silk stock; and, at the time of his return from questioning, he was already thinking of the manner in which Pichegru had, more or less voluntarily, ended his life. But in order to hang oneself it is necessary to find a point of support and sufficient space between the body and the ground for the feet not to rest on anything. Now, the window of his cell overlooking the prison yard had no hasp, and the iron bars fixed outside were separated from Lucien by the thickness of the wall, not allowing him to find his point of support there.

This is the plan which Lucien's inventive faculty quickly suggested to him as a means of accomplishing his suicide. If the hood attached to the bay prevented Lucien looking out on the prison yard, this hood equally prevented the warders from seeing what took place in his cell; now, although in the lower part of the window frame the glass had been replaced by two stout boards, the upper part contained, in each half, small panes separated and held in place by the cross-pieces which are proper to such glazing. By standing on the table Lucien could reach the glazed part of his window, remove two panes or break them, in such a way as to lay bare at the corner of the first cross-bar a solid point of support. He proposed to pass his neck-tie through at that point, to turn round so as to tighten it about his neck, after having knotted it securely, and then to kick the table away.

To this end, he moved the table close to the window without making a noise, he took off his frock coat and waistcoat, then he climbed on to the table and unhesitatingly made holes in the glass above and below the first slat. Once on the table, he could see down into the prison yard, a magic spectacle which he glimpsed for the first time. The governor of the Conciergerie, having received Monsieur Camusot's recommendation to show Lucien the greatest consideration, had caused him, as we have seen, to be led through the Conciergerie's interior passages by way of an entrance below street level opposite the Tour d'Argent, thus avoiding showing an elegant young man to the crowd of prisoners who walk about in the yard. We may judge whether the aspect of that place of exercise is of such a sort as to capture the lively attention of a poet.

Hallucination

THE prison yard of the Conciergerie is bounded on the embankment by the Tour d'Argent and the Tour Bonbec; the distance between these two exactly marks from outside the breadth of the yard. The long gallery, the one called after Saint Louis, which leads from the Galerie Normande to the Central Court of Appeal and the Tour Bonbec, in which, it is said, Saint Louis's study may still be seen, will show the visitor the length of the prison yard, for it covers the same extent of ground. The solitary confinement cells and the *pistoles* lie beneath the Galerie Marchande. On her way to appear before the revolutionary tribunal, which held its sessions in what is now the solemn audience chamber of the Central Court of Appeal or Court of Cassation, Queen Marie-Antoinette, whose dungeon lay under the present solitary cells, was taken up a fearsome staircase built into the thickness of the walls which sustain the Galerie Marchande, and which is now condemned. One side of the yard, along the first floor of which runs the Galerie de Saint Louis, presents to the eyes a succession of Gothic pillars between which the architects of I know not what epoch constructed two tiers of cells to house as many prisoners as possible, clogging up with plaster, grill and foundation blocks the shafts and ogees of this magnificent cloister. Below the supposed study of Saint Louis in the Tour Bonbec, a spiral staircase leads to these cells. This prostitution of one of the most glorious memorials of France is hideous in its effect.

At the height at which Lucien stood, he was looking slant-wise along this gallery and took in the details of the building between the Tour d'Argent and the Tour Bonbec, whose pointed turrets he could see. He stood astounded, his suicide delayed by a sense of wonder. Today the phenomena of hallucination are admitted by the science of medicine, and this mirage of our senses, this strange faculty of our mind, is no longer contested. Under the pressure of a feeling brought to the point of monomania by its intensity, a man often finds himself in the state produced by opium, hashish and nitrous oxide. Then appear spectres, phantoms, then dreams take on bodily form, things vanished revive in their pristine condition. That which in the brain was a mere idea becomes a living, animate creature or creation. Science has now begun to suppose that, under the influence of passions in a state of paroxysm, the brain is injected with blood, and that this congestion produces the terrifying play of waking dreams, so reluctant are scientists to regard thought as a living and generating force. Lucien saw the Palais in all its primitive beauty. The colonnade was slender, young, fresh. The abode of Saint Louis reappeared as it had once been, he marvelled at its Babylonian proportions and oriental fancies. He accepted this sublime vision as a poetic farewell to the created world of civilization. Taking measures intended to result in his death, he wondered how it was possible for this marvel to exist unknown in Paris. He was two Luciens, the Lucien who was a poet abroad in the Middle Ages, under the archways and turrets of Saint Louis, and the Lucien preparing to kill himself.

AT the moment when Monsieur de Granville finished giving instructions to his young secretary, the governor of the Conciergerie appeared, the expression on his face was such that the Attorney General had a foreboding of misfortune.

'Did you meet Monsieur Camusot?' he asked.

'No, sir,' replied the governor. 'His clerk Coquart told me to release Father Carlos from solitary confinement and to set Monsieur de Rubempré at liberty, but it is too late . . .'

'Good God! what has happened?'

'Here, sir,' said the governor, 'is a packet of letters for you which should explain the catastrophe. A warder in the prison yard heard the sound of windows breaking, in the *pistole*, and Monsieur Lucien's neighbour started shouting at the top of his voice, for he could hear the death agony of the poor young man. The warder returned pale from the sight which met his eyes, he saw the prisoner hanging from the window by his neck-tie . . .'

Although the governor spoke in an undertone, the terrible cry which Madame de Sérisy uttered proved that, in exceptional circumstances, our organs develop an incalculable power. The countess heard or guessed; and, before Monsieur de Granville could turn round, without either Monsieur de Sérisy or Monsieur de Bauvan being able to check movements so quickly made, she was off like a shot, through the door, and reached the Galerie Marchande along which she ran to the head of the staircase which descends to the rue de la Barillerie.

A barrister was handing in his gown at the door of one of the shops which for so long encumbered that street, where shoes were sold and where gowns and caps could be hired. The countess asked him the way to the Conciergerie.

'Along there and turn to the left, the entrance is in the Quai de l'Horloge, first archway.'

'That woman is out of her mind . . .' said the woman who kept the shop, 'she ought to be followed.'

Nobody could have followed Léontine, she flew. A doctor

might explain how society women, whose strength goes unemployed, are able to draw on such resources in moments of crisis. The countess dashed through the arcade towards the wicket so fast that the constable on sentry duty did not see her go in. She was swept against the grating like a feather in a gale, she shook the iron bars with such fury that she tore out the one she had seized. She struck her breast with the broken fragments, blood spurted, and she fell crying: 'Open! open!' in a voice which froze the warders.

The turnkey ran up.

'Open! I've been sent by the Attorney General, *to save the dead man!* . . .'

While the countess was on her way round by the rue de la Barillerie and the Quai de l'Horloge, Monsieur de Granville and Monsieur de Sérisy went down to the Conciergerie through the interior of the Palais divining the countess's purpose; but, in spite of their haste, they arrived only as she fell fainting at the first grill, and was lifted up by constables from the guardroom. At sight of the governor of the Conciergerie, the wicket was opened, the countess was carried into the record-office; but she pulled herself up, and fell on her knees with her hands joined.

'To see him! . . . only to see him! . . . Oh! gentlemen, I shan't do any harm! but unless you want to see me die where I am . . . let me look at Lucien, dead or alive . . . Ah! there you are, my friend, choose between my death or . . .' She sank down.

'You are very kind,' she continued, 'I will love you! . . .'

'Take her away? . . .' said Monsieur de Bauvan.

'No, let's go to the cell where Lucien is!' Monsieur Granville answered reading in Monsieur de Sérisy's distracted eyes what his wishes were.

And he took hold of the countess, raised her up, held her by one arm; while Monsieur de Bauvan held her by the other.

'Sir!' said Monsieur de Sérisy to the governor, 'the silence of the grave about all this.'

'There's no need to worry,' replied the governor. 'You've chosen the right course. This lady . . .'

'She is my wife . . .'

'Ah! forgive me, sir. Well! she will certainly faint at sight of the young man, and while she's in a swoon she can be taken away in a carriage.'

'That's what I thought,' said the count, 'send one of your men to tell my people, in the Cour de Harlay, to come round to the wicket, my carriage is the only one there . . .'

'We can save him,' said the countess walking forward with a courage and a strength which astonished the guards. 'There are ways of bringing people back to life . . .' And she dragged the two magistrates with her crying out to the warder: 'Faster, hurry, every second may mean the lives of three people!'

When the cell door had been opened, and the countess saw Lucien hanging as though his garments had been placed on a coat-hook, at first she sprang forward to kiss and enfold him; but she fell face down on the tiled floor, uttering cries that were stifled by a kind of dying gasp. Five minutes later, she was taken home in the count's carriage and laid on cushions, her husband on his knees beside her. Count Bauvan had gone off for a doctor to bring the countess first aid.

A tactful conclusion

THE governor of the Conciergerie examined the outer grating of the wicket, and said to his clerk: 'Nothing was spared! the bars were of wrought iron, they were tried, it was all very costly, and now it turns out there was a cleft in that bar? . . .'

The Attorney General, back in his office, was obliged to give new instructions to his secretary.

Luckily, Massol hadn't appeared yet.

A few moments after Monsieur de Granville had left to hurry round to Monsieur de Sérisy's, Massol arrived and found Chargeboeuf in the Attorney General's office.

'Ah, there you are,' said the young secretary, 'if you'd be so kind, perhaps I could dictate something to you and you'd put it in tomorrow's issue of your *Gazette*, in the column for News from the Law Courts; head it as please.'

'Right you are!'

And he dictated the following:

It is recognized that the Demoiselle Esther voluntarily took her own life.

Monsieur Lucien de Rubempré's arrest is all the more to be deplored in that he died suddenly while the examining magistrate was making out an order for his release, his alibi having been confirmed and his innocence established.

'There is no need, I imagine, my friend,' said the young probationer to Massol, 'to recommend the greatest discretion about the small service which is being asked of you.'

'Since you do me the honour of taking me into your confidence, I shall take the liberty,' replied Massol, 'of venturing a comment. This note will give rise to observations uncomplimentary to the Courts . . .'

'No doubt we shall survive them,' rejoined the young man attached to the Attorney General's office, with the arrogance of a future magistrate trained by Monsieur de Granville himself.

'Allow me, sweetheart, a couple of sentences will straighten that out,' said the man trained to the other side of the bar.

And he wrote:

This sad event is unrelated to the processes of Law. An immediate autopsy demonstrated that death was due to the rupture of an aneurism in its last stages. If Monsieur Lucien de Rubempré had been upset by his arrest, death would have ensued at an earlier stage. Indeed, we believe ourselves able to affirm that, far from being worried by his arrest, this regrettable young man laughed noisily and said to those who accompanied him from Fontainebleau to Paris that his innocence would become evident as soon as he had seen the examining magistrate.

'That puts it in perspective, doesn't it? . . .' the barrister-journalist inquired with an air of no less innocence.

'You are right, _maître_.'

'The Attorney General will be very pleased with you in the morning,' said Massol craftily.

Thus, as we see, the greatest events of life are translated into little Paris news items bearing some relation to the truth. It is the same with things on a far greater scale than this.

But even now, for the greater number, as indeed for the more select reader, this Study may perhaps seem not entirely to be completed by the deaths of Esther and Lucien; perhaps Jacques Collin, Asia, Europe and Paccard, despite the infamy of their lives, may be thought sufficiently interesting for us to want to know what became of them. This last act of the drama may further serve to round out our portrayal of the customs of the time and disentangle those interests which Lucien's life had so strangely brought together, mingling some of the most ignoble figures of the Underworld with others drawn from the very highest spheres.

PART FOUR

THE LAST INCARNATION OF VAUTRIN

'WHAT is the matter, Madeleine?' said Madame Camusot seeing her maid enter with the air which servants know how to adopt in critical situations.

'Madame,' replied Madeleine, 'Monsieur is just back from the Palais; but he looks so upset, really, he's in such a state, that Madame might do well to go and see him in his study.'

'Is he ill?' asked Madame Camusot.

'No, Madame; but we've never seen Monsieur with such a face, I think he may be sickening for something; he looks yellow, as if he was falling to pieces, and . . .'

Without waiting for the end of the sentence, Madame Camusot rushed out of the room and ran to her husband. She saw the examining magistrate sitting in an armchair, his legs stretched out, his head leaning back, hands hanging down, face pale, eyes vacant, absolutely as though about to pass out.

'What's the matter, my dear?' said the worried young wife.

'Ah! my poor Amélie, the most frightful thing has happened . . . I am still all of a tremble. Just think, the Attorney General, . . . no, Madame de Sérisy . . . I, . . . I don't know where to begin . . .'

'Begin at the end! . . .' said Madame Camusot.

'Yes, well, just as Monsieur Popinot, in the summary jurisdiction council chamber, had appended a final signature at the bottom of the nonsuit made out on my report discharging Lucien de Rubempré . . . At any rate, that was complete! the clerk was taking the minute-book away; I should have been quit of the whole affair . . . The chairman of the tribunal comes in and casts a cold eye on the bill and laughs a mocking laugh and says:

' "You're ordering the release of a dead man. The young fellow, as M. de Bonald puts it, must now appear before his natural judge. He has succumbed to a fatal seizure . . ."

'I breathed again, supposing that there had been an accident.

411

' "If I understand you, Mr Chairman," said Monsieur Popinot, "it must be a case of Pichegru's apoplexy . . ."

' "Gentlemen," the chairman went on with a solemn air, "you had better understand that, for public consumption, young Lucien de Rubempré died of a ruptured aneurism."

'We all looked at each other.

' "Important persons are mixed up with this deplorable affair," said the chairman. "May it please God, Monsieur Camusot, for your sake, though of course you have done nothing but your duty, that Madame de Sérisy shall not stay out of her mind as a result of the blow she has received! they have carried her out as though dead. Just now I met our dear Attorney General in a state of despair which really upset me. You boobed a bit, my dear Camusot!" he added in a private whisper to me.

'No, I must say, my dearest, on my way out, I found it difficult to walk. My legs were so shaky, that I simply daren't venture out into the street, I went back to my office to sit down. Coquart, who was putting the documents on this wretched case in order, told me that a fine lady had taken the Conciergerie by assault, that she'd hoped to save the life of Lucien with whom she was madly in love, and that she fainted on finding him hanged by his necktie from the window of his cell. The thought of the manner in which I questioned this unfortunate young man, who, as a matter of fact, between ourselves, was entirely guilty, has pursued me ever since I left the Law Courts, and I'm still very near fainting myself . . .'

'What, you mean you think you're a murderer, because a prisoner hangs himself in gaol just as you were going to discharge him? . . .' cried Madame Camusot. 'Why, in a case like that, an examining magistrate is like a general who has a horse shot under him! . . . That's all.'

'Comparisons like that, my dear, are at best good for a joke, and joking is out of place as things are. The quick and the dead have reversed roles in this instance. Lucien takes our hopes with him into the tomb.'

'Truly? . . .' said Madame Camusot in a tone of profound irony.

'Yes, my career is finished. For the rest of my life I shall be nothing more than a simple magistrate on the Seine bench. Even before its fatal outcome, Monsieur de Granville was somewhat discontented with the turn the inquiry was taking; what he said to our chairman made it quite clear that, while he remains at the head of Prosecutions, there will be no promotion for me.'

Promotion! that is the dread word now, the obsession which turns a magistrate into a civil servant.

Formerly to be a magistrate was itself sufficient. Three or four High Court presidential caps were all that the ambitious could expect under any one government. To be named councillor was enough for a de Brosses or a Molé, at Dijon no less than in Paris. Such a jurisdiction, a fortune in itself, required a private fortune in its holder. In Paris, outside Parliament, the gentlemen of the robe could aspire to no more than three superior modes of existence: as inspector general, at Seals and in chancery. Outside parliament, at a lower level, the incumbent of a presidial was a person of sufficient importance to keep him happy on his bench for a lifetime. Compare the position of a councillor at the royal court of Paris in 1829, who had nothing but his salary to live on, with a parliamentary councillor in 1729. Great is the difference! In modern times, when money is the sole guarantee of social position, magistrates don't, as formerly, need to be men of fortune; so they become deputies, peers of France, piling one form of magistracy on another, judges and legislators at the same time, borrowing importance from positions other than the one in which they ought to shine.

In short, magistrates think to distinguish themselves through promotion, as others do in the army or the civil service.

This thought, even if it does not weaken the independence of the magistrate, is too widely known and too understandably common, its effect too clearly visible, for the magistracy not to lose in majesty before the public gaze. The salaries paid by the State make the priest and the magistrate its employees. The grades to be scaled develop ambition; ambition engenders a subservience to power; modern equalitarianism then places the ordinary man and the judge on the same social footing. The two pillars of social order, Religion and the Law, are thus diminished in the nineteenth century, where the notion of progress takes precedence over all else.

'What's to stop you gaining promotion?' said Amélie Camusot.

She looked at her husband with a mocking air, feeling the need to restore energy to the man upon whom her own ambition rested, and upon whom she played as on an instrument.

'Why despair so easily?' she went on with a gesture which vividly depicted her lack of interest in the death of a prisoner. 'That suicide will please two women who are Lucien's enemies, Madame d'Espard and her cousin, Countess Châtelet. Madame d'Espard is on the best of terms with the Keeper of the Seals; and, through her, you will be able to obtain an audience of His Highness, at which you can tell him the inwardness of this matter. Once the Minister of Justice is on your side, what have you to fear from your chairman or the Procurator?'

'But what about Monsieur and Madame de Sérisy! ...' cried the poor magistrate. 'Madame de Sérisy, I tell you, is out of her mind! and she has been driven out of her mind by me, or so they say!'

'Well, if she's mad, she can't judge, can she?' cried Madame Camusot laughing, 'so she can't do you any harm! Look, tell me all that happened today.'

'Good God,' replied Camusot, 'just as I'd taken this young man's confession, including a declaration that the supposed Spanish priest was Jacques Collin, the Duchesse de Maufrigneuse and Madame de Sérisy sent in a message, by a footman, requesting me not to interrogate him. But it was too late ...'

'So you lost your head!' said Amélie; 'you can trust your clerk, can't you? all you had to do was call Lucien back, calm him down tactfully, and alter the report!'

'You're just like Madame de Sérisy, you don't take the Law seriously!' said Camusot who did. 'Madame de Sérisy picked up the report and threw it on the fire!'

'*There's* a woman for you! bravo!' cried Madame Camusot.

'Madame de Sérisy told me she'd sooner blow up the Palais than allow a young man, who'd been accepted socially by herself and the Duchesse de Maufrigneuse, to appear on the benches of the Court of Assize in the company of a convict! . . .'

'But, Camusot,' said Amélie, unable to restrain a smile of superiority, 'you're in a superb position . . .'

'O-ho, yes, superb!'

'You did your duty . . .'

'Unfortunately, and despite the jesuitical advice of Monsieur de Granville, who met me on the Quai Malaquais . . .'

'This morning?'

'This morning!'

'At what time?'

'At nine o'clock.'

'Oh, Camusot!' said Amélie joining her hands together and wringing them, 'I who never stop telling you to be on your guard all the time . . . Good Lord, it isn't a man, it's a cart-load of rubble I'm dragging! . . . Camusot, that Procurator General of yours was waiting for you on your way, he must have offered you advice.'

'Of course . . .'

'And you didn't understand! If you're deaf, you'll always be an examining magistrate who's examined nothing. At least have the wit to listen to me!' she said silencing her husband who had made as if to reply. 'Do you think this matter is finished with?' said Amélie.

Camusot looked at his wife like a country bumpkin gaping at a quack.

Amelia's plan

'If the Duchesse de Maufrigneuse and Countess Sérisy are compromised, you'll have to see that they are both on your side,' Amélie went on. 'Look, Madame d'Espard will make the Keeper of the Seals grant you an audience at which you let him into the secret of this matter, and he will use it to amuse the King; for all sovereigns like to know what goes on behind the curtains, and to be told the real motives for events which the public watches pass by open-mouthed. From that point, neither the Procurator, nor Monsieur de Sérisy are to be feared . . .'

'What a treasure a wife like yourself is!' exclaimed the magistrate picking up courage. 'After all, I have smoked out Jacques Collin, I shall send him to render accounts with the Assize Court, I shall unmask all his crimes. A case like that is always a triumph in an examining magistrate's career . . .'

'Camusot,' continued Amélie pleased to see her husband step out of the mental and physical prostration into which Lucien de Rubempré's suicide had cast him, 'the chairman told you just now that you had blundered; but you're still right off the track my friend, . . . in the opposite direction!'

The examining magistrate remained standing, looking at his wife with stupefaction.

'The King, the Keeper of the Seals will be very happy to know the inwardness of this affair, but they won't like to see lawyers with liberal notions dragging people as important as the Sérisys, the Maufrigneuses and the Grandlieus before the bar of public opinion and the Assize Court, with everybody who's involved directly or indirectly with the case.'

'They're all in it! . . . so I have them?' exclaimed Camusot.

Now on his feet, the magistrate paced about his study, like Sganarelle on the stage when he's seeking the way out of an awkward situation.

'Listen, Amélie!' he continued placing himself before his wife, 'I've just remembered something, an insignificant detail you might think, but really of capital importance. This Jacques Collin, try to imagine him, a man of quite colossal subtlety, dissimulation, trickery, . . . a man of such depth . . . Oh, he is . . . what? . . . the Cromwell of the convict settlements! . . . I have never met a rogue his equal, he very nearly caught me! . . . But, in criminal investigation, when you pick up what may look like a mere loose thread, you often find yourself with a whole clue with which you walk through the labyrinth of the most sinister consciences, or the most obscure facts. When Jacques Collin saw me turning over the letters seized at the domicile of Lucien de Rubempré, the scoundrel watched me like a man who wanted to see whether such-and-such a packet was among them, and when I'd finished he positively sighed with satisfaction. That look of a thief evaluating a haul, that mark of a prisoner saying: "I still hold trump cards," taught me a great deal. You women are rather like us and our prisoners, you can detect, in an exchange of glances, the enactment of whole scenes of deceit as complicated as security locks. Whole volumes of suspicions, you know, may pass through one's mind in a second! It is terrifying, a matter of life or death, in the blink of an eye. The fellow has other letters in his hands! I thought. Then I was preoccupied with countless other details of the affair. I passed over the incident, for I was thinking that I had to bring the two prisoners face to face and could return to that little matter later. But let us regard it as certain that Jacques Collin had deposited in a safe place, as these wretches always do, the most compromising of the letters addressed to this handsome young man by so many . . .'

'And you, Camusot, are afraid! You'll be chairman of your own court sooner than I thought! . . .' cried Madame Camusot, her face alight. 'Look, you must act in such a way as to keep everybody happy, for this is becoming so *big* a matter that if we don't watch out somebody'll *steal* it from us! . . . When Madame d'Espard instituted proceedings to deprive her husband of control over his estate, weren't they taken out of Popinot's hands and given to you!' she said in reply to a sign of astonishment from Camusot. 'Well, since he takes so lively an interest in the honour of Monsieur and Madame Sérisy, couldn't the Attorney General evoke this cause in the King's Court and get a councillor attached to start the judicial inquiry all over again? . . .'

'Oh, my dear, where ever did you do your criminal law?' cried Camusot. 'You know everything, you're better at it than I am . . .'

'What! you imagine that by tomorrow morning Monsieur de Granville won't be afraid of the pleading of some liberal lawyer whom this Jacques Collin will soon find, for they'll come offering him money to be allowed to defend him! . . .

These ladies know the danger they stand in as well, not to say better, than you think; they'll see that the Attorney General knows, too, and he already sees these families brought very close to the bench of the accused, in consequence of the convict's connection with Lucien de Rubempré, *fiancé* of Mademoiselle de Grandlieu, Lucien, Esther's lover, former lover of the Duchesse de Maufrigneuse, Madame de Sérisy's darling. So you have to behave in such a way as to gain for yourself your Procurator's affection, the gratitude of Monsieur de Sérisy, that also of the Marquise d'Espard and Countess Châtelet, adding the protection of the house of Grandlieu to that of the Duchesse de Maufrigneuse, then your chairman will pay you compliments. I'll take care of Mesdames d'Espard, Maufrigneuse and Grandlieu. Tomorrow morning, you should go straight to the Procureur Général. Monsieur de Granville is a man who doesn't live with his wife; his mistress for ten years or so has been a Mademoiselle de Bellefeuille, isn't that so, who has borne him adulterine children? Well, then, he's no saint, that leader of your profession, he's just a man like any other; he can be won over, a hold can be got on him, you find out his weak spot, you flatter him; ask his advice, make him see how dangerous the thing is; in short, see that other people are compromised with you, and you will be . . .'

'Truly, I ought to kiss the print of your footsteps,' said Camusot interrupting his wife, taking her by the waist and folding her to his heart. 'Amélie! I owe my salvation to you!'

'It was I who took you in tow from Alençon to Mantes, and from Mantes to the tribunal of Paris,' replied Amélie. 'Well, then, don't worry! . . . I want to be called Madame la Présidente five years from now; but, my lamb, always take time to think before you make up your mind. A magistrate's job isn't like a fireman's, your papers aren't going to flare up, you have time to reflect; in places like yours, stupid actions are inexcusable . . .'

'The strength of my position lies entirely in the identity of the sham Spanish priest with Jacques Collin,' the magistrate continued after a long pause. 'Once that identity has been established, even if the Court should take this case out of my hands, it will always be a solid fact which no magistrate, judge or councillor can put aside. I shall have done what a child does when it ties a tin can to a cat's tail; the proceedings, no matter who conducts the inquiry, will always give off the sound of Jacques Collin's irons.'

'Bravo!' said Amélie.

'And the Attorney General will prefer to come to an understanding with me, who alone could remove this sword of Damocles suspended over the heart of the Faubourg Saint Germain, than with anyone else! . . . But you don't know how difficult it will be to produce this magnificent result . . . The A.G. and I, just now, in his office, agreed to treat Jacques Collin as what he claims to be, a canon of the chapter of Toledo, Carlos Herrera; we agreed to acknowledge him as diplomatic envoy, and allow the Spanish embassy to claim him. It was as a consequence of this plan that I made out the report which set Lucien de Rubempré at liberty, and that I started to dictate new versions of the interrogation of my prisoners, showing them both as white as snow. Tomorrow, Messieurs de Rastignac, Bianchon and I don't know who else, are to be confronted with the supposed canon of the royal chapter of Toledo, they won't say he's Jacques Collin, whose arrest took place in their presence, ten years ago, at a boarding house, where they knew him under the name of Vautrin.'

A moment of silence reigned during which Madame Camusot reflected.

'Are you sure that the prisoner is Jacques Collin?' she asked.

'Quite sure,' the magistrate replied, 'and so is the Attorney General.'

'Well, without letting pussy's claws be seen, try to provoke a rumpus at the Palais de Justice! If your man is still in solitary, go at once to the governor of the Conciergerie and arrange things so that the convict shall be recognized there in public. Before you think about children and their tin cans, do what police chiefs do in states under absolute rule, inventing conspiracies against the sovereign so as to have the merit of foiling them and making themselves seem indispensable; put three families in peril so as to gain credit for saving them.'

'Ah, there we're in luck!' exclaimed Camusot. 'My head is in such a muddle I'd forgotten one little circumstance. The order to release Jacques Collin from solitary and transfer him to the *pistole* was taken by Coquart to Monsieur Gault, governor of the Conciergerie. Now, at the suggestion of Bibi-Lupin, an enemy of Jacques Collin, they've transferred from La Force to the Conciergerie three criminals who know him; and, if tomorrow morning he goes down into the prison yard, terrible scenes are expected . . .'

'Why?'

'Jacques Collin, my dear, holds in trust the fortunes possessed by the convict stations, which amount to very considerable sums; now, they say that he dispersed these to entertain the late Lucien in luxury, and accounts will be demanded of him. According to what Bibi-Lupin told me, it will come to the point of butchery, the guards will have to step in, and the secret will stand revealed. Jacques Collin's life is at stake. If I go to the Palais in good time, I shall be able to draw up a report on the identification.'

'If only his clients would finish him off! you would be thought a very capable man! Don't go to see Monsieur de Granville, wait for him in his office armed with this formidable weapon! It is a cannon trained on the three most important families at Court and in the Peerage. Be bold, suggest to Monsieur de Granville that he should rid you of Jacques Collin by transferring him to La Force, where the convicts know how to deal with informers. I shall go see the Duchesse de Maufrigneuse, who will take me to the Grandlieus. I may also call on Monsieur de Sérisy. Trust me to raise the alarm in every quarter. Send me a little note to let me know whether the Spanish priest has been formally recognized as Jacques Collin. Arrange to leave the Law Courts at two o'clock. I shall have fixed a private interview for you with the Keeper of the Seals; it may be at the Marquise d'Espard's house.'

Camusot stood firmly planted in a pose of admiration which made the subtle Amelia smile.

'Come, let's to dinner, and be gay,' she said in conclusion. 'Look! we've been in Paris only two years, and here you are in a fair way to becoming a councillor by the end of the year

... From that point, my pet, to a chairmanship of your own court, the distance to be covered is only a service performed in some political affair.'

These secret deliberations show to what point the actions and least words of Jacques Collin, the final character in our study, concerned the honour of the families in whose bosom he had placed his deceased favourite.

.

Observation on the subject of magnetism

LUCIEN's death and the invasion of the Conciergerie by Countess Sérisy had so upset the functioning of the machine, that the governor had forgotten to release the pretended Spanish priest from solitary confinement.

Although examples may be found in the juridical annals, the death of a prisoner in the course of the preliminary investigation of his case is an episode rare enough to disturb the tranquillity in which clerk, warders and governor normally work. For them, nevertheless, the remarkable thing was not the sudden transformation of a handsome young man into a corpse, but the breaking by a society woman's delicate hands of a wrought-iron bar in the first wicket-grating. Thus, as soon as the Procureur Général and Count Octave de Bauvan had departed in Count Sérisy's carriage, taking away with them the inanimate wife of this last, the governor, his clerk and the prison staff were to be seen grouped before the wicket in company with Monsieur Lebrun, the prison doctor, called to attest the death of Lucien and now on his way to arrange matters with the *dead persons' doctor* of the district in which that unfortunate young man resided.

The name *dead persons' doctor* is given in Paris to the medical office, in each mayoralty, whose function it is to verify decease and examine its causes.

With characteristically rapid calculation, Monsieur de Granville had judged it desirable, for the honour of the families compromised, to have Lucien's act of decease drawn up at the town hall for the Quai Malaquais, where the dead man had been living, and to have him taken from his residence to the church of Saint Germain des Prés, where the funeral service would be held. Monsieur de Chargeboeuf, Monsieur de Granville's secretary, was called and received orders to this effect. Lucien was to be moved during the night. The young secretary was instructed to arrange matters with the town hall, the parish and the undertakers. Thus, in the eyes of the world, Lucien would have died at home in a state of freedom, the procession would leave from there, his friends be called there for the last farewells.

In consequence, just as Camusot, his mind at rest, sat down at table with his ambitious better half, the governor of the Conciergerie and Monsieur Lebrun, the prison doctor, were outside the wicket deploring the fragility of iron bars and the strength of women in love.

'Few of us are aware,' the doctor was saying as he departed to Monsieur Gault, 'of how much nervous power there is in men excited by passion! Dynamics and mathematics lack the necessary symbols and calculations for registering that force. Only yesterday, for example, I observed an experiment which made me shudder and which shows the same kind of physical strength displayed a short while ago by the dear lady.'

'Do tell me about it,' said Monsieur Gault, 'it is one of my little weaknesses to be interested in magnetism, not that I believe in it, but it intrigues me.'

'A magnetizing doctor, for there are some among us who believe in magnetism,' continued Dr Lebrun, 'wanted me to try out on myself a phenomenon which he described and I was sceptical of. Curious to see for myself one of those strange nervous crises by which they demonstrate the existence of magnetism, I consented! This is what happened. I should very much like to know what our Academy of Medicine would say if its members were submitted, one after the other, to this experiment which affords no loophole to incredulity. My old friend . . .

'This doctor,' said Monsieur Lebrun opening a parenthesis, 'is an old man who has been persecuted by the Faculty for his views, ever since Mesmer; he is seventy or seventy-two, and his name is Bouvard. He is in our time the patriarch of the doctrine of animal magnetism. I am like a son to him, I owe to him all that I am. Well, now, the ancient and respected Bouvard proposed to demonstrate to me that the nervous force brought into play by the mesmerist was not infinite, for man is subject to determinate laws, but that it emanated like the forces of nature whose final principles are beyond our calculation.

' "Thus," he said to me, "if you abandoned your wrist to the grip of a somnambulist who in the waking state would not apply pressure beyond a measurable power, you would see that, in the condition foolishly called somnambulistic, his fingers would have the faculty of being able to act like a locksmith's shearing machine!"

'Well, sir, when I gave my wrist up to the grip of a woman, not *asleep*, for Bouvard does not accept that expression, but *isolated*, and the old man had commanded her to squeeze me unrestrainedly with all the force of her grip, I begged him to stop her just as blood was about to spurt from my finger-ends. But you can see for yourself! this mark will remain like a bracelet about my wrist for three months or more.'

'Good Heavens!' said Monsieur Gault examining a circular ecchymosis like that which burning might have produced.

'My dear Gault,' the doctor continued, 'if my flesh had been clamped in an iron ring which a locksmith had tightened up with a screw, I should not have felt the metal collar as painfully as I felt the fingers of that woman; her grip was inflexible steel, and I truly believe that she could have broken the bone and separated my hand from its wrist. The pressure, at first barely sensible, continued without respite all the time adding new force to the pressure of a moment before; in short, a tourniquet could not have been applied with more precision than that hand changed into an instrument of torture. It seems to me clear, then, that, under the empire of passion which is will-power concentrated upon one point and brought to an incalculable degree of animal force, as the various types of electrical current may be, man's entire vitality, whether for attack or for resistance, can be concentrated in any one of his organs . . . That slightly built woman, under the pressure of her despair, had brought all her vital power into her wrists.'

'It needs a devilish amount to break a wrought iron bar, . . .' said the head warder shaking his head.

'There could have been some flaw in the metal!' Monsieur Gault pointed out.

'For my part,' the doctor went on, 'I no longer venture to assign any limit to nervous energy. It explains, you know, the way in which mothers, to save their children, mesmerize lions, walk into a fire or along cornices where a cat wouldn't set foot, and bear the pain of a difficult childbirth. It explains the attempts prisoners and convicts make to recover their liberty . . . We still don't know the extent of our vital forces, they derive from the underlying power of nature, and we draw upon them from unknown reservoirs!'

'Monsieur,' a warder came to whisper to the governor as he conducted Dr Lebrun to the outer gate of the Conciergerie, 'Solitary No. 2 says he's ill and wants the doctor; he claims to be at death's door,' added the turnkey.

'Really?' said the governor.

'He's at his last gasp!' replied the warder.

'It's five o'clock,' said the doctor, 'I haven't dined yet . . . Still, here I am, ready for anything, so never mind, come along . . .'

The man in the cell

'SOLITARY Confinement Cell No. 2 means precisely the Spanish priest suspected of being Jacques Collin,' said Monsieur Gault to the doctor, 'one of the accused in the case in which that poor young man was implicated . . .'

'I saw him already this morning,' replied the doctor. 'Monsieur Camusot instructed me to pronounce on the fellow's state of health, and, between ourselves, he's in excellent shape and, moreover, could easily make his living by posing as Hercules in a troupe of mountebanks.'

'He might want to kill himself, too,' said Monsieur Gault.

'Let's take a stroll to the cells, the pair of us, I have to go there, if only to have him transferred. Monsieur Camusot has released this curious anonymity from solitary confinement . . .'

Jacques Collin, nicknamed Dodgedeath in the underworld, to whom from this point we shall give no other name than his own, had, from the moment of his return, by Camusot's order, to the cells, fallen prey to an anxiety which he had never known during a life marked by so many crimes, by three escapes from the penitentiary and by two verdicts of guilty before a Court of Assize. About this man, in whom the world of the convict stations is summed up, with all its thoughts, its energies and its passions, himself their highest expression, is there not something monstrously beautiful in his attachment, worthy of the canine race, to the one whom he had made his friend? Damnable, infamous and horrible in so many ways, that absolute devotion to his idol renders him so truly interesting, that our present study, though already long, would seem curtailed, incomplete, if the upshot of this criminal life were not added to Lucien de Rubempré's end. The little spaniel dead, one is led to wonder whether his dreadful companion, the lion, can live!

In real life, in society, facts of one kind are so fatally linked with those of another, that hardly anything can be safely ignored. The water of the river forms a kind of travelling platform; the most rebellious wave, to whatever height its column rises, must presently sink into the general mass, whose onward course is stronger and more rapid than any whirl or eddy that forms within it. Just as the flow of the water may be clearly seen despite the incidents on its surface, you may wish to measure the action of social forces on the vortex called Vautrin? see how long it will be before the mutinous wave is engulfed, what must be the fate of this truly diabolical man, who is yet attached to humanity by love? with such difficulty does that divine principle die in the most cankered of hearts.

The ignoble convict who yet embodied a poem shadowed forth by so many poets, by Moore, by Lord Byron, by Mathurin, by Canalis (that of a demon possessing an angel drawn into its circle of hell to refresh it with dew stolen from paradise), Jacques Collin, if one has truly penetrated this heart

425

of bronze, had for seven years renounced mere self. His powerful faculties, absorbed in Lucien, had been brought into play only for Lucien; his advancement, his loves, his ambition had been the source of the convict's only joy. Lucien had been his visible soul.

Dodgedeath had dined at the Grandlieus', slipped into great ladies' boudoirs, loved Esther by proxy. Finally, in Lucien he had seen a Jacques Collin, handsome, youthful, ennobled, in the position of an ambassador.

Dodgedeath had fulfilled the German superstition of the *Doppelgänger* by a phenomenon of intellectual paternity which will be easily comprehended by women who, in their lives, have truly loved, who have felt their soul pass into that of the man they loved, who lived with his life, whether it was infamous or noble, happy or unhappy, famous or obscure, who, in spite of the distance between then, have felt pain in their leg if he had received a wound there, who knew when he was fighting a duel and who, to sum up in a word what was more important still, didn't need to learn of his unfaithfulness to know it.

Taken back to his cell, Jacques Collin said to himself: 'The child is being questioned!'

And he shuddered, he who killed as a workman drinks.

'Was he able to see his mistresses?' he wondered. 'Did my aunt find those damned females? Did those duchesses, those countesses move, have they prevented the interrogation? . . . Did Lucien receive my instructions? . . . And if fate means him to be questioned, how will he *hold*? Poor child, I brought him to this pass! It was that brigand Paccard and that weasel Europe who caused this uproar, by snitching the seven hundred and fifty thousand francs' order given by Nucingen to Esther. Those two rogues made us stumble at the last step; but they'll pay dearly for that caper! Another day, and Lucien would have been rich! he'd have married his Clotilde de Grandlieu. I no longer had Esther on my hands. Lucien loved that wench too much, whereas he'd never have loved the drowning man's plank, that Clotilde . . . Ah, then the child would have been mine altogether! And to think that our fortune depends on a glance, on Lucien blushing in front of this Camusot, who sees everything, who isn't lacking in the subtlety of judges! for, when he showed me those letters, he exchanged looks by which we sounded each other, and he knew that I could blackmail Lucien's mistresses! . . .'

The monologue lasted three hours. The anguish was such that it gained ascendancy over that constitution of iron and vitriol. Jacques Collin, whose brain was as though on fire with madness, felt so devouring a thirst that, without noticing that he was doing so, he drained all the supply of water contained in one of the two buckets which constitute, with a plank bed, all the furniture of a confinement cell.

'If he loses his head, what will become of him? for that poor child lacks Théodore's strength, . . .' he wondered as he lay down on his guardroom bed.

A word about the Théodore who occurred to Jacques Collin's mind at that moment of extremity. Théodore Calvi, a young Corsican, sentenced to life imprisonment for eleven murders, at the age of eighteen, thanks to influence which had been dearly bought, had been Jacques Collin's chain mate from 1819 to 1820. Jacques Collin's last escape, one of his finest operations (he had got out disguised as one of the armed constabulary with Théodore Calvi walking beside him as a convict to be taken before the superintendent), that superb escape had taken place at the port of Rochefort, where the convicts die like flies, and where the authorities had hoped to see the last of those two dangerous individuals. Escaping together, they had been forced to separate by the hazards of flight. Théodore, recaptured, had been returned to the penitentiary. Having reached Spain and there transforming himself into Carlos Herrera, Jacques Collin was looking for his Corsican friend in the neighbourhood of Rochefort when he met Lucien on the banks of the Charente. The young hero of the bandits and the *maquis*, to whom Dodgedeath owed his knowledge of Italian, had then been naturally sacrificed to the new idol.

Life with Lucien, a young man without police record, guilty even to his own mind only of the very slightest transgressions, rose, furthermore, fair and splendid like the sun of a summer day; whereas with Théodore, Jacques Collin had foreseen no other outcome than the scaffold, at the end of a series of inevitable crimes.

The thought of some misfortune caused by Lucien's weakness, for solitary confinement might well cause him to lose his head, assumed dreadful proportions in Jacques Collin's mind; and, imagining the possible catastrophe, this unfortunate man felt his eyes fill with tears, a phenomenon which he had never once experienced since childhood.

'I'm sweating like a horse,' he said to himself, 'and perhaps if I got the doctor here and offered him a considerable sum he might put me in touch with Lucien.'

At that moment, the warder appeared with his dinner.

'It's no use, my son, I cannot eat. Tell the governor of this prison to send the doctor to me, I feel so unwell, I think my last hour has come.'

Hearing the guttural rhonchus with which the convict accompanied his words, the warder inclined his head and departed. Jacques Collin seized furiously upon the sudden hope; when, however, he saw the doctor and the governor enter his cell together, he saw the plan miscarried, and he coldly awaited the outcome of the visit, mechanically tendering his pulse to the doctor's fingers.

'The man is feverish,' said the doctor to Monsieur Gault; 'but there's always a bit of fever with accused persons at this stage, and,' he whispered to the sham Spaniard, 'to me it is always a proof that there is criminal guilt of some kind.'

At that moment, the governor, to whom the Procurator General had given the letter addressed by Lucien to Jacques Collin with instructions to hand it to the latter, left him and the doctor under the eye of the warder, and went to fetch the letter.

'Doctor,' said Jacques Collin seeing the turnkey at the door and without questioning the reasons for the governor's withdrawal, 'I should think nothing of going up to thirty thousand francs to get a few lines to Lucien de Rubempré.'

'I don't want to rob you,' said Dr Lebrun, 'nobody in the world will communicate with him again . . .'

'Nobody?' said Jacques Collin stupefied. 'Why?'

'He's hanged himself . . .'

Never did a tiger finding its little ones gone rend the jungles of India with so fearful a cry as that of Jacques Collin, who rose up on his feet like the tiger on its paws, who cast on the doctor a gaze burning like the lightning which accompanies a thunderbolt, then collapsed on his camp bed saying 'Oh! my son!'

'Poor man!' cried the doctor moved by this terrible outcry of nature.

The explosion was indeed followed by such total weakness, that the words: 'Oh, my son!' were little but a murmur.

'Is this one going to croak on us, too?' asked the warder.

'No, it isn't possible!' continued Jacques Collin raising himself up and looking at the two witnesses of the scene with an eye devoid of flame or even warmth. 'You've made a mistake, it wasn't him! You didn't look properly. There's no way of hanging yourself in a cell like this! Look, how could I hang myself here? All Paris will answer to me for that life! God owes me that life!'

The guard and the doctor were stupefied in their turn, they whom nothing had surprised for a long time. Monsieur Gault came back, holding Lucien's letter in his hand. At sight of the governor, Jacques Collin, crushed by the very violence of that explosion of grief, seemed to grow calmer.

'The Procurator gave me this letter for you, he said you could have it unopened,' Monsieur Gault indicated.

'It is from Lucien . . .' said Jacques Collin.

'Yes, indeed, sir.'

'This young man, sir, he's . . . ?'

'He's dead,' continued the governor. 'Even if the doctor had been here, unfortunately he'd have been too late . . . The young man died along there, . . . in one of the privilege cells . . .'

'Can I see him with my own eyes?' asked Jacques Collin timidly; 'will you allow a father to go and weep over his son?'

'If you want, you can take his room. I have orders that you're to be transferred to a room in the *pistole*. You're no longer in solitary confinement, sir.'

The prisoner's eyes, without warmth or life, wandered slowly from the governor to the doctor; Jacques Collin questioned them mutely, fearing some trap, and he hesitated to go.

'If you want to see the body,' the doctor told him, 'there's no time to lose, it has to be taken away tonight . . .'

'If you have children, gentlemen,' said Jacques Collin, 'you will understand me behaving like an imbecile, I can hardly see clearly . . . This blow has been more than death to me, but you can't understand what I'm saying . . . If you're fathers, you're only that and no more; . . . I'm a mother, too! . . . I, . . . I'm out of my mind, . . . I feel it, yes, this is madness.'

The leavetaking

ALONG passages whose massive doors open only before the governor, it is possible to go in very little time from the solitary confinement cells to the privileged prisoners' quarters. The two rows of dwellings are separated by an underground corridor formed by two big structural walls which support the vaulting on which rests that gallery in the Palais de Justice known as the Galerie Marchande. Thus, accompanied by the warder who took his arm, preceded by the governor and followed by the doctor, in a matter of minutes Jacques Collin reached the cell in which Lucien lay, on the bed.

At this sight, he fell upon the body and glued himself to it with a desperate embrace, whose force and feeling of passion made the three onlookers tremble.

'You see,' said the doctor to the governor, 'there's an example of what I was saying to you. Look! . . . that man is going to knead and mould the body, and you don't know what a corpse is, it's stone . . .'

'Leave me here! . . .' said Jacques Collin in a spent voice, 'I haven't got long to see him, they'll be taking him away from me, to . . .'

He stopped before the word *bury*.

'You will let me keep something of my dear child! . . . Be so kind, sir,' he said to Dr Lebrun, 'as to cut off one or two locks of his hair, I cannot . . .'

'It is his son, that's certain!' said the doctor.

'Do you think so?' replied the governor with a doubtful air which made the doctor reflect uncertainly.

The governor told the gaoler to leave the prisoner in this cell, and to see that a few locks of hair were cut off for the supposed father, before the body was taken away.

It was then half past five, and in May it is still light enough at that time, even in the Conciergerie, despite the bars and gratings and close-meshed wire netting over the windows, to read a letter. Jacques Collin therefore spelled out Lucien's terrible letter while holding the hand which had penned it.

The man has not yet been found who can hold a piece of ice for ten minutes, gripping it firmly in the palm of his hand. The chill communicates itself with deadly speed to the sources of life itself. But the effect of that cold so extreme it acts like a poison is hardly to be compared with that produced on the soul by the rigid, frozen hand of a dead man held thus, pressed thus. Then Death spoke to Life, it recounted black secrets destructive of many a human feeling; for, where feelings are concerned, to change is to perish.

If we read Lucien's letter again with Jacques Collin, the dying man's declaration may be seen for what it was to him, a poison cup.

TO THE ABBÉ CARLOS HERRERA

My dear abbé, I have received nothing but benefits from you and I have betrayed you. This unintended ingratitude must be my death, and so, when you read these lines, I shall no longer exist; you will not be there to save me this time.

You freely gave me the right to cast you off whenever it suited me, flinging you to the ground like a cigar butt, but I found another and totally senseless way of bringing about your ruin. To free myself from an awkward situation, taken in by the clever question of an examining magistrate, your spiritual son, he whom you adopted, allied himself with those who would murder you at any cost, by establishing an identity, which I know to be impossible, between you and a French criminal. Need I say more?

Between a man of power like yours and myself, of whom you tried to make a greater figure than I had it in me to be, there can be no silliness exchanged at the moment of final separation. You wished to make me powerful and glorious, you have flung me into the pit of suicide, that is all. I have seen this giddiness approaching for a long time.

As you once said, there is the posterity of Cain and that of Abel. Cain, in the great drama of Humanity, is the opposition. You descend from Adam by this line in which the devil still blows on that fire whose first spark was struck in Eve. Among that demonic progeny, there appear from time to time, terribly, one or two of massive constitution, who sum up in themselves all human energy, and who are like those feverish animals of the wilderness whose form of life calls for the vast spaces they find there. People like that are dangerous in society as lions would be in the heart of Normandy: they must feed on something, they devour common men and browse on the money of fools; their play is so perilous that they end by killing the humble dog they have made a companion of, an idol even. When God chooses, such mysterious beings may be Moses, Attila, Charlemagne, Mahomet or Napoleon; but when He allows these giant instruments to rust on the sea-bottom of a generation, they become only Pugatcheff, Robespierre, Louvel and Father Carlos Herrera. Endowed with immense power over tender souls, these are drawn to them and ground small. In its own way, the spectacle is great and beautiful. It is that of a brightly coloured poison plant which fascinates children in the woods. It is the poetry of evil. Men like you should dwell in caves and never come out. You made me live with your giant's life, and I have paid for it with my very existence. So I take my head out of the Gordian knot of politics and give it to the slip-knot I have tied in my cravat.

To make amends for my fault, I am sending the Attorney General a formal retractation of all that I said at my interrogation; you will know how to turn this document to your advantage.

According to the provisions of a will drawn up in due form, you will receive back, Monsieur l'Abbé, the sums belonging to your Order which you so imprudently laid out on my behalf, in consequence of the paternal tenderness you bore me.

Farewell, then, farewell, mighty monument of evil and corruption, farewell, you who, set in the right road, could have been greater than Jiménez or Richelieu; you kept your promises: I am become again what I was on the banks of the Charente, after owing to you the dream and its enchantment; but, alas, it is not now the river of my own countryside where I was going to drown the petty transgressions of my youth; but the Seine, and the deep pool I chose is a dark cell in the Conciergerie.

Don't feel regret for me: my contempt for you was no less than my admiration.

LUCIEN.

They came to fetch the body a little before one o'clock in the morning and found Jacques Collin kneeling before the bed, the letter on the floor, let go no doubt as the suicide lets go of the pistol which has killed him; but the unfortunate man still held Lucien's hand between his and was praying.

Seeing the man thus, the bearers stopped a moment, for he was like one of those stone figures set kneeling for eternity on the tombs of the Middle Ages, by the genius of some carver of images. This false priest, his tiger's eyes colourlessly pale, rigid with an almost supernatural immobility, made a great impression on them, so that it was very gently they told him to get up.

'Why?' he asked timidly.

The audacious Dodgedeath was as weak as a child.

This sight was pointed out by the governor to Monsieur de Chargeboeuf, who, respecting such obvious grief, and believing that Jacques Collin was indeed the father as he claimed, passed on Monsieur de Granville's orders respecting the order of service and funeral procession for Lucien, who must, without further question, be removed to his domicile on the Quai Malaquais, where the clergy waited to keep vigil over him for the remainder of the night.

'Yes, there speaks the great soul of that magistrate,' the convict cried in a voice of distress. 'Tell him, sir, that he may count on my gratitude ... Yes, I shall be able to do him great service ... Don't forget that phrase; it is very important *to him*. Ah! sir, great changes take place in a man's heart, when he has wept seven hours over a child like this ... I shan't see him any more, then? ...'

Brooding over Lucien with the look of a mother deprived of the body of her son, Jacques Collin sank down, in utter depression. As he saw them take up Lucien's body, he let out a groan which made the bearers hurry.

The Procurator General's secretary and the prison governor had already withdrawn in haste.

What had happened to this nature of bronze, whose power

of decision was as rapid as the eye's glance, in whom thought and action sprang together like a flash of lightning, whose nerves seasoned by three sentences of hard labour and three escapes had acquired the metallic hardness of a savage's? Iron yields to certain degrees of hammering or sustained pressure; its impenetrable molecules, purified and homogenized by human agencies, break down; and, without smelting, the metal loses its power of resistance. Farriers, locksmiths, the makers of edge-tools, all those accustomed to work the metal describe its condition then by a technical term: *'The iron is retted!'* they say, borrowing an expression otherwise used exclusively for hemp and flax, which are softened by steeping. In the same way, the human soul, or, if you prefer, the threefold energy of body, heart and mind may be reduced to a state analogous to that of iron under repeated shock. It may then be said of men as of hemp and iron: they are retted. Science, law and public opinion discover endless reasons for the fearful catastrophes which occur on the railways, by the cracking of a rail, the most appalling of which was that at Bellevue in 1842; but nobody thinks of asking the real experts on the matter, the iron-founders, who all say the same: 'The iron was retted!' The danger is unpredictable. The metal which has turned soft, the metal which is sound, look wholly alike.

Great criminals are often found in this state by their confessors and examining magistrates. The dreadful sensations involved in facing a Court of Assize and even more acutely in being trimmed up for the scaffold almost invariably bring about in the strongest natures a depression of the nervous system. Confessions are heard upon lips till then tightly sealed; the hardest hearts break; and, strangely, it happens when confession can serve no purpose, except to reassure the men of law, who do not like to see a condemned man die without admitting his guilt and who had been worried by his mask of innocence till that moment.

Napoleon knew just such a dissolution of all his human powers on the battlefield at Waterloo!

The prison yard at the Conciergerie

At eight o'clock in the morning, when the supervisor of the *pistole* entered the room in which Jacques Collin was, he found the man pale and calm, like one who has recovered strength by a violent effort of will.

'Time to go out into the prison yard,' said the turnkey, 'you've been shut up three days, if you want to stretch your legs and take a breath of air, you can!'

Jacques Collin, wholly absorbed in his thoughts, taking no interest in himself, seeing himself as a cast-off garment, a rag, did not suspect the trap which had been laid for him by Bibi-Lupin, nor the importance of his entry into the prison yard. The unlucky fellow, going out mechanically, followed the corridor past cells set into what had been cornices in the splendid arcades of the Palace of the Kings of France, supporting what is known as the Galerie Saint Louis, along which the outbuildings of the Central Court of Criminal Appeal may now be reached. This corridor meets the one by the privilege cells or *pistoles*; and, a circumstance worth mentioning, the room in which Louvel, the famous regicide, was confined, is that situated at the right angle formed by the two corridors. Beneath the prettily appointed chambers which occupy the Tour Bonbec lies a winding staircase upon which the gloomy passage opens, and by way of which the prisoners lodged in both classes of cell come and go to or from the prison yard.

All the prisoners, those to appear on indictment before the Court of Assize and those whose cases have already been heard, those newly committed but not in the cells, in fact everybody detained in the Conciergerie walks about this paved, confined space, at certain times of the day, but above all early in the morning in summer. This yard, ante-room to the scaffold or the penitentiary, ends there in one direction, but in the other abuts on society by way of the police station, the examining magistrate's office or the Assize Court. Its appearance is thus more chilling than that of the scaffold.

The scaffold may serve as a pedestal for mounting to heaven; but in the prison yard, all the infamies of the world are met together without issue.

Whether it is that of La Force, or that of Poissy, of Melun or Sainte Pélagie, a prison yard is a prison yard. The same features appear identically in each, with little variation even in the colour of the walls, their height or their extent. Our study would be incomplete if it did not closely describe this Parisian *pandemonium*.

Beneath the massive arches which support the audience chamber of the Appeal Court, there stands (it is under the fourth arch) a stone which, it is said, Saint Louis used for the distribution of alms, and which, nowadays, serves as a table at which a certain number of comestibles are sold to the prisoners. Thus, as soon as the prison yard opens to the inmates, they all group themselves about this display of prisoners' delicacies, brandy, rum, etc.

The first two arches on that side of the yard, facing the magnificent Byzantine gallery, sole vestige of the Palace of Saint Louis's former elegance, are reserved for consultation between those on indictment and their lawyers, the area being closed to the prisoners by a formidable wicket, its ways in and out constituted by high bars, set within the space of the third arch. These parallel means of access are like those set up with barriers at theatre doors when seats are in great demand and queues form. In effect a parlour, contiguous with the huge new wicket hall of the Conciergerie, formerly lighted from the prison yard by hooded openings, was later to be given glazed lights on to the wicket, from which the lawyers in consultation with their clients could be observed. This innovation was necessitated by the excessive influence pretty women could formerly exercise upon their defenders. Where is morality to stop? . . . Such precautions are like those ready-made examinations of conscience which deprave the pure imagination by suggesting to it monstrosities of which it had never heard. In the same parlour or consultation space, friends and relations are sometimes allowed by the Police to interview selected prisoners.

What the prison yard means to the two hundred prisoners

in the Conciergerie may now be understood; it is their garden, a garden without trees, or soil, or flowers, a yard in fact! Its extensions, the parlour and Saint Louis's stone, constitute its sole channels of communication with the outside world.

The moments spent in the yard are the only ones during which the prisoner is in the open air or in company; true, in other prisons there are the workrooms, where the inmates are together; but at the Conciergerie there is no occupation for anyone, unless he is a first-class misdemeanant in the *pistole*. There, everyone is preoccupied with the drama of the Assize Court, since nobody is in the Concergerie except for interrogation or trial. The spectacle in the prison yard is appalling; it is not to be conceived by the imagination, it must be seen, or have been seen.

First, the meeting, in a space less than fifty yards by forty, of a hundred indicted or convicted persons, hardly constitutes a select social gathering. These wretches who, for the most part, belong to the lowest classes, are poorly clad; their physiognomies are ignoble, if not downright horrible; for a criminal who comes from more elevated social spheres is fortunately quite a rare exception. Peculation, forgery and fraudulent bankruptcy, the only crimes which bring respectable people to such a place, in any case carry with them the privilege of being installed in the first-class misdemeanants' cells of the *pistole*, which the occupants then scarcely ever leave.

This place of exercise, surrounded by fine, massive blackened walls, by a colonnade divided into cells, by fortifications on the side towards the river, by the *pistole* window-gratings to the north, guarded by attentive warders, occupied by a herd of low criminals who distrust each other, is sad enough in its bare physical aspect; it is terrifying to anyone who finds himself the cynosure of all those eyes full of hatred, curiosity, despair, face to face with these fallen creatures. No sign of pleasure! all is gloomy, the place and the men. All is mute, walls and consciences alike. To these wretches, everything represents a danger; unless there already lies between them the kind of sinister friendship which a convict station may engender, they dare not trust each other. The Police, watching their every movement, poisons the atmosphere for them and corrupts all, down to the handshake of two guilty men who know each other well, perhaps with a shared guilt. A criminal who meets his closest friend there cannot know that the latter has not repented, has not made avowals to save his life. This lack of trust, this fear of the *stool-pigeon* ruins the already deceptive freedom of the prison yard. In prison jargon, he is an informer, who appears to be in serious trouble himself, and whose proverbial skill it is to persuade the other that he is a *chum*, a chum being an experienced, a consummate thief, who long ago broke with society, who intends to remain a thief all his life, and whose nevertheless strict code of law is that of the *swell mob*.

Crime and madness are not without their resemblances. To see the prisoners of the Conciergerie in the prison yard, or to see lunatics assembled in the garden of an asylum, is much the same thing. Both walk up and down avoiding each other, dart glances at each other at best strange, at worst atrocious, according to their mood and thoughts of the moment, but neither gay nor serious; for they either know or fear each other. The waiting to be sentenced, remorse, anxiety give the walkers in the prison yard the restless, haggard air of madmen. Only the most accomplished criminals display an assurance of manner which suggests the tranquillity of an easy conscience, the sincerity appropriate to a pure life.

The man of the middle class being exceptional there, and shame keeping the few exceptional cases in their cells, those commonly seen in the prison yard are dressed like workmen. The blouse, the overall, the velvet waistcoat predominate. The vulgar and frequently dirty clothes, harmonizing with the vicious or merely common faces, the oafish manners, a little subdued by the prisoners' sad thoughts, everything, not least the remarkable silence of the place, contributes to the impression of terror or disgust produced upon the occasional visitor, to whom highly placed connections have accorded the far from common privilege of studying the Conciergerie.

Just as the sight of an anatomy collection, in which foul diseases are represented in wax, may inspire chastity or pure and noble love in a young man who is taken to see it; so the sight of the Conciergerie and its prison yard, stocked with guests destined for the penitentiary, the scaffold or some other dishonouring penalty, impresses a fear of human justice upon those who feel none of divine justice, loudly as it speaks to the conscience; and they go away honest for a long time.

Philosophical, linguistic and literary essay on slang, prostitution and thieves

SINCE the walkers in the prison yard when Jacques Collin went down were destined to play their parts in an important scene in the life of Dodgedeath, it may not be out of place to portray one or two of the principal figures in that august assembly.

There, as wherever men are gathered together and, indeed, already at school, physical strength and moral force are both at a premium. At school as at the convict stations, aristocracy and criminality mean the same thing. The man whose head is in peril takes precedence over anybody else. The prison yard, as various authors have said, is a School of Criminal Law, taught more effectively there than in the Place du Panthéon. One of its regular games is to act the proceedings in the Assize Court, to appoint a presiding judge, a jury, a representative of the ministry, a defence lawyer, and to judge the trial. This dreadful farce is almost invariably enacted when some important criminal case is in the courts. At that period, the sensation of the day was the frightful murder of the Crottats, husband and wife, retired farmers, the notary's parents, who, as the unfortunate case had proved, kept eight hundred thousand gold francs at home. One of the authors of this double murder was the celebrated Dannepont, known as La Pouraille, a discharged convict, who, for the past five years, had evaded the active pursuit of the Police under seven or eight different names. This rogue's disguises were so perfect, that he had served two years in prison under the name of Delsouq, one of his pupils, a well-known thief, whose own recognized offences had never taken him beyond the jurisdiction of ordinary magistrates' courts. Since his initial discharge from the penitentiary, La Pouraille had scored up three murders. The certainty of a death sentence, as well as the amount he was understood to have salted away, made this prisoner an object of admiration and terror to his fellows; for not a bawbee of all that stolen money had been recovered. Despite the imminence of the events of July 1830, that bold stroke, which caused as much commotion in Paris at the time as the following year's theft of medals from the Mint's own collection, is still recalled by many; for the unfortunate tendency of our time to think of everything in terms of the figures involved causes any murder to appear more striking if a large sum of money is stolen at the same time.

La Pouraille, a short, thin, wiry man, weasel-faced, aged forty-five, one of the celebrities of the three convict stations which he had inhabited successively from the age of nineteen, knew Jacques Collin intimately, as we shall see. Transferred within the past twenty-four hours from La Force to the Conciergerie with La Pouraille, two other convicts had at once acknowledged and imposed recognition of the sinister royalty conferred on this *chum* by his certainty of the scaffold. One of these two, an old lag called Sélérier, variously nicknamed l'Auvergnat, Father Ralleau, the Roller and known, in the society which the underworld calls the *swell mob*, as Hair's Breadth, a cognomen due to the skill with which he evaded the dangers of his profession, had been a confederate of Dodgedeath's long ago.

Dodgedeath had long suspected Hair's Breadth of playing a double part, of being at one and the same time admitted to the counsels of the swell mob and in the pay of the Police, and it was to this man he had attributed his arrest at Ma Vauquer's in 1819. Sélérier, whom we shall now refer to as Hair's Breadth, just as Dannepont will be called La Pouraille, already convicted of breaking his ticket-of-leave, was also involved in a number of aggravated thefts which, though without a drop of blood spilt, would send him back to the penitentiary for at least twenty years. The third convict, called Riganson, formed with his concubine, known as la

Biffe, one of the most formidable combinations in the swell mob. In trouble with the Law from his tenderest years, Riganson was nicknamed le Biffon. Biffon was the masculine of Biffe, for nothing is sacred to those boys. The swell mob are savages who respect neither law nor religion, nothing, not even natural history, whose sanctified nomenclature they parody, as we have seen.

Here a digression is necessary; for Jacques Collin's entry into the prison yard, his appearance in the midst of his enemies, so carefully engineered by Bibi-Lupin and the examining magistrate, the curious scenes which must ensue, would be inadmissible and incomprehensible without some explanation of the world of thieves and convict prisons, its laws, its customs, and especially its way of speaking, the dreadful poetry of which becomes indispensable at this point in the narrative. First, then, a word about the language of these Greeks, swindlers, thieves and murderers, their lingo, cant, jargon, slang or *argot*, which literature has, recently, employed with so much success, that more than one word from that strange vocabulary may now be heard on the rosy lips of young ladies, spoken in marble halls, used to amuse princes, more than one of whom has been heard to describe himself as having been fleeced, bilked, fobbed, prigged or *floué*! Whatever people may think, there is no more energetic or colourful language than that of this subterranean world which, ever since the first empires and their capital cities were founded, has been tossed about in cellars, in ships' holds, in 'sinks of iniquity', in 'dives', in the below-stage, the trap-door area of the theatre of society, where the machinery is kept and the footlights are fed and from which, at the Opera itself, blue flames are belched and magicians emerge.

Each word of this language is a brutal, ingenious or fearful image. Breeches do, indeed, go up and down. Sleep is a gentle thing, kipping and dossing are not, they suggest the hunted animal, the Thief, flinging himself down, exhausted, to a deep and necessary oblivion, while the powerful wings of Suspicion plane overhead. The animal may snore, but his ears, nevertheless, remain pricked, anxious.

Everything is savage in this idiom. The prefixes and suffixes, the words themselves, shock, they are rough and rasping. From a moppet or a popsie or a doll, by way of a mere skirt, to a mab or an old bag, a woman may be almost anything and in Paris is a *largue*. And what poetry! Straw is a swede-basher's feathers. Midnight is rendered by the periphrase: knocking twelve, where a *plombe* is certainly a leaden hour. Doesn't one shudder? When you ransack a room, you 'rinse' it. One of the words for sleeping means changing your skin. What vivacity in these images! Eating is *playing dominoes*; how else do hunted men eat?

Slang goes everywhere, all the time! it follows civilization, it treads on its heels, it is enriched with new expressions at every discovery or new invention. The potato, brought into France by Louis XVI and Parmentier, becomes in thieves' cant a *pig's orange*. Bank-notes are invented, the criminal world at once calls them garatted flimsies, from the name of Garat, whose signature appeared on them. 'Flimsy!' don't you hear the rustle of tissue paper? The thousand-franc note was a male flimsy, the five-hundred a female. Presently, you will see, convicts will invent baptismal names for hundred-and two-hundred franc notes.

In 1790, in the interest of humanity, Guillotin invented the expediting machine which solves all the problems to which capital punishment gives rise. At once, the convicts, the former galley-slaves, took a look at the new machine, bridging a gap between the old monarchical and the new republican systems, and immediately they called it Mount Unwilling or Mount Against-the-Grain Abbey! They observed the angle at which the steel blade fell, saw that it was like the action of a scythe, and called it just that! When you think that the main convict settlements are called *meadows*, truly those who concern themselves with linguistics must admire the creation of such appalling vocables, as Charles Nodier would have called them.

Let us further acknowledge the high antiquity of slang! It consists one tenth of words from the Romanic language, another tenth of the old Gaulish tongue of Rabelais. *Effondrer* (to break in), *otolondrer* (to annoy), *cambrioler* (all that is done in a private room), *aubert* (money), *gironde* (beautiful), the word for a river in Languedocian, *fouillousse* (pocket) belong to the speech of the fourteenth and fifteenth centuries. *Affe*, for life, is very old indeed. To upset *affe* gives us *affres*, whence the word *affreux*, which we must translate as all that upsets life, etc.

At least a hundred words of slang belong to the language of Panurge, who, in the work of Rabelais, symbolizes the people, for his name is made up of two Greek words meaning: He who does all. The advance of knowledge changes the face of civilization with the railway; slang has already called it the *iron horse*.

The word for the head, when it is still on their shoulders, *la sorbonne*, indicates the ancient source of this language, but let us not forget that the name of the seat of the University of Paris is also, in chemistry, that of a fume-cupboard or fume-chamber, and that it is feminine. From remotest times, as in Cervantes, in the Italian writers of *novelle*, in Aretino as in early romance, in Rabelais, the daughter of joy, the harlot, has always been the protectress, the companion, the consolation of thief, Greek, coat-snatcher, confidence trickster, pickpocket.

Prostitution and theft are two forms of vital protest, male and female, of *the state of nature* against society. The philosophers of the eighteenth century, the reformers of today, all those humanitarians in whose rear trail the communists and syndicalists, agree, uncritically, on these two conclusions: prostitution and theft. It is not in sophistical books that the thief calls property, heredity, the social safeguards, into question: he suppresses them sharply. For him, to steal is to enter into his own. He doesn't discuss marriage, he doesn't denounce it, he doesn't, in printed Utopias, demand that mutual consent, that intimate alliance of souls about which it is useless to generalize; he couples with a violence whose links are incessantly hammered ever closer by necessity. Modern reformers write woolly, long-drawn, nebulous treatises, or philanthropic novels; but the thief acts! he is clear as a fact, he is logical as a blow with the fist. And what style! . . .

A further observation! The world of prostitutes, thieves and murderers, the hulks and the prisons comprise a population of some sixty to eighty thousand individuals, male and female. This world can hardly be ignored when the state of our society is depicted, when a literal reproduction of our way of life is attempted. The law, the constabulary, the police employ much the same number of people, is that not strange? The antagonism between all these people who reciprocally seek and evade each other constitutes an immense duel, eminently dramatic, sketched in these pages. Theft and the traffic in public prostitutes have much in common with the theatre, the police, the priesthood and the military. In these six conditions of life, the individual takes on an indelible character. He can no longer be other than he is. The stigmata of the sacerdotal function are ineffaceable, and so are those of the soldiery. It is the same with other conditions which are in strong opposition, the *contraries* in civilization. Their violent, strange, singular diagnostics, wholly *sui generis*, make the prostitute and the thief, the murderer and the discharged prisoner, so easily recognized that, to their enemies, the spy and the constable, they are what his game is to the hunter; a colour, a smell, in short unmistakable *properties*. Whence that profound understanding of disguise among the celebrities of the underworld.

The big boys

A WORD more on the constitution of this world, which the abolition of branding, the softening of penalties and the foolish indulgence of juries renders so menacing. In twenty years, Paris will be surrounded by an army of forty thousand discharged prisoners. The department of the Seine and its fifteen hundred thousand inhabitants being the only point in France where these unfortunates can hide, Paris is, for them, what the virgin forest is for savage beasts.

The swell mob, which is that world's Faubourg Saint Germain, its aristocracy, formed itself, in 1816, at the conclusion of a peace which put so many lives in question, into an association called the *Grand Fanandels*, which brought together the best-known gang chiefs and various bold individuals, then without other means of livelihood. The word *fanandels* means at the same time, brothers, friends, comrades. All thieves, convicts, prisoners are fanandels. The Grand Fanandels, the flower of the swell mob, were for twenty years and more the court of appeal, the academy, the house of peers, to these people. The Grand Fanandels had each his private fortune, capital funds in common and a code of behaviour of their own. They owed each other help-in-aid at need, they all knew each other. They were, moreover, beyond the ruses and seductions of the police, they had their own charter, their passwords, signs by which they recognized each other.

These dukes and peers of the underworld had founded, between 1815 and 1819, the famous society of the Ten Thou', so called from the agreement by virtue of which none of them undertook an operation in which the loot was less than *ten thousand* francs. At the moment we have reached in our story, in 1829 and 1830, there were appearing in print memoirs in which the exact strength of that society, the names of its members, were indicated by one of the great names of the judicial police. It was seen with alarm that there existed an army fully organized, of men and women; but so formidable, so clever, so frequently successful, that thieves like the Lévys, the Pastourels, the Collonges, the Chimaux, men aged between fifty and sixty, were there described as having been in revolt against society from childhood! ... The existence of thieves of that age was an avowal of impotence on the part of the Law!

Jacques Collin was the banker, not only of the society of the Ten Thou' but also of the Grand Fanandels, the heroes of the criminal underworld. It is admitted by competent authorities that the convict settlements have always had their funds. This curious fact is easily believed. Thefts are never recovered, except in unusual circumstances. Condemned prisoners, since they can't take anything with them to the hulks, are forced to have recourse to men of proved capacity and trust, to deposit their funds, as in society they are deposited with banking houses.

At one time, Bibi-Lupin, head of the detective force these ten years past, had belonged to the aristocracy of the Grand Fanandels. His betrayal had resulted from wounded pride; he had regularly seen Dodgedeath's high intelligence and prodigious strength preferred to his own. Hence the criminal investigation chief's unrelenting feud against Jacques Collin. Hence also certain compromising dealings between Bibi-Lupin and his former comrades, in which the magistracy had latterly begun to take an interest.

In his desire for revenge, to which the examining magistrate had given full rein in his need to establish the identity of Jacques Collin, the head of the detective force had therefore picked his helpers very cleverly, in setting against the bogus Spaniard La Pouraille, Hair's Breadth and Biffon, for La Pouraille, like Hair's Breadth, belonged to the Ten Thou' and Biffon was a Grand Fanandel.

La Biffe, Biffon's redoubtable *largue*, who was long to defy all the efforts of the Police, because of her capacity for disguising herself as a respectable woman, was at liberty. This woman, who could do you a marquise, a baroness, a countess to perfection, had her own carriage and servants. A sort of Jacques Collin in skirts, she was the only woman to rival Asia, Jacques Collin's right hand. Every leader of the underworld has, indeed, his devoted female double. The judicial archives, the secret chronicle of the Palais will tell you: no honest woman's passion, not even that of a church hen for her spiritual director, nothing surpasses the devotion of the mistress who shares the perils of a great criminal.

Passion is almost always, with these people, the original reason for their daring operations, their murders. The excessive love which draws them, *constitutionally*, say the doctors, towards woman, occupies the whole moral and physical strength of these energetic men. Thence the idleness which devours their days; for amatory excesses demand both rest and restoring meals. Thence that distaste for all work, which compels such people to adopt quick means to procure money. Even so, the need to live and to live well, itself so violent, is nothing in comparison with the prodigalities inspired by the female to whom these noble Medaros want to give jewellery, clothes, and who, always ravenous, loves good cheer. The wench wants a shawl, her lover steals it, and the woman finds in that a proof of love! That is how one proceeds to theft, which, if the human is examined with a magnifying glass, must be regarded as an impulse almost natural to man. Theft leads to murder, and step by step murder leads the lover to the scaffold.

The unruly physical love of these men would therefore, according to the medical faculty, lie at the origin of seven tenths of the crimes which are committed. The proof, indeed, is always furnished, striking, palpable, at the autopsy of a man just executed. This it is which procures to these monstrous lovers, society's scarecrows, the adoration of their mistresses. It is this female devotion squatting faithfully at the prison gates, constantly occupied in undoing the tangled ruses of the investigation, incorruptible guardian of the blackest secrets, which renders so many trials obscure, impenetrable. There lies the strength and also the weakness of the criminal. In prostitutes' language, *to keep one's self-respect* means not to fail in any of the rules of this attachment, to give every penny one has to the man inside, to see to his welfare, keep faith in every respect, do anything for him. The cruellest insult one tart can hurl into the dishonoured face of another is to accuse her of faithlessness to a lover under lock and key. A whore of whom that can be said is considered as a woman without heart! . . .

La Pouraille passionately loved a woman, as we shall see. Hair's Breadth, a philosophical egoist, who stole as a way of life, greatly resembled Paccard, Jacques Collin's henchman, who had gone off with Prudence Servien, the two of them richer by seven hundred and fifty thousand francs. He was unattached, he despised women, he only loved Hair's Breadth. As to Biffon, as we now know, he owed his very nickname to his attachment to la Biffe. These three exemplars of the swell mob had accounts to demand of Jacques Collin, accounts not to be established without difficulty.

Only the cashier knew how many of his clients survived, or what fortune each one had. The special mortality rate among his clients had entered into Dodgedeath's calculations, when he decided to make off with the cash to Lucien's benefit. Concealing himself both from his comrades and from the Police for nine years, Jacques Collin had a near-certainty of having inherited, by the terms of the Grand Fanandels' charter, two thirds of the principal. Could he not, furthermore, allege payments made to chums who were subsequently topped? No system of inspection could touch the head of the Grand Fanandels. He had to be trusted implicitly, for the wild animal's life that a gaol-bird leads necessitated, among the more respectable denizens of their savage world, a high degree of delicacy. Of the hundred thousand crowns he had made away with, Jacques Collin could perhaps acquit himself at that moment with a hundred thousand francs or so. As we have seen, La Pouraille, one of his creditors, had only ninety days to live. Provided elsewhere with a sum no doubt considerably in excess of that which his leader kept for him, La Pouraille might in any case be expected to be not unaccommodating.

One of the infallible signs by which prison governors and their minions, the Police and those in its pay, and even examining magistrates recognized the old lag, the horse back in its stall, the man who has already been fed on horse-beans, is his way of settling down in prison; the hardened offender naturally knows how things are done; he feels at home, nothing surprises him.

And so Jacques Collin, carefully watching his step, had till that moment played to perfection the part of an innocent and an alien, whether to La Force or the Conciergerie. But, stricken by grief, crushed by his double death, for on that fatal night he had twice died, he became Jacques Collin once more. The warder was stupefied not to have to tell the Spanish priest the way down to the prison yard. The accomplished actor forgot his part, he descended the winding stairs of the Bonbec tower as one accustomed to the Conciergerie.

'Bibi-Lupin is right,' the warder said to himself, 'he's an old lag, he is Jacques Collin.'

The boar at bay

AT the moment at which Dodgedeath appeared framed in the door of the turret, the prisoners, having made their purchases at the stone table called after Saint Louis, disposed themselves about the prison yard, never big enough for them: the new inmate was thus perceived by everyone at the same time, with all the more speed in that nothing can equal the precision of a prisoner's glance, when each stands or squats in the yard like a spider at the centre of its web. The comparison is mathematically exact, for the eye being closed in on every side by high, black walls, the prisoner is always aware, even without looking, of the door through which the warders enter, of the parlour windows and of the staircase of the Tour Bonbec, the only ways out of the yard. In the profound isolation in which he exists, everything is an event to the man awaiting trial, everything engages his interest; his boredom, which may be compared with that of a tiger in its cage at the Zoo, multiplies his faculty of attention tenfold. It is not perhaps unnecessary to point out that Jacques Collin, dressed like an ecclesiastic not altogether suited to the cloth, wore black breeches, black stockings, shoes with silver buckles, a black waistcoat, and a certain type of dark maroon frock coat, whose cut betrayed the cleric at any time, especially when these indications are completed by the characteristic haircut. Jacques Collin wore a superlatively ecclesiastical and wholly convincing wig.

'Look, look!' said La Pouraille to Biffon, 'here comes a bit of bad luck! a *wild boar*! how does one of that lot come to be here?'

'It's one of their dodges, a new sort of *kitchen-hand*,' replied Hair's Breadth. 'He's some marshalsea *old-rope merchant* in disguise, plying a trade in snares and bootlaces.'

The armed constabulary had a variety of cant names: on the tracks of a thief, he was a *marchand de lacets*, a corruption of *maréchaussée* or marshalsea, '*chaussé*' no doubt suggesting at once bootlaces and the snares in which a foot may be caught, as well as whipcord and the hangman's rope; with a man in

449

custody, he was something between a sea-swallow and a sand-martin, a *hirondelle de la grève*, but the Grève in Paris, like the Strand in London, was a place of assembly for malcontents by the river; then, taking his man to the scaffold, he became a guillotine hussar. A kitchen-hand, of course, is inevitably a spy, especially if he is also a *sheep* or prisoner planted to gain information among his fellows. In that infernal bestiary, the warder's returned horse had, it will be noted, become a wild boar, that being the cant term for a priest, nobody knows why.

To complete this picture of the prison yard, it is perhaps necessary to sketch in the two other *fanandels*, and first Sélérier, known as the Auvergnat or man from Auvergne, *alias* Father Ralleau, *alias* the Roller, *alias* Hair's Breadth (he had thirty names and as many passports), who will henceforth be known only by this last appellation, the one always used among the swell mob. This profound thinker, who detected a constable in the mock priest, was a merry fellow of five feet four, whose muscles bulged oddly. In an enormous head burned two small, heavily-lidded eyes, like those of a bird of prey, the pupils grey, dull and hard. At first sight, he looked like a wolf because of the breadth of his jaws, vigorously carved and delineated; but all that this similarity implied in cruelty, even in ferocity, was counterbalanced by the cunning, the vivacity of his features, badly pock-marked as they were. Even these scars added by their sharpness to the impression of keen wit. They gave out mockery. The criminal life, with all that it implies in the way of hunger, nights spent out of doors on quaysides, embankments, barges, bridges and streets, the orgies of strong liquor to celebrate some lucky stroke, had given this face as it were a coat of varnish. From a distance of thirty yards, if Hair's Breadth had appeared undisguised, any kind of constable or policeman would have spotted his natural prey; but he was the equal of Jacques Collin in the art of costume and make-up. At that moment, Hair's Breadth, in his everyday wear like an actor who troubles about his appearance only on the stage, wore a sort of hunting jacket without buttons, the frayed buttonholes showing the white of the lining, decayed green slippers, nankeen breeches turned grey, and on his head a cap without peak but with flaps through which passed the ends of a torn, much-washed, old Madras pinner.

Beside Hair's Breadth, Biffon formed a perfect contrast. This celebrated prig, of small stature, broad and fat yet agile, of livid complexion, eyes black and deep-set, dressed like a butcher, planted on two bandy pins, inspired fear by a physiognomy in which predominated all the signs of the constitution peculiar to carnivorous beasts.

Hair's Breadth and Biffon made a fuss of La Pouraille, who no longer had any hope. This double or triple murderer knew that he would be convicted, sentenced, executed within four months. Hair's Breadth and Biffon therefore never addressed him except as Canon, *i.e.*, canon of the Abbey of Mount Unwilling. It may be readily conceived why Hair's Breadth and Biffon made much of La Pouraille. La Pouraille had buried two hundred and fifty thousand gold francs, his share of the loot collected from the Crottats husband and wife at the time of their demise, as the bill of indictment put it. What a magnificent legacy to leave to two fanandels, although these two former convicts must in a matter of days return to the chaingang. Biffon and Hair's Breadth were to be sentenced for 'qualified' theft (*i.e.*, for theft with aggravating circumstances) to fifteen years consecutive to, not concurrent with, the ten years of a previous sentence which they had taken the liberty of interrupting. Thus, although one of them had twenty-two and the other twenty-six years of hard labour to look forward to, they both hoped to escape and pick up La Pouraille's gold hoard. But this Ten Thou' man had so far kept his secret, it seemed pointless to him to give it away before sentence had been pronounced. Belonging to the high aristocracy of his calling, neither had he given his accomplices away. His character was known; Monsieur Popinot, the examining magistrate in that appalling affair, had got nothing out of him.

This terrible triumvirate stood at the upper end of the yard, under the *pistole* or privilege wing. Hair's Breadth was just finishing a lesson he had been giving to a young man shopped for the first time, who, expecting a sentence of ten years' hard labour, was seeking information about the various *meadows*.

'Well, now, my child,' Hair's Breadth was telling him

sententiously, at the moment at which Jacques Collin appeared, 'the difference between Brest, Toulon and Rochefort is as follows.'

'Right, old un', carry on,' said the young man with all a novice's curiosity.

The young prisoner, son of a respectable family indicted on charges of forgery, had come down into the yard from the *pistole* adjoining that in which Lucien was.

'At Brest, sonny,' Hair's Breadth went on, 'you can be sure of finding a bean or two in the third spoonful, if you dig into the tub; at Toulon, it takes five scoops; and at Rochefort, you never catch any, unless you're an old hand.'

Having spoken, our philosopher rejoined La Pouraille and Biffon, who, much intrigued by the *wild boar*, began to cross the yard, while Jacques Collin, bowed down with grief, walked towards their end. Dodgedeath, given up to dreadful thoughts, thoughts appropriate to a fallen emperor, had not realized that everybody was looking at him, that he was the centre of attention, and he walked slowly, gazing at the fatal casement from which Lucien de Rubempré had hanged himself. None of the prisoners knew of this episode, for Lucien's neighbour, the young forger, from motives which we shall presently discover, had said nothing about it. The three mobsmen so arranged themselves as to bar the priest's way.

'He isn't *a boar*,' said La Pouraille to Hair's Breadth, 'he's an old *horse*. Look how he drags his right foot!'

Here it should be explained, for not all our readers have taken it into their heads to visit a penal settlement, that each convict is attached to another (always a young one and an old one together) by a chain. The weight of this chain, clinched to a ring above the ankle, is such that, after a year, it has permanently affected the convict's gait. Compelled to put more force into one leg than into the other to drag this manacle, for the old French word *manicle* is still used by convicts for that piece of hardware, the condemned man invincibly contracts a habit from the effort. Later, when he is no longer fettered, it is the same with the iron as with an amputated limb, from which an old soldier suffers to the end of his days; the convict always feels his manacle, he can never get rid of the effect it has had on his gait. In police terms, he always *drags his right foot*. This diagnosis, known among ex-convicts, as it is to the police, if it doesn't serve to establish the identity of a comrade, at least confirms it.

In the case of Dodgedeath, whose last escape had taken place eight years before, the movement had become almost imperceptible; but, in consequence of his absorbed meditation, he moved with a step so slow and so heavy, that, weak as the deformity of gait had grown, it might catch a practised eye like that of La Pouraille. It will be readily understood, moreover, that convicts, forever in each other's presence in the hulks, and having no other persons than themselves to observe, have so studied each other's physiognomies, that they recognize certain habits which escape their systematic enemies: the informers, the constabulary, police superintendents. Thus, for example, it was to a certain tugging motion of the maxillary muscles of the left cheek recognized by a convict, who was sent to observe a parade of the Seine legion, that the lieutenant-colonel of that body, the famous Coignard, owed his arrest; for, despite Bibi-Lupin's conviction, the Police dared not believe in the identity of Count Pontis de Sainte Hélène with Coignard.

His majesty the Dab

'IT's the boss, it's the Dab,' said Hair's Breadth on receiving from Jacques Collin that distracted look which a man sunk in despair casts on all around him.

'Faith, yes, it's Dodgedeath,' said Biffon rubbing his hands together. 'Oh, it's his build, that square frame; but what's he done to himself? it doesn't look like him.'

'I've got it,' said Hair's Breadth, 'I know what the plan is! he wants to see his queen who's due to be executed.'

For the benefit of those readers who don't know what a *queen* is, we may recall the words of the governor of one of the central prisons to the late Lord Durham, who visited all the prisons during his stay in Paris. This nobleman, anxious to learn all the secrets of the French penal system, even got the late Sanson, the public executioner, to set up his machinery, and asked to see a live calf executed so that he could estimate the action of that engine which the French Revolution made so famous.

The governor, having shown him round the whole prison, the yards, the workshops, the dungeons, etc., pointed to one building with an expression of disgust.

'I shan't take Your Lordship there,' he said, 'for that's the *queens'* quarters . . .'

'Really!' said Lord Durham, 'and what are they?'

'That's the third sex, my lord.'

'They're going to *shorten* Théodore!' said La Pouraille, 'a nice lad! what dash! what cheek! what a loss to society!'

'Yes, Théodore Calvi's taking the edge off his last appetite,' said Biffon. 'Ah, the *largues* are going to blubber their ogles, for they loved that little scamp!'

'So there you are, my friend?' said La Pouraille to Jacques Collin.

And, together with his two acolytes, with whom he had linked arms, he barred the way to the newcomer.

'Oh, Dab, so you've turned wild boar, then?' added La Pouraille.

'They say you've heaved our chink,' Biffon put in with a threatening air.

'There'll be some rhino coming from you, no doubt?' asked Hair's Breadth.

'Don't make fun of a poor priest brought here by mistake,' Jacques Collin, who immediately recognized his three comrades, answered mechanically.

'It's the tinkle of his bell all right, if it isn't the right mug,' said La Pouraille putting his hand on the shoulder of Jacques Collin.

This gesture, the looks of his three comrades, violently pulled the Dab out of his state of prostration, and restored him to contact with real life; for, during that fatal night, he had ranged through spiritual realms of unbounded feeling in search of a new way.

'Don't stew it up for your Dab!' said Jacques Collin in a

low voice, hollow and threatening as the growl of a lion. 'The cops are there, let them cut the pack at the bridge. I'm playing this lark for a chum at his last throw.'

His manner as he spoke displayed all the unction of a priest attempting to convert the unfortunate, and a glance starting heavenward nevertheless took in the prison yard, the warders under the arches, and spoke contempt for them.

'Skin your glaziers,' he said, 'and look at the narks. Don't let on you know me, use your bean and make out you think I'm a *wild boar*, or I'll scuttle you, you, your *largues* and the bawbees.'

'Who do you think we are?' said Hair's Breadth. 'You've come here to ransom your queen.'

'Madeleine is dressed for a bill on the Strand,' said La Pouraille.

'Théodore!' said Jacques Collin suppressing a start and a cry.

It was the last turn of the screw for this crumbling colossus.

'They're going to top him,' La Pouraille repeated, 'he's been two months stacked for the way out.'

Jacques Collin, near fainting, his knees giving way, was held up by his three companions, and he had the presence of mind to put his hands together and adopt an air of compunction. La Pouraille and Biffon respectfully sustained the sacrilegious Dodgedeath, while Hair's Breadth ran to the warder on duty at the wicket-gate which led to the parlour.

'The venerable priest wants to sit down, give me a chair for him.'

And so the trial shot mounted by Bibi-Lupin failed. Dodgedeath, like Napoleon recognized by his soldiers, obtained submission and respect from the three convicts. Two words had sufficed. They were 'your *largues*' and 'the bawbees', summing up all the objects of man's real affection. This threat was for the three convicts the index of supreme power, the Dab still held their fortunes in his hands. Still all-powerful outside, their Dab had not betrayed them, as false friends had said. The colossal renown for skill and deliberation of their chief aroused, moreover, the curiosity of the three convicts; for, in prison, curiosity becomes the only goad to these outcast souls.

The boldness of Jacques Collin's disguise, maintained against the very keys of the Conciergerie, further dazed the three criminals.

'I've been in solitary four days, I didn't know Théodore was so near the Mount, . . .' said Jacques Collin. 'I came to save a poor lad who hanged himself there, yesterday, at four o'clock, and here another misfortune faces me. I have no more trump-cards to play! . . .'

'Poor Dab!' said Hair's Breadth.

'Ah, the Baker has abandoned me!' cried Jacques Collin, using a cant name for the Devil, tearing himself away from the arms of his two comrades and holding himself formidably erect. 'There comes a moment when the world is too strong for men like us! The Stork' – the Palais de Justice – 'swallows us in the end.'

The governor of the Conciergerie, informed of the Spanish priest's fainting fit, came to the yard himself to spy on him, he seated himself on a chair, in the sun, watching everything with the fearful perspicacity which the exercise of functions like his augments daily, and which an air of indifference conceals.

'Ah, dear God!' said Jacques Collin, 'to be confused with people like these, the refuse of society, criminals, murderers! . . . But God will not abandon his servant. Dear Mr Governor, I shall mark my passage through this place with acts of charity whose memory will remain! I shall convert these unfortunates, they will discover that they have souls, that life eternal awaits them, and that, if they lost the battle here below, there is still a heaven for them to conquer, the heaven which is theirs at the cost of a true, a sincere repentance.'

Twenty or thirty prisoners, who had come up and grouped themselves behind the three terrible convicts, whose ferocious looks had kept the inquisitive at a distance of at least a few feet, listened to this allocution pronounced with evangelical suavity.

'That one, Monsieur Gault,' said the formidable La Pour-aille, 'well, we should listen to him . . .'

'They tell me,' continued Jacques Collin, addressing Monsieur Gault who was nearby, 'that there is a man condemned to death in this prison.'

'At this very moment,' said Monsieur Gault, 'the rejection of his appeal is being read out to him.'

'I do not know what that means,' Jacques Collin asked innocently looking about him.

'Gawd, is he a simp!' said the young fellow who had been consulting Hair's Breadth about the blooming of horse-beans in the meadows.

'Ho, well, today or tomorrow they'll *shorten* him,' said a prisoner.

'Shorten?' asked Jacques Collin, whose air of simplicity and ignorance filled the three swell mobsmen with admiration.

'In their language,' replied the governor, 'it means that the sentence of death will be duly executed. As the clerk is now reading out the result of an appeal, no doubt the executioner will presently receive his instructions. The unfortunate man has steadfastly refused the consolations of religion . . .'

'Ah, Mr Governor, it is a soul to be saved! . . .' cried Jacques Collin.

The sacrilegious impostor wrung his hands with a despairing lover's expression which to the attentive governor seemed like the effect of divine fervour.

'Ah, Monsieur,' went on Dodgedeath, 'let me prove what I am and all I can do by allowing me to cause the flower of repentance to unfold in that hardened heart! God endowed me with the gift of speaking certain words which effect a great change. I shatter the heart, and it opens . . . What do you fear? let me be accompanied by constables, by warders, by anybody you like.'

'I'll see if the house chaplain is willing to let you replace him,' said Monsieur Gault.

And the governor retired, struck by the perfectly indifferent, though inquisitive, manner with which the convicts and other prisoners regarded this priest, whose evangelical voice lent charm to his half-French, half-Spanish babbling.

'How do you come to be here, Father?' Hair's Breadth's young interlocutor asked Jacques Collin.

'Oh, it was an error,' replied Jacques Collin taking stock of the white-headed boy. 'I was found at the house of a courtesan who had just been robbed after her death. It was discovered that she had killed herself; but the authors of the theft, who were probably her servants, have not yet been arrested.'

'And was it because of that theft that the young man hanged himself? . . .'

'Ah, there is no doubt that the poor child could not bear the thought of being stigmatized by unjust imprisonment,' replied Dodgedeath raising his eyes to heaven.

'Yes,' said the youth, 'they were just going to set him at liberty when he did it. That was bad luck!'

'Only those who are innocent so catch the imagination,' said Jacques Collin. 'Observe that the theft was committed to his detriment.'

'How much was it?' asked the subtle and profound Hair's Breadth.

'Seven hundred and fifty thousand francs,' Jacques Collin answered gently.

The three convicts looked at each other, and they separated themselves from the group which all the other prisoners had formed round the supposed ecclesiastic.

'It's him rinsed that tart's cellar!' said Hair's Breadth in Biffon's ear. 'They wanted to put the wind up us about that lot we filed.'

'He'll always be the Dab of the Grand Fanandels,' replied La Pouraille. 'Our gelt hasn't hooked it.'

La Pouraille, who looked for a man he could trust, wanted to believe in Jacques Collin's good faith. In prison more than anywhere, people like to believe what they hope for!

'I'll bet you fifty pigs he fobs the dab at the Stork,' said Hair's Breadth, meaning that *his* Dab would outwit the Attorney General, '*and* he'll get his queen off.'

'If that happens,' said Biffon, 'I shan't think he's Meg altogether,' Meg being God, 'but I *shall* believe he's smoked a pipe or two with the Baker.'

'Did you hear him,' Hair's Breadth pointed out, 'say the Baker had abandoned him?'

'Ah!' cried La Pouraille, 'if he'd a mind to save my seat of learning, what a life I should have with my lick of the gelt, all the yellow billets I've got stowed away!'

'Do what he tells you!' said Hair's Breadth.

'Is that a giggle?' La Pouraille added looking at his mate.

'Are *you* a simpkin? You're already stacked rigid for Mount Unwilling. The only way you can rub, so you can stay on your stumps, hone your grinders, unsalt yourself and go on heaving, is to lend him your lugs.'

'That's about the size of it,' La Pouraille admitted, 'and not one of us'd cackle on the Dab, or I'll take him along o' me where I'm off to . . .'

'He'd do it just like that!' cried Hair's Breadth.

Even those who are least susceptible to any feeling of sympathy with this strange world may yet imagine Jacques Collin's state of mind, between the corpse of the idol he had worshipped five hours that night and the impending death of his old chain-mate, the future corpse of the young Corsican Théodore. If it were only to see this unfortunate, he had to use his wits in no usual degree; to save him, that would be a miracle! And he was already considering how.

To understand what Jacques Collin was now to attempt, it must be remarked here that murderers, thieves and the prison population in general are less redoubtable than is commonly supposed. With very few exceptions, the criminal classes are cowardly, no doubt because of the perpetual fear with which their hearts are contracted. Their faculties being incessantly alert to the opportunities for theft, and carrying out a theft requiring the employment of all their vital forces, an agility of mind equal to the bodily aptitude, an attentiveness which is a strain on their temperament, they become stupid, outside those violent exertions of the will, for the same reason as a singer or a dancer will sink back exhausted after an exacting solo or one of those formidable duets which modern composers inflict on the public. Malefactors are, indeed, so denuded of reason, or so oppressed by fear, that they become utterly childish. Credulous to a degree, the simplest ruse snares them. After the success of a venture, they are in such a state of prostration that, giving themselves up at once to the excesses they seem to find necessary, they get drunk on wine or spirits, and fling themselves wildly into the arms of their women, hoping to calm themselves by expending their last strength, to lose with their reason all memory of what has just taken place. In this situation, they are at the mercy of the Police. Once arrested they are blind, they lose their heads, and their need of hope is so great that they will believe anything, while there is no absurdity they cannot be led to admit. One example may serve to show just how far an arrested criminal's stupidity will go. Bibi-Lupin had recently obtained a confession from a murderer aged nineteen, by persuading him that minors were never executed. When this boy was transferred to the Conciergerie to undergo sentence, after the rejection of his appeal, that terrible agent came to see him.

'Are you sure you're not yet twenty? . . .' he asked the lad.

'Yes, I'm only nineteen and a half,' said the murderer with perfect calm.

'Ah, well,' replied Bibi-Lupin, 'don't worry, you will never be twenty . . .'

'Why?'

'Oh in three days' time they'll have topped you,' said the head of criminal investigation.

The murderer, who still believed, even after judgment, that minors weren't executed collapsed like a batter pudding.

These men, made cruel by the need to suppress witnesses, for they commit murder only to destroy proof (it is one of the arguments put forward for abolishing capital punishment); these giants of skill and cunning, with whom the action of the hand, the speed of the glance, the senses are exercised as among savages, become heroes of evil-doing only upon the theatre of their exploits. Not only, the crime once committed, do their troubles begin, for they are as bewildered by the need to hide their booty as they were formerly oppressed by poverty; but also they are weakened like a woman recovering from childbirth. Frightening in their energy at the time of action, they are like children from the moment of triumph. Their nature, in a word, is that of wild animals, easy to kill when they've fed. In prison, these singular men are human only in their dissimulation and by that discretion which gives way only at the last moment, when they are broken, worn-out by the length of their detention.

It may therefore be understood why the three convicts, instead of giving their chief away, wanted to serve him; they admired him because they suspected him of being in possession of the stolen seven hundred and fifty thousand francs, because they saw him still calm under lock and key at the Conciergerie, and because they believed him capable of coming to their rescue.

The condemned cell

WHEN Monsieur Gault had left the bogus Spaniard, he returned by way of the visiting-room to his office, then went in search of Bibi-Lupin, who, during the twenty minutes since Jacques Collin had emerged from his cell, was watching everything, ensconced at a Judas-hole in one of the windows overlooking the prison yard.

'None of them recognized him,' said Monsieur Gault, 'and Napolitas, who goes round among them all, heard nothing. The poor priest, after all that he went through last night, didn't utter a word to suggest that his cassock concealed Jacques Collin.'

'That shows how well he knows prison life,' answered the head of the detective force.

It was Napolitas, Bibi-Lupin's secretary, unknown to any of those currently detained at the Conciergerie, who was playing the part of the young man of family accused of forgery.

'And now he's asked if he can confess the man condemned to death!' the governor added.

'That's our last chance!' cried Bibi-Lupin, 'I didn't think of that. This Corsican, Théodore Calvi, was Jacques Collin's chain-mate: Jacques Collin at the *meadow* made him, I've been told, a set of beautiful *reamers*.'

The convicts make themselves pads which they insert between the iron ring and their flesh, to deaden the weight of the fetter on their ankle and instep. These pads, made of oakum and bits of linen rag, are so called after the opening of ship's seams for caulking, which is what oakum is for.

'Who's watching the condemned man?' Bibi-Lupin asked Monsieur Gault.

'The one they call Thimbleheart!'

'Good, I'll do myself up as a constable, I'll be there; I shall hear what they say, I take responsibility.'

'Aren't you afraid, if it *is* Jacques Collin, that you'll be spotted and that he'll strangle you?' the governor of the Conciergerie asked Bibi-Lupin.

'As a constable, I shall have my sword,' answered the chief superintendent; 'besides, if it is Jacques Collin, he won't do anything to give himself away; and, if he's a priest, I'm safe.'

'There's no time to lose,' Monsieur Gault then said; 'it's half past eight, Father Sauteloup has just read out the rejection of the appeal, Monsieur Sanson is in the hall waiting for orders from the Parquet.'

'Yes, it's today, the Widow's hussars are standing by,' replied Bibi-Lupin. 'I can understand why the Parquet hesitates, this boy goes on saying he's innocent, and, to my mind, the proofs against him have never been quite sufficient.'

'He's a real Corsican,' Monsieur Gault added, 'he won't say a word, he stands up to everything.'

The governor of the Conciergerie's last words to the chief of criminal investigation contained in a nutshell the sombre history of those condemned to death. A man whom the Law has removed from the number of the living belongs to the Parquet, which is the public prosecutor's office. His authority is absolute; he is responsible to nobody, he has only his own conscience to deal with. The prison belongs to the Parquet, which is its sovereign master. A great poet has seized upon this subject, eminently proper to strike the imagination, in Victor Hugo's *Dernier Jour d'un Condamné*! Poetry there is sublime as usual, prose has no other resource than reality, but the reality itself is terrible enough to vie with lyricism. The life of a man condemned to death who has not admitted his guilt or revealed the names of his accomplices is subject to frightful tortures. It is not a matter here either of a boot to break the feet, or of water ingurgitated into the stomach, or of the distension of the limbs by machines; but of an underhand and as it were negative torture. The Parquet delivers the condemned man over to himself, it leaves him in silence and darkness, with a companion, a *sheep*, of whom he must be careful.

Our well-intentioned modern philanthropy believes itself to have invented the atrocious torment of isolation, but it is wrong. Since the abolition of physical torture, the Parquet, naturally desiring to soothe the already delicate consciences of jurors, has seen what dreadful resources solitude offers Justice against remorse. Solitude is a vacuum; and the moral being, like physical nature, abhors it. Solitude is habitable only by the man of genius who fills it with his ideas, those daughters of the intellectual world, or by the contemplator of the divine works for whom it is illuminated by the light of Heaven, enlivened by the breath and voice of God. Apart from these two men, so close to paradise, solitude is to torture what the moral is to the physical. Between solitude and torture there is the same difference as there is between nervous and surgical illness. It is suffering multiplied by infinity. The body touches upon the infinite through its nervous system, as the mind penetrates it by thought. Thus, in the annals of the Parquet in Paris, criminals who never confessed are numbered.

The sinister situation, which assumes enormous proportions in certain cases, for instance in politics, when a dynasty or the State is concerned, will have its place in the COMÉDIE HUMAINE. For the moment, the description of that stone box in which, under the Restoration, the Public Prosecutor's office in Paris kept a man convicted of a capital felony, must suffice to show the horror of the last days before he pays the supreme penalty.

Before the July revolution, there existed at the Conciergerie, and, indeed, there still exists, a condemned cell, which is described as a chamber or bedroom. This room, set back to back against the registry, is separated from it by a thick wall entirely of freestone and flanked by the even more massive wall, seven or eight feet thick, which supports one end of the immense waiting-hall in the Palais de Justice. Its door is the first you come to along the dark corridor which meets your eyes in the middle of the vaulted entrance-hall, itself sizeable. Light enters this sinister room through a cellar-light, protected by a powerful grill and barely visible outside the Conciergerie, since it opens off the narrow space which remains between the registry window, which is next to the grill of the reception wicket, and the quarters of the clerk of the Conciergerie, which the architect thrust like a cupboard to the far end of the entrance-hall. Its very situation thus explains why this small room, set between four massive walls, was destined, when the Conciergerie and the Palais were reconstructed, to its baleful and ominous use. Any escape from it is out of the question. The corridor which leads to the solitary confinement cells and the women's quarter comes out facing the big stove, around which constables and warders are always grouped. The sky-light, the only way to the outside, set nine feet above the flag-stones, overlooks the first courtyard guarded by the con-stabulary on duty at the main gate to the Conciergerie. No human power could breach the massive walls. Moreover, a criminal condemned to death is at once put in a strait-waist-coat, a garment which, as is well-known, deprives him of the use of his hands; is chained by one foot to his immobile camp bed; and has a *sheep* to look after him. The floor of the room is paved with thick stones, and the light is so weak that one can hardly see.

It is impossible not to feel chilled to the bone as one enters, even now, although for sixteen years that room no longer serves any purpose, as a consequence of the changes introduced in Paris in the execution of the decrees of the Law. Imagine the criminal there in the company of his remorse, in silence and darkness, two sources of horror, and ask yourself if it would not have driven you mad? What a constitution it must be whose temper stands up against this situation to which the strait-waistcoat adds immobility, inaction!

The Corsican Théodore Calvi, then aged twenty-seven, shrouded there in almost total secrecy, had nevertheless for two months resisted both the effect of the dungeon and the stool-pigeon's captious jabbering! . . . Let us now look at the singular criminal proceedings which had resulted in the Corsican's condemnation to death. They were curious in the extreme, but to analyse them needn't take us long.

The matter was at that very moment still causing much distress of mind to the jurors in attendance at the session before which Théodore Calvi had appeared. It was a week since the criminal's appeal had been rejected by the Central Court. During that time, Monsieur de Granville's mind had been constantly occupied with the matter, and he had put off the execution from day to day, still hoping to be able to reassure the jurors by publishing the fact that the condemned man, at the threshold of death, had admitted his crime.

A singular criminal trial

A POOR widow of Nanterre, whose house stood isolated within the commune, situated, as is generally known, amid the infertile plain which extends between Mont Valérien and Saint Germain-en-Laye, between the hills of Sartrouville and Argenteuil, had been murdered and robbed several days after receiving her share of an unexpected inheritance. This share amounted to three thousand francs, a dozen pieces of silver tableware, a gold watch and chain and some linen. Instead of banking the three thousand francs in Paris, as she was advised to by the solicitor of the deceased wine merchant who had bequeathed her the legacy, the old lady wanted to keep it all with her. In the first place she had never seen so much money which belonged to her, in the second she mistrusted everybody in every kind of business, like most of the lower orders and especially those who live in the country. After some reflection and after discussion with a wine-merchant in Nanterre, her own kinsman and that of the deceased wine-merchant, the widow had resolved to buy an annuity, to sell her house in Nanterre and to take up lodgings at Saint Germain.

The house in which she lived, with its big, ill-fenced garden, was the sort of indifferent structure which small-holders around Paris have built for themselves. The plaster and rubble-stone so abundant in Nanterre, where the surrounding district is full of open quarries, had been, as they commonly are on the outskirts of Paris, made use of in haste and without the least architectural consideration. It is the hut of the savage in a civilized country. The house contained a ground floor and a first floor with attics above.

The quarryman, this woman's husband and constructor of the dwelling, had placed very solid iron bars in all the windows. The entrance door was of notable solidity. The dead man knew that he was alone there, in open country, and what country! His customers were big master builders in Paris, and so the best part of his building material had been taken in by cart. The carts would then have returned empty, but among the demolitions in Paris he picked out what best suited his purposes and bought it very cheap. Thus, windows, gratings, doors, shutters, much of the joinery, all were the result of authorized depredations, presents from his clients, good, well-chosen presents. Of two window-frames on offer he selected the better. The house, before which stood a very substantial yard, in which were the stables, was shut off by walls from the road. The gate was a massive grating. Moreover, several watch-dogs lived in the stables, and a smaller dog spent the night in the house. Behind the house was a garden of some two and a half acres.

Left a widow and childless, the quarryman's wife lived in the house with one servant. The selling price of his quarry had paid off the quarryman's debts when he died two years previously. The widow's only property was this isolated house, where she fed chickens and cows, selling the eggs and milk in Nanterre. No longer having a stable-boy, a carter or the quarry hands whom the dead man had put to work of every kind, she no longer cultivated the garden, but simply picked the few herbs and vegetables which grew of their own accord out of that stony soil.

The price of the house and the money from her legacy being sufficient to produce seven or eight thousand francs, the woman expected to find herself very well off at Saint Germain with the seven or eight hundred francs' annuity she imagined she would get for her eight thousand francs. She'd had several discussions with the notary in Saint Germain, for she'd refused to make a deed of gift of the money to the wine-merchant in Nanterre who'd asked her to do this. These were the circumstances when, from one day to the next, neither Widow Pigeau nor her servant were to be seen about. The farmyard gate, the door of the house, the shutters, all remained closed. After three days, the Law, informed of this state of affairs, descended upon the place. Popinot, as examining magistrate, accompanied by the district attorney, came out from Paris, and this is what they found.

Neither the grating which gave entrance to the yard nor the door of the house showed any signs of forced entry. The key was found in the lock of the front door, on the inside. Nowhere had an iron bar been forced. The locks, the shutters, all the fastenings were intact.

The outer walls showed no trace which might give a clue to the passage of malefactors. The chimney-pots and earthenware fireplaces were impossible of access, nobody could have got in and out that way. The ridge-tiles, sound and intact, showed no sign of having been disturbed. Penetrating into the bedrooms on the first floor, the magistrates, the constabulary and Bibi-Lupin found the Widow Pigeau strangled in her bed and the servant strangled in hers, by means of the neckerchieves they wore at night. The three thousand francs had been taken, as well as the silver tableware and jewels. The two bodies were in a state of putrefaction, as were those of the house-dog and a big yard-dog. The fencing about the garden was examined, it was nowhere broken. There were no footprints on the garden paths. It seemed probable to the examining magistrate that the murderer had walked on the grass to avoid leaving footprints, if that was the way he had come in, but how had he got into the house? On the garden side, the door had a fanlight protected by three iron bars which had not been tampered with. On that side, the key was equally found in the lock, just as it was at the main door on to the yard at the front.

Once these impossibilities had been fully acknowledged by

Monsieur Popinot, by Bibi-Lupin, who spent a whole day inspecting everything, by the district attorney himself and by the chief constable of the station in Nanterre, the murder became an appalling problem which defeated both politics and the Law.

This drama, reported in the *Gazette des Tribunaux*, had taken place in the winter of 1828 to 1829. God knows to what extent the strange adventure roused interest in Paris; but Paris, which has new dramas to digest every morning, soon forgets. The Police forgets nothing. Three months after that first fruitless search, a public prostitute, observed by Bibi-Lupin's men to be spending freely, and watched because of her known dealings with certain robbers, tried to get one of her friends to pawn a dozen silver dishes and a gold watch and chain. The friend refused. This fact came to the ears of Bibi-Lupin, who remembered the tableware and the gold watch stolen in Nanterre. Immediately the state pawnbrokers and all the known fences and receivers in Paris were questioned, and Bibi-Lupin subjected Manon-la-Blonde to constant watching.

It was presently learnt that Manon-la-Blonde was madly in love with a young man who was scarcely ever seen, for he was said to be deaf to all proofs of love from the fair Manon. The mystery deepened. This young man, subjected to the attention of spies, was presently spotted, then recognized as an escaped convict, the hero of Corsican vendettas, handsome Théodore Calvi, known as Madeleine.

One of those two-faced receivers, who equally serve robbers and the Police, was loosed on Théodore and undertook to buy from him the plate, the watch and the gold chain. Just as this scrap-iron dealer in the Cour Saint Guillaume was counting out the money for Théodore, disguised as a woman, at half past ten in the evening, the Police pounced, arrested Théodore and confiscated the objects.

The judicial inquiry started at once. With such weak evidence, it was impossible to secure conviction on a capital charge that would have satisfied the Attorney General. Calvi never contradicted himself, or gave himself away. He said that a country woman had sold him these objects at Argenteuil, and that, after he'd bought them, rumour of the murder committed at Nanterre enlightened him as to the danger of being found in possession of the plate, watch, jewels, which had been listed in the inventory made on the death of the wine-dealer in Paris, the uncle of Widow Pigeau, and so were known to be stolen goods. Finally, forced by economic necessity to sell them, he said, he'd hoped to get rid of them by way of some uncompromised person.

Nothing could be got out of the discharged convict, who, by his silence and the firmness of his resolution, succeeded in making the magistracy believe that the Nanterre wine-dealer had committed the crime and that it was this man's wife from whom Calvi had bought the compromising articles. Widow Pigeau's unfortunate kinsman and his wife were arrested; but, after a week's detention and careful investigation, it was established that neither husband nor wife had left home at the period of the crime. Moreover, Calvi himself did not identify, in the wine-dealer's wife, the woman who, by his account, had sold him the silver and jewellery.

As Calvi's doxy, caught up in the inquiry, was convicted of having spent something like a thousand francs between the date of the crime and Calvi's attempt to dispose of the loot, such evidence was considered enough to send the convict and the woman before a court of assize. That being the eighteenth murder committed by Théodore, he was condemned to death, for he seemed to be the author of the crime so cleverly committed. Although he did not recognize the wine-dealer's wife from Nanterre, he was recognized by her and by her husband. During the preliminary investigation, numerous witnesses had established the fact of Théodore's residence in Nanterre for a month or more; there he had worked on building sites, ill-clad, his face dusty with plaster. Everybody in Nanterre gave eighteen as the probable age of this boy, who must have been plotting his crime or, as they said, *feeding that baby*, for a month.

The Prosecutor's office believed in the existence of accomplices. The flues were measured for breadth, to see whether fair-haired Manon could have got in by the fireplace; but a child of six could not have been introduced through those chimney-pots, with which present-day architecture has replaced the open chimneys of former times. But for this singular and irritating mystery, Théodore would have been executed a week ago. The prison chaplain had, as we have seen, completely failed with him.

This affair and Calvi's name had escaped the attention of Jacques Collin, then preoccupied with his duel with Contenson, Corentin and Peyrade. Dodgedeath, in any case, wanted as far as possible to forget the mob and everything to do with the Law Courts. He shrank from any encounter which would have brought him face to face with a *fanandel* who might have demanded accounts which the *dab* would have found it impossible to furnish.

Charlie

THE governor of the Conciergerie went at once to the office of the Attorney General and there found the chief prosecution counsel talking with Monsieur de Granville, and holding the order of execution in his hand. Monsieur de Granville, who had just spent all night at the Sérisys' house, although overcome with fatigue and unhappiness, for the doctors did not yet dare to say that the countess would preserve her reason, was obliged, by this important execution, to devote several hours to the work of his office. After a few minutes' conversation with the governor, Monsieur de Granville took the order of execution from the barrister and gave it to Gault.

'Let the execution take place,' he said, 'unless exceptional circumstances arise, which you will judge; I trust in your discretion. The erection of the scaffold may be put off until half past ten, which will give you an hour. On a morning like this, hours are like centuries, and a great deal happens in a century! Don't hold out any hope of a reprieve. Let the prisoner be got ready, if he must, and if there is no confession, give Sanson his orders at half past nine. He can then hold himself in readiness!'

On leaving the Attorney General's office, the prison governor met, beneath the arched passage which led to the gallery, Monsieur Camusot on his way to the place he had just left. He exchanged a few words with the magistrate; and, having informed him about what was happening at the Conciergerie in respect of Jacques Collin, he went down to arrange the confrontation between Dodgedeath and Madeleine; but he did not allow the supposed ecclesiastic to communicate with the condemned man until Bibi-Lupin, convincingly disguised as an armed constable, had replaced the stool-pigeon who was keeping an eye on the young Corsican.

The profound astonishment of the three convicts, when they saw a warder come to fetch Jacques Collin, to lead him to the condemned man's quarters, can hardly be imagined. They pressed simultaneously about the chair on which Jacques Collin was sitting.

'It's for today, isn't it, Monsieur Julien?' Hair's Breadth asked the warder.

'Yes, Charlie's there,' replied the warder with perfect indifference.

Everybody in the prison world gives the name *Charlot* or Charlie to the executioner for Paris. This nickname dates from the revolution of 1789. The name produced a great sensation. All the prisoners looked at each other.

'It's all over!' the warder went on. 'The order of execution has reached Monsieur Gault, and the sentence has just been read out.'

'So,' said La Pouraille, 'pretty-boy Madeleine has received all the sacraments? . . .' and he gulped.

'Poor young Théodore, . . .' cried Biffon, 'he's a good lad. It's no joke to *sneeze in the bran* at his age.'

The warder made his way to the wicket, under the impression that Jacques Collin was following him; but the Spaniard walked slowly, and, when he found himself ten paces behind Julien, he appeared to stumble and with a gesture called for La Pouraille's arm.

'He's a murderer!' said Napolitas to the priest pointing to La Pouraille and offering his own arm.

'No, to me he's a man in misfortune! . . .' replied Dodgedeath with the presence of mind and the unction of the archbishop of Cambrai.

And he moved away from Napolitas, who at first glance had struck him as highly suspect.

'He's on the first step of the Abbey of Mount-Unwilling; but I'm the prior! I'll show you how I'm going to deal with the *Stork*' (the Procurator). 'I'll have that *seat of learning* out of his claws.'

'For the sake of its breeches!' said Hair's Breadth with a smile.

'I desire to give that soul to Heaven!' Jacques Collin answered with compunction seeing other prisoners gather about him.

And he rejoined the warder at the wicket.

'He came to save Madeleine,' said Hair's Breadth, 'we were right. There's a *dab* for you! . . .'

'But how? . . . the guillotine hussars are everywhere, he won't get the lad to himself,' cried Biffon.

'The Baker's on his side!' cried La Pouraille. 'Him, snitch my deeners! . . . He's a chum, that one, he needs us and he likes us. They wanted us to make 'em a present of him, like we was scabs! If he gets Madeleine off, I'll blab to him.'

This last statement, meaning that La Pouraille would let Dodgedeath know where his money was hidden, had the effect of augmenting the devotion of all three convicts to their deity; for at that moment all their hopes were pinned on the Dab.

Jacques Collin, despite the peril in which Madeleine stood, did not forget his part. This man, who knew the Conciergerie as well as he knew the three great convict settlements, took wrong turnings so guilelessly that the warder was obliged to say repeatedly: 'This way, no, along here!' until they reached the head gaoler's office. There, Jacques Collin at once saw, leaning against the stove, a big, heavily built man, whose long, red face was not without distinction, and he recognized Sanson.

'This gentleman is the chaplain,' he said going up to him with every sign of cordiality.

This mistake was so appalling that it froze the onlookers.

'No, sir,' replied Sanson, 'I perform other functions.'

Sanson, father of the last executioner of that name, dismissed in 1847, was the son of him who executed Louis XVI.

After four hundred years of discharging this duty, the heir to so many torturers had endeavoured to repudiate the hereditary burden. The Sansons, executioners in Rouen for two hundred years before they were invested with the first dignity of the kingdom, had been carrying out the decrees of Justice since the thirteenth century. Few families can show an office or a title of nobility handed on from father to son for six hundred years. At the moment when the young man, then a cavalry captain, saw himself with a fine career before him in the Army, his father demanded him as assistant at the execution of the king. Then he was appointed his father's second-in-command when in 1793 two permanent scaffolds were set up; one at the Throne gate, the other in the Strand. Aged, at the time of our story, about sixty, this awful functionary was noted for his excellent attire, his quiet and composed manners, and for the contempt he displayed towards Bibi-Lupin and his acolytes, the machine's provision merchants. The only indication, in this man, which betrayed the fact that in his veins flowed the blood of medieval torturers, was a certain breadth and formidable thickness in his hands. Sufficiently well educated, much concerned with his duties as a citizen and a voter, very fond, it was said, of gardening, this tall, broad-built man, who spoke in a low voice, always calm and of few words, his forehead broad, rather bald, far more closely resembled a member of the British aristocracy than a public executioner. Thus a Spanish canon might well make the mistake which Jacques Collin had made on purpose.

'He's no convict,' said the head warder to the governor.

'I begin to believe it,' thought Monsieur Gault nodding to his subordinate.

The confession

JACQUES COLLIN was introduced into the kind of cellar where young Théodore, in a strait waistcoat, sat on the edge of the dreadful prison bed of his room. Dodgedeath, momentarily catching the light from the corridor, at once recognized

Bibi-Lupin in the constable standing there, leaning on his sword.

'*Io sono Gaba-Morto! Parla nostro italiano*,' Jacques Collin said quickly. '*Vengo ti salvar*,' thus at once indicating to the prisoner who he was by his nickname, that there was some hope and that they must speak a language incomprehensible to the false *gendarme*, who, since he was supposed to be guarding the prisoner, could not leave his post. The fury of the head of the C.I.D. may thus be imagined.

Théodore Calvi, a young man of sallow complexion, fair-haired, with deep-set, ambiguously blue eyes, well-proportioned, of prodigious muscular strength beneath that lymphatic air which is often found in those from the South, would have displayed the most attractive physiognomy but for arched eyebrows and a somewhat low forehead, sinister in their effect, but for red lips of a savage cruelty, and but for a muscular habit in which is revealed that irritability peculiar to Corsicans, the explanation of their readiness to kill in a sudden quarrel.

Seized with astonishment at the voice, Théodore abruptly raised his head and believed in some hallucination; but, as two months of living in this freestone box had accustomed him to its darkness, he looked at the bogus churchman and sighed deeply. He did not recognize Jacques Collin, whose face scarred by the action of sulphuric acid did not in the least seem to him to be that of his Dab.

'It really is me, your Jacques, I'm dressed as a priest and I've come to save you. Don't show you recognize me or do anything stupid, and look as though you were at confession.'

This was spoken rapidly.

'This young man is very low-spirited, death frightens him, he is going to confess all,' said Jacques Collin addressing himself to the armed constable.

'Say something to prove to me that it's *him*, for you only have his voice.'

'You see, he tells me, the poor unfortunate, that he is innocent,' Jacques Collin said again speaking to the constable.

Bibi-Lupin did not dare to speak, for fear of being recognized.

'*Sempremi!*' replied Jacques returning to Théodore and murmuring the code word in his ear.

'*Sempreti!*' said the young man giving the agreed reply. 'It's my Dab all right . . .'

'Did you do it?'

'Yes.'

'Tell me the lot, so I can see how I can set about getting you off; there's not much time, Charlie's here.'

The Corsican at once knelt down and appeared ready to confess. Bibi-Lupin did not know what to do, for the conversation was so rapid that it barely took as long as it does to read. Théodore promptly went over the known circumstances of his crime, which were unknown to Jacques Collin.

'The jury convicted me without proof,' he said in conclusion.

'My child, you argue while they are coming to cut your hair! . . .'

'I need only have been charged with getting rid of the jewels. But that's how a case is judged, even now and in Paris! . . .'

'How did you manage it?' asked Dodgedeath.

'It was easy! Since the last time I saw you, I've got a little Corsican girl I met when I got to' – using the slang name for Paris – '*Pantin.*'

'Men stupid enough to love a woman,' cried Jacques Collin, 'always die for it! . . . They're tigers at large, tigers that prattle and look at themselves in mirrors . . . You were a fool! . . .'

'But . . .'

'Tell me, what use was she, this confounded *largue*? . . .'

'This moppet as big as a handful of sticks, as thin as an eel, as quick as a monkey, got through to the top of the oven and opened the house door for me. The dogs, stuffed with a horse-doctor's poison balls, were dead. I chilled the two women. Once I'd picked up the money, Ginetta shut the door again and got out by way of the oven.'

'An idea as pretty as that deserves a life,' said Jacques Collin, admiring the formation of the crime as a carver admires the modelling of a statuette.

'I was fool enough to lay out all that talent for a thousand crowns! . . .'

'No, for a woman!' Jacques Collin continued. 'When I told you how they take your intelligence away! . . .'

Jacques Collin turned on Théodore a look burning with scorn.

'You weren't around any longer!' replied the Corsican. 'I was on my own.'

'And do you love the child?' asked Jacques Collin sensible of the reproach contained in this reply.

'Oh, if I want to live now, it's more for you than for her.'

'Don't worry! I'm not called Dodgedeath for nothing! I'll see you're all right!'

'What! life! . . .' cried the young Corsican raising his swathed arms towards the damp roof of the dungeon.

'My dear little Madeleine, get ready to go back to the shop on a lifer,' went on Jacques Collin. 'You'll have to wait, they aren't going to crown you with roses, like a fat ox! . . . If they've already got us ironed-up for Rochefort, that was to get rid of us! But I'll get you sent to Toulon, you'll escape, and you'll come back to *Pantin*, where I'll fix up quite a nice little existence for you . . .'

Few such sighs can ever have resounded beneath that merciless vault, it was a sigh exhaled by the joy of deliverance, vibrant against the stone which sent the note back, a note unequalled in music, to the ears of a stupefied Bibi-Lupin.

'It is the effect of the absolution which I just promise him because of all he tells me,' said Jacques Collin to the chief of the detective force. 'These Corsicans, you see, constable, are full of faith! But he is innocent as the Christ child, and I must endeavour to save him . . .'

'God be with you, Father! . . .' said Théodore in French.

Dodgedeath, now more Carlos Herrera, more a canon than ever, left the condemned cell, hurried into the corridor, and presented a face of horror to Monsieur Gault.

'Mr Governor, this young man is innocent, he has told me who the guilty person is! . . . He was about to die for a false point of honour . . . He is a Corsican! Go, please, ask for me,' he said, 'five minutes of interview with the Attorney General. Monsieur de Granville will not refuse to hear immediately a

Spanish priest who suffers so much from the errors of French justice!'

'I shall go at once!' replied Monsieur Gault to the surprise of all who witnessed this extraordinary scene.

'But, please,' said Jacques Collin, 'meanwhile show me into the prison yard, for there I will finish the conversion of a criminal whose heart I have already touched ... They have a heart, those wretches!'

This speech affected everybody there. The constables, the committal clerk, Sanson, the warders, the executioner's assistant, who awaited the order to set up the machine, in prison style; all these, who are little subject to feeling, were moved by an easily imagined curiosity.

In which Mademoiselle Collin appears on the scene

At that moment, an equipage with fine horses was to be heard pulling up at the gates of the Conciergerie, on the quay, with an air of importance. The carriage door was flung open and the steps pulled out so briskly that everyone believed the arrival to be that of a person of great note. Presently, a lady, waving a piece of blue paper and followed by two flunkeys, presented herself at the wicket. Dressed magnificently all in black, a veil thrown back over her hat, she was dabbing her eyes with a large embroidered handkerchief.

Jacques Collin immediately recognized Asia, or, to restore to this woman her real name, Jacqueline Collin, his aunt. The atrocious old creature, worthy of her nephew, her thoughts wholly concentrated on the prisoner, whom she was defending with an intelligence and a perspicacity at least as powerful as those of the Law, held a permit made out the previous evening in the name of the Duchesse de Maufrigneuse's personal maid, on the recommendation of Monsieur de Sérisy, to see Lucien and the Abbé Carlos Herrera as soon as they were out of solitary confinement, and the divisional magistrate in charge of prisons had also scribbled a note on the form. Its very colour indicated that it carried authority; for these permits, like complimentary tickets at theatres, vary in appearance.

The turnkey therefore opened the wicket, the more readily at the sight of the footman with a feather in his hat, his green and gold livery as bright as that of a Russian general, evidence of an aristocratic if not indeed a royal visitor.

'Ah, dear Father!' cried the bogus great lady weeping copiously at sight of the ecclesiastic, 'how could they bring you here, even for a moment, so holy a man!'

The governor took the permit and read: *On the recommendation of His Excellency Count Sérisy.*

'Ah, Madame de San Esteban, Madame la Marquise,' said Carlos Herrera, 'how beautiful this devotion!'

'Madame, communication with prisoners is not quite so informal,' said worthy old Gault.

And he himself halted in passage that tun of black watered silk and lace.

'But from this distance!' protested Jacques Collin, 'and with you present? . . .' he added casting a glance round the assembly.

His aunt, whose costume must have dazed the office staff, the governor, the warders and the constabulary, smelled strongly of musk. Apart from a thousand crowns worth of lace, she wore a black cashmere shawl worth six thousand francs. The footman paraded about the courtyard of the Conciergerie with the insolence of a lackey who knows that he is indispensable to an exacting princess. He did not speak to his fellow-servant, who stood at the quayside gate, kept open during the day.

'What do you want? What am I to do?' said Madame de San Esteban in the slang used between aunt and nephew, a diplomatic code applied to popular speech.

'Put all the letters in a safe place, take out those which are most compromising to those two ladies, come back to the waiting-hall looking like a streetwalker, and await my orders.'

Asia or Jacqueline knelt as though to receive a blessing, and the sham priest blessed his aunt with evangelical compunction.

'*Addio, marchesa!*' he said aloud. 'Also,' he added in their private language, 'find Europe and Paccard with the seven

478

hundred and fifty thousand francs they've made away with, we need them.'

'Paccard is here,' replied the pious marchioness indicating the liveried footman with tears in her eyes.

Such promptitude of understanding caused Jacques Collin not only to smile but to start with surprise. His aunt alone could startle him like that. The false marchioness turned to the witnesses of this scene like a woman certain of her position.

'He is in despair because he cannot go to his child's funeral,' she said in broken French, 'for this frightful miscarriage of Justice has made the holy man's secret known to me! . . . I shall attend the mass for the dead in his place. There, sir,' she said to Monsieur Gault, giving him a purse of gold, 'it is something to relieve the wants of the poor prisoners . . .'

'That's a nice touch!' whispered her satisfied nephew.

Jacques Collin followed the warder who was taking him back to the prison yard.

Bibi-Lupin, chafing furiously, had in the end caught the eye of a real *gendarme*, to whom, since Jacques Collin's departure, he had been addressing significant throat-clearings and who in the end replaced him in the condemned man's room. But Dodgedeath's enemy could not arrive in time to see the great lady, who disappeared in her brilliant equipage, and whose voice, though disguised, carried to his ear its husky tones.

'Three hundred toshes for the boys on remand! . . .' said the head warder showing Bibi-Lupin the purse which Monsieur Gault had handed to his clerk.

'Let's have a look, Jacomety,' said Bibi-Lupin.

The chief of the secret police took the purse, emptied the gold pieces into his palm, examined them carefully.

'Well, it's gold all right! . . .' he said, 'and the purse is stamped with armorial bearings! Ah, the scoundrel! the clever sod! he thinks of everything! He bamboozles the lot of us, every time! . . . He ought to be shot like a dog!'

'What's the matter, then?' asked the clerk taking the purse back.

'The matter is, that woman's a common street whore! . . .' cried Bibi-Lupin stamping his foot with rage on the flagstone outside the wicket.

These words produced a lively effect on the spectators, grouped not too closely about Monsieur Sanson, who remained standing, his back against the big stove, in the middle of that great, vaulted hall, waiting for the order to get the criminal trimmed up and to erect his scaffold in the Strand.

Seduction

ONCE he found himself back in the yard, Jacques Collin walked up to his friends with a true old lag's gait.

'What's on your mind?' he said to La Pouraille.

'It's all up with me,' replied the murderer whom Jacques Collin had led into a corner. 'What I want now is a real mate.'

'Why?'

La Pouraille, having recounted all his crimes to his leader, in cant terms, told him all about the murder and theft at the house of the Crottat couple.

'I admire you,' said Jacques Collin. 'It was a first-class job; but it seems to me you were guilty of one mistake.'

'What?'

'Once it was done, you should have had a Russian passport, disguised yourself as a Russian prince, bought a fine carriage with armorial bearings, gone and boldly placed your gold with a banker, taken out a bill of exchange on Hamburg, posted there with a manservant, a lady's maid and your mistress attired like a princess; then, from Hamburg, taken ship for Mexico. With two hundred and eighty thousand francs in gold, you simpkin, a lad of spirit can do what he wants, and go where he wants!'

'Ah, you think of things like that, because you're a dab! . . . You never lose your seat of learning, you! But me, it's different.'

'Well, good advice to a man in your position, it's offering soup to the dead,' Jacques Collin went on fixing his *fanandel* with a hypnotic stare.

'Too true!' said La Pouraille uncertainly. 'Offer it to me all the same, that soup; if it doesn't feed me, I can wash my feet in it . . .'

'Well, there you are, the Stork's got you, with five classified thefts, three murders, the last of them two wealthy citizens . . . Juries don't like wealthy citizens killing. You'll be stacked for the long passage, you haven't a chance! . . .'

'They told me all that,' replied La Pouraille piteously.

'My Aunt Jacqueline, with whom I've just had a few words right in the gaoler's office, and who is, as you know, the Fanandels' mum, told me the Stork only wanted to be shot of you, they're scared of you.'

'But,' said La Pouraille with a simplicity which shows how deeply imbued thieves are with their *natural right* to steal, 'I'm quids-in right now, what are they worried about?'

'We haven't time to philosophize,' said Jacques Collin. 'Let's get back to the position you're in . . .'

'What can you do about it?' La Pouraille asked interrupting his Dab.

'You'll see! a dead dog is still worth something.'

'Not to itself!' said La Pouraille.

'I'll take you on!' Jacques Collin answered.

'That's something, anyway! . . .' said the murderer. 'Then what?'

'I'm not asking you where the money is, but what you want doing with it?'

La Pouraille studied the impenetrable countenance of his Dab, who went on.

'Is there some *largue* you're fond of, a nipper, a chum that needs looking after? I shall be out of here within an hour, I can fix it for anybody you'd like to see all right.'

La Pouraille still hesitated, bearing his indecision like a rifle at the slope. Jacques Collin then put forward a last argument.

'Your share in our exchequer is thirty thousand francs, are you leaving it to the *fanandels*, are you giving it to somebody? The money is safe, I can lay my hands on it this evening and give it to whoever you're leaving it to.'

The murderer allowed a feeling of pleasure to appear.

'I've got him!' said Jacques Collin to himself. 'But don't let's waste time, make up your mind? . . .' he went on speaking in the ear of La Pouraille. 'We've less than ten minutes, old friend ... The Procurator will be asking for me and I'm going to have a conference with him. I've got him, that man, I can wring the Stork's neck! I'm certain of saving Madeleine.'

'If you save Madeleine, old Dab, well, me, you can ...'

'Let's not waste breath,' said Jacques Collin abruptly. 'Make your will.'

'I'd like la Gonore to have the money,' La Pouraille answered with a piteous air.

'Ah! ... you lived with the widow of Moïse, the Jew who was on the *rollers'* trail in the Midi?' Jacques Collin queried.

Like a great general, Dodgedeath was admirably acquainted with the men in all the troops.

'Herself, yes,' said La Pouraille excessively flattered.

'A pretty woman!' said Jacques Collin who well knew how to manage these terrible machines. 'She's a fine *largue!* she knows everybody, and she'll have been loyal! a bright prigger, too. So! you picked up with la Gonore, eh? it's stupid to get yourself earthed up when you've a *largue* like that. Idiot! You should have started a little business and taken things easy! ... And what's her caper now?'

'She's set up in the rue Sainte Barbe, she runs a house ...'

'Well, then, you're making her your heir? Well, there we are, my lad, that's what happens when we're stupid enough to start loving these trollops ...'

'Don't give it to her till I've taken my tumble!'

'That's a sacred duty,' said Jacques Collin in a serious tone. 'And nothing to the *fanandels*?'

'Nothing, it was them 'at squealed,' La Pouraille answered with an expression of hatred.

'Which of 'em? Do you want me to do him?' asked Jacques Collin eagerly trying to awaken the last feeling which makes these hearts vibrate at the supreme moment. 'You never know, my old chum, I might be able to avenge you and make your peace with the Stork at the same time?'

At this, the murderer gaped at his Dab with sudden happiness.

'Don't forget,' was the Dab's response to this play of the man's features, 'that right now I'm putting on this stunt for nobody but Théodore. After that, if the act goes down well, well, tosh, for a chum, and you're one of mine, tosh, there might be a lot I can do.'

'If only I can see you get poor little Théodore's ceremony postponed, well, look, I'll do anything you tell me.'

'It's in the bag, I know I can get the Stork's claws off his seat of learning. To get out of these holes, you know, La Pouraille, we've all got to give each other a hand ... You can't do anything on your own ...'

'Too true!' cried the murderer.

Confidence was now so well-established between them, and his faith in the *dab* was so fanatical that La Pouraille no longer hesitated.

Last incarnation

LA POURAILLE gave away the names of his accomplices, the secret so carefully guarded till then. That was all Jacques Collin wanted to know.

'Here's the cackle, then! On that job, Ruffard, one of Bibi-Lupin's agents, went third man with me and Godet ...'

'Woolpicker? ...' cried Jacques Collin giving Ruffard his name among the mob.

'That's him. The scabs shopped me, because I know where their dump is and they don't know mine.'

'That's a bit of joy, my handsome!' said Jacques Collin.

'Eh?'

'Well, well,' the Dab answered, 'just look what you stand to gain when you put all your confidence in me! ... Your revenge is now part of my game! ... I'm not asking you where the loot is, you can cough that up last thing; but let me know everything about Ruffard and Godet.'

'You are and you always will be our Dab, I'll keep no secrets from you,' replied La Pouraille. 'My gold is in the cellar at la Gonore's.'

'Can you trust the *largue*?'

'Why, ay, she didn't know when I was monkeying about!'

La Pouraille continued. 'I got la Gonore drunk, though she's a woman who wouldn't blab with her head on the block. All that gold, though!'

'Yes, that curdles the milk of the purest conscience!' replied Jacques Collin.

'So I was able to work without anybody watching! The birds were all in the hen-roost. The gold is three feet underground, behind the wine-bins. There's a layer of stones and mortar over it.'

'Good!' said Jacques Collin. 'And where have the others put theirs?'

'Ruffard's pile is at la Gonore's, too, in the poor woman's bedroom, it's a hold he's got on her, because she could be made accomplice as a receiver and end her days at Saint Lazare.'

'The scab! that's how the dicks set you up for a thief!' said Jacques.

'Godet's lot's at his sister's, a washerwoman for the fine stuff, a good girl who might land herself up with five years' bird. The chum pulled up tiles in the floor, put them back, and scarpered.'

'Do you know what I want from you?' Jacques Collin now said fixing La Pouraille with that same hypnotic gaze.

'What?'

'I want you to say you did Madeleine's job . . .'

La Pouraille gave a violent start; but then at once took up his submissive stance again under the Dab's unmoving stare.

'So you're already kicking! you won't play the game my way! Look! four murders or three, what's the difference?'

'You tell me!'

'By the Fanandels' Meg, is it claret that runs in your vermicelli, or gnats' piss. And me thinking I could save you! . . .'

'That's a right way!'

'Imbecile; if we promise to give the gold back to the family, they'll let you off with a lifer on the big field. I wouldn't give a tanner for your nob if they'd got the rhino; but, right now, you idiot, you're worth seven hundred thousand francs!'

'Dab! Dab!' cried La Pouraille overflowing with happiness.

'What's more,' Jacques Collin persisted, 'we can plant the murders on Ruffard ... At one stroke, Bibi-Lupin comes unstuck ... I've got him!'

La Pouraille remained stupefied by this idea, his eyes grew large, he was like a statue. Arrested three months before, on the eve of his appearance before the Court of Assize, advised by *chums* at La Force, where he'd said not a word about his accomplices, he was so utterly deprived of hope after the preliminary investigation, that this scheme had quite escaped his depressed intellectual powers. Thus the new glimpse of hope plunged him into a state of near-imbecility.

'Have Ruffard and Godet been celebrating already? have they been throwing gold smackers around?' asked Jacques Collin.

'They daren't,' answered La Pouraille. 'The sods are waiting till after I've been topped. That's the message my *largue* sent by la Biffe, when she came to see Biffon.'

'Well, we'll collect their loot within twenty-four hours!' cried Jacques Collin. 'Those jokers won't be able to offer restitution then like you, you'll be as white as snow and all the blood will be on them! The way I'll work it, you'll be turned into an honest lad egged on by them. With your money, I shall be able to fix up alibis for you on the other charges, and once on the big field, because you *will* go there, it's up to you to escape ... It isn't much of a life, but it's life all the same!'

The eyes of La Pouraille showed his inner delirium.

'Old friend! with seven hundred thousand francs you're a hero, you can buy yourself a medal!' Jacques Collin was saying, making his *fanandel* drunk on hope.

'Dab! Dab!'

'I'll make the Minister of Justice's eyes shine ... Ah, Ruffard's the boy for the high jump, that nark wants rubbing out. Bibi-Lupin's goose is cooked.'

'You've said it!' cried La Pouraille with savage joy. 'Now give me your orders, I'll obey.'

And he folded Jacques Collin in his arms, unashamed tears of joy in his eyes so possible did it seem to him now to save his head.

'That's not all,' said Jacques Collin. 'The Stork's digestion is touchy, especially when it comes to new charges. What we've got to do yet is frame some *largue*.'

'How? And what's that for?' asked the murderer.

'Just put your mind to it! You'll see! . . .' Dodgedeath answered.

Jacques Collin rapidly told La Pouraille about the crime committed at Nanterre and made him see the need to have a woman who'd agree to play the part Ginetta had played. Then he went up to Biffon with a gay La Pouraille.

'I know how fond you are of Biffe . . .,' said Jacques Collin to Biffon.

The look on Biffon's face was a horrible poem.

'What will she do while you're out at grass?'

A tear crept into Biffon's fierce eyes.

'Suppose I shut her up for you in the Madelonnettes or Saint Lazare for a year, just long enough for you to be cased, packed off to the field, get there and escape?'

'You can't work miracles, they've nix on her,' replied Biffe's lover.

'Ah, Biffon my boy,' said La Pouraille, 'our Dab can do anything Meg almighty can do! . . .'

'What's the password between you and her?' Jacques Collin asked Biffon with the assurance of a master who can't be denied.

'*Pantin* by night. If you say that, she knows you come from me, and if you want her to do something, show her a ten-hog piece and say: "Clip it!"'

'She'll be sentenced alongside La Pouraille here, and released on confession after a year in the shade!' said Jacques Collin sententiously looking at La Pouraille.

La Pouraille understood his *dab*'s scheme, and promised him, with a look, to persuade Biffon to cooperate by obtaining Biffe's sham complicity in the crime he was going to admit.

'Good-bye, then, children. You'll be hearing presently that I've saved my youngster from the hands of Charlie,' said Dodgedeath. 'Yes, Charlie was there at the desk with his waiting-maids to perform Madeleine's toilet! Ah, but,' he said, 'I can see they're coming to look for me on the part of His Majesty the Stork.'

A warder had indeed appeared through the wicket and was making a sign to this extraordinary man, to whom the young Corsican's peril had restored all the savage power with which he battled against society.

It is not without interest to note here that, at the moment when Lucien's body was taken away from him, Jacques Collin had resolved, in a moment of supreme decision, to attempt a last incarnation, not with a living creature, but with a thing. He had as fatally made his last cast as Napoleon aboard the shallop which rowed him out to the Bellerophon. By a strange concatenation of circumstances, everything conspired to aid this genius of evil and corruption in his enterprise.

Thus, even though the unexpected outcome of this life of crime thereby loses a little of that air of the marvellous, which, in our time, is achieved only through the abandonment of all verisimilitude, we must, before we penetrate with Jacques Collin into the office of the Attorney General, follow Madame Camusot as she calls on various people, while all these things were going on at the Conciergerie. An obligation forever incumbent upon the historian of our changing customs is that of never spoiling the truth by supposedly dramatic contrivances, especially when the truth itself has been at pains to take the form of a novel. The natural history of man's society, especially in Paris, comprises so many freaks of chance, such tangling of conjecture and caprice, that the imagination of the inventor is left far behind. The boldness of truth rises to a level of coincidence forbidden to art, so improbable, so indecorous are its devices, so that the writer must tone them down, trim and prune them.

Madame Camusot's first call

MADAME Camusot endeavoured to get herself up for the morning in a style with pretensions to good taste, difficult work for the wife of a judge who had spent most of the past six years in the provinces. It was a question of avoiding criticism at the houses of the Marquise d'Espard and the Duchesse de Maufrigneuse, when calling on them between eight and nine o'clock in the morning. Amélie-Cécile Camusot, although, let us hasten to say, *née* Thirion, half-succeeded. In the matter of dress, may we not say that this is to deceive oneself twice over? . . .

It is difficult to over-estimate the value of Parisian women to those who are ambitious in any field; their participation is as necessary in society as in the underworld, where, as we have just seen, they play a very considerable part. Take, for instance, a man who, in order not to be left behind in the arena, must, within a given time, speak to the personage still known as the Keeper of the Seals, whose influence under the Restoration was enormous. A judge might be thought in a favourable position, almost a regular visitor. And yet such a magistrate is obliged to seek out some departmental head, or a private secretary, or the general secretary, and to persuade them of his need for an immediate audience. Is a Keeper of the Seals to be seen there and then without warning? During the day, if he is not in the House, he is at a cabinet meeting, or he is signing documents, or he has other callers. In the morning, one does not know where he is to be found in bed. In the evening, he has public and private engagements. If all the judges were able to demand their five minutes' attention, on any pretext whatever, the head of the legal system would be under constant siege. The purpose for which a prompt and private interview is sought must therefore be submitted to the consideration of one of the various intermediate powers, who become obstacles, doors to open, themselves beset by competitors. A woman, on the other hand, goes in search of another woman; she gains immediate access to a bedroom, arousing curiosity either in the mistress or her maid, especially when the mistress is labouring under external pressure or keen self-interest. The female authority known as Madame d'Espard, who held a ministry in her hands, had only to write a little perfumed note and dispatch it by a footman to the minister's valet. The missive reaches the minister as he awakes, he reads it at once. Whatever his business that day, the minister is delighted to call on one of the queens of Paris, one of the powers of the Faubourg Saint Germain, one of the favourites of *Madame*, of the Dauphin or the King. Casimir Périer, the one real prime minister after the July revolution, put everything aside to call on a former first gentleman of the bedchamber of King Charles X.

Such a view of the matter explains the effect of the words: 'Madame, here is Madame Camusot on an urgent matter, which Madame knows about!' said to the Marquise d'Espard by her maid who supposed her to be awake.

Thus the marchioness cried out that Amélie was to be shown in without delay. The magistrate's wife was listened to carefully, when she began with these words:

'Madame la Marquise, we are ruined for having tried to avenge you . . .'

'What, my little picture? . . .' replied the marchioness inspecting Madame Camusot in the penumbra cast by the half-open door. 'You look divine, this morning, in that little hat. Where do you find models like that? . . .'

'Madame, you are most kind . . . But you must know that the way in which Camusot interrogated Lucien de Rubempré reduced the young man to despair, and that he hanged himself in prison . . .'

'Whatever will happen to Madame de Sérisy?' cried the marchioness pretending ignorance so that she could hear all again.

'Alas! she is thought to have gone out of her mind, . . .' replied Amelia. 'Ah! if you can arrange for His Highness to summon my husband at once by courier to the Law Courts, the minister will learn the strangest things, the King will be most interested . . . Then Camusot's enemies will be reduced to silence.'

'Who are Camusot's enemies?' asked the marquise.

'First, the Attorney General, and now Monsieur de Sérisy . . .'

'Splendid, my child,' replied Madame d'Espard, who owed to Messieurs de Granville and Sérisy her defeat in the ignoble lawsuit she had brought to deprive her husband of the control of his estate, 'I shall defend you. I forget neither my friends, nor my enemies.'

She rang, had the curtains drawn, light flooded into the

room, she demanded her writing-desk, and her maid brought it. The marchioness rapidly scribbled a short letter.

'Tell Goddard to saddle a horse, and take this note to the chancellery; there is no reply,' she said to her maid.

The maid went out briskly, but, in spite of her orders, stayed at the door listening for a while.

'There are dark secrets, then, are there?' asked Madame d'Espard. 'Tell me all about them, my dear. Isn't Clotilde de Grandlieu mixed up in the matter?'

'Madame la Marquise will learn all that from His Highness, for my husband told me nothing, he only warned me of his danger. It would be better for us for Madame de Sérisy to die than to stay out of her mind.'

'Poor woman!' said the marquise. 'But was she *in* her mind?'

By the hundred different ways they have of pronouncing the same phrase, society women display to attentive ears the boundless range of musical modes. The soul reveals itself as much in the voice as in the look, it impresses itself on light as on the air, the elements upon which the eyes and the larynx respectively work. By her accentuation of those two words: 'Poor woman!' the marchioness allowed the contentment of satisfied hatred, the happiness of triumph, to be divined. Ah! how great the misfortunes she wished for the protectress of Lucien! Vengeance beyond the death of the hated object, never assuaged, produces a gloomy and fearful effect. Herself of a ruthless, vindictive and meddlesome nature, Madame Camusot was nevertheless dumbfounded. She could think of nothing to say, she remained silent.

'Diana told me, indeed, that Léontine had gone to the prison,' Madame d'Espard continued. 'The dear duchess is most upset by this sudden stroke, for it is one of her weaknesses to be extremely fond of Madame de Sérisy; but it is understandable, they adored that little idiot Lucien at much the same time, and nothing so unites or disunites two women as paying their devotions at the same altar. And so this kind friend yesterday spent two hours in Léontine's room. It seems that the poor countess says dreadful things! I'm told it was downright disgusting! . . . A respectable woman really ought not to be subject to such attacks! . . . For shame! It was a wholly physical passion . . . The duchess came to see me as pale as death, she's terribly brave! There is something about this affair which is utterly monstrous . . .'

'My husband will justify himself in telling all to the Keeper of the Seals, for they wanted to save Lucien, and he, Madame la Marquise, only did his duty. An examining magistrate is bound to examine those in solitary confinement, with no more delay than the law allows! . . . Questions of some kind had to be put to the wretched young man, who didn't understand that the interrogation was a formality, so that he started confessing at once . . .'

'He was an impertinent young fool!' Madame d'Espard said curtly.

The magistrate's wife held her tongue on hearing this decree.

'If the petition in respect of Monsieur d'Espard was thrown out, it was not Camusot's fault, I shall always remember that!' the marchioness went on after a pause . . . 'It was Lucien, with Messieurs de Sérisy, Bauvan and Granville who defeated us. In time, God will be on my side! All those men will end badly. Don't worry, I shall send the Chevalier d'Espard to the Keeper of the Seals so that he makes haste to send for your husband, if that will help . . .'

'Ah, Madame! . . .'

'Listen!' said the marquise, 'I promise you the decoration of the Legion of Honour immediately, tomorrow! That will be a signal witness to my satisfaction at your conduct in this matter. Yes, it will be a further censure on Lucien, it will declare him guilty! People don't often hang themselves for pleasure . . . And so good-bye, pretty one!'

Madame Camusot's second call

TEN minutes later, Madame Camusot entered the bedroom of the fair Diane de Maufrigneuse, who, having gone to bed at one o'clock, was still not asleep at nine.

However insensitive duchesses may be, they are women

who, despite their stucco hearts, cannot see one of their friends afflicted by madness without the fact making some impression on them.

Moreover, the bond between Diane and Lucien, though dissolved eighteen months ago, had left enough memories in the duchess's mind for the child's tragic death to deal her also a sufficient blow. All night Diana had been seeing that handsome young man, so charming, so poetical, so adept at making love, hanged as Léontine depicted him in her attacks and with the gestures of raging fever. She had kept eloquent, intoxicating letters from Lucien, comparable with those written by Mirabeau to Sophie, but more literary, more polished, for they were letters dictated by the most violent of passions, vanity! To possess the most ravishing of duchesses, to see her commit follies for him, and those in secret, such happiness had turned Lucien's head. The pride of the lover had truly inspired the poet. The duchess had therefore kept these moving letters, as some old men collect obscene engravings, for the sake of their hyperbolical eulogies upon what was least duchesslike about her.

'And he died in a low prison!' she said to herself fearfully clutching the letters as she heard her maid knock gently on the door.

'Madame Camusot, on business of the utmost gravity which concerns Madame la Duchesse,' the maid announced.

Diana at once got to her feet in terror.

'Oh!' she said looking at Amélie who had put on a face suited to the occasion, 'I can guess all! It is about my letters . . . Ah, my letters! . . . Ah, my letters! . . .' And she dropped on to a little settee. She remembered how, in her throes of passion, she had replied to Lucien in the same key, celebrating the poetry of the male just as he hymned the glories of womanhood, and not less dithyrambically!

'Indeed, yes, Madame, I have come to save more than your life! it touches your honour . . . Pull yourself together, get dressed, and come along to the Duchesse de Grandlieu's; since, happily for you, others besides yourself are compromised.'

'But Léontine, yesterday, burned, I was told, at the Palais, all the letters seized at our poor Lucien's apartment?'

'Alas, Madame, Lucien was coupled with Jacques Collin!' cried the magistrate's wife. 'You forget that frightful companionship, which, I am sure, is the sole cause of the death of that charming and regrettable young man! Well, now, that penitential Machiavelli, *he* never lost *his* head! Monsieur Camusot knows for a certainty that that monster has put away in a safe place the most compromising letters from the mistresses of his . . .'

'His friend,' said the duchess quickly. 'You are right, my pretty child, we must go and take counsel with the Grandlieus. We are all concerned in this affair, and we are lucky to have Sérisy with us . . .'

Extreme danger has, as we have seen from the happenings at the Conciergerie, as great an effect on the soul as powerful reagents on the body. It is a Volta battery of the mind. The day may not be far off when we shall discover by just what chemical means feeling is condensed into a fluid, similar perhaps to electricity.

The same phenomenon took place in the duchess as in the convict. Cast down, half-dead, this duchess who hadn't slept and who was always difficult to dress, recovered the strength of a lioness at bay, and the presence of mind of a general under fire. Diana herself then picked up garments and improvised her toilet with the speed of a seamstress who is her own maid. The achievement was so remarkable that the lady's maid remained standing where she was for a moment, astonished to see her mistress in a shift, possibly happy to let the judge's wife see, through the light mist of the linen, a white body as perfect as that of Canova's Venus. It was like a piece of jewellery wrapped in tissue paper. Diana had suddenly noticed her quick-service corset, fastening at the front, which saves women in a hurry all the time wasted in lacing. She had already comfortably disposed the lace of her petticoat and the splendours of her bosom, when the maid brought her underskirt, and completed the job with a gown. While Amelia, at a sign from the maid, fastened this behind and helped the duchess, the maid fetched stockings in Scotch thread, velvet half-boots, a shawl and a hat. Amelia and the maid each shod one leg.

'You are the most beautiful woman I have seen,' said Amelia with due calculation kissing Diana's fine, smooth knee rapturously.

'Madame is without equal,' said the maid.

'Come now, Josette, be quiet,' replied the duchess. 'Have you a carriage?' she said to Madame Camusot. 'Let's be off, my pretty, we'll talk on the way.' And the duchess ran down the great staircase of the Cadignan mansion drawing on her gloves, a sight which had never been seen.

'To the Grandlieus, with speed!' she said to one of her servants, signing to him to get up behind the carriage.

The footman hesitated, for it was a hackney carriage.

'Ah, Madame la Duchesse, you didn't tell me that the young man had letters from you! otherwise, Camusot would have set about the matter differently . . .'

'I was so preoccupied by Léontine's situation that I altogether forgot about myself,' said she. 'The poor woman was nearly out of her mind the day before yesterday, so you can judge the effect of this fatal upshot! Ah! if you only knew, my dear, what a day we had yesterday . . . No, really, it's enough to make one give up love. In the morning, dragged the two of us, Léontine and I, by a horrible old woman, a clothes dealer, very capable I must say, into that smelly, bleeding sink called the Law, I said to her, on our way to the Palais: "Couldn't one, really, fall on one's knees and cry out, like Madame de Nucingen, when, on her way to Naples, she was overtaken by one of those fearful storms in the Mediterranean: 'Dear God! save me, and I promise never again!' I shall certainly remember these two days! why do we write letters? . . . But there, one is in love, one receives pages which set the heart on fire by way of the eyes, everything bursts into flame! caution is thrown to the wind! and one writes back . . .'

'Why write, when you can act!' said Madame Camusot.

'All for love!' said the duchess proudly. 'Destroying oneself is a pleasure at the time.'

'Beautiful women,' modestly commented Madame Camusot, 'must be excused, they have more opportunities than the rest of us to succumb!'

The duchess smiled.

'We are always too generous,' Diane de Maufrigneuse continued. 'I shall do like that frightful Madame d'Espard.'

'What does she do?' the magistrate's wife asked curiously.

'She's written at least a thousand love-letters . . .'

'As many as that! . . .' cried la Camusot interrupting the duchess.

'. . . And you wouldn't, my dear, find a single compromising word in them all . . .'

'You couldn't keep up that coldness, that calculation,' Madame Camusot replied. 'You're a woman, you're one of those angels who can't resist the devil . . .'

'I have sworn that I will never write again. I never, in my whole life, wrote to anyone but the unfortunate Lucien . . . I shall keep his letters until the day I die! My dear child, it warms one, and one needs warming at times . . .'

'But if they were found!' said la Camusot with a shy little gesture.

'Oh, I should say they were the beginning of a novel. For I copied them all out, my dear, and burned the originals!'

'Oh, Madame, as a reward, let me read them . . .'

'I might,' said the duchess. 'You will see then, my dear, that he didn't write like that to Léontine!'

There spoke the whole of womankind, the woman of all ages and every country.

An important figure vowed to oblivion

LIKE the frog in La Fontaine's fable, Madame Camusot was bursting in her skin with pleasure at entering the Grandlieu house in the company of the fair Diane de Maufrigneuse. She was to forge, that morning, one of the links so necessary to ambition. She could already hear herself being addressed as 'Madame la Présidente'. She experienced the ineffable joy of overcoming enormous obstacles, the chief of which was her husband's incapacity, still unknown to the world, but clear enough to her. To bring success to a second-rate man! for a woman, as for kings, the pleasure is like that which appeals to so many actors, the pleasure of giving a hundred performances of a bad play. It is the intoxication of egoism! In a sense it is also the saturnalia of power. Power especially proves itself to itself by the singular abuse of itself which consists in crowning some absurdity with the laurels of success, thereby insulting genius, the only strength which power can never attain. The promotion of Caligula's horse, that imperial farce, has enjoyed an almost unbroken run.

Within minutes, Diana and Amelia had passed from the elegant disorder of the fair Diana's bedroom to the carefully ordered grandeur and severe luxury of the Grandlieu establishment.

The Duchesse de Grandlieu was Portuguese and very pious. She rose at eight every morning and went to mass at the little church of Sainte Valère, succursal of Saint Thomas Aquinas's, then in the Esplanade des Invalides. This chapel, later demolished, was moved to the rue de Bourgogne, to make way for a Gothic church to be dedicated to Sainte Clotilde.

At the first words murmured into the ear of the Duchesse de Grandlieu by Diane de Maufrigneuse, the pious woman went to Monsieur de Grandlieu's apartments and at once returned with him. The duke cast upon Madame Camusot one of those rapid glances with which great lords analyse a whole existence and often the soul. Amelia's costume helped him to sum up that middle-class course of life from Alençon to Mantes, and from Mantes to Paris.

If the magistrate's wife had understood the gift dukes have, she might have quailed before that look so politely ironical, in which she perceived only politeness. Ignorance shares the privileges of guile.

'This is Madame Camusot, Thirion's daughter, one of the royal ushers,' said the duchess to her husband.

The duke bowed *very* politely to the lawyer's wife, and his face lost a little of its solemnity. He rang, and his valet appeared.

'Go to the rue Honoré Chevalier, take a carriage. There, you will ring at a little door, Number 10. Tell the servant who comes to open the door that I beg his or her master to come along here; if this gentleman is at home bring him with you.

Use my name, it will do to smooth out any difficulties. Try not to spend more than a quarter of an hour over all this.'

Another footman, the duchess's, appeared the moment the duke's man had gone.

'Go from me to the Duc de Chaulieu's, have this card handed to him.' The duke gave the man his card turned down in a particular way. When these two intimate friends felt the need to see each other at once over some urgent and mysterious affair which could not be set down in writing, they summoned each other in that way.

As we see, customs do not vary at different levels of society, except superficially. High society has its own slang, but that slang is known as *form*.

'Are you quite certain, Madame, that there are indeed such letters written by Mademoiselle Clotilde de Grandlieu to this young man?' said the Duc de Grandlieu. And the look he now cast on Madame Camusot was like a mariner's lead.

'I haven't seen them, but it is to be feared,' she replied nervously.

'My daughter can have written nothing unavowable!' cried the duchess.

'Poor duchess!' thought Diana looking at the duke in a way that made him tremble.

'What do you think, dear little Diana?' said the duke in the Duchesse de Maufrigneuse's ear as he led her to a window embrasure.

'Clotilde so doted on Lucien, my dear, that she arranged a meeting before her departure. But for little Lenoncourt, she might have fled with him in the forest of Fontainebleau! I know that Lucien wrote letters to Clotilde that would have turned the head of a saint! We are three daughters of Eve enveloped by the serpent of correspondence . . .'

The duke and Diana turned from the embrasure and came back to the duchess and Madame Camusot, who were talking in low voices. Amelia, who in this was following the advice of the Duchesse de Maufrigneuse, pretended to be extremely devout in order to win the heart of the proud Portuguese.

'We are at the mercy of a vile escaped convict!' said the duke with a peculiar shrug. 'That is what comes of receiving

497

in the house persons of whom one is not perfectly sure! Before anyone is admitted, one should know all about his means, his kinsfolk, his antecedents . . .'

From the aristocratic point of view, that is the moral of our story.

'It is too late to think of that,' said the Duchesse de Maufrigneuse. 'What we have to do now is save poor Madame de Sérisy, Clotilde, and me . . .'

'We can only wait for Henry, I've sent for him; but everything depends on the individual Gentil has gone to look for. God grant the man be in Paris! Madame,' he said addressing Madame Camusot, 'I am grateful to you for having thought of us . . .'

This was Madame Camusot's dismissal. The royal usher's daughter had enough wit to understand the duke, she got up; but the Duchesse de Maufrigneuse, with the adorable grace which won her so many friendships and secrets, took Amélie by the hand and turned her significantly to the duke and duchess.

'On my own account, and as if she had not risen at dawn to save us all, I shall ask you to do more than remember my little Madame Camusot. First she has rendered me a service of the kind one doesn't forget; then she is altogether on our side, she and her husband. I have promised to help her Camusot to get on, and I beg you to afford him your especial protection, for my sake.'

'You have no need of such recommendation,' said the duke to Madame Camusot. 'The Grandlieus always remember the services they have been rendered. The King's people will presently have an opportunity of distinguishing themselves, of proving their devotion, there will be an opening for your husband . . .'

Madame Camusot withdrew proud, swollen to the point of suffocation. She returned home triumphant, full of admiration for herself, she laughed at the hostility of the Procurator General. She said to herself: 'Suppose we got Monsieur de Granville out!'

IT was time for Madame Camusot to withdraw. The Duc de Chaulieu, one of the King's favourites, passed this middle-class lady on the steps outside.

'Henry,' cried the Duc de Grandlieu when he heard his friend's name announced, 'hurry, I beg you, to the Palace, try to see the King, this is what it is all about.' And he led the duke into the window embrasure where he had already talked with the light and graceful Diana.

From time to time the Duc de Chaulieu looked sideways at the flighty duchess, who, as she talked with the pious one and allowed herself to be sermonized, responded to the Duc de Chaulieu's glances.

'My dear child,' said the Duc de Grandlieu when his talk aside was finally over, 'do try to behave yourself! Look!' he added taking Diana's hands, 'just keep the rules, don't compromise yourself again, never write letters! Letters, my dear, have caused as much private grief as public misfortune . . . What might be forgiven to a girl like Clotilde, in love for the first time, is quite without excuse in . . .'

'An old grenadier who has been under fire!' said the duchess pouting at the duke. The joke and the play of expression on her face brought a smile to the grieved faces of the two dukes and the pious duchess herself. 'I haven't written a love-letter for four years! . . . Are we saved?' asked Diana who was concealing a good deal of anxiety under this childish behaviour.

'Not yet!' said the Duc de Chaulieu. 'You don't know how difficult it is to perform an arbitrary action. To a constitutional monarch, it is much the same thing as infidelity in a married woman. That is his form of adultery.'

'His besetting sin!' said the Duc de Grandlieu.

'Forbidden fruit!' answered Diana with a smile. 'Oh! how I should like to be the government; for there's no such fruit left for me now, I've eaten it all.'

'Child! child!' said the pious duchess, 'you go too far.'

The two dukes, hearing a carriage draw to a halt before the outside steps with the noise and commotion of horses which have been put to a gallop, bowed to the two women and left them together, and went into the Duc de Grandlieu's study, to which the dweller in the rue Honoré Chevalier was shown in. This was none other than the head of counter-espionage at the Palace, the obscure and powerful Corentin.

'Come in,' said the Duc de Grandlieu, 'come in, Monsieur de Saint Denis.'

Corentin, surprised at the duke's long memory, bowed deeply to the dukes and went in.

'It still concerns the same person, at any rate it's connected with him,' said the Duc de Grandlieu.

'But he's dead,' said Corentin.

'There is still a companion,' the Duc de Chaulieu observed, 'a rough companion.'

'The convict, Jacques Collin!' answered Corentin.

'Speak, Ferdinand,' said the Duc de Chaulieu to the former ambassador.

'The wretch is still to be feared,' continued the Duc de Grandlieu, 'he's got hold, for purposes of blackmail, of the letters which Mesdames de Sérisy and Maufrigneuse wrote to this Lucien Chardon, his creature. It seems to have been a practice with this young man to obtain passionate letters in reply to his own; for Mademoiselle de Grandlieu, it appears, wrote one or two; we fear, at any rate, that it is so, and we can know nothing with certainty, she's abroad . . .'

'The young fellow himself,' replied Corentin, 'was quite incapable of so much forethought! . . . It was a precaution taken by Father Carlos Herrera!' Corentin propped his elbow on the arm of the chair in which he was sitting, and put his head in his hand to reflect. 'Money! . . . this man has more than we have,' he said. 'Esther Gobseck served him as bait to catch nearly two millions in that fishpond of gold pieces called Nucingen . . . Gentlemen, see that I am given full authority in the right quarter, and I will rid you of this man! . . .'

'And . . . of the letters?' the Duc de Grandlieu asked Corentin.

'Listen, gentlemen,' Corentin went on rising and showing his angry weasel's face. He thrust his hands into the front pockets of his long, black-flannel trousers. This great actor in the historical drama of the time had put on only a waistcoat and frock coat, he hadn't changed his trousers, so well did he know how appreciative the great are of promptitude on certain occasions. He walked familiarly up and down the study talking aloud, as though he had been alone. 'He's a convict! he could be thrown, without trial, into a cell at Bicêtre, deprived of all communication with the outside world, and left to rot . . . He might, of course, have left instructions with his followers, in case that happened!'

'He was put in solitary confinement,' said the Duc de Grandlieu, 'at once, after he'd been taken at the girl's house, without warning.'

'I wonder if any cell can confine that scoundrel?' replied Corentin. 'He is as full of tricks as . . . as I am!'

'What, then?' the two dukes inquired of each other by a glance.

'We can clap the rogue in the penitentiary at once, . . . at Rochefort, he'll be dead in six months there! Oh! without violence!' he said in reply to a gesture from the Duc de Grandlieu. 'What do you expect? a convict doesn't last more than six months in a hot summer when he's really made to work in the mists off the Charente. But this will only do if our man has failed to take precautions about those letters. If the joker thought what his adversaries might be up to, and it seems likely he did, we shall have to find out what those precautions were. If the letters are in the keeping of somebody poor, he can be bought . . . So we must get Jacques Collin to talk! What a battle that would be, I should lose! No, the best thing will be to swap one sort of letters for another! . . . letters of pardon, and let me have that man in my shop. Jacques Collin is the only man with the capacity to become my successor, since poor Contenson and dear Peyrade are dead. Jacques Collin killed me those two incomparable spies as if to make a place for himself. You see, gentlemen, I shall have to be given a free hand. Jacques Collin is in the Conciergerie. I'm going to see Monsieur de Granville in his office. Let somebody in your confidence meet me there; either I need a letter to show Monsieur de Granville, who doesn't know me, a letter which of course I should return to the head of the government, or else somebody important to speak for me . . . There's half an hour to spare, it will take me about that to dress, that is to say to become what I need to be in the eyes of the Director of Public Prosecutions.'

'Sir,' said the Duc de Chaulieu, 'I know how profoundly clever you are, and I only want a simple yes or no. Can you guarantee to succeed?'

'Yes, with unlimited authority, and with your undertaking to see that I am never questioned on the subject. I have my plan ready.'

This sinister reply provoked a slight tremor in the two dukes.

'Be off, then, sir!' said the Duc de Chaulieu. 'The matter is to be charged up to the accounts on which you usually draw in the course of your duties.'

Corentin saluted the two great lords and left.

Henri de Lenoncourt, for whom Ferdinand de Grandlieu had a carriage waiting, went round at once to the King, whom he was able to see at any time, by reason of his court functions.

Thus, the diverse interests caught up together, at the lowest and the highest levels, were all to meet in the Procurator General's office, brought all together by necessity and represented by three men: the law by Monsieur de Granville, family interests by Corentin, faced by his terrible adversary, Jacques Collin, who embodied social evil in all its savage energy.

The duel lay between justice and governmental power, united against the underworld and its wiles! The underworld, the penitentiary, symbol of the daring which overrides calculation and reflection, to which all means are good, which can dispense with the hypocrisy of formally constituted authority, hideous representative of the interests of the empty belly, the bloody, swift protest of hunger! These were the attackers and the defenders, theft and property, the dreadful question of the social and the natural states confronting each other in the narrowest possible space. In short, this was to be a terrible, living image of the anti-social compromises into which the feeble embodiments of legally constituted authority are forced to enter with the forces of revolt.

Troubles of a public prosecutor

WHEN Monsieur Camusot was announced to the Procureur Général, the latter made a sign that he should be shown in. Monsieur de Granville, who expected this visit, wished to come to an understanding with the magistrate on the way of concluding Lucien's affair. The arrangement he had made, with Camusot, the previous day, before the poor poet's death, could no longer stand.

'Sit down, Monsieur Camusot,' said Monsieur de Granville, himself sitting down heavily.

Alone with his subordinate, the senior magistrate made no attempt to conceal his dejection. Camusot looked at Monsieur de Granville and saw on that strong face an almost livid pallor, and an extreme tiredness, an air of prostration which denoted suffering possibly more acute than that of a man condemned to death to whom the clerk has just read out the rejection of his appeal. Yet such a reading means, in the language of law: Prepare yourself, your last moments have come.

'I will come back, Monsieur le Comte,' said Camusot, 'though the matter *is* rather urgent . . .'

'No, stay,' replied the Procurator with dignity. 'True magistrates, sir, must accept their moments of anguish and know how to hide them. It was wrong of me, if you observed in me signs of perturbation . . .'

Camusot did not speak.

'May God spare you, Monsieur Camusot, the worst of the necessities of our life! One might succumb to less! I have just spent the night with one of my dearest friends, I have only two such friends, Count Octave de Bauvan and Count Sérisy. We remained, Monsieur de Sérisy, Count Octave and I, from six o'clock yesterday evening till six this morning, taking it in turn to go from the drawing-room to the bedside of Madame de Sérisy, fearing each time to find her dead or irrecoverably mad! Desplein, Bianchon, Sinard with two attendants did not leave the bedroom. The count adores his wife. Think what a night I have spent between a woman mad with love and a friend mad with despair. A statesman does not show his despair like a fool! Sérisy, calm as though in his place at a meeting of the Council of State, writhed in his chair to show us a calm face. That forehead bent by such heavy labours was covered with sweat. I slept from five o'clock to half past seven, overcome by fatigue, and I had to be here at eight o'clock to give orders for an execution. Believe me, Monsieur Camusot, when a man in my position has lain all night in an abyss of grief, feeling the hand of God weigh heavy on human life and strike blow after blow on noble hearts, it is difficult for him to sit there, before his desk, and to say coldly: "Let a head fall at four! destroy one of God's creatures full of life, of strength, of health." Yet such is my duty! ... Bowed down with grief, I must give the order for the scaffold to be raised ...

'The condemned man does not know that the magistrate feels an anguish no less great than his own. At this moment, linked to each other by a sheet of paper, myself representing a society which exacts vengeance, he the crime to be expiated, we are the two heads of a single duty, two existences joined for an instant by the knife of the law. Nobody pities, nobody consoles the magistrate's sufferings. It is our glory to bury them deep in our hearts! The priest, with his life offered to God, the soldier and his thousand dead given to the country, seem to me happy beside the magistrate with his doubts, his fears, his terrible responsibility.

'You know,' continued the Procurator General, 'that we have to execute a young man of twenty-seven, handsome like the one who died on us yesterday, fair like him, whose head became forfeit against our expectations; since the only charges against him were for receiving. Under sentence, this lad hasn't confessed! For seventy days now, he's resisted every test, insisting all the time that he's innocent. For the past two months, I've had two heads on my shoulders! Oh, I'd give a year of my life to receive his confession, juries need reassuring! ... Think what a blow it would be to Justice if one day it were discovered that the crime for which he is to die had been committed by somebody else.

'In Paris, everything is a matter of great weight, the smallest judicial incidents take on a political importance.

'The jury, that institution which our revolutionary legislators believed in so strongly, has become an instrument of social ruin; it fails in its purpose, it doesn't afford society due protection. The jury refuses to take its function seriously. Jurors are divided into two schools, one of which wants to abolish capital punishment, and the result is to destroy all idea of equality before the law. With a dreadful crime like parricide, for instance, in one region a verdict of not-guilty will be brought in, while elsewhere what we may describe as an ordinary crime is punished with death! What would be the result if, under our jurisdiction, here in Paris, we executed an innocent man?'

'He is an escaped convict,' observed Monsieur Camusot timidly.

'In the hands of the Opposition and the Press, he'd be a Paschal lamb!' cried Monsieur de Granville, 'and the Opposition could whitewash him as it chose, for he's a Corsican fanatic with all the notions of his country, his murders would be the results of a *vendetta*! . . . In that island, if you kill your enemy, you still consider yourself, and are considered, to be an excellent fellow.

'Ah, what an unfortunate man your true magistrate is! You know, they ought to live outside the community, as pontiffs once did. The world should only see them when they emerged from their cells at fixed times, solemn, ancient, venerable, pronouncing judgment like the high priests of antiquity, combining in themselves the judicial and the sacerdotal powers! We should only be visible on the bench . . . Nowadays we may be seen amusing ourselves or in difficulties like anybody else! . . . We may be seen in drawing-rooms, at home, citizens, creatures of passion, and instead of being terrible we are grotesque . . .'

This superb utterance, punctuated by rests and interjections, accompanied by gestures which gave it an eloquence difficult to set down on paper, made Camusot shiver.

'MYSELF, sir,' said Camusot, 'yesterday I too began my apprenticeship to the pains of our condition! . . . The death of that young man almost killed me, he didn't understand that I wanted to help him, the unfortunate fellow gave himself away . . .'

'He shouldn't have been interrogated at all,' cried Monsieur de Granville, 'the best way to help somebody is often to do nothing! . . .'

'But the law!' replied Camusot, 'he had been under arrest for two days! . . .'

'Well, it is all over now,' the Public Prosecutor went on. 'I've done what I could to set things right. My carriage and my servants will be in the poor, weak poet's funeral procession. Sérisy's done the same, in fact more, he's undertaken what the unfortunate young man's last wishes asked him to do, he will be executor of the will. This promise elicited from his wife a look full of sense. Furthermore, Count Octave is to be present at the funeral himself.'

'Then, Monsieur le Comte,' said Camusot, 'let us finish the work! There is still a dangerous prisoner on our hands. You know as well as I do, he is Jacques Collin. This wretch will be revealed for what he is . . .'

'Then we are lost!' Monsieur de Granville cried.

'At this moment he is with your condemned man, who was formerly, at the penitentiary, for him, what Lucien was in Paris, . . . his . . . young friend! Bibi-Lupin has disguised himself as one of the constabulary to be present at their interview.'

'What are the judicial police mixing themselves up with now?' said the Procurator, 'they must act only on orders from me! . . .'

'The whole Conciergerie will know that we hold Jacques Collin . . . Well, what I came to tell you is that this powerful and daring criminal is supposed to have in his possession the most dangerous of the letters in the correspondence of

Madame de Sérisy, the Duchesse de Maufrigneuse and Mademoiselle Clotilde de Grandlieu.'

'Are you sure of that? . . .' asked Monsieur de Granville with an expression of troubled surprise.

'Judge for yourself, Monsieur le Comte, whether my fear is justified. When I went through the bundle of letters seized on the unfortunate young man's premises, Jacques Collin's eyes followed me incisively, and I saw on his face a smile of satisfaction, the significance of which could hardly escape an examining magistrate. A scoundrel as deep as Jacques Collin is very careful not to yield up weapons as useful as those. Can you not see those documents in the hands of some defence lawyer whom the rascal will pick from among the enemies of the government and the aristocracy? My wife, to whom the Duchesse de Maufrigneuse has shown kindness, went to warn her, and, at this moment, they are no doubt in consultation with the Grandlieus . . .'

'Then we can't put the man on trial!' cried the Attorney General rising and striding about his office. 'The documents will be in a place of safety . . .'

'I know where,' said Camusot. With these three words, the examining magistrate removed all the prejudices which the Public Prosecutor had conceived against him.

'Ah! . . .' said Monsieur de Granville again sitting down.

'On my way from home to the Palais, I thought very deeply about this distressing affair. Jacques Collin has an aunt, a real one, a woman, about whom the political police have sent a note to the Prefecture. He is the pupil and the deity of this woman, his father's sister, she is called Jacqueline Collin. The jade has a clothes dealer's business, and through trade contacts she picks up a great many family secrets. If Jacques Collin has confided those papers, which are to be his salvation, to anybody, it is to that creature; let us arrest her . . .'

The Procureur Général looked at Camusot with a quizzical glance which said: 'This man is not such a fool as I thought him yesterday; he is young after all, he doesn't yet know how to hold the reins of the law.'

'. . . However,' said Camusot as he went on, 'in order to achieve this, we must countermand all the measures that were taken yesterday, and I wanted your advice on that, your orders . . .'

The Procurator picked up his paper-knife and gently tapped the edge of the table with it, in one of those gestures familiar to all thinkers, when they abandon themselves completely to reflection.

'Three families in danger!' he cried . . . 'We can't make one false step! . . . You're right, the main thing, to follow Fouché's maxim, is: *Arrest them!* Jacques Collin must be put back into solitary confinement at once.'

'That makes him an avowed convict! The memory of Lucien will suffer . . .'

'What a frightful business!' said Monsieur de Granville, 'danger at every turn.'

At that moment, the governor of the Conciergerie entered, not without having knocked; but an office like that of the Attorney General is so well guarded, that only those known to the Parquet can knock at the door.

'Monsieur le Comte,' said Monsieur Gault, 'the prisoner bearing the name of Carlos Herrera is asking to see you.'

'Has he been in communication with anybody?' asked the Procurator.

'With the other prisoners, for he went out into the yard at about half past seven. He's seen the condemned man, who appears to have *talked* to him.'

Monsieur de Granville, at a word from Monsieur Camusot which came to him like a sudden glimpse of light, perceived just how much advantage could be taken, in the way of laying hands on the letters, of a confession of intimacy between Jacques Collin and Théodore Calvi.

A good entrance

GLAD of a reason for putting the execution off, the Procurator with a gesture called Monsieur Gault to him.

'I intend,' he said, 'to put the execution off until tomorrow; but I don't want this delay to be suspected at the Conciergerie.

Total discretion. Let the executioner appear to be making everything ready. Send to me here, under a stout guard, that Spanish priest, the Spanish embassy is making inquiries. The constabulary will bring Don Carlos up by way of your communicating staircase, so that he sees nobody. Warn your men, and see that two of them come up with him, one holding each arm; they are to leave him only at the door to my office. Are you quite sure, Monsieur Gault, that this dangerous foreigner has not had the opportunity of talking to anyone but the other prisoners?'

'Oh, just as he came out of the condemned man's room, someone appeared wanting to see him, a lady . . .'

Here the two magistrates exchanged a look, and what a look!

'What lady?' said Camusot.

'One of his penitents, . . . some marchioness,' replied Monsieur Gault.

'Worse and worse!' cried Monsieur de Granville looking at Camusot.

'She gave the warders and the constables a headache,' Monsieur Gault concluded lamely.

'No part of your functions will permit slackness,' averred severely the Attorney General. 'The Conciergerie is not surrounded by walls for nothing. How did this lady get in?'

'With a valid permit, Monsieur,' replied the governor. 'This lady, perfectly attired, accompanied by a footman and a runner, in a splendid equipage, came to see her confessor before going to the funeral of the unfortunate young man you had taken away . . .'

'Bring me the Prefecture's permit,' said Monsieur de Granville.

'It was made out on the recommendation of His Excellency the Comte de Sérisy.'

'What was this woman like?' asked the Procurator.

'It seemed to us that she was the most respectable of women.'

'Did you see her face?'

'She wore a black veil.'

'What did they say?'

'A pious lady with a prayer-book! . . . what could she say? . . . She asked the priest's blessing, kneeled . . .'

'Did they talk long?' asked the judge.

'Not five minutes; but none of us understood a word of what they were saying, they were clearly talking Spanish.'

'Tell us everything, sir,' the Procurator insisted. 'I repeat, the smallest detail is, to us, of capital interest. Let this be an example to you!'

'She was weeping, Monsieur.'

'Was she really weeping?'

'We couldn't see her, she was hiding her face in her hand-kerchief. She left three hundred francs in gold for the prisoners.'

'It must be someone else!' cried Camusot.

'Bibi-Lupin,' Monsieur Gault continued, 'cried out: "*She's a known thief*."'

'He would know,' said Monsieur de Granville. 'Make out a warrant,' he added looking at Camusot, 'and affix seals everywhere in her dwelling, at once! How did she obtain Monsieur de Sérisy's authorization? . . . Bring me the Prefecture's permit, . . . go at once, Monsieur Gault! Send the priest to me promptly. So long as we leave him there, the danger could not be greater. In two hours' talk, one may go far in a man's soul.'

'Especially a man of your authority,' said Camusot with delicacy.

'There'll be two of us,' replied the Procurator politely. And he resumed his reflections.

'In all prison visiting-rooms, there should be a position created for a supervisor, a well-paid job given on retirement to the cleverest and most conscientious police officers,' he said after a long pause. 'That's where Bibi-Lupin should end his days. Those places need closer supervision than they receive, we need eyes and ears there. Monsieur Gault could tell us nothing of the slightest use.'

'He is so busy,' said Camusot; 'but between the solitary cells and us, there is indeed a lacuna, which should not exist. When we come from the Conciergerie to our offices, we pass along corridors, through yards, up staircases. The attention of our agents can't be everywhere, while the prisoner is thinking all the time of his own case.'

'I'm told that a woman was already there in Jacques Collin's path, when he left the cells to be interrogated. This woman reached as far as the guardroom, at the top of the little stairway to the Mousetrap, the ushers told me, and I've scolded the constabulary about it.'

'Oh, the Palais needs altogether rebuilding,' said Monsieur de Granville; 'but it will cost twenty or thirty millions! ... See if you can get thirty millions out of the two Houses for the convenience of the Law.'

The footsteps of several persons and the sound of arms were heard. It must be Jacques Collin.

The Attorney General covered his features with a mask of solemnity beneath which the man disappeared. Camusot imitated the head of the Parquet.

As they had anticipated, an office messenger opened the door, Jacques Collin appeared, tranquil and quite unsurprised.

'You wanted to speak to me,' said the magistrate, 'I am listening.'

'Monsieur le Comte, I am Jacques Collin, I give myself up!'

Camusot gave a start, the Procurator remained calm.

Conversation between Crime and Justice

'You must think that I have a motive for acting like this,' Jacques Collin continued, embracing the two magistrates with a mocking look. 'It must be a great embarrassment to you; for if I'd remained a Spanish priest, you could have had the constabulary take me to the frontier at Bayonne, and Spanish bayonets would then have relieved you of me.'

The two magistrates remained impassively silent.

'Monsieur le Comte,' the convict went on, 'my reasons for acting thus are graver even than that, though they're devil-ishly personal to me; but I can only speak of them to yourself ... If you were afraid ...'

'Afraid of whom? of what?' said the Comte de Granville.

At that moment, the stance, the facial expression, the carriage of the head, the gesture, the look, of that great Attorney General presented a living image of the Magistrature, which should give the finest examples of civic courage. Then, briefly, he stood at the level of the old judges of the ancient parliament, at the time of the civil wars when the presidents of courts faced death like the marble of which their statues were to be made.

'Afraid of being alone with an escaped convict.'

'Leave us, Monsieur Camusot,' the Procurator said briskly.

'I was going to suggest that my hands and feet should be tied,' Jacques Collin persisted coldly, his gaze upon the two magistrates formidable. He paused, then continued solemnly: 'Count, I only esteemed you before, now I admire you . . .'

'Do you then think yourself redoubtable?' asked the magistrate with a look of contempt.

'*Think myself* redoubtable!' said the convict, 'what use would that be? I am and I know it.' Jacques Collin took a chair and sat down with all the ease of manner of a man who knows himself to be his adversary's equal in a discussion in which he is to speak from a position of strength.

Just then, Monsieur Camusot, about to close the door on whose threshold he stood, came back into the room, went up to Monsieur de Granville, and handed him two papers, folded . . .

'There we are,' said the judge to his Director of Prosecutions showing him one of the papers.

'Recall Monsieur Gault,' cried Count Granville as soon as he had read the name of Madame de Maufrigneuse's maid, whom he knew.

The governor of the Conciergerie entered.

'The woman who came to see the prisoner,' the Procurator said in his ear, 'describe her.'

'Short, strongly built, stout, stocky,' replied Monsieur Gault.

'The person for whom the permit was made out is tall and thin,' said Monsieur de Granville. 'What age was she?'

'Sixty.'

'Does this concern me, gentlemen?' said Jacques Collin.

'Look,' he went on cheerfully, 'there's no need to make inquiries. The person in question is my aunt, my real aunt, a woman, an old woman. I can spare you a lot of embarrassment ... You'll only find my aunt when I mean you to ... If we flounder about in this way, we shall never make any progress.'

'Monsieur l'Abbé no longer speaks French like a Spaniard,' said Monsieur Gault. 'He's given up jabbering.'

'Because things are jumbled up enough without that, my dear Monsieur Gault!' replied Jacques Collin with a bitter smile and addressing the governor by name.

Monsieur Gault hurriedly went up to the Procurator and said in his ear:

'Watch out for yourself, Count, the man is in a rage!'

Monsieur de Granville studied Jacques Collin deliberately and found him calm; but he very soon recognized the truth of what the governor said. That deceptive attitude concealed the frigid and terrible nervous irritation of a savage. In Jacques Collin's eyes a volcanic eruption brooded, his fists were clenched. He was very much the tiger gathering itself to spring at its prey.

'Leave us,' went on the Director of Prosecutions with a solemn air addressing the governor of the Conciergerie and the examining magistrate.

'You did well to send Lucien's murderer away! ...' said Jacques Collin without caring whether Camusot heard or not, 'I could stand it no longer, I was about to strangle him ...'

And Monsieur de Granville shuddered. Never had he seen so much blood in a man's eyes, cheeks so drained, forehead so covered with sweat, and so great a contraction of the muscles.

'What good would such a murder have done you?' the Procurator asked the criminal quietly.

'Every day you avenge or believe you're avenging Society, sir, and you want me to reason about revenge! ... You never felt vengeance, then, sharpening its knives in your veins ... Don't you realize that that idiot of a judge killed him for us; for you loved him, my Lucien, and he loved you! That dear child told me all, every evening, when he came in; I put him to bed, as a serving woman puts her brat to bed, and I made him tell me everything . . . He confided everything to me, even his slightest sensations . . . Ah! never did a good mother tenderly love her only son as I loved that angel. If only you knew! goodness was born in that heart as the flowers spring in the fields. He was weak, that was his only fault, weak like the string of a lyre, so strong when it's stretched . . . The finest natures are like that, their weakness is a blend of tenderness, wonder, the gift of expanding in the sun of art, of love, of the beauty which God has made for man under so many forms! . . . In short, Lucien should have been a woman. Ah, when I think of all I said to the brute beast who has just gone out . . . Ah! sir, what I did, as an accused person before a judge, was what God would have done to save His Son, if He had wanted to save him and gone before Pilate with him! . . .'

Théodore's innocence

TEARS flooded from the convict's pale, yellow eyes which till then had burned like those of a wolf famished by six months' snow in the heart of the Ukraine. He continued: 'That blockhead wouldn't listen, and he destroyed the child! . . . Sir, I washed the lad's body with my tears, imploring *Him Whom I don't know* but Who is over us! I who don't believe in God! . . . (If I were not a materialist, I shouldn't be what I am! . . .) I've told you all there in a word! You can't know, no man can know what grief is; I alone know it. The fire of grief so dried up my tears, that last night I could not weep. I'm weeping now, because I feel that you understand me. I saw you there just now, the very figure of justice. Ah! sir, may God, . . . (I am beginning to believe in Him!) may God keep you from becoming like me . . . That damned judge has taken my soul from me. Monsieur! sir! at this very moment, my life, my beauty, my virtue, my conscience, all my strength, are being buried! Imagine a dog whose blood is drained off by a chemist . . . Look at me! I am that dog . . . That is why I came to you and said: "I am Jacques Collin, I give myself up! ..." I had decided to do that this morning when they came to take away from me the body I was kissing like a madman, like a mother, as the Virgin must have kissed Jesus at the entombment ... I wanted to place myself unconditionally in the service of Justice ... That is what I must now do, and you shall learn why ...'

'Are you speaking to Monsieur de Granville or to the King's Attorney General?' said the man of law.

These two men, CRIME and JUSTICE, regarded each other. The convict had profoundly moved the magistrate who was seized with divine pity for the man of misfortune, aware of his life and his feelings. Finally, the magistrate (a magistrate is always a magistrate) who knew nothing of Jacques Collin's conduct since his escape, thought he knew how to make himself the master of this criminal, against whom after all nothing more than a single forgery had been proved. And what he proposed was to exercise generosity upon a nature variously composed, like bronze, of the metals of good and evil. A man who, moreover, had reached the age of fifty-three without ever having succeeded in inspiring love, Monsieur de Granville admired sensitive natures, like all men who have never been loved. It was perhaps that despair, the lot of many men to whom women grant only their friendship and esteem, whose intimate bond secretly united Messieurs de Bauvan, de Granville and de Sérisy; for a shared misfortune, like shared happiness, tunes souls to its own diapason.

'There is a future for you! ...' said the Procurator casting upon the heavy-hearted villain an inquisitorial look.

The man made a gesture expressive of total indifference with regard to himself.

'Lucien left a will in which he bequeathes you three hundred thousand francs.'

'Oh, the poor child! the poor child!' cried Jacques Collin, 'always the same, *too* honest! The bad feelings, that was me; him, the good, the noble, the beautiful, the sublime! Fine souls like that don't change! all he'd taken from me, sir, was my money!'

This profound, this total abandonment of the personality

which the magistrate was unable to revive, was such un-
deniable proof of what the man said that Monsieur de Granville found himself taking the criminal's side. Was he still
Attorney General!

'If nothing is of interest to you any longer,' asked Monsieur
de Granville, 'what have you come to see me about?'

'Wasn't it already something that I gave myself up? You
were *warm*, but you hadn't got me; besides, you found me an
embarrassment! . . .'

'What an adversary!' thought the great Procurator.

'Mister Attorney General, you are about to cut off the
head of an innocent man, and I have discovered the guilty
one,' Jacques Collin went on solemnly drying his tears. 'I
have not come here on their account but on yours. I came to
spare you remorse, for I love anyone who interested himself
in any way on Lucien's behalf, just as I shall pursue with
hatred all the men and women who brought his life to an
end . . . What does any convict mean to me?' he continued
after a slight pause. 'A convict, to me, is barely what an ant is
to you. I'm like those proud Italian brigands, if a traveller
carries about with him more than the cost of one shot, they
stretch him out dead! I thought only of you. I confessed this
young man, who had only me to confide in, I was his comrade
in the chain-gang! Théodore's nature is good; he thought he
could do a mistress a service by undertaking to sell or otherwise dispose of stolen objects; but he is no more criminally
involved in the Nanterre affair than you are. He is a Corsican,
revenge is a custom with them, they kill one another like
flies.

'In Italy and in Spain, they don't treat a man's life with
respect, for the simplest of reasons. They believe that we are
possessed of a soul, a something, an image of ourselves which
goes on living, perhaps eternally. Try to explain a crack-
brained notion like that to one of our analysts! It is only in
atheistical or philosophy-ridden countries that human life
must be paid for dearly by those who disturb it, and this is
quite right among people who believe only in matter, only in
the present!

'If Calvi had informed against the woman from whom the

stolen goods came, you wouldn't have known who the guilty person was, for he is already in your clutches, but only an accomplice whom poor Théodore doesn't want to harm, for she's a woman . . . What would you? every condition of life has its point of honour, the penitentiary and the thief on the street have theirs! Now I know who killed those two women and carried the whole bold scheme through, a strange, quite peculiar affair, I've been told it in all its details. Stop Calvi's execution, you shall learn everything; but give me your word to return him to the convict station, commuting his sentence . . . In my state of grief, it is too much trouble to tell lies, you know that. What I have just told you is the truth . . .'

'With you, Jacques Collin, although it diminishes the dignity of the Law, which itself would never compromise in this way, I think I can soften the rigour of my duties and refer the matter back to the right quarter.'

'Do you grant me this man's life?'

'It seems possible . . .'

'Sir, I implore you to give me your word, that will do.'

Monsieur de Granville's gesture was one of wounded pride.

The society file

'THE honour of three great families is in my keeping, and in yours only the life of three convicts,' Jacques Collin persisted, 'I am stronger than you.'

'You can be returned to solitary confinement; then what could you do? . . .' the Procurator asked.

'Ah! so this is a game!' said Jacques Collin. 'I was speaking *without frills*, me! I was speaking to Monsieur de Granville; but if the man before me is the Attorney General, then I pick up my cards and *stick*. Well, there we are, if you'd given me your word, I was going to hand you the letters written to Lucien by Mademoiselle Clotilde de Grandlieu!' This was said with a steady emphasis, a coldness of manner and a look which revealed to Monsieur de Granville an adversary against whom one false step was dangerous.

'Is that all you are asking me for?' said the Procurator.

'I shall be plain with you,' said Jacques Collin. 'The honour of the Grandlieu family is what I am offering for the commutation of Théodore's sentence: the gain is all yours. What is a convict serving a life sentence? . . . If he escapes, you can soon be rid of him! you draw a note of hand on the guillotine! The only thing is, as he'd been bundled off, not with the kindest intentions, to Rochefort, you'll promise to redirect him to Toulon, recommending that he should be well treated. But now, for myself, I want more; I have files on Madame de Sérisy and the Duchesse de Maufrigneuse, and what letters those are! . . . Listen, count: when whores write they express themselves with some taste and a display of fine feelings, well! society women who go in for taste and fine feelings all day long, write as whores behave. Philosophers could no doubt explain this *set to partners*, I shan't try. Woman is an inferior being, she is too much governed by her organs. To me, a woman is only beautiful when she is like a man!

'And so these little duchesses who are men in their heads have written masterpieces . . . Oh, it's wonderful stuff, from end to end, like that celebrated ode of Piron's.'

'Really?'

'Do you want to see them? . . .' said Jacques Collin with a smile.

The magistrate looked ashamed.

'I can let you read them; but, there, we aren't joking! This is a straight game? . . . You'll give me the letters back, and you'll give orders that the person who brings them won't be informed on, followed or even looked at.'

'It will take time, won't it?' said the Procurator.

'No, it is half past nine, . . .' Jacques Collin went on with a glance at the clock; 'well, in four minutes, we can have a letter from each of these ladies; and, after reading them, you'll countermand the guillotine arrangements! If I were pretending, you wouldn't see me so calm. These ladies have, moreover, been warned . . .'

Monsieur de Granville did not conceal his surprise.

'At this very moment, they must be taking steps, they'll be putting the Keeper of the Seals to work, they may go, who knows, as far as the King ... Look, do you give me your word to pay no attention to who comes, not to follow or have the person followed for an hour?'

'I promise you that!'

'Very well, a man like you wouldn't try to trick an escaped convict. You are made of the metal of men like Turenne and you keep your word even to thieves ... Well, in the waiting-hall, there is at the moment a beggarwoman in rags, an old woman, standing in the centre of the hall. She's there to speak to one of the public scriveners about a case to do with some party wall; send a boy for her, and tell him to say: *Dabor ti mandana*. She'll come ... But don't be cruel without need! ... Either you accept my proposals, or you won't compromise yourself with a convict ... I'm only a forger, you know! ... Well, then, don't leave Calvi in the frightful anguish of a man togged up for execution ...'

'The execution has already been countermanded ... I don't,' said Monsieur de Granville to Jacques Collin, 'wish Justice to subsist beneath your level!'

Jacques Collin looked at the Attorney General with a kind of astonishment and saw him pull the cord of the bell.

'Will you be so good as not to escape? Give me your word, and I am content. Go and find this woman ...'

One of his staff appeared.

'Félix, send the constables away, ...' said Monsieur de Granville.

Jacques Collin admitted defeat.

In this duel with the magistrate, he wished to be the greater, the stronger, the more magnanimous, and the magistrate crushed him. Nevertheless, the convict felt himself to be superior in that he was playing with the Law, which he would convince that the guilty was innocent, and from which he meant to win a disputed head; but that superiority had to be dumb, secret, concealed, while the Stork conquered him in full daylight, and with majesty.

Jacques Collin's first appearance
in comedy

As Jacques Collin was leaving Monsieur de Granville's office, the general secretary of the Cabinet Office appeared, himself a deputy, Count des Lupeaulx, accompanied by a small, sickly-looking old man. This character, wrapped in a purple-brown quilted overcoat, as if it had still been winter, his hair powdered, his face cold and pale, walked as though full of gout, unsteadily, on feet made to seem larger by shoes of Orleans calfskin, leaning on a stick with a gold knob, hat in hand, a row of seven decorations on his breast.

'What is it, my dear Lupeaulx?' asked the Public Prosecutor.

'I come from the prince,' he whispered in Monsieur de Granville's ear. 'You may take whatever measures you like to recover the letters of Mesdames de Sérisy and Maufrigneuse, and those of Mademoiselle Clotilde de Grandlieu. You may deal with this gentleman . . .'

'Who is he?' the Procurator asked des Lupeaulx in a whisper.

'I have no secrets from you, my dear Attorney, this is the famous Corentin. His Majesty wishes you to tell him yourself all the details of this affair and what hangs on it.'

'Do me the further favour,' replied the Procurator still in des Lupeaulx's ear, 'of going and letting the prince know that the matter is at an end, that I had no need of this gentleman,' he added indicating Corentin. 'I shall go for orders to His Majesty, at the end of this matter which concerns the Keeper of the Seals, for there are two reprieves to be made out.'

'You acted wisely in going ahead on your own,' said des Lupeaulx shaking the Procurator's hand. 'We are on the eve of great things, and the King doesn't want, at this point, to see the peerage talked about, tarnished . . . It isn't a low criminal action now, it's an affair of State . . .'

'Tell the prince that, when you came, it was all done with!'

'Are you sure?'

'I think so.'

'Well, then, my dear, you'll be Keeper of the Seals, when the present Keeper becomes Chancellor . . .'

'I'm not ambitious! . . .' replied the Procurator.

Des Lupeaulx went out laughing.

'Beg the prince to solicit me ten minutes' audience with the King, at about half past two,' added Monsieur de Granville, as he saw Count des Lupeaulx out.

'So you're not ambitious!' said Lupeaulx casting a perceptive glance at Monsieur de Granville. 'Come, now, you have two children, you would like to be made a peer of France at least . . .'

'If the Attorney General already has the letters, there is no need for my intervention,' Corentin pointed out, when he found himself alone with Monsieur de Granville, who looked at him with understandable curiosity.

'A man like yourself is never superfluous in so delicate a matter,' replied the Director of Prosecutions seeing that Corentin had either understood or simply heard all.

Corentin's inclination of the head was almost condescending.

'Do you know, sir, the individual with whom we are concerned?'

'Yes, Monsieur le Comte, he is Jacques Collin, head of the Ten Thou' society, treasurer to all three penitentiaries, a convict who, for five years, has managed to conceal his identity under the cassock of the priest Carlos Herrera. How did he come to be entrusted with a mission from the King of Spain to our late King? We all lose our way in seeking out the truth of this matter. I am waiting for a reply from Madrid, where I sent letters and a man. That convict is possessed of two kings' secrets . . .'

'He's a man of lively temper! There are only two things to be done: to make him work on our side, or to get rid of him,' said the Procurator.

'Our thoughts were the same, and I am deeply honoured,' answered Corentin. 'I am compelled to think so much on behalf of so many people, that I am bound statistically to meet a man of wit from time to time.' This was offered so drily and in so icy a tone, that the Attorney General said nothing and addressed himself to one or two other pressing matters.

When Jacques Collin appeared in the reception hall, the astonishment of Mademoiselle Jacqueline Collin can hardly be imagined. She remained planted firmly on her two feet, her hands on her hips, for she was dressed as a costermonger. Habituated as she was to her nephew's unexpected accomplishments, this surpassed all.

'Dear me, if you go on looking at me as though I were a show-case of natural oddities,' said Jacques Collin, taking his aunt's arm and leading her out of the hall, 'they'll think we're both very odd, they might arrest us, and that would be a waste of useful time.' And he descended the staircase of the Galerie Marchande, which leads into the rue de la Barillerie. 'Where's Paccard?'

'He's waiting for me outside la Rousse's, walking up and down the Quai des Fleurs.'

'And Prudence?'

'She's inside, pretending to be my godchild.'

'Come on, then.'

'Watch we aren't being followed . . .'

The red-headed lady's story

LA ROUSSE, who kept a hardware shop on the Quai des Fleurs, was the widow of a famous murderer, one of the Ten Thou'. In 1819, Jacques Collin had faithfully restored over twenty thousand francs to the wench, on behalf of her lover, after his execution. Dodgedeath alone knew of the private life of this young woman, at that time a milliner, and her *fanandel*.

'I'm your man's *dab*,' he, then living at Ma Vauquer's, said to the girl, whom he'd arranged to meet in the Botanical Gardens. 'He must have talked to you about me, little one. Whoever betrays me dies within the year! those I can trust have nothing to fear from me. I am the *chum* to die without saying a word that will compromise anybody I wish well.

treat me as though I were the devil you'd sold your soul to, and you'll benefit by it. I promised your poor Auguste I'd see you in luck, he wanted you to be set up; he got sliced for you. Don't cry. Listen to me: nobody in the world except me knew that you were a convict's moll, a killer who got put down Saturday; nobody'll ever know. You're twenty-two, you're pretty, and there you are with twenty-six thousand francs; forget Auguste, get married, become an honest woman if you can. In return for that cushy life, I want you to be ready to help me, me and anybody I send to you, without hesitation. I shall never ask you to do anything compromising, either to yourself, or your children, or your husband, if you have one, or your family. Sometimes, in my profession, I need a place where I can talk without risk, or where I can hide. I need a woman who can post a letter or run an errand discreetly. You would be one of my letter-boxes, one of my porters' lodges, an occasional messenger, nothing more, nothing less. You are blonde to a fault, Auguste and I always called you *la Rousse*, you'll keep that name. My aunt, a dealer in the Temple, to whom I'll introduce you, will be the one person in the world you must obey; tell her everything that happens; she'll find you a husband, she'll be useful to you in a lot of ways.'

Thus they concluded one of those diabolical pacts of the same kind as that which, for so long, had bound Prudence Servien to this man and of which he formed many; for, like the devil, he had a passion for recruiting.

Jacqueline Collin had married la Rousse to the head clerk of a rich wholesale ironmonger, in about 1811. This head clerk, having bought the commercial side of his master's undertakings, was on the way to prosperity, father of two children, and deputy mayor of his district. La Rousse, now Madame Prélard, had never had the least grounds for complaint, either against Jacques Collin, or against his aunt; but, each time her assistance was sought, Madame Prélard trembled through all her frame. Thus, when she saw these two dreadful individuals enter her shop, she turned pale.

'We have business to discuss with you, Madame,' said Jacques Collin.

'My husband is at home,' she replied.

'For the moment, your own presence won't be much needed; I never disturb people needlessly.'

'Send out for a cab, child,' said Jacqueline Collin, 'and tell my goddaughter to come down; I'm hoping to place her as maid to a great lady, and the steward of the house wants to take her along.'

Paccard, who looked like one of the constabulary in plain clothes, was at that moment talking to Monsieur Prélard about a large order for steel cable for a bridge.

A shop-assistant went to look for a cab, and a few minutes later, Europe, or to substitute her real name for the one under which she had waited on Esther, Prudence Servien, with Paccard, Jacques Collin and his aunt, were, to the great joy and relief of la Rousse, sitting together in a cab, whose driver Dodgedeath instructed to make for the Ivry barrier.

Prudence Servien and Paccard, trembling before the Dab, were like guilty souls in God's presence.

'Where are the seven hundred *and fifty* thousand francs?' he, the *dab*, asked them, fixing upon them one of those lucid glances which so disturbed the blood of such damned souls, when they were caught out in a fault, that the hairs of their head seemed like so many pins.

'The seven hundred and *thirty* thousand francs,' Jacqueline Collin replied to her nephew, 'are in a safe place, I handed them this morning to la Romette, in a sealed packet . . .'

'If you hadn't given them to Jacqueline,' said Dodgedeath, 'that's where you'd have found yourselves, . . .' and he pointed in the direction of the Strand, by which the cab was passing.

Prudence Servien crossed herself, as she might once have done at home in the country, as though she had seen a thunderbolt strike.

'I shall forgive you,' the Dab pursued, 'on condition that you don't attempt anything of the kind again, and that from now on you act like these two fingers of my right hand,' he said showing them the index and the middle finger, 'for the thumb is that good *largue*!' And he tapped his aunt's shoulder. 'Listen to me. From now on, Paccard, you have nothing to

524

ear, and you can follow your nose anywhere in Pantin as you please! I allow you to marry Prudence.'

How Paccard and Prudence are to set themselves up

PACCARD took Jacques Collin's hand and kissed it respectfully.

'What do I have to do?' he said.

'Nothing, you'll have an income and women, without counting your wife, for you're too Regency, old friend! . . . That's what it is to be as handsome as you!'

Paccard blushed at this mocking compliment from his sultan.

'As for you, Prudence,' Jacques continued, 'you need a career, a condition, a future, and to remain in my service. Listen carefully. In the rue Sainte Barbe, there exists a nice little establishment belonging to the Madame Saint-Estève, whose name my aunt sometimes borrows . . . The shop has a good custom, it brings in fifteen or twenty thousand francs a year. The place is managed for Saint-Estève by . . .'

'La Gonore,' said Jacqueline.

'Poor La Pouraille's *largue*,' said Paccard. 'That's where I slipped off with Europe the day poor Madame van Bogseck died, our mistress that was . . .'

'It's usual to chatter when I'm speaking, is it?' said Jacques Collin.

Deepest silence reigned in the carriage, and Paccard and Prudence no longer dared to look at each other.

'The firm, then, is run by la Gonore,' Jacques Collin went on. 'If you went to hide there with Prudence, I can see, Paccard, that you've got enough sense to fob the dicks off, but that you're not wide enough to bamboozle Mom, . . .' he said pinching his aunt's chin. 'I can see now how she managed to find you . . . Well, the coincidence is fitting. You're going back there, to Gonore's . . . I proceed: Jacqueline will see Madame Nourisson to negotiate the purchase of her establishment in the rue Sainte Barbe, and you'll be able to make a fortune there, if you behave yourself, little woman!' he said looking at Prudence. 'Mother Superior at your age, eh? just the ticket for a true daughter of France,' he added in biting tones.

Prudence flung her arms round Dodgedeath's neck and kissed him, but with a sharp push which betrayed his extraordinary strength, the Dab flung her so abruptly away that but for Paccard, the wench's head would have gone through the cab window.

'Paws down! I don't like that sort of behaviour!' the Dab said drily. 'It shows a lack of respect.'

'He's right, my love,' said Paccard. 'Look, it's as if the Dab gave you a hundred thousand francs. The shop's worth that. It's on the main road, opposite the Gymnase. You get people coming out of the theatre . . .'

'And I'll do better than that, I'll buy the house as well,' said Dodgedeath.

'In six years we shall be millionaires!' cried Paccard.

Tired of being interrupted, Dodgedeath fetched Paccard a kick in the shin which might have disabled him; but Paccard had nerves of rubber and bones of tinplate.

'All right, Dab! we'll shut up,' he replied.

'Do you think I'm talking nonsense?' Dodgedeath went on, observing that Paccard had drunk too many little nips. 'Listen. There are two hundred and fifty thousand francs in gold in the cellar of that house . . .'

The deepest silence reigned once more in the hired carriage.

'That gold is solidly bricked in . . . The sum has to be got at, and you've only three nights to do it in. Jacqueline will help you . . . A hundred thousand francs will pay for the establishment, fifty thousand will buy the house, and the rest you leave.'

'Where?' said Paccard.

'In the cellar!' echoed Prudence.

'Silence!' said Jacqueline.

'Yes, but to move a load like that, you need a bit of good will from the coppers,' said Paccard.

'You'll get it,' said Dodgedeath drily. 'What are you worrying about? . . .'

526

Jacqueline looked at her nephew and was struck by the strain evident in his face beneath the impassible mask with which this man of such remarkable strength habitually concealed his feelings.

'My child,' said Jacques Collin to Prudence Servien, 'my aunt is going to let you have the seven hundred and fifty thousand francs back.'

'Seven hundred and thirty,' said Paccard.

'All right, seven hundred and thirty,' Jacques Collin went on. 'Tonight, you'll have to find some pretext for going back to Madame Lucien's house. You'll get up by a skylight on to the roof; then you'll let yourself down by the chimney into your late mistress's bedroom, and you'll stuff the packet she made into her mattress . . .'

'Why not by the door?' said Prudence Servien.

'Imbecile, the seals are on!' replied Jacques Collin. 'The inventory'll be made in a day or two, and the two of you'll be innocent of theft . . .'

'Long live the Dab!' cried Paccard. 'Ah, what kindness!'

'Driver, stop! . . .' Jacques Collin called out in his powerful voice.

The cab had come to the cab-rank outside the Botanical Gardens.

'Take yourselves off, little ones,' said Jacques Collin, 'and don't do anything silly! Be on the Pont des Arts this evening at five o'clock, and there my aunt will tell you if any of these orders has to be changed. No chances have to be taken,' he added in an undertone to his aunt. 'Jacqueline will explain to you tomorrow,' he went on, 'how to set about removing the gold from the cellar. That is a very delicate operation . . .'

Prudence and Paccard danced on the king's highway, happy as discharged thieves.

'Ah, what a man, the Dab!' said Paccard.

'He'd be the king of men, if he didn't act so contemptuous to women!'

'Oh, he's a darling!' cried Paccard. 'Did you see what a kick he gave me! We deserved to be packed off *ad patres*; for after all it's we who put him in this difficulty . . .'

'So long,' said the subtle and witty Prudence, 'as he doesn't bundle us into some crime to get us sent *into the country* . . .'

'Him! if that was his fancy, he'd say so, you don't know him! What a pretty load he's fixed you up with! There we are, solid citizens. What luck! Oh, when he likes you, that man, there isn't his equal for kindness! . . .'

The quarry joins the hunt

'My pet!' said Jacques Collin to his aunt, 'you take care of la Gonore, she must be put to sleep; in five days from now, she will be arrested, and in her room they'll find a hundred and fifty francs in gold, part of one share in the murder of the aged Crottats, mother and father of the notary.'

'That'll get her five years in the Madelonettes,' said Jacqueline.

'About that,' replied Jacques Collin. 'So there's a reason for the Nourrisson to get rid of her house; she can't run it herself, and you can't pick up a manageress just like that. You'll be able to arrange the matter without difficulty. Then we shall have an *eye* there . . . But these three operations are all subordinate to the bargaining I've started with regard to our letters. So unpick your dress and give me your trade samples. Where are the three packets?'

'Good Lord! they're at la Rousse's.'

'Driver!' cried Jacques Collin, 'go back to the Palais de Justice, and get a move on! . . . I promised speed, here I've been away half an hour and it's too long! Stay at la Rousse's, and give the sealed packets to the messenger you'll see appear and ask for Madame *de* Saint-Estève. It's the *de* that'll be the password, and he will say to you: *Madame, I come from the Attorney General's office for what you know of.* Take up your stand before la Rousse's door watching what goes on in the Flower Market, so as not to arouse the attention of Prélard. As soon as you've passed on the letters, you can set Paccard and Prudence in action.'

'I see what you're up to,' said Jacqueline, 'you want to

take Bibi-Lupin's place. That boy's death has turned your head!'

'And Théodore, whose head they were going to crop in order to *slice* him at four o'clock this evening,' cried Jacques Collin.

'It's not a bad idea! we shall end up as honest, prosperous folk, on a fine estate, under clear skies in Touraine.'

'What else could I do? Lucien took away my soul, my entire happiness; I may still have thirty years to drag out, and I haven't the heart. Instead of being the Dab of the convict stations, I shall be the Figaro of justice, and avenge Lucien. It's only in the skin of the police that I can demolish Corentin. To have a man to eat, that gives me life again. The parts we play in the world are mere appearances; the reality is the idea!' he added striking his forehead. 'What have we left in the kitty?'

'Nothing,' said the aunt appalled by her nephew's accent and expression. 'I gave you everything for the boy. La Romette has no more than twenty thousand francs in the business. I took everything from Madame Nourrisson, she had about sixty thousand francs of her own. . . . Ah! the bed-clothes we lie in haven't been washed for a year. The boy devoured your Fanandels' loot, our own funds and all the Nourrisson had.'

'That made?'

'Five hundred and sixty thousand . . .'

'We have a hundred and fifty in gold, that Paccard and Prudence owe us. I'll tell you where you can pick up two hundred more . . . The rest will come out of what Esther left. Nourrisson must be paid back. With Théodore, Paccard, Prudence, the Nourrisson and yourself, I shall soon have formed the unholy batallion I need . . . Listen, we're nearly there . . .'

'Here are the three letters,' said Jacqueline who had just given the last scissor snip to the lining of her dress.

'Good,' replied Jacques Collin, taking the three precious autographs, three sheets of woven paper still scented. 'Théodore did the job at Nanterre.'

'Him, was it? . . .'

'Shut up, time's precious, he wanted to offer a beakful to a little bird from Corsica called Ginetta . . . You can make use of la Nourrisson to find her, I'll get the information out to you in a letter Governor Gault will let you have. Come to the wicket at the Conciergerie in two hours from now. That little girl has to be turned loose on a laundrywoman, sister of Godet, and she must be ready to take over . . . Godet and Ruffard were La Pouraille's accomplices in the murder and theft at the Crottats'. The four hundred and fifty thousand francs are intact, one third in la Gonore's cellar, that's La Pouraille's share; the second third in la Gonore's room, that's Ruffard's; the third share is hidden at Godet's sister's.

'We shall begin by taking a hundred and fifty thousand francs out of La Pouraille's lot, then a hundred each out of Godet's and Ruffard's. Once Ruffard and Godet have been stowed away, it'll be they who made off with what's missing of their shares. I'll make Godet believe that we've put a hundred thousand francs aside for him, and I'll tell Ruffard and La Pouraille that la Gonore still has it for them! . . . Prudence and Paccard are doing the job at la Gonore's. You and Ginetta, who strikes me as a bright little piece, you'll do what needs to be done at Godet's sister's. For my beginnings in the art of comedy, I present the Stork with four hundred thousand francs from the Crottat theft, and the guilty parties. I give the impression of throwing light on the Nanterre murder. We pick up our lot, and we're in with the boys! They used to hunt us, now we hunt them, that's all. Give the cabby three francs.'

They were at the Law Courts. Jacqueline payed, dazed. Dodgedeath climbed the staircase on his way back to the Attorney General.

Let the English gentlemen shoot first

A TOTAL change in one's life is so violently critical a matter that, in spite of his decision, Jacques Collin climbed slowly up the staircase which, from the rue de la Barillerie, leads to the Galerie Marchande off which, beneath the peristyle of the

Court of Assize, open the sombre premises of the public prosecutor's department, semi-officially known as the Parquet. Some political matter had occasioned a confluence of people at the foot of the double staircase to the Assize Court, so that the convict, absorbed in his reflections, was delayed for some time by the crowd. To the left of this double staircase stands, like an enormous pillar, one of the close buttresses of the Palais, and let into its mass may be seen a small door. This little door leads to a spiral staircase communicating directly with the Conciergerie. It is used by the Attorney General, the governor of the Conciergerie, presiding judges of Assize, prosecuting counsel and the head of the security police. It was by way of a branch of this staircase, now condemned, that Marie Antoinette, the queen of France, was conducted before the revolutionary tribunal, which sat, as we know, in the great hall used for solemn hearings of the Central Court of Criminal Appeal.

At the sight of this dreadful staircase the heart contracts on reflecting that the daughter of Maria Theresa, whose attendants, whose dressed hair, the hoops of whose petticoats filled the great staircase of Versailles, passed that way! ... Perhaps she was expiating her mother's crime, Poland hideously partitioned. Sovereigns who commit such crimes evidently give no thought to the price at which Providence will ransom them.

Just as Jacques Collin reached the vaulted head of the great staircase, on his way to the Attorney General's department, Bibi-Lupin emerged from that door hidden in the wall.

The chief of the detective force on his way from the Conciergerie was also going to Monsieur de Granville's. Bibi-Lupin's astonishment on seeing before him the frock coat of Carlos Herrera, whom he had so closely watched that morning, may be imagined; he quickened his pace to a run. Jacques Collin turned. The two enemies stood face to face. On either side, each stood motionless, and the same glance left each of the two pairs of eyes, themselves so different, like two pistols which, in a duel, fire at the same moment.

'This time I've got you, brigand!' said the chief of the security police.

'Ah, ah! . . .' replied Jacques Collin, in a tone of irony. His first thought was that Monsieur de Granville had had him followed; and, strangely! he was hurt at finding the man less great than he had supposed.

Bibi-Lupin leaped bravely at the throat of Jacques Collin, who, his eye on his adversary, delivered a sharp blow which sent him hands and feet in the air three paces away; then Dodgedeath went deliberately up to Bibi-Lupin and stretched out a hand to help him to his feet, much like an English boxer who, sure of his strength, asks nothing better than to go on with the fight. Bibi-Lupin was too much master of himself to start shouting; but he got up, ran to the entry to the corridor, and signed to a constable to stand there. Then, with the speed of lightning, he returned to his enemy, who had watched him calmly. Jacques Collin had made up his mind: Either the Procurator has not kept his word or he has not taken Bibi-Lupin into his confidence, in which case the situation needs explaining.

'Do you mean to arrest me?' Jacques Collin asked his enemy. 'Say so without accompaniment. I know that here at the heart of the Stork's precincts you are stronger than I. I could kill you with a couple of boxer's kicks, but I can't take on the constabulary and the regular troops. Let's have no fuss; where do you want to take me?'

'To Monsieur Camusot's.'

'Let us go to Monsieur Camusot's,' replied Jacques Collin. 'But why shouldn't we go to the Parquet itself? . . . it's nearer,' he added.

Bibi-Lupin, who knew himself to be out of favour at the higher levels of judicial authority where he was suspected of having made his fortune at the expense of criminals and their victims, was not displeased by the thought of presenting himself before the Director of Prosecutions with such a catch.

'Come along, then, that suits me!' he said. 'But, since you're giving yourself up, allow me to fit you up, I don't trust you not to lash out!' And he took a pair of thumb-cuffs out of his pocket.

Jacques Collin held out his hands, and Bibi-Lupin fastened his thumbs.

'Well, now, since you're behaving yourself,' he continued, 'tell me how you got out of the Conciergerie?'

'The same way as yourself, up the little staircase.'

'So you showed the constabulary a new trick?'

'No. Monsieur de Granville let me out on parole.'

'Are you kidding?'

'You'll see! ... Perhaps they'll put thumb-cuffs on *you*.'

An old acquaintance

At that moment, Corentin was saying to the Prosecutor General:

'Well, sir, it's just an hour ago since our man went, aren't you afraid he's been making game of you? ... He may be on his way to Spain, where we shall never find him again, for Spain is a country with its own curious ways.'

'Either I don't know men, or he'll come back; all his interests lie that way; he has more to gain from me than he has to give ...'

At that moment Bibi-Lupin appeared.

'Monsieur le Comte,' he said, 'I have good news for you: Jacques Collin, who had escaped, has been recaptured.'

'So that,' cried Jacques Collin, 'was how you kept your word! Ask your two-faced agent where he found me?'

'Where?' said the Procurator.

'A few yards away from this office, under the archway,' replied Bibi-Lupin.

'Free this man of your trappings,' Monsieur de Granville said severely to Bibi-Lupin. 'Know that, until you're ordered to arrest him again, you are to leave him at liberty ... Get out! ... You're too much inclined to go about acting as though you alone were the law and the police.'

And the Procurator turned his back on the head of the security brigade, who turned pale, especially when he caught a glance from Jacques Collin, in which he read his downfall.

'I didn't leave my office, I was waiting for you, and you're in no real doubt that I kept my word as you kept yours,' said Monsieur de Granville to Jacques Collin.

'I doubted you for a moment, sir, and perhaps in my place you'd have thought as I did; but reflection showed me that I was being unjust. I bring you more than you are giving me; it wasn't in your interest to deceive me . . .'

The magistrate exchanged a quick glance with Corentin. This glance, which could hardly escape Dodgedeath, whose attention was fixed on Monsieur de Granville, made him take notice of the curious little old man, sitting on a chair, in a corner. Immediately, warned by that quick, vivid instinct which betokens the presence of an enemy, Jacques Collin examined this individual; he saw at first glance that the eyes were not of an age to match the costume, and he recognized that this was a disguise. A second glance was enough to give Jacques Collin his revenge on Corentin for the rapidity of observation with which Corentin had seen through him at Peyrade's.

'We are not alone! . . .' said Jacques Collin to Monsieur de Granville.

'No,' the Attorney General answered briefly.

'And the gentleman,' said the convict, 'is one of my closest acquaintances, . . . I believe?'

He took one step that way and recognized Corentin, the real and avowed author of Lucien's fall. Jacques Collin, whose complexion was brick-red, turned, for a rapid and imperceptible instant, pale and almost white; all the blood rushed to his heart, so frenetically ardent was his desire to leap upon this dangerous animal and destroy it; but he drove back the brutal impulse and held it in check with the strength which made him so terrible. He adopted a friendly air, a tone of obsequious politeness, of which he had formed the habit while playing the part of a highly placed churchman, and he greeted the little old man.

'Monsieur Corentin,' he said, 'is it to chance that I owe the pleasure of meeting you here, or is it my good fortune to be the object of your visit to the Parquet?'

The Procurator's astonishment was extreme, and he could not fail to examine the two men confronting each other.

Jacques Collin's evident feelings and the way he enunciated his words betokened a moment of crisis, and he was curious to penetrate its causes. At this sudden and miraculous recognition of his identity, Corentin rose up like a snake on whose tail someone has stepped.

'Yes, it is I, my dear Abbé Carlos Herrera.'

'Did you come here,' Dodgedeath inquired, 'to interpose between Monsieur le Procureur-Général and myself?... Have I the happiness of forming the subject of one of those bargains in which your talents so brilliantly shine? Look, sir,' said the convict turning to the Procurator again, 'in order not to waste your precious time, read this sample of my merchandise ...' And he tendered to Monsieur Granville the three letters, which he drew from the side pocket of his frock coat. 'While you are taking cognizance of them, I shall, if I may, talk a little with this gentleman.'

A position in prospect

'IT is a great honour for me,' replied Corentin, who could not repress a shudder.

'Sir, you were wholly successful in the matter between us,' said Jacques Collin. 'I was beaten ...,' he added lightly in the tone of a gambler who has lost his money; 'but you left certain of your men on the field ... It was a victory gained at some cost ...'

'Yes,' replied Corentin, accepting the pleasantry; 'if you lost your queen, I lost both my castles ...'

'Oh, Contenson was only a pawn!' Jacques Collin answered in the same tone of raillery. 'They're soon replaced. You are, allow me to praise you in this way to your face, you are, *upon my word*, a prodigious fellow.'

'No, no, I bow to your superiority,' replied Corentin, who had adopted the air of a professional wit (seeming to say, 'All right, you want to crack jokes, well, let's crack them!'). 'Why, everything was on my side, while you, so to speak, you were all on your own ...'

'Oh! oh!' said Jacques Collin.

'And you almost brought it off,' said Corentin noticing the exclamation. 'You are the most extraordinary man I have encountered in my life, and I have seen many who were extraordinary, for those with whom I do battle are all remarkable for their daring, the boldness of their designs. I was, unfortunately, very intimate with the late Monsignor the Duke of Otranto; I worked for Louis XVIII, while he reigned, and during his term of exile for the Emperor and the Directory ... You have the temper of Louvel, the finest political instrument I have seen; but you are as supple as the prince of diplomats. And what auxiliaries! ... I'd give many of the heads to be cut off to have in my service poor little Esther's cook ... Where do you find creatures as beautiful as the wench who understudied that Jewess for a while on Monsieur de Nucingen's account? ... I never know where to find them when I need them ...'

'Oh, sir, my dear sir,' said Jacques Collin, 'you overwhelm me ... Coming from you, such compliments turn a man's head ...'

'They are deserved! What, you deceived Peyrade, he took you for a peace officer, him! ... Look, if you hadn't had that little idiot to protect, you'd have taken us all in ...'

'Oh, but, sir, you're forgetting Contenson disguised as a mulatto ... and Peyrade as an Englishman. Actors have all the resources of the theatre at their disposal; but perfect performance in the full light of day, no matter what time it is, only you and people trained by you ...'

'Ah, well, there we are,' said Corentin, 'the two of us, both convinced of each other's worth, of our mutual merits. There we are, the two of us, each of us now somewhat on his own; I've lost my old friend, you've lost your young *protégé*. I'm the better placed of the two for the moment, why shouldn't we do what they do in the play of the *Auberge des Adrets*? I give you my hand, and I say: *Let us embrace and make an end*. I offer you, in the presence of Monsieur le Procureur-Général, full and entire letters of pardon, and you will be one of my men, the next after me, my successor perhaps.'

'So, it's a position you're offering me? ...' said Jacques

536

Collin. 'A nice position! I leave the brunette for the blonde . . .'

'You will operate in a sphere in which your talents will be appreciated, well paid for, and you take action only in your own time. The political and governmental police has its dangers. I myself, the man before you, have been twice imprisoned, . . . I don't feel any the worse for it. But one gets about! one is what one makes oneself . . . One stage-manages political dramas, one is treated with consideration by great lords . . . Well, now, my dear Jacques Collin, would that suit you?'

'Have you received orders in the matter?' the convict asked him.

'I am fully empowered, . . .' replied Corentin, pleased with his sudden happy thought.

'You're trifling, you're a powerful man, you know very well that people might distrust you . . . You've sold more than one man tied up in a sack you'd got him to enter of his own accord . . . I know your fine battles, the Montauran affair, the Simeuse affair . . . Ah, those were the battles of Marengo in police work!'

'Well,' said Corentin, 'you regard Monsieur le Procureur-Général with esteem?'

'Yes,' said Jacques Collin bowing respectfully; 'his fine character, his firmness of purpose and his nobility fill me with admiration, and I would give my life to make him happy. For that reason, I shall begin by putting an end to the dangerous condition in which Madame de Sérisy lies.'

A feeling of gladness betrayed itself in the Procurator's eyes.

'Why, then, ask him,' Corentin went on, 'whether I am not fully empowered to remove you from your present shameful state, and to attach you to my person.'

'It is quite true,' Monsieur de Granville said watching the convict.

'Really true! I should have a pardon for my past and the promise of succeeding you if I proved my capacity?'

'Between two men like ourselves, there can be no misunderstanding,' Corentin continued with a greatness of mind which must have attracted anybody.

'The price of this transaction no doubt is my return of the three files of letters? . . .' said Jacques Collin.

'I had not thought it necessary to say so . . .'

Disappointment

'My dear Monsieur Corentin,' said Dodgedeath with an irony worthy of that which made Talma's triumph in the part of Nicomedes, 'I thank you, I am obliged to you for teaching me what I am worth and what importance is attached to depriving me of my weapons . . . I shall never forget it . . . I shall be forever and at all times at your service, and instead of saying, like Robert Macaire: "Let us embrace! . . ." I shall simply embrace you.'

He so quickly took hold of Corentin by the middle, that the latter could not defend himself from the embrace; he pressed him like a doll to his heart, kissed him on both cheeks, lifted him like a feather, opened the door of the office, and put him down outside, bruised by so rough an enfoldment.

'Good-bye, my dear,' he said in a low voice, not meant to be overheard. 'Three corpse lengths separate us from each other; we have measured swords, they are of the same temper, the same fashion . . . Let us respect each other; but I mean to be your equal, not your subordinate . . . Armed as you would be, you seem to me too dangerous a general for your lieutenant. Let a ditch lie between us. Woe to you if you cross on to my ground! . . . You call yourself the State, just as lackeys call themselves by the same name as their masters; I wish to be called Justice; we shall often see each other; let us always treat each other with the dignity, the decorum, appropriate to . . . the frightful riff-raff we shall always be,' he added in a whisper. 'I am setting you an example by kissing you . . .'

Corentin remained stupefied for the first time in his life, and allowed his terrible adversary to shake him by the hand.

'If that's the way it's to be,' said he, 'I fancy it is in both our interests to remain *friends* . . .'

'We shall be stronger each on his own side, also more dangerous,' added Jacques Collin in a low tone. 'So tomorrow perhaps I shall ask you for a deposit on the deal . . .'

'Well, then,' said Corentin affably, 'you are taking your affairs out of my hands and turning them over to the A.G.; it will help in his career; but I can't resist telling you this, you're on the right lines . . . Bibi-Lupin's limits have become clear, he's on his way out; if you replace him, you will be in the one place that suits you; and I shall be delighted to see you in it . . . upon my word . . .'

'So long, then, see you soon,' said Jacques Collin.

Turning, Dodgedeath found the Procurator at his desk, head in hands.

'Really, you can stop Countess Sérisy going mad? . . .' asked Monsieur de Granville.

'In no time at all,' replied Jacques Collin.

'And you can let me have all the letters from these ladies?'

'Did you read those three? . . .'

'Yes,' said the Procurator quickly; 'I am ashamed for the ladies who wrote them . . .'

'Well, we're alone: secure the door, and let us negotiate,' said Jacques Collin.

'Allow me . . . The Law must in the first place follow its course, and Monsieur Camusot has orders to arrest your aunt . . .'

'He'll never find her,' said Jacques Collin.

'A search is to be made in the Temple, at a Demoiselle Paccard's who runs her establishment . . .'

'They won't find anything but old rags, costumes, diamonds, uniforms. Still, Monsieur Camusot's zeal ought to be checked.'

Monsieur de Granville rang for an attendant, and told him to bring Monsieur Camusot along.

'Look,' he said to Jacques Collin, 'let's make an end! I can't wait to hear your prescription for curing the countess . . .'

In which Jacques Collin abdicates as Dab

'Monsieur le Procureur-Général,' said Jacques Collin turning grave, 'I was, as you know, sentenced to five years' penal servitude for the crime of forgery. I love my freedom! . . . This love, like all loves, has defeated its own purpose; for lovers, too much adoring each other, quarrel. Alternately escaping and being recaptured, I have done seven years in the penitentiary. Thus you only have to pardon me for penalties I further incurred *in the country* . . . (sorry!) at convict stations. In reality, I have served my sentence, and until some other crime has been laid at my door, which I defy the Law and even Corentin to do, my rights as a French citizen should be restored to me. Excluded from Paris, and under police supervision, is that a life? where can I go? what can I do? You know my abilities . . . You've seen Corentin, that magazine of ruses and betrayals, pale with fear before me, pay justice to my talents . . . That man took everything from me! for it was he, he alone, by what means I do not know or in whose interest, who overturned the edifice of Lucien's fortunes . . . Corentin and Camusot brought all this about . . .'

'Let's avoid recrimination,' said Monsieur de Granville, 'and come to the point.'

'Well, then, this is the point. Last night, holding in my hand the cold hand of that dead young man, I promised myself to give up the senseless struggle I have waged for twenty years against the whole of society. You won't expect a dull monkish sermon from me, after what I've told you of my religious views . . . Well, then, for twenty years, I've seen the world from below, from its cellars, and I recognize in the march of events a force which you call Providence, which I have always called *chance*, which my companions call *luck*. Every bad action meets retribution somewhere, however quickly it hides. In this battler's trade, when your luck's in, when you hold both a quint and a quatorze, the taper falls over, the cards burn, or the player is struck with apoplexy! . . : That was Lucien's story. That boy, that angel, hadn't committed the

540

shadow of a crime; he did what he did, he let things take their course! He was going to marry Mademoiselle de Grandlieu, be made a marquis, he had a fortune; well, then, a tart poisons herself, she hides the proceeds of a registered income, and the so-painfully erected edifice of this fortune crumbles all at once. Then who takes the first cut at us? a man covered with secret infamies, a monster who in the world of tangled interests has committed such crimes that every penny of his fortune is bathed in some family's tears, a Nucingen who was a legalized Jacques Collin in the world of money. But you know as well as I do the liquidations, the tricks for which he deserved hanging. My chains will forever mark all my actions, even the most praiseworthy. To be a shuttlecock between two battle-dores, one called the penitentiary, one the police, is a life in which victory means endless labour and tranquillity seems to me impossible. Jacques Collin now lies buried, Monsieur de Granville, with Lucien, upon whom holy water is being sprinkled at this moment prior to his departure for the cemetery of Père Lachaise. I, too, must have somewhere to go, not to live there, but to die . . . As things are now, you don't want, you, the representatives of justice, to concern yourselves with the conditions of life for an ex-convict. The law may be satisfied, but society isn't, it keeps up its mistrust, and it does all it can to justify that mistrust to itself; it makes life impossible for a freed convict; it should give him back all his rights, but it forbids him to live where he chooses. Society says to the wretch: Paris, the only place where you can hide, and the surrounding district for so many miles around, you shan't inhabit! . . . Then it submits the ex-convict to police supervision. Do you think one can live under those conditions? In order to live, you must work, for you don't leave prison with a private income. You so arrange things that the convict shall be clearly marked, recognized, hemmed in, then you imagine that people are going to treat him with confidence, when society, the law, the world about him show none. You condemn him either to hunger or to crime. He can't find work, he is inescapably driven back to his old trade which brings him to the scaffold. Thus, while I wanted to abandon my struggle against the law, I have failed to find a place in the sun for myself. There is only one for me, that is to serve the power which weighs on us all, and when the thought came to me, those other forces I was speaking to you of rose up around me.

'Three great families are in my hands. Don't think I want to blackmail them . . . Blackmail is one of the most cowardly forms of murder. Indeed, murder itself seems mild by comparison. The murderer has need of a frightful courage. I append my signature to these views, for the letters which are my only security, which make it possible for me to speak to you as I do, which at this moment put me on an equal footing with yourself, me who am crime and you who are justice, those letters are yours when you want them . . .

'A messenger from your office can go out for them on your behalf, they will be given to him, . . . I ask no ransom, I'm not selling them! Alas! Monsieur le Procureur Général, when I put them on one side, I wasn't thinking of myself, I was thinking of the danger in which Lucien might find himself one day! If you do not fall in with my request, I have more than enough courage, and more than enough distaste for life, to blow my own brains out and rid you of me . . . I could, with a passport, go to America and live in solitude; I have all the capacities that a savage needs . . . Such are the thoughts which passed through my mind last night. Your secretary should have repeated to you a message I gave him . . . When I saw the precautions you were taking to save Lucien's memory from all reproach, I gave you my life, a poor gift! I no longer cared for it, life seemed to me impossible without the light shining on it, the happiness in it, the purpose which gave it meaning, the prospects of that young poet who was its sun, and I wanted you to receive those three packets of letters . . .'

Monsieur de Granville inclined his head.

'WHEN I went down into the prison yard, I discovered the authors of the crime committed at Nanterre and my youthful chain-mate's neck under the knife for involuntary complicity in the crime,' Jacques Collin went on. 'I learned that Bibi-Lupin is deceiving the Law, that the murderer of the Crottats was one of his agents; it was, you might say, providential ... This gave me the idea I might do some good, using the qualities with which I am endowed, the unfortunate acquaintances I have formed, in the service of society; I could be useful instead of doing harm, and I ventured to count on your intelligence, as well as your kindness.'

His own air of kindness, directness, simplicity, of a man speaking freely without bitterness, without that philosophy of vice which till then made him so terrible to listen to, caused it all to seem like a transformation. This was no longer the same man.

'I so believe in you that I wish to place myself entirely at your disposal,' he continued with the humility of a penitent. 'You see me with three ways before me: suicide, America and the rue de Jérusalem. Bibi-Lupin is rich, he has served his time; he works for both sides, and if you cared to let me act against him, I'd pick him up *on the job* within a week. If you give me that scoundrel's place, you will have performed a great service to society. I'm not out for what I can get, I shall play straight. I have all the qualifications. I'm better educated than Bibi-Lupin; I was made to study up to the top classical form; I shan't be as clumsy as he is, I have manners when I want. I have no other ambition than to be an instrument of law and order, instead of a corrupting influence. I shall never again recruit anyone into the great army of vice. When in war you take an enemy general, you see, sir, you don't shoot him, you return him his sword, and give him a town for his prison; well, I am the general of the convict stations, and I surrender ... It wasn't the Law, it was death that defeated me ... The sphere in which I want to live and operate is the only one that will suit me, and there I shall develop the strength I feel in me . . . Decide . . .'

And Jacques Collin adopted a submissive, modest stance.

'You have placed those letters at my disposal? . . .' said the Public Prosecutor.

'You can send for them, they will be handed to the person you dispatch . . .'

'How?'

Jacques Collin read the Procurator's heart and went on with the game.

'You promised me to commute Calvi's death sentence to twenty years' hard labour. Oh, I'm not reminding you of that to strike a bargain,' he said briskly, noting the Attorney's gesture of impatience; 'that life must be saved for other reasons: the boy is innocent . . .'

'How do I put my hand on those letters?' the Procurator insisted. 'I have the right and the obligation to know whether you are the man you say you are. I want you without conditions . . .'

'Send a man you trust to the Quai aux Fleurs; he will see on the steps of an ironmonger's shop, at the sign of the *Shield of Achilles* . . .'

'The house of the *Shield*? . . .'

'It's there,' said Jacques Collin with a bitter smile, 'that I keep my shield. There your man will find an old woman dressed, as I was saying, like a well-to-do dealer in fish, wearing ear-rings, a figure at the markets; he will ask for Madame *de* Sainte Estève. Don't forget the *de* . . . And he will say: "Madame, I come *from the Attorney General's office for what you know of* . . ." He will at once be given three sealed packets for you . . .'

'Do they contain all the letters?' said Monsieur de Granville.

'That's clever of you! I can see you don't hold your position for nothing,' said Jacques with a smile. 'So you think me likely to draw you on and then deliver blank paper . . . You don't know me!' he added. 'I trust you as a son trusts his father . . .'

'You will be taken back to the Conciergerie,' said the Pro-

curator, 'and wait there for a decision to be made about you.'
He rang, his messenger appeared, and he said: 'Ask Monsieur
Garnery to come here if he's in.'

Apart from the forty-eight police superintendents who
watch over Paris like forty-eight little providences, and without counting the detective force – and that's why in thieves'
slang a superintendent is called a *quarter eye*, there being four
in each district – there are two superintendents attached at
once to the Police and the Law Courts for missions of particular delicacy, sometimes replacing examining magistrates.
The office of these magistrates, for police superintendents do
belong to the magistracy, is called the delegations office, for
they are in effect delegated each time and formally empowered
to carry out either searches or arrests. The job calls for men of
ripe years, proven capacity, high moral standards, absolute
discretion, and one of the miracles Providence performs on
behalf of Paris is that such men are always to be found. A
description of the Law Courts would be inexact without
some mention of these *preventive* magistracies, as we may
call them, the most effective auxiliaries of Justice; for if, by
the march of events, Justice has lost some of its ancient pomp,
its former richness, material gains have to be acknowledged.
Particularly in Paris, the machinery has been admirably
perfected.

Monsieur de Granville had sent Monsieur de Chargeboeuf,
his secretary, to join Lucien's funeral procession; he had to be
replaced, for the present mission, by a sound man; and Monsieur Garnery was one of the two superintendents in
delegations.

The funeral

'Monsieur le Procureur-Général,' Jacques Collin went on,
'I have already given you proof that I have my point of
honour ... You let me free and I returned ... It is almost
eleven o'clock, ... Lucien's funeral mass is almost over, he
will be leaving for the cemetery ... Instead of sending me to

the Conciergerie, let me accompany that child's body to Père Lachaise; I shall return as your prisoner ...'

'Be off, then,' said Monsieur de Granville with an inflection of voice all kindness.

'One last word, Monsieur le Procureur Général. The money of that wench, Lucien's mistress, wasn't stolen ... In the few moments of liberty you granted me, I was able to question the servants ... I am as sure of them as you are of your two delegations superintendents. When the seals are lifted, you're certain to find in Mademoiselle Esther Gobseck's bedroom the money due to her for the bonds she sold. Her maid told me that the deceased was, as she put it, given to hiding, suspicious, she must have put the bank-notes in her bed. Let the bed be carefully searched, let them take it to pieces, open the mattress, the pillows, they'll find the money ...'

'Are you sure of that? ...'

'I'm sure of the relative probity of my own rogues, they don't play tricks on me ... I have power of life and death over them, I judge and condemn, and my sentences are carried out without the formalities you need. I work to some effect, as you will see. I shall find you the sums stolen from *Monsieur et Madame* Crottat; I shall turn in one of Bibi-Lupin's agents, his right-hand man, and you will learn the secret of the crime committed at Nanterre ... That's my deposit! ... If now you take me into the service of Justice and the Police, at the end of a year you will congratulate yourself on what I reveal, I shall have become what I should be, and I shall find means to succeed in all the tasks confided to me.'

'I can promise nothing, except my good will. What you ask doesn't depend on me alone. To the King only, on a recommendation from the Keeper of the Seals, belongs the right of pardon, and the position you would like to occupy lies in the gift of the Prefect of Police.'

'Monsieur Garnery,' the office-boy announced.

At a gesture from the Director of Public Prosecutions, the delegations superintendent entered, looked at Jacques Collin with a connoisseur's eye, and suppressed his astonishment at hearing:

'*Be off, then!*' addressed by Monsieur de Granville to Jacques Collin.

'Will you allow me,' replied Jacques Collin, 'not to leave until Monsieur Garnery has brought you what constitutes my only strength, so that I can take away with me evidence that you are satisfied?' The Procurator was touched by such humility and utter good faith.

'Be off!' this magistrate repeated. 'I am sure enough of you.'

Jacques Collin bowed deeply and with the total submission of an inferior before his superior. Ten minutes later, Monsieur de Granville had in his possession the letters contained in three packets sealed and intact. This matter's importance and Jacques Collin's effective confession, however, had made him forget the promise about curing Madame de Sérisy.

Jacques Collin experienced, once outside, a sensation of incredible well-being. He felt free and born to a new life; he walked swiftly from the Law Courts to the church of Saint Germain des Prés, where mass was over. Holy water was being sprinkled on the bier, and he was in time to pay this Christian farewell to the mortal remains of the child so tenderly cherished, then he climbed into a carriage and followed the boy to the cemetery.

At funerals in Paris, unless there are unusual circumstances, or in the rare cases of the natural death of a celebrity, the crowd at the church thins out as the procession moves towards Père Lachaise. There is time enough to show one's face in church, but everyone has business to pursue and returns to it as soon as possible. Thus, of the ten mourners' carriages, not even four were full. When the procession reached Père Lachaise, the followers numbered no more than a dozen, among whom was Rastignac.

'You are right to have kept faith with *him*,' said Jacques Collin to his old acquaintance.

Rastignac showed surprise at seeing Vautrin there.

'Don't be alarmed,' said the former lodger at Madame Vauquer's, 'you enslave me by the mere fact of your presence here. My support is not to be despised, I am or shall be more powerful than ever. You've slipped your cable, you have been very clever; but you may yet need me, and I shall always be at your service.'

'What are you to be, then?'

'Purveyor to the penitentiary instead of being its tenant,' replied Jacques Collin.

Rastignac's features expressed disgust.

'Ah, you might be robbed one day! . . .'

Rastignac walked quickly to place a distance between himself and Jacques Collin.

'You never know what circumstances you may find yourself in.'

They had reached the grave dug beside that of Esther.

'Two creatures who loved each other and were happy!' said Jacques Collin, 'are reunited. It is still a form of happiness to rot together. They shall put me there, too.'

When Lucien's body was lowered into the grave, Jacques Collin fell stiffly, in a faint. So strong a man could not endure the light sound of the spadefuls of earth which the gravediggers throw upon the body before they come round asking for a tip. At that moment, two agents of the security brigade appeared, recognized Jacques Collin and lifted him into a cab.

In which Dodgedeath comes to an arrangement with the Stork

'WHAT is the matter now? . . .' asked Jacques Collin, when he had recovered consciousness and looked round the interior of the cab. He saw that he was sitting between two police agents, one of whom was precisely Ruffard; on this man he cast a glance which plumbed the murderer's soul as deep as the hiding-place of la Gonore.

'It's just that the A.G. was asking for you,' Ruffard answered, 'that we looked everywhere, and that we only found you at the cemetery, where you nearly toppled head first into that young man's grave.'

Jacques Collin was silent for a while. Then, 'Was it Bibi-

Lupin who sent you out looking for me?' he asked the other agent.

'No, it was Monsieur Garnery who booked us.'

'Did he say anything to you?'

The two agents looked inquiringly at each other in expressive dumb show.

'Look! how did he give you the order?'

'He ordered us,' said Ruffard, 'to find you at once, saying you were at the church of Saint Germain des Prés; and that, if the procession had already left, you'd be at the cemetery.'

'The Attorney General was asking for me? . . .'

'Might be.'

'That's it,' replied Jacques Collin, 'he needs me for something! . . .'

And he relapsed into silence, which greatly disquieted the two agents. At about half past two, Jacques Collin went into the office of Monsieur de Granville and there saw a person new to him, Monsieur de Granville's predecessor, Count Octave de Bauvan, now a presiding judge at the Central Court of Criminal Appeal.

'You forgot the dangerous state of Madame de Sérisy, whom you promised me you could save.'

'If, Monsieur le Procureur Général, you cared to ask these two jokers,' making a sign to the two agents to enter, 'what state they found me in? . . .'

'Unconscious, Monsieur le Procureur Général, beside the open grave of the young man they were burying.'

'Save Madame de Sérisy,' said Monsieur de Bauvan, 'and you shall have everything you are asking!'

'I am asking for nothing,' Jacques Collin went on, 'I have submitted unconditionally, and the Attorney General should have received . . .'

'All the letters!' said Monsieur de Granville; 'but you promised me to preserve Madame de Sérisy's reason, didn't you? Wasn't that idle boasting?'

'I think I can do it,' answered Jacques Collin modestly.

'Well, then, come with me,' said Count Octave.

'No, sir,' said Jacques Collin. 'I won't sit in a carriage at your side . . . I am still a convict. If my purpose is to serve

Justice, I won't begin by dishonouring it ... Go you to Madame la Comtesse's house, I shall be there shortly after you ... Tell her that Lucien's best friend, Carlos Herrera, is coming ... The mere expectation of my visit will inevitably produce on her the kind of impression to relieve her crisis. You must forgive me if I again take on the false character of the Spanish canon; it is in order to perform a very great service!'

'I'll see you there at about four,' said Monsieur de Granville, 'I have to go with the Keeper of the Seals to see the King.'

Jacques Collin went to find his aunt, who was waiting for him on the Quai des Fleurs.

'Well, then, so you've turned yourself over to the Stork?'

'Yes.'

'It's risky!'

'No, I owed poor Théodore his life, and he'll get a reprieve.'

'What about yourself?'

'Me, I shall be what I should be! I shall always be feared in our world! But we must set to work! Go tell Paccard to dash off at full speed, and Europe to do what I ordered.'

'It won't be much trouble, I know how to handle la Gonore! ...' said the terrible Jacqueline. 'I didn't waste my time picking daisies!'

'Ginetta, that Corsican moppet, has to be found by tomorrow,' Jacques Collin went on smiling at his aunt.

'How do I pick up her trail?'

'You start with Manon la Blonde,' replied Jacques.

'We'll have it this evening!' his aunt said. 'What a hurry you're in! This is it, then?'

'I want by these first efforts to surpass anything Bibi-Lupin has done. I've had my little bit of conversation with the monster who killed Lucien for me, and I live only for my revenge on him! By reason of our positions, the two of us will be equally armed, equally protected! It will take me several years to deal with that wretch; but when I strike, it will be to the heart.'

'I dare say he's got the same thing in mind for you,' said the aunt, 'for he's taken Peyrade's daughter into his house, you know, the kid we sold to Madame Nourrisson.'

'Our first trick will be to find him a servant.'

'That won't be easy, he'll be good at picking servants!' said Jacqueline.

'Go to it, hate gives you new life! to work!'

Jacques Collin took a cab and went at once to the Quai Malaquais, to the small room where he lodged, which didn't connect with Lucien's apartment. The porter, very surprised to see him again, wanted to tell him everything that had happened.

'I know it all,' said the priest. 'I was compromised, despite the sanctity of my character; but thanks to the intervention of the Spanish ambassador, I was released.'

And he went up quickly to his room, where he picked up, between the covers of a breviary, a letter which Lucien had addressed to Madame de Sérisy, when Madame de Sérisy had banished him, after seeing him at the Italiens with Esther.

The doctor

In his despair, Lucien had omitted to send this letter, believing himself lost for ever; but Jacques Collin had read the masterpiece, and as everything Lucien wrote was sacred for him, he had kept the letter pressed in his breviary, because of the poetical expressions used about that vain love. When Monsieur de Granville had told him of the state in which Madame de Sérisy lay, it immediately occurred to this deep-minded man that the despair and madness of the great lady were due to the quarrel she had allowed to subsist between her and Lucien. He knew women, as magistrates know criminals, he divined the most intimate feelings of their hearts, and he at once thought that the countess must attribute Lucien's death in part to her own severity, and reproach herself bitterly. A man filled with love for her would manifestly not have relinquished his hold on life. To know that, in spite of harsh treatment, she was still loved might restore her reason.

If Jacques Collin was a great general to the convicts, it must be acknowledged that he was nevertheless a great doctor of souls. This man's arrival in the apartments of the Sérisy house was at once a source of shame and of hope. A number of people, the count himself, the doctors were in the little drawing-room which led to the countess's bedroom; but, to avoid all spot of dishonour to his soul, Count de Bauvan sent everybody away to be alone with his friend. To a privy councillor, to a vice-president of the Council of State, it was already something of a blow to see the gloomy, sinister individual enter.

Jacques Collin had changed his clothes. He had put on long trousers and a frock coat of black cloth, and his bearing, his looks, his gestures, all was of a perfect appropriateness. He greeted the two statesmen, and asked whether he might go into the countess's room.

'She awaits you with impatience,' said Monsieur de Bauvan.

'With impatience? . . . Then she is safe,' said the dreadful enchanter. And in fact, after half an hour's discussion, Jacques Collin opened the door and said: 'Come along, Monsieur le Comte, you need no longer anticipate any fatal outcome.'

The countess held the letter to her heart; she was calm, and seemed reconciled to herself. Seeing her thus, the count gave visible expression to his happiness.

'That's what they're like, then, the people who decide our fate and that of whole peoples!' thought Jacques Collin, who shrugged his shoulders when the two friends had come in. 'A sigh breathed amiss by some female turns their intelligence inside out like a glove! They lose their heads for a glance! A skirt raised or lowered by a fraction, and they rush all over Paris in despair. A woman's fancies affect the whole State! Oh! what strength a man acquires when, like me, he eludes that childish tyranny, that loyalty overturned by passion, that candid malice, that primitive cunning! Woman, with her executioner's skill, her torturer's gifts, is and always will be man's ruin. Attorney General, minister of State, look at them, all blind, twisting everything for the letters of duchesses and little girls, or to save the reason of a woman who will be madder in her right mind than out of it.' He assumed a proud smile. 'And,' he thought, 'they believe me, they act upon my disclosures, and they will leave me standing where I did. I shall always reign over this world, in which, for twenty-five years, I have been obeyed . . .'

Jacques Collin had employed that supreme power which he formerly exercised upon poor Esther; for he possessed, as we have many times seen, the way of speaking, the looks, the gestures which tame madness, he had presented Lucien as having borne away the countess's image with him.

No woman can resist the idea of being the only beloved.

'You no longer have a rival!' was the last mocking word of this cold man.

He stayed a whole hour, forgotten, there, in the drawing-room. Monsieur de Granville arrived and found him sombre, erect, lost in the dream of those who have attained the 18 Brumaire of their lives.

The Attorney General walked as far as the threshold of the countess's bedroom, stayed there a moment or two; then he came up to Jacques Collin and said to him:

'Do you hold to your intentions?'

'Yes, sir.'

'Right, then, you shall replace Bibi-Lupin, and the sentence on Calvi will be commuted.'

'He won't be going to Rochefort?'

'Not even to Toulon, you can take him into your service; but these reprieves and your nomination depend on your conduct over a period of six months during which you will act as Bibi-Lupin's deputy.'

Conclusion

WITHIN a week, Bibi-Lupin's deputy recovered four hundred thousand francs on behalf of the Crottat family. He also turned in Ruffard and Godet.

The proceeds of the sale of Treasury scrip by Esther

Gobseck were found in the harlot's bed, and Monsieur de Sérisy placed to Jacques Collin's account the three hundred thousand francs left him in Lucien de Rubempré's will.

The monument ordained by Lucien, for Esther and himself, is regarded as one of the finest in Père Lachaise, and the plot on which it stands belongs to Jacques Collin.

After having exercised his functions for some fifteen years, Jacques Collin retired in 1845 or thereabouts.

MORE ABOUT PENGUINS
AND PELICANS

For further information about books available from Penguins please write to Dept EP, Penguin Books Ltd, Harmondsworth, Middlesex UB7 0DA.

In the U.S.A.: For a complete list of books available from Penguins in the United States write to Dept CS, Penguin Books, 625 Madison Avenue, New York, New York 10022.

In Canada: For a complete list of books available from Penguins in Canada write to Penguin Books Canada Ltd, John Street, Markham, Ontario L3R 1B4.

In Australia: For a complete list of books available from Penguins in Australia write to the Marketing Department, Penguin Books Australia Ltd, P.O. Box 257, Ringwood, Victoria 3134.

In New Zealand: For a complete list of books available from Penguins in New Zealand write to the Marketing Department, Penguin Books (N.Z.) Ltd, P.O. Box 4019, Auckland 10.

BALZAC

Translated by Marion Ayton Crawford

EUGÉNIE GRANDET

Eugénie Grandet, completed in 1833, is one of the earliest and finest novels of Balzac's Human Comedy. The story, told with classical simplicity yet with constant awareness of the wider setting of post-revolutionary France, centres round a house in provincial Saumur. There the miser Grandet lives with his wife and daughter Eugénie under the stifling shadow of his obsession with gold. But with the arrival of her cousin, Charles, Eugénie has her own obsession, and the tragedy which follows is described by Balzac (1799–1850) with irony and psychological insight.

OLD GORIOT

Old Goriot is the tale of a young man's temptation by the world, the flesh, and the devil. The devil is represented by a character founded on the criminal Vidocq, who later became Chief of the Paris Sûreté; the world and the flesh by Paris in the early nineteenth century and the lovely aristocratic women of the Faubourg Saint-Germain.

It is also the tale of a working-class Lear whose daughters, to whom he has given his all, leave him to die in poverty while they live in the world of fashion.

These are the chief among many threads of the story, which are intertwined through the intersecting lives of a group of people who by various chances come to live in a boarding-house in an old but obscure corner of Paris.

THE PENGUIN CLASSICS

A Selection

Livy
ROME AND THE MEDITERRANEAN
Translated by Henry Bettenson
with an introduction by A. H. MacDonald

Flaubert
BOUVARD AND PÉCUCHET
Translated by A. J. Krailsheimer

LIVES OF THE LATER CAESARS
Translated by Anthony Birley

Aretino
SELECTED LETTERS
Translated by George Bull

THE MABINOGION
Translated by Jeffrey Gantz

Balzac
URSULE MIROUËT
Translated by Donald Adamson

EGIL'S SAGA
Translated by Herman Pálsson and Paul Edwards

THE PSALMS
Translated by Peter Levi